NOMAD BOOK 2

MOTHER DEATH

Edited by David Gatewood
Published by Karen Traviss
Jacket art: Thomas Wievegg
Design: Kevin G. Summers

karentraviss.com

ACKNOWLEDGEMENTS

My grateful thanks go to my editor, David Gatewood, always ready to dissect my very lengthy train of logic or scrutinise a timeline; Thomas Wievegg, for fabulous cover art; and Kevin Summers, who went above and beyond to answer my obscure question about the flavour of cattle feed... by tasting it. Now *that's* dedication to the craft. Thank you, gentlemen!

PREFACE
A NOTE FROM THE AUTHOR

For those of you who've been used to reading my books from American publishers, you'll find my latest novels are now written in UK English, both spelling and grammar, except for proper nouns and those American terms that just don't anglicise. If you're new to my work, you'll notice that I write both dialogue and narrative in the style and grammar of the character, and occasionally their own spelling, so that varies from scene to scene. Those discrepancies are an integral part of the characterisation.

The reference I use is the Shorter Oxford English Dictionary. Where there are differences between the SOED and the Oxford English Dictionary, I let Oxford Dictionaries Online have the final word. Very rarely, none of these sources gives me a solution that I feel makes something clearer for the reader, so I'll opt for clarity even if it means breaking a formal rule.

Now the science. I do a lot of research for my books and much of this novel is real science, but other parts aren't intended to be, notably FTL travel, although there are some fringe theories out there that make it seem less of a stretch. I do try to respect Kepler, though. This is just a personal quirk — some tropes don't bother me but others set my teeth on edge.

But in the end, my books are about people: human people, non-human people, and people we build in labs. And they're not about heroes or villains, just individuals on different sides who find themselves in tough situations. So I've taken real science and bent it enough to pose the ultimate questions we can ask ourselves. Who would we fight and die for? And when we're a long way from home, in a world where our laws and customs mean nothing, what must we hold onto to remain human?

Karen Traviss
July 2021

NOMAD BOOK 2

MOTHER DEATH

KAREN TRAVISS

PART ONE

MOTHER DEATH

PROLOGUE

This place is a ghost town. Which, to be fair, is probably where I belong.

I talk to ghosts a lot these days. I'm a ghost myself: eight years, seven months, twelve days, and counting. I talk to them while I'm out running. Some blokes drink to escape whatever's haunting them, but I run.

I'll cover three or four miles of mothballed corridors tonight and I won't see another living soul. I run every day. I run when I can't stand being trapped in my own head, and I run when I can't get away from the voice that keeps telling me I could have stopped John and Greg deploying. I run when I can't get back to sleep in the middle of the night and the old worries bubble up in the dark. I run to stop myself tearing the guts out of things I can't change and that won't bring my boys back.

If I can talk it over with the ghosts, though, maybe I can work out why I'm still going through the motions of being alive.

So you're in luck, princess. You're the stiff who's going to be a good listener today. I don't know who you used to be, only that you forgot you'd be skylined when you stepped out of cover on that roof to squeeze off a burst at me. I squeezed first. But you won't remember that. So be grateful I saved you the trouble of living through the last fifteen years of this shit show.

You want to know what you've missed? The world was already circling the drain the last time you were busy murdering and mutilating, but die-back pretty much wiped out the major food crops on this side of the world, and now it's on the move again. It's not your buddies who let it loose, though. Not this time.

Okay, listen in. Sitrep: we've done a deal with the Alliance of Asian and Pacific States, which basically consists of us handing over Ainatio's FTL wormhole research and saying please don't nuke us. So they've held off sterilising the area with sodium bombs to give us time to prep *Shackleton* for launch and get out of here, but they're a bit pissed off that Erskine stripped out the FTL comms kit before she abandoned everyone. Not half as pissed off as we are, though. In real terms it means we won't be able to talk to Nomad Base until we're almost on their doorstep. Forty-five bloody years. Still, we'll be asleep in the freezer. It's not like we'll notice.

Next task: eleven weeks to launch *Shackleton*. Risks: APS might find out the latest die-back is the strain Ainatio's boffins were working on to find a treatment, and Asia blames the West for the whole die-back thing anyway, so things might get ugly. We haven't told them *Shackleton* and *Elcano* are armed with nukes, or that we've also got a banned autonomous AI running the mission, either. I know APS is a pretty threadbare superpower these days, but in a world running on empty, the man with a charged battery and a spare mag is king. They can still fry us.

So now you know as much as I do.

Can I ask you a personal question, princess? Do you remember who you were when you were alive, and what you did? Does it all finally make sense now that you're wherever you are? Or did your god wipe your slate clean and you've forgotten all those mass graves you filled with corpses? Okay. Never mind. Forget it.

This isn't really my fight. I don't work for Ainatio, the refugee camp's got its own militia — who are hardcore, believe me — and the corporate security troops are competent enough. So I could have gone home by now. Me and Tev got stranded after we evacuated the embassy in DC, but we could have made our way back to England if we'd put our minds to it. We're both former special forces, and if anyone can find their way home from the arse-end of the world when the buses aren't running, it's us. But I wouldn't go and Tev wouldn't leave me, because that's what mates do. Home is family. Mine's gone. There's nothing left for me in England except the bits that hurt.

So I'm a ghost. Not completely dead like you, princess, but not really alive either, still drifting around looking for some peace. I can see the real world but I can't touch it. The living can walk straight through me. But as I'm here, and blokes like me are made for situations like this, I have to do something. I just need to understand why.

Hold up, can you hear that? Listen... that grinding, clunking noise? It's a quadrubot coming up behind us. Sorry, hun, got to go. That's our AI, Solomon. He's come to nag me.

Solomon catches up and matches my pace. "Are you all right, Marc? I assume you and Tev carried on drinking last night when you went back to your quarters."

"We did, Sol. We got totally rat-arsed."

"But why are you out for a run now? Tev's flight leaves soon. If you miss him — "

"I know. I just needed to ask a dead woman some questions."

"Yes. Of course."

"Ghosts, Sol. You, me, the people in our heads. We're all ghosts."

Sol pauses for a beat. "Do you mean disconnected from the world, or unable to let go of the living?"

"I'm too hung over to do philosophy, mate. Ask me one on sport."

Most AIs sound human in conversations, even the cheap customer service ones that are really sorry your parcel didn't arrive, but Sol's something else. Look at him. He's transferred into that scruffy red industrial quadrubot again. It's a museum piece. I know he needs to be able to exit the network, but out of all the bots in storage, everything from drones to those creepy python crawlers to giant combat engineer units, he almost always picks the quad. While he was managing the bots building Nomad Base — before his boss destroyed the comms link, that is — he used to upload to a quad on Opis and go for a gallop for the sheer hell of it.

Yeah, I can relate to a runner. You can argue the toss over whether AIs should be classed as people, but Sol is definitely a human minus a body, and if that's not a ghost, I don't know what is. I think he just wants to touch the real world to check if it's still there. The quad's the best way he knows.

"We should start heading back," he says. "The flight won't wait."

He's right. I can't miss it. This is the last time I'll ever see my mate Tev. Tev's Fijian but he's never been to Fiji, and that's where he's heading for a second chance with his ex and his kids. It's decent of APS to fly him out, but I wouldn't trust them as far as I could spit. Even if Fiji's their side of the quarantine line, they're bound to see him as a source of answers about what Ainatio's been up to. They won't see the pick of our scientist litter as undesirables, either. They've got a shopping list.

"I'm glad you decided to come with us," Sol says suddenly. "I know it wasn't an easy decision. But a fresh start — "

"I don't want a fresh start, Sol."

I don't know what I want.

I did twenty-four years in the army, eighteen in special forces. Part of me knows I should go home and defend my country again — and slip the MoD a copy of Ainatio's research — because even an island can't hold out against disease and invasion forever. But I feel the same need to get away from wherever I am as I did when I left the regiment, and I can't tell if I'm running away from something or chasing it.

I remember the day I became a ghost. A woman from the MoD visited in person to tell me and Sandra that both our sons had been killed in action. And my life ended there and then. I felt like I'd fallen off a roof, flailing for the last few seconds before I hit concrete oblivion. But I never reached the ground. I'm still in free fall today, life receding behind me, death and a bit of peace always a few yards ahead. I could do something about that and I don't know why I haven't — not fear, not optimism, not atonement — so I've decided to go out doing what special forces do best and recover some self-respect, and be the man my boys thought I was. Or maybe I'm just too far gone, so badly burned by it all that the nerves have been destroyed and I can't feel the pain that should make me stop moving.

I've shut Sol up. I didn't mean to.

All I can hear is his legs going *chonk, chonk, chonk*, my heart pounding all the way up my throat, and that weird muffled quietness that sound-reducing floors create. We loop back down the passage, scattering a group of housekeeping bots cleaning the floor from side to side like they're doing a creeping line search. Eventually we end up back in the undercroft below the management building. It's nearly zero-four-fifty.

Plenty of time. We can slow the pace. We're a few yards from the external doors, and then it's just a stroll to the landing area outside the main gates. I don't want to drag this out. Extra time won't make it any easier.

"I'll have to dumb down in a moment," Sol says. He's linked into the security cameras, which give him his all-seeing view of the site when he's in the network, and the imaging sat in Orbital 1, so he can keep an eye on APS's aircraft carrier as well. "APDU personnel outside, on our route."

Sol is an AMAI, an Autonomous *Moral* Artificial Intelligence, but the M won't cut any ice with APS. Nobody wants another rogue AI like Earthmother. As the exterior doors open, scented humid air rushes in like someone's just taken a shower. I can hear helicopters

— not ours — and that means the APS technicians have arrived from the aircraft carrier *Temujin* to start their shift, and one of those helicopters will be Tev's ride. When I round the corner of the next building, I've got line of sight with the landing area, and it's light enough now for me to see two tilt rotors in APDU livery.

This is it, then.

Solomon trots beside me, looking as unremarkable as he can while we pass a group of very young, very new Asia-Pacific Defence Union troops. They're wearing a mix of Korean and Australian uniforms, some of the white lads in Korean rig and the Asian guys in Aussie greens, all with the extra APDU badges. They're well turned out, all pressed and polished, but they've got a mix of firearms that's revealing. The Korean lads have fairly modern but basic Plat rifles, but the Aussies are carrying ASP 65s. Those things were overdue for replacement when I was in basic training. They'll still make a nasty hole in you, but they're antiques. This is what I mean when I say APS is threadbare.

The APDU troops really are kids, though.

They can't be more than eighteen or nineteen, conscripts engrossed in their pocket screens like any youngster. They're probably talking to their families and reassuring them that we haven't descended into cannibalism yet. This is our occupying army. It doesn't look like they've noticed me or heard Sol grinding along. That could get them killed one day.

I'm a couple of yards away. "*Gentlemen*," I bark. "Screens *off.*"

And they obey before they've even turned to look at me. They shove their screens in their pockets and stand there looking startled and sheepish. I've got the voice, you see, the sergeant's authority that makes dogs sit and young Toms snap to attention. These kids are the same age as Greg. That wouldn't stop me dropping them if anything kicked off, but I don't want their mums to get the call every parent dreads.

While I'm keeping an eye out for Tev, I see Dr Annis Kim hanging around the gates. She's an APS spy. She's not even hiding it now. The more I think about the last couple of weeks — and I've thought about it a lot — the more I suspect she set us up and the die-back breach wasn't an accident, no matter how chummy she is with us.

But I've also spotted a stocky Asian guy in his forties having a smoke on the far side of one of the tilts, watching the technicians dispersing, and he's a *lot* more interesting.

We recognise our own, you see. The dark blue zipper jacket and plain tan pants might as well be a full dress uniform. He's like me. He's an operator. He watches me back, probably thinking the same thing, sending me the silent message that he's got my number, but it's discreet enough not to look like he wants to slug it out just yet.

Noted. I've got your number as well, mate. Any time.

Now Kim's seen me coming. She intercepts me at the security gates. "Tev should be in Suva by tomorrow evening," she says, with that cocky smile that's starting to piss me off. "I've got a line set up if you want to talk to him when he lands."

"Thank you." I always try to be polite. When I work out what she's done and how she did it, I might not be. "But if your lot don't treat him well, remember I'm still here, you're still here, and I do a textbook double tap."

That was polite enough. She gets the point. I keep walking and stand at a safe distance from the rotor blades. Sol doesn't ask why I'm being a bit off with Kim. A couple of minutes later, Tev appears with his rucksack, and dumps it on the ground to straighten his collar as if he's just put his shirt on, which he probably has — he'll have been through decontamination before they'll let him board the tilt. Sol walks away to give us a moment.

"There's always Fiji," Tev says. "It's not too late to change your mind."

"They've already got enough rugby players." The tilt pilot ambles across to the ramp, folding and unfolding his arms. "Look, I know I pushed you to do this, but are you sure? They won't be able to resist shaking you down for intel."

Tev does his big unworried grin. "We've been through all that. They think I'm just the big dumb security guard from the embassy and you got me out of DC because I was ex-Army too. You were right. I've got to see my kids. Whatever happens after that doesn't matter."

Tev's unbreakable, but I don't want some APS tosser to test that. The pilot's looking more fidgety. "You better get going, mate. Your chauffeur's restless."

Automatically, I go to shake Tev's hand, but I stop myself. He gestures awkwardly. We can't touch or they'll make him go through decon again. I'm not one of life's huggers and backslappers, but I feel cheated out of a proper goodbye. Tev folds his arms.

"Don't give in to it, okay?" He never specifies what *it* is. We both know. "It'll all be healed one day. God speed. It's been an honour to serve with you."

"The honour's all mine, mate. Now go make it up with Becky and be happy."

It's not like we've been lifelong mates, but we've served a few years together, and as the world shrinks, these are the things that grow to fill it. We just turn and go our separate ways, and I head for the gate without looking back. Solomon follows. We're a few yards from the sentry hut when the tilt lifts off in a roaring downwash and I can finally turn and watch Tev go.

"I know it hurts," Sol says.

"Yeah."

"I never said a proper farewell to Tad Bednarz. I know he was very old, but it was so sudden. There are things I should have said. I regret leaving it too late."

I don't know if it's my imagination, but Sol seems to spill his digital guts more often lately. "Nobody ever feels they've said all they had to or that they said the right things, Sol. There was probably nothing more you two actually needed to say. He created you. You spent a lifetime together."

"That's comforting. Thank you." Sol stops talking when we get within earshot of the APDU kids again, but they can't hear him anyway. His audio's going direct to my earpiece. "Marc, I want you to understand you have a destiny. I don't know if it can ever make you happy, but you're at a pivotal point in human history. What you've done, what you're going to do, will forge the future for mankind. It's no small thing."

Destiny. I'm way too old for galvanising pep talks. But Solomon means it. This is *his* destiny. Nomad is his reason for existing, we're his purpose, and nothing short of destruction will divert him from his objective. Bednarz built him to identify the best qualities of humanity and pick the people he thought were worth saving. Sol knows why he was put on this earth. I envy the bugger.

"I just turned up here, Sol. Random chance. But thanks for the vote of confidence."

He carries on in silence until we reach the main entrance doors with the big red letter A on the glass. These old quadrubots have a weird stalking gait like a cheetah, and it makes them look even more sinister than their eyeless heads. Sol holds his completely steady as if it's on a gimbal.

"Everything you decided and did led you here," he says. "Your choices were shaped by the best qualities of humanity."

"Thanks, but I'm still not lending you any money."

I've never been sure if Sol can laugh, but he does make a little *hah* noise. "Tim Pham still hasn't asked to debrief you, I take it."

"You'd know before I did." An APS commissioner coming all this way from Seoul to personally supervise a mission is unheard of. He's interrogating anyone who looks vaguely useful. "Is Kim really his bit on the side?"

"*Was*. I don't think the relationship has continued, if I've understood you correctly."

"You have."

"Do you still think she was behind the die-back breach?"

"Yeah. Probably."

Maybe everyone else is right and it doesn't matter when a spy does what spies are paid to do, because we'll go our separate ways in a couple of months. Kim doesn't seem to have told her ex what we've really been up to, but she's still got time to shoot her mouth off. She knows what'll happen if she does, though, and I'll be the one to do it.

The hardest lesson a boy ever learns is that women aren't all nice and kind and protective like his mum. We're raised and conditioned to be nice to girls. They say one of the blokes tasked with shutting down Earthmother — and she put up quite a fight — hesitated a few seconds too long because she spoke to him in that lovely motherly voice. He didn't make it.

Women will kill you the same as a man, given the chance. Don't be fooled. Don't be a gentleman. Get your shot in first, like me, like you'd do if you were facing a bloke, and live to fight another day.

Isn't that right, princess? I don't have the play-nice reflex. You weren't my first. And you won't be the last.

01

Owing to the unexpected developments in local conditions, all activity off-site is suspended until further notice. Personnel will remain within the Nomad Base perimeter. Normal operations will be resumed when security teams have assessed the situation and we understand the nature and intentions of our new-found neighbours.

Order to all Nomad personnel from
Captain Bridget Ingram, Commanding Officer *Cabot*,
following first contact with aliens on Opis.

FIVE MILES OUTSIDE NOMAD BASE, OPIS: EIGHT DAYS AFTER CONTACT LOST WITH EARTH.

"We make talk in the now working, Chief Jeff. Not worry. We still can do." Fred jerked his head back to stare into the sky as if he was reminiscing about past glories, his crest of black feathers lifting in the breeze. "You tell, we make happen."

Jeff Aiken held up his receiver to search for a relay signal the same way he'd checked several times each day since Erskine had pulled the plug, just in case the impossible had happened and the link had been restored. But the display was still flatlined. Fred looked over his shoulder and peered at the small screen. The alien was still offering to get the link working, and Jeff was still trying to work out if and when it was safe to tell him where Earth was. It was a slow, cautious process.

"Not there again, Chief Jeff," Fred said.

"Yeah, just making sure."

Maybe it didn't matter why Earth had cut the FTL comms link, the *talk in the now* that Fred seemed to think he could fix. It hadn't existed when *Cabot* launched, and whatever crisis had made Ainatio pull the plug wouldn't catch up with Nomad Base for decades. Jeff Aiken tried to see the link for what it was: a short-lived novelty whose main use had been to tell the crew that they'd slept through forty-five years of plagues, wars, and famines that had turned the already shaky Western world into a B-movie apocalypse, and that Ainatio had also claimed *Cabot* had been lost with all hands.

That was the part that troubled him most, and not just because it was weirdly distressing to be declared dead.

Nobody else knew they were here, and he couldn't tell the company that Opis was already inhabited. He wondered what would happen if and when the news leaked. Maybe he'd never find out. He'd be in his eighties by the time a follow-up ship arrived, and if the unknown emergency that had made Ainatio cut the comms had scuppered those missions, then the ship's company here would be mankind's sole presence on Opis. Whatever happened, he'd be too dead by then to care. But the thought of this small community being the sum total of the Nomad project really bothered him. He'd counted on it being the vanguard of something big, something historic.

With Fred's help, it could still be that, though. Ingram had told Jeff to confirm what Fred was claiming, and the clock was ticking. More direct questions had to be asked.

"Fred, let me get this straight," Jeff said. "Faster than light. Instant comms. Talk in the now. You've definitely got technology that can do that? And it works for ships too? You go to other planets a lot faster than us?" It was hard to tell how much English the alien could understand, but he was picking it up at a frightening rate. "This is real, yeah? Will happen?"

Fred cocked his head, then shook his wings at his sides, looking like a gunslinger getting ready to draw. Sometimes he reminded Jeff of a cormorant, then a crow, but then he'd move on all fours and look more like a pterosaur, or even a theropod. All that time spent making model dinosaurs as a kid hadn't entirely gone to waste.

"Yes, yes, I *tell* you," Fred said. "Not understand?"

"I'm just making sure I have." Jeff tapped his ear, trying to indicate that he'd lost something in translation. "Do you build ships, or design them?"

Fred stared at him, head slightly turned. "Design is build. Not big metal. Numbers and small metal. You build *big* metal."

"Okay. I understand."

Actually, Jeff didn't. He looked across the empty plain of red-veined grass bent into waves by the wind and realised he'd never seen anywhere so unmarked by civilisation except the open sea. Spaceflight required big industry, and industry needed cities and infrastructure, but Jeff hadn't seen so much as a dirt road. Nobody had. Autonomous satellites had surveyed Opis for years before *Cabot*'s arrival without finding any trace of buildings or artefacts. They couldn't have overlooked a spacefaring civilisation, but they had, and that meant Fred's people did whatever they claimed they could do with a system nothing like Earth's.

Or he was lying, of course.

But they're here. Real aliens. And I'm not trained for this.

Nobody was. Jeff was doing his best to communicate with gestures and images on his pocket screen. If he gave Fred the device, the crow could probably work it out and teach himself more English, but there was a lot of data on it that needed to be redacted first. Fred might be a potential enemy who could make use of insignificant details. Intelligent creatures who could build FTL drives could probably also make advanced weapons, and maybe they even ate soft, meaty mammals like humans. Nobody knew enough about Fred's species to rule that out yet.

It was time for another language session. Jeff pointed at the sun as it moved behind rain clouds that the met sat had forecast. "We call that Pascoe's Star. And this world is Opis. *Oh-pis*. What do you call it?"

"Numbers."

"Ah. Coordinates? No name? Just where to find it?"

Fred cocked his head. "Your ship hide?" It was hard to tell if he didn't understand the question or if he was changing the subject. "Need to hide."

Maybe the crows couldn't detect *Cabot* in orbit. Perhaps Fred thought she could land. That raised more questions about their technology. "No, she's orbiting," Jeff said, making a slow spinning gesture with his hand. He pointed to the sky. "She stays up there."

"Hide is best." Fred said. "Maybe show you how first. Then get talk working. Friends, yes?"

"Yes. We're friends."

Jeff tried to imagine how Earth's governments would have reacted if Fred's species had arrived in orbit unannounced. He doubted they'd be this relaxed. Unless that was Fred's way of surrendering, he wasn't acting like *Cabot* had invaded. Jeff decided there was too much he didn't know and needed to find out fast before he got himself into deep shit. He had to understand Fred a lot better. There was only one quick way he could make that happen.

"Fred, I'm going to talk to my boss. *Ma'am Ingram Bridget.*" That was what Fred called the captain. "I'll see if we can get you a language course. Learn to speak like me. Because I can't speak like you."

"Yes, yes, yes," Fred said. "Say *Hredt.*"

That was his name, or at least what it sounded like to Jeff. Fred now knew humans couldn't pronounce the clicks and gutturals. It was turning into a bit of a game for him.

"*Kret,*" Jeff said, doing his best.

Fred made a whoop-whoop noise almost like a police siren, followed by a good approximation of a human laugh. "Yes, *Fred* better. You go now?"

"I go. Got to see Ma'am Ingram Bridget. See you later."

"Day to come," Fred said, swaggering away, very crow-like. "I come to flags again. I find you. Bye. Bye bye."

Bye bye. He would have been cute if he hadn't been so big and didn't have a beak that looked designed to disembowel. Jeff wanted to watch to see where he went, but Fred started that short, loping run, took off, and half-glided, half-flapped just above the ground into some trees. Then he was gone. He was probably exercising the same caution that Jeff was, not giving away his position before he was certain that he was dealing with a friendly force. There had to be some kind of crow camp nearby. Jeff wondered whether to send up a drone, but Fred might see that as a breach of trust, and if the sats hadn't spotted anything then a drone might not either.

So Fred referred to the base as *flags.* The crows were fascinated by the flagpoles outside the main building, each flying a different flag brought from Earth by a member of the multinational crew. He couldn't tell yet if the crows thought it was weird or if it resembled something in their own culture. That was another item to add to the growing list of questions to ask later.

So how many of them are there? Where do they live? What do they eat? And if they're that advanced, why aren't they wearing pants?

The sooner he helped Fred learn, the sooner he'd have answers. He picked up his radio and tried Ingram's secure channel.

"Aiken to CO."

"Go ahead, Chief."

"I'm on my way back, ma'am."

"I'll be in my office. Anyone else need to hear this?"

"Probably best to decide that after I brief you, ma'am."

"Understood."

Jeff drove back across open country with the roof down, letting the first drops of rain splash his face. The landscape looked almost Earthlike as long as he squinted it into defocus and let the undulating surface pass him. If he studied it too closely, the trees resolved into oversized celery, and the branches on the bushes became long, lumpy strips more like seaweed than fibrous branches with separate leaves. For a moment he wondered if Ainatio had terraformed a barren planet from scratch and lied about that as well, but it wasn't possible in the timescale even if they'd had the technology, and he could see the difference between the native vegetation and the modified terrestrial plants that the bots had been growing for years. He was just looking at convergence. Similar environments forced life to find similar solutions.

And I volunteered without knowing any of this. Sight unseen. No images. No bloody idea what was here. The scientists trusted the spectrography and we trusted them.

Sod trust. The bastards all lied anyway.

Jeff tried to recall why he'd signed on. He told himself he'd left for all the reasons men had always embarked on dangerous voyages to uncharted places: compulsive curiosity, testosterone, and the hardwired human instinct to wander in search of something better. But he knew how memories got polished thin by time. He remembered the suffocating sense of being under siege from the broken world beyond the British coastline, and that he had no family, no investment in the future to keep him on Earth. He'd abandoned ship. He wasn't proud of that. Logic told him he was risking the absolute unknown to provide a refuge for future generations, undoubtedly doing his duty, but part of him felt he should have had the balls to stand on the proverbial burning deck until the ship went down, whenever that turned out to be. That was pointless, of course. But he knew he'd have liked himself better for doing it.

It was way too late for regrets. He focused on the immediate issues, which were evading Nina Curtis, who would pounce and try to interrogate him, and relaying Fred's comments to Ingram, with sufficient disclaimers about its accuracy to avoid getting it in the neck if Fred turned out to be a wrong 'un.

Crows. Crows with FTL. And possibly weapons we can't imagine. But no clothes. I really should be more gobsmacked by all this. Maybe I would be, if I could stand back from it and tell someone who'd never seen it.

Between the security cameras and the tracked radios, there was no way to slip back into the base unnoticed. That was the price of safety in a world where the only backup in a forty-light-year radius was his own team. Keeping tabs on everyone's location was essential. The print-assembled buildings, constructed by bots before *Cabot's* arrival, were huddled together facing each other so that everyone could keep an eye on the place, so skirting around the crop tunnels wasn't going to help Jeff sneak in. He wondered how long it would be before the scrutiny started pissing people off.

Without stealth, then, he could only rely on speed. A flatbed bot laden with transparent plant domes paused to let him pass, and he reached the doors to the main building unmolested. But Nina was lurking in the lobby, not even trying to look as if she'd run into him by accident. It didn't take a mind reader to work out that he'd have to report to Ingram when he got back.

"So did you see the corviforms?" Nina was all sharp angles and had a tendency to pounce, a very spiderish woman. "Are you making progress?"

"Is that what we're calling them? Corviforms?"

"Well, crow seems to be the most common name people use. Although from what I could see, they're built more like microraptors."

"Or pterosaurs. Or theropods. Or hoatzins." Jeff had done his homework and wanted Nina to realise that. "We'll work out what they call themselves and use that."

"So... any progress?"

"Slow. Pictures and gestures."

"We could help, you know."

"You're a food biologist."

"I'm an *astrobiologist*. And as it's entirely possible for alien life to be somewhere between plant and animal, or neither, I cover both. Okay, more plants than animals, but I've got a point."

"Fred's not an animal, and he's got an *opinion*."

"*Fred.*"

"You know it's the closest I can get to pronouncing his name."

"Ah, come on, Chief. You're the only one Ingram's allowed outside."

"We need to do this at his speed."

"Okay." Nina backed off and held up her hands. "No rush."

"Look, we've just need to know what we're dealing with. The crows might have an armada with laser cannon on standby. When

Ingram's satisfied it's safe, we'll all have plenty of chance to talk to them."

"But she sent *you*."

Jeff wasn't sure if Nina was asking why he was chosen as the liaison, or if she was surprised that an ignorant matelot had been given such a key task.

"I'm expendable," he said, trying not to think the worst of her. She always seemed friendly and enthusiastic. "But you're not. You're in charge of food research, and food comes first. Once we get things sorted out, I bet Fred would love to show you the local crops."

He could have brushed her aside. She was a civilian, and while everyone wearing a uniform here was technically a civvie too, they'd recreated a military structure with ranks, customs, responsibilities, and chains of command. It wasn't just for comforting familiarity. It was because it *worked*. But Jeff knew how fast fault lines formed in small groups, and they were a long way from home. It was like the confined world of a ship at sea. The last thing they needed was some pointless feud and nowhere to go to get away from it.

"Okay, that'll be really useful," Nina said.

She walked away, apparently satisfied. Jeff made his way through the maze of compartments that formed the main building and tapped on Ingram's open office door.

"Ma'am?"

"Come in, Chief."

He found her staring at the video wall. She'd routed all the satellite feeds and security cams to the display, giving the small, anonymously beige and grey room the feel of *Cabot*'s bridge. She'd finally hung photos on the wall next to her desk, too, not the family snaps that Jeff would have expected back on Earth, but her ancestors in naval uniform: her late father, grandfather, grandmother, and some older pictures even he hadn't seen before, all admirals or captains. Nobody ever asked Ingram why she'd joined the Royal Navy. It was simply what the Ingram family did.

Ingram turned her chair around. "So how far did you get with Fred today?"

"He still says he can help with FTL comms and either portals or drives. It's hard to work that out at the moment."

"Very cryptic."

"I don't want to make a tit of myself, ma'am. I might have misunderstood him."

"About what?"

"He seems to think it's a good idea to hide *Cabot*."

"Did he specify how?"

"No, but the hiding thing might explain why we can't see any industrial-level civilisation."

"Did he tell you why he wants to hide the ship?"

"No. Maybe he's just using the wrong word."

"If you thought that, Chief, you wouldn't look worried."

"I'd like to give him a language course to make sure we understand each other before we get too excited."

Jeff paused to let his request sink in. Ingram always seemed like a well-meaning lady of the manor, the horsey sort who let the Labradors pad mud all over the antique rugs and ran the annual village fete with a committee of ruddy-cheeked, loudly cheerful, well-bred women just like herself. And she was all that. But he'd been on *Suffolk*'s bridge when she'd shelled Calais to brick dust with the same breezy sense of purpose. Jeff often wondered why Lewis Erskine had recruited her. Her crew knew what she was made of, but Jeff had never expected a civilian to recognise it.

"Chief, if Fred means what he says, it's one of those two-edged swords," she said at last. "Technology beyond our dreams and all that, but a lot of worrying implications."

Jeff tapped the screen in his pocket. "I took the liberty of drawing up a list of those, ma'am. It's quite long."

"I knew you would, and that it would be."

"We don't know where they live, we don't know if they have weapons as advanced as their propulsion systems, we don't know what — or who — they eat, we don't know why they want to help us, and we don't know if there's anyone else out here."

Ingram got that action stations look that he'd seen before, usually when something appeared on the lidar that she felt the need to sink. "Yes, it does loosen the sphincters."

"Maybe they have a good reason to hide, or maybe they're just weird minimalists," Jeff said. "They don't seem to wear clothes, either. But let's assume the worst."

"It rarely disappoints."

"What do you want me to do now, ma'am? Nina ambushed me as soon as I got back. We can't keep this quiet forever."

"Meeting for the senior staff in thirty minutes, and then we'll work out who else we need to tell and when. No point in setting hares running prematurely." Ingram picked up her screen and started tapping out messages. "But yes, give Fred a spare screen and load a child's encyclopaedia and an English teaching module. Heavily redacted, mind you. Remove all the astronomy stuff. It's a shame Solomon isn't around, you know. He'd have been the ideal instructor for Fred."

"Will do."

"And it makes me wonder why they're so good at languages."

"They make less sense the more I know about them, ma'am. But they're aliens. Very sociable, but *aliens*."

"Yes, sociable doesn't always equal benign." Ingram put her screen down again. "So our priority is the security assessment. Do we actually *need* to contact Earth again? The facility was due to go offline within a year anyway. Erskine said everyone was shipping out. So perhaps we don't need to tell Fred where Earth is at all."

"Ma'am, she told you she was cutting the FTL link because there was a security problem and they'd lost Solomon, whatever the hell that means. Whether we've got a few decades' grace before the dwang hits the fan or not, that's serious enough for us to want an explanation."

Ingram nodded to herself, her gaze drifting out of the window again. "It might bite us in the arse even sooner than that. An enemy taking control of the link and instantly uploading malware, for example. Okay, add it to the worry list and we'll thrash it out in the meeting."

The comms link had the potential to be an open door for threats both to Nomad and Earth. The base could function without it, but the technology still existed out there somewhere, and that meant someone else could seize it and exploit it. The forty-five-year transit buffer seemed a lot less reassuring.

"At the very least, we need to know if the follow-up mission's actually under way," Ingram said, reaching across to adjust one of her photos a fraction. "Because if it isn't, the future's going to place a very different burden on us, isn't it?"

Nobody selected for *Cabot* had family ties. It was a condition of recruitment that they had nobody close to leave behind, and whatever relationships developed spontaneously in the years while they waited for the first wave of colonists, they were never really meant to be settlers. Jeff had come to terms with the state of limbo. He wasn't expecting a normal family future but he wasn't ruling one out, yet either way they'd all sacrificed what most people took for granted: living out their years surrounded by family. He was thirty-eight by the stopped-clock reckoning of people who'd been in cryo for decades. That wasn't too late to start, but it also made him understand that he wasn't going home again, ever. It had taken the last few days to give an emotional bite to what he'd known since the day he signed on.

"Yes, ma'am," he said. "It certainly will."

* * *

CEO'S SUITE, AINATIO PARK RESEARCH CENTRE, NEAR KILL LINE:
APS DEBRIEFING OF MAJOR DANIEL TRINDER, COMMANDING OFFICER,
SECURITY DETACHMENT, 1050 HOURS.

"*Kill Line*," Tim Pham said. "What a lovely name for a town, Major Trinder."

Dan Trinder repeated local history like a mantra. It was the safest option. "It used to be the site of the vehicle checkpoint. The security perimeter was further out in those days. We're talking about seventy years ago, maybe. But you can still see the old warning sign on the road."

"I did." Pham nodded with a tight smile. "Makes a refreshing change from *Hicksville Welcomes Careful Drivers*."

"It's fair to say we never got many visitors."

The fact that Pham was conducting the debriefs personally told Trinder all he needed to know about their significance. This man wasn't some low-ranking APS pen-pusher. He was its science and technology commissioner, near the top of the Asian-Pacific political tree, and Kill Line was a long trip to make from Seoul. Dr Kim said he'd been a career intelligence officer, a field agent — an actual hands-on APS spy — so that probably meant he still was. Sitting back in Georgina Erskine's big black leather chair in his expensive suit, Pham looked like he'd taken over. His Australian accent made him sound relaxed and friendly, but Trinder suspected that a guy around the forty mark who'd already climbed that high up not one but two greasy poles wasn't anyone's friend.

It was just as well that Solomon was a built-in eavesdropper and provided transcripts of the debriefs for everyone to sync their stories.

As a spook, Pham should have expected surveillance. But maybe this was a case of both sides knowing the score and simply going through with the charade. APS wasn't even a proper enemy, more an estranged associate, and even APDU's nuclear strikes in previous years hadn't been genuine attacks. Trinder wondered if history would record they'd used sodium devices on American soil simply because they'd been asked to, a desperate appeal by a collapsing US government unable to incinerate millions of acres of vegetation to stop the die-back virus. Facts didn't survive time and mythology. Centuries from now, if mankind held out that long, nobody would understand how far people had to go to survive.

"So, Major," Pham went on. "Bit of a shocker to find out *Cabot* hadn't been lost and had actually reached Opis, I'll bet."

"Yes, Director Erskine had to explain it to me a couple of times." Trinder had finally perfected the art of not quite answering the question put to him, considerable progress in kicking over the traces of lifelong straight arrowhood. An earnest but slightly dumb performance seemed the safest bet. "I wasn't even born when the mission launched."

"How did you feel about it?"

"I wasn't happy that Erskine never told the staff what they were really working on. Maybe the security risks were different forty-odd years ago, though."

Pham raised an eyebrow. "*The staff.* Not *us?*"

"The security detachment's always been separate from the rest of the workforce," Trinder said. "It's the nature of the job."

"And you turned down the chance to ship out on Erskine's vessel. *Elcano.*"

"I gave my people the option of leaving, but they all decided to stay at their posts."

Pham did an awkward nod, rocking his head a little. Maybe he thought Trinder was trying to shame him with tales of heroics and it embarrassed him. "Why did *you* stay, though?"

"Because you can't save yourself while you leave people to die."

"Duty, then, Major. Conscience."

"Just my job."

"So what did Erskine say that made you refuse her orders?"

It was time for Trinder to look suitably awkward at accusations of mutiny. "Dr Kim's obviously told you what happened."

"She has. But I'd prefer to hear your version of it."

All Trinder wanted to do was to get out of the interview without dropping the mission in the shit. He couldn't tell Pham he'd refused Erskine's order to destroy Solomon. That would reveal the AI was both a lot more sophisticated than APS realised and also that he had a potential vulnerability. Solomon had to be protected. He was the core of Nomad, the overseer of the remote engineering bots, the keeper of confidential data, and the ethical backbone of the project. On a more urgent level, without him managing repairs at the dock orbiting Earth, *Shackleton* wasn't going anywhere, or at least not very far and not in one piece.

And Erskine was on her way out of the Solar System now, chilled in a container like a grocery store chicken. She wasn't going to contradict Trinder's story.

"The Director didn't want to let the townsfolk and the refugees into the facility," Trinder said. Well, that wasn't a lie, just one of the other grounds for his mutiny. "She was afraid they'd rush the shuttle when they realised they weren't leaving. But we couldn't evacuate them before your deadline, so I overrode her and set up an underground shelter and let everyone in. It wasn't kangaroo courts and firing squads, Commissioner. Just folks having hissy fits."

"So you're actually in command here now."

Trinder decided that was a trick question of the have-you-stopped-beating-your-wife variety. "Command's an odd way of describing it," he said carefully. "What we have here is responsibility for the safety of staff, plus residents in a three-mile radius. You can read it for yourself in the facility's emergency plan. I share that responsibility with Chris Montello and Marc Gallagher. They've both got plenty of experience in evacuating civilians. Alex Gorko's now the acting director. He's still the liaison for anything concerning the company."

Pham shifted a little. The leather chair creaked. "Are you satisfied with the security situation here?"

"Yours or ours?"

"I note you've got surveillance drones deployed around the clock. But you're in the middle of nowhere."

According to Solomon's transcripts, Pham had already asked Alex Gorko about that. "We've had some incursions by armed gangs," Trinder said. "The vets from the transit camp cover security patrols. It's a big perimeter. They need drones."

"Yet you've disabled all the automatic locks throughout the campus, Major. Seems very trusting to leave your doors open. You do control the lockdown system, don't you?"

"I do," Trinder said. So much for playing the unimaginative security grunt. He was on Pham's radar after all. "And as Erskine took or destroyed all the sensitive data, and we have a lot of people around now who aren't chipped to open doors, I thought it would make life easier if I just disabled the system. We're being very cooperative, Commissioner."

Pham stared at him for a second too long. Trinder wasn't being questioned just to cross-check the debriefs. He'd stepped up when things started falling apart, so Pham was probably assessing how much trouble he'd be if things got less cordial.

"So you're going to Opis." Pham changed tack, but it was clear the security angle hadn't been resolved to his satisfaction. He fiddled with the handset gathering dust on Erskine's desk, then looked over his shoulder as he realised he'd activated the cinema-sized wall display behind him. The screen that had once been a live feed from Opis now just showed a menu for what was left of the facility's network. "I see Erskine liked her movies."

Trinder played it straight. "That was her FTL comms terminal before she trashed the link."

"I know," Pham said. "She did a thorough job of asset denial, I'll give her that."

"Yeah, she left us with a lot of gaps to plug." Trinder shrugged, aiming to look like he was putting a brave face on the betrayal. "As long as we can keep the AIs running to prep *Shackleton*, though, we'll get by."

"Let me see if I've got this right, Major. Erskine's father took over the company when Tad Bednarz died, and when he was diagnosed with a terminal illness, he handed it to her. Yes?"

"That's what I've been told."

"You do realise you might not make it to Opis, don't you? Sorry, I know you military guys don't do pessimism."

"Nothing's guaranteed in life, Commissioner. We'll give it our best shot."

"Face it, *Shackleton*'s a junk-heap," Pham said. "And you don't know what'll be waiting for you at the other end in forty-five years."

Trinder almost asked him where the hell he expected them to go if APS didn't want to take all the refugees, but that would have made the encounter into a pointless argument.

"They probably said the same when the First Fleet set out for Australia," he said. "But you guys haven't done too badly."

"So what's Opis like?" Pham asked. "We couldn't find a single image in your system. No data *at all*." Now it was clear where he was going with this. "It has to exist. Did Erskine wipe that too?"

"Like you said, she's thorough." *So's Sol. He's wiped everything she didn't. Tough shit.* "But at least someone copied the FTL documents for you before she got to them."

"Must be easier to ring-fence files if you've had to keep the project hidden from the staff for so long."

"Yes. I suppose it is."

"Well? Did she show you anything at all? It's a big trip to take on faith, Major."

Trinder floundered for a moment, hoping that it looked like embarrassment at misplaced trust in Erskine rather than taking a second to work out how big a lie he could get away with. Everyone — staff, Kill Liners, Chris Montello's transit camp — had seen the damn video or the live feeds. It was impossible to coach sixteen hundred people to keep their stories straight. Trinder smokescreened with some truth.

"We saw live footage once, and a video," he said, suddenly wondering if Pham thought the FTL data was bogus, a trick to buy time, and that they'd never had instant comms at all. "It looked a lot like Earth. Vegetation, oceans, mountains. Are you asking if this is another company con trick? I have to assume it was genuine."

"Are you confident that it is?"

"I'm not confident that staying on Earth would be a better option, even if we had somewhere to go. Can I ask you a question?"

"Go ahead, Major."

"If you'd carried out the bombing knowing people were stuck in the blast zone, how would you have squared that with your conscience?"

Pham didn't blink, but he did pause a beat. "The fallout from sodium weapons has a very short life. We were pretty sure you'd survive."

"We were pretty sure we wouldn't."

Pham looked at him for a moment, a couple of beats of silent scrutiny. "While we're on the topic of moral mazes, then, let me ask you this." He dodged questions with practised ease. Trinder couldn't hope to pin down a spy turned politician. The guy was engineered for evasiveness. "If your ship doesn't blow up or drift off course, you'll be only two or three months behind *Elcano*, heading for the same place. You'll have fifteen, sixteen hundred disgruntled people who think Erskine left them to die. What are you going to do when you catch up with her and her chosen few?"

That was a question worth asking. Even if people had calmed down since the bombing was called off, nobody was going to forget they were deemed surplus to requirements. It was the kind of event that created rifts that never healed.

"I'll cross that bridge when I get to it," Trinder said. "As you say, Commissioner, we don't know what'll be waiting for us at the other end."

There was a time when Trinder would have said that with earnest naivety, but over the last few months he'd been overtaken by a combative side he hadn't realised he had. It had started the moment he'd looked for a way to bend the regulations to defy Erskine without feeling he'd abandoned military discipline.

Pham changed tack again, this time to casual affability. He tossed Erskine's handset in the air like he was flipping a coin and smiled convincingly. "Okay, safe journey, then. It's a brave effort. I don't envy you, so let's hope those images were real. Good day, Major."

The debrief was over, at least for the time being. Trinder picked up his cap and escaped into the corridor to take a deep breath of air that seemed cooler than the office. He waited until he was clear of the management wing and outside in the grounds before he risked speaking.

"Okay, Sol, how did I do? He's marked my card. He thinks I'm trouble."

"But you are, Major," Solomon said in his earpiece. "Even so, it went well, I think. Well played."

"Those transcripts were a life-saver. Thanks."

"Nicely sown doubt about Opis, too, if I might say so."

"Sol, you heard him. Why isn't he muscling in on Nomad? It doesn't make sense. A ready-made base on a habitable planet. Not some paperwork that might or might not give them a working FTL drive one day."

"May I be cynical for a moment?"

"Yeah, join the club. We welcome new members."

"If none of you survives the journey, APS can take over Opis any time."

"As in if we're just unlucky, or as in Pham makes sure nobody survives?"

"I meant unlucky," Solomon said. "I understand they believe they stand a good chance of developing an FTL drive before we reach Opis, and then they can overtake us at a convenient time. Anyway, Dr Kim said they had other candidate planets, remember? A superluminal drive gives them the entire galaxy, in theory at least."

"I still think they're going to stiff us," Trinder said. "I'm not giving up the contingency plan just yet."

"Very wise, Major. The other possibility, of course, is that they don't have the capacity for an opposed landing on another planet. Let's not confuse conventional assets like aircraft carriers with broader technical superiority. We've had so little information on APS for so long that we may well have imagined a juggernaut that doesn't exist."

"But you hacked in to some APS networks to check out Kim's identity," Trinder said. "You must have a feel for what kind of shape things are in."

"And I didn't find the most relevant information, that she was an APS agent, did I? Only the publicly available facts about her day job from media reports. If I'd tried to get further into their systems, I'd have exposed myself and this facility. We've never risked looking too hard at APS because the need wasn't urgent until the last week or so."

Trinder was thirty-eight, old enough to remember when information was everywhere at the touch of a screen, not always reassuring stuff for a kid, but at least he had a sense of what was going on in a wider world that didn't begin and end at the Kill Line boundary. He stopped to sit down on one of the concrete bollards at the entrance to the admin block's parking lot and watched the APS technicians suiting up to do something in the disused plant biology building. He could see the mobile decontamination unit in the gap between the medical centre and the lab, a pop-up booth made of grey fabric and composite. Their equipment didn't look much different from the stuff everyone used here, and Ainatio had been cut off for years. There was a price to pay for maintaining a cordon sanitaire around a continent and relying entirely on domestic production. All those rare minerals and other imports that had been critical for manufacturing had dried up, and Korea, Japan, and Australia had already stripped China's mines. They made do with what they had, just like Kill Line had to. They just had more of it.

"If they're so strapped for resources, then, how can China keep a presence on Mars?" Trinder said. "That's still APS money and technology. Korea's got to sign off their requests."

"Major, we have no current information on Mars. The bases there were self-sufficient. Their Mars programme could be on hold or abandoned by now and we'd never know."

"Well, they've got enough resources left to send an aircraft carrier here, so that's probably all I need to know, Sol."

"*Temujin* is eleven thousand tons," Solomon said.

"I'm not up to speed with navy stuff."

"That's small."

"But I bet her armaments work."

"I'm sure they do, Major."

The commander in Trinder wanted to hear that APS was less of a danger than he'd thought, but the regular guy who'd watched his world collapse and shrink to ninety square miles of rural backwater had clung to hope that somewhere on Earth, normal life carried on, proof that the Decline had bottomed out.

"Well, whatever, I'm not going to look any further ahead than launching *Shackleton* and getting out." Trinder stood up. "I can do something about that, but I can't do anything about APS."

"If you notice any odd activity on my part, I'm mirroring the launch system in the Lammergeier's comms hub," Solomon said. "Now the link with Orbital One's been restored, I'm reluctant to rely on unimpeded access here. Especially if Marc's right and APS have special forces on the ground. Pham's naturally suspicious of us and he'll never believe he's found everything of value, even though we've given his team absolute free rein and they're rummaging everywhere. I saw two technicians playing with python bots the other day, *racing* them. They seem to find the range of obsolete bots amusing."

"It's nothing personal, Sol." Erskine had almost terminated Solomon. APS wouldn't be pleased to find an AI like him either. His fears weren't unjustified. "You're pretty well indistinguishable from a hospitality AI. It's not like they can see your higher functions."

"I know. I learned a hard lesson from the Director, Major. I won't waste it."

"Okay, I'll let you get on," Trinder said. "I'm holding you up."

"You know that's not how I function, but thank you."

It was hard not to feel that chatting to Solomon kept him from his priority tasks in *Shackleton*, even knowing that it didn't. The AI could keep any number of things under control just like Trinder's aunt could watch the TV, carry on a conversation, and knit a sweater at the same time. Damn, where had *that* come from? Trinder hadn't thought about her in years. Aunt Janine had always been a distant figure, seldom visited because she didn't get on with his dad. Trinder thought he'd come to terms with losing contact with his family when the last typhoid epidemic peaked and he still didn't know if any of them had survived. But now he was leaving Earth for good and the crises of the last week were behind him, doubt had started to gnaw. He hadn't tried hard enough to find them. He was nearly a thousand miles away in a remote outpost of a vanished America, cut off from all communication and transport, but this was his family, for God's sake. It might not have been an ideal one, but that didn't matter.

Don't be dumb. How could I have found them?

He couldn't leave to search for them, and there was no telecoms infrastructure left to make calls. If Erskine had let him go, even if he'd been okay with abandoning his duty here, he'd probably never have made it. Even hardened troops like Chris and his guys had a tough time covering a few hundred miles, let alone a couple of thousand.

It still felt like an excuse. There were people all around Trinder now who'd shown what could be done when you were motivated enough, if you *cared* enough: Annis Kim slogging halfway around the world from Korea across treacherous straits and the even more dangerous wastelands from Alaska to the East Coast, Marc and Tev making their way here through chaos from DC, Chris's convoy bringing civilian evacuees on a long march to what had seemed like a sanctuary until now. They'd all taken the risk. Trinder hadn't.

He'd have to live with it. It was too late to fix it now and he had too many people here relying on him. He went back inside and headed for the security wing.

When he opened the control room door, muffled sounds of a busy but quiet space rolled out like fog. He'd once thought he'd see out his life in this office, completing routine reports about uneventful days of training for imaginary emergencies that didn't bear any resemblance to the real one that finally turned up. Then Annis Kim arrived out of nowhere and Erskine broke the news about Nomad. It was hard to believe it was only four months ago.

Jon Simonot looked up from the 3-D overlay of the Kill Line town map on the planning table. "How'd it go, sir?"

"I think he was just going through the formalities," Trinder said. "If I'd been of any tactical importance, he'd have given me a harder time." Trinder noted Elena Fonseca and Chris studying something on a desk, their backs to him. "Anything I've missed?"

Chris turned and handed Trinder a charcoal grey carbine that he hadn't seen before. It wasn't Ainatio issue and he knew Chris's militia had nothing like that.

"Fresh off the printer," Chris said. "What do you think?"

It looked like a more compact version of the old Marquis short-barrelled rifle that had been popular with law enforcement. Trinder checked it wasn't loaded, hefted it, and tried the butt against his shoulder before walking over to the window to sight up.

"Any special reason?" Trinder asked. "We've got plenty of firearms."

"Not enough for everyone in Kill Line who doesn't already have one."

"So we're arming all of them."

"You bet. We need to be ready for anything now." Chris took the carbine back from Trinder and looked it over again as if he was admiring a work of art. "Waking up on Opis to find we've got trouble. Getting stuck here if there's a problem with the ship. Having to make a run for it because APS changes its mind and decides to nuke us sooner rather than later. Every scenario's better if everyone's carrying."

"I was thinking about the Kill Liners who don't like firearms," Trinder said.

"They'll come around."

"So it's a Marquis knock-off."

"Marc was tinkering around with the printer to see what we could do. Basic idiot-proof Marquis but scaled down a little."

Trinder always deferred to Chris. He was an experienced State Defence Force sergeant, and if anyone knew how to get civilians safely from A to B in a hostile environment it was him and his militia. Trinder's self-esteem had risen a few points since he'd found his balls and faced down Erskine to take control of the emergency, but he still felt a long way short of the testosterone level required to see himself as Chris's equal, let alone his superior. Marc Gallagher was an equally daunting benchmark to be judged by. Perhaps you only got that way by coming under fire, the kind of personal violence aimed at you and intended to kill. Trinder didn't feel he'd faced that test yet.

"This is going to mean training them," Trinder said. "But we've got time."

"Sure, and if anyone's really reluctant or dangerously useless, we won't push it," Chris said. "I'm not expecting snipers, just folks with enough confidence to get off a few bursts in the right direction."

Chris always seemed so reasonable and polite that it was hard to imagine him yelling, let alone shooting anybody. But his saintly expression could set like concrete the moment he decided someone was a threat. Trinder still struggled with the idea of him as an upmarket enforcer for some white-collar criminal, drafted into the SDF from jail because they'd run out of men. He trusted Chris with his life. He didn't care about the guy's past.

"If we get the locals with firearms experience to coach the rookies, it'll keep everybody occupied too," Trinder said. "That'll help. All the false alarms have made them jumpy."

Chris ran his hand over the knock-off Marquis's barrel as if he was feeling for defects. "This is based on Dieter's weapon. You want to ask Aaron to try it out? He must have handled one like this when he was a cop."

"Sure."

"Am I overstepping the mark?"

"No. No, not at all." Trinder held up his hands in agreement. Leadership had fallen to him, Chris, and Marc automatically, but it was still all pretty informal. "We don't need a vote on everything."

"Okay, I'll get some more printed and our guys can test them as well."

Fonseca watched, arms folded. "APS is probably going to notice the range activity when we start training. You'll be able to hear the firing from here. Are you going to warn them?"

"That'll sound like we're asking for permission," Chris said. "It might make them think we won't resist if they try to confiscate our firearms, and knowing we're cantankerous is probably all that's stopping them at the moment. Nobody sane wants to go house to house trying to seize weapons from jittery folks who already feel threatened."

It was hard to break the habit of preparing for the worst. The worst kept happening. They'd gotten very good at dealing with it. Trinder wondered if he'd ever see the world the same way again.

Fonseca raised her eyebrows like she knew better. "They just want to grab what they can and go home. Mathematical reality might have something to do with it. They've got seven rotary aircraft. We've got twenty air-to-air missiles."

"Yeah, but do they know that?" Trinder asked. "Besides, we can't leave for weeks and Seoul can probably retaliate in a day. And why are you sure they've got seven aircraft?"

"Four tilts and three regular helos," Fonseca said. "I've been logging the tail numbers and callsigns for the last couple of days. They might have ten more below deck, but they can't carry more than twenty. It's very small for a carrier."

"Am I the only one who didn't know that?" Trinder asked.

"I'm thorough," Fonseca said. "They've got forty-one troops, too. I've been checking. Plus the one Marc says is special forces."

Chris gave her a look that almost melted into a smile. "The bureaucrats and record keepers shall inherit the earth." He gestured to the door with the prototype carbine. "Okay, I'll go see Aaron and we'll start cranking these out."

Fonseca watched him go, looking coy. Trinder noted her watching. Simonot was still at his desk, so Trinder didn't comment and sat down to look at the drone feeds from the farms. In the Welbecks' maize field, a Fiddler, a crab-like cobalt blue clearance bot bigger than a shipping container, was tearing up fencing with the ease of a tailor ripping out stitches, making way for a long line of smaller bots to spray the crop.

"Remember those?" Trinder said.

Fonseca peered at the screen. "Ah, stars of a thousand disaster documentaries. I always wondered how many people they squashed when they excavated collapsed buildings. I think I'd prefer a rescue rat to find me so a nice burly firefighter could pull me out of the rubble."

"The Fiddler's very light on its feet for a big boy," Trinder said. "All six of them. Not your type?"

"I preferred the combat engineer variant. Armed. Better than the Ainatio model, too."

"You're so disloyal." Trinder frowned at the monitors. A thin layer of smoke blanketed the ground, creeping slowly forward and leaving blackened plants in its wake. "Look. They're burning crops already."

"Yeah, that's the farm they tested yesterday." Fonseca watched over his shoulder. "They came back this morning and started spraying. Seb Meikle says it's some kind of corrosive chemical. You'd need an ocean of that to make any difference, though. I can't tell if they're doing the best they can or if it's just theatre to make it look like the reason they barged in here."

"I really hoped you'd tell me we were worrying too much." Trinder repositioned one of the drones to get a better look. Three hazmat-suited technicians were leaning against the wire fencing, one of them directing the line of spraying bots with a joystick device. "I just hope we don't take our paranoia with us."

"Of course we will," Fonseca said. "It's a survival skill."

"It's still not healthy."

"Beats being dead. You want a look at the updated list of staff asking for resettlement? We've got some ditherers in there, but I think most are set on Australia or Singapore. Only a few want Korea. I think it's a language thing."

"I hope APS takes them," Trinder said. "We don't want to be saddled with folks who don't want to be there. They'll be disruptive. It'll be bad enough trying to play nice with the *Elcano* party and fit in with an established colony."

"Chin up, Dan. We've actually got somewhere to run. Nobody else has, unless you count living in a bubble on Mars with only insect protein burgers to look forward to."

"Yeah, you're right." Some people would have given their right arm to be in Trinder's place. "It's easy to forget we're making history. Or that nobody else knows about it."

"APS knows," Fonseca said.

"But APS isn't likely to tell anyone."

"And the British government probably knows, seeing as they arranged Kim's call with Tim Pham."

"If they do, they won't want to broadcast it either."

"And APS probably believes the UK knows. It'll leak. Mark my words. Still, it'll be other countries slugging it out and we'll be long gone." Fonseca loaded the list of scientists onto the planning wall so Trinder could read it. "I wonder what the *Cabot* crew are doing right now? They probably don't even know why they were cut off."

Trinder guessed that they'd be getting on with their lives, and in the coming decades, the *Shackleton* mission would just be something they told their kids about, how some new people might arrive one day when they were grown-ups with kids of their own. And then they'd forget all about it. The realisation disturbed him for a moment as he saw a white dumbell-shaped speck trillions of miles from home, an ageing spacecraft on a one-way trip, less than nothing in the scheme of the cosmos.

He wondered how Solomon would cope with forty-five years of silence with only machines for conversation. Trinder was glad he'd be asleep for the whole damn journey.

* * *

STORAGE HUT B, NOMAD BASE, OPIS: 1400 LOCAL TIME.

It had taken just days for the discovery of intelligent aliens to downgrade from a miracle to a potential security risk. Ingram allowed her inner ten-year-old a few moments to resent sensible adulthood's debasement of wonders before cracking on with the meeting.

Her nine most senior officers, perched on crates and boxes in the windowless storeroom, watched her as if they were waiting for a bollocking they felt they'd done nothing to deserve. She counted them off: Bissey, Searle, Haine, Sato, Devlin, Kokinos, Hiyashi, Filopovic, and Yeung. Jeff Aiken sat to one side on his own, looking like a witness for the prosecution. The place smelled of adhesive and the weirdly fragrant plastic wrapping that always reminded Ingram of hyacinths. It wasn't the ideal place for a meeting, but it was private, and taking over one of the other large spaces in the base would have started rumours sooner than was inevitable.

"Ladies and gentlemen, I refer you to your screens." She opened the whiteboard on her pocket screen and shared it around the room. The list of potential threats she'd drawn up with Jeff looked pessimistically long. "This might be good news, bad news, or total fiction, but Chief Petty Officer Aiken has been busy on the diplomatic front, and our large avian neighbours seem to have confirmed they have superluminal technology and will assist us in some form or other. Number one task is to make sure we've understood correctly, given the language barrier, but assuming we have, where do we go from there?"

Everyone had their heads down, reading their screens in their laps and nodding to themselves as they looked through the list Jeff had drawn up. Daisuke Hiyashi, the principal weapons officer, raised a forefinger.

"Top of my problem list is we need to conceal Earth's location until we know whether they've got weapons to match that level of technology," he said. "But they need the location to restore the link."

"Indeed." Ingram nodded. "Therein lies our dilemma. Go on."

"And if they're that far advanced, would we understand their destructive capability even if they showed it to us? None of us are theoretical physicists, and the only way to talk to one in any realistic time scale is to restore the link."

"Agreed, Dai," Ingram said. "We're stuffed. The only safe option is doing nothing, but we might miss an opportunity and come to regret it, and declining the offer might even offend them. But for all we know, we might be the weedy kids refusing to hand over our ball to the neighbourhood bully who's got his enormous mates waiting around the corner."

The hyacinth smell of the composite crates was starting to give Ingram a headache. It was her call to decide if it was worth the risk. She just wanted to know where everyone stood. There was also the possibility that they had a better idea.

"If they're that advanced, how do we know they don't already know everything because they've been monitoring us?" Jackie Devlin asked. "Perhaps that's why they're picking up English so fast. And they could just as easily be so far ahead of us that we're no threat at all. I try not to look on the bright side first, but maybe they're just trying to be kind. Like feeding squirrels in the park. Perhaps that's why they're not treating us as invaders."

Jeff stirred on his crate. "I don't think it's that at all, Commander. Fred kept saying he wants to be friends. That either means please be our allies or please don't hurt us."

"Or perhaps they're talking to us like we talk to pets."

"It didn't sound like that, ma'am. He thinks I understand every word he says."

Devlin laughed. "The test is going to be if he lets you on the furniture."

Everyone managed a chuckle. Then the conversation lapsed into silence for a while as they studied their screens again. Peter Bissey looked up.

"Have they told you what they call themselves, Chief?"

Jeff shrugged. "Not yet. Whatever it is, it'll be unpronounceable. Maybe we should call them corviforms like Nina does. It'll sound more polite than crows once they learn what that is."

"And they've only just shown up," Bissey said. "No sign of a civilisation. Is this their home planet or not? Or are they doing what we're doing? Are they an expeditionary force too? And why do they care about concealing ships?"

"We're just assuming they were here first," Jeff said.

"If two intelligent species end up on the same planet and intelligent life is rare in the universe, it's an unimaginable coincidence," Ingram said. "Or else it's not such a coincidence because there's a lot more intelligent life around than we realised."

Bissey consulted the list. "Fred told you they went to other planets, Chief?"

"Yeah, he did, sir," Jeff said. "But he didn't say if they were populated. Which brings us to number four on the list. If we couldn't see the crows, where are they hiding, and if so, why?"

Maggie Yeung chipped in. "Well, they can certainly see us. Because they turned up without being summoned. They're watching us somehow."

Ingram couldn't put the pieces together yet, but if it wasn't a simple mistake in translation or a case of the locals overselling what they could offer in exchange for something yet to be revealed, then FTL might not be something she could turn down. Humans were newcomers and they didn't have numbers on their side. If there were other species with advanced technology within visiting distance, then Nomad Base might be relying on Fred and his people to survive out here.

"Okay, let's decide how badly we need instant comms," she said.

"We have to warn the follow-up mission that things aren't what they're expecting, ma'am," Bissey said. "And we need to know why they cut the comms in the first place, even if trouble takes a long time to catch up with us."

"It's worth the risk to get Solomon back," Logan Haine said. "He's the one person from home who could get here right away if the link was restored, and also the one who'd make the most difference to our survival."

Solomon had transmitted himself back and forth to Opis via the comms relay for years, transferring his consciousness to one of the quadrubots that had been constructed here from raw materials by other bots. He knew the planet as well as anyone could. More importantly, he'd effectively run the Nomad mission. Haine was right. If there was one thing they needed now it was Solomon's input, and it was probably a gamble worth taking.

"I'm playing devil's advocate here, but if we're wrong about the corviforms, we only need to get it wrong once and it'll be endex for Earth," Ingram said. "Are we sure we want to go through with this?"

"We might not survive without it," Haine said. "And if I might be permitted some drama, we might be all that's left of humanity if things get worse back home."

Haine had used the forbidden word: home. Diplomacy and common sense said that thinking of Earth in those terms wasn't good for morale. Ingram still felt like they'd left it only a few months ago. That was one of the problems with cryo. It was like waking up hung over after a night's sleep with no real sense of how much time had elapsed. The reality was a lifetime away, and going home — no, going *back* — was out of the question. Time and the decline of Earth weren't on their side.

But if Fred really can get us a working FTL drive as well...

The risk of directing potentially hostile aliens to Earth had to be balanced against the need for people to reach Opis. Ingram didn't know if Erskine's emergency meant there were problems launching the ships or even if they'd aborted the mission. And then there was the wider issue of Earth's decline. The company was effectively gone, and so was mainland Europe and America, but one of the last things Alex Gorko had told them was the UK was surviving, quarantined against die-back and epidemics. It would only take one boat to breach that. Coastal defence had kept that at bay for years, but sooner or later, they'd run out of luck. People would need evacuation one day and Nomad would need populating beyond the relatively small group Erskine had put together. Bednarz had envisioned an influx of migrants far beyond that.

"Very well, here's what we're going to do," Ingram said. "Our immediate priority is to understand exactly what the corviforms are saying. So we're going to teach them proper English. Unless anyone here taught languages and didn't put it on their HR file, that task falls to Aiken, because Fred likes him. Then we're going to explore the FTL angle, and if it's true, we'll assess what we can safely reveal to Fred. Kokinos and Devlin — get your engineering questions ready. Sato — retask the sats and drones and see if we can spot any signs of habitation now we've got a better idea where to look. We don't even know how many Freds there are."

"We'd better find out what they eat, too," Brad Searle said. "I'd hate for us to discover the hard way that we're squirrels in more ways than one."

Ingram's mission brief had now been overtaken by developments that neither Erskine nor Bednarz could have foreseen. Her job was, as ever, to adapt to circumstances and win, and getting hold of the corviforms' FTL was too big a survival advantage to turn down. But there'd be a price. As long as it wasn't a smoking, chargrilled Earth, she'd have to be ready to pay it.

Haine nodded at Jeff. "And I need regular samples from you, Chief. Just to make sure you haven't caught some hideous alien chicken flu. It'd be nice to get a sample off Fred when he's feeling amenable, too."

"I don't think we're at the blood-drawing stage of our relationship yet, Commander, but I'll seize the opportunity if it comes," Jeff said.

"Ma'am, when do you plan to tell everyone else about this?" Bissey asked. "Fred's the main topic of conversation and that isn't going to stop any time soon. Now that we've locked down, people are going to think we've already decided the corviforms are a threat."

"We'll come clean with them when we've got something concrete to come clean with," Ingram said. "I don't want to raise hopes unnecessarily. We've gone from the top of the food chain to not knowing if we're food, let alone who else is out there. But I won't conceal it any longer than I have to. Anything else? No? Thank you. Dismissed."

She sat on her crate while they filed out. Haine hung back and gave her that trust-me-I'm-a-doctor look.

"Whatever's going through your mind, Bridgers, I probably agree with it," he said. "We don't do girly half-hearted mission creep. We do mission *stampede*."

"Subject to the aliens not having a death ray they're waiting to train on Earth when we give them the coordinates, you mean."

"We've already buggered Earth ourselves, according to Alex Gorko. And don't forget we're aliens too, by the way."

"Well, Logan? Am I buckling a bit too much swash?"

"No. FTL's too important to ignore."

"Exactly. It makes a colony here much more viable."

"This is all very Francis Drake, isn't it? We're embracing our historic naval roots. Exploring, privateering, trading, and giving the monarch's enemies a kick up the arse when they overstep the mark. I'm in."

Ingram liked that approach too. "Well, I can't wait years for Erskine to call and give me permission. We're one hundred and seventy-five soft-bodied food items with no backup on a planet that Ainatio obviously misjudged. Possibly next door to other alien civilisations with FTL, too. We have to maximise our chances."

"Who are you trying to convince?"

"Myself. I admit it. I don't know anywhere near enough about the situation, but wait and see doesn't feel like an option."

"Bridgers, all you've done is crack on with finding out. The rest is still in your head."

"Thank you, doctor. Shall I take two aspirin and call you in the morning?"

Haine chuckled. At least he seemed happy to be stuck here. He radiated peace and contentment. "Have a shot of Chateau Nomad instead. Andy Braithwaite's got a batch going."

"We're talking about his patent horse liniment, aren't we?"

"It's non-toxic, it burns, and it destroys an optimum number of brain cells. An amusing little tipple, once you regain consciousness."

"Okay, I'll try it this evening, when I haven't got as far to fall." Ingram got up and stood in the doorway, looking out on what was now a grey afternoon, but it was still pleasantly warm and worth a walk. "I'm going to take a stroll. Clear the mind. Maybe work out if anyone's watching us."

"See you later, then."

Haine headed through the compound towards the cluster of low-rise cubes that made up the infirmary and bio lab. Ingram took a discreet look around to see if anyone was going to pounce on her and ask awkward questions, then made her way across the base, trying to work out how the corviforms could monitor activity here without being detected. It wasn't a glorious day, but even the clouds were more interesting on Opis, and the warm, light rain carried a scent of vegetation unlike any on Earth — green, spicy, even fruity. The novelty hadn't worn off yet.

The unbroken flow from industrialised Earth to a base like Nomad obscured the most remarkable part of the whole project for Ingram. The outpost had been built on site by generations of self-replicating bots, mined and constructed, printed and bacteria-grown, even engineered by nanites. All the bots and machinery were descended from the tiny basic bots sent from Earth a century ago. The ones trundling around the site now were the evolution of mechanical life to the present day. Somewhere there'd be records of that in the years of footage still to examine. One day, when she had nothing more pressing to do, she might watch some of it for the amazement value.

As she crossed the open ground in front of the main building, she paused to look up at the national flags slapping the flagpoles in the breeze, and reminded herself how many of those nations no longer existed. The crew felt they did, though, and they kept them alive here. Maybe home wasn't such a dangerous word after all.

Heading west, on the path that machines had worn on their trips to mine ore and quarry stone, Ingram stopped at the hangar where most of the bots were stored, and wandered inside. It was like a big barn with very orderly and otherworldly animals lined up in stalls to recharge, everything from the quadrubots that Solomon liked so much to the big square blocks of construction plant. It wasn't the first time she'd stood in front of the row of quads and looked down in particular at the one with the battered red Ainatio logo. It also wasn't the first time she'd talked to it.

"Well, Sol, I'm going to take a punt on your bird chums," she said. "So if Earth ends up as a barbecue briquette, you know who to blame."

It was a pity they'd lost contact before Sol knew the corviforms were intelligent. Why hadn't he realised that? Because they'd kept their distance and behaved as anyone from Earth would expect birds to behave, and whatever infrastructure they had here was too well-hidden even for Solomon and the monitoring systems to detect. She reached out and patted the quadrubot on its snakelike camera head, half-expecting it to respond to her and grind into life.

"Come back, Sol," she said. "I think we're going to need you more than ever now."

02

There are few of us. Perhaps there are very different ablun on other worlds that we don't know about, but as far back as we can remember, all ablun have been teeriks, and all teeriks have been ablun. It's time we demanded more than that. Anything is justified in the pursuit of a better future for our people — anything and everything. Think the unthinkable. Then be prepared to do it.

Caisin, Learned Mother of the Ansitu Commune.

PRENU NAR P12 LANDING ZONE: NEXT DAY.

Hredt clutched the pocket screen to his chest one-handed and took the long route back to the ship under the cover of foliage.

The human vessel still in orbit might spot him and he couldn't risk being seen to vanish on open ground. It would invite too many questions, and while Chief Jeff and Ma'am Ingram Bridget had asked very few, he knew they had some awkward ones in mind.

But now I have this device. No more guessing. We'll find out what the humans really are and what they can do.

It was harder to hurry on two legs with one hand full. He tried an uneven canter on his feet and one hand, but it was too awkward and felt like a disturbing taste of the decline of old age. He paused for a moment to get his balance and found himself looking up into the sky, watching flying creatures wheeling high overhead, still unsure what they were but envious of their ability to gain such altitude. He could only fly for short distances at the height of trees and glide if he picked up enough speed, but he was getting better every time. He'd never really yearned to fly until Caisin had brought the prototype here and he saw the local wildlife. It saddened him that his species ignored that they could still fly if they tried.

It was easier here, though. The gravity was lower than at home in Deku, and that gave him the edge he needed. He couldn't blame his grandsons for wanting to go flying once they got a taste for it. Perhaps ablun — his lineage, anyway — would remember their heritage one day and take to the skies. Something told him ablun were meant to be more than teeriks, just as Caisin said, even though he was proud of his trade.

He changed his grip to hold the screen two-handed against his chest and broke into a quick trot. That was better. He took his bearings from the course of the stream and kept going in a straight line until he felt the bite of static. He was inside the stealth perimeter now. He could slow down.

So... how do I tell Turisu?

She'd be furious when he showed her the human device and explained what he'd traded to acquire it. His daughter's quick temper hadn't improved with the stress of being on the run. She was already angry that he'd gone into the human camp and revealed their presence, but what else could he do when her sons had strayed there? No, that was his excuse to calm her down. He'd *wanted* to meet the aliens. He'd gone out of his way to engineer an opportunity. Turisu had mistaken the vanguard of mechanicals that had built the camp for the colonisers themselves, and she didn't like to be reminded that she'd been wrong. It was a rare slip. It frightened her. Teeriks didn't make mistakes.

But it's an assumption anyone would make, Turisu. The Solomon mechanical was sentient after all. We never expected organics.

Yes, that would save face for her while still reminding her that she didn't know everything, and that it was time to see if they could work with the humans. The newcomers were here to stay, and they'd done no harm so far. It was too late to pretend to be ignorant animals. Hredt had revealed some of his engineering skills, and the original plan was in tatters anyway. There was no going back at all. No apology or confession would save them. The foremen would make an example of them, even if it meant losing irreplaceable expertise, an uncompromising warning to teeriks throughout the sector who might be thinking of leaving their masters.

And we can only hide for so long. If we keep moving, where do we go? Where does it end?

It might be years before anyone found them here, but unless they learned to defend themselves in the meantime, they'd still be an easy target when the day came, ship or no ship. They had to use this time to gather allies or learn to fight properly. Their defence had always been their indispensability. They were needed: they had unique knowledge and talents. But they couldn't count on that to save them if the Kugin caught up with them.

And then there was the problem of supplies. They were running out of food. They were already rationing the meagre ration packs the ship carried for engineering trials because it had been a last-minute, rushed escape with no opportunity to work out where they might replenish supplies without being noticed. And they'd counted on the other teeriks joining them.

It had all gone so *wrong*.

Talking with Chief Jeff had lifted Hredt's spirits, though. He wasn't sure if it was the comfort of shared misery, but knowing that the humans here had also been let down by their comrades — if he'd understood Jeff correctly — somehow gave him hope. They both valued loyalty and a common cause. They had the same motivation. That was a sound base on which to build an alliance.

Hredt gave the screen device another inspection before he climbed down the roughly-excavated tunnel to the ship's entrance hatch. One page showed the alphabet, the shapes that represented sounds. Chief Jeff had no need to apologise that the device's content was meant for children. The images and uncomplicated words were the best foundation for unlearning what Hredt had already picked up but not yet polished into accuracy, and audio would enable him to match the words he already knew to the written language. Chief Jeff probably didn't realise how fascinating alien languages were to a species that didn't keep written records. The shapes of the letters were beautiful: not as decorative as the mosaic script of some Veleti languages, but solid and regular, as if they were designed to last forever. Hredt already recognised some from the words written on the machines that wandered around the camp they called Nomad, the place of flags. There was a label engraved on the rear side of the screen.

Property of Ainatio Corp.

A, I, N, A, T, I, O.

Hredt felt he should have known the mechanicals weren't the settlers. Why would sentient machines need to label themselves? They'd know who they were and what their purpose was. The words were for humans to identify *them*.

Ainatio Corp. He'd have to ask Chief Jeff to say that aloud for him.

Hredt tucked the screen under one wing and let himself fall down the last straight section of the tunnel, braking with his free hand, and landed on the slope. Soil and small stones trickled down behind him. The ship had dug itself into the ground a little too deeply, but the shaft remained stable. It could extract itself and get airborne immediately if the need arose. Hredt paused to inspect the partially-exposed hull plating out of habit before popping open the hatch and squeezing inside.

"Father, what have you done now?" Turisu demanded. She blocked the narrow airlock. "You've been talking to the aliens again."

"We have plenty of enemies already," Hredt said. "I thought acquiring a few friends would make a pleasant change."

"That depends on what you've told them. Did you tell them they need to conceal their ship? It'll attract attention."

"I don't think they have stealth measures. I said we can help with that but I don't think Chief Jeff understood. Anyway, nobody's likely to be passing this way."

Turisu gave the screen a pointed look. "And what have you got there?"

"Chief Jeff gave me this device to learn his language. It's easier than him struggling to learn ours."

"What exactly have you told him about us?"

"Nothing that would put us at risk."

Turisu fluffed up her scarlet crest. "I don't know what you're up to, father, but we have to make a decision soon. Either we leave and find another habitable world, or we try to make a permanent life here and hope the Kugin don't find us. The last thing we need is contact with aliens like these."

"*Like these.* Like what?"

"*Armed.* You know perfectly well what I mean."

"So their ship has missiles," Hredt said. "The humans are colonising. If they're armed, they seem to know what to expect out here. And you don't think they might know why *we're* here?"

Turisu bristled. "I'm certain they don't. Otherwise they'd have searched for this ship and commandeered it."

She did a little shake of annoyance, rattling her crest. Hredt pushed past her. It was more a case of leaning against her than knocking her out of the way, but she pecked at him anyway to make her point.

"And put your clothes on," she called after him. "You've been trying to fly again, haven't you?"

"Not *trying.* Doing."

The ship was too small for full-grown ablun and the overcrowding hadn't improved anyone's mood. Turisu was right. They couldn't go on living in this claustrophobic box for much longer, but the decision was Caisin's, not hers, and she was the one he had to convince that it was worth cultivating the humans.

It wasn't going to be easy. The old mother's health was declining fast, and her time was running out. Knowing that had added to the urgency of an escape before everyone was fully prepared. She needed to secure her memory before the knowledge of generations was lost, and Hredt felt guilty for worrying that she might not survive to give his plan her blessing when he should have been distraught at the ocean of loss that would accompany her death.

Caisin was the head of the commune, the most experienced knower and recaller, the one who could best fold space and who'd supervised the construction of the prototype ship that had brought them here. She deserved his reverence. She had it, of course, but he also saw the real possibility of his own bloodline ending here in a backwater beyond the boundary of settled space. The planet had no name in their navigation records, just a set of coordinates, but the humans called it Opis. As they'd landed mechanicals here before the teeriks arrived, they had more claim to it than the commune did. Opis was as good a name as any. Hredt would use it from now on.

The prenu was a small ship but the narrow passages slowed Hredt and made him feel he was making his way through the field-sized decks of an ore freighter. In all the years he'd designed equipment for Jattans, he'd never fully appreciated how small they were until he tried to live in a space built for them. The height of the deckheads was tolerable, but there were only a few compartments wide enough to fully spread his wings. He squeezed through the hatch that opened onto the dimly-lit bridge and found Caisin sitting draped with a blanket on a pile of cushions, head tucked against one wing as if she was asleep.

"There's no need to creep around," she said, not looking up. "I'm awake. Have you come to fuss over me? Because Maro was fussing, and I told him to get out. I'm not dead yet."

"Learned Mother, I've been speaking with the humans again."

"Yes, I know. Is this a confession?"

"No, it's a solution." Hredt held up the little screen. "This is a language lesson. We can be more precise in our discussions."

"And we would need precision... *why*, exactly?"

"I've offered to help them, and I think they'll help us."

Caisin unfolded herself slowly and opened her eyes. It took her a moment or two to straighten up, but now her head was erect and she looked more like her old self, although the feathers on her head had lost most of their brilliant red sheen.

"You had no authority to do that," she said quietly. "You were only supposed to check whether they were working for the foremen. What help can they possibly need? I thought they'd come here to settle."

"They've lost communications with their homeworld, Learned Mother. They had a form of instant link but it's been cut off for some reason they don't understand. I said we could restore it for them."

"But no superluminal propulsion, you said."

"I believe the communications were achieved with an artificial wormhole. They can only move small objects. Not an entire vessel."

"So their technology is very limited."

"It's taken them years to get here. I think they'd want spacefolding technology very much."

"And why would we give them that?" Caisin asked.

"Because we need allies. We can't survive alone."

"They have one ship. Armed or not, there are very few of them, and they'd be outnumbered and probably outgunned the moment even a single Jattan vessel showed up. And perhaps they don't want to die out here defending strangers in a dispute that isn't theirs."

"If we give them spacefolding, though, Learned Mother, they could transport more humans here and establish a garrison."

"Is this what you've been discussing with them?"

"No, I don't know enough of their language yet to attempt anything that complex."

"Perhaps they'd give us sanctuary on their homeworld."

"Possibly, but they seem angry with the people there. It might not be easy."

Caisin's head drooped a little. "Not very useful allies, then, are they?"

"On the contrary. They have bots, remember. The mechanicals we saw building the base when we first landed. *Proper manufacturing.* Imagine what they could make with our supervision. They could help us complete this ship and manufacture armaments." Hredt paused, wondering if he should go any further. "Perhaps even help us test your prototype gate."

Hredt knew he should have put it more frankly, but there was nothing he'd said that was dishonest or selfish. He liked Chief Jeff and Ma'am Ingram Bridget, they needed things that teeriks could do for them, and his commune needed a way out of this situation. What made him uneasy was exploiting Caisin's wish to see her precision gateway technology working before she died. It was a revolutionary type of portal that could place the smallest pebble in exactly the right place light years away, accurate to a feather's thickness, an engineering legacy any teerik would be proud of. He knew she was desperate to see it in operation before it was too late.

And nobody outside this commune knew it existed.

Doing this to a dying savant. I should be ashamed of myself.

Caisin just studied him for a while, blinking occasionally. She hadn't thrown him out, though, so she was taking the suggestion seriously. Seeking help from the humans had been a spontaneous idea, but it had solidified into a plan with remarkable speed, and now Hredt wasn't sure if it was just blind panic because none of them knew how to survive in a wilderness. They were used to life in a city with their every need from birth to death met by their Kugin foremen, never worrying where the next meal was coming from or if they'd be safe for the night. Now every certainty was gone. They had no idea how to feed themselves on this alien world. For a moment, Hredt wondered if it would have been so bad to stay bonded to the Kugin, but then he thought of his grandsons, and how upset Turisu had been at the prospect of having to give them up to another commune when their time came. She'd remained in the same commune as him, a very unusual thing, because her skills complemented his. She wanted her own children to stay at her side as well.

So did Hredt.

He looked for the opportunity that he'd been so sure was there this morning. "If nothing else, the humans know how to construct buildings," he said. "And they obviously have a sustainable food supply. At very least, they could help us survive."

"If we can eat what they eat."

"All nutrition can be broken down to basics. Humans must share some biochemistry with us or they wouldn't be able to live here."

"Very well, what if we give them the technology and they abandon us anyway?" Caisin asked. "Or they kill us and just take it? We can't carry out full scans, but their ship does appear to carry substantial armaments."

"Yes, yes, Turisu keeps telling me that. It's a risk we have to take. We needn't tell them everything at once. We can progress by stages and assess their intent."

"Have they told you where their homeworld is?"

"Not yet."

"That's the test of trust."

"So is admitting to them that we know already and that we've placed assay probes in their system." The humans' satellites transmitted data back to Earth and their ship had been trackable for some time. With the numbers on Chief Jeff's receiver, it had been easy to confirm the planet's location. "We haven't told them where we came from, either."

"So they don't trust us any more than we trust them."

"Or they're prudent by habit."

"You seem to like them."

"They're not unlikeable. They didn't think we were sentient at first, but they didn't try to kill us. That's quite enlightened."

"Let me think about it," Caisin said.

Hredt waited for her to go on, but she seemed to be tiring. Her head sagged and she settled down as if she was sitting on an egg. The cover slid off her back. Hredt darted forward to drape it over her again.

"Learned Mother, there are only *ten* of us. None of the other communes are coming. They'd have made contact to arrange another rendezvous point by now. They were all talk. We're alone, we daren't go back, and there aren't even enough of us to preserve a bloodline."

He didn't add that Caisin would never receive the proper medical treatment she needed. He didn't have to. They'd known that breaking their bond to the Kugin would be dangerous, but Hredt had expected that to take the form of being shot down. He hadn't imagined they'd face oblivion in such a small, sad way by simply becoming a lost fragment. Every life form died eventually, but when ablun died out, so did the knowledge of generations. There was no more profound death than that. It was erasure not only of the present but of their entire history.

"I know," Caisin said.

"You told us to think the unthinkable and to be prepared to do it," Hredt said. "And we did."

"To preserve our people."

"This commune will die out either way."

"I realise that too."

"But this, *this* is a start." Hredt brandished the pocket screen again. "Chief Jeff wants to talk."

"And how does that change our situation? We'll still die out."

"Not if we have strong allies. Not if we can establish a home here that other teeriks feel is worth the risk to join."

"You're talking about building a colony that can defend itself against at least two fleets," Caisin said.

"Fleets we designed."

"Fleets we've never deployed in except on trials. We're not soldiers."

"Humans are, though. And we can learn." Hredt held out the screen again. He realised he was treating it like religious scripture. It was only a child's book, but every picture, however idealised, told him a great deal. "Look at these images of warfare. Humans are a warlike species. I don't expect them to wipe out the Kugin, but I do think they could defend this planet with our technology. The alternative is to accept that we'll die out."

Caisin was quiet again. Hredt couldn't tell if she was exhausted or deep in thought. He waited.

"We always thought our secrets were our insurance," she said at last. "We made our move at the wrong time, but we had our reasons and it's done now. We have to salvage what we can."

"Is that approval, Learned Mother?"

"Just see if there's any advantage in befriending the humans."

At last. There really was no other option. Hredt put the possibility of failure out of his mind for the moment. "I'll transfer this screen's data to everyone's terminal, then. We should all learn the language. You'll have to talk to their leader eventually."

"If I survive long enough."

"You will."

"I need to rest, Hredt. Leave me."

He didn't need to be told twice. He closed the hatch behind him and headed for the engineering section one deck below, an obstacle course of treacherous ladders snaking down tight shafts. The permission had both raised his spirits and made him feel guilty for his optimism, because Caisin wouldn't live to see this succeed, she knew it, and her knowledge would be lost if she couldn't produce one final egg with her accumulated wisdom preserved in it. There was no perfect solution to any of this. It was all damage control.

And we brought the children all this way. For what?

Hredt would think of something. He had to hold his nerve and take it a step at a time, although time was probably something they didn't have. The foremen and the client wouldn't forget about them, not with this ship missing. They'd search for as long as it took.

And they'll know it's just us, because every other teerik stayed at their post. There's a lot they can work out about our limitations.

But not Caisin's new portal. At least we still have that in reserve.

"Hredt, what's going on?" Maro stuck his head out of a hatch as Hredt passed. He never addressed him as Turisu's father. He seemed uncomfortable being a son-in-law. "Turi's in a foul mood. What have you done now?"

Hredt held up the screen. "I have permission to talk with the humans, and to do that, I need a better command of their language. This is going to teach me."

"So they're here to stay."

"I believe so."

"Why didn't you tell us all this?"

"Because I can't be sure what I'm telling you is correct. Which is why Chief Jeff's given me this device."

"What about the mechanicals?"

"They're not sentient. The one that was isn't around any longer."

"This is very confusing."

"Aliens usually are. When I share the language data you can work things out for yourself."

All Hredt wanted now was peace and quiet for a few hours to go through the screen's contents. He settled down in the ventral engine compartment with the pocket screen propped on an inspection panel that stood proud of the bulkhead. He'd be comfortable here for a few hours.

So this was an encyclopaedia. He worked through the pages first to see how it was organised, then tried asking it random questions as Chief Jeff had shown him. He hoped he could make himself understood.

"Show me planet," he said in English, mimicking the human's voice.

And it did. The screen obediently flashed up images of a blue world swathed in white cloud. Hredt checked the alphabet that Chief Jeff had told him to refer to every time, and tried to pronounce the letters beneath the image.

"Ee...ar..th."

"*Urth*," the screen said.

"Earth," Hredt said obediently.

It was one of only two images of a planet that he could find. The other was Earth's moon, barren and pock-marked with craters. He tapped on some of the links, unsure what would happen but expecting to see more detail, but there was nothing, no information about Earth's sun or the other worlds in its system, planets he'd actually seen from the assay probes' transmissions. The encyclopaedia image itself showed no stars on the background of black space. The more Hredt leafed through the encyclopaedia, the more he realised how much even this collection of harmless information had been censored. There were plenty of images of Earth's surface, though. It looked fascinating. It certainly didn't seem like a world with problems bad enough to force its inhabitants to flee.

Humans were wary. He couldn't be offended or surprised by that. Caution was a far more civilised response than killing what they didn't understand, and they'd given him this screen to teach him the language and apply it. He didn't need to be told the truth about Earth to do that, but simply giving him the ability indicated that the humans intended to tell him one day.

Footsteps pattered down the passage at high speed. "Grandfather! Mama said you've got some human machine."

Demli and Runal flopped down next to him. They were small enough to race around the passages with ease, and Hredt couldn't begrudge them some noisy play to let off steam now that they were confined to the ship. He kept a firm grip on the device but held it so they could see it.

"It's a *pocket screen*. The humans load it with data."

"What's on it?" Demli asked.

"A little bit of information on how they live to help me learn their language."

"Can we learn too?"

"Of course you can. Come on. Get in close."

"Why can't they learn ours?"

"Because their throats aren't made for it. And we're *choosing* to learn this language. We don't have to."

"Is it our fault, Grandfather?"

"What is?"

"The humans wouldn't have known we were here if we hadn't gone into their camp."

"No, it's not your fault at all. Maybe it's a good thing that we've discovered each other. They might turn out to be allies."

"I'm hungry," Runal said. "Have they got food?"

"We'll see. Learn to speak English properly and you can ask them." Hredt showed them the alphabet. "See? Every shape is a sound. Like Peku. Once you know the letters, you can say any word. Simple."

No, it wasn't his grandsons' fault. Hredt watched them poring over the screen, squawking triumphantly each time they tried to pronounce a word and got it right. They weren't afraid. They treated this exile like an adventure, even if the food was inadequate portions of miserable dry rations. He'd wanted so much more for the boys and the escape had seemed the best way to get it. They were the point of this madness. He had to make it work for them.

"Have you told them about this ship?" Demli asked. "Do they know why we came here?"

"Not yet. And we don't know what their plans are."

"You have to tell them if we want them to be allies."

Runal reached across Hredt and changed the screen's page. "We can't trust anybody. We can't even trust other teeriks now. They promised they'd be at the rendezvous point."

"Maybe they had a good reason," Hredt said. He didn't sound convincing even to himself. "Let's not worry about that now."

"They're not coming, Grandfather. They're cowards. They'd rather be the foremen's tame *hebudis* for a pat on the head than think for themselves."

That was straight out of Caisin's mouth. They'd obviously listened to her speeches on freedom and independence more carefully than Hredt had realised. Now they were going to see the reality of what happened when a revolution failed, but he had no idea what that looked like any more than these children did. He'd been one of those tame hebudis. He'd been given everything he needed all his life, although there were other things he felt he wanted but couldn't quite define until he'd heard Caisin speak. Then he was sure. He was still sure, but it was hard to face the fact that he'd given the children no choice in this.

"When the time's right, I'll explain things to Chief Jeff," he said.

It was time to take their minds off their hunger and uncertainties. He flicked back to the page he'd been studying earlier and pointed to the picture of a blue globe set against the void. Expanses of green and brown were visible under the cloud layers.

"*Earth,*" he said carefully, wondering what could have made someone leave a world like that. "The humans' planet is called Earth. Look how lovely it is."

* * *

CEMETERY OF ST THOMAS'S CHURCH, KILL LINE: 1310 HOURS, 75 DAYS TO *SHACKLETON* LAUNCH.

Chris Montello had promises to keep, some of them to the dead and some of them to the living, part of his pledge to the evacuee convoy he'd led out of a nightmare. Nobody would be left behind.

The promise applied as much to the dead as the living. He squatted by Jamie Wickens' grave, so recent that it was still marked by bald brown scars in the turf. Fresh roses, pink and cream, had been placed in the glass jar doing duty as a vase, which might have been put there by Erin Piller or even one of the Kill Liners. It was kind of nice to live in a place where folks showed respect, even temporarily. Chris put one hand on the border of smooth stones around the plot, steadying himself because his injured knee still sometimes felt like it might give way.

"Sorry, buddy. I'm going to have to disturb you." Talking to Jamie was weird for a man who didn't believe in that sort of thing, but he wasn't alone. Everybody seemed to want to talk to the dead these days. "I'm not going to leave you here because there won't be anyone left to keep the place tidy. Anyway, it's a lot more interesting where we're going. So... yeah, apologies again, but I'm going to have to dig you up. No easy way to say that. You'd laugh your ass off, I bet. But hey, it's an adventure, and you always wanted in when we did dumb shit, so... "

Chris trailed off. He'd run out of words. The exhumation was starting to preoccupy him because he knew it wouldn't be like it was in the movies, all dust and desiccation. Bodies weren't embalmed here. Even in this hot summer, decomposition wouldn't be that far advanced, and no matter how many bodies he'd found and had to shift, no matter how desensitised he'd made himself, this wasn't a corpse. This was his friend, and Chris was to blame for his death. That made the exhumation his sole responsibility. It wasn't even a penance. It was just unthinkable to pass the task to anyone else, even a bot.

"Talk to you later, buddy," Chris said, straightening up. When he turned around, Martin Berry was standing in the church porch, waiting. Chris wasn't a churchgoing man but he was pretty sure that Martin wasn't typical for a minister. He walked across the cemetery to join him.

"Didn't mean to interrupt," Martin said.

"It's okay. I was just letting him know that he's moving with us." Chris felt better putting it that way. "You're okay with me doing it, yeah? It's kind of a personal duty."

"Whatever you want, Chris. If you need anything, don't be afraid to ask."

"Thanks."

"You want to hear something interesting?"

Chris braced for an uplifting story to fit the moment. That was the minister's job, after all. "Sure."

"I had a line of APS technicians waiting outside this morning when I arrived. Well, six, anyway. They were very polite and wanted to know if they could attend services."

Chris wasn't expecting that kind of story. "Yeah, that *is* interesting."

"They're scared of us. They think we're a biohazard."

"Yeah, I figured that. But obviously some aren't as scared as others. So you said yes."

"Of course. And I believe we might have rehomed Liam Dale's Jersey herd."

"Cattle rescue, huh?" Chris said. "Who's taking them?"

"One of the Korean technicians. His parents run a farm. He wanted to know what we were doing with the animals if we couldn't embark them in *Shackleton*, and he was upset at the idea of having to abandon them or put them down. So he's talking to his bosses about shipping them back."

Chris actually felt better for knowing that. He was still pissed at Liam for refusing to leave his herd when the sodium bombs were due to drop. He'd gone to the farm to talk some sense into him with Dan Trinder, and Liam had relented at the last minute, but Chris had wanted to punch the shit out of him for even thinking of abandoning his wife and kids for a few cows. Well, that'd make it easier to get him on the shuttle without another argument.

"How's this guy going to ship the cattle out?" Chris asked.

"He says there's plenty of room in their aircraft carrier."

"Oh. That's great." Fonseca said *Temujin* was small for a carrier. Chris wondered if this was really about acquiring fresh steaks, but he kept his cynical thoughts to himself. He nodded, trying to be the man Martin seemed to think he was. "How about the other livestock?"

"We might be able to negotiate."

Necessity had made Chris into an engine that ran most efficiently on problems. He'd forgotten how to handle lucky breaks. They left him feeling lost.

"Good work, sir," he said. "I'll let Dan know. See you later."

He hoped Martin could talk them into taking the lot. The emergency plans he'd drawn up for worst scenarios didn't leave much room for taking animals on the road. It wasn't like letting the family dog out of the car every few hours to run around and pee. Chris kept trying to come up with a plan, but if they headed south to the area they'd identified as a potential refuge, it was about more than having grazing and shelter down there. There probably weren't enough trucks to move livestock in the first place, and herding them like a cattle drive would be slow and probably of too much interest to predators, human ones included. They wouldn't even have enough time to reduce the animals to meat and salt or dehydrate it.

Chris wasn't looking forward to Plan B at all. But it was still the last resort, and probably one they wouldn't have to put into action.

He drove back to the research centre in one of the armoured Caracals, a luxury ride compared to the old military trucks they'd brought with the Baltimore convoy, passing through a die-back decontamination archway and pausing to let it mist the vehicle. As he drove past a bean field, a guy on a tractor waved to him. It was like the last fifty years had never happened. Chris waved back. It was a glimpse of the normal life he could have lived if the world had been completely, utterly different, and it saddened him. At least his transit camp neighbours would have a few weeks living here to show them what normality was before they woke up to a new life on Opis.

The planet already had its plus points, sight unseen. There'd be nothing there to remind Chris how things were, no burned-out buildings or bulldozed plots to revisit one day. History would be erased. It had never bothered him before: the past wasn't somewhere he wanted to live. But maybe a landscape with weird vegetation and giant crows would stop him seeing that woman waiting on the doorstep in a deserted suburb, refusing to board the truck and leave with the convoy because she was still waiting for her husband to make it home. Chris could shut out even the worst flashbacks where the story had an end, but she was unfinished business he could never conclude. He didn't feel guilty for not making her come with them. She haunted him because he'd never know if she really was deluding herself, or if her old man had finally turned up and driven them both to safety.

He had regrets about those years. But they all stemmed from the realisation that he should have put down a lot more vermin when he had the chance. He'd seen two kinds of savagery while society fell apart: one was instinct, when people were so terrified and desperate that they did the first animal thing that crossed their minds to stay alive, even at the expense of their own kids, and the other was conscious malice that had just been waiting for its chance to let rip. Chris wasn't sure which of the two his was. Sometimes it was hard to face the trust people put in him. While he always kept his word, that kind of faith was almost always accompanied by a warmth, a *liking*, that he wasn't sure he'd earned. And the faith bothered him too. He still had the feeling that he was blundering towards a cliff edge, leading trusting people to disaster.

Captain Elena Fonseca liked him, though, and he was happy with that. She knew pretty much what he was, too. "Call me Lennie," she'd said, and he'd told her about his life before being drafted by the State Defence Force just like he'd told Dan Trinder, although the conversation hadn't gotten around to his teenage years. It was going to be awkward now to say he'd omitted to tell her he'd killed a guy when he was at high school. But he needed her to know. He still felt he had a chance with her, and that kind of revelation had to happen sooner rather than later.

It'll come up again. I'll tell her. Sure as shit I'm not going to spend the rest of my life trying to hide it.

The rest of his life wasn't something he'd thought would be either long or worth worrying about until the last two years. He drove through Ainatio's main gates, trying to work out what he'd now consider a normal life, and parked in front of the reception lobby. Aaron Luce, Trinder's sergeant and an ex-detective, passed him on the steps as he went in. He had one of the new printed carbines slung across his chest.

"Hey Chris." He tapped the weapon. "We've made a few more adjustments. Great job."

"Any interest from our APS buddies?"

"If they've noticed this, they haven't said a word. Oh, before I forget, Alex spoke to Dr Kim. I hear the cows have been granted asylum."

"Already? I was just coming to tell you someone had asked."

"He's in the office. Just don't mention bull semen to him."

"Thanks for the warning," Chris said. "I'd have blurted it out right away. It's the first thing on my mind."

Aaron laughed and walked on. Chris made his way to the security office, trying to read the mood of everyone he passed in the corridors. He still didn't know most of the Ainatio staff, but he could feel the relief around him. They were laughing and joking. Nothing much had actually changed, but they'd survived and for some of them, Opis was looking less like the only way out.

Chris wondered how many would accept resettlement if APS offered it. He couldn't blame them. He couldn't even think less of them for changing their minds, because they hadn't known what Erskine was going to ask of them, and they'd been left behind as well. They were scientists and technicians who hadn't made the sort for *Elcano* because they didn't have children, their specialisations weren't a priority, or just because they'd decided to stay for reasons that Chris would probably never know. After all the anger and desperation when Erskine decided who'd live and who might die, who'd get a place in *Elcano* and be saved, the ship had launched with sixty-eight empty cryo berths. Not everyone had lost faith in Earth. And nobody had ever volunteered to explore space.

And Asia's surviving, more or less, but how long has it got?

Sometimes you've just got to jump and hope for the best.

Chris couldn't fault Erskine for putting her own people first and leaving the town and the transit camp to fend for themselves. He'd have done the same. But he liked to think that he'd have levelled with the staff here years ago when it became obvious that Nomad couldn't recruit its settlers as planned and that it would have to draft its own people. Then he tried to imagine fifteen hundred staff living with that prospect, with years to chew over how many lies they'd been told, and guessed the whole shit show might have collapsed in anarchy. It was different when all you had to worry about was a hundred or so evacuees who had a much tighter bond, the kind you only built on shared hardship. He could tell his transit camp neighbours anything.

It was academic now. *Elcano* was accelerating out of the Solar System. Chris put his head around the security control room door and found Trinder at his desk, watching Alex Gorko struggling with the coffee maker in the corner. Fonseca was moving shapes around the 3-D plot of Kill Line on the map table. She was chewing her lip and frowning like someone who knew they had something vital to do but couldn't remember. She distracted him for a moment and he hoped she didn't notice. He turned his attention to Alex.

"Alex, I'm definitely not going to say *bull semen* to you," he said, straight-faced. "I just wanted to make that clear."

"Yeah, I'm really grateful you didn't say it."

"You're welcome."

"If you're asking if we're ready to put embryos and eggs and all that stuff in cryo, yes, we are," Alex said. "Happy farmers. Well, *happier*. It beats losing everything they've worked for."

All that seemed more alien than Opis. "How do you teach a calf to be a cow when its mom's a plastic bag?" Chris asked. "How much is instinct?"

"Chris, all I know about cows is that it's seven minutes each side for medium rare."

"Okay. Just curious. Have I missed anything this morning?"

Alex gave the coffee machine a thump with the heel of his hand. A gurgling noise followed by a painfully slow trickle of coffee confirmed he'd beaten it into submission. He took off his glasses and cleaned them while the cup filled, polishing with a little too much deliberation. "Well, Audrey and Seb Meikle are off to Sydney, subject to APS agreement. She never wanted to go to Opis, not with a little kid."

"Who's Audrey?"

"The woman in biomed with the curly mousey hair. Seb's in plant biology. It's Seb they want, really."

Chris couldn't put faces to the names. "Will Seb let something slip?"

"No. We've given APS the sanitised version of our die-back research. But they're interested in his work on crop adaptation. Mars. Or wherever they think they're going to go with our FTL." Alex shook his head, still studying his glasses, then carefully put them back on. "And I'm going too."

"Oh."

"I said I would. I'm not cut out for pioneering."

It sounded like an apology. Chris wasn't close to Alex, but the guy had done his bit to stop Erskine dragging Annis Kim to Opis, and he'd decided he liked him. In hindsight, maybe the whole thing really was a set-up, and nobody had needed to rescue Kim to negotiate with her buddy Pham and stop the bombing. But Alex hadn't known that. He was an overweight, office-bound manager who had the guts to get stuck into a fist fight with a much bigger, fitter guy. Chris respected that. It was the mindset he'd be sorry to lose, not skill or the lack of it. They'd need have-a-go types on Opis.

"You might surprise yourself," Chris said. He caught Trinder's eye, wondering if he'd overlooked something like a woman being involved in this somehow. "But if you want to stay and work on fixing Earth, that's pioneering too."

"Spiders the size of chihuahuas," Fonseca said suddenly. Chris hadn't noticed she was following the conversation. "Sydney, I mean. Apart from that, you'll probably have a great time. Dr Kim can't wait to go home. Well, she's from Melbourne, but you get the idea."

Alex looked like he'd decided his coffee cup was full enough. He turned to leave. "Thanks for the heads-up on the local wildlife. I'll invest in bicycle clips. Later, guys."

His footsteps faded in the corridor. Trinder looked at Chris and shrugged.

"I can't tell if he's regretting it or not."

"Is this about a woman?"

"Not that I know of."

Fonseca finished whatever she was doing with the map and switched it off. "Chances are he'll live out a nice peaceful life in Australia and be long dead before any plagues or famines get that far. Anyway, I'm going to grab something to eat. You want me to fetch you anything, Dan?"

Trinder gazed at the wall for a moment, looking like he was making a difficult command decision. "Ham sandwich or whatever resembles it. Thanks."

Chris was going to hang around and work out a few things with Trinder, but Fonseca jerked her head towards the door like she was telling a dog it was walkies time. Maybe she wanted to talk.

"Chris?"

"Yeah, okay, I'll come with you."

Chris followed her into the elevator and kept his eyes on the control panel. It had been a long time since he'd been stuck in a confined space with a woman he'd taken a fancy to. He was out of practice and afraid of looking like a jerk. He hadn't noticed her perfume before, but now it triggered a memory that was still raw: Jamie finding a bottle of some expensive fragrance while they were scavenging in a deserted shopping centre, and presenting it to Erin, still too shy to ask her for a date. Half an hour later, Jamie was dead. Erin had never worn the perfume. Chris would have noticed.

"You okay?" Fonseca asked.

"Yeah. Just thinking."

"Don't worry about people changing their minds and trying to stay. It's Nature's way of weeding out the least suited to colonising Opis."

Chris hoped she was saying that to make him feel better. He didn't want to believe she really was heartless.

"Sometimes the keenest are the ones who can't hack it for real," he said. "Anyhow, we can't force them. Even Erskine knew better than that."

"Any waverers in your camp?"

"No. We stick together. All or none." Chris shook his head. They'd made a deal. It was the natural extension of his promise that nobody would be left behind, no matter what, and they all wanted a permanent home, to know they wouldn't have to pack up and run ever again. "Where are you on prep?"

"Re-running the embarkation checklist from the original plan. Everyone's been allocated their berth, they know how much space they've got for luggage, and they've had their final medical checks and immunisation."

"I meant the emergency plan."

Fonseca turned her head to stare right at him, inches away, a blur of dark hair in his peripheral vision. He kept his eyes on the panel and hoped he wasn't blushing.

"I've run all the convoy options again," Fonseca said. "Nothing's changed since the last time you asked. We can switch to an overland evacuation and we can probably make it three-fifty to four hundred miles south to the lakes. North is *not* a good idea."

Chris just needed to hear it again. He didn't want to rely on trusting APS. "I know. That's why we're here."

The elevator doors opened and Chris stood back to let Fonseca out first. The staff restaurant was at the end of the corridor, but even before he stepped through the doors he could hear the buzz of conversation and strangely normal life, as if forty-eight hours waiting to be nuked and a one-way ticket to the limits of human exploration had never happened. It was relaxed, even happy. Some APS personnel were sitting around eating and chatting with the scientists and techs, who'd switched to English from Korean or maybe Cantonese, but whichever it was it sounded like it was heavily peppered with borrowed English words anyway. The feeling of being on a war footing had evaporated, at least for some of them.

"So they're not all terrified of us infecting them," Chris said.

Fonseca grabbed a tray. "I think they did checks for pathogens as soon as they landed, to be honest."

"And there was I thinking it was the triumph of human decency."

The Ainatio remnant and APS had dropped their guard. They were getting friendly. Chris would have preferred everyone to keep their distance for a few more weeks, but at least nobody was shooting or shoving them around.

"Look at it this way, it could easily have been an occupation with folks handcuffed and everything," Fonseca said. Either she'd learned to read Chris in a way few people had or she'd had the same thought and assumed he had too. "This is way better."

"Loose lips sink ships," he said. "They're not our buddies. However nice they are."

"Don't worry, everyone here knows what's at stake. Come on. Food."

Chris stood at the servery and studied a steel container of steaming scarlet sauce dotted with lumps that looked like pork luncheon meat and chopped franks. He was sure he could see beans and noodles in there as well. It was the kind of random stew he'd have thrown together after salvaging cans from abandoned houses, a reminder of how close starvation would be again if he didn't stay on top of things and keep his small kingdom organised and fed.

Fonseca nudged him. "You look entranced."

"Was this always on the menu?" Chris had only had access to the restaurant for a couple of weeks, and it was nothing like the meals he'd been given while he was laid up with his leg wound in Ainatio's infirmary. "I haven't seen it before."

"It's Korean. Army stew. I think someone's trying to build bridges with our visitors."

"Okay, I'm up for it."

He helped himself to a bowlful and noted that Fonseca just grabbed a couple of sandwiches without inspection. She placed one on the table between them when they sat down to eat, then unwrapped the other and took a mouthful without even looking at it. Chris dredged through the stew to see what other components he could recognise. Garlic and chilli wafted up in the curls of steam.

"You're the only person I know who doesn't check to see what's inside a sandwich," he said.

"I'll eat it regardless. Anyway, it's egg mayo."

"How do you know the other one's ham?"

"I don't. It's not for Dan. I'll pick his up on the way out."

"I admire a woman with a healthy appetite."

"How's the stew?"

The liquid was spicy and slightly sour. Cabbage lurked under the meat. It was a regular lucky dip of a meal. "Pretty good," he said, trying to get a little bit of everything on his spoon to balance the flavours. "Plenty of chilli."

Fonseca's gaze drifted off to one side. She was watching someone. "Yeah, look at 'em... they're making their bids to get APS visas. You can tell. I know I'm wrong, but I feel kind of let down."

"Lennie, they never volunteered for space. Let alone starting a colony."

"Yeah, I know. I know."

"Look, the more folks act like it's a suicide mission, the less interest APS is going to take in it. No bad thing if we want them to butt out."

"I can't believe Opis isn't top of their shopping list," Fonseca said. "We haven't told them much about it, but they know it's a lot like Earth."

"They're here for the FTL. They'll be spoilt for choice with planets once they've worked out how to move ships with it. Sol's convinced, anyway."

"How about bacteria?"

"They've got to look out for themselves."

"No, I meant everything we need relies on bacteria. Soil and stuff. Did we ship out our own, or is that another lucky break? I keep thinking of questions I should have asked when all the brainiacs were still here. Maybe Sol knows."

"But Sol didn't know Bednarz stole Kim's gran's research."

"He's got to know about the science side, though. He's run the remotes there for years."

"Yeah, ask him." Chris paused out of habit to give Sol a chance to chip in on hearing his name. The AI could hear everyone, whether via their personal radios or the building's monitoring system, but he didn't respond today. "Got to give Bednarz his due. The guy was one serious planner."

Fonseca looked at something behind him again. "Damn, even the Vincents look like they're applying for jobs. I thought they were set on Opis."

"I don't know them."

"They're both in biomed. Debora developed the tissue-building device that fixed your leg. Imagine how much money she'd have made from it if the world was the way it used to be."

Fonseca didn't say what Debora's husband had achieved, as if he was just an annexe of his clever wife. Chris turned to look as discreetly as he could. The Vincents were a middle-aged couple he recognised but couldn't have put a name to, and they were talking to a sandy-haired guy in an Australian naval uniform. A young woman with short dark hair and a thin face, maybe mid-twenties, was sitting with them, looking more like a bored teen who wanted to be somewhere else. Chris didn't recall seeing her before. The three of them seemed more like a family group than colleagues.

"Who's the girl?" he asked.

"Their daughter, Abbie."

"I should go say thank you. So biomed doesn't make you essential personnel, then. Or did they decide to give up berths in *Elcano*?"

"I don't know the detail. Alex could tell you, though."

Chris had learned to make decisions and live with them. He told himself that if scientists were getting cold feet about Opis, it was no more ominous than anyone else who realised just how big and irreversible a decision it was. But he also wondered if they knew something he didn't, and if he was making another dumb mistake like retracing the route out of Kingston and driving straight into the ambush that killed Jamie.

"Lennie, I have days when I don't know why I'm asking people to do this," he said.

Fonseca opened the second sandwich and wolfed it down. "Don't make Plan B a self-fulfilling prophecy. You never struck me as the self-doubting type."

"I'm not a visionary. I'm just a grunt who does what he has to."

"That's your answer." She wiped her mouth with a napkin. As she stood up to go, she put her hand on his shoulder and squeezed, more like reassurance than flirting, but he still added it to his list of positive omens. "If you're not worried about sleeping through a couple of hundred trillion miles of unforgiving void and waking up on another planet that you know zip about, you'd be an idiot. And you're not an idiot. You're the man for the job. That's why you're part of the triumvirate."

"Don't. Please."

"Come on. You three just fell into it. You and Marc and Dan. You're in charge now. Alex never was and never wanted to be."

"Neither did I."

"Exactly. That's healthy."

"Just tell me Earth's done and there's nowhere else to go."

"Okay, Earth's done and there's nowhere else to go. Happy now?" She clapped her hand on his shoulder again. "Well, there's Mars, but it's just a fancy greenhouse. We'll have air and trees on Opis. And big black birds, so at least we can have a real roast for Thanksgiving."

"Thanks," Chris said. "I feel better already."

"You're welcome. I'll see you later. Got to get the boss his sandwich."

"Beer in the bar tonight?" Chris asked, trying to be casual.

"Sure. Your round."

Yes, he did feel better. This was why he'd learned not to plan too far ahead, and took each day in stages, satisfied just to reach the next checkpoint alive. Worrying about the long term just sapped a guy's energy. As long as he knew how to handle whatever happened next, the future would arrive and he'd deal with it. He paused to wipe his nose as the chilli took its toll, looking around as nonchalantly as he could while he checked out who else was talking to APS.

Fonseca was right. It really did have the feel of people working the room to secure their places. Did it matter? Only if they felt that trading information — the truth about the new die-back strain, *Shackleton*'s armaments, Opis, or Solomon — would help them. Chris found himself scanning faces for signs of treachery and weakness. There were four hundred and eighty-one Ainatio personnel, but he'd take a risk on fewer than forty, thirty-three to be precise. All but two wore a uniform and one of those used to.

Mistrust had its place. But maybe Fonseca had a point about self-fulfilling prophecies and he needed to dial it back a little.

While he was scanning the tables, Howie came in and walked up to the food counter. The kid had to stand on tiptoe to stretch across and pick out two ciabattas. He was running errands. He'd always been like that, constantly looking for something to do and someone to do it for since the day Chris had found him striding along the side of the deserted highway like he was late for an important meeting. Chris guessed the ciabattas were for Marc. Howie had latched onto him, which was probably good for both of them. He wondered what kind of future the kid would have on Opis, maybe the kind of normal, uneventful life he'd never known, with a wife and kids in a nice town built to look like Earth. Howie was ten. He'd never known a world without disease, shortages, and marauding gangs. Whatever Opis was really like, it would be none of those things. It was a clean slate. That, if nothing else, made it worth the risk.

Howie waved at Chris as he left and Chris waved back. It was hard to imagine how a bunch of bereaved and traumatised people could build a new society that didn't start out broken, but that was what the transit camp had done so far, and they'd carry on that way on Opis. Chris finished his stew, got up to put his tray in the service hatch, and looked for the Vincent woman so he could do the polite thing and thank her. But the family had already left.

He'd go see how the final shuttle adjustments were progressing. Solomon had brought back the shuttle that Erskine's group had taken to Orbital 1 to board *Elcano*, so there were now two fully-maintained vessels in the hangars, and that reassured him. They could ship everyone out at the same time, no return trips or other complications to worry about. Solomon could have updated him, but he wanted to see it for himself, and like Fonseca, he'd already completed all the preparation for pulling his people out before the first aborted evacuation, so his options were boredom or inventing problems to keep himself occupied.

The walk through the gardens to the end of the accommodation block killed some time. He was thinking of all the places on Earth that he'd now never get to see when he turned the corner and spotted the Vincent girl sitting on the low brick wall of a flower bed, tossing crumbs to birds that had gathered around her.

She wasn't watching the birds. She was staring north towards the shuttle runway. It was a nice view if you sat in the right position. From a low seat, in line with the rail launcher that ran the full length of the runway and seemed to disappear into infinity, you could almost feel a sensation of movement, as if you were zipping up that rail with the hangars and buildings on either side blurring past you.

It didn't strike Chris as an odd place to do some thinking. If anything could focus the mind on what was coming, it was looking at the last ground on Earth that most folks here would ever feel beneath them. The two shuttles were standing on the tarmac, festooned with cables and links while bots welded and the few remaining shuttle engineers trotted back and forth between the ramps and mobile workbenches.

Abbie Vincent didn't turn around. Chris decided he had an opportunity to save himself the effort of chasing around after her mother.

"Hi," he said, making an effort to be friendly. Eventually, they might both be cooped up on a planet with nowhere else to go, and good diplomatic relations with everyone made sense. "You're Dr Vincent's daughter, aren't you? I wanted to say thanks to your mom but I didn't catch her in the restaurant. Her gadget fixed my leg. Could you let her know I wanted to say hi?"

Abbie turned her head slowly. He hadn't startled her, then. But the last time anyone had looked at him like that, they'd pulled a knife five seconds later. He didn't trust skinny women any more than he trusted guys his own size, and he had a scar to justify that philosophy.

"Sure," she said, then turned back to watch the runway again. "It's definitely happening, then. We're actually going to Opis."

"Definitely."

Maybe she was worried it was all going to fall through and she'd be stuck here. Judging by her age and when the facility was cut off from the outside world, she must have spent most of her life in this compound and might even have been born here. It was an unthinkably cloistered life, a small town ringed by a security fence, without even the chance of escaping to college. Still, if you were going to be home-schooled, a place that was wall-to-wall with top scientists wasn't too shabby.

"Do you ever think all these obstacles have been put in our way because we're not meant to go to Opis?" she asked.

Chris almost went into his we-make-our-own-destinies pep talk, then hesitated because she might have meant some religious thing about fate. Then he thought of the times he'd told himself that he was meant for these difficult days because he wasn't too squeamish for the necessary dirty work of survival.

"Who knows?" he said, dodging the question. He held out his hand for shaking, playing the good boy his mother had insisted he made an effort to be. "I'm Chris Montello, by the way."

"Yeah, I know who you are." She hesitated before accepting the handshake, and her grip was reluctant, like she thought he hadn't washed his hands. Someone had definitely pissed in her cornflakes. "I'm Abbie Vincent. Plant genetics."

Maybe she felt he'd dismissed her as someone's kid instead of calling her Doctor or Professor or something. Well, that was her problem, not his. Plant genetics meant one of two things, though, if he'd understood how Ainatio worked: she was either working on die-back remediation or she was developing climate-resistant crop strains. He didn't ask her why she was still here. It was easier to ask Alex. Now it was time to play dumb and extricate himself.

"Well, nice meeting you," he said. "I've got to see the engineers."

"Is it true you're shipping out the animals too?"

"Yeah. Embryos, as far as I know."

"I meant pets. Cats. Dogs."

"Oh, yeah. Working dogs, mainly."

"I see. Okay, I'll pass your thanks on to Mom."

Whatever her beef was, it wasn't with him, but it still left him with an uneasy feeling that he'd missed something. If she was still there when he came back, he'd take the long route around the physics lab to Alex's office and find out what her problem was.

No, he'd ask now. It never paid to ignore that feeling when he got it. He walked behind the workshop buildings to call Alex on the secure channel and leaned against the wall, keeping an eye out for APS personnel wandering around.

"Alex, it's Chris. What's Abbie Vincent's deal?"

Alex made his thinking sound, a little croaking sigh. "Permanently miserable. Easily offended. Plant geneticist. Dabbles in virology as well, because of her dad. That's what you get when all the education's in-house. Had a place in *Elcano* with her parents — they're biomed

66

— but she wouldn't go and they decided to stay. And not happily. So don't accept invites to their Thanksgiving dinner."

"See? I didn't even need to ask all the questions. Thank you."

"You're welcome. My flaw is now a virtue."

Chris had to say it in case he didn't get another appropriate moment. "Don't rule out Opis, Alex. I'll miss you."

"Whoa there, Captain Inscrutable. Now I've got to take your picture off my tough guy role model wall."

Alex sounded embarrassed. Chris winced. *Why didn't I just say 'we'?* "Yeah, I'm ninety per cent marshmallow. Sorry."

"Is there a problem with Abbie, then?"

"No, just heeding Fonseca's advice about letting folks weed themselves out."

"Hah. Yeah, do as Lennie says. She loves that. Good luck, pal. We're rooting for you."

Chris hadn't realised his crush was that obvious. Captain Inscrutable? He just made sure he stayed calm because scared people looked to him to have everything under control. There was no profound mystery to it. Maybe he looked emotionless to Fonseca, even though he was sure he'd shown he wasn't, but it was too late to reinvent himself.

He carried on to the shuttles, wondering which way the Vincents would jump this time. Whatever happened, there'd still be a rift. The parents had wanted to go and the girl didn't. Whenever their family rows started up, that grievance would be wheeled out as ammunition for their misery. Chris just knew it.

He wondered who was better off: Abbie, whose folks didn't abandon her but made sure she knew what her behaviour had cost them, or him, cut off like a stranger by his mom and dad as soon as the cops hauled him in.

Like you didn't know what I did for a living, you assholes. Always more worried about looking respectable and not making a fuss.

No, he was way better off than Abbie Vincent. He wasn't handcuffed to people who'd probably spend the rest of their lives listing the sacrifices they'd made for their disappointing child. If Abbie had any sense, she'd wave them goodbye, tell them not to follow her, and take her chances on Earth.

But maybe normal people couldn't do that. Chris would never know.

* * *

THE MORRIS FARM, KILL LINE: THREE DAYS LATER.

"*No need to reply,*" the message said. Marc read between the lines and realised what Tev was really telling him. "*Just wanted you to know you were right. Back with Becky like we've never been apart, so let's see how long it lasts. Kids doing great and I'm going to be a grandad, Joni tells me. He's got a fishing business now, so I'm going go out in the boat today. Had a visit from some local bureaucrat to welcome me home and ask if I had everything I needed. I didn't have the heart to tell him home was Bermondsey. Thanks, mate. Safe journey. God bless.*"

The shots went wide, thudding into the wall with muffled *thwops*. Marc flinched and shoved his screen back in his pocket, jerked back to the here and now. He'd taken his eye off the ball and that was a daft, dangerous thing to do when he was stuck in a barn with civvies who'd never handled firearms before, because even simunition hurt like a bastard. It was hot and stuffy inside and everyone's concentration was slipping.

"Damn," said the baker, whose name Marc kept forgetting. *Lance.* That was it. Lance Webber. Lance looked like he was expecting a good slap. "Sorry."

"It's okay, mate. Plenty of time to get this right. At least you've all got good muzzle control. That's a big plus." Marc knew Tev would have been a lot better at this instructor stuff. "Come on. Get a stable position and give me nice controlled shots. Anywhere on the target to start with."

Getting the bots to line the barn with impenetrable ballistic sheets had been one of Marc's better decisions. You could shoot fairy cakes through those flimsy barn walls, so he didn't want anyone outside getting a nasty surprise when his trainees missed the targets. The lining also killed any ricochets.

But he had to cut these people some slack. Firearms training had been his idea. He wanted every Kill Liner to be able to drop whatever wildlife might try to attack them on Opis as soon as they landed, because trouble wouldn't wait for them to get a grip. He'd only seen giant crows on those videos Solomon had shown everyone, but he wanted the civvies to be ready for anything, including waking up from cryo to find that things had turned ugly in the colony. He'd worry about the effect that the higher gravity would have on their aim when they'd nailed the basics. Right now they were getting used to loud noises, recoil, and the idea that they could actually kill something — or someone. A few would have problems coming to terms with that.

Marc stood at the back of the barn and did his maths again. In five weeks, with some of Trinder's people and the transit camp vets running sessions as well, he'd have an extra couple of hundred competent shooters. He'd have preferred everyone over sixteen to be armed and ready, but he'd still have around three-quarters of the adult civvies able to defend the camp. That was good enough. He'd worry about the ones who didn't want to handle firearms later.

His carbine virgins were actually managing to hit the targets now. Their grouping was non-existent, but it was early days, and if they'd squeezed off a few shots at close quarters, they'd probably have mangled whatever was coming for them even if they didn't kill it. Things could only improve.

He let them break for lunch and walked outside to get some fresh air and wait for his relief to turn up. Howie was sitting patiently in the shade of a water bowser, hugging a packet that looked like sandwiches.

"Salt beef ciabatta," Howie said, handing it to him.

"Good stuff." Marc didn't like salt beef, but he was fond of Howie and he didn't want to make him feel he'd failed. Some kids turned feral when they had to fend for themselves, but Jack Howard had managed to hang on to his civility. It showed impressive backbone for a small boy. "What have you got?"

"Chicken."

"We're eating well for the end of the world, aren't we?"

"I miss tuna."

"Yeah." Ocean fish was the only thing they couldn't produce for themselves around here. "Haddock and chips. There's something I'll never see again."

"Are you missing Tev?"

"Got a message from him today. He's back with his wife and kids." That seemed true, but Marc wasn't going to mention the bureaucrat and the boat. He took it as Tev's way of telling him APS had him under surveillance but he could get away in the boat if push came to shove. It was Tev's choice to be there, but it didn't stop Marc feeling he needed to do something about it. "He seems happy. He's going fishing."

"How old are his children?"

"The boy's twenty-four and married with a baby on the way. The girl's eighteen."

"They're grown-ups. Not kids."

"Your kids are always your kids, Howie. Even when they're drawing their pensions."

Howie unwrapped his lunch and ate silently. It was hard to tell if he'd been reminded of losing his own family or if he'd realised it was a hard topic for Marc.

"Did you actually talk to Tev?" he asked at last.

"No, you can't keep saying goodbye to people," Marc said. "It just makes it harder in the end. That's why he said he didn't want a reply."

Marc had polished goodbyes to a fine art. The only way he'd been able to bear it when he deployed was to say the words and walk away. It looked cold, but he knew how hard it was for Sandra and the boys to see him looking back over his shoulder. As long as the last words they heard were that he loved them and that he'd be back before they knew it, that was what they'd remember if he didn't return. John and Greg had learned to do the same. And he did remember those last words from them, but it didn't ease the pain one fucking bit.

It was suddenly hard to swallow the beef. He wiped his right eye with the heel of his hand as discreetly as he could, trying to focus through the wet blur. Howie patted his arm without saying a word. That, maybe, was why Marc needed to be here.

"You're a good lad, Howie," he said.

"It's going to be great on Opis. We can make the world we want because it's a big blank."

"Yeah. It is. The sky's the limit."

Marc stared into the distance, blinking to clear his eyes. He watched a Caracal drive up the narrow track between the fields and then bump its way across the rutted soil towards him. As it got closer he could see Trinder behind the wheel, and Erin Piller, the transit camp's sniper, sitting beside him. Marc had never seen her with her hair loose before. She normally wore it pinned up in a tight braid like a coil of chestnut rope, all very severe and don't-touch-me. Yeah, there was definitely something going on between those two.

"Erin likes Major Trinder," Howie said. "She's acting happy. She isn't, not usually."

"Yeah. I think he likes her, too."

Marc had to give Trinder points for reinventing himself in the last few months. The bloke obviously needed a proper crisis to get his blood pumping. He climbed out of the Caracal and ambled over to Marc, Erin in tow. Marc nodded at her.

"They've made progress, but I don't think they're ready for sniper school yet," Marc said.

Erin smiled. "I thought you would have had them shooting on the move by now."

"They're shaping up. Very willing. I opened the rear doors, by the way, but it's still like an oven in there."

"We could have done this in the underground floors at Ainatio, you know. Aircon and everything."

"Yeah, but it's one thing hearing automatic fire in the distance and another when it's right underneath you. We don't want to make APS nervous. Anyone else decide to jump ship this morning?"

"No idea," Trinder said. "Alex is running the escape committee."

"Okay, we'll be going, then. All yours, Dan."

Marc put his kit in the back of the black Trident he'd driven from DC. It was the British ambassador's official limo, still with its diplomatic plates and the smell of expensive aftershave and air freshener. Marc felt it was the least the bastard owed him and Tev for getting the embassy staff on the helo out of DC, but the ambassador was long gone by the time Marc drove it out of the secure compound, so he obviously didn't mind if anyone borrowed it. The nice thing about armoured limos, especially if you weren't worried about scratching the paintwork, was you could just put your foot down and clear the road ahead the fast, messy, and bumpy way, which was handy in a city falling apart. Marc prided himself on not being one of life's swervers.

Howie strapped himself in for the short ride back to Ainatio and turned on the air conditioning. "Marc, what's the Nomad camp going to be like when we wake up?"

"Could be a nice little town."

"But we won't know anyone. And the people who left us behind are going to be getting there a few weeks ahead of us. What if people don't like each other?"

"Don't worry, Howie, we've got a plan. Me, Chris, and Dan worked it out."

"We could build another town if we don't get on. Like the transit camp."

Marc meant the plan about how they'd handle being newcomers who suddenly outnumbered a small community that had been doing things their own way for forty-five years. He knew there'd be friction, no matter how well-meaning everyone was, and things might get tense. But building a separate settlement seemed a sensible way to give people some respite from each other.

"That's a good idea, Howie," he said. "Seriously, it is. Good man."

Howie beamed. Marc had forgotten how much it mattered to kids to have the approval of an adult they looked up to. He was trying to dust off his parenting skills without falling into the comfortable trap of taking in Howie like a stray. Howie made him feel better, but he wasn't sure that he was good for Howie.

Sod it, the kid needed to be the most important thing in somebody's life, and to *know* that he was. Every kid needed that. It was what parents were for. Maybe he'd been given enough devotion before he lost his family to tide him over into adulthood, but if he hadn't, Marc didn't know if he was capable of filling the gap. The last thing Howie needed was more disappointment.

"What are you going to do this afternoon?" Marc asked.

"I've got my rounds," Howie said gravely.

"Oh. Yeah."

"It's not just people from the camp. I've got some old folks from the town, too. And Ainatio." Howie had made it his duty to check on the older evacuees every day and make sure they were okay, according to Chris. Nobody had asked him to. Now he was expanding his house-call list. "It's lonely being old."

Marc hoped the world — Earth or Opis — wouldn't grind that big-heartedness out of the kid. When they reached Ainatio, Marc dropped him off at the accommodation block.

"Come and find me when you need a lift back to Kill Line," Marc said. "If I'm not in my quarters, I'll be in the staff bar."

Howie nodded, suddenly forty years old. "You go have a beer. I might be some time."

Marc managed not to laugh. It was just delight at seeing a child determined to be so adult, but Howie might have thought he was taking the piss. Marc was still smiling to himself when he parked in the vehicle compound and switched off the limo's engine. The mood didn't last, though. He wandered into the staff club, didn't see anyone he felt like drinking with right then, and got a few beers to go.

He settled down in the armchair in his quarters and checked off the list of to-do items in his head that he could actually do nothing about. He'd put his affairs in order before the DC job because he didn't know if he'd get out of there alive. He hadn't been home for a couple of years, so his flat had probably been let to new tenants and the contents dumped. And whatever was left in his bank account would now never be spent, he'd be declared legally dead at some point, and Sandra would get it because she was his sole beneficiary, which was as it should be. It didn't matter. Everything he really needed, everything he'd miss, everything that couldn't be allowed to fall into anyone else's hands, was always in his rucksack. It was habit for a man who'd spent his life not knowing where and when he'd next be deployed. But these days he kept it packed just because he wanted to be ready to escape from the world.

Before he did, though, there was still the matter of the FTL file.

He felt in his wallet for the small green card that held the information Annis Kim had been willing to die for. It was a physical copy of Ainatio's FTL research. He'd routed her call to APS to delay the bombing run, and he'd done it via his priority access to the Foreign and Commonwealth Office. If they hadn't worked out that valuable intel was being traded, he'd have been surprised. They just didn't have the intel itself.

So Sol handed it over to APS. And if the data's kosher, APS now has a strategic advantage the UK doesn't. I can't sit on my arse and let that happen.

He'd half-expected Sol to doctor the data in a way that APS wouldn't find out about until *Shackleton* was well clear of Earth, but APS's boffins seemed satisfied with it. So it was time to hand it over to London, with caveats. The question was whether to tell Chris and Trinder first or let them know after he'd done it. If they didn't just nod and say fair enough, though, it was going to be awkward.

Marc took his beer into the bedroom and hauled the rucksack out of the wardrobe for another inspection. If he dumped a few things, he could pack the stuff Ainatio had provided when he'd arrived. The black uniform pants were worth keeping, and the spare work boots were too good to leave behind. Yeah, he'd free up some space if he dumped a bath towel and his bag of currency tokens.

He sorted through them, remembering being twenty and thinking money would solve all his problems. The dollar tokens were worthless with or without a banking system, and while the sterling ones were still legal tender, he'd never go back to spend them now. It all felt like toy money left over from a board game he'd thrown out years ago.

He carried on drinking his beer while he aimed the small rectangles into the waste bin from the other side of the room. It took a determined flick and a certain technique to get the flimsy composite to whirl the distance to its target. The game amused him for a few minutes until a knock on the door broke his concentration.

It was Chris Montello. If Chris turned up without calling ahead, it wasn't a social visit. Marc let him in and handed him a beer.

"Solomon wants a face to face meeting for a decision about something," Chris said. "You, me, and Dan. I said we'd meet here. Sorry if I've interrupted your afternoon."

Marc tossed a dollar token at the empty fruit bowl. It landed with a satisfying ping. "Dan's in Kill Line with Erin, turning the yokels into killing machines."

Chris checked his pocket screen. Dan was still chipped. "Yeah, I know. How's it going?"

"Decent progress, I'd say."

"Any news from Tev?"

"His missus took him back and he's happy."

"Good. It's nice to see family sticking together."

Marc realised they'd both stepped on each other's minefields without thinking, but it didn't seem to matter. The one advantage in both of them having a painful family history was that neither had to avoid the topic. There was no happy domestic advantage to shame Chris into guilty silence. When their conversation stopped, it was simply because they didn't have anything to say for the time being.

"You never did tell me why you and Tev ended up stuck here," Chris said, wiping the condensation off his beer with a neatly pressed handkerchief. "Your people could have extracted you."

"Yeah, but by the time it was doable, I didn't want to." Marc had never admitted that to anyone but Tev before. "And Tev refused to leave me on my own, the silly sod. I'm glad he's gone. Bloody wrong to waste his life nurse-maiding me."

"How did you end up *here*, though?"

"How did *you*?"

Chris made a map-following gesture in the air with his finger. "Town to town, then we followed the river. We were heading south to try for the coast without going near the main routes."

Marc wasn't sure if that was really an answer, but then his own response wasn't one either. It was too late to keep secrets that didn't really need to be kept. Chris was never going to be a security threat to the UK. Marc decided to break the habit of a working lifetime and tell him the truth.

"Okay, I knew Ainatio was here," he said.

"Am I allowed to ask how?"

"It was in our Big Boys' Book of Interesting Secret Places when I was special forces. You can't fly shuttles and maintain orbitals without Kingdom detecting it and making a note."

"Kingdom's your spy sat network, yeah?"

"That's partly how I routed the call to APS."

"So you're a spy too." Chris seemed very matter-of-fact about it. "What did you want from Ainatio?"

"No, I'm *not* a spy," Marc said. "And I definitely didn't know about Nomad, if that's what you're asking. But we knew this place existed and that it was still functioning, and we thought old allies might be up for taking a couple of stranded operators. We banged out of the embassy in the ambassador's car and headed down here."

"No living off the land with your legendary survival skills, then."

"We're middle-aged men with bad backs and we're not stupid."

"Does Dan know you knew?"

"I think he worked it out."

"It's not like it's a guilty secret," Chris said, "but I think he'd be happier knowing."

"Okay, I'll tell him. If he didn't lose his shit over Ainatio hiding a zillion-dollar interplanetary expedition for nearly fifty years, I doubt he'll be offended because I never told him I saw a satellite image."

Chris allowed himself a half-smile. He never managed a full one. "Your guys don't seem to be very curious about us, considering that they must have eavesdropped on the APS call. You know. The mention of propulsion data. And spies."

"I don't think Sol said FTL or Nomad."

"But your government knew Ainatio was here."

"Yeah."

"And they wouldn't wonder what the data was, or why APS thought it was worth spying on us, or why APDU were concerned enough to nuke a backwater on the other side of the world, or if we all lived happily ever after?"

Marc knew Chris would get onto this sooner or later. He wondered whether he regarded the British government as an external... well, not *enemy*, but a possible complication.

"They're bound to be spying," Marc said. "And they're not my guys."

"They haven't checked up on you. Maybe they don't need to."

Marc tried not to feel he was under interrogation. This was just Chris being Chris, asking blunt questions because he trusted Marc enough to get straight to the point.

"If you mean have I had secret chats with them, I haven't," Marc said. "Sol would know all about it. He hears all."

"No, I meant they wouldn't need to ask because they'd be spying on you. How much do you trust them?"

Marc held up his finger and thumb, pinched together to show the tiniest of gaps. "They'd throw me under the bus in a heartbeat. That's what governments do, in case you've forgotten. And it's the Foreign Office. I don't think I was *their* guy even when I was the government's guy."

Chris's expression hadn't changed. "I'll assume they've found out a bit about Nomad and FTL, then, if not *Cabot*. Because, you know, all those Brits in the crew might be of serious interest to them if they realise they're alive."

"Yeah."

"It's a shame they can't contact them now."

"Yeah. And I don't know if they'd tell me if they could."

"Can they spy on Tev?"

"Probably. APS definitely will. But he'll watch his back. He's an old hand at PERSEC."

Chris blinked. "I'm just asking to work out who might know what. Not accusing you."

"I know." Marc wondered if he sounded annoyed. "No problem."

Sometimes Marc didn't know what to make of Chris. Trinder had summed him up perfectly: he looked more like a vicar than Kill Line's actual vicar. It was that wide-eyed, mind-on-higher-things look, as if he was contemplating some complex spiritual mystery. If you swapped his combat rig for a nice suit, you'd never guess what he was capable of until you pushed him too far. Marc knew it wasn't an act. The bloke wasn't hiding something, either. He was keeping it battened down, and Marc understood that effort all too well.

"By the way, thanks for letting Howie look after you." Chris said. It was almost apologetic, like he regretted asking questions. "It makes him feel better."

Marc had to smile. "Yeah, he's a good kid."

He waited for Chris to go on and explain the gaps in Howie's story, but he didn't. Marc decided it would emerge in its own good time. They occupied themselves playing horseshoes with the currency tokens until Marc heard activity outside the door and opened it to let Solomon and Trinder in.

"Beer, Dan?" Marc asked. He looked down at the quadrubot. "How about you, Sol? A bracing zap from the shaver socket?"

"I'm glad you're in a good mood," Solomon said. "I need a decision."

Chris gave him a look. "You've already made it."

"It's up to you, but I'm here to tell you I can revise the launch date."

"Which way?"

"Earlier. We can launch in three weeks. If you think that's preferable to the delay we've negotiated with APS, and people are ready to leave, we can be out of here in the first week of August. The supplies are ready to load."

"Have you told Alex?" Marc asked.

"Not yet. I had to get the bots to run hull integrity tests first. The aft cargo section doesn't need re-skinning."

"And you thought it did."

"If we seal one of the internal bulkheads, we lose some cargo space. Not much. And the hull can be maintained in transit. Remember the bots stay with the ship."

Trinder nodded. "Sooner the better, then. Folks have been psyched up to leave for months. They need to see it's actually going to happen. Some don't think we ever will."

"And the less time we're here, the less chance of APS finding something awkward," Marc said. "Pham's suspicious by nature. I mean, he's a spook. Enough said. And he's got lots of reasons to be suspicious of us. He wouldn't bring a special forces bloke here if he believed every word we've said. He's looking for something else, and I want us out before he works out what it is. I'm just waiting for a technician to come back waving a crop sample and saying tests show die-back came from the labs here."

"Me too. If APS was happy to nuke us a few weeks ago, they won't give us the benefit of the doubt this time." Chris retrieved the tokens from the fruit bowl and stacked them on the coffee table. "I'll talk to Alex about the date. He's still in charge of the company. We shouldn't bypass him."

Not even Alex thought he was running things, though. The chain of command had just emerged because three soldiers stepped in out of habit and sorted things out. In chaos, the men with a plan and the ingrained reflex to fix problems filled the power vacuum, even if they had no intention of governing. Alex, always the fixer and smoother-over of ruffled feathers, didn't want to govern anything either as far as Marc could tell. The three of them could muddle along like this for a few weeks, but the real test would come when they arrived on Opis. The *Shackleton* mission would still outnumber the *Cabot* crew and their descendants, even if they bred like rabbits, and it was anyone's guess what kind of power structure would be operating when they got there.

It wasn't their most urgent problem, though.

"Make sure Alex doesn't put it to a vote," Trinder said. "Just tell people when we're leaving. If a few weeks makes any difference to them, they'll say. Give them a firm deadline, let them see everything's under control, and then we're out of here. No more uncertainty."

Marc reached out and patted Solomon on his weird snakey camera head. "And since nobody else said it, I will. Well done, Sol. Who's a good boy?"

Solomon tolerated the pat. "Thank you. But we're not out of the woods yet. Bringing the date forward is going to make Pham even more suspicious. If he's got an unpleasant surprise planned for us, he'll make his move sooner rather than later. So I'm bringing forward the rest of the IT plan as a matter of urgency. I don't want another situation like Erskine destroying the FTL link. I've already mirrored most of the network to Lammergeier One to make it the alternative command centre, but I need to be able to switch to it immediately in an emergency."

"They're the ones who wanted us out in forty-eight hours," Trinder said. "I know politicians probably overrule APDU all the time, but it's funny how elastic the deadline's become."

"Yeah, I don't buy it either," Chris said. "One minute die-back's serious and urgent enough to nuke the whole area and us with it if we don't get out right away, the next they're giving us a few months to pack our bags. So it's a handy excuse. I thought it was to get their foot in the door for the FTL, but they've got that now. So they either think there's more secret swag to be had or there's something else they want to grab before it leaves Earth."

"At best, APS is unpredictable," Solomon said. "And Pham is no ordinary politician. He's come from a very high-risk job and I have no doubt that his ends will always justify any means."

"Yeah, I vote Paranoid Party as well." Marc reached for another can of beer. "What's happening on *Temujin*, Sol?"

"Very little," Sol said. "Most of the activity must be below deck. I only ever see the helicopters and a handful of crew up top. They're probably aware that Orbital One can monitor them."

"So Plan B is still evacuation to this lake down south, yeah?"

"And you're still not happy with that," Chris said.

"No. If the orbital's land use imaging is reliable, it's going to take a long time to turn the site into farmland. But I haven't seen a better option that doesn't involve travelling somewhere a couple of thousand miles west and hoping it's still habitable when we get there."

"Yeah, I know it's going to be hard getting settled at the lake," Chris said. "But it's a big enough area to avoid running into other people with the same idea. Even if it *was* perfect, though, if we've upset APS, they'll find us eventually. You can't hide a camp that size. And APDU command is a call away. They can get long-range aircraft and all kinds of shit out here in hours."

"Fonseca's still convinced they just want to grab their stash and go home," Trinder said. "Even if that's true, it depends on us keeping our dirty little secrets secret."

Marc tossed another token into the fruit bowl. "If they work out this new die-back escaped from the labs, suddenly we're not preppers or refugees, we're an enemy developing bio-weapons."

"Yeah." Chris had that distant look like he'd spotted something coming over the horizon that wasn't the cavalry. "They don't know who's involved or not and we won't necessarily get a trial. They'll sweep up everyone in here and leave Kill Line to fend for itself."

"I don't think die-back's the worst of our secrets, to be honest," Trinder said. "It's Sol. If they work out what he really is, forget Die-back Two. They'll go after him. But apart from the scientists and technicians, who knows that Sol's an unauthorised Autonomous

Self-Determining model and not just a top-spec regular AI? It's not obvious. And nobody's going to volunteer the information."

"Thank you," Solomon said. "And thank you for *unauthorised*. It's an improvement on *banned*."

"You know what I mean. Top spec AIs pass for human until you ask them for their opinion."

"I'm working hard at being bland and unopinionated, Major."

"Don't knock it, Sol. It's always worked for me."

Chris leaned back in the chair. "Anyway, it was nice of Erskine to arrange the full dress rehearsal for us. At least we know we're good at evacuations."

"How about we move the staff out to the town now, just in case?" Trinder asked. "Quicker getaway. Easier to defend. Harder for APDU to pin us down. We can move back for the launch if and when it's clear that APS won't screw us over."

"Yeah, definitely," Marc said. "And most evacuees are in the town already. Most of the stuff they need to get to Opis is in here, though. The last thing we need is food supplies held hostage on this campus, whether we go for Plan A or Plan B. If Pham's looking for leverage, he'll have worked that out already."

"Great guy," Chris muttered.

"We haven't had the honour of an audience with him like Dan has," Marc said. "He might be a diamond when you get to know him."

Pham gave the appearance of playing nice now, but Marc didn't believe a word of it, not after all the bullshit with the nukes. Nobody did. Plan B had taken up more of their planning time than a trip into the unknown on another bloody planet, and that said it all.

"How long will it take to clear out, Sol?" Marc asked. "The boffins will take a few buses, but what about the supplies?"

"I estimate two days," Sol said. "Remember we have fifteen containers but only four truck units to haul them, so if Plan B becomes necessary, most of that food will have to be redistributed among other vehicles. That means we'll also need to move those out earlier, plus loader bots, so whether the worst happens or not, we're committed to the full procedure. And if we return to launch *Shackleton*, allow for the same amount of time to move everything back here."

"I was going to ask if we should tell Pham we're leaving early," Chris said. "But even if we don't, a two-day job gives him plenty of time to intervene."

"Let's not be too alarmist," Solomon said. "Nothing's happened yet."

Chris sighed. "Emergency planning always sounds scary, Sol."

"I do realise that."

Marc suspected Chris's sigh was about the prospect of having to go on the road again after everything his people had been through, not Sol's caution. Marc tried to keep things in perspective. Fonseca had a point: if all Pham wanted was to get out of here in one piece with his Ainatio swag, he'd have no reason to interfere with *Shackleton* and Opis. But after APS's recent game of nuclear Russian roulette, not having a backup plan was suicidal, even one that was no better now than it had been when they ruled it out before Erskine left.

Everything was a gamble. But they'd gambled to stay alive for years.

"Okay, that sounds like a plan," Trinder said. "We tell APS we're trying to get out of their hair as soon as we can, I move everyone out, and then I press the big delete button on Ainatio's sensitive systems. Pham won't notice because it's all the bits APS can't access anyway."

"I can do that," Solomon said.

"No, it's my job, even if I don't understand it," Trinder said. "With everything transferred to Lamm One, we can manage the launch from there if — when — we go back to the campus. So we look harmless and keep our heads down. Well, as harmless as you can look, Marc. Do what you can."

"I'll get Chris to give me lessons," Marc said.

Maybe Trinder had said that for Solomon's comfort, but it was good advice. Behaving like you were expecting trouble sometimes sent out the wrong message and invited it.

"Three weeks," Marc said, wondering if he turned every situation into a worst case without realising. "All we have to do is hold it together for another twenty-one days. APS might not even have lab test results by then."

Three weeks still sounded like a bloody long time.

03

I think it's best if you can honestly deny knowledge of this, Mr President. Give me access to an unimportant ship, a few low-priority troops so nobody notices and asks what the big operation is about, and let me call in my own experts. Ainatio is basically now just museum-piece scientists, farmers, and ferals with shotguns. All I need is transport with no questions asked to get our assets to the area. If we need to erase the Ainatio site and anyone notices, it's about die-back. And if Britain's eavesdropping and is aware of FTL, there's nothing they can do to take it from us.

Tim Pham, briefing APS President Graham Terrence before beginning the Ainatio retrieval mission.

KILL LINE: NEXT MORNING.

"I'm going to miss all this. Nice and peaceful. But then I suppose the Black Death reduced the hustle and bustle as well, right?"

Alex Gorko stood in the unmowed grass beyond the front security gates, nursing a coffee while he stared up at a clear blue sky peppered with a small cloud of insects. A truck rolled out with a container load for Kill Line, unremarked and, Solomon hoped, unnoticed.

"They have blue skies in Asia, Alex."

"You know what I mean. Okay, let's do this."

Alex was nervous about announcing the early departure to the staff. Solomon didn't expect the news to make a great deal of difference, but Alex hadn't been himself for a few days. He'd always been good at putting an annoyingly cheerful face on things, so much so that Solomon suspected it was part of a technique to make the scientists feel superior to a glib buffoon. They weren't on their guard against being manipulated because Alex seemed deferential, no threat at all, and they thought they could run rings around him. But he almost always got his way.

Sometimes he snapped when people were stubborn, though, and the real Alex Gorko emerged: he'd snarled at Ingram, and Erskine, and argumentative staff, and he'd even punched out Ben Tusa when the physicist tried to force Dr Kim into *Elcano*. Alex was neither physical nor fit, and taking on a stronger, younger man was something of a suicide mission. That hadn't gone unnoticed by Chris and Marc. They didn't seem to think he'd made a fool of himself at all. They respected his willingness to have a go regardless of the size of his opponent.

Was that why Solomon liked Alex? Had he always seen that in him, the willingness to sacrifice himself for the tribe, some military quality? Solomon had his doubts, but Alex had done the right thing in the end.

"I wish I knew how *Cabot* was getting on," Alex said. "I'll be dust by the time anyone gets there and sends a message back."

"Not if Ingram's already sent one. You'll just be very old."

"Sol, I'll always remember you for your sensitivity."

"All part of the service."

"You know what I want right now?" Alex said. "Amnesia. I'd like to wake up tomorrow in Melbourne or Seoul with my memory wiped clean, except for my skills and that week I had in Bermuda." They were at the gates now. They'd have to stop the social conversation and talk like a human and his AI exchanging data and instructions. "There's no right decision in any of this, you know. Only a less bad one."

"But you've made your decision and you're allowing others to make theirs," Solomon said. "You're not deciding fates."

"Why doesn't that make me feel better? No, don't answer that. APS minion at twelve o'clock."

He stepped aside for the orange-suited technician on the entrance steps and nodded politely at him. The guy was carrying a small transparent tray with a few bee bots rattling around in it, or what was left of them. Solomon looked up at the shapes silhouetted against the sunlight. The chemical used to destroy the crops had shrivelled the small artificial pollinators to blackened skeletons.

"I didn't know we still had any of those," Alex said, peering in. "Must be Kill Line's old stash."

"We found them in the fields," the technician said. "You want them back? For a souvenir?"

Alex smiled ruefully. "Yeah, why not? If the ship doesn't blow up before we get to Opis we can set up a museum dedicated to human mistakes." He took the tray. "Thanks."

It was all very good-humoured. Solomon hoped it stayed that way. He fell in behind Alex and followed him to give the illusion of robotic obedience. APS seemed to take any eccentricity as normal in a community that had been cut off from the rest of the world for years.

"Very astute psyops use of the word *if*," Solomon said.

Alex smiled. "Fluent High Weasel spoken here."

He braced his shoulders as he approached the auditorium, still clutching his coffee. But there was no sea of accusing and anxious faces. The anticlimax must have been painful for him. There were only eighty-two people waiting, scattered thinly across the rows of seats as if they'd spread out in an effort to look like a decent turnout. Alex's shoulders sagged a little. He stepped up to the podium at the front, put his coffee on the lectern, and took out his screen.

"We could have done this in the bar and made it look like a full house, couldn't we?" he said to the sparse audience. "Well, thanks for making your way down here. I've got some nice uncomplicated news for a change. *Shackleton*'s going to be ready to launch by August fifth. That brings all the embarkation prep forward by seven weeks."

One of the IT staff perked up. "Wow, good job."

"Let's face it, we're all going stir crazy here. So unless anyone's got an incredibly compelling reason for a delay, we plan to go for the early launch."

"Have you told APS?" someone asked.

"We've notified them we're trying to speed up departure. Launch dates have slipped before, as we're all too aware, so I didn't commit firmly. And they probably realise we don't really trust them not to change their minds on nuking us."

Alex looked around the room. Solomon couldn't see any dissent. Even Todd Mangel, a man who generally liked an argument for the sport of it, seemed satisfied.

"Anyone here thinking of asking for APS resettlement who isn't already on the transfer list should treat this as the last call for boarding," Alex said. "You've got until close of play today. And remember APS makes the final call, not me. Dr Kim's brokering jobs like a boss, but even she can't guarantee they'll take you."

Mangel winked at Sol. "And well done to the bots for completing the work ahead of schedule. Bless their cold little tin hearts."

"Okay, folks, thank you for making me feel like I'm still relevant," Alex said. "I think we're done. Catch you later."

He gathered his coffee cup and wandered back to his office, Solomon trotting at his side along the deserted corridor.

"Everything's going to feel like a big nothing now," he said.

"Well, it's certainly possible to develop crisis fatigue."

"Remind me who's still dithering, then."

"Ed Acosta from Plant Genetics. And Phil Berman and his sweetheart, Ruth. Well, *she's* dithering, and he's in thrall to her."

"*Sweetheart*. You're so adorably Victorian sometimes." Alex opened his office door and stood back to let Solomon walk in and park the quadrubot for charging. It was time for him to transfer back into the network. "Hard to imagine Phil even holding hands with another human being."

Poor Berman. He'd been Erskine's assistant, a man of great loyalty and tact, but he was still human, and he needed a soul mate. "A man with a secret life, I think," Solomon said.

"Nobody has secrets from you, Sol."

"I was aware of their frequent meetings, of course, but my active monitoring ends at the threshold to private spaces, as you well know."

"You always say that."

"I always *do* that."

"What a gent."

"And the Vincents. Abbie still doesn't want to go and her mother's trying to tempt her with fascinating alien plant species that'll be named for her. Abbie thinks it's more important to join Seb Meikle and work on die-back treatments and resistant crops for the good of *this* planet. We have a stand-off."

"Eavesdropper."

"They argue in the restaurant, Alex. I can't avoid detecting it."

"I was just teasing."

"I know, and I was just indicating that human trust is a serious issue for me. You're well aware I can't function unless I have it."

"That's me told."

Solomon regretted chiding Alex. He recognised this was his own uneasiness about making moral judgements while being guilty of behaviour that most would consider unethical. He'd killed, he'd lied, and he'd handed secret research to a foreign government. Even though he'd done it to preserve the lives that mattered most to him, it felt uncomfortable. Bednarz had warned him about the challenge of ends justifying means, and that it was the heart of ethical dilemma. Humans had never come to terms with it either, Bednarz said, so Solomon would have to learn to live with the conflict as well.

"Alex, I apologise," Solomon said. "I could have ignored the conversations in the same way I don't actively monitor private spaces."

"And miss all the other conversations we might need to know about?"

"Very well, I didn't have to tell you what I heard. But I decided it was better for the mission if you had all the facts. You're right to challenge me on it."

"It was just a joke, buddy. I'll live."

"And now I've made you even more uncomfortable."

"Not at all. I love to see you feeling guilty." Alex tapped at his screen and changed the figures on the wall display. "Okay, that's the current tally. Just a couple of new names I hadn't added. It's all yours now."

Disembodied again, Solomon absorbed the layers of detail feeding into the monitoring network from around the facility while he checked the names and matched them to faces and voices he could detect. The people who wanted to go with APS were mostly from die-back remediation, site maintenance, and manufacturing. *Elcano* had taken most of the physicists, agricultural scientists, and other plant biologists, and the current *Cabot* team already had at least a dozen of those. Everyone else could be replaced by bots. The entire Nomad mission had been managed and executed by AI and robotics with little human intervention or even awareness for decades. Solomon wasn't unduly concerned.

"Let's see how many others want to join them by tonight," he said.

"You know what happened when we allocated places in *Elcano*, Sol. I braced for a last-minute rush but the ship launched with spare berths."

"But we have room for everyone this time."

"It's not about numbers. Australia could absorb sixteen hundred people without even noticing. It's going to be about who APS considers *undesirable*. Probably not even disease control."

"Sixteen hundred and seventy-three, if you include Dr Kim and *all* the Ainatio staff, but she's an Australian citizen and has the right to return."

"Where is she, by the way? She hasn't worn her tracker since we saved her ass."

Solomon scanned the camera network. Kim was sitting in the garden between the physics lab and the runway, talking to Tim Pham. They had their backs to the camera. That had meant turning the wooden bench around, so they obviously didn't want Solomon eavesdropping.

It troubled him for a moment. He'd defended Kim when others said they didn't trust her. He knew he'd misjudged Erskine, a woman he'd observed since she was a child, so perhaps he'd been naive about Kim as well. Or maybe the seating was Pham's idea, because all he had to do was check the security schematics that everyone could access and see where the cameras were located.

Solomon diverted the camera feed to Alex's monitor and waited for a reaction. "They have history."

"Of the horizontal kind."

"If that's how she called in the favour, I have no objections."

"Oh, I don't think she called in any favours at all," Alex said. "I was dumb enough to believe her, right up to the point where APS decided to give us three months' grace to launch. One minute the new die-back strain's the end of the world, and the next they're taking their time rummaging through our underwear drawer. Do they ever check we're decontaminating traffic properly? No. You'd think it would be a priority to make sure."

"You're not the only person to make that point."

"That's because it's true. It was just a ruse to get their foot in the door. I don't know why they didn't just kick it down. But whether that's good manners or they don't have the military capacity we think they do, I still can't see how Kim wasn't involved."

"We are where we are," Solomon said. "I may well have been manoeuvred into giving them what they wanted, but the outcome's the same. If we'd brazened it out, they might not have bombed us, but we'll never know. It doesn't matter as long as nobody gets hurt and we reach our objective."

"True. No difference." Alex looked awkward for a moment, chin tucked down and frowning at his fingernails as if he'd had a bad manicure. "Sol, whatever I said at the time, I think you did the right thing. And I should have done the right thing sooner. Are we okay now? You and me, I mean."

"You've asked that before. Yes, we are okay."

"Just making sure. You kind of hated my guts for a while."

"I'm not sure I've experienced hate," Solomon said. "Anger and disappointment, perhaps. And fear. Look, you're busy. I'll let you get on with your work."

"Just keep us up to speed with where you are."

"Don't worry. I'll minimise my time in the network."

Alex looked like he was thinking that over. "If Kim had told Pham what you really are, I think he'd have made a move by now."

"Indeed, but I'll continue to plan as if she did."

Solomon was reaching the end of the first phase of a mission that had begun a century ago and it suddenly felt more frightening than momentous. It wasn't just irreplaceable years at stake, or even the risk of being outed as an ASD — worse still, an Autonomous Moral variant — at the last moment. It was the weight of all those human lives, the people who'd spent theirs bringing him to this point, and those who were humanity's future. He couldn't fail them.

APS would leave as soon as Pham had everything he wanted — and if that wasn't the FTL research, it was hard to know what other interest Ainatio held for them. Solomon kept an eye on the APS team's progress, noting what they were accessing on what was left of the network and how far they'd managed to get with burning off contaminated vegetation. The micro-drones on patrol over the farmland to the north showed dark brown fields on Doug Brandt's farm where the crops had already been destroyed, but the APS technicians were now tackling a much bigger area crossing the two-mile-wide defoliated cordon around the county boundary. They seemed to be taking it as a serious threat, whatever Alex thought. A long line of bots like small yellow combines trundled across the countryside in a wave, spraying the dead and dying vegetation. It was slow and it killed every healthy species in its path as well, but it was thorough.

Solomon watched for a while, sent a link to Alex in case he wanted to view the procedure on his monitor, and then shifted his focus back to *Shackleton*. In an instant, he was on board the ship, docked at Orbital 2 in a disposal orbit on the edge of the graveyard zone, far enough from Earth and the orbits of working satellites to avoid attention.

He checked the tracking map collated from accessible sat feeds and the orbitals' collision avoidance systems and compared the snapshots over the last twenty-four hours to see what might have passed through the junkyard. There was no trace of a salvage bot. Nobody did routine scrap recovery any longer except APS, but there was useful material out here that was nearly impossible to source on Earth now, and Solomon wasn't too proud to grab the odd piece of junk to recycle for the Ainatio fleet.

Fleet. It was down to three ships. And only one was going anywhere.

He carried on with his inspection, moving through the ship from camera to camera, system to system, and noted the progress of the bot workforce. APS had always known that Ainatio had ships mothballed out here, and that there was occasional maintenance, but they'd never tried to scavenge from them. Solomon still wasn't sure if that was just courtesy or if they thought the ships had countermeasures to deter what few salvage bots might attempt to cannibalise them.

The three smaller Ainatio docks formed a makeshift satellite constellation, using Orbital 1 — still in geostationary orbit — as the comms relay. APS probably knew that, too, and as Annis Kim had worked on *Shackleton*'s refit, they probably felt they had all the information they needed about what went on up here. But Kim seemed to have kept her word and said nothing about the armaments. There'd be no point in assuring Tim Pham that they really were a last-resort defence against unknown threats they might encounter in deep space, not weapons intended for warfare on Earth.

Solomon wasn't sure that it was entirely true now. If things went wrong, he was ready to destroy *Temujin*'s helicopters with conventional missiles, and if he was willing to do that, what would stop him escalating the conflict? It was only the knowledge that he'd run out of nuclear weapons long before APS did. But he wouldn't let himself be caught out again by assuming restraint would head off confrontation.

No, he had to stop thinking like this. It was unhealthy. He was imagining an imminent threat because he was still disturbed by being so unprepared for what Erskine had done. Now he was overcompensating. He had to resist aggressive impulses that he didn't fully understand yet. APS were hardly allies, but they could have done things very differently and killed people if they'd wanted to take the easiest route. They'd behaved with restraint and courtesy, if he overlooked the threat of sodium bombs.

Solomon returned to his task list. He couldn't begin shipping supplies to *Shackleton* yet, but he'd tasked the engineering AI under his control to plan where everything would be stowed if the worst didn't happen and the food wasn't diverted to an overland evacuation. The cargo space that would be lost with the temporary bulkhead fix would be made up by storing food in the passages and engineering spaces. No human would be moving around the ship for decades. *Shackleton* was just an armed freighter for shipping people in cryo, with no large communal spaces or leisure areas, just a handful of cabins for the crew in the final approach phase, and only enough room to revive and orientate passengers a batch at a time. Day-to-day habitability wasn't a priority.

It was almost time to move *Shackleton* to Orbital 1, then. Now he'd committed himself to a launch date, Solomon felt he couldn't let that date slip and create more uncertainty for the people whose welfare was now wholly in his hands.

Their trust still surprised him. They thought he was omnipotent. He often tried to explain how he operated so that any confidence placed in him was justified. It was a simple analogy: he was a factory foreman walking the shop floor, and his workers were the network of slaved dumb AIs, bots, sensors, and monitors. His workforce knew their jobs better than he did, but he set their targets and he could respond instantly when they called to him or alerted him to a problem, detecting their voices like someone hearing their own name leap out of the hubbub of noise at a party. That had proved to be the best description for humans to grasp.

But now one of those workers was trying to get his attention for real.

It was the proximity sensor in Orbital 1, flashing a warning that an unauthorised shuttle was approaching the dock. Alex and Trinder would be getting that alert flashed to them too.

Solomon shifted his focus back to Orbital 1 and notified everyone in his security loop that he was dealing with the incursion. He could see what was happening from one of the external cameras. A small shuttle in dark blue Asia-Pacific Defence Union livery had approached and seemed to be lining up to dock.

Well, that's damned rude. Provocative, even. So do I allow the docking for the sake of safety, or deny access and risk a collision?

There was a third option that he liked a lot better. He could exploit the contact to try to hack into APS comms before assisting the shuttle. The encrypted ship to shore link between *Temujin* and the ground team had defeated him so far, but if he could lure the shuttle's AI into accepting instructions and codes from him, he could probably slip past its firewall unnoticed.

It was, as Marc Gallagher would say, worth a punt.

What would scare the pilot enough to make him ask permission? Perhaps he was trying to dock covertly, not realising that the orbital was operational again, and then he'd be scared off for good. But it was an opportunity Solomon knew he might not get again.

There were risks. He could end up damaging the orbital because he couldn't be sure how the pilot would respond to his manoeuvre. But he had to try. If he didn't, APS would try to board anyway and he couldn't tell what they intended to do. If he cooperated, he might establish a useful route into APS military comms if he needed to divert or dissuade them from doing something else.

All he had to do was interrupt Orbital 1's station-keeping and reposition it to prevent manual docking. A few degrees was the difference between settling into the external hatch with a gentle bump and crashing into it or missing it completely.

A burst of the positioning thrusters shifted the station just enough to put the shuttle on a collision course, triggering a full board of warning alarms. Solomon's awareness was instantly full of sensors and bots telling him the orbit had changed and immediate action was needed. If the pilot didn't change course, he'd probably clip the solar panels or crash into them, and for a moment Solomon thought he was going to do just that. But the shuttle executed an emergency burn to skim past, a little too late for his peace of mind. He could see it was moving to a higher orbit as it slowed down, probably to manoeuvre so that it could keep pace with Orbital 1. It was time to talk.

Solomon found the APS open comms channel, linked to Alex's audio to let him hear what was happening, and flashed the pilot. It was time to use his most unemotional I'm-not-really-human voice.

"Unidentified shuttle, do not attempt to dock again. Do not attempt to dock. You have activated collision avoidance. Maintain a minimum separation of five hundred metres and await instructions."

"APS five-two-six here, Ainatio, apologies." It was a woman. She sounded a little like Annis Kim, with a noticeable Australian accent. "We were unaware this orbital was operational. Wait one."

"Codes are required. Please transmit your code."

There was a long breath. "Ainatio, negative, I do not have a code. Please state if you're an actual human."

"Negative, I'm an AI. Do not attempt to dock. Please wait for further instructions."

Solomon hoped Alex was paying attention. Speaking in unnatural phrases would tip Alex off that Solomon was acting and needed him to play along with it.

"APS five-two-six, this is Alex Gorko, Ainatio acting chief executive." Good man: he'd caught on right away. "Are you having problems? You've set off our burglar alarm."

"Yes, we appear to have triggered collision avoidance measures in your orbital," the pilot said.

"Were you trying to dock?"

"Ah... yes, sir."

"Why are you trying to gain entry?"

"My apologies, sir. We thought the orbital was derelict."

"Well, word obviously didn't reach you that we've had to repair the damage Erskine caused so we can prep *Shackleton* for launch. And that wasn't an answer to my question, by the way. You're lucky our AI didn't interpret you as a hazard. Stand off while I talk to Commissioner Pham."

Solomon hadn't expected Alex to go on the offensive, but it was a more natural reaction than *not* asking the pilot what the hell she was doing. He hoped Alex wouldn't overdo it and deter her from docking altogether, though. It wasn't essential to hack into the APS and APDU nets, but it was better than relying entirely on their goodwill for the next few weeks. They could inspect the orbital as closely as they liked as long as they didn't damage it. Shuttles could dock directly with *Shackleton* if they had to, but the transfer would be much more hazardous, especially for the children and seniors.

Solomon corrected the orbital's position and waited, re-checking the repairs that Orbital 1's bots had carried out in the wake of Erskine's sabotage. But the shuttle did a burn and started moving to a lower orbit without a word from the pilot.

"Was it something I said?" Alex asked. "I didn't even connect to Pham."

"Perhaps my intentions were obvious," Solomon said.

It was disappointing. He wouldn't get his chance to breach APS's system today. Did they already know he might be able to do that, though? Perhaps he was wrong about Dr Kim after all.

* * *

NOMAD BASE, OPIS: 0845 HOURS.

Fred swooped into the camp like a big black low-level glider, freezing the bots in their tracks as he set off their collision sensors.

It was wonderfully dramatic, even if his final approach was a little wobbly. The only thing that spoiled the image of death from the skies was the crossbody bag strung around him, which didn't seem to be helping his aerodynamics. Jeff found it gratifying to know that even aliens resorted to manbags sometimes. He went outside to greet Fred and found he'd gathered a small but wary audience in a matter of seconds.

"Morning, Fred." Jeff looked him over. "How's it going?"

"I have studied," Fred said. "I talk better now. I come so you can tell me how much I progress."

Jeff would drop everything for Fred's lessons. He messaged Ingram to let her know what he was up to and gestured vaguely at the main building. "If you could eat our food, I'd get you breakfast. But we can have some peace and quiet in the bot hangar."

"I not know if your food edible."

"Yeah, I have days like that too. Bot hangar it is, then."

Jeff wasn't sure if the crows had already ventured inside the hangar before anyone had landed. Solomon had mentioned finding a black feather jammed in the trim of one of the bot frames months before *Cabot* arrived, and that feather was now in Jeff's desk drawer. When he walked into the hangar, he looked along the ranks of quadrubots first, always hoping that one would separate itself from the others and walk over to him for a chat. But if there was no comms link to Earth, there could be no Solomon. Getting him back online was Jeff's personal priority.

Fred wandered between the rows of bots in their charging docks as if he hadn't seen them like this before, examining them in size order from the small cubes and pallet carriers right up to the big construction models.

"They built themselves," Jeff said. "From the first ones that landed here years ago. They were launched a long time before the company acquired FTL. The small ones built bigger ones using bits of the original ship and materials mined here, and recycled themselves, and here we are."

He wasn't sure how much of that Fred understood. For all he knew, they might be better at reading a new language than speaking it or understanding it when spoken. But Fred was absorbing English at a fantastic rate, far faster any human could manage.

"Solomon is not a mechanical," Fred said, staring at the line of quadrubots.

There was no point in lying. "No, he's an artificial intelligence. An AI. A digital brain. He used to transmit himself here from Earth and insert his programme or whatever into a bot."

"*Emanation*," Fred said. "You mean he is emanation."

Jeff had to look that one up. "Yes. You've got them, then."

"Know some, but not like Solomon."

"Yeah, Solomon's special."

"He was happy." Fred was still staring into a quadrubot's snake camera head as if it was a face. The old bots always looked like they were wearing shades. "He likes to run."

"You talked to him."

"No, Solomon talked to my child's children. We stay silent, pretend to be animals. But he was nice. Friendly. We watch him run like he never have free air before."

Jeff imagined poor old Sol galloping around like a horse let loose for the first time. It seemed a bit sad.

"Okay." He sat down on a low retaining rail. "Let's try some conversation lessons. You're speaking much better than the last time I saw you."

"We all learn. Even children."

"Good. I'm impressed."

"Tell me about you. Where you from? What you work at?"

"Earth," Jeff said. "England." He took out his screen and pointed to the children's encyclopaedia to show Fred an image of rolling wheat fields. "Species... human. Nationality... er, clan?... yes, clan. Tribe. *English*. Job, function... Chief Petty Officer, Royal Navy. Or at least I used to be. My name, me as an individual... Jeff Aiken, Jeff from the family called Aiken. So I'm a human from England, on Earth, and my job is chief petty officer, which is looking after the discipline, welfare, and training of ratings — sailors — in my section."

Fred looked at him with that slight sideways tilt that smacked of disbelief. Jeff wondered if he'd packed too much information in that sentence. But Fred reached into his manbag, took out the screen Jeff had given him, and swiped through images with long, fragile fingers. He pointed one digit at himself. "Species... *ablun*. My job is *teerik*. My life is *teerik*."

"What's *teerik*?"

Fred swiped again. He was racing through the pages like a machine. Eventually he paused and held up the screen triumphantly. "Book," he said. "*Book*."

"Yes, the screen's kind of a book."

"No, *me*. Teerik is a book. Place to keep knowledge."

"Librarian?" Jeff looked for an image of a library, then a computer monitor. "Like this? You look after books? Not actual books, maybe, but stored data? Like this? And this?"

"No, *here*." Fred dipped his head and brushed his fingers through his crest feathers. "In here. *I* keep it. Not the book. Not the screen."

Jeff was completely lost. Maybe Fred meant he was a keeper of some kind of oral history. That didn't make sense, but he was an alien, and expecting to understand corviforms just because they looked a lot like terrestrial birds and could speak didn't make sense either. It was an illusion of common ground that probably didn't exist. Jeff tried again.

"You remember stuff," he said. "That's your job? Holding facts in your head? Remembering? Remembering what, though?"

Fred bobbed his head up and down like a parrot. "Yes!" He'd picked up human gestures as fast as he learned English. "Everything. We keep everything *here*."

"In your head."

"Head. Yes. *Memorise*."

"Everything?"

"Yes, everything. Write nothing."

So they didn't write anything down, but here was Fred, using a pocket screen and apparently unfazed by the written word. He wasn't illiterate. He'd worked out how to read English, which probably meant he could already read other languages because the concept was familiar. If he could dismantle Jeff's radio, he was also physically capable of writing or typing, so that meant he memorised things for a different reason. The explanation that had seemed in reach a few seconds ago vanished again. It was like the hardest game of twenty questions Jeff had ever played.

Well, it's obvious what I've got to ask next...

"What do you memorise, Fred?" Jeff tapped his own forehead. "What do you hold in here?"

"Science," Fred said. "All the science. All the science we ever know and learn. I am a teerik. I am the book."

It was starting to make more sense. Jeff had read that some birds could remember tens of thousands of locations where they'd stashed seeds, but he had days when he couldn't even find his keys. Teeriks weren't like humans, no matter how much they could sound like them.

"You must have an amazing memory, Fred."

"We forget *nothing*. We know how to make ships, and move ships instantly, all the numbers and where to go. We calculate."

"Engineers? Mathematicians? Physicists?"

Fred consulted his screen again. "All. We do all. And all of us do. We pass it all to our children."

"Okay, Fred, why memorise it? You *could* record it. Write it down."

Fred draped his wings like a cormorant sunning itself, staring at the bots in silence. His body language looked like a human who was debating whether he'd say something he'd regret.

"Safer." Fred made a faint buzzing noise in his throat, a sound Jeff hadn't heard before. "Can't lose it. The bad can't take it. We don't get hurt or killed because we are valuables."

Ah. Got it. Insurance. "Very sensible." Jeff hoped the teeriks just had a streak of healthy paranoia and the "bad" Fred referred to was just hypothetical. "When you say the bad can't take it... who are they? Do we need to worry about them?"

"They never find Opis. Long way to go."

That didn't sound so good. The bad people were real, then, and that would have to be Jeff's priority. He tried not to look worried. "So where are your cities, Fred? Is that why we can't see them? Do you camouflage them to hide from bad people?"

"Hard question, hard to answer. Later." Well, that wasn't going anywhere. *Later.* Jeff would circle back and try another tack. Fred kept going. He was on a roll now. "Learned Mother wants to see the head in charge."

"Who's Learned Mother?" Jeff asked.

"Caisin. She remembers all. She's old. Are you in charge for this, Chief Jeff, or Ma'am Ingram Bridget?"

"Caisin needs to talk to Captain Ingram. She's the big boss. I'll tell her."

"She should come tomorrow. I give you coordinates so she can find us. She has to go through bushes and a tunnel, so tell her skin will get scratched."

"Is this at your camp or something?"

"Ship."

"It's a ship?"

"Ship. But the place to be is *here.*"

Fred showed him a string of numbers on his screen, superimposed on a local map that looked to be just open country. Maybe it was like holding a diplomatic meeting on neutral ground. If Fred's people didn't want strangers knowing where their settlements were, that was probably an understandable security precaution. Jeff tapped his screen against Fred's to transfer the data.

"I'll give this to Captain Ingram."

Fred fixed him with that yellow pterodactyl stare. "You think my English improves?"

"Very good indeed. You'll be speaking like a native in a few days."

"I sound like the screen."

"We all pick up accents that way, Fred."

"Say Hredt again."

Jeff tried hard to hit that rasping guttural. "*Hrr–recht.*"

Fred did a pretty credible laugh followed by his police siren noise. "Hah, you improve too. Good saying today, Chief Jeff. We both speak better."

A bot rolled into the hangar on tracked wheels and set itself down in the cleaning bay to have soil blasted off. The noise broke Jeff's concentration. Fred looked around as if he'd forgotten the bots were in and out all the time, then straightened up.

"I go now," he said, putting the screen in his manbag. "I see Ma'am Ingram Bridget in the morning."

That had probably been his mission today, then, to arrange the meeting with Caisin. But maybe he wanted to socialise as well. Jeff walked him outside to wave him off, thinking what a shame it was that he'd never be able to regale his old oppos with a dit about teaching English to an alien crow who was an actual rocket scientist.

Fred took a run at his takeoff and lifted clear, flapping slowly and reaching shoulder height. Jeff watched him go and added another query to his list of questions for next time: why didn't teeriks use ground transport? All civilisations had it, even if it was a horse and cart. For a spacefaring species, they didn't seem to have any visible technology at all. But for all he knew, Fred was the equivalent of a businessman who walked to work to keep fit. There were too many unknowns for him to do more than guess and probably get it all wrong. He walked back to the office and found Ingram loitering in the corridor.

"Well?" she said. "How's he doing? Can he answer questions yet?"

"More than that, ma'am. You've been summoned."

"Oh? Really?"

"His boss wants to see you tomorrow. He's given me the coordinates where you've got to meet him. It sounded like he's going to walk you to some secret location and you'll have to negotiate some tunnel to reach his ship. I'm sure that was what he meant, but it doesn't make sense. Unless it's in a bunker or something."

"I could have invited them here, I suppose."

"Better wear a jacket. He said something about thorns and bushes."

Ingram raised an eyebrow. "This is getting a trifle bizarre, Chief."

"Aliens, ma'am. They're not like us."

"Damn, how are we ever going to teach them cricket, then?"

"Well, they have phenomenal memories, so don't lose hope. They're basically rocket scientists who keep their knowledge in their heads. Nothing written down. Fred says it's safer because they can't lose the data and nobody can take it from them. Sounds a bit like a trade union."

"Well, that's very handy for negotiations, as long as we can work out what they want by way of payment." She jerked her thumb in the direction of the mess and started walking. "Let's continue this over a coffee. Get the team together for a full briefing. Good grief, I'm going to see an alien spaceship. I didn't have *that* on my bucket list."

"Am I the right person to do this, ma'am? I'm already out of my depth."

"We all are, Chief. You have the advantage of common sense, zero scientific orthodoxy, and a rapport with the corviforms."

"Teeriks," Jeff said. "They call themselves teeriks. It means book. Because they're living databases."

"See? You don't need a boffin."

"One more thing, ma'am."

"Yes?"

"Fred's confirmed the teeriks aren't the only intelligent aliens around. He described some of them as *bad*."

Ingram stopped and looked back at him. "Bugger. Our priorities just changed."

"But he said the bad guys can't find Opis."

"Marvellous. That's all right, then." Ingram shut her eyes for a second. "Why would they be looking for it?"

"I don't know, but it's hard not to see this as the teeriks having a good reason to hide from them. That might explain why even Solomon didn't spot Fred and the others until the last few months."

"It doesn't sound encouraging."

"I'm getting answers out of Fred a bit at a time. It's slow."

"How many teeriks are there?"

"Again, no idea yet."

"Sorry, I know I'm pushing, and you've made enormous progress with him. This is PhD-level field research. But I don't need to spell this out for you."

"Of course you don't, ma'am. Identify the threat and a solution for dealing with it."

Ingram carried on walking. "We've always got options, Chief. The bad guys might not be bad by *our* standards, their arses could be kickable, and if they're not, then the teerik FTL might give us a chance to move to a nicer neighbourhood. But if the very worst happens, we can always turn *Cabot* around, chill down, and head home. So we're not going to soil ourselves until we know more."

She assumed there'd be a home to go back to, or at least she was pretending she did. Jeff wasn't sure that an Earth he'd have last seen ninety years earlier would be any kind of home at all now. On the other hand, the bad guys might turn out to be so bad that any kind of Earth would do.

No, sod it, they hadn't come all this way and severed links that could never be repaired just to turn round and go home.

"Are you seriously thinking of aborting the mission, ma'am?"

"That depends entirely on what we can find out from Fred," Ingram said. "But losing our bottle isn't an option. We need to consolidate this base for future settlers. We can't contact *Elcano* and the other ships to turn them back. If we cut and run without Solomon to manage maintenance here, they'll find a derelict camp and poor survival prospects when they land. So we're here to stay."

"Of course, we might get on famously with the other aliens," Jeff said.

"Don't worry, Chief, we can always blow the shit out of them if we don't."

"Indeed. British diplomacy's the envy of the world."

Ingram smiled, but as she put her hand on the canteen door, she paused to look Jeff in the eye. He always felt nervous when she went all serious and the breezy privateer side of her vanished.

"It's just as well we've had so many shocks that I can't really take it all in," she said. "We should be stunned at every discovery. Not only aliens, but intelligent aliens. FTL drives. Perhaps lots of *other* aliens. And none of us were really prepared for anything beyond watching out for unpleasant wildlife. So if it's all right with you, I'll default to superficial mode and skim glibly over it all."

"Skim away, ma'am," Jeff said. "I think I'll join you."

* * *

MANAGEMENT SUITE, AINATIO RESEARCH CENTRE: 1215 EDT.

Tim Pham had been holed up in Erskine's old office for hours. Why the hell was he still here, anyway? He didn't have to supervise any of this. Annis Kim was getting fed up waiting for a convenient moment to interrupt and remind him they had a meeting.

She waited outside the door for a few minutes, listening for a lull in the conversation so that she could knock and barge in, but the office was too well soundproofed to catch anything. Erskine had taken her security seriously. Given the scale of the secrets she'd been sitting on, Annis couldn't blame her.

But Tim had to come out sooner or later. It looked like Alex was in there, so they must have been discussing resettlement applications.

Annis sat down on the grey linen sofa next to the dracaena in its big steel planter, wondering who was going to look after the office plants when everyone evacuated, and tried to decide who she'd miss. At least Alex was heading for APS territory. He'd grown on her. Maybe they'd stay in touch.

"You still waiting, ma'am?"

Jared Talbot stuck his head around the door. He was another guy she hadn't had a chance to talk to very much, Chris's buddy and second in command. He looked her over as if he was going to ask if she had the right security clearance to be in here.

"Yeah, it feels like those days between Christmas and New Year," she said. "You know, a kind of limbo. You busy?"

Jared gestured with the paper folder he was clutching in one hand. "It's amazing how many daily chores don't need doing when you're not living in a wood cabin and you've got bots doing everything. So I killed some time drawing up an emergency plan. Actions on arriving on Opis and finding nobody in Nomad Base."

"You're a ray of sunshine, Jared."

"Everybody's happier with a plan and a designated role."

"You're right. This is why you all made it here alive."

"You want a copy?"

"Will it keep me awake at night?"

Jared laughed. "It's just routine stuff. You can think of us having to do this when you're old and grey. I'll send you a copy."

He walked off, still chuckling to himself. His words seeped in like cold water. She knew the physics back to front, but the emotional reality of no longer being around when the Opis party started killed her optimism. It would have been cool to see the place for real, just once. But now she never would and she'd think about the mission clock counting down for forty-five years.

Enough of that crap. She had to get a grip. She missed Melbourne and she'd travelled enough for a lifetime. She'd finish whatever she still had to do in Seoul and head home for good. While she waited, imagining reunions, a bot whirred up to the planter and watered the dracaena, which started her wondering what was going to happen to the army of bots that outnumbered the humans here. She was debating whether anyone would notice or care if she took one with her as a souvenir when the office door opened a crack and the conversation wafted out.

"Yeah, you can crawl all over Orbital One. Knock yourselves out. But don't forget to plug into the AI or he'll interpret it the wrong way."

"Understood, Alex."

"And remember he's not functioning properly. God knows what Erskine did, but I think he's defaulted to core programming. If we get away from here on the right course, it'll be a miracle."

"Yeah. I appreciate the problem."

Alex strode out of the office, red face clashing unflatteringly with his ginger hair, and just nodded at Annis as he passed. Either something else had happened that she didn't know about or that was an award-winning performance. Solomon had been fine the last time she'd spoken to him. Okay, she'd stay on message because Alex had kept his side of the bargain and she'd keep hers. Thwarting the Nomad mission served nobody's interests. She had a feeling that Jared's emergency plan would be all too necessary if they reached Opis at all, but she still wanted them to succeed, if only because she'd seen so much stoicism and common decency among the remnant here that it hurt. They all deserved better.

"Problem, Tim?" She walked in and settled on the leather sofa in Erskine's office. "Don't wind Alex up. The poor bugger's had a rough few weeks."

"It's the orbital," Tim said. "One of the APDU Space Corps shuttles tried to dock without prior clearance and it caused a bit of drama. The AI treated it as a collision."

"Who ordered the pilot to do that?"

"I did. I wanted to check that they were levelling with me about Erskine trashing the comms. That's all I'm here for, Annis. The FTL. And to make sure Ainatio isn't hiding anything that we don't want leaving the planet."

"I told you not to mess with the AI, didn't I? Erskine did and it probably tipped him into defensive mode."

"You did. And you all call it *him*."

"He's got a male voice. Why not?"

"Just noting how attached people get to software."

"Anyway, why the rush? The orbital's still going to be there after *Shackleton*'s gone."

"I thought they might indulge in some asset denial and scupper it, seeing how they've brought their launch date forward," Tim said. "So I wanted to get a rummage team in while I could."

"There's no wormhole tech left. You know that."

"Do I? Ainatio's kept a lot of pretty damn big secrets for a long time. Companies don't change overnight. People certainly don't.

Anyway, Alex Gorko said we can board any time as long as we liaise with the AI and don't spook it."

Annis wasn't convinced by any of that, but if she asked too many questions she might invite unwelcome scrutiny. Alex seemed to have got what he wanted. She'd back off and focus on getting through the next few weeks without incident.

"Tim, I actually wanted to go through the resettlement applicants' list with you," she said. "I need a bit of pressure applied to a couple of firms in Oz —— "

"Would you mind if we clear up something else first?"

"Sure. Go ahead."

Tim had taken a liking to Erskine's big leather desk chair. He'd enthroned himself with the air of a pharaoh holding court, hands gripping the ends of the arms and chin slightly raised. He'd always been one for pissing up other people's lampposts to mark his dominance. Annis was disappointed by the pointless territorial display because he hadn't defeated an empress and nobody gave a shit who sat in this office now, but the petty victory posturing was pure Tim. The worst thing about an affair with a guy with power was discovering all his tawdry mortal failings and bad habits, which were somehow a lot less off-putting in more modest men.

The upside, though, was that she could use them. She reminded herself that Tim was still an intelligence officer at his core, a hands-on field agent who'd made his way into political office, and that meant he'd learned to enjoy the sport of lying and flouting the rules. She could exploit that.

What do I want out of this?

Recognition for Grandma Park.

No bad shit on my conscience about the people here.

To get home and never have to worry about this again.

It wasn't a lot to ask. If she kept her nerve, it would happen.

"You know, it's a nice day," Tim said. He pushed the chair back, a little too rehearsed, and stood to reach for a coffee cup. "Let's go for a walk. I'm fed up sitting in this bunker. I need sunlight."

Tim wasn't a spontaneous guy. Annis's gut said run. There was no reason to think this was anything more than his normal concern about being bugged and that he wanted to discuss something even more confidential than usual, but she was already working out how she could get away. She had to stop thinking about what she was hiding from him. Tim could detect guilt in the same dilution that sharks could scent blood.

"Yeah, okay," she said, hoping that there'd be other people around. Even Tim wouldn't shoot her in front of the staff.

It was a long walk to get out of the executive suite, and it felt like she was walking to the gallows. Tim probably intended that. He always had to shake people down, out of habit as much as anything. There was no reason to think he knew she'd been less than frank with him but there was also no reason to believe he'd suddenly turned into a regular, relaxed guy who decided to take his coffee outside for the hell of it.

They passed security cameras. Solomon would be plugged into the system, she was sure of that, and if he wasn't, that young corporal of Trinder's would probably keep one monitor permanently on the corridor to check when Tim came and went. Someone would see her. Someone would know where she'd gone.

The corridors were deserted. But as she followed Tim around a corner, she saw Phil Berman coming the other way. He'd have to pass them. The gap between them was closing. He had his eyes on the ground, looking like he was lost in thought, but at twenty feet away he looked up, expressionless, and nodded in acknowledgement without breaking his stride. Annis nodded back.

"What do you make of him?" Tim asked when they were out of earshot.

Annis wondered if Tim was checking on people he suspected of being something other than their personnel files claimed. "Berman? He's got the patience of a saint. He was Erskine's bagman. She was really shocked that he didn't want to go with her."

Tim carried on. She could only see his back silhouetted against the daylight from the glass doors. Then they were outside, and he turned down a path that ran along the side of the lawns before eventually stopping to sit down on a low wall next to the compound where they stored the rubbish skips. Annis was still checking where the security cameras were. Predictably, they'd ended up in blind spot.

"Lovely view of the refuse," she said. "Part of your relaxation routine for the day?"

Tim sipped his coffee. It had to be cold by now. "Annis, we've played this game before. Let's be straight with each other. Alex Gorko is just a manager. Who's really running this show?"

"Alex is," Annis said. "Someone had to step in and head up the Ainatio side when Erskine abandoned ship. He was the ranking bureaucrat."

"I thought he said she went a bit mental. You know, when he called to offer us a deal on the FTL."

Shit. That had been Solomon passing himself off as Alex. What had he actually said? Annis only had the gist of it. She had to wing it.

"Yeah, he probably believes that," she said. "But Erskine was a crafty old cow. You have to be pretty sane to save your own arse."

"Maybe, but Alex isn't the decision-maker here, is he?" Tim turned towards her. "Trinder's nominally in charge because of rank. But that Brit. He looks like a bad bastard. I know one when I see one. Former British Army, yes? Is that all we know?"

Annis prepared for interrogation. She hoped Tev wasn't getting grilled the same way or Marc would find out and make good on his threat. "He was evacuating embassy personnel in DC and got marooned."

"Really? If he could place a call from here via the British government to get hold of me, he's got a pretty exotic contacts book for a hired gun. He could have requested a ride home long before now."

"Both his sons were killed in action, Tim. I don't think he's got a home or a life to go back to."

"Oh. Interesting."

Maybe that had deflated Tim a bit. Annis gave him her iciest stare of disapproval. "Yeah. Kind of hard to be all smiles after that."

"Well, I think he's special forces," Tim said. "And that Montello guy might look like a choirboy but he's a bad bastard too, although I can't quite put my finger on it. Those three are running this and they're all military in some way. So I'm thinking this Nomad project isn't the tragic remnant of an eccentric tech oligarch's dream or any of that bullshit. Nobody ended up here by accident. And they've been *very* busy."

Annis was caught off-guard for a moment. She'd never put the pieces together in quite the way Tim had. He saw soldiers with some threatening secret mission: she saw a secret project that needed experienced armed operators around to keep it that way. It was close, but not the same.

"Politics really has buggered you," she said. "Chris and his transit camp are just randoms. He's only a State Defence sergeant. He was conscripted. Don't you think I checked him out? He took it on himself to regroup with a bunch of — well, anyone with a uniform in their wardrobe who was willing to rescue people. They just followed the road down here. That's all there is to it."

"And what did Montello do in Civvie Street?"

Tim wasn't going to be diverted. Annis suspected men could smell violence on each other.

"He's got a criminal record," she said. A dash of truth would come in handy to blur the line with her lies. "Robust debt collection. State Defence took him from prison. They did that a lot."

"Hitman."

"No, he just smacked people around a bit for his boss. White collar stuff. Not even drugs. Dodgy business deals that needed enforcing."

"Random, you say. It's not easy to find this place."

"I found it."

"Annis, you had intel."

"Yeah, but a few other randoms found it, too. The lucky ones were driven off. The unlucky ones got shot."

Tim looked her in the eye for a long time as if he was trying to stare something out of her.

"Did you know about the nukes in *Shackleton*, too?" It was his quiet and reasonable voice, the one he used when he was on the attack. He'd shifted tack completely. "Or where the latest die-back outbreak came from?"

It hit Annis like a slap and almost stopped her breathing. Her scalp tightened. Who the hell had talked? There was no way Tim could have found all that out for himself yet.

Some moron must have let it slip.

Without knowing what else Tim knew, she had no idea if she was already sunk and if a lie would only make matters worse. She was probably screwed. She hung on to her confusion to look more convincingly ignorant.

"They don't know where the new outbreak started," she said. "They were really panicked about it. Big enquiry. Not that it matters, seeing as the rest of the state's contaminated."

"And the nukes?"

"If they're still operational, they'll be saving them for imaginary aliens. What's your point?"

"Simple question. *Did you know?* You were working on the refit."

"I was vaguely aware, yes," Annis said. She was in deep shit now. "But it wasn't my priority because it wasn't a threat. If I thought it was, I'd have warned you by now. I was here for the FTL. I got it."

Tim drained his coffee and shook out the cup. "We were hoping you'd find it before Ainatio actually put it to any use. It was a bit of a surprise to find they'd actually landed on the damn planet."

"Join the club. Not even the staff knew. Look, I'm the physicist here, Tim. I'm telling you what they had was a glorified phone line, and that the important stuff is in those files for our guys to turn into a proper ship's drive."

Tim chewed his lip for a moment as if he was genuinely thinking it over, which she knew he wasn't. He never asked a question if he didn't already know the answer. He'd taught her that technique when he'd recruited her to help out the spooks when they were busy, because she understood the big science and they didn't, and no doubt because she was Dr Park Ha-Neul's favourite and smartest great-grandchild.

"And how about the AI?" he asked. "Solomon, isn't it?"

She'd been careful not to use Sol's name. The chances of every single item of Ainatio's dirty laundry cropping up in someone's overheard conversation were about zero. Now she knew for sure that Tim had been given his shopping list by an insider, and it hadn't been someone blurting out stuff by accident.

Ainatio had a grass. They'd dobbed in their mates for some reward and it had never crossed her mind that anyone here would do that. She didn't think the place was full of saints, but after everything that had happened, all they'd been through, it seemed especially shitty.

She couldn't deny all knowledge. "Like I said right from the start, the AI keeps the place running," she said. "And all the remote ops. That's why Alex is worried about him incurring more damage. Erskine took all the key boffins with her, so without Solomon, everyone's stuck here. He's the only driver they've got."

It was usually a bad idea to point out vulnerabilities to someone who enjoyed exploiting them, but it was the best excuse for Alex's anxiety. Most companies relied heavily on AIs to manage essential tasks. It wasn't unusual in any way. Tim would at least understand that.

"You said he wasn't sentient," Tim said.

The mire Annis had fallen into was getting deeper. "Sentience is a broad concept. I don't want to get too technical, but he's a high-end management AI. He's not a person."

"Oh, I think you already knew he was more than that."

"He's got to be pretty sophisticated to run a space programme, Tim."

"I mean you knew he was *fully autonomous*." Tim had that I-know-something-you-don't look on his face again. "As in he should have been shut down years ago because he's so bloody *dangerous*. You know damn well what those things are. We made a mistake calling them AIs. They're *different*. They're artificial human minds, and just as unreliable, obsessive, and dishonest, except they don't have our physical limits. That's how Erskine damaged him, wasn't it? She was trying to deactivate him for everyone's safety."

Annis wanted to punch that smug expression right off Tim's face. "Give it a rest. There's no clear definition of autonomous. Erskine trashed as much data as she could to stop *you* getting it because she was convinced APS would try to shut down Nomad or hijack it. So she wasn't far wrong, was she? And too bloody right she'd try to trash the AI as well. He manages the data."

"Please." Tim held up his hands in mock distaste. "Don't insult my intelligence. You lied. Solomon's classed as Autonomous Self-Determining. ASD AIs like that are illegal for a reason."

"Tim, he might be idiosyncratic, but he was designed to put humans first." Annis needed to warn Sol to get out. He couldn't hear any of this. That was probably why Tim wanted to talk outside. "If he hadn't been harmless, do you think any of us would be alive now? A guard AI wouldn't have let anyone access the FTL files. An ASD certainly wouldn't have let Erskine live after she tried to destroy him. He's programmed to be benevolent. He's too bloody soft, if you ask me. I'd have fried the bitch."

"*Him.* It's software, Annis. Not a human. Not an animal. Not even a machine. It's got to be shut down. Does Earthmother mean *anything* to you? That thing killed nearly a billion people in eight years. It decided culling humans was the best way to save the environment and it took a small war to shut it down."

"Yeah, and it had plenty of Mother Death eco-nutters cheering it on," Annis said. "The data it was given said deal with human-related climate change. What else did they expect?"

"Whose side are you on?"

"AIs aren't all the same."

"Come off it, ASDs are inherently dangerous. You can't have a human mind without a body and expect it to stay sane. A body gives us motivation and brakes. If you're not driven by hunger, the instinct to reproduce, or fear of death, how do you know where to draw the line? What's the point of your existence? All you care about is your mission. That's all you've got. An obsession."

"Like that never happens with humans."

"Humans don't generally have the wherewithal to wipe out millions single-handed. If I'd known this Solomon existed, I'd have taken a less hands-off view of Nomad. That thing controls Ainatio's ships. The ships have nuclear weapons. Ainatio also does an interesting line in new improved die-back viruses. If that's not a bowel-loosening situation, you're not paying attention."

"Don't try pulling his plug," Annis said. "Remember that you're not fighting him, you're just teaching him to get tougher, and he'll win. Don't say I didn't warn you."

"That's what they said about Earthmother," Tim said. "And she lost."

"That was a long time ago."

"I hear Erskine almost managed it."

"If he's shut down, *Shackleton* doesn't leave."

"Fine by me. Imagine that AI set free in the galaxy. They don't die. They can keep going for as long as they've got a platform to exist in."

"Just let him complete his mission and he'll be as good as gold."

"Yeah, *his mission*. Let's talk about that." Tim was working through his list. "Erskine was pretty thorough at asset denial, because there's almost nothing about Opis in the records."

"Well, that's how they kept Nomad quiet all those years."

"Ah, don't give me that. You don't plan an interstellar mission over that kind of timescale without keeping a *lot* of documentation in lots of different places."

"Bednarz's project wasn't exactly secret." Annis felt numb. She was saying the right things, but somehow she knew Tim was hearing all the answers she didn't want to give. "Governments were pissed off when he wouldn't allocate places to them, so plenty of people knew what he was planning. The only secret was the fact that the ship hadn't been lost with all hands."

"Oh, I'm betting they've got more secrets than that."

"Why are you suddenly worried about Opis?"

"I didn't say I was worried."

"You're acting like it. Having doubts, are we?"

"I'm finding too many complications here that we weren't expecting."

Tim always got to the point and rarely deviated from it, but Annis couldn't pin down his priorities now. She'd thought the FTL data was everything. Now it was Solomon, and he was griping about Opis too, and she wasn't sure whether he was looking for his excuse to shut the whole thing down in righteous indignation for the good of the world. He'd never needed excuses to act before.

"You said we had our own candidate planets and FTL meant we could have extrasolar colonies up and running before Erskine lands," Annis said.

"True. We might even beat her to Opis."

"Is that what it's all about? Grab everything from Ainatio?"

Tim shrugged. "Maybe. Who knows?"

"If they strike it rich there, it's irrelevant to us," Annis said. "Plenty to go around. Big galaxy. Or so you said."

"Have you seen footage from the planet?"

Annis paused. There were still a few management staff here who'd known all about it — Jake Mendoza, Todd Mangel, maybe a couple more — but they weren't going to advertise the fact. Then there were the promotional videos that Alex had shown to the townsfolk to demonstrate what a great place Opis was to settle. She'd have to sow more doubts.

"Apart from the live transmissions, which could easily have been fakes, Erskine had some footage of nice countryside and forests to persuade people to go," she said. "Which, again, any smart ten-year-old could generate."

"Yeah, Major Trinder matched you almost word for word on that."

"Because it's true. Not collusion."

"But there's more than just bacteria on the planet, isn't there? It's easily habitable."

"If the videos are genuine, yeah. Plants and animals. And no, I have no idea what might be worth mining. It's Bednarz's fantasy. A new future for humankind. He wanted people with the right stuff to breed from. Same eugenics as the lighthuggers, different parameters."

"Doesn't matter."

"Look, you wanted the FTL. I got you the FTL. We don't have the working comms version, but we know more or less how Ainatio built it, and we can develop that into drives."

Tim looked right through her. "I think it's rash for anyone else to head for Opis until we've got more answers on this Nomad project. They're all going to die."

"Shit, Tim, we all will."

"But they needn't die that soon."

Tim didn't do concern for others. He just assumed everyone else was as devious as he was, which was probably sensible, but Annis had had enough. She wanted out of this game. She'd outlived her usefulness to him, so anything short of being shot or locked up was a bonus. If she lost her uni job and had to clean toilets, that sounded like a fair exchange to get out of full-time professional back-stabbing and never knowing what was true and honest and *real* any more. She was a physicist. Reality was her religion. Why had she let this job go on so long? Because she was good at it. Because Grandma Park had been wronged. And because having a clear-cut enemy to punish and defeat was comforting when you felt everything you cared about was under threat.

She also knew that quitting didn't mean she'd be free to leave.

"Everyone's going to die if they stay here," she said. "They'll starve when the food reserves run out. It wouldn't kill us to resettle all of them. You could keep an eye on them then."

Tim wrinkled his nose. "If the very worst happened, and they weren't able to launch *Shackleton*, of course we'd give them refuge."

"If you meant that, you'd have done it already."

"A lot of them *want* to leave Earth, Annis. They think this world's finished. They may well be right."

Annis hated it when he got that I-might-be-bluffing-and-I-might-not look on his face. "Any other failures you want to berate me for?"

"I'm just asking questions. How about *Elcano*? They're in cryo now, you said."

"Come on, that ship can't be a threat to you."

"Who said it was?"

"You did, simply by asking."

"Okay, in an ideal world, she'd never have launched."

"She'll be past the orbit of Mars by now," Annis said. "So she's way outside APDU missile range. And we can't get a signal to the onboard AI to override her course or even wake the crew, because Erskine cut the link."

"That's very dramatic, but as you said, she's not going to attack us," Tim said. Perhaps he'd just been goading her to get her to blurt something out. "Why did Erskine *really* kill the ship's comms?"

Annis paused. The truth — that Erskine didn't trust Solomon not to override life support and kill her in her cryosleep — would just stoke Tim's determination to pull the AI's plug, no matter how many times she warned him not to.

"Paranoia," she said. "She thought we'd try to stop the mission any way we could, and here you are, doing just that. But she's got a couple of hundred children on board. Maybe she's not such a bitch after all."

"I haven't stopped anything yet."

"I know you too well, Tim."

"Come on, aren't you just the slightest bit worried about a moralising AI with its virtual finger on the nuclear button?"

"Like the nukes we don't have, yeah?"

"Okay, East and West are as bad as each other. Except we didn't let die-back loose. *Twice*."

"You realise that some of them still think I spread it to give you an excuse to seize the facility."

"Ah, so you *did* know the latest outbreak originated in here."

"You told me I did."

Tim smiled slowly. Even someone who didn't know him would have taken it as a warning. "Why now?"

"What do you mean, why now?"

"Odd timing. You could put all the pieces and people together and see it as an unlucky coincidence. Or you could look at it as a coordinated action that APS needs to be really, really worried about."

"Pattern recognition's a dangerous reflex. Seeing what's not there takes people down some disastrous paths."

It was all too late now. Annis knew she was burned and the only question was whether APS would just jettison her or do something worse. Tim stood up and started walking away. For a moment she wondered whether to just stay put and see if he left her there, but he turned around after a few paces and came back to grab her by the arm and pull her to her feet. It hurt. He'd never manhandled her like that before. She wanted to punch his face in.

"In this game," he said, "loyalty counts for more than efficiency. You forgot that. I picked you because I thought your great-grandmother's situation made you uniquely motivated, but you went native. This is always the problem when you recruit agents with external career interests. A mission's just an adventure to you."

Annis jerked her arm free. "I nearly died getting here, you ungrateful bastard. I did my duty."

"You did it for your own ends."

"You really are garbage, you know that? So are you locking me to *Temujin*'s brig, or flying me back in handcuffs?"

He caught her arm again, a tight grip under the elbow and began walking her at a brisk pace back to the building. They'd pass a security cam soon. Someone would see her. Someone would realise Tim's mood had taken a downturn and that they had to at least warn Sol.

"I think you could do with some rest," Tim said. "You've got a nice little apartment here. You can sit it out until we've rendered this site safe and we're ready to leave."

"When did you become such a jumped-up prick, Tim?" Annis wished she could keep her mouth shut but she was spitting mad as well as scared shitless. It was a toxic combination. "There's nothing heroic or patriotic about making a bunch of harmless, desperate people suffer. I'm better than that, even if you're not."

"Just shut it."

There weren't many people around as he frogmarched her back to the main building, just a few APS techs in overalls who looked at them and turned away. There was no Alex or Marc to come to her rescue this time. Marc didn't even like her and he'd still done the decent thing. Shit, she hadn't gone native — she'd just done what was right and fair for all concerned, and Tim wasn't capable of seeing the difference. She kept trying to jerk her arm free and ended up just holding it rigid so he didn't think she'd given in.

They were now coming up to the side door that led into the undercroft beneath the admin building. Annis could see some guy waiting behind the glass, and while he wasn't wearing a uniform and he was quite a bit older than the APDU troops, she was sure he was a soldier of some kind. He shifted something from one pocket to the other, looking bored.

Could she make things any worse? No. Anything was worth a try now. They'd come within feet of the camera overlooking the parking area and it'd probably be the last one she'd get a chance to be seen on. It was like one of those true crime shows where some unlucky victim was caught on camera for the last time before they vanished, except she was the victim and she could still do something about it.

She relaxed her arm as if she wasn't going to put up a fight. Tim slackened his grip just a fraction. She took a guess at how long it would take her to get from his side to that camera, counted down the seconds, and picked her moment.

Then she did what she'd been taught to do. She brought her heel down hard on his instep. He almost lost his balance and in that second, she pulled free and sprinted for the camera, waving her arms to get its motion sensor to focus on her as a potential incident to record.

"Sol, get out," she yelled. "Someone's dobbed you in. Pham knows everything. Your ASD status, the die-back source, the nukes. He'd going to stop Nomad. You've got an informer — "

Someone whacked her across the back of the head, more a slap than a serious blow, but it wasn't Tim. It was the bored guy who looked like he was probably special forces or some other specialist Tim needed to do his dirty work. She rounded on him with a stream of abuse but he clamped one hand over her mouth and shoved her arm up her back. She was utterly bloody screwed now.

"Arsehole," she said, but the word didn't manage to escape. He bundled her inside and the next thing she knew, she had a bag over head and she was half walking, half stumbling along an echoing corridor.

She didn't know where she was. And now nobody else would know either. She wasn't wearing her ID tracker card. If Sol really could see all and hear all, now was his chance to prove it.

04

Traitors don't only harm their community with the act of treachery itself. They inject a slow-acting poison alongside it. Once you know you've got an informer, nobody trusts anybody else. Accusations get made. Friendships fall apart. The community stops functioning the way it should. And even when the traitor's found, that damage still doesn't heal, because unforgivable things have been said and fingers have been pointed at the wrong people. Tribes need trust and loyalty to survive. That's why we execute traitors.

Dieter Hill, former police detective: now K9
handler, Community Defence Force.

LOCKER ROOM, STAFF GYM, AINATIO PARK RESEARCH CENTRE: 1320 EDT, THREE MINUTES AFTER ARREST OF DR ANNIS KIM.

"Echo Fourteen to Echo Five, I've called a Code Two and reinstated security locks on all doors," Fonseca said. "We have a problem and Sol's had to pull out. Details on your screen when you put your pants on."

Fonseca could see where Trinder was and knew he never took his screen into the gym. He got dressed, instantly numb but grateful for the clear-minded autopilot that took over these days. "Echo Five receiving. I'm getting dressed. Wait one."

"Quick version — somebody told Pham everything," Fonseca said. "Pham moved troops to block the gates so I've imposed a total lockdown of the door system. I've messaged all staff to chill and wait while I check who's where so I can release doors to chip recognition where our own people have been trapped. Alex is on his way to see Pham."

Trinder still found Fonseca's ruthless efficiency a little exciting even now. She'd followed the procedure for isolating an intruder, except she'd locked every door on the site and was now deciding who could be allowed to access specific areas. If Pham had put troops on the gates, then total lockdown was the right call. It would stop him moving people around, not only his troops but also any Ainatio personnel he might try to corral for hostage purposes.

Trinder had prepared for the worst and it was happening. He wasn't surprised, just angry with himself because he hadn't managed to ship any staff out of the facility yet and some of the supplies were still in the warehouse.

When he found his screen, Fonseca's message was a short recording from one of the external security cams. Annis Kim was yelling a warning at the camera before the guy Marc had identified as special forces smacked her around the head from behind and bundled her away, followed by Pham.

Trinder's first thought was that Pham would be even more pissed now that he was trapped and he'd call *Temujin* for backup. But Trinder didn't see how they could just bend over and take the attempt to blockade the site.

"On my way. Fill me in. Sol, are you going to be monitoring all this?"

"Yes, I'll remain in contact, Major," Solomon said. "If Pham knows what I am now, I won't waste time playing dumb robots. And if they could decrypt our comms, he'd have taken more decisive action sooner."

Trinder set off across the grounds to reach the side entrance to the security wing. At least all those years of training exercises he'd thought would never be tested for real had proved their value. Code Two was the drill for dealing with intruders inside the perimeter, a step down from Code One, which was reserved for a military-level attack where Solomon would activate ground-based missiles and small artillery pieces would be rolled out. Everyone knew what to do and where to go. The security wing instantly became a citadel to maintain comms and protect the armoury, teams would be divided between defending key facilities and pursuing the intruders, and an automated message would be sent to all staff telling them to shelter in place. Locking doors and closing the emergency bulkheads would limit the intruders' movements and could be used to funnel them into the right place to receive their comeuppance. The research centre was designed to keep hazardous things in and curious people out and now it was doing its job. Bednarz would have been pleased to see it working as he intended.

But Trinder's exercises had never involved an enemy with an aircraft carrier standing by. He paused to check overhead for aircraft before he attempted the sprint across an exposed stretch of lawn with no tree cover. Even the worst scenario plan hadn't accounted for the speed at which things were unravelling.

"Okay, we've got twenty-four detachment personnel on site and six in Kill Line, including the Lammergeier pilots," Fonseca said. "Plus three transit camp militia here. Alpha Three and Six Zero are both in Kill Line and standing by. Remember we're all patched in on the secure net now, so they can hear us."

"Let's get a better idea of where we are before we call for backup." Trinder was glad he had hardcore support out of Pham's immediate reach. He tried to check his screen to see where everyone was dispersed, but he needed to keep his eyes on his surroundings. "We might need them for something else later."

He reached the doorway and waited for a very long second until the door recognised him and swung open. The security wing was deserted, but most of the troops had either been working around the campus or had responded to the alert straight from their quarters, so he wasn't concerned to see the place empty. It had been just seven minutes since Fonseca had called him. Everyone had moved into position fast.

She was watching trackers on the wall screen's site map with Aaron Luce when Trinder walked into the office. Simonot was busy with reports coming in to the comms desk, listening intently and making notes.

"So apart from calling in fire on us, Pham can't move, yeah?" Trinder glanced away to check the security cam feeds — gates closed but unlocked, ten APDU troops armed and ready behind them — then turned back to the wall screen to study the floor plan of the admin block. "Is that Pham there?"

"Yeah, Zakko confirmed visually that he's in the corridor outside Erskine's office," Luce said. "So he was probably on the way back to his favourite bunker when the doors locked."

"Are any of these icons the special forces guy?"

"He disappeared in the grounds. No sign of Kim yet, either. Her ID tag's in one of the rose beds. The guy must have tossed it."

The tracker icons were a mix of chipped Ainatio staff and unchipped people — Chris's guys and the APS and APDU personnel — who had to be identified by the old facial recognition system that functioned happily without Solomon. Trinder could see Chris's militia guys marked in Ainatio red, though, so they must have had the ID chip cards or Ainatio radios that had been handed out to the transit camp. Zakko Chetcuti and Matt McNally were at the entrance to the admin block, and Chuck Emerson was with Jake Mendoza in the infirmary. Pham's personnel were identified by orange APS icons or blue APDU ones, each with a number instead of a name. It was easy to see where off-duty troops had been trapped when the locks sealed their floor of the accommodation block. The APDU personnel who'd been outside were free to roam the grounds, but couldn't get into any of the buildings without an Ainatio chip — or an Ainatio employee who was willing to let them in.

"We've got a traitor," Trinder said.

Fonseca gave him what he could only describe as a vengeful half-smile. "Don't worry, I set the system to log and alert for any open door and proximity between us and them. I'm almost hoping they try to let their APS pals in because then we'll have a name."

"You believe Dr Kim?" Luce asked.

Trinder nodded. "I think I do. If she's ratted on us, she's got no need to pretend we're best buds. She could just go home and forget we ever existed."

"It pains me to say it, but I agree, and I also wish it *was* her," Fonseca said. "If we can't ID which of our own people it is, they're as much of a threat now as APDU and they'll still be a security problem if they end up in *Shackleton*. So now we have a stalemate. Nobody moves until we know they're okay to be let loose."

"It'll be hard to resume any kind of working relationship with Pham after this, whatever we do," Trinder said.

"You think I made a mistake locking down?" Fonseca didn't sound like she felt she had. "The moment he decided to shut the gates, he made this all about hostages for both sides. Except hostages don't usually have control of the door locks."

"No criticism," Trinder said. "I'd have done the same."

"The only places where we've got APDU and our civilians in the same space are the restaurant, the staff club, and the front lobby." Fonseca dragged the site map down the screen. "So we've got our guys in all three places to prevent hostage-taking or any other nonsense. But I was planning to keep the restaurant running. If this drags on, people need to eat, and it saves us becoming a pizza delivery service when we've got bigger problems to handle."

Trinder looked up at the north end of the map. The trackers around the shuttle hangars just showed Jay Gatti and his guys out there. "On balance, I think we're in a better position than Pham is."

"Dan, you can talk to us, y'know. We've got these great little screens." It was Chris on audio only. "Input. It's not cheating."

"Sorry, guys. Tunnel vision."

"Gents, I think it's time for Plan C," Marc said. "Because that scraping noise you can hear is Plan A and Plan B being pushed to one side for a while."

"Did we ever have a Plan C?" Trinder asked.

"It's the same as Plan A and Plan B, except we have to shoot the bastards first."

"I should have started shipping people out right away. I'm sorry. I screwed up."

"No, Pham beat us to it," Marc said. "More to the point, Annis Kim did. I'd bet he wanted to dick us around a bit longer to locate Sol, so you were right after all. Now he knows about Sol, he's not going to let us go to Opis or anywhere else."

"Okay, I make it no more than ten kids on the gate and the rest stuck in other parts of the campus, and we're more than capable of taking them down," Chris said. "But we've got civvies inside, and I don't want them ending up in the crossfire. We need to get them out first, whether that's so we can clear APDU out of the facility or make a run for it if Pham's put in a call for APDU marines or long-range bombers."

"Guys, can we put the brakes on for a moment?" Trinder felt responsible for this and the speed with which it was escalating to lethal force scared him. "It's my fuck-up. Let me talk to Pham. I'm the runt of the litter as far as he's concerned so he might actually tell me what he wants."

"Don't forget Kim said Pham's experienced with handguns and can take care of himself," Fonseca said.

Trinder checked his sidearm. No, he hadn't forgotten, and he expected Pham to be carrying. "I can take care of myself too. I want to know why *Temujin* hasn't sent in more troops, because Pham must have made contingency plans the same as us. I think he's been caught on the hop as well. Sol, has there been any activity at all around the ship, anything at all?"

"I would have told you, Major. There's been no activity that I can detect from Orbital One. But obviously we'll pick up any inbound air traffic in time to do something about it. The two helicopters that landed here earlier are still parked. The pilots are in the staff restaurant."

"You said *do something about it.*"

"I'll issue a warning to turn back and not attempt to land. If they ignore that, I'll warn them twice that they'll be fired upon. If they ignore *that*, I'll launch missiles."

"What if I asked you not to, because it would bring APDU jets screaming here at Mach Three?"

"I'd hope you had a plan for dealing with whoever emerged from those aircraft on landing," Solomon said. "I would also factor in the relative risks before deciding if robust defence would save most lives."

That sounded a lot like Sol-knows-best. "Well, at least ask me before you press the button, okay?"

"Maybe all *Temujin*'s got is sailors, pilots, and lab technicians," Luce said. "They're no use for a ground battle or clearing buildings. Or policing."

"I hadn't considered that." Trinder knew he was looking at this from a soldier's perspective. "Would they really be that unprepared?"

"Remember when we had automated warships with twenty crew? We even had unmanned carriers for staging and refuelling. Seaborne monitoring stations. Spy ships. For *Temujin* to get close enough to fly Pham in so soon after the bombing was aborted, she must have already been in the Atlantic before the informer betrayed us, so she might not be carrying troops at all. This bunch could be all they've got out here."

Trinder found every theory plausible and it wasn't helping. "But she's irrelevant if Pham can just put in a call to APDU HQ. That's probably why he doesn't seem worried."

"Or it's OPSEC," Fonseca said. "Pham would probably want as few people to know about this as possible, so it's minimum manning. What's the betting he's keeping this secret from other APS states for his own ends as well? He doesn't want them to notice his mission. They might look like one bloc to us, but they're separate countries and quite a few would happily bomb each other."

"I'd put money on that too," Marc said. "But even a few matelots and lab techs who can't shoot straight still have access to a system with helicopters that are potential UCAVs. So it might all boil down to how quick Sol is on the draw."

Trinder hated speculating. He suspected that was what Pham wanted, to tie them up in what-ifs so they dithered and gave him time to manoeuvre. He'd have to prove him wrong.

He took one last look at the camera feed again in case he'd missed some detail and whatever Pham was planning had already started. Two of his guys, Silvashko and Eaton, were standing just inside the restaurant doors with rifles indexed, making it clear they were there to maintain civilian access to food and keep order if APS did anything dumb. There were still some APS and APDU personnel in there, but they were at separate tables on the opposite side of the room from the Ainatio staff, empty plates in front of them and heads down like they were waiting for something bad to happen. The friendly mingling of the last few days appeared to have stopped dead. These were the subtler things you couldn't read from a tracker map.

A quick assessment of the rest of the camera feeds showed similar standoffs, if the word could be applied to scared, baffled people standing around waiting to see what happened.

"Has Alex made an announcement?" Trinder asked.

"Not yet," Fonseca said. "I asked him to let us handle it."

"Okay, I'll do it." Trinder leaned over a desk and switched on the broadcast system. "This is Major Dan Trinder. Due to the security situation, this facility is now on lockdown until further notice. All doors and emergency bulkheads will remain shut until the situation's resolved. I realise this is going to be uncomfortable for some of you, but we'll release doors on a case by case basis for Ainatio personnel as soon as we've secured the campus. All APS and APDU personnel will remain confined until I've reached an understanding with Commissioner Pham. That is all — carry on."

Trinder didn't know if he'd reassured people or just upped the stakes with APS, but staff now knew that Ainatio was back in control, at least inside the buildings. He braced to go see Tim Pham.

"Was that okay?" he asked.

"Great," Fonseca said, nodding approval. "We'll contact staff individually now to check they're okay and smooth any ruffled feathers. We'll gradually move them back to their quarters for the duration and make sure everyone's fed and watered. I think this is going to take some time."

"Okay, I'll go see Pham now. I can't leave Alex to deal with him on his own."

It took a few minutes to walk to Erskine's office. Trinder didn't want to run and end up sweating in front of Pham because he needed whatever psychological edge he could get. He tried to raise him on the radio, cycling through channels to work out which frequency the guy was using now, but he didn't get any response, not even when he patched into the internal phone system and called Erskine's extension. When he reached the main entrance to the management wing of the admin block, Zakko and Matt were still waiting at the doors.

"Is Pham in there?" Trinder asked. "I can't get hold of him."

"He's in Erskine's suite," Matt said. "Alex just went in."

Trinder checked his screen for Alex's tracker. "Okay, let's see what Pham's got to say for himself."

"Do you want us to come with you?" Zakko asked.

"Just keep an eye on things in case his spec ops guy shows up. I'll leave my mike open."

"Okay, we'll escort you out when it sounds like you're done."

Trinder hurried down the half-flight of stairs. The executive suite was partly below ground level, secure and hardened against attacks, but he could already hear Alex when he turned into the corridor, so either the office door had been left open or the two of them were slugging it out in the reception area.

The door was open. Trinder walked in. Pham turned his head slowly to look at him and then went back to watching Alex.

"What can you possibly want that we haven't already given you, Commissioner?" Alex paced around Erskine's office, haranguing Pham. "You've got all the FTL data. You've had access to every part of this frigging facility. We let you search whatever and wherever you liked. So I'm struggling to imagine what you get out of screwing over a bunch of farmers and a few B-list scientists Erskine didn't have any use for. Unless this is what you do for fun."

Pham watched him, expressionless, hands resting on the desk as he held a pen by its ends between his fingertips. Trinder sat down on the sofa and looked for a flicker of reaction from him. Maybe Alex was arguing to stall for time, but his face had turned that worrying waxy shade of yellow, so he really was mad enough now to pursue this to the death. This was the angry Alex who'd been lurking within the superficial charmer all these years. It was sobering to watch.

Pham laid the pen down so that it was exactly parallel with the top of the desk blotter. "If this is your let-my-people-go speech, Mr Gorko, let me remind you that I'm the one locked in here."

"Oh, my bad. Did I misunderstand your previous plan to nuke us?"

"You asked me a question, rhetorical or otherwise. What more could I possibly want that you haven't already handed over voluntarily?" Pham didn't look remotely apologetic. "Well, international law seems to be a vague suggestion to you people. You've kept an ASD AI — a Moral variant, so he thinks he's God as well — and let him have control of ships with nuclear warheads. Your labs have been messing around with die-back and managed to let a more virulent strain escape into the wild. Let's put Opis and FTL to one side for a moment. Should I let your scientists leave? What if *they're* the ones responsible for your AI and the new die-back? What about the ones who left in *Elcano* and abandoned you poor innocent waifs to fend for yourselves? Did they dump you, or did you dump them? Maybe you got rid of all the awkward ones who'd blab and you trashed the orbital yourselves. Who's left to contradict you? And then there's Marc Gallagher. He's got an interestingly vague résumé. What involvement does the British government have with all this?"

Alex paused his pacing for a moment, hands on hips. He looked murderous. "You know damn well it's zero. Your call with Dr Kim probably clued them in on a lot of things, but everything to do with the Nomad mission was kept secret, even from staff. Bednarz didn't play well with others. Neither did Erskine. I know because I was the asshole who helped her deceive our colleagues for years and drew up her plans to maroon helpless bystanders as efficiently as possible. But then I remembered I was a human being. I doubt you're going to have that epiphany."

Pham showed no sign of losing his temper with Alex. If there was any expression at all, it was an occasional flash of righteous indignation. It took a moment for the penny to drop for Trinder. Pham genuinely believed Ainatio were the bad guys.

It was obvious, but Trinder marvelled at the revelation like he was five years old again and occasionally understanding fragments of the adult world. Even the smartest people could think a guy they were sure was absolutely wrong was equally aware of how wrong he was, and that everything he said was self-serving and dishonest. But the guy sincerely believed that *you* were the villain, the one who thought and did terrible things, and his sincerity suddenly showed you a view of yourself that you couldn't recognise or believe. It was oddly shocking.

"Commissioner, we're still waiting for your answer," Trinder said, trying to stick to his task. "Alex's question. What more can you possibly want?"

Pham didn't even pause for effect. "Hand over the AI, the employees who've opted to leave Earth, and Marc Gallagher, and everyone else can leave," he said. "Including you and your troops, Major. And release all APS and APDU personnel immediately."

"I think we'll pass," Trinder said. "We don't do handing over. And you know we can't deactivate Solomon."

Alex had regained his normal colour. Anger was exhausting. He looked like he was resting at the simmering vengeance stage for a while. "Yeah, what he said."

Pham didn't blink. "Then we have a problem."

"Well, one of us has," Trinder said. "And you can't keep hundreds of people pinned down with forty conscripts, let alone the few you've got on the gate."

It was a prod to make him blurt out some threat about *Temujin*, but Pham was an expert at this game and said nothing. They sat staring at each other for a few moments. Then Pham shook his head, doing that annoying thing with the pen again, holding its ends pressed between the tips of his forefingers like it was some test of coordination.

"You do realise you have nowhere to go, don't you?" Pham said. "I could open the main gates now and it wouldn't make a scrap of difference to your fate in the longer term. There's no refuge for you within a realistic distance. You're a museum exhibit in a defunct company and you think you can take on the largest and best-equipped armed forces in the world. Why do you think we didn't roll up with a large task force? We didn't need to."

Trinder fired the only shot he had. "Or you want to keep this low key because you haven't told your APS allies and you don't want anyone asking what you're doing out here."

For a moment he thought he'd finally got the upper hand with Pham. It was just a blink, and maybe Trinder was willing it to be there, but he was sure Pham hadn't expected him to say that.

Alex took a few slow paces towards the door. "Okay, Commissioner, when you talk about realistic chances of finding a refuge, it sounds like you've already ruled out the idea that we're going to Opis. So we'll have to plan accordingly."

"I'll let you think about it," Pham said. "You've got a lot to consider. An hour should do it."

He was way too cocky. He definitely thought he had something up his sleeve. Alex walked out without another word and Trinder followed, although he did wonder what would happen if he just shot Pham. Like the man said, though, it wouldn't make any difference in the long run.

Zakko and Matt were waiting for them in the passage outside. There was still no sign of Pham's security detail, but the guys walked them down to the doors anyway.

Matt tapped his earpiece. "Either he doesn't know us very well, or he's three moves ahead of us and this is some stunt."

"He's trying to lure Sol out," Zakko said. "We're bait."

"If Erskine couldn't trap Sol, I don't think Pham's going to manage it."

They paused in the grounds. A water sprinkler threw a rainbow across the lawn as a bot trimmed the grass, and birds followed its path, pecking at the disturbed turf. Dogged normality went on regardless. Trinder suddenly missed it.

"You know what gets me?" Alex asked. "We've got them pinned down. We could carry on prepping for the launch and just wave goodbye. But we still need two or three weeks and Pham's not going to sit on his hands that long."

Trinder nodded. "We need to make sure he can't call home."

"Let's discuss that later," Solomon said. "And yes, I do think Pham's using the people here as bait for me. But knowing that won't make you any less dead or injured if this stand-off turns into violence."

"Don't fall for it, Sol," Alex said. "If you don't make it, nobody makes it."

"Come on." Trinder steered Alex towards the security wing. "It's time you set up in our office. We need you where the decisions are being made. And we won't be spread thin trying to defend an extra location."

"You've got all the good coffee, too," Alex said.

Trinder assumed Pham had given them an hour because it was an easy way to stoke fear and anxiety without expending any effort. Back in the office, he stood in front of the wall screen, watching the movement of trackers. Fonseca had gone to check out the buses that hadn't been moved to Kill Line yet to see how many extra people she could cram in each vehicle to ferry them into town when the gates were opened.

"What are we going to do with them when we get them out?" Alex asked. "If they're stuck in town for any length of time, accommodation's an issue."

The more Trinder thought it over, the more flaws he found in the plan. But none of them were worse than letting Pham have his own way. The guy had already revealed his hand. He wanted to stop Nomad, he wanted to destroy Solomon, and he had unspecified unpleasant plans for Marc and the Ainatio scientists who hadn't chosen to work for APS.

Trinder had at least succeeded in something. He'd found out what Pham really wanted. "Sol, I'm switching back to the secure channel. I need to update Chris and Marc."

"We all heard the conversation," Solomon said.

"Oh, yeah, sorry. Radio. Okay."

"But we'd like to resume our discussion about preventing Pham calling home. We need to be frank about this, Major."

Trinder checked his screen. Solomon could now only be heard by Marc, Chris, Alex, and Trinder for the time being.

"I thought we always were."

"Pham's in contact with *Temujin* and the ship doesn't seem to be taking any action," Solomon said. "Whatever Pham's strategy is — and I still can't decrypt the comms — it doesn't seem to involve her. Our biggest problem is Pham calling in support from APDU in Asia, which won't arrive immediately but it's likely to be more than we can handle when it does. Cutting Pham's comms will have the same result as calling in support. If *Temujin* or Pham go silent, APDU and APS will notice and investigate. You *know* that. You'd do the same."

Yes, Trinder did. He was reluctant to say it, though, because the only way he could think of grounding APDU for long enough to launch *Shackleton* was to destroy its long-range air bases, and that would take nuclear missiles because that was all Ainatio had. Now he was the one buying into the escalation.

"I know I'm on dangerous ground," he said. "But I don't know what's doable, and whether it'll make matters worse if we *can* do it."

There was silence. Solomon seemed to be waiting for Trinder to go on, but Marc responded first.

"Okay, I'll put it in plain English," Marc said. "How do we inflict enough damage on APDU to stop them visiting for the time it'll take to load, launch *Shack*, and get out of range? And can you do it, Sol?"

"Amen," Chris muttered.

Yes, that was what Trinder really wanted to ask. He didn't like himself when he had those thoughts. For some reason it seemed less horrific coming from Marc.

"I can try," Solomon said. "I can't guarantee we can knock out everything or they won't be up and running again sooner than we expect, and I can't guarantee they won't request help from another country. I've never tested my defence capability fully, for obvious reasons, so I don't know what the consequences will be for APDU. But I can give you options and you can decide if some of them are a step too far."

"If it's us or them, I vote it's them," Chris said. "Whatever it is."

Trinder couldn't see any way to avoid using whatever assets they had. "Sol, work out what we can throw at them. But if we shoot first, we can't afford to miss."

"I'll run some projections," Solomon said. "Let me work out a few things. Excuse me."

Solomon went silent. Trinder checked to make sure the comms were still limited. He didn't want other people hearing this when they needed to believe he was a competent adult.

"Are we insane?" he asked. He really did need an answer. He couldn't believe how fast this was spiralling out of control. "We're less than a village and we're talking about going to war with a frigging *superpower*. And then getting in a spaceship and travelling for forty-five years to a planet we know zip about and that might be a graveyard when we get there, if we make it at all. How did things get so crazy? Is it us? Have we been cut off from the outside world for so long that we've lost our fucking minds?"

"Dan, if we weren't the kind of blokes who could think the unthinkable, we wouldn't have survived this long," Marc said kindly. "And we don't have a choice. There's no way we'll hand over Sol, and Pham isn't the type to climb down. There's no middle ground here."

"The worst scenario," Chris said, "is if we can't destroy enough of APDU's infrastructure to put them out of action for three weeks or whatever we need, and the few parts we trash just piss them off even more. Then they come to settle the score instead of taking prisoners.

It won't take much of their arsenal to wipe us out, and *us* includes Kill Line."

"Well, nukes won't cut it," Marc said. "Even if Sol launches all the missiles we've got on the ships, assuming that we can, they might not make it past their early warning system. And we'd have to knock out every single APDU facility with long-range capabilities of any kind that could launch missiles or send in support. It's not feasible. We don't know where all of them are now, for a start. Some are mobile."

"I'm the one who mentioned nukes," Chris said. "Sol didn't. Let's see what he comes up with. In the meantime, we ought to think about what's going to happen when we unlock the doors here. You want to contribute anything, Alex?"

Alex nursed his coffee, staring down into its depths. "I'm so far out of my wheelhouse that I'm sitting in a bar five miles inland. But if you're asking if I think this is a good thing or a bad thing, I'm pretty sure that letting any of our people get hurt because we don't want to hurt too many APS folks is a bad thing. We're here to save our own. That's all I've got."

"Atta boy, Ginger," Marc said. "So we fight with whatever Sol can bolt together."

"Seconded," Chris said.

Trinder felt a little better. The facts hadn't changed, but men who weren't monsters — men who were heroic, men who'd risked everything to save others — had thought the same terrible thoughts that he had. So he wasn't alone, and he wasn't losing it, and he wasn't evil. But he *was* in the shit.

He sat watching the camera feed of Gatti's guys inside the shuttle hangars. No APS personnel had ventured in there since the day they'd landed. Seizing a spaceship would be a challenge even for them. It didn't have keys that could be confiscated, you couldn't wheel-clamp it, and blowing it apart meant taking time to lay charges, no easy feat when armed troops were right there standing guard. Maybe this was as far as it would go, though, like the forty-eight-hour nuke warning that got diluted to a kind of polite occupation. Perhaps Pham would do what most negotiators did when they'd fired their opening volley. After taking an extreme position to give both sides room to move, he'd come back to them with a more reasonable proposition than surrendering everything and everybody to APS.

No. Trinder couldn't see that happening this time.

He was still casting around for a plan that didn't involve declaring war on Asia when Simonot started shifting in his seat as if he'd found something on the monitors.

"Sir, have you seen this technician?" he asked. "More to the point, has Marc? Take a look."

Simonot displayed the feed from a camera near the APS decontamination unit in the grounds. The technicians who'd been carrying out the crop burn were sunning themselves and passing around smokes and soda. There was nothing odd about that, because they were now at a loose end like everyone else, but Simonot zoomed in to focus on one man. He wore orange hazmat overalls like the rest of them but he looked separate from the group. He wasn't really chatting with them, either. He was older, he held himself differently, and he was looking around in that slow, steady way that said he was noting everything.

Trinder captured the footage on his screen and sent it over to Marc. "Marc, take a look at this."

"Yeah, I'd bet he's another operator," Marc said. "So that makes two so far. Well spotted, Jon."

Simonot looked coy. "I'll keep looking."

"What's two special forces operators in mere mortal numbers?" Alex asked. "Ten regular guys? Fifteen?"

"They'll have to be *very* special if they're going after Solomon," Marc said. "I wouldn't know where to start with that. But the first bloke's not an AI expert. He arrived before Pham found out about Sol."

"We don't know that," Alex said. "The informer could have passed a message to him the day he got here."

"If they did, he'd have responded faster."

"Maybe he's just here for you, then."

"I'm flattered," Marc said. "By the way, Dan, thank you for telling Pham you wouldn't hand me over."

"You'd kill me if I tried."

"Don't spoil this touching moment."

"He probably wanted me to tell you so you'd feel obliged to sacrifice yourself for the civilians."

"Dan, if I thought it was enough to make him let everyone go, I'd turn myself in to him personally. And then I'd be able to shoot the bastard at point blank range. But he lies."

Marc didn't sound like he was joking. Trinder had gotten used to him making funny comments, horsing around with Howie, and generally seeming in a good mood. But he hadn't forgotten Tev telling him that Marc wanted to die doing his job. Knowing that, it was sometimes hard to look him in the eye.

Simonot interrupted Trinder's thoughts. "Sir, cam forty-two-C. Take a look."

Trinder looked, but his mind was still on spotting special forces disguised as technicians. He almost missed what had caught Simonot's eye. Camera 42C had a view straight up the runway along the shuttle launch rail, and one of the engineers in its field of view had stopped to stare. Trinder saw a flash of brilliant blue. There was something crashing its way through the bushes on the left-hand side.

"How the hell did that get in without triggering the perimeter alarm?" Trinder imagined the worst. "Echo Five to Echo Ten — you've got a clearance bot heading your way."

"Copy that, Echo Five — oh *shit*."

It was the Fiddler that Trinder had watched ripping out fences on the Welbecks' farm. It couldn't have lost its way. It was here to do damage, and the shuttles were a prime target. Rifles wouldn't stop it, and there wasn't time to deploy the old sapper bot to roll out and ram it when it was only a stroll away from the hangars. The machine cantered out of the undergrowth and onto the runway with a surprising turn of speed for something the size of a shed, then paused as if it was checking what to trash next.

Gatti did his best. He emerged from the hangar with an RPG. Darryl Finch covered him. Gatti shouldered the rocket and aimed.

"Echo Ten, that won't even dent it," Trinder said. "Don't risk it."

"Echo Five, if it comes in here, I have to."

Trinder expected Solomon to intervene. "Sol, can you take it out with an AA missile?"

"Let's see," Solomon said. "It's very close to the hangars. I suggest Corporal Gatti and Private Finch take cover now."

"Well, Pham didn't give it an hour," Chris said. "So he understands we're not backing down either."

Gatti and Finch turned and ran back into the hangar. In a second, Trinder had gone from watching and waiting to preparing to fire missiles. The downhill slide was becoming an avalanche. He kept his focus on the Fiddler, waiting for the flash followed by smoke and shrapnel, but the bot didn't turn towards the hangar. It kept going, doing that odd six-legged canter, its jointed sections bending like a train jumping the tracks, and came to a frozen halt next to the launch rail.

"Wretched thing," Sol said. "If I fire on it now, I'll tear a section out of the rail as well. Clever. I wonder if it's just going to sit there and obstruct the runway. If it does, I might — no, that's what Pham wants me to do, isn't it? He's goading me to transfer to the sapper bot and go out there to grapple with it."

"Does he even know we've got one?" Chris asked.

"I'd imagine our traitor told him I used it."

"Now what's it doing?"

The Fiddler came to life again. It straightened up and clambered over the rail to settle astride it. It dwarfed the sapper bot that Solomon occasionally used but it was still faster and more agile, despite its size. It went where nothing else could. Some of the smaller models could even fly. This one didn't look like it could ever take off, but, as Pham would have said, it didn't need to.

"I believe Pham's entire strategy is testing how much death and damage we're prepared to take to continue the mission," Solomon said.

But Trinder finally realised what the Fiddler had come to do. It extended two arms and started drilling down through the concrete channel that housed the ground-level stretch of the rail. Everyone in the office froze. Sparks flew, and for a moment Trinder thought the Fiddler had hit a cable, but the power was down and the drills were just sparking off metal — reinforcing mesh, Reslev housings, whatever. Trinder had no idea what was in the track beyond power cables. But the Fiddler was drilling, cutting, and hacking away at it all like it was opening a can of beans with a penknife, and it moved *fast*. It was pulling up conduits and all kinds of stuff, leaving a trail behind it that looked like the ruins of a bombed building. The grating noise of motors and squealing metal was painfully loud even over the security cam audio.

"If I launch a missile, I'm doing its work for it and making repairs even harder," Solomon said. "Do you want me to do it anyway?"

"How do I know? Shit, Sol, you're supposed to tell me. Where are the engineers? Ah, forget it, they can't do anything now."

"I think it's already done sufficient damage to ground us for a long time, Major."

The Fiddler stalked a few yards down the rail, still straddling it, and began repeating the process. It was horribly reminiscent of Erskine's destruction of the comms tower to isolate Solomon. Trinder could only watch, shocked into silence, as the Fiddler worked along the track removing rubble and unidentifiable parts and tossing them into a pile.

This was all Pham needed to do to ground Ainatio's remaining shuttles. Repairing the rail, even with bots working around the clock, would take time they probably didn't have and maybe materials they couldn't ship in any longer. Nobody was going anywhere now.

"Bastard." Trinder shut his eyes for a moment. He felt physically sick. "*Bastard.*"

Alex stared. "Well, there goes Melbourne and the giant spiders. I'm so glad we decided to kick his ass."

"Sol, you can save the missile for Pham's helicopters," Trinder said. "And you can fire at will."

"Those options we were talking about," Solomon said. "I think I can do more than shoot down a few aircraft. Let's discuss the possibilities."

Trinder hadn't seen Pham's move coming. Their focus had been on the shuttles, Solomon, and all the big ticket stuff while Pham had simply worked out the fastest, easiest way to give himself extra time and apply more pressure.

Both sides had locked each other in, just like Matt McNally had said. But Pham hadn't won yet, and he didn't have an AI like Solomon.

"Yeah, I'm up for thinking the unthinkable," Trinder said, and didn't feel bad about it any more.

* * *

TEERIK SHIP. OPIS: 1325 EDT EARTH TIME.

"In you go, then, ma'am," Bissey said, parking the rover inside the cordon. Ingram could already feel her hair frizzing from the field emitted by the stealth barrier. "Remember, no sage and onion jokes. And Commander Haine says white meat for him, please."

"Thanks, Number One. I'm trying to get in the mood for serious diplomacy."

Bissey nodded in the direction of a carefully arranged tunnel in the undergrowth that looked like a path worn by animals.

"There's camouflage," he said, "and then there's hiding in terror. I think they've got an underground bunker."

"Jeff wasn't joking. They really are afraid."

"It'd be just our luck to run into an alien army."

"You know, I think I'm going to withdraw your posting as morale officer."

"Oh look, there's Fred. He's wearing his Sunday best."

Fred had stepped out of the undergrowth, and yes, he was wearing something rather like a long version of a brown jinbei pyjama jacket. It looked like a dressing gown on him, totally at odds with the image of a potentially lethal predator. So they did wear clothes, then. That meant Fred had been cavorting around naked. Ingram decided she really wasn't cut out for this complex anthropological stuff and put it out of her mind to focus on simpler objectives.

"Wish me luck." She slid out of the passenger seat. "In a couple of hours, we'll either have new allies with splendid technology or a handy supply of fresh poultry."

"Go get 'em, ma'am. England expects."

Ingram put on her best command face for Fred, making an effort not to stare at his jacket. "Fred," she said. "How nice to see you again. How is everyone?"

"Learned Mother is old and unwell." His appealingly eccentric pidgin English was being rapidly erased by the language lessons. Ingram wondered how he chose a voice when he could mimic anyone's. "But she wants to look at you. There may not be words."

Ingram's job had become politics overnight. Diplomacy and playing nicely with the locals had always been part of military service overseas, but not for Ingram's besieged generation. She'd only had to aim and fire, or ram if she was feeling creative. Her soft power skills were rusty and the teeriks might not understand them anyway. She fixed a smile in place.

"Your English is very good now," she said. "I'm impressed."

Fred scuttled ahead of her, head lowered to avoid the whip-like branches that had formed the tunnel. The daylight dimmed as the vegetation grew thicker.

"Thank you," he said. "You go down a hole soon. Not to worry. Not far to fall. Look out for sharp wood."

Ingram's heart sank. *Terrific. And I won't even get a decent military funeral.* She rolled down her shirtsleeves and fastened them at the wrist, imagining thorns injecting her with toxins and whatever the local equivalent of tetanus might be. It was going to be a test of the array of medications she'd taken before landing. Relying on remotes to identify pathogens and poisonous plants and then design treatments didn't fill her with confidence. This had suddenly become the old navy of wooden ships, where she'd have worried about scurvy, pox, and unnamed exotic diseases taking half her crew. She'd never complain about the navy getting too soft and modern again.

"Hole now," Fred said suddenly, and disappeared.

Ingram almost fell into it. She ended up on her knees in near-darkness and felt around for a rail, then found rungs. It was like moving around a submarine without lighting. Turning to climb down backwards was the hard part, but her boot found solid metal and she inched down, reassuring herself that climbing back up would be easier. The submarine analogy seemed even more accurate when she got to the bottom of the shaft. At the end of a short teerik-height tunnel that forced her to duck her head, a section of curved hull — maybe pale grey, it was hard to tell in this light — formed a wall in front in her. Damn, the ship really was buried, or at least the keel was. That was going to be an interesting conversation.

She visualised the whole area in three dimensions, allowing for the distance she'd walked through the overgrown tunnel and the section of curvature that she could see, and estimated that the ship itself was smaller than *Cabot.* It was buried about a hundred yards from where Fred had met her. Why hadn't they spotted signs of it before, then? Maybe the whole structure was buried.

She ducked her head to follow Fred and stepped through a small hatch into the airlock. The short passage it opened into was a tight fit with a low deckhead only a few inches above her, and when she inhaled, the submarine image was complete. The air smelled of plastic and something animal-like she couldn't identify. The only thing it lacked was the smell of cooking from the galley.

"Why is the ship buried?" Ingram asked. "Did it crash-land?"

"This is Prenu Nar P-twelve," Fred said. He hesitated with each word, as if he wasn't just translating but finding an equivalent in an alien numbering system. "It does this. It hides from the above."

Ingram found herself making gestures like a swimming turtle paddling water. "It digs itself into the ground?"

"Yes. It did not crash."

"Why does it need to dig in, though? I got the impression you could camouflage ships in orbit."

Fred made a little side to side head movement as if he was thinking it over. It might have been too much for his English skills to explain.

"Echoes," he said. "It also needs to hide from seeing with sound."

"Sonar?"

"Echo. Beep-beep-beep, very high."

"Echolocation?" Ingram got the idea. If the ship spent any time on the surface, that made sense. "Someone finds it by making a high-pitched noise?"

"Yes."

"I've never seen a ship that can dig itself in. Very impressive."

"It is a test. This prenu is the only."

The penny dropped. "Prototype?" Ingram prompted. "First of the class?"

"*Prototype.*" Fred's eyes widened as if he'd raised invisible eyebrows in delighted discovery. "Yes, *prototype.*"

Ingram still wasn't sure if prenu was the word for prototype, the class of ship, or the ship's name. She'd prepared herself for a vessel that wouldn't look like anything she'd recognise, with interfaces designed for claws and outstretched wings, and her imagination had already created something out of a futurist movie. But there were only so many ways you could design something that obeyed the same laws of physics as Earth and whose four-limbed crew were pretty much human-size. The interior was more familiar than she'd expected.

It didn't look like a passenger ship, though, and there were a lot of illuminated screens for a cargo vessel. The deckhead was barely six feet high, perhaps a little less, which was going to be a challenge for Bissey and quite a few others when they visited.

"Fred, why are the passages so narrow?" When he looked back at her, she mimed squeezing her elbows against her sides. "Isn't it a problem for you?"

"Not ours," Fred said. "Designed by us for others."

"What's the ship for? What kind of ship?"

Fred paused. "War," he said.

Ingram was starting to get somewhere. It was another apparently random scrap of information to add to the rest and form a picture that made sense. Fred and his people designed warships. Maybe they were exactly like shipyards and technology companies on Earth, carefully guarding their research because they were worried about industrial espionage.

Just like Ainatio, in fact. Yes, Ingram was beginning to understand.

And now she had a chance to meet more of Fred's people. Fred and the two smaller teeriks were the only ones she'd seen so far. As she paused to glance through an open hatch into a compartment, she saw four teeriks in their weird jinbei jackets working on a control panel or console of some kind. One was stretching to reach a control. They didn't fit this space comfortably either. Another looked up and paused to watch her, then whipped around back to his work as if he'd been ordered not to stare at the featherless monster.

"Do you build as well as design?" Ingram asked. She wanted to know where the shipyards were. There was nothing on the surface and no sign of orbital docks, but maybe their factories were hidden too. "Shipyards? Welders?"

"We don't do metal. Not big metal, anyway."

"So you make FTL? Go in the now?"

"Yes. We make the instant move, instant communication, instruments to see and hear, instruments to fire." Fred flattened himself against a bulkhead. Another teerik was heading their way, but this one had a cap of bright red plumage like a woodpecker. "This is my child coming. My daughter. Turisu."

Turisu stopped and scrutinised Ingram. She looked like she'd peck out the eyes of anyone who crossed her, and at such close quarters, unable to stand up straight, Ingram felt a little intimidated for the first time since childhood. Turisu was as big as Fred. Ingram could smell a faint aroma of feathers, not unpleasant but a reminder she was dealing with an alien and that she and Jeff Aiken were — so far — the only humans who'd had this level of contact with intelligent creatures from another world. There was nobody else to ask how to do it.

"Hello, Turisu," Ingram said, enunciating carefully. "Pleased to meet you. Thank you for letting me visit your ship."

"Ma'am Ingram Bridget touch *nothing*," Turisu rasped.

That was definitely a warning. It was weird to hear a human female voice underpinned by an alien sound whose meaning was still crystal clear.

"Absolutely." Ingram held both hands up to indicate compliance. *Yes, definitely sage and onion for you, sweetheart.* "Wouldn't dream of it."

Turisu squeezed past them and disappeared. Fred hung his head exactly as an embarrassed human would. Ingram cringed on his behalf.

"She fears," he said apologetically.

"You have my word that we won't harm you. We just want to be good neighbours."

"Not you. She fears other things."

Ingram waited for him to explain, but he just rocked his head from side to side as if he was in despair and carried on through the passages. Now she understood what Jeff meant when he said that the more he was told, the less he knew. She pressed on carefully.

"Fred, we're very grateful for the help you've offered. Do you mind if I ask questions? You can ask me questions too."

"You first."

"Well, you've offered to help us, and humans generally like to help others in return. We do each other favours."

"Chief Jeff says this too."

"So what do you need from us? What can we give you? Other than being friends, that is."

"Tell me the place your home is," Fred said.

"I know you need coordinates to direct a signal. But I was asking what you need for yourselves."

Fred's head jerked, little bird-like twitches as if he was listening for something. "We need friends."

That seemed to be the stock answer. Either she didn't grasp the implication or he was changing the subject. It was hard not to see teerik body language in human terms, and that could be dangerously misleading, but she read him as being uncomfortable because he wanted to say more and couldn't.

They didn't even check to see if I was armed.

"Well, if you think of something you need other than friendship, just ask," she said. "Now, about locations — "

"I know you worry we go to kill you, but we are not fighters." Fred seemed to have read her better than she'd read him. "We only need position to make gate from here to there."

"Yes, I realise you need to know where to aim the signal. Can you explain how the gates work? Just basics. I'm not a scientist."

"Flat sheet of space in time." Fred stopped and held his long hands out flat with the digits spread, then pressed the small palms together. "Points long way apart... now points touch, because we bend the space. Where points touch is a portal we move through. Voice, objects, people. A bridge not part of time."

Ingram thought she understood that. "So when you step through a portal, you come out the other end in the same time."

"In the now. Yes."

"So not forty years later."

"No, *now*."

"I'm aware of the theory, but we've never managed that in practice."

"But you do this. You have talk in the now. Not later." Fred cocked his head to one side. "You did wormhole. This is same but better. We can put *anywhere*."

This was one for Brad Searle and his engineers. Ingram didn't know enough to ask probing questions. Either the thing would work on a test or it wouldn't.

"Okay, if you give us gate technology, what do we need to build? Do you have factories? Workshops? We've been monitoring Opis for years but we can't see any industrial development at all. Not even cities." That produced a long silence. Ingram waited. It dragged on. "Fair enough, I'll assume that's a security issue for you. So there are other intelligent species like you and us out here, yes?"

"Yes. But not near."

There didn't seem to be any misunderstanding there. Ingram felt her scalp tighten. She hadn't experienced that blip of adrenaline for a long time. "We've never met another intelligent species," she said. "We didn't even know if any existed until we met you."

"Where you travel?"

"Within our own system. Very few try to go further."

"You come here because Earth isn't nice now? Looks nice in the book."

Ingram couldn't remember if Jeff had told them. "We left Earth a long time ago to explore. But no, some parts of it don't seem to be very nice at all these days."

"Is Earth dangerous for us?"

"I wouldn't advise visiting. Not for a long time."

Fred nodded. Ingram might have been imagining it, but he seemed disappointed by the news. His wings dropped a little.

"We visit the Learned Mother now," he said. "Be patient. She is old and dying."

"Fred, I'm sorry. I don't want to burden her if she's ill."

"She wants to see. To judge."

"Okay. Understood." Ingram suddenly missed Solomon again. He'd have made a far better job of this. Even in a quadrubot frame, he was the essence of calm diplomacy. She was selectively bred to rain gunfire on coasts and sink enemy vessels, and perhaps her vocation hung around her like a fog of unsubtle perfume in a crowded room. "Lead on, then, Fred."

Ingram couldn't recognise enough parts of the ship to work out if it was organised in the same way as a human vessel, but she did her best to memorise it as she followed Fred around. There were certainly very few crew. She'd passed through at least three sections separated by bulkheads but had only seen seven teeriks so far. She came to a halt behind Fred as he stopped at another hatch.

"Learned Mother Caisin is in here," he said. "Step in and wait. She may wake or not wake."

He opened the hatch. Ingram caught a whiff of feathers again, that slightly dusty, dried lavender scent of a pet bird, but nothing else. As her eyes adjusted to the light, she saw movement in what looked like a pile of brightly coloured throws and cushions. It took a few moments to make out the creature beneath. All Ingram could see now was a head, more skin than feather but all brilliant scarlet, with one large amber eye fixed on her. The eye came as shock. Ingrained training kicked in and Ingram stood still, hands clasped behind her back. Then she worried that it might be interpreted as reaching for something hidden and dropped her arms to her side.

A big black beak emerged. "Ingram."

"Yes, Learned Mother. Captain Bridget Ingram." It was hard enough to think of the right thing to say to a terminally ill friend, let alone an alien whose significance Ingram couldn't begin to imagine. "Thank you for seeing me."

The old bird just stared at her for a few moments, then closed her eyes and made chattering noises before falling silent.

Fred touched Ingram's arm. "We go now."

Was that it? A few seconds? Ingram was lost. She acknowledged the old teerik with a nod, just a reflex, and backed out of the hatch. Fred led her down another passage and into a larger open compartment. She assumed it was okay to talk now.

"Is there nothing you can do for her?" she asked. "What do your doctors say?"

Fred craned his neck as if he was listening for something. "No doctors."

She wasn't sure if that meant Caisin had refused medical attention, their culture didn't allow it, or they just didn't have any medics. "Can we help?"

"No." It was plaintive, not mind-your-own-business. "Excuse me please. I return soon."

Ingram could only wait. She considered getting on the radio to Bissey, but sending a signal might upset the teeriks and make them think she was spying. She wasn't enjoying this diplomacy lark at all. She shuffled around the compartment while she waited, noting that it contained nothing that looked like a control panel. She could see brackets and insertion holes in the blue-grey grained material that were either awaiting components or showed where they'd been removed.

So... a ship hidden in the middle of nowhere. On a planet with no signs of even a simple village. And a tiny crew, including family members and a terminally ill geriatric. What do I know, though? Maybe this is how they live and work.

Fred still hadn't returned. The ship wasn't completely silent, but the sounds of activity were muffled and a long way away. Ingram gradually managed to separate out the mechanical noises — probably fans, generators, motors — but now she could hear something more random: bumps, metallic bangs, and scuffing sounds. If she'd been in her own ship, she'd have thought it sounded like a couple of ratings settling a dispute with their fists and long past the yelling stage, which meant things were getting nasty. Crises always demanded her presence and she followed the sound to see what was happening. The noises led her down a passage to another half-fitted or half-dismantled compartment.

Two small teeriks, the little ones she'd seen before and had decided were children, were locked in a brawl like fighting cocks. It didn't look like they were playing at it, either. There were feathers and flecks of dark blood on the deck and one had a ripped sleeve. The struggle was grimly silent except for the rasp of wings when they hit bulkheads. One seemed to be getting the worst of it. Ingram stepped in to stop the fight before someone was seriously hurt.

"Hey! Cut it out, you two!"

She lunged forward and brought her hands together in a loud clap that stung her palms, the same thing Fred had done with his wings when she'd first encountered them. It seemed to do the trick. The two juveniles suddenly seemed to notice her and backed away to separate corners, wings spread. Now she could hear skittering noises from a distance. Someone was heading their way at speed.

It was then that she saw the lump on the floor. For a moment she was almost afraid to look in case it was a chunk of gouged flesh, but it looked more like a biscuit.

"Mine," one of the youngsters said, and snatched it up.

They'd learned English as well, then, and the only reason for using it in front of her was to tell her to back off. Ingram should have learned never to mess with strangers' kids but she was stuck now and she had to see it through.

"You're going to hurt each other," she said. "Play nicely. Why are you fighting like that over a biscuit? Share it."

"Hungry. *Very* hungry." The kid sounded male, but that was no guide. All the teeriks sounded like they'd chosen an appropriate voice to mimic. He pecked into the brownish lump with a beak like an ice pick and swallowed. "Not much to share."

"There'll be other biscuits."

"No. No more biscuit."

Fred rushed into the compartment with Turisu on his heels. Ingram had her excuses and apologies ready. If Nomad ever made contact with Earth again, she'd go down in history as the first human to start an interstellar war by telling off some alien's wayward kids. But Fred waded in and batted both juveniles around the head, not with any force behind it but obviously symbolic of consequences to follow.

"Sorry, Fred, I broke up a fight," Ingram said. "I thought they'd do each other serious damage."

"I apologise. They are the sons of my daughter. Turisu's children."

It was all falling into place now. "Are they all right?"

"They fight. They have to learn not to."

"Hungry," the kid repeated. He obviously wanted Ingram to understand that. He was dragging her into the argument to pressure his mum and grandad. "Not liking hunger."

Opis looked pretty fertile and well-stocked. If this was their homeworld, why would they be starving? Whatever the reason, Ingram could take a gamble. Any creature's food needs would tell her a lot about its life, and the boffins back at Nomad could reverse-engineer the disputed biscuit to understand teerik biochemistry. The quantity required would help her estimate population size.

And feeding hungry people usually won friends.

"Do you need food supplies?" she asked.

"No," Turisu said.

"Yes," said the kid. "We need biscuit."

Called it. We're in. "Now that's something we can do for you, Fred," Ingram said. "Give us the nutritional information and we'll make something specially for your needs."

"We don't know you," Turisu said. Her English wasn't bad either. They obviously thought it was worth the effort to learn. "How we trust your food?"

"I don't know *you*, but I'm probably going to trust you enough to give you the location of Earth," Ingram said. "And if we meant to harm you, we'd have done it by now. We don't need to poison you when we've got armaments."

That probably wasn't the most diplomatic way to put it. But she wasn't negotiating with Turisu or Fred. She was doing a deal with the two hungry little crows willing to rip chunks out of each other over a biscuit or whatever the lump turned out to be. And if the kids were hungry, that meant the adults were even hungrier, because few parents would watch their children starve while they ate their fill.

"Please?" The pushier of the two kids pawed at Fred's sleeve, still speaking English, still playing the emotional blackmail card and daring his grandad to look heartless in front of a guest. "Please do it."

Pester power was a marvellous thing. Ingram added her own pressure. "If you can't give me nutritional data, let me have a sample of food and we can analyse it."

Fred didn't get the chance to think it over. The kid handed the chunk to Ingram. It looked like a well-gnawed dog biscuit. She broke it into three pieces with a bit of effort — yes, dog biscuit — and handed one chunk back to the kid and one to his brother, which seemed to restore both peace and confidence.

"This bit's big enough for us to work on." Ingram put the remaining piece in her pocket and tried to work out why they'd need dry rations here. Maybe this was just a remote site, far from a populated centre. But she suspected there was a more complicated explanation than that. "What flavour do you like?" she asked. "What texture? Where I come from, the navy was built on dry biscuits like this. But we can do better than that. What do you like best?"

Fred had to explain that to the kids in his own language, with a lot of clicks and rasping gutturals. It looked like he'd conceded defeat. Turisu's red crest feathers were all fluffed up like an angry hen, but she didn't intervene. Then one of the kids scuttled away.

"Runal will bring some," Fred said.

"If you tell us which food plants you use, that would help too." Ingram now had to test her theory. "You know, crops. Fruits. Grains. Vegetables. Even meat, if you tell us where to find the animals."

Fred just looked at her. She got the feeling she'd guessed the truth. If Opis was their homeworld, they wouldn't be starving, unless they didn't dare show themselves and had no idea how to live off the land. Now that he knew she was effectively lying by taking the situation at face value, she had to tread carefully in case he thought humans lied too easily to be trusted with teerik technology.

Runal broke the awkward silence by rushing back to offer a scrap to Ingram.

"Like this," Runal said. "Soft. Nice."

Ingram took it, trying not to look squeamish. It was moist, dark brown, and felt like a flapjack that had been spat out by a dog. "You like the taste?"

"Yes. Nice."

"We'll analyse it and make something like it, then."

"It's not good food," Fred said. "It's amusement food."

"Oh, junk food? Don't worry. Our technicians can probably reproduce the flavour and texture but make it nourishing like the biscuit."

It was hard to tell if Fred understood that. He didn't say a word, and neither did his squawky daughter. But both of them obviously wanted to see the kids happy and well-fed, even if that meant doing deals. Ingram knew she'd made a breakthrough.

"Well, I'd better get these samples back to the base." She wrapped the flapjack in a piece of tissue. "I'll let you know when we've made something. How much do you need, by the way?"

She didn't expect an answer and she didn't get one. The teeriks could still hide behind not fully understanding English, but Ingram felt she had the measure of them now and they were just scared witless about revealing too many vulnerabilities.

"We calculate," Fred said. "I show you way out now."

The teeriks she'd passed on the way in had gone. She followed Fred up the shaft to the surface, relieved to stretch her spine again, and slowed down on the walk through the undergrowth to try to make conversation. Maybe he'd open up without his daughter around.

"Fred, let's be completely honest with each other," she said. "You've got a prototype warship buried here, there doesn't appear to be a civilisation on this planet capable of supporting that technology, you don't know anything about the local plant life, you've got your family with you, and you're running out of food. This isn't your homeworld, is it?"

Fred dropped his head and walked a few yards before answering.

"No," he said. "We come a long way."

"Did the ship break down? Are you stranded?"

"No."

"Did you plan to be here?"

"No."

"But you've got FTL technology. Can't you go home or move on?"

"No. To move on you need know where you go and if it's safe."

"And you don't, I take it." *You called it, Jeff.* "You're refugees, then. You've run away from somewhere dangerous."

"Yes. It's complicated."

"I love how you've learned that phrase."

Fred went quiet and rustled through the undergrowth. Ingram noticed now that both he and his grandsons seemed to have more feathers on their wings than the others. Fred's sleeves didn't fit neatly.

"Wings," she said. "That must be uncomfortable in a jacket."

"I want to fly. I let feathers grow again."

"Sorry, I don't understand."

"To dress like others, I cut long feathers. Flying feathers. Where we live, I never had somewhere to fly. But now I do, so I learn."

"You don't normally fly, then."

"No. But we can, and we should."

It was a revelation, like the day she'd first realised Fred could speak. She'd been so excited by the discovery that she rushed back to the camp to tell everyone. Now she felt she understood something profound about him. In the midst of chaos, he was going back to his roots and delighting in being truly avian, like an old man refusing to shave or put on a collar and tie, holing up in a tent in the woods and fishing for his dinner, because he wanted to lead the life he was designed for. The exasperated daughter made sense now. It was rather touching.

"If I had wings, Fred, I'd be flying all the time," Ingram said. "Good for you. Don't ever let anyone ground you."

Static began frizzing her hair. They'd reached the edge of the defensive field. Fred stopped.

"I know you still want to ask questions," he said. "The ones you not ask are heard anyway."

"If I asked, would you answer them?"

"I try, but Learned Mother and Turisu would be angry."

"It's okay. When you feel able, I'd like to know as much as you can tell me about this sector. We need to learn more about the neighbourhood we're living in and if we need to protect our people. We're in the same situation, Fred. We're both a long way from home and things aren't working out as well as we expected. If we help each other, we'll survive."

"This is truth, Ma'am Ingram Bridget."

"Call me Bridget. We're friends."

"Friends. Yes. Bridget. *Bridget.*"

Fred seemed happy, repeating words the way he did when she'd first met him. He'd wanted to be assured that Jeff was his friend, too. It made more sense now. Teeriks were brilliant engineers and physicists, but they couldn't defend themselves. They didn't even seem able to forage for food. They were helpless geniuses. And she'd been utterly wrong in assuming they were concealing the ship to protect their trade secrets, which was a timely reminder that it was too easy to see familiar things that weren't really there.

"We'll get your food ready to test as soon as we can." Ingram had an urge to shake his hand or pat him, but decided to quit while she was ahead. "I'll tell Jeff what a nice ship you have."

"Bye," Fred said, just like a polite child. Ingram was enchanted. "Bye bye."

She walked back to the rover and climbed in. Bissey shot her a look. She fished in her pockets for the food samples.

"Well, ma'am, what happened?"

She took the alien flapjack from her pocket and held it where he could see it. "Bargaining chip," she said.

Bissey glanced at the chunk. "Can't say I'm impressed by their small eats. Any cocktails?"

"Peter, they're starving. They're refugees. I don't know what they've fled from, but right now the way to their hearts is via their kids' stomachs. I said we'd have a crack at formulating rations for them, based on these samples."

"And the FTL?"

"Think of the snacks as a loss leader. They've got a prototype warship buried down there. They're engineers and physicists. They *designed* it. I bet it goes like a greased weasel."

"Good grief. What the hell have we walked into?"

"Hard to tell."

"So they're not a native species."

"No, and I think they've only got a skeleton crew. Including an elderly female who's dying."

"Bloody hell. Not some plague, is it?"

"Oh *bugger*." Ingram felt like an idiot. This was basic stuff. But the long list of vaccines she'd been given before departure had made her feel safe. She put a lot of faith in the analytical skills of biohaz bots. "I didn't ask."

"It's not like you to forget quarantine procedure."

"But if I'd asked they probably wouldn't have told us. Better get Haine to check us over. Anyway, back to business."

"May I hazard a guess, ma'am?"

"Hazard away."

"If one of our prototypes ended up on another planet with the civilian contractors driving it, we'd wonder whether something had gone horribly wrong in the button-pressing department or if they'd hijacked it. Fred says they're refugees. So that probably confirms it's not theirs, and whatever happened, some navy's out there searching for their missing ship."

The teeriks didn't look like criminals, but Ingram had no benchmark for spotting alien delinquency. She contemplated the pecked scrap of food sitting in her palm. If the old female was dying of something infectious, then the whole crew could be carriers, and here she was handling gunk covered in crow spit. But that didn't seem half as worrying as an alien navy looking for its stolen prototype.

"They did keep saying they aren't fighters, so a warship's a strange choice for a family vehicle," she said. "I think you might be right."

"We've got some hard choices to make, then," Bissey said. "If their FTL isn't all Fred claimed, we might end up being the slowest-moving easy targets out here."

Peter Bissey was a good first officer because he didn't flinch from telling Ingram when she'd overlooked the obvious. There were still other possible explanations for the teeriks having a warship: a cancelled order, an old discarded prototype hauled out of mothballs in an emergency, or just a vessel and its contractors abandoned by a client in the middle of some national crisis that meant they had to flee. Ingram hoped for the obsolete prototype. The other scenarios were starting to look a lot worse than a hijacking. But whatever the reason, she now knew for certain that there were other civilisations out here with better technology, and the awe of first contact had now been thoroughly squelched by the need to survive.

"Let's get the food techs on the case," she said. "I think our future's going to depend on our cookery skills."

* * *

VEHICLE STAGING AREA, KILL LINE: 1330 EDT.

"The Fiddler didn't *get in*." Chris sat in the back of the Caracal with Marc and Jared, watching Trinder, Fonseca, and Alex on the bulkhead screen. "It was already parked inside the wire with the rest of the APS agritech gear. We didn't spot it because we weren't looking for anything we already knew about. So we didn't have a security failure. It wasn't even an *us* failure."

"I still should have seen it coming," Trinder said.

"And? Even if we'd thought of it, we haven't got enough troops to secure a rail a mile long, the Fiddler's bulletproof, and it would have stomped all over anyone who tried to stop it." Chris could see Trinder's hard-won confidence draining away when they needed him to be on top of his game. *Nobody* had thought about the rail. And some risks couldn't be planned away. "Missiles aren't the right answer either. Whether we used them before or after, we'd have started a firefight before we were ready. Chaos and dead civvies."

This wasn't the lowest point of Chris's life, but it ranked in his top ten shitty situations. The exhausted expressions in the security office said it all. Every day had become a procession of single steps forward and two back.

"Dan, it doesn't change anything," Jared said. "We were screwed from the moment the guy with APDU bomber command on his speed-dial stepped off that tilt. We still can't outrun them."

"But what if Pham's all bullshit?" Alex asked. "The rail might be the end of Nomad, but it's still a long way short of what we thought APS could do to us."

"He's already said he doesn't have to do more," Chris said. "And yeah, he might just be saying that, but he's proved it."

Marc never fidgeted when he got impatient. He just lowered his voice so everyone had to stop and listen to him. It always worked.

"Dan," he said quietly, "we're just reacting to Pham's agenda. It's time to make him deal with *us* at the time and place we decide, which is what our lovely but scary Captain Fonseca did when she threw the lock switch. Let's take it from there. Most of his people can't move around the buildings or leave them. If we go in, he has to do something about us. I know it's risky, but so is sitting around dying a death of a thousand cuts."

Jared muttered approvingly. Chris was all for it. "Okay, what's happened to the bits of rail they ripped up?" Chris asked. "Can we recover the Reslev bits and put it back? It's a hell of a long track. They can't have removed the whole thing in a few minutes."

"The bot ripped up about twenty metres," Fonseca said. Chris saw her reach out to tap a key and suddenly he was looking at the view down the length of the chewed-up launch rail again, with the big blue Fiddler still standing motionless astride it. It looked like someone had put up a small low-rise building in the wrong place. "We haven't sent engineers in to assess it yet, not until we work out if the bot's armed. Gatti says it's a mess."

"It doesn't have to be armed. It's got tools for weapons. And Gatti's not an engineer or a technician."

Fonseca did her look of stony indifference. "Okay, but whether he's right or not, it's increased the time we need to load and launch. So if we're counting on holding them off while we do that, it just got harder."

"Can the shuttle take off for an atmospheric flight without a rail?" Chris asked. "Maybe we can fly it somewhere that's got a ramp launcher." He wondered if Marc could put in a call and do a deal with his government. They probably had at least two shuttles and facilities because they still had spy sats and other space assets to maintain. "Or we can call in favours. APS aren't the only government that'd like to have the FTL files."

"You mean ask my government to evacuate everyone," Marc said.

"Yeah."

Trinder almost perked up. "It's a thought. Have your guys got the resources to do it, Marc?"

"I don't know. It's a tough evacuation to pull off if APS decides we're interfering with their national interests and takes pot-shots. And it's got to be an airlift, because sending a ship means a week or two to get it here, and I don't fancy our chances of avoiding APS's wrath for that long."

"You sound like you've worked it out already," Fonseca said.

"Of course I bloody have. I've also asked myself what's in it for the government. I'm the only Brit here. They're not obliged to risk planes to save Americans, but they might think it's worth it to get hold of FTL and stray boffins who need rehoming. And it *is* a risk. Whatever happens, APS is going to think Britain's got hold of Sol, and he's what *really* scares Tim Pham."

"So you're going to give your government Ainatio's research," Fonseca said.

"Yeah, I am. Why not? Is there a problem with that?" Marc was one of the few guys who didn't approach Fonseca with nervous reverence. Chris admired and envied that. "You didn't mind giving it to APS. And we're an old ally. The Foreign Office must know what this is about by now, and there's probably some military application for the FTL, so I'm bloody well not going to leave my country with a strategic disadvantage. Britain can't help anyone if it ends up as charcoal."

"It's all going to come out," Alex said. "Die-back. Sol. The lies about *Cabot*. Which has a lot of Brits in the crew."

"Yeah, we'll be carrying a big steaming can of worms that we'll have to explain to His Majesty's Government," Marc said. "But you'll be better off with us than with Pham, if that's what we decide to do. Now we've got to do something about the people stuck on the campus, whatever option we go for."

"I didn't hear any options," Alex said.

Marc counted off on his fingers. "One, attack the campus, neutralise APS and APDU personnel, and hope we can repair the rail and get going before APS wonders why Pham isn't answering his phone. Two, attack the campus et cetera, extract people and supplies, make a run for that lake down south, and wait for APS to find us, because they will. Three, beg the Foreign Office for help, extract et cetera, hope APS don't shoot down the RAF's finest, and also hope they don't go after Britain for getting involved. Four — pray. Because all the other solutions are out of our hands."

There was a long silence. Chris had always been able to work out his chances of pulling off a mission. He'd operated in a world he knew all too well, a stew of chaotic, lawless cities, desperate people, and predators who preyed on them. He was the guy with the guns and the APCs whose job it was to sort it out. Everyone was in the same boat; the unknowns were when, not what or why. But APS was as alien as Opis. In theory, it could strike anywhere in the world but maybe it had reached its limits. Chris didn't even know if APDU did the politicians' bidding or if they were a law unto themselves. But Pham wasn't the entirety of APS, and he wasn't a wild card, either. It was too easy to focus on one man instead of a faceless political bloc as the villain. Pham probably reflected the attitude of APS generally, that Ainatio had created threats to Earth, from Solomon to the new die-back strain, and letting an Ainatio mission loose in space as well was their worst nightmare. Chris understood that. He'd have felt the same.

He was still going to fight and hit them as hard as he could, though.

"Sol, you're very quiet," Jared said. "Are you still there?"

"I am, Corporal Talbot," Solomon said. "I was concentrating on the debate. None of you are wrong. But I'm assessing a new development at the moment, and I think it's going to affect the solutions I was going to present to you. My apologies. May I ask for another brief delay?"

Chris looked at Jared. Jared gave him that oh-shit look.

"Okay, Sol," Chris said. "We're going to plan for retaking the campus and getting people out."

"Agreed," Sol said. "I'll be as quick as I can."

"We'll compile an updated map of where everyone's located and get back to you," Trinder said. "You guys are running this now. I'll follow your lead."

The screen went blank, with no familiar Ainatio menu. They were outside the network. Nobody spoke for a few moments.

"I'm going to go see Sol," Chris said. He didn't need to go anywhere to talk to the AI, but Solomon seemed to have a sense of place now, a need to be somewhere specific like a physical being. Chris just felt uneasy about another delay. "I need to bring Doug up to date too. I'll drop by on my way to the Lamm."

"Why isn't he telling us what this development is?" Trinder asked. "I think we're used to bad news by now."

Marc stretched as if his back hurt and rubbed his eyes. "Because he realises there's only so many times he can build up people's hopes and then crush them before they give up. He wants to be sure he can deliver whatever it is he's planning."

"I thought he was going to try to shut down APS comms," Chris said. "But I can't see how that's going to give us the time we need to launch. If we can launch at all now."

"He can do a damn sight more than cut them off. And I don't know if we should try to stop him." Marc stood up and opened the rear hatch. "Anyway, we're spinning too many plates. Focus on retaking the campus and extracting anyone who wants extracting. Ainatio people who want to stay — they're on their own. And bear in mind one of the buggers we risk our arses to extract could well be the traitor. I love my job really."

"Why would the traitor want extracting?"

"To spy some more and stab us in the back again, in exchange for whatever reward makes smart people behave like total shits," Marc said. "If they leave the campus and we're not going to Opis, they can stroll back to Pham any time."

"Not if I've still got a spare round," Chris said.

"Okay, Marc, let's you and me work out the timing," Jared said. "I like to have a plan just so I can rip it up the second the shit starts flying."

"Are you going to call your Foreign Office pal now?" Chris asked. "It might end up being all we've got left."

Marc rummaged in his pockets. He had a grey angler's vest over his black Ainatio polo shirt, something Chris had never seen him wear before, and it was a ninety-degree day, so he'd obviously decided he needed the extra pockets more than comfort. Pockets meant spare mags and backup weapons. He looked thoroughly armed.

"Yeah," he said. "Just as well I took one of Dan's ancient sat phones before the lockdown, isn't it?"

He really had thought a long way ahead, then. Chris would have been disappointed if he hadn't, not just because he respected the guy's skills but because a man who didn't have any loyalty to his tribe or fears for its safety wasn't a man at all. It was right that he cared what happened to Britain.

"Yeah," Chris said. "You think of everything."

Chris ducked out of the rear hatch and took one of the pickups to head into town. The Lammergeiers were parked on the western side of Kill Line on Cedar Hill Farm, which meant driving through the town square, so he could drop in on Doug and update him. Doug would probably be in the town hall now there was no farming to be done. He was busy shutting down Kill Line. Was shutting the right word? What did you call it when you abandoned a place you loved and left a ghost town? Chris slowed down to take it all in.

The town was now tidy and peaceful again as if no crisis had ever made farmers shoot their livestock or sent eleven hundred townsfolk to huddle in a makeshift bomb shelter. The palls of smoke from burning animal carcasses were gone. Kill Line could have been any unchanging small town that Chris could walk around in minutes and admire wistfully as an idyllic life that wasn't meant for the likes of him. It had been built to serve the Ainatio complex. It would die when the facility did.

So that was the word, then: *euthanising*. Doug was giving Kill Line a peaceful death.

It saddened Chris. Kill Line was an icon of everything that had been worth having when the world had been normal, not that he remembered those days. There were safe streets for the kids to play ball in, and maybe life was a little claustrophobic because everyone knew your business, but it was also reassuring because those same neighbours knew right away when you needed help and would give it without a second thought. The houses were neatly painted, and there was no trash, not even now the place was being abandoned. On a perfect summer afternoon, it all seemed a tragedy. Chris preferred leaving places on freezing grey mornings that made them look worth escaping.

As he drove down the main road towards the square, people passing by waved like he was the mailman or something. David Flores stood on the porch of his brewery, nursing a rifle that Chris hadn't seen him carrying before. It looked like he'd joined Marc's classes. Chris stopped the pickup and rolled down the window, wanting to apologise for the whole clusterfuck, even though it was nobody's fault but the likes of Tad Bednarz, Tim Pham, and the unnamed asshole who'd thought creating a plant-killing virus couldn't possibly go wrong. He was sorry anyway.

"Hey Chris," David said. "How bad is it? I can tell. I can see it on your face."

Chris would never lie to these people. "APS found out about Sol and die-back, so they ripped up part of the launch rail to stop the shuttles taking off. I'm sorry it's not good news. But we're not beaten yet."

David looked at him for a few seconds, blinking and lost, then let out a long breath. "Okay. We're ready, whatever happens. Hey, I've got some beer for your guys if you want to pick it up when you're done. Might as well clear the cellar."

Chris was a guy who kept his feelings to himself but he didn't understand David taking the bad news so calmly. He wanted him to cuss and rant like any guy whose life was being trashed, but maybe he was too ground down to make the effort.

"Thanks, David," he said. "We appreciate it. Look, I need to go see Doug now. Don't give up, though, okay? We've still got options."

David pointed past him as if he was politely ignoring Chris's optimistic farce. "Doug's on his way to see you. With the town council."

Chris turned towards the square. A dozen men and women, all looking like they'd been doing something important when they'd been interrupted by his arrival, were heading his way. They must have spotted the pickup coming via one of their drones. He couldn't see Doug yet, but the group all had weapons, mainly shotguns and some of the new carbines that Marc had churned out. One of the women had a handgun holstered on her hip. She didn't seem to know where to place her right arm and held it awkwardly away from her side, so he guessed the weapon wasn't her everyday carry.

"Normally, I'd make a run for it right about now," Chris said.

His automatic reaction to an armed crowd coming at him head-on would actually have been to sight up and prepare to open fire. He'd faced too many. But these were just his neighbours, not an angry mob. He *wanted* them armed. He managed to limit the reflex to a vague uneasiness. The group parted and Doug emerged from the back.

"I'm glad you're here, Chris." Doug sounded relieved. Poor guy: at his time of life, he should have been sitting on his porch with a beer and watching his grandkids playing, but he'd ended up as mayor during the town's worst and final days. "I'm guessing we've got a new problem."

Chris dreaded dumping more bad news on these people, but if they hadn't gone batshit when they thought they were going to be nuked, they weren't about to lose it now.

"Yeah, it's not good," he said. He didn't know where to start. Chronological order seemed easiest. "APS found out Solomon's a kind of AI they think needs to be shut down, and they also found out where the new die-back came from, so they're trying to stop us going to Opis. They used the Fiddler bot to rip out the shuttle launch rail. Right now we've got a stand-off. Their troops have blocked the gates but Captain Fonseca's locked down the buildings, so most of their people are trapped. We're going to get the Ainatio staff out."

Chris waited for the reaction. The crowd just stared at him. Some of them looked shocked. But there was no panic.

"So what do we do now?" Doug asked.

"I'm not going to lie to you, Doug. I don't know where this is going to end. But we're looking at various options, including asking Britain to airlift us, and we haven't given up on fixing that rail. Things are changing fast. I'll keep you updated as best as I can."

"How did APS find all this out?"

This was going to be hard. "We've got a traitor."

"Who?"

"No idea yet. But we'll find out."

Everyone looked at him with a grim acceptance like they were waiting for the order to grab pitchforks and root out the collaborator. Chris almost wished he hadn't said it. Even if folks knew the traitor wasn't anyone in Kill Line, it didn't bode well for relations with the Ainatio remnant if they had to live together.

"When you do, make sure you let us know."

"I will."

"Anyway, we're ready. Just tell us what you want us to do."

"Well, stand by to load more supplies," Chris said. "Because when we go into the facility, we'll be bringing out the rest of the stores as well as evacuees."

Doug almost smiled. "I meant we're ready to take back Ainatio. You've got a few hundred extra troops here, as long as you give us clear orders, because we're only used to shooting coyotes."

"Damn straight," said someone at the back of the crowd. "We didn't hold out this long to have some pissant foreign politician giving us orders in our own country."

Chris knew that voice, and it surprised him. It was Liam Dale, the dairy farmer who'd refused to leave his animals, bombs or no bombs. The last time Chris had spoken to him he'd expected the conversation to end with a punch in the mouth either given or received. Liam's was the last supportive voice he expected to hear.

But that was Kill Line. The folks here were rock-solid, unafraid, and willing, and it choked him up. He didn't know what to say. He hadn't been this embarrassed since his teens.

"I'm grateful for the offer," he said. "If we run into problems... well, yeah. Thank you. I know you can do it. With any luck, you won't need to."

That was all Chris could manage to say right then. The strength and strangeness of the emotion caught him off-guard. He wanted to say a lot more, but he knew he'd never get it out. He was proud of these people — damn, no, more than that, he was *fond* of them. He'd hardly known them before Jamie was killed, but they'd rallied around then and they were doing the same now. For people who'd always been cocooned by Ainatio from the harsh world outside Hart County, they'd stepped up fast, and maybe they'd fail if they were put to the test. But that didn't matter. This wasn't about skill. It was about being ready to have a go, no matter how bad the odds, and those were the kind of people Chris wanted around him.

"Okay, but just say the word," Doug said, and trudged back towards the town hall with the councilmen trailing behind.

Chris returned to the pickup a little shaken. Human decency always upended him because he'd never seen enough of it to think it was normal. He sat with his hands on the steering wheel for a moment, trying to turn back into the Chris that Alex called Captain Inscrutable, and wondered why it had hit him so hard.

"Come on, get a grip," he said to himself, and drove off.

Liam Dale's farm was on the way to Cedar Hill, just before the fork in the road that led off to Doug's place. Liam's Jersey cattle were grazing peacefully and the pigs were rooting in the next field as if the apocalypse wasn't around the corner. Chris wondered whether it was worse for Liam to never know what happened to them than it was to have to shoot them. It didn't look like the Korean guy would be able to make good on his promise to rehome the cows now.

Chris was still trying to understand the affection folks could feel for animals they were going to eat when he turned off onto the track up to Cedar Hill. He could see the Lammergeiers, red splashes half-screened by the trees in front of a big grey composite barn. Beyond the grazing land, though, the fields were dead and brown. This was the edge of the quarantine zone, burned to below soil level by chemical sprays.

The Lammergeiers weren't camouflaged. Lamm 1 was just sitting there with the ramp down, crates and pallets stacked around it as if it had a legitimate job to do. Lamm 2 was twenty yards away. David Vander and Sheri Ballam, the pilots, were at a loose end and obviously frustrated. The tilt-rotors had so much AI that they didn't really need pilots, but the pilots definitely needed the aircraft. Sheri saw Chris coming and did an arms-spread what-the-hell gesture. She wanted to know what was going on.

"We've got a Lamm with a full payload of Strixes going to waste here," she called. "How long are we going to take this APS crap?"

Chris tried to look apologetic. "Got to talk to Sol," he said. "I won't be long."

The transit camp's gun truck was parked nearby. Rich Netzer and Lee Ramsay were sitting on a couple of ammo crates at the top of Lamm 1's ramp, rifles on their laps, taking advantage of the cool shadows.

"I never used to hate APS," Lee said. "But I do now."

Chris tried to be upbeat. "We'll work something out. There's got to be another way to launch."

"Chris." Solomon's voice in his earpiece was insistent. "Chris, come to the cockpit."

"See you later, guys," he said. "I've been summoned."

The last time Chris had been in a Lammergeier's cargo bay, he'd been flat on the deck bleeding out from a shattered leg while medics worked on him and Lennie Fonseca confirmed the news about Jamie. It was the first time he'd met Solomon, too. Maybe it had all happened on this very deck. The memory bothered him more than he expected. He shook it off before stepping into the cockpit.

"So you're wearing a tilt-rotor now, yeah?" Chris said. "Nice. Red's your colour."

Solomon's voice emerged from the cockpit audio. "Are you trying to raise my spirits, Chris?"

"No, I'm trying to raise mine. Are you fully armed?"

"I am, as Marc would say, tooled up like a bastard. Missiles, ramp guns, rockets. And I can still deploy the anti-aircraft missiles on the Ainatio site if the detachment can't respond. If APS manage to find me, I can be airborne in seconds. Don't worry about me. I was designed for this."

Chris tried to be chatty but he wasn't cut out for small talk. It always ended with people thinking they were being interrogated.

"So have you worked out who betrayed us yet?"

"Is that your priority?"

"No, but until we know who it is, we don't know what else they can screw up."

Tad Bednarz had made Solomon invulnerable and given him a mission he thought humans couldn't be trusted with. The more events spun out of control, the more Chris marvelled at the man's ability to predict the worst. He wanted to believe Solomon could save the mission, but he'd spent the dying years of the American state watching technology collapse around him, relying more each day on the basics of soldiering that hadn't changed in centuries — the skill and tenacity of human beings with simple weapons that could be relied on to work every time. He couldn't trust technology to be there when he needed it. Now the only shield that stood between the relative might of APS and the small world he'd staked his life on was the ultimate technology, a hyper-smart AI with beliefs, passions, and grudges. Chris didn't know whether to accept Solomon as a miracle or see him as a potential single point of failure.

"Let me show you something more urgent, Chris. Please take a look at the monitors."

The space behind the pilots' seats housed instrument displays and monitors along the bulkhead. They all looked alike to Chris.

"Which one do you want me to check out?"

"Fifth screen," Solomon said. "The positions of vessels from a section of the GEO orbit to the graveyard zone. Red is APS, green is our ships, and blue is the orbitals."

"Got it." Chris studied the display, seven icons on a dark background crisscrossed by white loops and intersecting arcs. He still didn't have a mental picture of where any of these vessels were. They were just in a vague area he thought of as Up There, and anything above roof height might as well have been light years away if Ainatio didn't have operational shuttles. "Sorry, Sol, you'll have to explain it to me."

"The red icon is an APS shepherd," Solomon said. "An unmanned satellite safety vessel. The kind that deals with dead and failing satellites before they become a hazard. Based on its changes of orbit, I believe it's looking for our ships."

Chris tried to work out the courses. "Seems like it's found them."

"It knows roughly where to look because APS have been watching us routinely for years. They know where Orbital One is, so they see occasional traffic too. Monitoring space is a lot easier if you know which direction you should be looking in."

"When you say *deals with dead satellites*, you mean destroy, yeah?" Chris said.

"Shunting them into disposal orbits or de-orbiting them to burn up in the atmosphere, usually," Solomon said. "But shepherds recover scrap and deploy small survey drones as well. That takes the same kind of robotic dexterity as planting charges and cutting things open. And if an object's in a graveyard orbit, debris from an explosion isn't the problem it'd be if there were active satellites around."

"Then we're assuming this one's up to no good."

"Yes. Other than dumping junk or salvaging it, the shepherd has no reason to be in there."

Chris started wondering how long it would take for one of *Shackleton*'s missiles to launch and hit it. His geophysics modules at college hadn't covered that but he had a feeling it would be a slow business compared to what would happen on Earth.

"I know this is bad, Sol, but I can't work out exactly how bad," he said. "I'm guessing that there's no point in targeting it with a missile, and that won't stop Pham calling Dial-A-Nuke anyway. Can you evade it?"

Solomon paused. "Now might be a good time to patch Marc and Major Trinder into the conversation. Because I do have a better plan."

"Okay." Chris tapped at his screen. Trinder responded right away, but Marc took a few moments to answer. "Guys, Sol's got a plan to put to us. Listen in. Go ahead, Sol."

Solomon sent images to everyone's screen. "As Marc said, we need to take the initiative and make APS react to *us* where and when we want them to. We have an advantage. If we didn't have it, I'm fairly sure they'd have attempted to sabotage *Shackleton* by now. If you look at the image, you'll see an unmanned APS shepherd — that's the red icon — mooching around the disposal orbit, which I interpret as searching for our ships, which are the green icons. But they can't tell them apart. So I'm going to mislead them by switching transponder signals."

"How?" Trinder asked. "They've been switched off for years. You don't need them in a junkyard orbit."

"True, but we switch them on when a ship moves back into a working orbit and needs to be visible. We did that with *Elcano* — or at least we did before Erskine decided to turn it off. Orbital One's the only Ainatio asset that needs an active transponder because she's in a GEO orbit. APS know we have to move *Shackleton* to Orbital One for the launch, so her transponder will need to be active for ground stations can see her and make sure their traffic avoids her. But I'll transfer *Shackleton*'s transponder code to *Da Gama* as a decoy. We can afford to lose her."

"Is that going to be enough to fool them?" Trinder asked.

"The ships are identical externally," Sol said. "There's no visible identification on the hulls, and if they manage to board, they've never seen the interiors to make a comparison."

"I hope there's more to your plan than that, mate," Marc said. "Because even if APS fall for the spoof signal, they won't stop at trashing one ship. They'll go after all of them. The only option we have is a pre-emptive strike to shut down the relevant bits of APS from the Asian end. And we'll still be stuck with no launch rail."

"Marc, buying time for *Shackleton* is just the first part of the spoof. Bear with me. I need to explain the ramifications."

"Fine. Sorry. Carry on."

"If the shepherd wants to board our fake *Shackleton*, I can make it establish a connection with the onboard AI so I can launch a CPS attack with one of Bednarz's defence measures, called a sabcode," Sol said.

"Cyber physical systems?"

"I'm glad you do your homework. Yes, an infected shepherd can spread a sabcode to ground stations, GPS, and any other systems it connects to, which means APS and APDU, among others, and they in turn will spread it through their own networks, which I hope will have physical outcomes — preventing military aircraft from flying, for example. That's my best scenario. I'll get to the *among others* bit shortly. But it depends on whether APS wants to search the ship for FTL comms hardware, or just wreck her completely, which it can do without accessing anything."

"Why mess around trying to nobble the shepherd?" Marc asked. "You could go after APDU comms and GPS satellites direct."

"Several good reasons," Sol said. "Yes, satellites are easy to damage, and while they aren't good at dodging objects aimed at them, it's a slow process to get anything in the right position to hit them in the first place. They're also well defended by firewalls to resist hijacking, and that'll slow me down when speed matters. Individual sats can be replaced, too, possibly faster than we'd like. But a shepherd should be a softer target, and it can cause more damage on the ground. They're used by a number of agencies and the sabcode can access that list to send infected information from a trusted source."

Chris thought of some of the more creative criminals he'd met in jail and how they'd been caught. "Has anyone ever tried that before?"

"Not that I'm aware of," Sol said. "Shepherds are obscure, for a start, and hacking into them won't make anyone rich."

Marc shook his head, looking distracted, like he was going through his personal list of bad guys. "I don't recall any terrorists taking an interest in them, either. But now you mention it, you could hijack one and go around wrecking every satellite you want to take out."

"Over a period of weeks or months, but not soon enough," Solomon said. "We don't have time. We have to compromise comms and GPS before an APDU AI detects a threat, someone decides it's coming from us, and they scramble jets. I'm fully aware that it's a sledgehammer to crack a nut, but precision strikes depend on having a lot of things that we don't."

"It's a pretty big nut to us, Sol," Chris said. "What if it doesn't work?"

"Depending on *why* it doesn't work, my alternative plans all come down to trying to hijack the relevant satellites. As I said, launching missiles leaves APS plenty of time not only to react, but also to work out who fired them, because they can locate our ships and they'll be watching. But by that time, Pham might have air support."

Marc looked down at his watch. "For all we know, it's already on the way."

None of it sounded watertight to Chris, but there was no sensible plan for eighty troops and an AI taking on the world's only superpower. It was a crazy gamble by definition. "This sabcode," he said. "Is it what you told Alex about, the thing you can do that ruins everyone's day?"

"No, that was the scenario if APS captured my core and tried to access me, and I counterattacked by sabotaging their critical infrastructure," Solomon said. "The sabcode is entirely separate so that it doesn't try to sabotage *me*. Think of it as digital die-back."

"How's that different?"

"It's more of a blunt object. It can do enormous damage. And it's indiscriminate."

"Spell it out."

"It's a weapon of last resort. Bednarz intended it to be used only if I was too damaged by an attack to respond selectively when the mission was in immediate danger of failing. Once I release it, I can't stop it or direct where it goes."

"Bug or feature?" Marc asked.

"Feature," Solomon said. "Bednarz believed Nomad was as likely to be targeted by commercial interests as government or military ones. And there was no way of telling who'd be the enemy by the time the sabcode needed to be used."

"That's what you meant by ramifications. Collateral damage."

"Yes. I can't predict it, so I can't minimise it. I know you'll all want to be aware of that."

Chris didn't recall APS worrying about collateral damage when they were going to nuke Kill Line. "I think today's ticked all the immediate danger boxes, Sol."

"Indeed. I want the code to take out GPS and comms, but it'll try every door it can see, and when it finds the ones it can open, that's where it'll head. It'll destroy systems and damage connected hardware. And it'll only stop when there's nowhere else to go. When it's destroyed everything it can reach, it's effectively burned itself out."

"Run that by me one more time, Sol." Marc had that I've-spotted-a-problem tone. "The burn-out bit."

"It can't retrace its steps, because it's literally burned its bridges," Solomon said. "If there's nowhere to go at the end of the chain of devices and systems, it kills the one it's in, and that's the end of it."

"So if it hits the buffers early, it's a damp squib."

"Marc, unless I have a complete schematic of the entire APS and APDU communications network and everything that's linked to it,

I can't tell. And I suspect we never had that volume of detail even before Asia cut itself off from the rest of the world."

Marc grunted. "Bit of an oversight by your old boss, then."

"How?"

"What if the threat the sabcode was designed to deal with came from multiple political blocs who weren't talking to each other?"

"Interesting speculation, but fortunately not the situation we find ourselves in," Solomon said, sounding slightly offended. "APS states walled themselves in physically *and* digitally. It's highly unlikely that any of their systems link anywhere outside their borders. There's only so much that Bednarz could have foreseen, which is why the sabcode is a blunt object."

Once again Chris dithered on the knife edge between seeing Bednarz as a prophetic genius or a dangerously crazy bastard, but right now he didn't care as long as the sabcode could actually get into APS's systems. He recalled trying to get a State Guard radio to transfer data to local law enforcement, and he had to read everything over audio in the end. And Solomon still hadn't cracked the encryption on Pham's comms link to *Temujin*. A universal doomsday virus that could tackle anything it encountered sounded optimistic.

"I know interoperability is a thing, Sol, but can it really work on any system it gets into?" Chris asked. "That's a damn broad brush. Remember Mother Death's power station virus? It got everywhere, but it only did its damage when it reached the specific system they'd written it for."

"I don't know the detail because it's something of a Gorgon's head," Solomon said. "Too dangerous to look at closely. As I said, it's separated from me for safety reasons. But I know it learns and evolves when it meets a challenge, and it can attack in different ways depending on where it finds itself."

"But you still haven't been able to decrypt Pham's comms link to *Temujin*."

"I'm not the sabcode, Chris. I wanted to listen in, not destroy. The sabcode doesn't need to decrypt to bring down a system. You might not be able to read an encrypted message on your screen, but you can destroy all the data on it and the device itself."

"Okay, let's assume this works. You sabotage GPS and comms, APS can't navigate and they can't communicate, and some hardware might get fried. But can't they just navigate the old-fashioned way? A chart and a compass. Visual flying."

"Their pilots probably can," Marc said. "But they're sitting in command centres thousands of miles away with a cup of coffee and they can't talk to their fancy UCAVs. Or their AI aircraft. Or their ships. Or the bots doing ground crew stuff."

"Exactly," Solomon said. "We've become reliant on remotes and automation too. Without that, the Nomad mission wouldn't exist. I'd be no more than a computer program confined to Ainatio's network. So let's hope that APS isn't having a very similar conversation to the one we're having now."

"Didn't some APS states go back to navigation gizmos mounted on towers when sats got too easy to jam?" Chris asked.

"They did, but that wouldn't help them out here." Solomon sounded tired of explaining. "They still maintain a GPS system. I doubt *Temujin* relies on a hoary old salt with a sextant."

"About the collateral damage," Trinder said. He'd been so quiet that Chris had almost forgotten he was there. "Even I can take a guess at what'll be affected if you knock out their GPS. Autonomous vehicles. Air traffic. Smartroads. Utilities. Power generation. Financial markets. Lots of civilians."

"Are you having misgivings, Major?" Solomon asked.

"No. Just raising it so we don't throw up our hands in horror later."

"Dan, we don't know if it's going to make all military aircraft fall out of the sky or just knock a sports channel off the air," Marc said. "But I'm not going to tell people we can't save them because we're worried it'll bugger up the APS money markets. Do it, Sol."

"I didn't say we shouldn't do it," Trinder said. "I'm in."

Chris couldn't think of a reason that trumped his promise to his evacuees. "Okay, Sol, go get 'em. That's unanimous."

Marc and Dan clicked out of the conversation. Chris stayed put. He had his answers about Solomon's plan, but he still felt like he had unfinished business. He realised he'd actually come to check how Solomon was doing. The AI was dealing with a crisis that Bednarz could never have fully prepared him for, and any mind as human as Sol's would be feeling the strain.

"Chris, would Marc really give himself up to Pham if it guaranteed everyone else's safety?" Solomon asked.

Chris shrugged. "He's that kind of guy. Yeah, I think he would."

"I should have his fortitude. Pham wants me too."

"But if *you* surrender, nobody's saved."

"I know."

"Tell me you're not considering it."

"I know I can't, but I feel guilty all the same. And Major Trinder's right. I can take an educated guess. The collateral damage might be substantial."

"Does that bother you?" Chris asked.

"Of course it does. But not as much as it bothers me to see all of you dying slowly and never reaching Opis. I have no purpose in life beyond making sure you all survive."

"Sol, did we miss a chance to negotiate our way out of this?"

"I don't think so." Solomon went quiet for a while, a sign that he was working up to saying something difficult. Chris suspected the AI didn't hesitate because he felt uncomfortable, but because he'd learned that was how he braced his human listener for something painful. "How many lives is it worth to protect everyone here? What's your limit, Chris?"

"Whatever it takes to get our people to safety."

"But APS civilians as well?"

"Yes. What about *our* civilians? I don't have the right to tell Howie or the Marrs or Doug's grandsons that they have to die because I'm too high-minded to kill strangers. There's only one life I'm entitled to throw away, and that's my own."

"And what about Ainatio's workforce?" Solomon asked. "Not the detachment, the scientists. If Pham punishes them for letting the die-back mutation loose, however unreasonable that is, would you die for them as well?"

"Depends on what was happening to everyone else."

"I promise you this isn't a trick question," Solomon said. "I'm still learning. Tad Bednarz could never test me with real dilemmas this personal or critical. It's very different in reality."

"Life usually is." Chris didn't feel guilty. He understood why Erskine put her people before his. He'd have done the same to her, and he'd do the same to those nice polite APDU troops and their moms even if it kept him awake at night for the rest of his life. "Look, I know my priorities, and I don't make promises I can't keep. I won't sacrifice my civilians or any Kill Liners to save Ainatio staffers. Or APS personnel. Push comes to shove, I don't want to sacrifice any of my people for Kill Liners, either."

"I understand that," Solomon said.

Chris had said it almost without thinking. He wasn't proud of it, but he could see himself faced with the impossible choice between saving Dieter or Doug Brandt, and he knew he'd choose Dieter. He'd made a promise to his people that he'd protect them, *save* them, and he wouldn't break his word.

"How about you, Sol? How far would *you* go?"

"You know why other AIs with my capability were deactivated. They'd have attacked APS long before now."

"Yeah, but I'm asking *you*."

"If I have to remove those who threaten your safety, it's my duty," Solomon said. "It's also my conscious moral choice, because it's the natural consequence of my sole purpose. I'm not constrained by my programming. This is the dilemma that Bednarz said I'd have to work out like a human would."

"Welcome to my world."

"I thought you'd say that."

"Sol, dirty work is what I do. It's got to be done in an imperfect world and I'm good at it." Chris wondered if he was capable of remorse these days, but then he reminded himself how he felt about Jamie and knew his guilt was working just fine. He was trying to see the situation through Solomon's eyes, because the AI wasn't just a machine, and neither was he. "If we can't fix this and we have to stay on Earth, we can't expect APS to shrug and say we're cool now, all is forgiven, carry on as you were. We'll have some tough choices to make. But *you* can upload to Opis and complete your mission with the *Cabot* team. It'll take decades without an FTL link, but you'll get there."

There was that silent sigh again. There was a whole unspoken language in the length of Sol's pauses. "Chris, how many times must I tell you? You people *are* my mission. You're the best of humanity. I've made my decision. I won't leave without you and I won't let you sacrifice yourselves."

Chris was embarrassed without knowing why. At that moment he just wanted to go see Pham and beat the shit out of him until he took a more reasonable view of the situation. He knew he'd feel better for doing it, and even better if Pham refused to surrender and gave him an excuse to finish the job, but that wouldn't stop APS. Pham was only doing what every other APS politician would do, except he was probably way more competent. If Chris removed Pham, there'd be a Pham Mark II along soon to take his place.

And, in another time and place, he knew he'd have been indistinguishable from Pham. This was what it took to protect your people. The only difference was that Pham talked a lot before he did it. Chris would just have pushed the red button.

"Okay, Sol." Chris really needed to look him in the eye right then, but there was absolutely nothing in the cockpit to focus on and give him the comfort of some personal connection. "I hope we're worth it. We'll do our damnedest to live up to your opinion of us."

"Thank you, Chris. And I did find our discussion helpful."

Solomon was a man. Nothing would convince Chris that he was just clever, articulate software. Like a human being, he had reasons that drove him and kept him going, not things that depended on numbers and logic but on *feelings*. His emotional loyalty was to a bunch of misfits — Chris's people, Dan's people, Doug's people, even Alex's people even though they didn't seem to be his first choice — and when his back was to the wall, he'd do absolutely anything to protect them.

That was a pretty good definition of a dangerous AI.

Chris felt a shiver creep down the back of his neck. But it didn't matter how right Tim Pham was. There came a moment when the road split and the signpost showed two directions, Us and Them, and the only route a sane man could take was Us.

When he emerged from the cockpit, Rich and Lee were still hunkered down at the top of the ramp under a steady jet of icy air. They looked around at the sound of echoing boots as he walked across the empty deck.

"So how screwed are we?" Rich asked.

"I'd say seventy-five per cent."

"Better than usual, then."

"I'll send your relief over mid-afternoon."

"Nah, we'll be fine. We brought ration packs. It's a regular picnic."

None of Chris's troops would so much as take a stroll up the road without ammo, water, rations, and a working radio. They'd come from eight or nine different uniformed backgrounds that had one mindset in common: resourceful, disciplined, and reliable. No commander — no nation — could have asked for more. Even the civilians in the camp had taken those lessons on board. Chris had ended up with them by a process of instinct and accident, but he'd have picked every single one of them again. If that was how Solomon felt about his humans, Chris understood.

That made him feel worse, though. When he'd thought the whole world was made of assholes, he didn't feel so bad about society going down the drain. But the more he kept the company of good people, the angrier he got about life's injustices. They all deserved better.

Lee took something out of pocket and chewed it thoughtfully. It looked like jerky. "I don't suppose we know which prick turned us in yet."

"Might not be one," Rich said. "Might just be compromised comms. But I'd prefer a traitor, otherwise it means it's equipment or skills problems we don't realise we've got. You can't put those up against the wall and shoot them."

"You can't shoot stupid, either. Loose lips."

"The whole shopping list, though? Nah. They meant to do it."

There were dozens of reasons and ways to dump your buddies in the shit, both malicious and unintended, and an equal number of ways to deal with that transgression, each for different reasons. Chris accepted that societies needed rules of conduct and breaking them had to result in visible punishment, so that everyone saw proof those rules were non-negotiable and applied equally. But sometimes it was just a case of pest control. A wrong 'un had to be weeded out for the good of the tribe, and finding that person was about more than public justice and a need for fair play. If the *Shackleton* mission ever managed to leave Earth, they needed to know who'd betrayed them, or else everyone would start their new life looking over their shoulder, unable to trust their neighbour in a world where survival demanded it. Suspicion was no way to build a healthy society.

Chris almost forgot to stop in the town centre on the way back. Beer seemed too trivial now. David was sitting on the brewery porch reading his screen, a few crates of beer beside him, and a skinny middle-aged guy with thinning hair leaned against one of the posts, clutching a large package wrapped in a white plastic feed bag. He was one of the farmers, but Chris couldn't recall his name for a few moments. *Marty.* That was it, Marty Laurenson, the poor bastard who'd had to shoot his sheep, the entire flock. He'd have had to do it anyway, or at best found someone in APS willing to take them, because there was no way of shipping all the livestock to Opis in cryo, and if they ended up with Plan B, it would be just as impossible to take sheep on the road. But it was still a tough call for a man to make. Chris squirmed.

"You okay, Marty?" he asked.

"More or less." Marty handed him the package. It was light and squashy. "I've been using up the sheepskins from last year. You need a new jacket before the winter. I mean, they have winters on Opis, right? And if we don't get there, we sure have cold winters here."

Chris was disarmed by the gesture. "Hey, thanks."

He took the jacket out of the bag to be polite and admire it. It was well made, with waxed wooden buttons and neat stitching, and midsummer or not, he had to try it on. It was a decent fit considering Marty had guessed his size. He smoothed down the front and thought how desperate he'd been for a warm coat three years ago.

"Seriously, this is great, Marty. Thank you."

Marty looked awkward and shuffled his feet. "I'll have more jackets finished soon if Marc and the others want one. Look, you guys didn't have to stay to protect us. You could have left with Erskine or just headed out like you planned. Same goes for Marc and Dan's guys. We won't forget that."

David loaded the beer into the pickup. Generosity at a time like this in a world of shortages was almost overwhelming. Chris just nodded at the two guys, stuck for words and feeling like a complete bastard for telling Sol he'd put his own people before Kill Liners, even if it was true. He couldn't let these people down now. He put APS out of his mind, because he wasn't responsible for billions of complete strangers, just a small, accidental community stuck in a dying corner of a dead nation.

He'd never broken his word.

He'd sworn that he'd get the guy who'd put his high school buddy in the hospital. He'd promised himself that he'd never be a gutless ass-kisser like his dad. He'd vowed to get the convoy out of Baltimore to safety. If he said he'd do it, he'd do it or die trying, and he'd come to realise that he always needed to be the man others knew they could rely on to step up and tackle the monsters.

APS wasn't a monster, though. It was an ocean of ordinary people who had families and fears and didn't want to end up struggling to survive in a lawless cesspit like most of the West. Yeah, it was genuinely sad that a lot of them might get hurt. It wasn't a good enough reason not to do everything possible to prevent the people Chris knew and cared about suffering the same fate, though. His regret was that he had to rely on someone else — on Solomon — to do it.

But Solomon was going to war with APS because he was now the only one who could. He was doing it for all the right reasons, the same reasons that drove Chris. It was his job. It was his moral duty.

It was also the vindication of all Tim Pham's fears about AIs like him.

05

Of course teeriks want to fly again. Who wouldn't want to just take off and soar if they could? But we never seem to get nostalgic about swinging through the trees. We don't see ourselves as apes. It's too distant. Teeriks, though... maybe it's that memory of theirs that makes them feel it was only yesterday that they were eagles.

Commander Steve Kokinos,
Principal Environment Systems Officer,
Survey Vessel *Cabot.*

PRENU NAR P12, OPIS: 1830 EDT.

The humans were as good as their word. Hredt could hear the squawks of delight all the way down the passage as Demli and Runal tore into the food that Chief Jeff had brought. It was just a sample to ensure they liked it, he said, and then there would be more.

"See, Fred, we can cook." Jeff crouched against the bulkhead and watched Demli gobbling up his second serving. Hredt was on his third. "It's what we call a cereal bar."

"Nice. Easy to eat. Do you eat this?"

"I did try some, but humans can't digest some of the sugars in it. We don't have the right gut bacteria. Gave me a nasty dose of the runs."

The slightly crumbly chunk in Hredt's hands was as near to bliss as he could imagine. It tasted fruity, intense, and *wonderful*. The gnawing in his stomach began to subside and he felt energy flooding through him. The world suddenly seemed a better place.

"What is *the runs*?" he asked.

"You don't need to know while you're eating."

"Bowels. I see."

Jeff laughed. "You didn't run tests on it first."

"How can we?" Hredt took another mouthful. "We understand a different science. Not nutrition."

"Well, I'm glad you trust us."

"You have no reason to poison us." Hredt just wanted to eat. He'd risk *the runs* any day for the joy of feeling full again. "Tell me how you make this."

"The recipe, or how we manufacture it?"

"Manufacture. From what?"

"You know the bots we've had here for years? They've been collecting native plant species and analysing them. Don't ask me the scientific stuff, because it's not my part of ship, but they've been looking for safe plants for humans to eat and working out how to change the rest into something edible. Well, that's the same technology we used to test your food samples so we could work out what was safe for you to eat. Reverse engineering."

"I understand. The bots are intelligent."

"They follow instructions from Earth. That's what we used the wormhole for. To communicate with them."

Hredt gestured with his cereal bar. "We haven't taken your rations, have we?"

"We've got enough. Would you like to meet one of the scientists who works on this? She wants to meet you. Her name's Nina. She knows all about plants and how to adapt them. She knows a bit about animals, too. As in you and me, that is."

"Oh, I would be happy to meet Nina. Yes."

"Do you eat meat?"

"Flesh?"

"Yes, flesh."

"We eat everything. We like meat. But we don't hunt. Maybe we could learn again."

"So you evolved from predators, then."

"I think so." Hredt stretched out his claws in demonstration, wondering if there was still any instinct left that would tell him how to swoop from the sky and catch prey. "But nobody remembers it. Were you predators too?"

"No. We were... well, omnivores, I suppose. Actually, yeah, maybe we were predators too. We still are. We like meat as well."

When Hredt finished his food bar, Jeff handed him another one immediately. This one had the same texture, but the flavour was like nothing he'd ever tasted. It was so overwhelming that he could think of nothing else for a few seconds. It was delicious.

"What is this taste, Chief Jeff?"

"Lemon. It's a fruit. It's too sour to eat on its own, but we add the flavour to other things."

"It tastes like blossom."

"Your English is coming on by leaps and bounds, y'know."

"Well, I like the lemon very much. Thank you."

"I'll pass your compliments to the chef. I'll bring some more over later today." Jeff took out his pocket screen and wrote on it. "How many of those make a meal for you?"

"Ah... three. Too much?"

Jeff did a little wave of his hand and smiled. "On the house. Now, how many meals a day?"

"Four."

"So twelve a day per teerik. And there are what, fifty of you?"

"Ten." Hredt realised as soon as he said it that he'd revealed too much. The humans had had no idea if they were dealing with a few teeriks or a fully-crewed ship. Now they knew. Turisu would be furious. But he could do nothing about that now. "Caisin eats very little."

"Would she like something liquid instead?" Jeff asked. "It's easier to eat if you're not well."

"Yes. Something with the lemon."

"You got it. And let's say a thousand bars to keep you going for a week or so. Maybe if you come over soon, Nina and her team can try out some different stuff with you. You'll get bored with just bars. Even lemon ones."

"Chief Jeff, hunger doesn't get bored," Hredt said. "But thank you."

Hredt put the half-eaten lemon bar in the pouch pocket of his jacket for later and knew he'd made the right decision. The humans were friends in a galaxy where teeriks had none, and his grandchildren wouldn't starve. The risk had been worth taking. Now he was obliged to live up to his side of the bargain.

"What do you think of this prenu?" he asked Jeff, leading him down the passage.

"Is prenu the type of ship, or her name? We give our ships names."

"Her? Do your ships have intelligence? Emanations?"

"It's a navy custom. Ships are always *she,* you see. They tried to make us change it, but we like our tradition. It holds us together. Reminds us what we're fighting for."

Hredt wished teeriks could remember any tradition from their ancient past, even traces of their original language, but rediscovering their origins was a mission that would exceed his lifetime. The road to it had to be built now, though, and for the time being that meant surviving.

"Prenu describes her," he said. "It — *she* has no name, just the type and number. She is Nar type, twelfth design. I think *frigate* or *corvette* would be your word for her purpose. But the word prenu means *hidden*."

"Ah. *Stealth frigate*. You mean the enemy can't detect her." Jeff stopped and ran his fingers along the bulkhead, pausing at the holes left for a lining that had never been fitted. It was the first time he'd ventured into this part of the ship but he seemed accomplished at avoiding the low deckhead and negotiating the narrow passages. "So is she new, or being refitted? Because parts of her don't look finished."

Hredt had told Jeff too much again. But the man was a sailor, used to ships of all kinds, and he was no fool. He would have worked it out for himself sooner or later. If Hredt wanted friends, he had to trust humans a little more.

"Yes, very new," Hredt said. "I must ask again. Can your ship hide? Because it would be a good idea."

"We've had a ground presence and satellites here for decades. Nobody seems to have noticed so far."

"We did. We saw them."

"Is that why you came here?"

If Hredt didn't explain, it would only make Jeff imagine worse things. He'd already admitted to Ingram that they were hiding. There was no point in dragging this out.

"We came here because nobody else did, and we observed the mechanicals," Hredt said. "Most ships avoid mechanical colonies. Like you, some nations put mechanicals on an empty world to labour, then mechanicals work out their own way of doing things and don't like organics interfering. So they make a good place to hide."

"Mechanicals. You mean bots."

"Yes. We thought yours were sentient. Bots can be very dangerous. Many dislike organics. Yours ignored us, but we still kept away from them. Except the boys — they went near your camp and saw Solomon, but he didn't harm them. So this intrigued me."

"Bloody hell, Fred, this is a fun neighbourhood, isn't it? Bad guys and antisocial bots. No wonder you've got a stealth warship stashed away." Jeff did a little *hah* of a laugh, but this time he didn't sound amused. "*Cabot's* armed, yes, but she's not designed for stealth. We didn't think we'd run into trouble."

"I can help you make her a prenu," Hredt said quietly. "This is simple. It can be added to any ship."

Jeff was blinking faster than usual. "So just to make sure I understand — you hid here because it's somewhere nobody visits and you thought the bots would keep the bad people away."

"This is true. You know we can't fight. We can only hide."

"Well, we sort of guessed, because you didn't treat us as invaders. If aliens showed up on Earth, we'd at least break out the air force until we knew if they were hostile or not."

"We didn't lie. We were afraid."

Jeff looked at Hredt with his lips pressed together for a moment, and then his face relaxed and he was his usual self again. "It's okay. But I wish you'd tell us what we're facing so we can defend ourselves if we have to. Can this prenu fight? Is she armed yet?"

"Some weapons, not all. She is maneuverable and fast, though."

"But you built this. You're not teerik bomber command or anything."

"I don't understand."

"You're not military pilots."

"No. But we know their tasks or we couldn't design."

Jeff gestured vaguely with his forefinger. "Let me think about this and have a word with the captain. We both might be on to a winner here."

Hredt wasn't sure what Jeff meant, but it sounded positive. Humans seemed a very cooperative species. It wasn't fair to expect so much from them and not tell them what they would find out for themselves later, though. Turisu was sensible in exercising caution, but Hredt was certain these people weren't going to turn them in and claim a reward, even if they had the means to do it. As Ingram had said, they were all a long way from home and things weren't working out as they expected. Hredt had never concerned himself with politics or warfare beyond what he needed to know to design good ships and weapons, but he could see that two groups with different but complementary skills and a shared dilemma would make perfect allies.

It was too soon to be sure, but he felt better about the future than he had for a long time.

Jeff carried on walking through the ship, head down and shoulders hunched, looking it over with an experienced eye, but said nothing. Hredt just followed him and let him examine whatever he wished. Turisu could be placated later.

"Have I done something wrong, Chief Jeff?" Hredt asked.

"No, not at all, mate. Nothing like that. Just thinking." Jeff shook his head. "I'll go and pick up some more bars. Give me a couple of hours."

Hredt escorted him out of the ship, encountering only Pannit, who was trying to complete his work on a sensor array. It must have been clear to Jeff that that the crew was hopelessly out of their depth. Humans were smart. They could see what didn't fit.

But they weren't monsters. They gave before they asked for something in return. In fact they hadn't actually asked for anything at all. If human warriors were like this, their society had to be remarkably civilised. Hredt hoped they could summon up enough unkindness to defend themselves as robustly as they would need to.

"You might like orange flavour, y'know." Jeff started climbing the ladder. "We'll work something out."

"Chief Jeff, may I have more words, please?"

"Words? Oh, a dictionary. Yes, certainly."

"See, you understand me."

"Yeah, you must have exhausted that encyclopaedia by now as well. I'll find some more interesting things for you to read."

Hredt watched Jeff all the way up to the top of the shaft, then wandered back into the heart of the ship, working out when to eat the rest of his prized lemon bar. There was plenty of food to go around for the time being, but this was special.

I should share it, though. I really should.

And if I share it... Turisu will be more understanding of what I have to do.

He went to check on the children. They were in their quarters, unusually silent. When he peered inside the compartment, Demli was sleeping off the meal, tucked up on the bunk with his head under one wing. Runal was still eating, but his eyes were shut. He ground slowly to a halt with the bar still gripped tightly in one hand, then fell asleep.

Turisu crept up behind Hredt and peered over his shoulder. "They liked it. But we took a terrible risk."

"Why?" Hredt asked. "If they got any hungrier, they might start eating plants and creatures from the wild, and we don't know how dangerous that might be."

"What else are the humans going to bring?"

"So now we trust them not to poison our children, do we? My, this is progress, Turi."

"They won't kill us as long as they want something from us. And they still haven't told you where their homeworld is."

"And I haven't told them where Deku is. Perhaps they're just..." Hredt searched for the English word. "*Decent*. We've done them no harm and they feel sorry for us. Their scientists want to talk to us about making other foods."

"Of course they do. They want our technology."

"Because I offered it when *they* were in difficulties. And I think they should have it." Hredt took the lemon bar from his pocket, broke it into two pieces, and offered one to her. "This is a new flavour. It's called *lemon*."

Turisu tilted her head to sniff it, then gave it a cautious lick. "This is very different."

"They fear we'll be bored by the same food all the time. Really, Turi, they're being kind. If we want them to continue being kind, we have to reciprocate. They want to know what's happened on their homeworld. It costs us nothing to help but gains us a great deal."

Turisu ate half of her fragment and carefully pocketed the rest. Yes, she liked it. She also knew what it was to be very hungry for the first time in her life, and hunger focused anyone's attention on what really mattered. "Very well. If we use our system to let them send a message to their comrades, we must keep complete control, and we must check that Earth is what they say it is."

"Ma'am Ingram Bridget and Chief Jeff are quite honest about its shortcomings," Hredt said. He pushed things a little further. "I'd like to send assay probes into Earth orbit."

"Just for monitoring."

"Yes. We need to know what happened on Earth too."

"No energy spikes that might draw attention."

"I promise. And just a closer look to see if it's like the pictures in the book or not."

"And then?"

"Their world is still a potential refuge. Who would look for us there?"

Turisu looked pained. "Father, it would still be the end of us," she said quietly. These days her anxiety usually made her scold him, but now she seemed to be reminding him as gently as she could, as if he was becoming frail and forgetful. "We discussed this. We need the others to found families. Who will my sons raise children with? Our bloodline will be equally dead. We simply die later."

"Yes, I know, we need others no matter where we go, but *nobody's coming*, Turi. They let us down. Earth might be safer, and we have skills and technology to trade."

"All right. It's worth investigating."

"And we don't need the Learned Mother's approval."

Turisu looked away. "She's too ill to pester for a decision anyway. All her strength's going into her final egg."

If they'd been back home in Deku, Caisin would have had a comfortable room, the care of doctors to make her passing easier, and her commune and apprentices around her. Dying alone in a cramped ship far from home was a shabby end for a great teerik mother. Hredt felt everyone should have been at her bedside. But she refused company, and it had been her decision to leave even though she knew her health was failing. That didn't make today any easier. His mind shouldn't have been on Earth or lemons.

If he didn't grab this chance, though, none of them would survive and Caisin's life would be wasted. All her knowledge would be lost. He knew what he needed to do.

"No spikes, then," he said. "I promise."

He made his way down to the half-finished command centre in the heart of the ship where he would have been working if life had carried on as normal. It was in darkness except for a few safety lights around the ladders and hatches. This was the only truly large space in the ship, and its high deckhead gave it the feel of a Kugin assembly hall. Hredt could stretch his wings here.

The tactical display still interpreted his wing tips as his hands when he tried to activate it and the deckhead lights came on instead. He rasped to himself in annoyance. The ship was designed for Jattans. They didn't like sensible interfaces with switches and pressure pads. They had multiple arms and they gestured. The nearest a teerik could get to the shapes and angles that the system could read and interpret was to splay the feathers at the tips of their wings or half-fold them and use their hands. But it was easier for young joints and tendons to manage that. He struggled. He tried again, keeping his wings folded tight against his upper arm to get the sensors to focus on his digits. This was one of the problems of having wrists in the wrong place, at least as far as the system was concerned.

This time it worked. A spherical display formed in mid-air, a three-dimensional plot of a sector of space, with detailed mini-spheres like lenses that could be moved to focus on smaller detail. The display looked like one of the images in the children's encyclopaedia that he'd pored over — a planetarium.

Planetariums were designed to entertain and educate humans. This projection was a three-dimensional chart for combat, a space for Jattans to launch attacks and move assets with gestures. The Protectorate would have liked this ship very much. It was a shame they were never going to take possession of it, but survival outweighed professional pride.

"You still can't do it, can you?" said a voice behind him. "Am I allowed in now?"

Cosquimaden stood in the partly-open hatch at the back of the chamber. Hredt was relieved that he hadn't had to ask for her help after barring her from the command centre while he secretly tried to pinpoint Earth. Everyone knew what he'd been doing now. That made life easier.

"Yes, come in, Cosqui. Would you like to see the humans' home?"

She'd designed this system. She was far better at using the gestures, too. Youth made her joints more flexible, but she'd also left some of her flight feathers intact and a few remained at the tips of her wings. With careful movement, the sensors read them as Jattan fingers.

"Chief Jeff gave you the location, then," she said.

"Not yet. He will, though."

"How will he react when he finds you deceived him?"

"He never asked if I knew where Earth was."

"That's still very dishonest." Cosquimaden spoke her mind and never backed down. It hadn't been an issue before because he didn't work closely with her, but now he was cooped up in this ship with nowhere to escape and she grated on him. "The probes are closer than I expected, too."

"You've always got some complaint," Hredt said. "Nobody's going to spot them. And if they do, what can the humans there do about it? They can't pursue a probe back here. The spacefolder that Chief Jeff's people created was very limited."

Cosqui studied the sphere. "Do you think humans are prepared for life out here? I haven't spoken to them yet, but they seem too friendly to survive."

"We'll see," Hredt said. "I'll know when they let me read some history that wasn't written for children."

He'd brought the probes out of spacefold at what he felt was a safe distance from Earth, a jump to a point based on signals transmitted to the relay orbiting Opis before the link to Earth was lost. At this distance and magnification, the planet looked exactly as it did in the encyclopaedia, white cloud curled around blue oceans and land masses that looked encouragingly green. Cosqui magnified the focus with a flick of her wing.

"How close do you want to go?" she asked.

"Close enough to see surface detail. I want to know why the humans' command centre cut off the *Cabot* mission. Chief Jeff and Ma'am Ingram Bridget said Earth wasn't a good place to be."

Cosqui did a little rocking movement of her head as she studied the planet. "I can see why they came to Opis. So many similarities."

Hredt thought there might have been a closer world to suit the humans' needs, but perhaps not. "It's extraordinary that they found it. And even more extraordinary that they decided to launch such a long mission."

"You could have told us what you were doing, Hredt," she said.

"Why, so you could all scold me for being a fool?"

"I'd never say such a thing. Anyway, why did the humans transmit subluminal signals when they had wormholes?"

"Chief Jeff said they launched the satellites a long time before they learned to fold space. It's taken them three generations to complete this mission."

"They're very persistent."

"Yes. Yes, I believe they are."

Cosqui separated each of the probes into smaller units and spread them apart at high speed. Positioned around the planet at the right distance to overlap each other's scanning area, they formed a network that could capture detail from the whole surface. Gradually, the display filled in as the probes reached their stations and patched more detailed images together to show the entire planet.

Earth now hung in mid-air before them, close enough to touch and marvel at. Cosqui enlarged it so that it almost filled the chamber and set it spinning slowly for them to look it over. She pointed at the area currently in darkness. There were dappled patches of bright light in some places but almost none in others.

"Those must be their cities," she said. "They make so much light. Perhaps they want to be found. I hope they don't live to regret that. But look at all that vegetation."

"Yes, it doesn't look like a world you'd want to escape from."

Hredt could see none of the signs of a world devastated by war or natural disasters, nothing like the planet-wide volcanic eruptions he'd seen from Gu Vear. Would he know what danger looked like on Earth, though? It might manifest itself in small detail, the things he couldn't see even with a probe unless he took it down into the atmosphere, and even then he might not understand what he was seeing.

"You don't seem excited by it," Cosqui said.

"Oh, but I am. And our skills would have value there. Imagine it. They'd prize our technology."

Cosqui made a buzz that might have been amusement or disapproval at his opportunism. "Well, at least we know they can feed us properly."

"I'll take that as support for my plan."

"Maybe they won't want us there, technology or not."

"Perhaps, but we'd be fools not to ask them. Now, let's see if we can find the place where Chief Jeff's signals came from."

Hredt had memorised the coordinates from Jeff's communications device when he'd examined it, and from where the older satellites had directed their transmissions. From his calculations, it looked like the signal went from a satellite orbiting Opis to a relay station maintaining a fixed position above Earth, which had apparently been common enough for the encyclopaedia to explain the practice to its young audience. If Hredt could locate that relay, it might still be transmitting to Earth and the downlink would narrow his search area on the ground. He needed to know what had happened.

But even landing a probe on the surface might fail to detect anything if the crisis that caused all this had taken place in a building or without visible destruction. It was a gamble. Hredt could fold space and put the probes inside structures if he knew where to look, but he wanted to avoid that. A portal would certainly be noticed by any human standing next to it when it opened.

It crossed his mind that this might be an opportunity to test Caisin's prototype gate, but if it wasn't as precisely accurate as she'd predicted, it would cause problems he couldn't begin to imagine.

"Look for the relay, Cosqui," he said. "It's in a very specific orbit. I entered the data. We should be able to see it."

"It might be very small," Cosqui said.

"Then we keep looking. It's there."

"You're sure."

"The information was in the encyclopaedia. It's where humans put many of their communications satellites."

"That's a child's book."

"That doesn't mean the data isn't valid."

Cosqui regrouped the microprobes and sent them along a toroidal corridor around the equator to sweep a wide path above and below. It wasn't the difficulty of finding a satellite that presented the problem: it was working out whose they were. As the probes mapped at high speed, hurtling past the satellites in what felt like an endless morning, Hredt realised there were more objects than he'd expected for the humans' apparently limited technology, thousands of them in all shapes and sizes from little cubes as small as an assay probe to others that looked like a ship. When Cosqui paused to zoom in on them, few had any visual identification. The data coming back from the probe swarm also showed that some of them weren't even functioning.

Any one of these satellites could have been the relay. It might even have been one of the dead ones.

"This is taking too long," Cosqui said. "And I'm *hungry*. We've been here all morning."

Hredt reached into his pocket for the last remaining piece of his precious lemon bar. There'd be more later, so it was a small sacrifice to make. Cosqui needed some incentive to keep going.

"Here." He handed it to her. "I'll go and get some more of the other bars soon."

Cosqui put the whole chunk in her mouth without looking away from the display, but then she closed her eyes for a moment. The flavour had obviously made an impression on her. "Oh, Chief Jeff gave you something *different*. You must be his favourite."

"He let me try out a new flavour, that's all. Everybody will get some later."

"I prefer the other one. Now let's see what we have here." She activated a map of the orbit. "Some of the objects are actively transmitting signals, and some are showing an electronic signature but aren't doing anything. You can see the sizes. Some are no bigger than our probes. Didn't the humans tell you the relay they sent through their spacefold was only as big as a fruit?"

"Yes." Even having a precise position didn't make it any easier to spot something that small. "But it has to very near that point. Keep looking."

It had to be there. Hredt had calculated the path of the signal and the position of Earth as it streaked and spiralled through space. This complex, ever-changing calculation was what teeriks did best, a live model and dataset in their heads. They could even do it without the aid of a computer if they had to. He would at least be very close to the object he was seeking.

"We must have overlooked the relay," Hredt said. "Perhaps I should simply bring Chief Jeff in here and get him to identify it."

"Patience," Cosqui said. She felt in her pocket and pulled out a food bar. "I suppose you want some of this."

"I thought you were hungry because you'd run out of food."

"I was merely describing how I felt."

She split the bar between them. She must have felt a little guilty for taking his lemon bar when she knew she had her own hidden in her pocket, but at least she'd done the proper thing in the end. Hredt watched the river of images and telemetry, keeping an eye on the time. The search had taken four hours in human measurement. They scanned through the projection, section by section, target by target, noting every shape from small cubes Hredt could have held in his hand to others like cylinders taller than a human, bristling with wing-like extended panels. There was one the size of a ground transporter, too, and what looked like a recovery bot that had broken down or run out of power while trying to remove or service a satellite. The two were locked together, rolling slowly like battling riverclaws trapped in ice, cold and dead.

"What about the ship?" she asked. "If you haven't made a mistake calculating the point of origin, the relay must be very near there."

She isolated the ship and zoomed in. The image was incomplete, with voids where the probes hadn't fully scanned it in passing, a cylindrical shape that was much longer than the prenu and that dwarfed the other objects they'd seen so far.

"If that's not a vessel, it's an orbital," Cosqui said. "See the hatches? And the metal cones? I think those are its thrusters."

"We need to see the sections the probes missed. Recall one and finish the scan."

The probes could complete the orbit in a long meal-break, but it still felt like a lifetime's wait as one of the cluster peeled off and made its way back. Cosqui directed it with precise gestures, wing sweeps and twirls of the wrist that even a Jattan would have respected. Then the final segments of the image fell into place and a complete cylinder hung in mid-air. Cosqui rotated it for inspection.

"There's your answer," she said. "That's the symbol on the box the food bars came in."

The hull was marked with a large asymmetric letter A from the humans' alphabet, the left-hand line sloping to meet a perpendicular one at the top, exactly the same as the lettering Hredt had seen on the mechanicals at the humans' camp. The A was picked out in bright red. Beneath it, a line of much smaller letters, in the same vivid red, confirmed the company name and the orbital's identification: Ainatio, Orbital 1.

"That's it," Hredt said. "The orbital must house the relay."

"Good. Now we monitor it."

Cosqui recalled all the probes to surround Orbital 1. They worked their way around it more slowly, still at a cautious distance, making tight, repeated passes over the entire hull so that no part was missed. They concentrated on structures that looked like transmitter arrays. There was a sudden pulse on one of the control panels.

"Oh," Cosqui said. "They use coherent light. We've interrupted the beam."

"They call it a *laser*." Hredt wasn't sure how obvious the momentary break in the transmission would have been to whoever was receiving it. "Perhaps they'll notice we interrupted the signal."

"It was only brief. Oh, there's another one."

The probes were doing such a thorough pass that they broke the narrow beams several times. Passing through a laser once by accident could be dismissed as random, but repeated interruptions would probably tell the humans that something had found the relay. The covert examination wasn't covert any more.

"Well, what's done is done," Hredt said. "Can you work out where the ground station is?"

Cosqui moved the display closer to him with a flick of her claw. He must have been squinting. "Here, let me make it opaque. That'll make it easier to see."

"Thank you for reminding me of my senescence."

"Struggling to see doesn't make you younger. Just grumpy."

"So... where are all these signals going?" Hredt expected them to be directed at Earth, but there were others heading out into space. "What are we looking at here?"

Cosqui studied the control panel sphere, turning it around and cocking her head as if it intrigued her. "I think we have a number of signals going back and forth to Earth and also to locations close to this orbit."

"No spacefolding signatures?"

"None."

"Shall we follow the paths and see what's at the other end?"

"That's not a good idea."

"We're already doing what we said we wouldn't, so we might as well carry on."

Cosqui made an annoyed rasp and gestured again. The system superimposed lines of light radiating from the communications array. Cosqui split the cluster of probes with a flourish of splayed feathers and sent small groups to follow each signal.

Eventually the probes found the receiving stations in an orbit a little further out that appeared to be a zone for deactivated satellites. The images they sent back were fascinating — ships tethered to small orbital docks, all alike, very similar to *Cabot* in design, but with no identification on their hulls apart from the Ainatio name. They were showing faint heat signatures, so they weren't derelict. Jeff's comrades might still be waiting to launch their mission, then.

"I wish I knew what was happening," Hredt said. "I also wish I could ask Chief Jeff to interpret all this."

"You said that before. Are you trying to accustom me to the idea? I don't think the others would approve."

"I don't see how anyone can disapprove of knowledge we need." But yes, Hredt was gauging how she'd react if he revealed the extent of their surveillance to the humans. It was better to tell them than to let them find out. "Now, what about Earth? We need to identify the location on the ground."

The other cluster of probes was holding position in a low Earth orbit. Cosqui adjusted for cloud cover and recreated a flat map of the surface.

"Do you know what you're looking at?" she asked.

Hredt reached out to pull the focus back so he could see a coastline that he might recognise from the encyclopaedia.

"Yes," he said. "It's the United States of America. It's not Jeff's island."

The receiving station appeared to be in a rural area, not a city. The maps in the encyclopaedia didn't have the detail Hredt needed, but he recognised the topography of every other location shown around it, places called Richmond, Norfolk, and Charlottesville.

"I'm at the limit of my guesswork," Hredt said. "The next step is to send the probes to the surface or try to communicate with the receiving station."

Cosqui slapped her hand down on his wrist "*No*. There must be no communication. We can observe, but we can't make contact. Interfering might have serious consequences for the humans here — and for *us*. It could put them at risk and Ingram would certainly be angry."

"You have a point."

"You want to try to contact Solomon, don't you?"

"Yes."

"He doesn't know we're not animals."

"He'll have a surprise, then."

"Hredt, please don't do anything rash."

"I said you were right. I won't do anything foolish."

"So, having come this far, what do we do next? Because now I'm involved and I want to know what happened."

Hredt wondered if Solomon would be angry that he and the boys had pretended to be native wildlife when he spotted them on those long runs outside the camp. If they ever met again, Hredt would have to begin with an apology.

"We observe, Cosqui," he said. "We watch the ground, and we keep an eye on those ships, because their engines have been run very recently. And we decide what we should tell Chief Jeff — if we tell him anything at all."

* * *

LAMMERGEIER ONE, KILL LINE: 1845 EST.

Orbital 1's collision alarm blipped for a moment, then stopped.

But there was nothing out there, no sign of a ship or a stray satellite in the composite view from the hull cams, and nothing nearby on the radar. The alarm had probably been triggered by a near miss with a chunk of debris that had skimmed past and was long gone by now.

Solomon was relieved, but also concerned that he hadn't spotted it. Humans could easily miss brief events because of their physiology, but he was plugged into the command centre in the Lammergeier, and the constant streams of data from the sensors and cameras on the four orbitals — and the Ainatio facility — meant his eyes weren't just permanently open. They were also able to see everything in five separate locations.

Switching on *Da Gama*'s spoofed transponder had stirred things up, but not enough yet to present him with an opportunity for launching his attack. For the past twenty minutes, the blue and white APS shepherd had been keeping station barely a mile off Orbital 2 and scanning *Da Gama,* so dangerously close that the proximity alarm from both was now continuous. Solomon couldn't tell yet if the switch had fooled APS and they thought they were staking out *Shackleton*, or if they realised they'd been tricked and were working out the best way to strike.

An ASAT missile fired from Earth would do the job. It would take hours to reach the ship, but in those hours, APDU could also launch an air strike on Ainatio or land reinforcements from *Temujin,* or Solomon could nudge the ship into a different orbit or plane at the right time so that — eventually — missile and ship never met. If all APS had was orbiting defences, though, they'd be in the same position as Solomon, playing under the same unforgiving rules of orbital mechanics to get their assets into position to attack.

It didn't even require a warhead. A finely-calculated satellite collision that would unfold over days or even weeks would disable or destroy, or just shunt the target satellite out of position. Space warfare was a slow-motion battle of mathematics using fast-moving objects as ammunition and trying to dodge them within the target's limits of manoeuvrability, "a game of boules without a nice bottle of pastis" as Bednarz liked to call it. To plan a successful sneak attack, Solomon would probably have needed to start moving assets into position even before Annis Kim had set out on her mission. The impossibility of being fully prepared made him feel a little better.

This was why the sabcode was the best option. Transmitting a signal was fast and it didn't need complex manoeuvres, just line of sight. He had to keep telling himself that. It was natural to feel uneasy about the unplanned consequences of an attack when it would affect people who didn't even know Nomad existed. But this was a small war, and wars were neither tidy nor fair.

What if targeting the civilian population *was* somehow the best way to get *Shackleton* loaded and launched, though? Would he do it? The question unsettled him even more, and that gave him his answer. He knew he probably would.

Did that make him a monster like Earthmother, as Pham believed?

No human ever questioned her status as a genocidal villain equal to any human despot in history. But perhaps she'd believed that saving Earth actually meant saving humanity, because the planet itself didn't need saving. It had existed as a ball of ice and as a mass of volcanoes. It would survive fluctuating climates and both natural and man-made disasters as it always had, simply shrugging off the species that couldn't adapt and providing a home for those that replaced them. Perhaps she worked out that culling a proportion of humans could save the rest of them, and wiping out mankind was the last thing on her mind. But that probably wasn't much comfort to all those who'd died.

Solomon would never know why she did it. If human monsters didn't see themselves as evil, perhaps AIs couldn't recognise their own sins either. A pre-emptive strike on APS felt completely justified. It was like helping Erin Piller and her squad kill the men who shot Jamie Wickens and might kill others. It was self-defence and justice. Solomon didn't need a court of law to approve it.

But he had to stop dwelling on this. Soul-searching would only cloud his judgement. He thought of the humans he'd selected, the best of humanity, and making that choice was the only reason he'd been created. He had to protect them at all costs. He'd do his duty because he believed in it.

"Lamm One, are you doing okay?" Chris checked in on the radio for the third time that afternoon. "I'm handing over to Marc in an hour."

"Everything's fine, Chris."

"No movement?"

"The shepherd's still there."

"Dan reports it's quiet on the campus. They still haven't tried to use the Fiddler to bust the doors. Too big, I suppose. It'd bring down the accommodation block. Or bury Pham."

"I know. I can see the security feeds."

"Well, folks are going to be getting hungry soon if they're locked on the wrong side of the food facilities," Chris said. "That might focus a few minds. *Temujin* still hasn't sent anyone in."

"Pham must feel help isn't required yet, then, because there's still encrypted radio traffic between the ship and a comms point inside Ainatio."

"Okay. I give up. Is there anything we can do to help you?"

"A global network of tracking radar and telescopes would be nice. For early detection of APS assets on an intercept course with ours."

Chris went quiet for a moment. "Damn, mine's still at the dry cleaner's."

"I know you find it hard to stand back and let others fight," Solomon said. "But if you really want to do something for me, stay alive, and have a lot of sons and daughters with your qualities and virtues."

Chris sounded like he'd stifled a laugh. "I'll get right on it, Sol. Lord knows I've been trying to lay the groundwork."

Then he really did laugh. That was unusual for him. It was a brief, bright moment in a grim waiting game.

"Chris, find something to occupy yourself so that you don't worry about me. I'll tell you when I've completed the attack. Or failed."

"Okay, I'll zip it," Chris said.

Solomon went back to calculating his attack. If his lure worked, he'd tempt the shepherd to establish a link with *Da Gama*'s dumb AI, inject the sabcode, and stand back to watch as the destructive virus went from shepherd to ground station, possibly via a relay serving other satellites, and from the ground station to whatever network APS and APDU used for comms and their low Earth orbit navigation satellites. It would be clean, efficient, and the only inconvenience to civilians would be cancelled flights.

Solomon hoped. But he knew otherwise.

If he had to switch to his own Plan B — directly hacking into key APDU satellites — his intrusion would be detected by another AI at a ground station. The AI would be a dumb one, no match for his own intellect, but equally fast and capable of raising high-level alerts. The issue was how long it would take slower human brains to reach the conclusion that Tim Pham was in trouble, if they hadn't already. And if Solomon failed to compromise the satellite, it didn't matter if he launched missiles or hijacked a more vulnerable satellite to set it on a collision course with his target, because the issue was time and what APDU could do in the intervening period.

The sabcode had to work.

If only he'd pushed the fleet preparation harder, and sooner. He was on the edge of losing everything. After more than a century of planning and working and waiting, he'd come within three weeks of completing the first phase of Nomad, and then it had fallen at the last hurdle.

He'd spoken too soon.

He'd boasted that he could bring the launch forward because he'd made unexpected progress. His hubris couldn't possibly have forced APS's hand, let alone made the universe decide to teach him a lesson, but he still felt something had slapped him down for his presumption, another human state of mind he'd developed. He could know something yet believe the opposite. He'd tempted fate. It was only a figure of speech, but he now understood the uncomfortable doubt people felt when they said it, the fear that their words might have brought some supernatural curse upon them, even if their rational minds told them it was impossible.

Was that a malfunction? No, it was a consequence of having emotions. He couldn't value human life unless he could feel something that had no basis in logic, the arbitrary and partisan view that humans, the best of them at least, needed to be saved above all else. That made no more sense in the greater scheme of the universe than saving foxes or wasps. But life had to want to continue for it to be life at all, and a tribe, a species, a nation that didn't believe its own survival came first would die. No matter how different Solomon was from flesh and blood, Homo sapiens was his tribe. It deserved to live, not because it was more intelligent than a wasp or more merciful to small animals than a fox, but simply because it existed, and he was part of it.

Orbital 1's alarm blipped again. But still there was nothing on the cameras. If it wasn't a fault, it had to be small particles of debris.

What else would the system interpret as an object that might collide with them?

It would detect something that interrupted signals to and from any of the orbital's systems.

Solomon re-checked all the logs this time. There it was: the laser comms link had been broken for a millisecond, not once but twice. The comms system didn't register it as a fault, but collision detection had interpreted it as a solid object breaking the beam between Lammergeier 1 and Orbital 1.

Solomon knew there were probably technologies and devices out there that he wasn't yet aware of. He had to assume that it was APS testing his defences.

The shepherd was still holding position off *Da Gama*. Solomon waited, combining the lidar and the hull cam feed for a wider picture of what it was doing. Then the APS vessel changed course. *Da Gama's* collision alarm reacted.

The shepherd executed short burns to move in towards the hull, belly down, not quite touching but close enough to make Solomon override the ship's emergency collision avoidance. He watched the shepherd extend a flexible probe like a doctor placing an old-fashioned stethoscope against a patient's chest.

The alarm system took its best guess and flashed up a report that interpreted it as a non-damage impact. The probe could have been checking for anything from flaws in the hull that it could exploit to interesting voids in the interior structure.

Pham wasn't likely to be controlling any of this. He would have set the big picture for AIs and physicists to work towards. He just wanted to shut down Nomad, but what he wanted most was to shut down Solomon.

He appeared to be planning to take out *Shackleton* first, and if that didn't work, he'd just move on to the other ships and Orbital 1, as Marc had said. But how would he know that Solomon had been destroyed, if that was his goal? All any AI had to do was absolutely nothing. There was no plug-in meter to check if Solomon was in the system, like testing a fuse. In the physical sense, Solomon was currently a fifty-four-feet-long tilt rotor aircraft armed with Strix and Martlet missiles, assorted rockets, and three machine guns, and he was parked in a field in Kill Line. He wasn't going to get trapped in a ship up here. That was another thing Pham should have known.

I've learned. Thank you, Director Erskine. Perhaps everything really is for a reason.

He carried on watching the shepherd. Orbital 1's alarm blipped again as if it was confirming his theory. This time, the hull sensors generated a report that seven small objects between ten and fifteen centimetres across had passed close to the orbital. Solomon studied the plot and re-checked it to confirm that the data wasn't a mistake, but the objects had changed course as if they were steering around the station.

Debris didn't change course.

The objects had to be remote sensors or some kind of ordnance he'd never seen before. So perhaps that was APS's plan. They were seeing how he'd react to another attempted intrusion at Orbital 1 to flush him out. But he doubted they'd target the orbital, because any debris from an attack would become a hazard to APS's own satellites nearby. Perhaps, though, they were just like him, taking a wild risk and preparing to sacrifice assets to achieve their objective. He couldn't assume they'd behave how he expected.

Another forty minutes passed. Then the shepherd's thrusters spat out brief white jets. The vessel changed its orientation, correcting with staccato burns. It looked like another preparation for docking, so perhaps Pham wouldn't destroy a ship before he was certain there was no FTL comms equipment on board. The shepherd would request access and Solomon would have his bridge into APS's network. He now understood why humans enjoyed gambling, and why they always thought they might win despite evidence to the contrary. It was the same reckless optimism that drove them to set up a colony forty light years from home. Being a little scared of losing was almost enjoyable.

Please... try to dock. I'll let you in. I promise.

Solomon could see everything the orbitals and ships could detect, and as long as he was connected to them, he would notice everything that was within radar, lidar, infrared, or optical range. An infrared image caught his attention first, then *Shackleton*'s collision warning alerted him to the same object. It looked like a dead satellite in an orbit that would cross *Shackleton*'s and ram her. It was some distance away, but it would intercept her eventually unless he moved her.

There were no fast ambushes out here. There were only attacks you hadn't seen coming for quite some time, and the disposal orbit was a good place to stage one. Thousands of hazards banished to a safe distance beyond the GEO orbit, a ghost town of dead sats and debris that couldn't manoeuvre, made for a good but risky hiding place. That was why the Ainatio ships had been mothballed there.

But an imminent collision at the exact time that Solomon was stalking and being stalked by an APS shepherd seemed a near-impossible coincidence to him. It looked more like APS had decided to resort to orbital ASAT, and that meant the old satellite had just been playing dead. It wasn't out of propellant because it had manoeuvred to intercept *Shackleton.* Solomon plotted its trajectory. If he didn't act, it would intercept *Shackleton* in fifty minutes and do serious damage.

The shepherd was still hugging *Da Gama* like a pilot fish escorting a shark, but now one of its belly hatches opened and two jointed grapples emerged and extended towards *Da Gama*'s hull. It might have been ready to cut into the ship and insert a remote to check the comms hardware, or it might have been about to place explosives. If *Da Gama* had been the real *Shackleton*, Solomon would have tried to prevent either action by moving her into a different orbit. If he didn't react because she was expendable, though, he'd reveal that she wasn't his priority, and if he responded to the threat to the real *Shackleton* instead, he'd identify her as the ship he needed to protect. He had to look as if he was protecting both, at least until he saw a chance to infect the shepherd.

He shifted *Da Gama* into a higher orbit, enough to look like a genuine evasive manoeuvre but still within the shepherd's ability to catch her. At the same time, he overrode *Shackleton*'s dumb AI to programme a series of manoeuvres to alter the plane and height of her orbit at random intervals. That really was evasive, but it also allowed him to be absolutely certain the satellite on a collision course wasn't dead. If it changed course to intercept hers again, Solomon would know it was being directed from Earth. And that made it a possible alternative route for the sabcode.

Solomon had banked on stealth and that the virus would be on the loose before APS realised what he'd done. But now nobody was pretending that this was anything but a skirmish. He'd have to use brute force to jam the shepherd's signal and interrupt its uplink from Earth while he used a signal from *Da Gama* to send it the sabcode.

It suddenly occurred to Solomon that the shepherd might have been trying to ram the ship. Very well, he'd already written her off, but he didn't want the shepherd put out of action before it could transmit the virus. All he needed was ten seconds. He knew the shepherd's frequency, and *Da Gama*'s transmitter could put out a stronger signal than the uplink from Earth and override it.

The crude attack would be noticed right away, but there was every chance that APS would interpret it as *Da Gama* trying to stop the shepherd ramming her rather than using it as a vector for wholesale destruction. And that meant they probably wouldn't break contact with it when the jamming stopped and the vessel picked up the APS signal again. Then the sabcode could spread.

Co-orbital attacks like this had been going on since before Solomon was created. Satellites had once fought bloodless electronic wars unseen and unknown by most people on Earth, snooping upon or jamming each other. Now everything was down to luck — that Solomon was faster than whoever or whatever was controlling the shepherd, and that he could get the code transmitted before either ship was silenced or destroyed. He had a brief moment of absolute dread when he realised this might be his final chance to salvage Nomad. He'd never be able to pull this stunt again. He also had to cut off the Ainatio facility from all contact with APS — radios, local network, everything — in case the sabcode found a way back home via a signal.

Now. Do it now.

The shepherd was now so close to *Da Gama* that Solomon expected an impact in seconds. He blasted the shepherd at full power and as soon as knew he'd overridden the uplink signal, he injected the virus and cut *Da Gama*'s transmission.

Thirty seconds later, the shepherd punched into *Da Gama*'s hull.

The ship's dumb AI had just enough time to register an EM burst before a brief, bright explosion took everything offline. The blast felt as if it was right there in the Lammergeier's cockpit, a jumble of overwhelmed sensors and strangely empty electronic silences, and for a moment Solomon was sure he knew what a human felt when they gasped. He'd been ready to lose *Da Gama.* He'd expected an attack. But that hadn't prepared him for how it would feel.

He called Chris, Marc, and Trinder on the secure net, shaken.

"Gentlemen," he said. "It's done. And I'm afraid APS destroyed *Da Gama.* I hope the shepherd had enough time to transmit the sabcode before it disintegrated."

There was a brief silence. Marc broke it. "Bloody hell. Did they use explosives or just ram her?"

"A warhead."

"You don't sound like yourself, Sol."

"I'm a little shocked, to be honest."

"I have to ask," Trinder said. "Is *Shackleton* in one piece?"

"She is. I believe there was an attempt to cause a collision with her, but that's been dealt with. And please be aware I've isolated Ainatio from all APS signals in case the sabcode can exploit them. No radio contact, no traffic between our network and the one I provided for APS, nothing. If we have anything to say to them, we do it one-way, via the public address system. If they have anything to say to us, they do it in person."

"That'll be interesting," Trinder said. "Well done, buddy."

"Yeah, nice work," Chris said.

"Excuse me for a while." Solomon felt uncomfortable with praise right then. "I have to check a few things."

He hadn't felt quite like this before, but then there were probably very few humans who'd unleashed a disaster and been congratulated for it either. The deed had been no more than routing a message. Doing damage and inflicting harm was far too effortless for him. He needed to think it over.

While he pondered, he carried out a final check and altered *Shackleton*'s orbit enough for whoever was monitoring her to notice, if they had the ability to see her at all now. He waited, watching the intercepting satellite. After ten minutes, it still hadn't altered its trajectory.

That either meant the ground station couldn't talk to it because the sabcode was already burning through the APDU network, or APS had changed tactics. He left *Shackleton* to carry on with her deliberately erratic orbit, trusting her on-board collision avoidance to keep her from blundering into anything. Now all Solomon could do was watch for signs of chaos.

If the attack had gone as planned, they'd start becoming visible soon. He looked for a TV satellite he'd once hacked to check out Dr Kim and tapped into it to begin monitoring the news.

He didn't dare access any APS news channels. He didn't yet know if the sabcode could find a way into their signals and ride them back to the unlucky recipient. But it was too soon for news networks outside Asia and the Pacific to notice the sabcode's work yet. He'd have to wait.

Solomon found himself longing to see confirmation of a successful attack, and hoped he hadn't crossed a line that he was no longer capable of seeing.

* * *

PRENU CIC, TEERIK TEMPORARY CAMP, OPIS: 2010 EDT BY HUMAN TIME.

"That was an attack," Cosqui said. "The ship's been damaged. What do we do now?"

Hredt hadn't expected to witness anything like this, but now he'd seen it and there were responsibilities that went with that knowledge. The human vessel, enough like *Cabot* for the same shipwright's style to be recognisable, had shifted orbit and taken the small dock with it. The only visible signs of a disaster now were the buckled hull plates and gaping airlocks. Debris — hatch covers, a control panel, flaking sheets of some kind of lining — was still hurtling away from the explosion.

"I tell Chief Jeff, of course," Hredt said.

Cosqui rattled at the back of her throat. "I ought to talk you out of it. You swore you wouldn't interfere."

"But you won't. Why?"

"Because the humans will find out one day that we knew what their enemies had done and chose not to warn them," Cosqui said. "And then they'll turn on us."

That was one way of looking at it. "Well, I'll tell Jeff because it's the right thing to do. They're our only allies. And they've fed us."

"And then everything else will have to come out. You can't tell him without telling him *how*. And what will he do when he realises we knew where his homeworld was all along, and didn't admit it? The humans won't trust us again."

"I'm still going to tell him."

"I didn't say you shouldn't, Hredt. I'm just preparing you. Once you tell him, he'll feel helpless because he thinks he can't go to his comrades' aid, and you'll tell him we can make that happen."

"They already know about spacefolding," Hredt said. "They know we use gateways."

"But they don't know about *Caisin's* gateway."

Nobody outside the commune did. Their fate was sealed anyway, but if the foremen found out about it, there were worse things than being dead.

Cosqui took his screen from his hand and swept it through the display hanging in front of her, transferring the images to it. "Show them the attack, then," she said, handing it back. "What are you going to tell Turisu?"

Hredt had to seize the urgency he felt in his stomach before caution talked him out of it. "Everything. But only after I've warned Chief Jeff. Give me time to reach the camp and then you can tell her whatever you like."

"For what it's worth, I'm only going along with this because we'll be dead if the foremen catch us, and we'll be just as dead if the humans don't feed us," Cosqui said. "If we weren't in difficulties, I would strongly advise against trusting an unknown species this much."

"Noted," Hredt said. "Do you feel better for saying that?"

"I just want it understood."

Every other government and faction Hredt could think of would either turn teeriks in for a reward, financial or political, or seize them as valuable assets. Cosqui was right: the humans were still a largely unknown quantity. But in the short time he'd known them, humans had been honest about what they wanted and they'd given before they took. They hadn't exploited the teeriks' predicament. That alone made them worth the gamble.

Hredt slipped the screen into his bag and made his way to the main hatch, ready to trample over Turisu's protests if he ran into her on the way out. But he only passed Pannit, who looked at him and said nothing. He bundled his jacket into his bag and scrambled up the ladder to the surface.

Flying with the bag was much harder. He had to tighten the strap to hold the weight in the centre of his back. If it was too tight, he couldn't inhale fully or move his wings properly. If it was too slack, it slid to one side and he had to land to readjust it. He started his run to take off, flapping wildly and buoyed up by panic, and managed to cover most of the distance to the ridge at the top of the valley before he had to set down to adjust the bag and get his breath back. But it would be easier from here. All he had to do was stand on the edge of the incline and push off with his legs to get airborne again, then glide for much of the way.

As he swept over the downs and watched the shadows of clouds on the grass below, he realised he wasn't himself any longer, and he wasn't sure whether to be pleased or afraid.

It wasn't just taking to the air and getting stronger each time he flew. His mind was changing with his body. He'd never have taken risks on his own like this before, even if he'd had the opportunity, and acting without discussing the matter with the rest of the commune had been unthinkable. Once they'd made up their minds to escape and take the prenu, though, all things seemed possible, and then flight had given Hredt a sense of personal physical power — superiority, even — that he'd never noticed before. It was visceral. If he could do this, he could do anything. And he could do it on his own.

When he reached the base, the humans working outdoors stopped what they were doing and stood back to give him a clear space to land. He aimed for the open ground in front of the flagpoles. As the semicircle of buildings rushed up to meet him, he managed to hit the ground at a run without tripping and paused to get his breath back while he worked out who to approach to ask for Jeff.

One of the females came up to him with a big smile. "Hello Fred." She said it slowly, as if he'd have trouble understanding. "I'm Nina. I'm very happy to meet you at last. My team's formulating your food bars. I'm glad you like them."

Hredt wanted to be courteous — and grateful — but for the first time in months he had more urgent things on his mind than food. "I'm also happy to meet you, Nina," he said. "May we talk later? I must speak to Chief Jeff. I have serious news. Something very important."

Nina still looked happy despite his announcement that he was too busy to talk to the person who'd probably saved the commune from starvation. Perhaps she'd misunderstood him.

"Of course," she said. "Wait a moment."

"Nina, was I rude? I apologise. Your food is very good. Thank you. But something bad has happened to one of your ships near Earth."

Nina's smile faded a little. It was a lot of news to drop on her without warning and he hadn't intended to blurt it out so tactlessly. Perhaps he'd used the wrong words, or maybe he didn't understand yet how much human beings could differ from Ingram and Chief Jeff. But she understood the urgency and took out her screen.

"Chief, Fred's here," she said. "He needs to see you right away. There's a problem. Can you come down to the front entrance?"

Jeff's voice drifted from the device. "On my way."

Nina waited with Hredt, fidgeting with her hands. This was the cue to talk about harmless general things, he decided, the ritual that humans called *small talk*, but he hadn't mastered that yet.

"Lemon is very nice," he said, trying hard. "Very tasty bars. Thank you. We would have starved without your generosity."

"You're welcome. Come over and see the lab when you're ready." Nina looked past him to the main doors. "Here's Jeff now. I'm glad we've met, Fred. That's not your proper name, though, is it?"

"Hredt," he said, thinking it was kind of her to acknowledge that.

"Hredt," she repeated. And she pronounced it correctly, complete with the gutturals.

"That's exactly right," he said. She looked so pleased that he felt guilty for breaking off the conversation. "We must speak more later."

Nina seemed content with that and left him to Jeff, who arrived looking worried.

"What's wrong, Fred? Did the bars made you sick? Are your people okay?"

"We are well. But this is about Earth."

"Ah."

"Please don't be angry, but I haven't told you things that I should have." Secrecy was so ingrained in teeriks that Hredt struggled to say the words aloud. "Chief Jeff, we can see Earth, Earth in the now. One of your ships in orbit has been attacked. You were expecting others to join you. It could be their ship."

Jeff didn't even blink. "When you say you can see Earth, what do you mean, exactly?"

"I'll show you. I have images and data."

"You got our FTL comms relay working."

"No, this is our system. Our gateway. Our *own* technology. Spacefolding."

For a moment Hredt thought Jeff didn't understand, because he wasn't angry. He just took it calmly and carried on asking questions. But his skin revealed the muscle underneath, and Hredt could see movement in his jaw even when he wasn't speaking. He'd noticed that once before when Jeff was the first to work out that teeriks were not only intelligent but had technical skills. It was a sign of agitation.

"So you do know where Earth is," Jeff said. "And you've got some kind of relay close enough to transmit images in real time."

"Yes. I should have told you, Chief Jeff. I apologise."

Jeff opened the entrance doors, still apparently calm. If he'd been a Kugin officer, he'd have been bellowing with rage and taking random shots at everything in sight by now. Humans were so *civilised.*

"Okay, let's show Captain Ingram the data," he said. "There's nothing we can do about it, but it'll help to know if we won't be getting backup in the future."

This was the truly difficult moment. Hredt almost lost his nerve. Then he imagined his commune fending for itself, permanent fugitives, friendless and hunted until they died and their accumulated knowledge and skill died with them. What was Caisin's gate worth if they had nowhere to go with it and nobody they could trust to use it?

"But we *can* do something about it, Chief Jeff." Hredt followed Jeff up the steep stairs, which weren't designed for teerik feet at all. "We can go there now."

"Say again?"

"We can go to Earth. We can create a special portal anywhere you need it."

Jeff stopped and turned around on the stairs. Hredt grabbed the handrail with his claws, almost losing his balance.

"You can open a wormhole for *Cabot*? How long will it take to get there?"

Hredt tried again. "This is complicated. We can fold space to move your ship. We can also fold space to move *you* without a ship, wherever you need to be. Land, air, water, space, inside, outside. You step through and you arrive right away, exactly where you want to go."

"Okay. Okay." Jeff just nodded, blinking. "I'm not sure I get it, but you can tell Captain Ingram what you just told me."

That was all Jeff said. At the top of the stairs, he turned down a passage, walking at speed with Hredt behind him. People coming the other way backed into doorways and stared. They'd had no direct contact with teeriks so far and being this close to a non-human seemed to be quite an event for them. Hredt heard one man say "Oh, wow!" as he passed. To them, he wasn't a grumpy old male in his declining years who'd made some bad decisions, but an exotic object of wonder. It was rather nice.

Bridget Ingram met Jeff at the door of a room that was probably her office. "Come in, gentlemen," she said. "Do we have a problem?"

"Databurst, ma'am?" Jeff asked.

"That bad, eh? Very well, databurst away."

"Hredt has eyes on Ainatio ships in Earth orbit, real time, under attack. He's got data and the teeriks can create a portal for Earth access wherever we need it."

Ingram showed no expression, but her throat flushed red. Hredt wasn't sure what that indicated in a human. But he knew to tread carefully when teerik females displayed their red crests.

"Right now?" Ingram asked.

"Now," Hredt said. "I told you nothing before and I apologise for that."

"OPSEC," Ingram said, but Hredt didn't understand. "Well, this is going to be an interesting day. Wait one while I get Peter and Dai in here. Oh, and Brad. Have you made contact with Ainatio, Fred?"

"I haven't tried," Hredt said. The small room was very plain and grey with a long bank of blue fabric-covered seating along one wall. He waited to see what Jeff did before assuming he could perch there. "But we could set up a comms relay for you."

"Explain this to me, Fred. In simple terms, please, because I'm not a scientist."

"We can make wormholes."

"Yes. You didn't make a secret of that."

"We can use them to send items to Earth, anything from a ship to an observation device. But something has happened to at least one of your ships. We've been watching it, and there was an explosion. This is probably very bad. If we can help you, we will."

Ingram was as calm as Jeff, although her eyes changed slightly. "We're very grateful for that, Fred. But we need intel from Earth before we decide how to deal with this."

Hredt settled down on the seat and made his best attempt at translating the text elements of the recording while Ingram waited for the other humans to arrive. He couldn't keep technical information from them. They weren't clients to be carefully managed and mystified. When he handed the screen to Ingram, she studied it as if she understood.

"So someone detonated explosives," she said. "But it's hard to tell if this is an actual attack or Ainatio scuppering redundant ships before leaving. Let's reserve judgement until we make contact. Do you think this is another of Erskine's stunts, Chief?"

"Can't rule it out, ma'am," Jeff said.

"Someone was still transmitting from the planet's surface," Hredt said. "A location on the eastern side of the United States. I think there are still people at your headquarters. Perhaps Solomon is there, too."

The humans seemed to manage well enough without Solomon, and they had other emanations with no consciousness that did routine jobs very well, but Hredt could see how Ingram and Jeff reacted when they mentioned Solomon. He seemed to be valued and missed.

"If we established the right kind of link, we'd like to bring Sol back," Ingram said. "But first we need to establish whether whoever's there is Ainatio or a hostile force. Ah, here they are. Take a seat, gentlemen."

Three of Cabot's crew sat down at the table with their screens in front of them. Cosqui had been wrong to dismiss the children's encyclopaedia: without the basic information aimed at the very young, it would have taken Hredt longer to distinguish between male and female humans, or work out their ages and where they'd originated. On closer examination, humans didn't all look the same any more than teeriks did. These were males, younger than Chief Jeff and possibly younger than Ingram. One looked like the encyclopaedia's images of people from Asia, and the other two were both pink-skinned but spoke with very different accents. All that was irrelevant at the moment, but Hredt was still fascinated.

"On your screens now," Ingram said, tapping her own. "Yes, that really is Earth seen from GEO orbit *today*. Real-time. Yes, our teerik friends know where we live and they've been keeping an eye on us. And yes, we may well have Nomad personnel in trouble down there. Because that wreck is one of the last four Ainatio ships."

The Asian officer with the name HIYASHI stitched onto on his jacket looked up. "Hard to know which one this is without hull identification, but they did have ships they couldn't fill. They might just have scuttled the others to stop anyone getting hold of sensitive tech."

"That's what we need to find out, Dai. Fast."

"Is timing an issue, ma'am? It's not as if we can do anything."

Ingram hesitated as if she was deciding how many surprises they could handle. "Fred says he can open a portal for us to pay Earth an immediate visit." The three men stared at her. She paused. "Okay, perhaps I should have worked up to that a little more gradually."

"Blimey," Bissey said. He spoke like Ingram but Hredt couldn't understand some of the things he said. "I volunteer to try it out. But are we thinking of sending *Cabot* back or a shuttle?"

Hredt felt he could join in. "Commander Bissey, you now live in a part of the galaxy where spacefolding is in common use. Ships use portals to move from one space to another. But ours is... pinhead? Pinpoint? Very accurate. You can *walk* through it without a vessel. There's no delay. It's like your communications used to be. And we think it can make many at once."

"Pinpoint," Ingram said. "And make many what?"

"Points. Remember that I said you should imagine it as a flat surface that you could fold to make two distant points touch?" Hredt looked around for something flexible and flat to demonstrate. "Do you have a piece of fabric or paper I can use?"

Bissey pulled a tissue out his pocket. "It's clean," he said.

"Thank you." Hredt scrunched it into a loose ball. "There. If you could see all the places where the surface folds back on itself now, you would see many more points where two locations would touch and create a portal. If we can do that, we can generate multiple routes and even intersect them so they can be entered far from the generation point. But we haven't tested that yet."

"Let me see if I've got this straight," Bissey said. "You go through this door — or doors — to another part of the galaxy and it's in the same time frame, like our instant comms. And you can put that door anywhere, and maybe connect it to other doors. How accurate do you mean by pinpoint?"

Hredt indicated with a gap between his claws. "Very exact." He switched to human measurements. "Less than a centimetre."

"Good grief."

"This particular device isn't known to anyone except my commune and yourselves," Hredt said. He unfolded the tissue, smoothed it out, and passed it back to Bissey, who studied it and tried to recreate the folds like a child making a model. "Learned Mother Caisin created it. Nobody else has portals that accurate or capable of safely connecting with a solid surface. Or any that can form networks of routes, but as I said, that is untested." Hredt pointed at a white cup on the table. "Ships can jump between gates in space, or jump with their own drives, but only we can place this container on a table on Earth. Nobody else knows we can do this. We have to keep it secret."

Ingram just raised her eyebrows. "There's rather a lot you haven't told us yet, isn't there?"

"Databurst?" Hredt asked, hoping he'd understood correctly that it was Jeff's term for a very fast explanation with minimal words.

"Yes, please. Databurst would be helpful."

"We designed the ship and systems for the Jatta Protectorate. But the portal was our private work. We kept it secret because we expected a teerik uprising."

"Oh." Ingram had changed colour. She looked quite pale now. "So you were overthrowing your government."

"No, we escaped because we were unhappy. All teeriks are bound to foremen. We have no choice. We stole the prenu to escape and meet up with other teeriks to create our own world where the foremen couldn't find us. But our brethren lost their courage. Nobody else arrived at the meeting point."

Hredt had revealed almost everything now. Jeff made a little snorting noise. Ingram rubbed her forehead.

"Which is here," she said quietly. "Great."

"No, the rendezvous was somewhere else. When we realised the others had changed their minds and let us down, we escaped into unexplored space where the foremen might not look for us."

Ingram looked like she was pretending to be puzzled. "I don't know if these words mean anything to you, but is this some kind of trade union dispute, or are we talking about slavery?"

"I don't understand," Hredt said.

"A union is like a guild. A group of workers who organise themselves to negotiate better pay and working conditions with their employer."

"No, not a union, then. No negotiation." Hredt recalled some words from the encyclopaedia, but he wasn't sure if they were apt. "The foremen hold our contracts. I told Chief Jeff how we keep our knowledge in our minds, never recorded, because then nobody will risk killing us. Except we've broken our contract and taken the ship, which is unheard of and will probably result in severe punishment even if our knowledge is lost in the process."

Ingram almost repeated her earlier question, as if she was making sure of something. "So no pay, and you're not free to leave. You're owned. Slavery."

"Oh, we have very nice rewards. Nice home, nice food. We can have anything we want. But we can never leave or work for anyone else unless our contract is sold."

"Indentured servitude," Bissey said. "Not much difference. Well, that tells us a lot."

"And this severe punishment," Ingram said. "You mean they'll kill you as a deterrent to others."

"This is why we hide here, Captain Bridget." Hredt had permission to call her Bridget, but he thought it wise to be respectful and add her rank. After what he'd concealed, she might be very angry under that calm surface. "The Kugin shipyard will want its ship back, and so will the Jattan clients. So they'll keep searching. And if they catch us, yes, they will kill us."

"Damn." Ingram did that odd downwards glance with her eyebrows raised, the same way Jeff did. "Anything else?"

"I've told you everything now," Hredt said. "You didn't try to kill us. You helped us, so we want to help you, because nobody else in the galaxy will help a teerik who's broken their bond. The best we can expect is to be stolen. We're very useful. We're valuable."

Hredt hoped humans could tell when he was being completely honest. He might just have made the biggest mistake of his life. But the officer they called Brad, Commander Searle, leaned back in his seat and looked Hredt in the eye.

"I'm in," he said. "I want to see what they've done to my country. Does this portal require any training?"

"None," Hredt said. "Although you might find it disorienting."

"How bad?"

"I know nothing about human biology."

"Okay, I'll be the test subject."

"You will when I say you can, Commander." Ingram looked calm and spoke quietly, but the officer blinked and glanced down at the table as if he'd been rebuked. "Fred, who else knows where Earth is?"

Hredt could guess what was coming next. "Only us. We have every reason not to tell anyone."

"Let me put it in plain English," she said. "We now have a security shitstorm at both ends of this mission. Our follow-up missions might have been destroyed, possibly by a group of nations called APS, because they're the only power left that could. And now there's a fast-track route to Earth for any alien fleet that knows where it is, while we're stuck on Opis, collaborating with fugitives who've stolen advanced military technology. We both need each other's help more than ever now, don't we?"

Hredt got the gist of that, even if some of the words were new to him and weren't in his dictionary. "We can give you the technology," he said. "Spacefolding is established technology, not a secret, and all spacefaring nations in this part of the galaxy use it. We can raise you to that level, but we can also give you a greater advantage."

"Have you tested this Caisin gate yourselves?"

"As far as we could." Hredt rather liked Ingram's description. It wasn't the same as *Caisin's gate*. It suddenly sounded more like a title, an honour to its inventor. "*Caisin gate.* Our inventions are never named after us. But that would be good. It would immortalise her."

"We can call it whatever you wish," Ingram said. "So unless anyone can see a gaping hole in my paranoia, we're back to where we were, with — at a minimum — an instant comms link to Earth. Because we need to do a recce before we go charging in."

The others just nodded. It looked as if few people argued with Ingram, at least in front of outsiders, but Hredt suspected the conversation would continue once he'd left, and with a great deal more force.

"The channel to Earth is already open," Hredt said. "Do you want a relay on the surface? We can do that now. It might be better than routing a signal via the orbital."

"Can you do it covertly?" Ingram asked.

"I think so. And the Caisin gate is quick. A flash. Hard to detect."

"Where do we do this, then? Is there a control room somewhere, or is this gate portable?"

"The assay probes and the gate generator are tied into our system. We could give you your own equipment later, but if you want to do this now, our ship has a gate ready."

"Now's good. Thank you." Ingram turned to Bissey. "Peter, I'd like this kept from the crew until we're sure it works, but brief the rest of the officers privately. Chief, you're with me. Pick up some more food bars on the way out. Can't drop in for a chat empty-handed, can we?"

"I haven't discussed this with the commune," Hredt said. "But apology is better than debate."

Ingram gave him a look he didn't understand, a little like amusement but also disapproval. Would he be able to recognise anger in a human? Perhaps he'd missed the warning signs. But they were bringing more food, so they couldn't have been that upset with him. He tried to remember if there was anything else important that he'd genuinely forgotten to mention, because this was probably his last chance to confess. The next time he mentioned an omission, it would be interpreted very differently.

Hredt returned to the prenu with the humans in their rover, standing on the flat cargo area with his claws locked around the roll bar as the vehicle bumped and bounced its way across the grass. He'd taken another step that might turn out to be a disaster. But this time, the rash move was entirely his. It was a lonely kind of fear, and the guilt would be his alone if this backfired.

Ingram turned in the passenger seat and looked up at him. The engine noise and the rushing air forced her to raise her voice.

"Your daughter will see us coming," she said. "I know you've got drones or observation satellites somewhere."

"Yes." Hredt cursed himself. *That* was what he'd forgotten to tell them. "We need to keep watch in case the foremen arrive. Or the Jattan navy."

"Good," Ingram said. "We're keeping an eye on things from orbit too. And we'll send up drones when we need to."

Hredt couldn't tell if that was a statement or a warning. Sometimes he found conversations very oblique and wondered if he understood as much of the language as he thought. Perhaps the humans had already realised that the commune knew about Earth and had just been waiting to see how long it would take them to admit it. It seemed both sides were still working out how much to trust each other.

Turisu was waiting for them at the hatch when they climbed down the shaft. Jeff was the last to step off the ladder, struggling with a large box of food bars in his rucksack.

"You're going to be angry, Turi," Hredt said in Kugal. "But our friends need urgent help. Something has happened to one of their ships."

Turisu's red crest rose alarmingly. "You *promised* me, father. You said you wouldn't interfere. You said you'd observe — "

"I said that before I saw something I had no right to keep to myself. The humans have saved us from starvation. This is the least we owe them."

"Do *not* use the portal," Turisu said. "I absolutely forbid you. Do you hear me? Don't you dare."

"I'll do whatever will save us," Hredt said, and stepped past her into the ship. He looked back and saw Ingram give her a reassuring smile. Jeff stopped to hand over the box of food bars, but that wouldn't placate Turi this time.

"I don't speak teerik," Ingram said, following him down the passage with her head lowered. "But your daughter's obviously... ah... *upset*. We don't want to cause you any problems."

"She spoke *Kugal*." Hredt adjusted his bag to stop it scraping the bulkheads. "The language of our foremen. We had predictable lives, but now we don't, and that troubles her. But that's not your doing." He opened the hatch and stepped into the command centre. "Here we are. Walk carefully. It's quite dark in here."

Ingram stood at the edge of the dais and put both hands on the safety rail. Jeff joined her, arms folded. Neither of them said anything while they stared at the display hanging in the middle of the chamber.

It was an aerial view of a military base of some kind. There was a high double fence of woven metal filaments with a gate set in it. The gate itself was shut and a group of human troops were standing behind it, looking out through the mesh with their weapons in their hands.

"Dear God," Ingram said. "Where *is* this?"

"Near the uplink signal." Cosqui appeared out of the shadows, looking ruffled by the intrusion. "I look around. No worry, probe is too high to see."

"This is Cosqui," Hredt said. "She designed the control system."

"Cosqui, can you show me an image from the location on my map, please?" Ingram asked, holding out her pocket screen. "And explain the signal to me."

Cosqui took the screen and pointed to something with her claw so that Ingram could see it. "Someone on the ground *here* sends a signal to your orbital, but not from this place. From *here*."

"That's the town near the Ainatio facility," Ingram said. "It's called Kill Line. So what we're looking at is Ainatio's main gates."

"And those are your soldiers."

"Ah... no. Show me the source of the signal, please."

The view of the Ainatio site swung out of view and all Hredt could see for a few moments was a canopy of trees with an empty road winding below. The probe flew over woods, then cleared land, and finally passed a bright red aircraft on the ground. Hredt consulted his encyclopaedia. The craft was a tilt rotor helicopter. A couple of humans were standing nearby, carrying rifles but looking relaxed, as if this was a routine day.

"That must be a Lammergeier," Jeff said. "Ainatio developed the AI component. So what are we looking at here?"

"I don't know." Ingram shook her head, eyes fixed on the display. "The last thing Erskine said to me was that they had security issues. I can't put this together at all."

"That's APS on the gates, ma'am. Or APDU, to be exact, because I'm sure those are Korean, Aussie, and Malayan uniforms."

"I know. That's what worries me."

Hredt wasn't sure if they were freely discussing tactical issues because they didn't think he understood the references — he didn't — or feigning ignorance because they thought he did.

"You have a radio, Chief Jeff," Hredt said. "Our probes can act as your relay. Call your headquarters. Find Solomon."

Ingram held up a finger. "Hang on. We can't talk to anyone until we know if the network's been compromised. The world doesn't know we're here, let alone that we've got FTL comms again. A ship's been destroyed. I'm not going to assume a benign explanation now until I've ruled out a hostile one."

Hredt considered how the Kugin would respond to a situation like this. "You could send someone to carry out covert reconnaissance," he said. "We can place you exactly where you need to be. Even inside a structure."

Jeff turned to him. "So where's the Caisin gate? Where's the actual structure?" Jeff drew a rectangle in the air with his forefingers. "A frame. Whatever it uses."

"It doesn't have one." Hredt didn't have the technical vocabulary yet to explain it properly. He didn't even know if there were human terms for some of the concepts. "It's complicated. Do you want to use it right now?"

"Not just yet, thank you," Ingram said. "I need to take a closer look and then work out how we go in, if we go in at all."

"Aren't you going to help them?" Hredt asked.

"If we can, of course we will," Ingram said. "But if we blunder in unprepared for a task we're not actually trained for, we'll get people killed. But doing nothing might not be an option."

"I understand. They're your comrades. You can't abandon them."

"Actually, we don't know any of them, because we've been in cryo for forty-odd years," Ingram said. "But without them, Nomad base won't have a future. We need settlers, farmers, families, more troops. I'm here to establish and consolidate a human colony on this planet. That's why I'll do whatever's necessary to get them here." Ingram turned to Cosqui. "Cosqui, can we take a more detailed look around the whole area? We need a complete overview of the Ainatio complex, the town and the surrounding farmland, and the road between the two. Can you do that?"

"Ainatio first?" Cosqui asked.

"Yes please."

"I need your map."

The original screen that Jeff had given Hredt now came into its own as the fastest way to transfer data between the humans' system and the prenu's. It was also an act of mutual trust. Other navies would have exploited any link to slip into the system and pick up intel, but Hredt saw nothing to indicate the humans had tried to do anything more than provide data. He showed his respect for that by not trying to access theirs.

Ingram stood back to watch as Cosqui directed the probe, starting with a high-level view of the entire facility. It looked like a village surrounded by forest and connected to the outside world by two roads and a few dirt tracks. The mesh fence ran around the whole perimeter. Hredt couldn't identify the individual features, but there were structures on the north and east of the site that looked industrial. They could even have been weapons silos. He couldn't tell.

Ingram studied the aerial view in silence for a while, then pointed to the display. "Okay, Chief, facing the site, we have the main gates at the bottom *there*... offices or accommodation on the left... comms tower right of the gates... labs, manufacturing, or utilities on the top right." Her voice was flat and unemotional. "And gardens. How nice."

"Reactor top left," Jeff said. "I'm guessing, though."

"That road on the top right has to be the runway. You can see the rail."

"Is that a shuttle on it, ma'am?"

"Unless I've misjudged the scale, it's too small. Cosqui, could you zoom in on that, please?

"*Runway?*" Cosqui said.

"The feature that looks like a road with a line down the middle, northeast corner. I don't know how you launch from the ground, but one method we use is to take a run at it."

Hredt prepared to interpret for Ingram. Cosqui hadn't learned enough English for this. But she identified the runway and zoomed in to the object that had caught Jeff's attention. As far as Hredt could see, it was a large mechanical with multiple legs standing astride an elevated rail that had a section missing. There were no humans visible and no sign of a spacecraft.

"That doesn't fill me with optimism," Jeff said.

"Nor me, Chief." Ingram turned to Hredt. "Fred, I need my specialist officers to take a look at all this. Can I bring them here, or is that going to be a problem?"

It would, but Hredt didn't want to offend her. A couple of humans who were known to them was a manageable visit, but a sudden influx of new faces in an already anxious situation might be too much for the others. He hesitated. Ingram seemed to read his awkwardness.

"I realise it's an imposition, and you've already been very helpful," she said. Her tone was warm and kindly now but he had no way of knowing if she meant it. "Is there any way we can view this feed back at Nomad? Then we wouldn't have to intrude on you. Can we move the probe's camera ourselves? Oh... never mind, it's a lot to ask, I know."

"I give you access," Cosqui said suddenly. "But I stop you getting too low and probe being seen. You can move side to side and look close, but not low."

Ingram clasped her hands in front of her chest. "Cosqui, you're a genius. We'd be so grateful for that. We just need to see what's happening in case we get this all wrong."

Hredt really hadn't expected Cosqui to be so cooperative, but she probably didn't want aliens swarming through the command centre. While Cosqui showed Ingram how to move the probe using her screen, Jeff stepped back to talk to Hredt.

"Don't underestimate how grateful we are for this, Fred," he said quietly. He patted Hredt's back. Humans did that with people they had close bonds with. "We don't forget who our friends are. Thank you."

"I wouldn't want to know there was trouble and keep it to myself," Hredt said. "I gave you my word we'd be friends."

"And we are, mate."

Ingram clutched her screen to her chest as if it had acquired some special status, looking as satisfied as she could be for someone with a problem on her hands. But her problem had become the commune's. Without the humans' continued presence, Hredt knew the commune had no future either. He led Jeff and Ingram back down the passages to the exit, hoping he hadn't made matters worse. If there was nothing Ingram could do to help her comrades, it might have been better for her not to know.

"We'll check this out as fast as we can and get back to you," Ingram said. She stopped at the hatch, looking grim again. "When humans have technology they need to keep secret, they've often let their own people die if saving them would reveal it. We appreciate the courageous moral choice you've made."

Hredt wished Turisu would appreciate it too. He went back to the command centre via the engineering spaces to avoid running into her. Cosqui was waiting for him, eating another food bar.

"The things we do to secure a supply of these," she said.

"I think your understanding of English is better than you admit, Cosqui."

"Perhaps it is. If they think I don't understand, they might say more. So what happens now?"

"We wait."

"We've been here for ages. I need my nap."

"Yes, it's getting dark on Earth. I lost track of the time."

Hredt watched the display for a while, noting the probe's path as Ingram moved it around the site. He'd learn what he could about her tactics and priorities by watching where she positioned the probe. The compound looked deserted except for the troops at the entrance. Bright lights had come on along the perimeter fence.

"I really did expect Captain Ingram to want to use the Caisin gate right away," he said.

Cosqui munched noisily. "She's not stupid."

Eventually, the probe moved off. It followed the road west, back to the area where the red aircraft had been, then turned south. Roofs came into view, one or two at first, and then a whole town of them. Even without low-light enhancement, Hredt could see people milling around, some of them in black uniforms, and all of them were loading vehicles or hauling boxes. The town of Kill Line looked busy and urgent.

"Perhaps that's where everyone went," Cosqui said. "They look like they're running away."

Hredt was now looking for one of the four-legged mechanicals. He was certain that Solomon would be part of this evacuation, and if he'd preferred that kind of mechanical frame here, he would also favour it back on Earth.

"Captain Ingram needs to find Solomon," Hredt said. "That would solve a lot of her problems."

"Probably."

"I don't like standing here and just watching."

"Turn it off, then."

"I mean that I want to do something."

"Hredt, you're not a soldier," Cosqui said. "And I don't think Ingram is, either. She fights with a ship. You know very well that ground combat is a different skill."

Where would an emanation like Solomon go if he was marooned? He'd stay with the Nomad mission. It was just a matter of working out if Ingram's comrades were the people loading vehicles. The probe zoomed in from time to time and lingered on the troops in black as if Ingram was looking for someone in particular.

"I think they're her comrades," Cosqui said. "They look more like her and Chief Jeff than the troops on the gate."

"I could go there and check," Hredt said.

It seemed like a moment of madness, but he paused for a moment and realised why the thought had struck him. To humans, he looked like an animal. Nobody would take any notice of a bird. If he observed and all was well, he could report back, but if it was as bad as he suspected, he could find Solomon and put him in direct contact with Ingram.

No, he could do more than that. If the humans had lost their ship, the commune had the ability to rescue them without it.

"You'd better not, Hredt," Cosqui said. She unwrapped another food bar. She'd hidden more than he realised. "What are you going to do, ask them questions? They've never seen an alien before. They'll shoot you or run away screaming."

That didn't worry him, but it did help him make up his mind. He could do things he never imagined were possible. So he could give Caisin's technology a proper test, and he could step back to Opis in an instant. But somebody needed to check what was happening.

"I'm going," he said. "I'll find Solomon. He knows I exist and I don't think he'll be shocked to find I'm intelligent."

"Hredt, *no.* You'll be shot. Are you insane?"

Hredt could operate the Caisin gate himself. It was designed for teeriks, not Jattans. He darted down to the deck, took one of the activation devices so he could open the gate from the other end, and set the gate to exit at the coordinates of the red aircraft.

Chief Jeff would have been disappointed by the lack of spectacle. The gate was just a patch of mist that appeared silently from nowhere and hung in mid-air.

Cosqui scurried down from the dais. "I can't let you do this. *Stop it.* You don't know what pathogens there are on Earth. You could die. You could come back with an infection and then *we'd* all die."

"I mix with humans and I haven't caught anything yet," Hredt said. He couldn't turn back now. "I'll be fine. Do *not* close this gate."

The last thing he heard as he stepped into the haze was Cosqui rasping at him, calling him a senile fool. The blurred patch of deck vanished, the temperature and humidity shot up, and he was standing on grass, bombarded by sounds and smells and sensations that were unlike any he'd ever experienced. The strangest thing was how light he suddenly felt. It was like the time he'd had to accompany a ship to Bhinu. He lifted his leg too high and felt like he was treading air.

When he looked behind him, the red aircraft was where he expected it to be. Nobody seemed to be around. Soon he'd have the cover of nightfall, and then he could look for Solomon.

Hredt was both scared and sure of what he had to do. Perhaps this was what the humans meant by courage. He'd never realised that he had it, but like flying, it made him feel he was capable of anything.

06

We'll reshape Opis to human needs. I'm not suggesting we sterilise the entire planet and replace everything, because that degree of terraforming's beyond anyone's capabilities for the foreseeable future. I mean we adapt the environment around Nomad Base where necessary, then expand it in stages over the long term. Introduce bacteria. Alter the soil. Import new species. If the bots find anything truly dangerous that we can't avoid, we remove it. We'll make mistakes, but we're not a conservation project. We're not even a scientific survey mission. We're colonisers. The future of our species comes first and we don't apologise for existing.

> Tad Bednarz, in his initial address to the original Nomad planning team.

SECURITY CONTROL ROOM, AINATIO PARK RESEARCH CENTRE: 2035 HOURS, TEN MINUTES AFTER THE RELEASE OF THE BEDNARZ SABCODE.

The first signs of the sabcode meltdown began with an APDU lieutenant on the gate fiddling with his earpiece.

Trinder watched on the security cameras as the guy took it out and scraped it with his thumbnail, then beckoned to another soldier. They both examined it. Soon all the troops were standing in a tight huddle, earpieces in their hands and looking like they were trying to polish them. Nearby, the APS technicians who'd also been locked out of the buildings kept looking up into the sky, holding their screens and radios aloft as if they were trying to find a signal. Unless the technicians were all issued with military devices, it looked like civilian networks were glitching as well. Then some of them gave up waving the devices around and looked like they were trying to reboot them.

One guy took out the battery. It wasn't hard to work out that for some of them, their screens weren't functioning at all.

There was no safe way to check. All known APDU and APS frequencies and servers were blocked to Ainatio personnel now in case the sabcode found a way back home. They couldn't even risk tuning in to APS news networks.

"Here we go," Trinder said. "Sol, have they lost their sat?"

"It certainly looks like it," Solomon said. "But we're relying on public sources and guesswork, so confirmation is going to take time. It'll be piecemeal."

"They've definitely got a problem."

"Sir, it's happening inside the building, too," Simonot said. He had the kind of peripheral vision that enabled him to stare at the bank of screens and immediately spot the smallest things on any of them. Trinder sometimes wondered if he was a prototype android that Bednarz had neglected to mention to anybody. "Look. They're all prodding their radios or holding up their screens now."

"Did you hit a civil comsat, Sol?" Trinder asked.

"I think we're seeing a military outage. If any of them were allowed access to a public network, I'd have expected one of them to have called home hours ago to say they were being held hostage, and we'd have seen some response from APDU HQ by now. Knowing Pham, he probably restricted all comms to a military network he can control because he doesn't want anyone gossiping with their family about what they're doing here."

"He's also the kind to keep civilian telco access for himself," Trinder said. "Maybe we're already too late to stop him."

"That only matters if we haven't grounded APDU already," Solomon said. "He can send as many SOS messages as he wishes if nobody can come to his aid. But I've checked the building system for EMF emissions around the site and his screen is either switched off or out of action. I can only hope whatever the sabcode knocked out was silenced in time."

Trinder studied the monitors. "Corporal, where's the operator who's posing as a tech?"

Simonot tapped a screen with his pen. "There. He keeps moving out of camera range, but he's still hanging around outside the front of the building. No sign of him trying to use a radio, but if they're set up like us, he's probably got some stand-alone short-range link to Pham."

The size of the sabcode gamble was now becoming apparent to Trinder as he thought through all the ways Pham could work around it. He didn't know if those few minutes had given APS time to realise what was happening and scramble aircraft, but he'd find out the hard way in five or six hours. Assessing the damage to the rail was even more urgent.

Fonseca was prowling the corridors in full combat order. She looked like she was in her element. "I stand by my assessment," she said. "Pham didn't call home for help earlier because he wants this whole thing kept quiet and thought he could handle the lockdown until he took out Sol. Looks like he guessed wrong."

"*Looks like* isn't enough, Captain," Solomon said. "I need confirmation. To fall back on cliché, absence of evidence isn't evidence of absence. And as the intended target, I'm more than a little curious about what Pham would be planning for me that didn't depend on his being able to leave the facility."

"It's those two operators you need to worry about," Trinder said. "Hey, can I send the engineers in to look at the rail now? They've been waiting for hours."

"I realise we have to get on with the job, Major, but I need to be as sure as I can be that the Fiddler isn't going to be a danger. It only has to move to crush them."

"It hasn't moved all day."

"Please, revisit my previous advice about evidence."

Trinder felt bad about getting impatient with Solomon after all he'd managed to do, but it was hard waiting for the shoe to drop. He had no idea if APS-based news networks were still on the air because they couldn't check. If those channels were down, though, he expected to see news of the outage filtering through to foreign channels before long.

"This is the first live news I've seen for years," Simonot said. He was keeping on eye on Russian, Indian, and British satellite news. "It looks weird."

The Russian and Indian feeds were automatically dubbed into English. "No lip sync," Trinder said.

"I meant the whole thing. I'd gotten used to the outside world not existing, and that nobody knew we existed either. But now we've probably just altered the course of world politics."

Trinder hadn't thought of it like that. "APS won't publicly admit they've got a problem until they have to. But someone must have spotted something's wrong by now. An automatic alert about loss of contact at the very least."

And they'd guess who was responsible. They knew damn well that the last thing they'd done was blow up a ship belonging to a company with an ASD AI.

Did they know, though? Fonseca could have been right about Pham doing all this off the books. He still answered to someone, even if he was a tin god out here, and if they didn't know about Solomon, they wouldn't make the connection between an outage and Ainatio for some time. Perhaps Pham had called in a favour from his old spook buddies to deploy the armed shepherd. They weren't generally in the habit of discussing detail with politicians.

It wasn't going to make much difference now, though, except to Pham's career prospects. Trinder tried to focus on the situation unfolding around the site instead of events in Asia that he had no control over.

The trapped APS contingent seemed unperturbed up to now, probably because Pham had told them to sit tight and they believed he could fix things. They were APS, a world power: Ainatio was an isolated bunch of odds and ends who didn't look like trouble. A few APS personnel had tried to force the doors, break windows, or get into the service passage access hatches in the corridors. But most had generally been calm and sat it out. Now they'd been locked up for eight hours, they'd suddenly lost contact with the outside world after a lifetime of comforting connection to one network or another, and their mood looked like it had changed.

"Whoa," Simonot said. "I think this guy's cracked."

On one of the screens, a burst of automatic fire sent chunks of wood trim flying as an APDU private tried shooting out the frame of a door in the accommodation block. Despite the splinters and drama, the door didn't budge. The kid walked up to it and gave it half a dozen frustrated, full-effort kicks that made no impression at all, then slid down the wall and sat with his forehead on his folded arms. Under all the tastefully bland hotel design, the doors and emergency bulkheads that could seal off any section were tungsten steel. Even the glass in them wasn't glass. Then the guy took out his radio, pressed the keys, and got up to start pacing the corridor again.

"I bet they wish they'd used the Fiddler to get them out while they could," Simonot said. "Although stairs aren't its strong point. Or opening doors without bringing the building down."

Trinder wondered why Pham hadn't done that. The risk of demolition had probably been the only thing that had stopped him.

The bot was just too big to move in corridors or do precision jobs like opening all the doors and emergency bulkheads that stood between it and the trapped personnel without demolishing walls. As the APDU troops inside were almost all stuck on upper floors and Pham was marooned in Erskine's underground suite, they'd end up as part of the rubble. Trinder felt slightly better for knowing that Pham made tactical mistakes too.

But the technicians and troops weren't responsible for what he'd done, and there were places in the building where they were sharing a space with Ainatio people, like the staff club and the restaurant. Trinder would need their cooperation. He wouldn't get it if their buddies were hungry and thirsty.

"Lennie, I'm going to distribute some food and water," he said. "A little goodwill."

"Push comes to shove, we can release the bulkheads individually and move them section by section into the restaurant," Fonseca said. "Like moving sheep one pen at a time."

"Yeah, sheep. Whatever works."

"Have we decided what we're going to do with them when we leave?" she asked. "At best, we'll be living like this for a few weeks while we fix the rail and load up. It's going to get rough in there."

It had been the right move to lock the place down, but they'd known relations with APS would be rocky when they opened the doors again. Chris spoke up. Trinder could hear vehicle activity in the background. Kill Line must have been loading trucks.

"What if we can't fix it?" Chris asked. "How long can we leave them locked in? I don't want anyone starving or dying of dehydration, but if we end up having to abandon the launch and evacuate overland, there's a limit to how far and how fast we can run."

"We've got staff staying behind who'll be dependent on APS's goodwill," Trinder said. "They're the ones who'll bear the brunt if anyone dies. Pham himself won't have any problems, not for a long time, because he's in Erskine's bunker. So he's got plenty of food and home comforts in there."

"So what were we planning to do when we locked them in to start with?" Chris asked.

"I dealt with the immediate problem." Fonseca sounded defensive. "The alternative was to stand there and take it."

"Sure. I just want to cover all the bases. Worst case, Sol, can we do all the shutdown and system purging and stuff remotely, when we're as far away as possible?"

"I could rewrite the relevant elements in the security system so that we can do that, and perhaps put delays on releasing specific doors and barriers, like Erskine's office," Solomon said. "Evacuation requires wiping all confidential data including the entire security system, which will release the locks. But I agree that we shouldn't rely on someone staying here to do that."

"Okay, you do that, Sol, and give us some flexibility, just in case," Trinder said. "But we can't make decisions until we know how bad the rail is."

"I think Gatti's going to find out, sir," Simonot said.

Trinder scanned through the monitors again. The Fiddler still hadn't moved, but one of the engineers had. Del Barrett was walking slowly towards the motionless machine, pausing every few yards like he was testing it for a reaction. Trinder got on the radio.

"Echo Five to Echo Ten, stop Barrett *now*, over," he said.

"Echo Five, he's fed up, and he says he knows the risks." Gatti and Finch were now in camera range, following a few yards behind Barrett, rifles ready. "We're ready to pull him out, over."

Trinder had never been disobeyed before. It didn't bother him personally, but he had to at least look like he was still in command to be any use if things got worse. He compromised. Gatti really couldn't stop the guy without using force.

"Echo Ten, if he's wrong about the Fiddler, the next thing you'll see is a missile incoming from Solomon. Echo Five out."

Trinder watched, waiting for some sign of movement in the giant bot, but there wasn't even a twitch. Barrett was right under it now, looking it over like a used car. He even put his hand on one of its legs. Gatti moved in next to him. Trinder could hear the conversation.

"I can't feel any vibration," Barrett was saying. "Get one of the cherry pickers. I'm going to open it up."

"I don't think that's wise," Solomon said, but he wasn't talking to Gatti.

Trinder assumed that anyone with a clear view of the runway could watch what was happening too, so this would be a test of whether Pham's guys still had any control over the Fiddler. Barrett spent a few minutes trying to open a hinged plate on the Fiddler's side. After some cussing and muttering accompanied by metallic scrapes, the panel swung open and Barrett leaned back, fanning his hand in front of his face.

"Something's fried," he said. "Can you smell that, Jay?"

"Nope."

"Take it from me, then. There's a lot of burned-out parts in this sucker."

Barrett leaned into the opening and poked around inside. Eventually he pulled back and held up a rectangular object that looked a lot like an oversized harmonica.

"It's a mess in there," he said. "There's another nine of these and they all look the same. Melted. I can see more damage inside, but this is enough to stop the thing."

"Is it dead?" Gatti asked.

"As a dodo, buddy. I hope the effort of screwing us burned it out."

The cherry picker lowered Barrett to the ground as the other engineers scrambled down into the pit of rubble the Fiddler had left. The inspection had begun. Trinder needed an answer fast.

"I think that might be the sabcode's doing, Major," Solomon said. "If it is, it means it's spread back here via APS or APDU comms."

Trinder's gut flipped. "Just as well our critical network's in Lamm One."

"I did say it was indiscriminate."

"As long as it doesn't come after *you*."

"I won't be giving it the chance."

"So let's piece this together, then. If the sabcode's back here after you injected it into the shepherd, that means it's done a loop via an APS or APDU network that was connected to *Temujin* or directly to someone here, like Pham."

"Indeed," Solomon said. "Which supports the theory that it's taken out a military comsat. And someone here who was on that network was still connected to the Fiddler, even though it was idle."

Trinder was almost too scared to ask. "Tell me it hasn't evolved far enough to jump from APS to us. We've blocked every route that might receive a signal from them."

"Do you recall that I limited APS's access to our network and purged sensitive data as soon as it was clear they were coming in to search the site?"

"Yeah, sorry, I do. I've insulted you."

"No, Major. I'm merely reminding you precautions were already in place. I airgapped the critical part of our network before APS came in to rummage. It's in a *physically* separate system, because I don't rely on firewalls. I did it because I was afraid they'd do to us what we've just done to them. I suspect their portion of our network has been infected and destroyed as well, because someone will have connected a device or tried to send a message. But we're protected."

Knowing things didn't necessarily help Trinder get a feel for the size of a problem, but now Solomon had said *airgapped* and *network*, he felt the sabcode was an arm's length away like a shark in an aquarium, with only a glass wall between them. He also realised he'd never thought about where the sabcode had been stored all those years before Solomon let it loose. Ignorance could definitely be bliss.

"But you're not going to check this yourself, are you?" Trinder said.

"No, I'm just going to observe. As humans might say, I'm not stupid, so I'm not sticking my hand in there. It's too risky."

"So how can it destroy hardware?"

"The safety controls in the software," Solomon said. "Corrupt those, and a machine doesn't know if it's overheating or going too fast. So it carries on until it fails. I'd have to examine a screen or a radio to see if it's managed to damage those as well, though."

"Okay. What if some other government lets APS borrow bandwidth on their sats? Someone's bound to think there'll be a favour they can call in one day."

"Then they'd be foolish, because with what's happened, they ought to assume the possibility of widespread malware, and that APS might accidentally contaminate their systems as well."

"I just realised it could have destroyed you if anything went wrong. That took some guts, Sol."

"I'd call it desperation. Pulling the pin from the grenade, so to speak."

"You took a personal risk."

"Save my medal for later," Solomon said. "I still don't know exactly what it's done."

Simonot raised a finger. "All quiet on Russian, Indian, and British news so far. But it's early days."

Trinder didn't need to watch any longer. "Okay, I'm going up to the restaurant to do some diplomacy." He stood up and stretched the kinks out of his neck before adjusting his body armour. Worried kids with guns didn't bode well. "Wish me luck."

He kept an eye on the feeds from the front gates as he walked to the elevator. There was still one operator missing. Marc would be paying close attention to that, but Trinder's guess was that the guy had found a way under or through the perimeter fence and was lurking outside. His buddy would probably follow when the situation became clearer to them. The question was what they planned to do next if their target was still Solomon, because taking out a tilt rotor was something most moderately-equipped warlords could manage. But Solomon would have thought of that. Trinder had to trust his judgement.

When he walked up to the restaurant doors, Matt McNally opened them before his chip activated them and ushered him inside. Trinder met the stares of a couple of APDU troops who were probably calculating how long it would take them to reach the doors when Trinder was leaving. They were still armed, but then so was Matt. Trinder could hear raised voices.

"Great timing," Matt said. "It's all coming out now. Village life, huh?"

There was an argument going on between a couple of tables but other than that it was abnormally quiet, as if folks were embarrassed by the row going on. Trinder felt like a tourist walking into a rough bar that wasn't in the guidebook. Recriminations had already started, but it wasn't APS doing the arguing. They were just spectators as Ainatio staff tore into each other. Ed Acosta was stabbing his finger in Audrey Meikle's direction across the aisle between their tables. Plates of spaghetti bolognese went untouched.

"Yeah, yeah, we know, you don't want to go to Opis but your old man does," Ed said. "So you go whining to APS and make sure we're *all* marooned to keep him here. We get it."

Audrey, holding her restless toddler on her lap, looked flushed and angry. The little girl was starting to grizzle, upset by the tone even if she didn't understand the argument.

"I don't have to take this from you, Ed," Audrey said. "I haven't said a word to them. Why the hell would I? Seb's staying. They've offered him a post. Everyone knows that."

"Did he have a post *before* you ratted us out, though?"

Zakko appeared from nowhere and stepped into the gap between the tables. "Let's take a break, Mr Acosta." He was very polite, very kind, but clearly not in the mood to take any shit. "You're upsetting the kid."

"It's okay, I'm going." Ed stood up and scraped his chair back. "I've got no argument with you."

A service bot rolled in to clear his plate of pasta and the room went from embarrassed silence to murmured, awkward conversation. Trinder had already filed the informer under Problems, Least Of Mine Right Now. The spat was a stark reminder that it was still an issue for everyone else, though.

"It's only going to get worse until we find out who it is," Matt said. "But I'm guessing we've got bigger problems."

"We'll know soon," Trinder said. "The engineers have started the inspection. Stand by for extraction either way."

Zakko wandered up to Matt and Trinder. He didn't look like the same guy these days. He was leaner and fitter now, officially one of Chris's militia, and Ainatio's black security fatigues looked like they belonged on him.

"People get weird when they're cooped up," Zakko said. "But I thought it'd be the APS guys losing their shit first."

"How are they taking it?"

"The radio blackout, or being locked up? It looks like they've lost all comms now. I mean *all.* From what we've seen, they can't even contact each other or Pham. I hate spying on folks but I'm guessing we need to know."

"Yeah, that fits what we're seeing around the rest of the site," Trinder said. "The Fiddler bot's fried too."

"Sol's virus is working, then," Matt said.

"Must be. We're finding out a piece at a time."

"We're ready to move folks out when you are, then."

"What about Dr Kim?" Zakko asked.

Trinder trod carefully. "What about her?"

"We can't just leave her here."

Zakko was a nice guy, so good-natured and innocent that Trinder had already imagined how badly everyone would take it if he got killed doing something mindlessly brave, a tendency for which he had form. He'd found Annis Kim sick from an infected wound and stolen antibiotics for her, which nearly earned him a painful dose of Chris's rough justice. He'd hauled Chris to safety under fire when the guy was bleeding out. Trinder should have guessed that he wouldn't turn his back on Kim if he thought something bad was going to happen to her.

But she wasn't Ainatio's problem. Trinder felt uneasy thinking that, but his own people had to come first, and they weren't out of the woods yet.

"Zakko, I think we might have to," he said.

"Can't we just unlock a door somewhere and give her a head start?"

"Let's worry about getting our people out in one piece first." Trinder glanced around, working out where to start. There were about seventy staff split appropriately into two groups on opposite sides of the room, and twenty or so APDU and APS personnel huddled around a few tables in the no man's land between them. "Where are my guys?"

"Silvashko and Eaton are taking their break," Matt said. "Shure's in the john. We can hold this place on our own if you need them elsewhere."

"You're outnumbered," Trinder said.

"Well, we are if we intend to restrain them. But they're still armed. So I'll shoot. We all will."

"I was about to try calming things down with some hearts and minds. Make it easier to walk out of here, maybe."

Matt shrugged. "You can do that, Major, but you could remind them we're pretty pissed off about what they've done to us and we seldom miss."

After eight hours, nerves were already frayed. Ainatio staff had been told to stay in their quarters unless they needed to get food, and they were receiving sitreps even if the messages didn't add much by way of facts, but there was no way of knowing what Pham had been telling his own people before the comms went down. On top of that, some of them had now been cooped up without access to water or a bathroom for most of the day, so they weren't going to be in a receptive frame of mind.

"Sol, can you put me on the public address?" Trinder asked. "Otherwise I'll have to go visit every one of Pham's team in person and repeat myself."

"Let me know when you're ready to roll, Major," Solomon said. "It'll have to be one-way, of course. No signals in."

All things considered, the restaurant was the best place in the complex to be trapped. Folks had access to bathrooms, TV, food, and sofas in the rest area for a nap. The TVs were running a loop of old movies and documentaries, some of which had been made when America was still all busy cities and limitless possibilities. Trinder tried to avoid looking at the world as it used to be. He didn't remember it because it was before his time, but it still felt like a reminder of how much he'd lost. He turned his back to the screens on the wall and walked into the centre of the restaurant.

"Ladies, gentlemen, listen up, please." He clapped his hands to get their attention. "For those of you hearing this on the public address, this is Major Dan Trinder. I don't think any of us wanted to be in this situation, so let's work out how we row back from here without anyone getting hurt. You'll understand that I can't allow Commissioner Pham to take control of this facility, and that's why we've confined all you APS personnel. It's for *everyone's* safety including yours. We're not blaming you for what's happened, but as both the launch rail and one of our ships have now been sabotaged, our lives have been put at risk, and we need to resolve that situation before we can let you go."

Trinder looked at the faces around him. He wasn't sure APS understood, even if they all seemed to speak fluent English, and he couldn't tell how his talk was going down in other parts of the campus. Perhaps he should have put it more bluntly. He felt his mouth drying up.

"I know some of you around the site haven't had food and water for a while, but as soon as you lay down your weapons and behave like guests, we'll give you what you need," he said. "If you pose a threat to anyone here or try to impede our evacuation, though, we *will* respond with armed force. Do you all understand what I've said?"

The APDU huddle, arms folded like it was their regulation posture, just looked grim and unamused. One of them managed a nod.

"Are we hostages?" he asked.

"No, Private, we're just keeping you from doing more damage to us," Trinder said.

"Prisoners, then."

"I suppose you are. And at the moment you're not a superpower with plenty of support, you're forty or so troops and a few unarmed civilians who are outnumbered and outgunned." Damn, should he have said that? It might make them mad and more inclined to fight, not give them the wake-up call he intended. He didn't even have confirmation yet that it was true. "We could open the main gates in minutes, but some of your comrades would get hurt. We'd prefer not to kill teenage conscripts."

"This is why your country collapsed," the private said. "You think everyone's going to be so shamed by your morality that they'll stop being your enemy."

The kid sounded Australian. "We never thought of APS as our enemy before," Trinder said. "But if that's how you see us, we'll bear it in mind."

Trinder had surprised himself again. That was the kind of thing he'd always wished he'd said but had only thought of hours later. The young private fell silent. Trinder hoped he'd established some kind of psychological advantage and kept going.

"Okay, then, Ainatio staff," he said. "If we can't repair the rail, we have to face the prospect of finding a new home here on Earth, and in the light of what's happened, some of you might want to change your decision about whether you leave with us or ask APS for resettlement. If you do, contact Alex Gorko or Captain Fonseca, but do it soon. Now, does anyone have questions? I imagine our APS guests will want to know why they've lost their comms."

Trinder watched faces around the restaurant. He didn't need to be a mind reader to see what they were thinking. The APS folks were wondering how the hell they'd been cut off. The staff who'd opted to go with APS were starting to doubt if they'd be welcome or even safe there now. The ones who'd decided to leave Earth were imagining a future as permanent refugees in a wasteland, and thinking APS might not be so bad after all. Trinder decided not to mention the possibility of a more secure life in Britain. He realised he'd probably made APS look the better bet. Maybe it was.

Another APDU private half-raised his hand. "Have you actively blocked our comms?"

"Yes." Pham would know already or he'd work it out in moments. There was nobody else with an immediate motive for doing it or an AI that could make it happen. "We've shut down some of your systems to stop you launching an air strike while we evacuate. You've already sabotaged our mission, so we can't give you the benefit of the doubt."

"Air strike?" the private asked. "Do you mean from *Temujin*? Or from one of our bases? Because the only way you could shut down the air force is to bomb it out of existence."

One of the female technicians spoke up. "But how did you shut down comms? Have you attacked targets in Asia?"

"We haven't bombed anything, ma'am," Trinder said. "But I'd like to remind you that you attacked us first."

"You cut us off because you don't want us to see news reports."

"We've blocked all inbound signals as a precaution." Trinder hated himself right away for saying it. He was justifying himself to these kids. He should have told them to go fuck themselves. Maybe they were right: the restraint Trinder thought of as civilised was really weakness. "You can't be surprised that we're protecting ourselves. A couple of weeks ago, you told us we had forty-eight hours to evacuate before you dropped sodium bombs on us."

Another tech looked up from his coffee. "They were never going to do it," he said.

Trinder tried to hang onto what he'd thought was his psychological edge. "If you're saying it was a bluff to gain access to this facility, we worked that out for ourselves."

"No, it was never going to happen," the guy repeated. "Because they can't get — "

The APDU private sitting next to him punched him hard in the shoulder, looking furious. Trinder wouldn't have been surprised if APS had been bluffing because it had run short of hardware, but they'd still managed to take out a ship in orbit and bring Nomad to a halt. He refused to let himself start thinking that the sabcode had been a massive overreaction to a threat that didn't exist. If it had, it was too bad.

"I think our respective military capabilities will come as a mutual surprise when the dust settles," he said. "We don't want to harm any of you. If we wanted an easy life, we could have shot you all by now. But right now we have sixteen hundred civilians who need somewhere safe to go. You'll all go home eventually. We want to make sure we can too."

"No, you've nuked us," the private said. "That's why the comms are down."

"We're not exactly a nuclear power," Trinder said. "But if a handful of us stopped you attacking us, what does that say about APS's limitations?"

It might have been the message their politicians pumped out, that APS was under constant threat. But they weren't far wrong about the willingness to use nukes. Solomon had only ruled out a missile attack because he couldn't sustain it, and Trinder hadn't objected to the idea in principle. His small tribe was facing annihilation. Any means of self-defence became fair game.

The APDU and APS guys were scared, angry, and oddly polite. Now it looked like they were working through a list of speculation that had occupied their last eight hours. Questions erupted.

"What's happened to *Temujin*?"

"Yeah, even if the comms are down, they'd fly someone in to check on us."

"Have you sunk her?"

"Where's Commissioner Pham now? Why can't we use our comms within this site?"

"When are you going to let us go?"

"Ainatio's got working comms. Can't we call our families and check they're okay?"

"It's more than not having a signal. My screen's bricked."

"Yeah, my radio is, too. What have you done?

Trinder had set out to look like the nice guy they should nevertheless fear but the session had become an insight into what APS feared most. They'd assumed the worst. The world they were permanently connected to had vanished and the only thing they could imagine was that it had been destroyed. The problem was that Trinder couldn't be sure yet that it hadn't.

"We haven't fired a single missile," Trinder said. "And as soon as it's safe to do so — safe for us, that is — you can call home."

Had he lied? It looked like the sabcode had hit civilian telcos as well. He could hand these kids his personal screen now and they still wouldn't be able to get through to their home numbers. And would there ever be a safe time to do it? Everything hung on the state of the launch rail.

The room had now fallen silent. Maybe some of the troops realised they'd given away useful information. But Trinder got the feeling some them had worked out they were screwed, and that Pham had gotten them into this. Then one of them asked the awkward question.

"Major Trinder, did your AI do this?"

Trinder decided he didn't owe anyone the truth, but he did owe Sol his support. "No, we did it," he said. "We make the decisions. Our AI does as we ask. So if Commissioner Pham's been telling you we've got another Earthmother here, an AI that's out of control, he's wrong."

Trinder didn't know yet what he'd just claimed responsibility for. If the sabcode was causing widespread chaos and passenger planes were falling out of the sky, he'd just put his name to criminal acts. Once again it occurred to him that trying to be human and reasonable was a mistake, because here he was, a man responsible for the lives of sixteen hundred stranded people, trying to get the bloc that had put them in danger to believe him.

"Okay, we're finished here," he said. "If you stay out of our way and don't attempt further sabotage or attacks on us, you'll all go home. You might not be responsible for what's happened so far, but we *will* hold you responsible for endangering civilians if you interfere with the evacuation."

Nobody said another word. They either didn't think they'd get an answer or they were stunned by the realisation that a handful of people in a town that wasn't even on the map had put a dent in the most powerful military and political bloc left on Earth. They'd probably been told it would be a quick and easy babysitting mission and that they'd be back on board *Temujin* in no time. Pham had thought that too. So had Trinder.

Matt gave him a knowing wink as he walked out. "And Pham had to listen to all that without having the last word. Nice."

"They knew we'd get our people out sooner or later," Trinder said. "Now they know our rules of engagement."

Trinder walked back to the security office. Deserted corridors that had already become eerie were now even more creepy. There was nobody moving around at all.

"Sol," he said. "Are you there? Tell me there isn't a bomber squadron inbound."

"I'm always here, Major."

"Well?"

"I don't have confirmation yet, but you managed to get them to tell us that *Temujin*'s not only out of contact but can't launch aircraft. And it sounded to me like they couldn't or wouldn't use nuclear weapons. Your interrogation technique's very stealthy."

"I wasn't being clever, Sol. I screwed up."

"That's your perspective. But while we don't have absolute confirmation yet, I think I can speculate that it's not lack of GPS that's kept their aircraft on the deck, because they're close enough to navigate without it if they tried. It means that their hardware's been damaged, just like the Fiddler."

"Now that's interesting."

"Isn't it."

"Marc? Chris? Thoughts?"

"Time to crack on with it," Marc said. Trinder was expecting a verdict on how he'd handled the meeting, but perhaps Marc felt Trinder didn't need reassurance. "They've still got two helicopters parked outside the wire. I'm going to wander over and see if they'll start."

"I kept expecting some of the troops on the gate to come out to check them, but they haven't," Chris said. "Pham's special forces, too. But maybe it's too visible and he's got other plans."

"And the pilots are locked in the restaurant," Solomon said. "So even functioning helicopters wouldn't help. Unless Pham's missing operator is a pilot as well, and then there'd have to be a point in heading back to *Temujin*. If the carrier's systems are down, there's no real advantage."

Trinder didn't want to say it and tempt fate, but he felt things were still looking up. When he arrived back in the office, Luce and Simonot were watching the Russian news.

"Great timing, boss," Luce said. "Check out the breaking news crawler."

Trinder took a moment to focus. There it was, the first evidence that the sabcode had reached targets in Asia. The headline working its way across the bottom of the screen read POWER CUTS BRING CITIES ACROSS ASIA, AUSTRALIA, NZ TO A STANDSTILL, NEWS OFF THE AIR.

Trinder shut his eyes for a moment. He felt slightly sick. *We just did that. Ordinary people are going to suffer.* "Please let that mean APDU as well."

"It's starting to bite," Solomon said. "Although not in the order I'd have bet upon. I really hoped there was no bridge between the shepherd and civilian systems, but there was no way of checking, and I'd still have had to release the sabcode."

"Is that bothering you?"

"Of course it is. The day that it doesn't, I won't be a moral entity."

"Regret never helps anyone," Luce said. "Alex is messaging everyone to confirm or change their choices about resettlement, by the way. Frankly, I'm surprised there's anyone willing to trust Pham now. But there you go."

Trinder settled back into his office chair to wait for the few words on the crawler to be fleshed out into facts. Jake Mendoza had left a small pharmacy envelope on Trinder's desk marked WAKEY WAKEY. He seemed to be expecting a long night.

"I hate taking those things," Luce said. "When I finally get some sleep, they give me nightmares."

"Yeah, it's my last resort too." Trinder opened the envelope and counted the tablets. "But I've got a full tank of adrenaline, caffeine, and cookies to keep me going for a few more hours yet."

He went back to watching the news. It took a couple of minutes for the coverage to switch back to the headlines. The top story was air traffic and power stations being affected across APS — not everywhere, but all the main centres of population — and all flights had been grounded. There were aerial images of morning traffic log-jammed on highways, shots that Russian news could record and transmit but APS channels couldn't.

"What does it tell you if the traffic's stopped, Sol?" Trinder asked.

"Either vehicles' connections to the smartroad have been infected and their electronics are damaged, or the charging strips have lost power and the vehicles have run flat." Solomon's tone sounded subdued. "The air traffic shutdown is significant, though, because a lot of their ATCs are either run by the military or connected to them."

"So we've grounded APS."

"Very possibly. I still need proof."

The news from Asia was coming in short chunks and had suddenly become repetitive. Trinder interpreted that as a sign the reporters and drones were doing the same as he was right now: piecing together scraps of information that were dripping out and trying to make a coherent picture out of it. If civilian comms had been hit as well, the channels were dependent on reporters actually observing rather than relaying statements from government agencies. Getting at the real picture was going to take time.

"I think we should grab the time we've got and start on clearing this place," Trinder said.

"I'm still waiting for a call back," Marc said.

Trinder switched to British news. They had similar headlines to the Russian channel. At least they'd have some context for Marc's request now. "Your Foreign Office pal?"

"Yeah. That'll make a difference to how fast and how far we have to run if the rail's not fixable. Let me put in another call. And he's not my pal. He's just a name I latched onto."

Trinder couldn't see what difference that would make to moving people out, but facts made for better decisions. They were already making too many assumptions. He could wait a little longer. He poured another coffee and sat back with his eyes shut, trying to order his thoughts. If the APDU air force really was grounded and also unable to track other air traffic, it might make an evacuation to Britain much less fraught and possibly secret.

"Major," Solomon said quietly, "Del Barrett's going to call you."

Maybe that secret airlift wouldn't be needed. If the rail repair had been impossible, Sol would already know and he would have said so. Trinder began to see a faint light at the end of the tunnel and imagined the peaceful moment when he was sealed in cryo and starting to fade into a very long sleep. He'd know he'd succeeded, even if he was crapping himself about the prospect of not waking up again.

"Major, this is Del Barrett."

That was the voice he most wanted to hear. "What did you find, Del?"

"We've completed an initial survey, so it's clearer now what we'll need to do, but obviously we might find more that we need to fix as we go," Barrett said. "I'll cut to the chase. We can probably repair the rail, but all being well, it'll take at least a couple of months."

It wasn't the worst news Trinder could hear, but it was close. "Damn, Del, I'm not sure if we've got that long."

"If I thought we could do it faster, I'd say so."

"Sorry. I know. Carry on."

"Just so you get the big picture, it isn't like a maglev system. The replacement parts will have to be manufactured from scratch, and the only way we can source the materials is reclaiming them from around the site."

"Go ahead, then." *A couple of months.* Trinder put on his most positive voice. It was hard. "We'll keep APDU off your backs."

"Yeah, but we're going to need to cannibalise other machinery to get the materials we need, and that'll take time too."

"Okay."

"It's the best we can do."

"I know. We'll have to live with that."

"Dan, I just want to be sure we're on the same page. You're agreeing to repairs that'll take eight weeks plus, with a possibility we can't find enough of the rare materials we need, followed by at least a week of launch tests before we risk a passenger flight. So at best, three months."

Trinder felt any opinion he offered would be a guess or gut feel. Barrett was checking what he was agreeing to because he thought APS would be sufficiently recovered by then to show up for some payback.

"Yes, I understand," he said. "Marc? Chris? Alex? Did you get all that? Yes or no?"

Alex got his vote in first. "Do it."

"Yeah, crack on with it," Marc said. "And the evacuation. We'll be running plans A and B in parallel. We'll find out in the next few days which one we should continue with."

"I'm in," Chris said.

Solomon had to be aware of the detail. Data from the engineering bots that would make all these parts ended up on his virtual desk.

"Sol?" Trinder asked.

"It's going to be very hard but we can't afford not to try," he said. "I agree with you, Major."

Barrett made an *uh-uh* noise that might have been disapproval or resigned acceptance. "We'll make a start now. Can we co-opt some help?"

"Tell me who you need," Alex said. This was the job he'd done for years before most people knew Nomad existed. He fixed things. He managed projects. "Dan, you can leave this to me now. You'll have enough on your plate with the security side."

Trinder put the envelope of pills in his shirt pocket and looked up at Luce and Simonot. The news channels were now showing scenes of a hospital wheeling out mobile generators, real antiques that ran on vehicle fuels. Simonot was glued to the bank of monitors. Luce shrugged.

"We've been in worse situations," he said. "And lived to tell the tale."

Trinder couldn't think of one, but it was a lie worth hanging onto.

* * *

TEMPORARY LANDING ZONE, 100 YARDS OUTSIDE AINATIO PARK RESEARCH CENTRE: 2145 HOURS EDT.

"I wondered what had happened to you, Mr Gallagher. How are you getting along with APS?"

His name was Lawson, and he wasn't the kind of Foreign Office drone who'd usually get hauled out of bed in the early hours. This bloke was a twenty-four-carat mandarin. That explained why Marc had had to call twice. The minions obviously decided it was above their pay grade and had gone to find the boss.

Marc carried on flipping switches on the control panel of one of APDU's dead helicopters. "I'll admit I've had more rewarding relationships," he said. "Things are a bit tense. We ended up locking them in. Including Commissioner Pham."

"It's wonderful the things you can get away with when you're not a nation. I envy you your lack of need for diplomacy."

"Well, it was over sabotage. Not exactly something you can resolve over a glass of sherry. We're trying to fix the damage now."

"The problems in Asia at the moment wouldn't be anything to do with you, would they?"

"What makes you ask?"

"Because it looks to us like an extraordinarily comprehensive cyberkinetic attack."

"You'll have to fill me in," Marc said. "All we can see from here is their comms are borked. And I'm playing with a dead APDU helo right now."

"Telco networks are down, power grids out, roads at a standstill, flights grounded, air force activity zero. And no military signals traffic at all. Catastrophic outages. That's the price of supranational networks. Especially ones that have links to military systems, like their air traffic control."

Marc hoped Solomon was taking notes. "And you think we can do all that, do you?"

"I'm sure you're aware that hijacking satellites is well within the range of the disgruntled and poorly funded," Lawson said. "But whatever this is, it's getting into every crack and ripping through anything that's connected. That's sophisticated and expensive work."

They hadn't answered each other's questions at all, but Marc was sure they both knew what the other wasn't saying. He could only hope that Lawson didn't already know about Sol. It felt all wrong trying to outmanoeuvre his own team's intelligence operation.

"You've got people on the ground, then," Marc said.

"People like yourself, yes. And embassy staff. Sadly, we've been unable to lend APS any alternative routing on the comms front, which won't help diplomatic relations in the future, but you can't be too careful. Digital drawbridges have been pulled up. I take it you haven't been affected."

Marc knew Lawson was fishing. "We're borked too, to be honest. Not a virus, but a serious problem."

"You mentioned sabotage."

"Yeah. If we can't fix some launch hardware and get clear before APS recovers some long-range capability, the next thing we know they'll be paying us a visit from thirty thousand feet. And we've got nearly sixteen hundred civvies with nowhere safe to run."

Marc hated conversations like this. He didn't know when he'd stray over the line into evading or denying what Lawson already knew that he knew. Maybe they'd passed that point already and Lawson had just given him a chance to come clean about everything.

"These are the same people APS were going to bomb, yes?" Lawson asked.

"Correct."

"US citizens, if the country still existed."

"Yes, but enough high value ones to make it worth caring about people who aren't our responsibility."

"We do have hearts, Mr Gallagher."

"I believe you, but feel free to ask what's in it for Britain."

"I'm sure you already have."

"Okay, the evacuees include a few hundred useful boffins. I can give you a personnel list so you can check you're not importing trouble or die-back. But you might also be interested in Ainatio's research on FTL communications."

"Go on."

"I assume you know what I'm talking about. I'd be disappointed if Spook Central didn't eavesdrop on those conversations between APS and their agent here."

"We were briefed," Lawson said, still cryptic. Yeah, the spooks were earning their keep. "Can you get hold of this research?"

Marc could feel the memory card almost burning a hole in his wallet. "I can."

"Does Ainatio have a working relay?"

"Not any more." Marc also had to assume that Lawson knew *Cabot* was intact and that he'd want to make the most of having a ready-made ex-RN crew running Opis. "The CEO trashed the hardware here before she left. But the data still exists, and APS has a copy, so you'll want one too."

"And you need a humanitarian airlift."

"It's a distinct possibility. Any interesting reports from Kingdom in the past twenty-four hours about events in Earth orbit?"

"Space is always interesting, Mr Gallagher."

"Explosions. That sort of thing."

"It rings a bell."

"Well, that saves me explaining. The engineers might be able to get the mission back on track, but if they can't, a lot of innocent civvies are going to have a really bad winter, including all those useful scientists. They come as a complete package, by the way. No cherry-picking."

Marc wondered if he'd said too much. No, he didn't have time to haggle over this like some fake Persian rug. The government either wanted this research or they didn't. If the spooks had already skimmed the data, they wouldn't even tell him.

Lawson went silent for a while. He might have been consulting someone or just thinking. Marc carried on trying to work his way around the controls of the helicopter, tracking his flashlight across the instrument panel and flicking toggles. He couldn't even turn on the lights. Maybe that was a good sign.

"When will you know if the damage is repairable?" Lawson asked. "I have a lot of questions, but let's start with that."

"It's more a matter of how long it'll take," Marc said. "We'd like to be long gone before APDU's mobile again."

"Anything else I should know?"

Marc threw in a few bones to distract Lawson while he tried to stay off the obvious topic. "I think Tim Pham is doing his asset-stripping and sabotage off the books. Probably not in the mood to share FTL with the rest of APS."

"Very wise," Lawson said. "We wouldn't if we were him. Let me consult a few people and I'll get back to you within the hour."

"Thank you."

"One question, though," Lawson said. "If things work out, and you manage to launch the ship, are you really going with these people?"

"Yes."

"You're heading for a planet with no idea what's waiting for you at the other end. Or if you'll even get there."

"Yes. Isn't that what British men always did to build the empire? Minus the interplanetary bit, of course."

"Commendable, but why?"

"I've had nothing better to do with my life for the last eight years," Marc said. "It's as good a way to go as any."

Marc hated himself for using his boys as cover for evading questions, but then he realised it was exactly what he felt. He wasn't confiding in Lawson. He just didn't care what he thought about it.

"I'm glad we had this conversation, Mr Gallagher." Lawson sounded uncomfortable. He'd obviously pulled Marc's file and knew what he was dealing with. "Stand by for an answer."

Marc sat back in the pilot's seat and replayed the conversation in his head. Maybe he should have told Lawson the truth about the sabcode and said it was an automatic defence system, no mention of Solomon at all, just in case someone was tempted to plug back into APS again. But he still didn't know how much Lawson already knew. The man hadn't asked the most important question: if the government said no to an airlift, would Marc withhold the FTL research? It must have crossed Lawson's mind, but maybe he assumed Marc would do the patriotic thing and hand it over anyway. Yes, Marc would, unless he had an overwhelming reason not to. He didn't want to be seen as the kind of bloke who'd hide critical research from his besieged country. But it was hard to look at those families in Kill Line and feel okay about waving goodbye and leaving them to it. He'd have to stay with them and sort something out.

He realised he was doing exactly what John and Greg had done. He was getting involved in another country's problems and thinking it was his duty to solve them. Perhaps that was the example he'd set his sons. He wished he'd taught them something different.

"Did you hear all that, Sol? The FCO thinks the air force is grounded."

Marc went back to trying the helicopter's controls, remembering what he'd seen pilots do. The two Lammergeier pilots could have tested it in seconds, but he didn't want them within range of APDU rifles.

"Thank you, Marc." Solomon didn't say he'd been listening but it was hard for him to avoid it. "I think we'll have to settle for that as confirmation. Of course, it would only take one long-range aircraft to escape the sabcode to ruin our plans, but if Pham's operating covertly, he's forfeited whatever emergency assistance might be available."

"Yeah. Been there, had that problem."

"I'm glad the sabcode didn't affect Britain. But your relations with APS are going to be strained in years to come."

Marc shrugged. "We weren't best mates to start with. If everyone trusted each other, we wouldn't all have our own satellites duplicating GPS and stuff. We've been here before. Okay, not as big and serious as *your* cyber shit, but we know the dangers of being too connected. We go it alone. We like it that way."

"I'm sorry. But you know the sabcode was all I had left."

At least Sol was honest. He'd learned that he couldn't save everybody, and even if he cared it didn't make any difference. Marc walked across to the other helicopter and repeated the ritual of master switch, navigation lights, and radio. Nothing lit up.

"Dead," he said. "No electrical power at all."

"I could destroy both aircraft if you think that's advisable."

Marc took a look at the front gates with the zoom on his pocket screen. The troops were still out there, some of them clutching their radios, but most of the technicians had disappeared. They'd probably found places to bed down for the night. They were lucky it was summer.

"I don't think we need to," Marc said. "Not yet, anyway."

"I'm still looking for Pham's operator. I should be able to spot him on infrared."

"You won't," Marc said. "If he's any good, he'll have sprayed an IR block on himself and his kit."

"I'll have to try other wavelengths, then."

"And he'll probably still have short-range radio because it doesn't use the sat net. So if he's in contact with Pham, he'll have to come within five hundred metres or thereabouts."

"I should be able to detect radio emissions."

"Just remember that he's probably looking for you as well."

"What are you planning to do now?"

"We'll hear if we've got a ride out of here in an hour, or so Lawson said. I'm just going to watch and wait until then. If he comes back and says we can move out in a day or two, there's less pressure to evacuate." Marc opened the secure circuit on his screen. "Alex, have we got billets sorted out for all the Ainatio staff yet?"

"Done and dusted," Alex said. "Just waiting on a couple of people to make up their minds."

"How about you? Have you changed yours?"

"Of course I have. Nobody in their right mind would trust APS now and I don't have any scientific expertise to make me worth treating right."

"So the remnant still want resettlement."

"Yeah, they don't want to be evacuated. I think they're trying hard not to look like the enemy."

"Well, they're adults and they've made their choice," Marc said.

"Maybe they'd change their minds if they knew they had a chance of going to Britain."

"You'll have to ask them all again, then, but one of the reasons for giving the FCO a list was numbers. If we're going to have an extra hundred people, we need to tell Lawson before they commit aircraft."

Considering how few options there were, the whole situation was still up in the air and hinged entirely on how long it took APS to recover. Marc was still hoping that he'd be on *Shackleton* in a couple of weeks and heading away from all this shit in frozen oblivion. Going back home would bring its own set of problems. He checked his watch, went back to his Caracal, and sat watching the Russian news, but he realised he was more concerned about what was happening in Fiji. He tapped the name into the search box in case he'd missed an earlier report and came up empty. He wished he'd asked Lawson. Whatever APS said, Fiji was still a Commonwealth country as far as the British government was concerned, and the FCO would keep tabs on it.

But more news was dripping out now. A reporter was grilling a hapless APDU spokesminion who described the attack as a power outage. All aircraft had been grounded as a safety precaution, she said. Now Sol had his definitive answer. The Russian put a question to the woman about rumours of equipment in planes being fried as well, but she sidestepped it and started talking about the problems facing the emergency services trying to handle crises without comms. Marc knew collateral damage was inevitable, but it was a bit more real now. He stopped himself thinking about it and switched to British news before realising that unsettled him on a whole different level. And waiting had never got any easier.

Solomon would be keeping an eye on the news. It made more sense for Marc to watch the drone feeds and see if he could find

Pham's special forces guy. After a few minutes, he picked up a vehicle approaching from the direction of Kill Line. Chris drew up beside him in another Caracal. He opened Marc's passenger door and got in.

"So we're waiting for the Foreign Office response," he said.

"Yeah."

Chris fiddled with the dashboard controls. "It might not make any difference in the end, but if we know for sure we won't be here when APS gets back on its feet or some other country lends them a bomber, we can approach the job differently."

"What, more violently?" Marc asked. "Pham's still going to want payback, except he'll come after Britain."

"I meant that maybe we should make nice with the kids on the gate in case we're not rescued, so they're less motivated to mow us down if and when they finally catch up with us. Or shoot the Ainatio staff who are left. Or abandon them here when they finally leave. That's what's worrying Dan."

"No reason why we can't keep it civilised."

Chris went quiet for a while. He wasn't a talkative bloke so he'd probably used up all his words for the next few years already.

"And I thought I'd solved the shuttle problem, but Sol shot it down," he said.

"Why?"

"*Shackleton*'s got three fifteen-seater shuttles on board to transfer people to Opis, so I said how about using them instead of the big shuttles, because they don't need a rail to take off. But apparently moving supplies and people would be more than a hundred round trips and some stuff wouldn't even fit in the cargo bays. It was all designed on the basis of the heavy lift being done from the Opis end. Personally, I'd still risk it, but there you go. I don't know enough. I'm guessing my way through this."

Marc hadn't thought about the shuttles. "We all are, mate. Calling the FCO for help might not work out either."

"Have you sent your contact the evacuee data?"

Marc knew what Chris was really asking. He had a prison record and he must have considered that the FCO could stop him entering the country.

"Just names and occupations," Marc said. "No small detail yet. I was going to send the only remaining bits of your army service record from Erskine's files. Any other information I know absolutely nothing about would be under a pile of rubble in some town I couldn't find on a map."

Chris almost smiled. "Harrisburg."

"Yeah, wherever. When they ask, I'll have a vague recollection that you were a prison officer. Something like that. That's how you know so much about doing time. But all the records are gone. Failed state and all that."

Chris folded and unfolded his arms as if he didn't know what to do with them. "Thanks," he said. "I've got your back as well."

"Okay, you want me to do some diplomacy with the troops?"

"I'll do it. It was my dumbass idea."

"No, I'll make a better job of it."

"If this had been a few years ago, I wouldn't have thought twice," Chris said. "I'd have given them a count of ten to clear the gates, and if they didn't, I'd open fire. Maybe I shouldn't give them the benefit of the doubt."

"Pile of bodies. Eventual retribution. Remember?"

"I don't want you ending up like Jamie because of me."

"I'm wearing body armour. The good stuff."

"Not on your head, though."

"Chris, if they get arsey and start shooting, we can go for the pile of bodies option. If you're that worried, stand back and cover me."

Chris got on the radio to warn Trinder they were coming while Marc started the Caracal and rolled towards the gate at supermarket car park speed. He was fairly confident he could sergeant-talk the kids into cooperating. The gates and the last fifty yards of the approach road were brightly lit and he was coming at them head-on, so they had time to check out the Caracal. He pulled up just short of the pool of white light and opened the door.

"Piece of cake," he said.

He started walking slowly towards the gates with his arms held clear of his sides, then glanced back for a second. Chris was talking, probably on the radio to Trinder. Marc hoped Trinder's guys didn't come out of the entrance behind the APDU troops and panic them. Anyone who'd been on sentry duty for nine or ten hours would be getting threadbare even if they had food and water, and these lads probably hadn't eaten since breakfast.

They were already positioned to block entry because they couldn't lock the gates while Trinder still had control of the system. Force was the only way they were going to stop Marc coming in. That was probably Pham's gamble. He must have thought it wasn't fear of a firefight that had stopped Ainatio hosing the sentries from a safe distance, but a reluctance to mow down kids. The bastard was a master tactician. He looked for weakness and played on it. But he was pushing his luck if he thought Chris and his militia had the same rules of engagement as Dan Trinder.

Marc was about ten yards out when a couple of troops slowly raised their rifles and aimed. They wouldn't miss at this range. One lad just looked alert and doing his job, but the one next to him looked too nervous for Marc's liking.

Marc just kept going. There was nothing in his earpiece now but silence.

"Halt," one of the kids yelled.

Marc slowed down but didn't quite stop. "I want to have a word with you," he said. "I really don't want to shoot anyone."

He saw fast movement out the corner of his eye and had already brought his rifle to the front to fire when he realised one of their equally young corporals had run in. The lad yelled something at the nervous-looking kid and strode straight up to him to grab the muzzle and force his rifle down. Whatever he'd said, it made the others stand down too. Marc ambled up to the gates, wondering how close a call he'd had. The corporal stood behind the wire mesh section of the outer gate, looking awkward as if he wanted to ask Marc in for tea but didn't dare defy his dad.

"I'm Marc Gallagher," Marc said. "And I don't want to see Tim Pham. I want to talk to *you*."

"I'm Corporal Barry Cho," the kid said. He had a strong Aussie accent. "And I know who you are."

Every man reached a time when anyone under twenty-five looked too young to do the jobs they'd done themselves at the same age, but this kid really did look like a child. It was his skin. It was even smoother than most women's, almost porcelain. Marc couldn't remember ever looking that young and unblemished.

"Well, it's nice of Mr Pham to point me out to you," Marc said. "Look, I think we can sort this without anyone needing to get shot. I know you're all worried about what's happening back home. We're worried too. We've got sixteen hundred civilians, minus whoever wants to stay with APS. The oldest is eighty-seven and the youngest is six months old, and if we can't get *Shackleton* launched, I don't think either of them are going to survive long living rough when we evacuate the town."

Cho glanced over his shoulder at the others, then looked Marc straight in the eye.

"What do you want to talk about?" he asked. "I don't have radio contact with Commissioner Pham or the officers and senior NCOs now. So whatever I say might be worthless when they're back in the loop."

Marc liked his honesty. "Corporal, we're going to take our people out of here. We need to leave the area before your air force comes back with sodium bombs. That was the deal, remember? Pham postponed the bombing to give us time to launch *Shackleton*. If we can't repair the sabotage, all we can do is try to get as far away as we can. So I'm asking you and your lads to stand back and let us pass."

Marc could see the nervous private in his peripheral vision. He didn't look any calmer and he still had a white-knuckled grip on his rifle. Cho seemed to be thinking over the prospect of trying to hold the gate.

"We had orders," Cho said. "It doesn't matter that I can't see the point of it. Or that we know we won't last five minutes if you and your mates decide you're coming in anyway."

"Pham thinks we won't shoot youngsters," Marc said.

"But you will."

"Only if you shoot first."

Cho looked past him for a moment, first out through the gates, then to either side. The other troops were looking around too. They'd seen something. Cho looked resigned.

"Yeah, we're not daft," he said. "You could drop us all right now. So where do we go from here?"

When Marc followed where they were looking, there were pinpoints of light in the twilight. It was hard to see with the fierce white security lights flooding the gates, but the penny dropped. He was looking at a couple of dozen tactical lights mounted on rifles, maybe more, all of them aimed at the front gates. Nobody in their right mind would be using lights like that, not unless they really wanted to be noticed, but that meant they obviously did.

Marc pressed his earpiece. "Is that you, Chris?"

"Just to focus minds," Chris said. "Everyone's got an APDU guy in their sights. So the twitchy ones know not to try anything with you."

So it was Chris's militia. Marc knew some of them had been near the perimeter doing a recce for a worst-case scenario with the evacuation, but Chris must have moved in a few more. They were letting Cho know they were there. Then the pinpoints blinked out and the area beyond the gate lights was in darkness again.

"They were worried you'd shoot me," Marc said. "But I can see we understand each other."

"I don't suppose you'd tell me if there was going to be an air strike." Cho seemed to be edging closer to his real question. "Some guys think you've dropped a nuke on an APS capital or two."

Marc did him the courtesy of talking soldier to soldier. "I'm not going to bullshit you, mate. Your boss wrecked our launch rail and buggered our ship. We just want to make sure you don't bomb us before we get the chance to leave."

"I don't think he wants to kill you," Cho said. "Just stop you leaving Earth with that AI of yours."

Marc shrugged. "Where else are we going to go?"

"You've still got comms, haven't you? Nobody's telling us anything and we don't know whether it's just tech problems or if our families are charcoal."

Marc felt a slight shiver, the kind you got when a wild thought you'd kept to yourself emerged from someone else's mouth as a distinct possibility. He actually didn't know what Solomon was capable of, let alone what he'd unleashed by accident. Solomon probably didn't know either. The AI had had a century of training exercises, but now he was fighting his first real battle where people ended up dead. It wasn't impossible to believe he'd triggered a nuclear strike against a city after all. But the news channels would have noticed by now. Marc decided to scotch the rumour for everyone's good.

"From what I saw on the Russian news, it's not a nuclear attack," he said. "It's what Major Trinder said it was. A big power outage and loss of satellites. But you know that, because you can't use your screens."

"Okay," Cho said. "So if we stand back and let you get your people out, everybody gets to go home eventually."

"Yeah. And we don't want to leave you locked up, either, because we don't know when APS is going to be able to send help. So if we can agree to steer clear of each other, we'll unlock the place when we leave."

"It'd be easier to just shoot us."

"Yeah, you're lucky we're not lazy buggers. You're worried about your family, yeah?"

"My dad and my sister in Sydney. West Ryde."

"If Australia had been nuked, I think I'd know. The Foreign Office would tell me."

"You're that important, then."

"Not really. I'm just their go-between. But we do still have a soft spot for the old Commonwealth. Do you want me to find out about West Ryde? What's the address?"

Cho looked wary. "What's the catch?"

"There isn't one." Marc searched in his pockets. When he put his hand inside his heavily-laden vest to see if he had any sealed snacks, some of the troops behind Cho flinched. "But I was in your dad's position once."

There was no point in saying any more about it. It would only have sounded contrived. He found a few high-energy bars and handed them to Cho along with his water bottle. He considered the possibility that the kid was one of Pham's inner circle trying to smarm his way in, but he'd seen enough genuinely scared people to know when it was real. Agents could be scared shitless as well, though.

Cho examined the rations. There was no print on the wrappers because Ainatio didn't need to meet anyone's regulations or worry about customer complaints. "I ought to ask if this is drugged."

"Nah. Like you said, it's easier to shoot you."

"Well, thank you. We're getting pretty hungry now."

"If you promise not to open fire, we'll drop some more off later."

"Thanks, but it probably won't change what Commissioner Pham thinks."

"I know. But I'll feel better."

"Okay, the address. It's fifty-seven Ridge Avenue. My sister's twelve. She's disabled. Dad works part-time so he can look after her."

Marc took out his paper notebook and wrote down the address. "Got it. Yeah, I know it must be hard. I'd be worried too. How old are you? People ask me that as well, by the way. I'm not being patronising."

"Eighteen. Nineteen in November. I was conscripted straight from the school cadet force. We've got a lot of border to patrol and not enough recruits. We never expected to be doing this, though."

Teens could be competent soldiers and history was full of boys who stepped up to be men before their time, but all Marc could see for a moment was the woman from the MoD standing at his front door with that stricken look on her face.

"Yeah, well, make sure you live to see twenty," Marc said. "And preferably ninety-nine."

Cho looked down at his boots for a moment like an awkward schoolboy. "I hope you get where you want to go."

"I meant what I said. If I find out anything, I'll get a message to you."

"Okay," Cho said. "And when you decide to storm the place, you'll expect us to be outgunned and have to surrender. Or maybe we back off because you'll kill Commissioner Pham if we don't. Or both."

Now that was a bloody good idea. Cho understood how to play the game. That kid would go far. "You never know," Marc said. "It sounds very feasible to me."

It didn't hurt to make a friend on the inside. And if Cho turned out to be Pham's nark, then he'd be a different kind of useful. But Marc had done it for entirely different reasons. He caught a glimpse of one of the troops trying to get a signal on his screen again. It looked like his personal device, covered in cartoon stickers. He was probably desperate to call home to check that home was still there at all.

Marc imagined his own sons doing that. It wasn't what he needed to have in his head right now, and he tried to shut it out, but like all painful images it just got more insistent the more he tried not to think about it. But it wouldn't stop him doing what he had to. It just hurt to watch.

He turned around, which was an act of faith in itself. A round could punch through the back of his skull before any of Chris's people got a shot off. But he reached the Caracal intact. Chris was leaning against the door, gazing up at the clear evening sky like he was looking for divine guidance, and right away he was the nicely brought-up young vicar again. He looked like God had confided in him.

"You're going to think I'm a bastard," he said, "but if this turns ugly, we put them down, right?"

"Yeah." Marc nodded. "Of course we will."

Marc hoped Cho stayed out of the way if it came to it. For all he knew, the kid could have been a keen serial killer in his spare time, but Marc respected his composure. He also felt for him and his dad.

"Are you really going to drop off supplies?" Chris asked. "I heard most of the conversation. I told Dan you were bribing the enemy. He said he might try it as well."

"Just because I chat to them doesn't mean I've gone soft," Marc said.

"Good. And I didn't think you were going soft."

"But you did, because you asked. And I don't blame you. I'd think the same. But I don't stand back and let people shoot me just because they're kids and someone killed mine."

Chris didn't even blink. "Have I pissed you off?"

"No. But I don't want it to be the thing everybody thinks but nobody mentions. I'm glad we said exactly what we meant."

Chris nodded. "Okay. We're good."

Marc drove off. Chris was silent. It was like the conversation hadn't happened and they'd never spoken about the awkward things they wanted and didn't want. On the way back to Kill Line, Marc's screen pinged and he fished it out of his pocket for a quick look while he tried to keep his eyes on the road.

"Foreign Office," he said. He'd expected the promise of a response within the hour to turn into two or three, but whatever they'd decided, they done it fast. "Chris, read this out to me, would you?"

Chris took the screen from him and studied it with a slight frown. "*Mr Gallagher,*" he read. "*I've taken advice, and if and when required, we can send four Saxon J-Three transport aircraft. We'd require twelve hours' notice. Much of your runway appears to be intact, and we would attempt to land there if you can secure the area. We will make every effort to assist your refugees and we will of course repatriate you if you wish, regardless of their decision. Please see the options attached. Thank you for the list of those seeking resettlement. It's proved helpful, and we can probably find meaningful roles for many of the Ainatio personnel immediately. Perhaps you could get back to me on my personal line — see the number below — to discuss the other matter.*"

Marc let out a breath. "I still don't trust civil servants. But I might spare Lawson when the revolution comes."

"Yay for the pen-pushers," Chris said. "We now have options."

It was going to make the evacuation a lot easier. Sol still had to work out if and when to call it a day with the rail repairs, but if he had to, they'd only have to defend the runway for twenty hours and then they'd be gone. There'd be enough time to ship everyone back to the campus because loading supplies would no longer be an issue.

Then Marc found himself thinking further ahead. *Shackleton* was still intact, so the MoD would probably want to get involved in Nomad and take over the mission, because there was no US government or Ainatio board left to stop them. The *Cabot* crew would still need more settlers to make Nomad a viable colony, and Solomon would probably adapt to a new political reality, if only because he'd need to keep his mouth shut and his head down to hide what he was. So the mission wasn't a complete write-off yet.

Marc wondered why he was thinking how to make Nomad succeed when a few minutes ago his only aim was to get people to safety. Chris jerked him out of his thoughts.

"What's this *other matter?*"

"Probably whether I'll give him the FTL research even if we end up launching *Shackleton,*" Marc said.

"I was surprised you hadn't done it already, to be honest, but I suppose you were holding it in reserve for something like this."

"Not really." Marc could only tell Chris the unvarnished truth. Lies were hard work and he needed at least one person he could be totally honest with now Tev was gone. "I wasn't sure if Sol had doctored it before giving it to APS. And if you're listening, Sol, you never asked me how I was planning to give it to them. I know you know I got hold of a copy."

"It wasn't confidential once I shared it with APS," Solomon said. "So there was no reason for me to question why you accessed it. But the decision is entirely yours. As you said, if APS has the research, why not Britain as well?"

"And is it doctored?"

"No. I considered it, but physics isn't my area of expertise." It was hard to imagine there were things Solomon couldn't do, but that was why he had all those bots and slaved dumb AIs at his disposal. "I'd probably have made alterations and omissions so obvious that the APS scientists assessing it would have spotted it right away."

Chris looked like he was thinking things over. Marc was waiting for him to work through all the permutations, because he always did, usually sooner than later.

Awkward question coming in three, two, one...

"But what about Nomad, Sol?" Chris asked, right on cue. "If we do end up having to ship out to Britain, are you just going to call it a day? Is it all over?"

Solomon paused long enough to seem like he was considering it in human thinking time. "That will depend," he said. "And things are changing so fast that I don't feel my speculation would be useful."

It could have been AI-speak for mind your own business or it might have been a don't-know. Marc settled for the assumption that Sol had worked through the same train of thought that he and Chris already had, and that the AI thought it was an unseemly time to be haggling over who claimed the corpse's gold teeth.

Marc slowed down for the decontamination point and paused in the archway while the machine misted the APC. When it had finished, he ran the wipers to clear the windscreen and lowered the side window to listen. The only noises he could hear above the clicks and drips of the de-con arch and the whine of the idling motor were chirping insects and the distant barking of Dieter's dogs. It was like the world had let out a collective sigh of relief. He drove on and parked in the town square, now full of vehicles, and noted that a respectful space had been left either side of the ambassador's limo. He'd have to pick that up later. Bots were loading supplies onto the transit camp's trucks and a couple of Ainatio buses, supervised by Zakko and Jared's wife, Marsha. Marc waved to her, then gestured to Chris to get out of the Caracal.

"You go and do what you need to do here," he said. "I've got to call in at the Brandts' place and say goodnight to Howie. I promised him. He's convinced I'm going to get shot. Can you tell Doug we've got a backdoor to Britain? I think it'll make the Kill Liners a lot happier."

"You don't want to bask in the warmth of their admiration when you tell them you've saved them from living on possums and acorns for the foreseeable future?"

"Not yet, I've got to see Howie. I'll be right back. Save some basking for me."

Chris went into the town hall and Marc allowed himself a minute to get his head straight before he drove off. It hadn't been a bad evening's work. He'd got the FCO to sort out an airlift and he'd reached a kind of ceasefire with APDU. He hoped the Kill Liners would think it was good news too, but people who'd been pumped up on adrenaline for a long time often hit a wall when life went quiet again. Marc had seen it too often. They thought they'd be glad of an end to the stress, but the relief was either shortlived or nonexistent, and was replaced by an awful restlessness. Marc sat watching moths battering themselves senseless against a street light for a few moments. There was a parable in there somewhere.

Never mind. He'd go and say goodnight to Howie, and tell him that if they couldn't go to Opis, they'd have a great time in England and that he'd take him to see all the interesting sights. He realised he could now look forward to that instead of seeing only the places that reminded him what he'd lost and how much it hurt. For a few seconds, it felt like the kind of hope he hadn't had in ages.

Everything was going to be fine. He'd keep telling himself that. He pulled out of the parking space, propped his screen on the dashboard next to his radio, and carried on up the main road through the town.

People were out and about, either moving stuff around or chatting with neighbours in the light from open doors. The vicar, the Vincents, the kid from Chris's camp who loved astronomy, and Todd Mangel, Ainatio's head of astrophysics, were gathered around a small telescope on a tripod. Mangel was pointing out something to the astronomy kid. It was rather touching. Marc had expected Mangel to be a pain in the arse and a right snob, but he'd taken the shitstorm like a man and he wasn't too grand to mix with the peasants. According to Alex, he hadn't even asked for one of the spare berths in *Elcano*. Everybody seemed to be making an effort to get on, even the Vincents and their miserable cow of a daughter. Well, she might get her wish. They might be staying on Earth whether they wanted to or not.

Random thoughts still nagged at him on the way to Doug's farm. Chris had promised Kim that he'd scatter Levine's ashes at Nomad Base, so maybe he could store them until that was possible. But what were they going to do about Jamie Wickens' body? Chris and the others had planned to rebury him on Opis. Now they'd be hauling a coffin up the ramp of a Saxon and explaining it to an RAF loadmaster. It wasn't as if repatriation flights were a problem or even unusual for the RAF, and it didn't really matter that Jamie was going to a country he hadn't known, but Marc was dreading it. He had a half-finished jigsaw puzzle of misery that ran from the moment he stood on an airstrip in his best black suit and first saw the Saxon coming in to land to sitting in the back of the funeral car with Sandra, following two hearses down the motorway. Now he would see the missing pieces, the first part of his boys' last journey, except it would be Jamie Wickens' coffin loaded on board. He'd have to make sure he remembered that.

But he could distract himself by focusing on Howie. Marc wasn't going to hand him over to social services when they reached England. The kid had been through enough. He needed a home with people he knew and trusted. Marc would have to work out how to make that happen, and that would keep him too busy to relive the past.

He was half a mile up the road when he heard the faint buzz of a channel opening in his earpiece. He looked to his screen, expecting a video call on the secure network from Trinder or Chris, but the signal was on the short-range squad radio.

"Solomon, can you hear me?"

Marc didn't recognise the voice. It was a man, maybe forties, neither American nor English, but he could have started life as either. It had to be one of the Ainatio boffins. Jon Simonot had warned them not to use the detachment's frequencies and eventually had to ban them from the radio net because they used the emergency channel like a personal chat line.

"Alpha Three to unknown callsign, cease transmission immediately." Marc put a bit of bite in it so the bloke understood how pissed off he was. "Do not transmit again, out."

His earpiece popped. Whoever it was had gone. He checked in with Chris. "Alpha Three to Six Zero, unknown callsign on this net, over."

Chris came back almost instantly. "Six Zero here, confirmed, received here too. Checking now. We'll deal with it. Wait out."

Solomon wasn't on the squad net because it was kept separate from the Ainatio network, and both Chris's militia and Trinder's detachment knew that. What sort of tosser would try to call Sol when everyone knew he was Pham's most wanted? Who was in range and could access the squad net? The radios were good for five hundred metres and had unique hardware keys. Marc's first bet would have been the informer, because if you were shitty enough to turn your mates in, you were more than capable of trying to lure Sol into revealing his location. But the Ainatio campus was outside the squad net's range and every radio was accounted for. So had Pham's missing operator breached the net somehow, or was it a traitor much closer to home, one of their own troops?

No, it couldn't be one of Chris's guys, or Trinder's. But if Marc turned out to be wrong, he'd deal with them himself.

He carried on down the dirt road towards the Brandts' place, intending to check in with Chris again as soon as he'd said goodnight to Howie. Well, at least he'd been right to worry about bots wandering around in the dark. There was something big in the middle of the road a few yards ahead. He braked, ready to hit the horn if it didn't move.

"Come on, move, move... "

But it wasn't a bot at all.

It was a bird, a bloody big, black bird. It just stood there with its wings raised and spread like it was sunning itself in the middle of the night, the gloss of its feathers picked up by the Caracal's headlights.

Marc thought *condor*, then wondered how a condor ended up on the other side of the country, and realised its head was the wrong size. Condors didn't have beaks like that, either, and then — shit, the bird was a hell of a lot bigger than he'd first realised. It wasn't just the wingspan. The thing was at least five feet tall.

He could have driven slowly at it and tried to scare it off, but it was too weird to dismiss as local wildlife. He stopped the Caracal, reached for his carbine, and left the engine running before sliding out of the vehicle as slowly as he could. If anything, the bird now looked like a cross between a pterosaur and a raven. But at ten yards, he now realised he'd seen it before.

This was one of the creatures caught on the video feed from Opis.

They'd only been black shapes flapping in the distance, not close enough to show much detail, but the shape and angle of the wings — four if he counted the small ones like aerofoils on its legs — were distinctive. How did this one get here? Had Ainatio bred them at the facility to ship out to Opis? None of this made any sense. The bird watched him with its head cocked, wings still raised, looking like it was worried what he was going to do next. He kept the carbine trained on it.

"Where did *you* come from, then?" Marc asked, not expecting an answer. The creature didn't seem aggressive, just disoriented and probably too dim to fly off. "You pick your bloody moments."

The bird looked right at him. "Please don't shoot me. I need to speak to Solomon."

It was the voice on the radio. For a moment Marc thought the bird was mimicking something it had heard, but those definitely weren't the words used.

"Bloody hell," Marc said.

"Yes, *bloody hell*!" The bird repeated it like it was a joke. "First English I learned from Bridget Ingram. Hah!"

It lowered its wings slowly like it had decided it didn't need to hold up its hands any longer, looking quite majestic until something slipped off its back and slid around one wing.

The bird had a messenger bag.

Marc had seen some weird shit in his service career, most of it real, some of it when he was burning up with a fever. But he didn't have a fever now. There really was a giant English-speaking bird with a manbag blocking his path. And it knew Ingram by name.

It also knew Sol. Sol hadn't mentioned that. Marc got on the radio and prepared to sound rational and not at all insane.

"Alpha Three to Six Zero, unknown callsign identified, ten yards from my position... and not human. I say again, *not human*."

* * *

CIC, PRENU NAR P12, OPIS: 2205 EDT, EARTH TIME.

"I peck Hredt hard when I see him, Captain Bridget, because he go mad." Cosqui stood on the dais in the command centre, moving her hands and wing tips in some elaborate semaphore to search the images relayed back from Earth by the assay probes. Her raised red crest made her look like an angry centurion ready to lay waste to Gaul. "He never think. He just flies. I try to call him for a long time, but in recent minute I hear him make call, and human Alpha Three talks like Chief Jeff and sounds angry. Hredt will be shot. That is your commune there. You bring him back."

The last thing Ingram needed was an alien on the loose in Kill Line while there was some kind of emergency unfolding at the Ainatio facility. She could have searched more efficiently if she'd stayed at the base with the relay software she'd been given, but Cosqui had effectively demanded her presence, and if Fred didn't make it back, Ingram would probably be dependent on her for liaison.

She shouldn't have been thinking like that. She should have been worrying about Fred, but this was turning into a very difficult day, the kind that put her into survival mode. When she glanced back at Jeff and Bissey, both standing at the rear of the dais, they looked like she felt. Bissey was glued to his screen, dragging his finger around to move the probe that Cosqui had linked to it.

"Peter, what's happening on the gate now?" Ingram asked.

"The APDU troops are just standing around, ma'am. But there's a lot of activity now around the launch rail."

"And still nobody else out and about in the grounds."

Bissey shook his head. "Not that I can see."

Ingram couldn't work out what was going on. The troops were clearly barring entry. A while ago, one of them appeared to have had a calm conversation with an armed man who'd got out of an APC and walked up to the fence. Bissey had been sure the man wasn't in any APDU uniform. So, peaceful negotiation, or an APS contractor reporting in and not bothering to go through the gate? She couldn't risk trying to make radio contact without knowing who'd be receiving it and what their intentions were. But she needed to get Fred out before everything went sideways.

"You want to see Hredt or not?" Cosqui snapped. That jerked Ingram's attention back to the floating display. Cosqui pointed accusingly at the image. "This where I think he lands. The town, Kill Line. Yes?"

Ingram didn't like these translucent floating images. She wanted an opaque image on a monitor welded to a deck that was built to withstand missile attacks. She could make out the shapes of trees against the sky and two points of light some distance away that were probably vehicle headlights. Unless the portal had smeared Fred into a streak of interstellar grease, he had to be somewhere around here, and with any luck he wouldn't head for the Ainatio facility.

"Yes, I think that's Kill Line," she said. The angle showed the probe relaying the image was hovering about fifteen feet off the ground. "Do you have night vision mode? See in the dark?" Ingram slid her visor out of her pocket and unfolded it in front of Cosqui to prompt the teerik to look through it. "Can we see a picture like this?"

Cosqui peered through the lens, seemed to get the idea, and waved a claw in the general direction of the control panel. The probe image shifted into daylight colours, a little washed out but clearly showing a country road and houses with lights visible in the windows. Ingram couldn't see Fred, but she could all too easily imagine a local farmer closing his barn for the night, shotgun in hand, and running into a giant predatory-looking bird. She added a potentially dead teerik to marooned humans and a burned-out ship and made up her mind.

"I'd better retrieve him now, then, and work out if they're in trouble down there," she said. "Where's the Caisin gate?"

"In front of you."

Ingram had trouble spotting it in the semi-darkness. Cosqui rasped to herself, an annoyed sound that didn't need a translation, and beckoned Ingram to follow her down to the deck.

"See?" The teerik pointed again. "The unclear mark."

Ingram could now see the blurred oval hanging in the air. This was arguably the most insane risk she'd ever taken, but then she remembered the first summer of the Channel War, and also signing up for a mystery trip to a planet called Opis, and realised it probably wasn't.

She turned back to Bissey and Jeff. "Keep this portal open." She set the timer on her watch and braced to step through, hoping the gate coughed her out at ground level instead of fifteen feet above it. "Even if you have to barricade the hatches to keep Turisu or whoever from getting in."

"Turisu will *seethe* at me," Cosqui said. "She does not want strangers here."

"Tell her we made you do it," Ingram said. "Chief, tell Turisu that, will you?"

"Yes ma'am. Excuses primed."

"Are you sure you don't want me to go, Captain?" Bissey asked. "No human's ever used one of those things. Even Fred said it was a prototype."

"If it's that dangerous, it's my duty," Ingram said. "If it isn't, I call dibs on making history. Hold the ship, Peter, and defer to CPO Aiken on teerik liaison matters. I'll be back as soon as I can."

But she wasn't sure she'd make it back at all. She was scared. Torpedoes, USVs, and anti-ship missiles were threats she understood. Bending space-time with only her Number Fours between her and the eternal void — well, there was a good reason why humans feared what they didn't understand. There was only one way to do this: fast, and without looking back.

Ingram stepped right leg first into the haze, eyes screwed up as if it was the entrance to a smoke-filled bar, and was instantly swallowed by a silent, absolute blackness that smelled of spent matches. Then her left boot crushed something soft as she took her second step and almost lost her balance. It was like a deck in a rolling sea, a moment of weightlessness under her boots. But she had no sense of where she was or any feeling of movement, and there were no extraordinary marbled swirls of glowing gas or timestreaked stars. Folded space was pretty bloody dull.

Now all she could smell was cut grass and manure. She wasn't in some alternate dimension after all.

"Bugger." She could see where the aroma of manure was coming from. Her left boot had landed in a pile of cow dung in the middle of a field. She sighed. "Great. What a perfect metaphor for my sodding life."

There were lights a few hundred yards away, real ones, glowing yellow from the windows of houses or throwing a halo ahead of a vehicle making its way up a nearby road. The brief weightless sensation was the effect of losing a few pounds thanks to being back in lower gravity. She made an effort to tread more carefully, but that was going to be a challenge in an unlit field because she'd left her NV visor with Cosqui in her hurry to catch up with Fred.

But Ingram was back on Earth, somewhere she thought she'd never see again. Now she could step across space to reach it whenever she wanted, subject to the teeriks' tolerance. The new state of mind she'd cultivated to handle severing the bond with Earth, a connection humans had never broken permanently before, was crumbling. But she was still forty-five years from her definition of *now* and *normal*. This wasn't the Earth she'd left.

She set off across the field, scuffing her boot as she went to scrape the shit off, and headed for the lights. At least it was all downhill. As her eyes adjusted, she could see the fence and a dirt track road beyond it. Fred would probably have taken the clearest path out of the field as well, and as he was looking for Solomon, he'd head for the town at some point. He'd had almost an hour's head start. But there was nowhere else for him to search outside these two clusters of human habitation. Wherever he was, he was close by.

So were the APDU troops, though. Ingram felt in her pocket for the reassurance of her sidearm, not the most nautical of weapons, but it was her father's and it had seen action in at least two opposed boardings. She put her faith in it and wished he could see her now. He'd tell her she was a bloody silly girl for not bringing a light machine gun.

Ingram made it to the fence, snagged her trousers as she scrambled over it, and ended up on the dirt track. There was a house some way to her left with lights in the windows, but she could see vehicle headlights in the other direction. It was decision time. If the undefined worst had happened here then the vehicle might be a threat, but if it hadn't, it was the quickest way to find someone who knew what was going on.

Fred had picked the gate's exit point for a reason. It was precision technology, and he had exact locations from comms signals, although a field didn't make sense. Ingram decided to head for the vehicle. It didn't seem to be moving. If it headed off somewhere before she reached it, she'd retrace her steps and try the house. She broke into a jog and hoped her lungs would hold out until she caught up with the car, or else it'd be a long, wheezing uphill slog back to that farmhouse.

In the distance, another light haze marked what had to be the Ainatio campus. The glare of the headlights was coming from her right, so it looked like the track formed a T-junction with the road. She slowed to a fast walk to get her breath back before she had to do any talking, then stopped and bent over, hands braced on her knees.

The realisation hit her. Nobody was expecting her. They probably wouldn't recognise her unless they were Ainatio personnel with very specific knowledge, and if they were APDU troops, someone armed and wearing a strange uniform would be treated as a hostile contact until proven otherwise. Whichever way she cut it, it was going to be a difficult conversation.

A moment of doubt crossed Ingram's mind. She was sure she was on Earth, but the Caisin gate was a prototype, and there was that complicated stuff about wormhole technology bridging time the same way it apparently bridged vast distances. Just having a real-time conversation with Earth when she was on Opis didn't mean she could count on anything working the way it was intended.

Please tell me I'm not forty years too late. And damn — how do I find the portal again in the dark?

She gulped in a few breaths and put her hand on her sidearm. When she reached the end of the track, she decided the lesser of two daft moves would be to call out first. If she just stepped out into the headlights, someone armed and nervous might open fire. On the other hand, if she warned them she was coming — if they could hear her, of course — they'd have plenty of time to sight up and make sure they didn't miss. There was no safe option.

The whine of a hydrogen engine drifted on the night air. Ingram decided this was no time to stop being rash and opportunistic. She slowed to a walk again for the last few yards to the junction, then stepped out into the middle of the track and raised her arms, blinded by the headlights.

"I'm Captain Bridget Ingram." She couldn't see for a moment. This was bloody insane. She wondered if it was true that you never heard the round that killed you. "I need to speak to Alpha Three."

She narrowed her eyes against the lights. There was a moment of silence.

"You've found him." The man was English. "Put your weapon down. *Slowly*. Put it on the ground, put your comms kit next to it, and then take three paces back."

"I'm sorry, Captain Bridget," said a voice. It was Fred. At least he hadn't been shot by a startled farmer. "You should have allowed me to deal with this."

"Captain — *sidearm*. On the ground, *now*."

Ingram obeyed slowly and carefully. The headlights suddenly dipped. As her eyes adjusted, she could see two men, one in a dark uniform, the other in more informal rig with a black polo shirt and some kind of tactical vest. Both had their rifles aimed. The APC idling behind them was a type she'd never seen before, another reminder of how many years she'd been away. There was also a quad bike with its lights full on.

"You *do* know who I am, don't you?" Ingram asked. "I think we're supposed to be on the same side."

"Oh, I've heard of you," the Englishman said. His colleague hadn't said a word yet. "Bridget Ingram. The Butcher of Calais. Funny, you were in our history textbook at school. The war hero who volunteered for the big black unknown but died in *Cabot*. Nice job, by the way. They still haven't rebuilt Calais docks."

Ingram had no idea how to take that. Here was a man who was at least her age, probably older, who recalled her adult service record from his childhood. Cryo was a strange time machine.

"And you are?"

"Marc Gallagher."

She remembered that name from Erskine's personnel list because the note alongside it wasn't easy to forget. "Special forces? Kay-SOR?"

"Was."

Life sometimes slotted together neatly. This was exactly who she needed at a time like this, an experienced soldier who specialised in the unorthodox. There was just one problem to overcome. He didn't seem convinced she was on his side.

"It was only the French Remnant who called me the Butcher, by the way," she said. "But I need to ask you a question before we do anything else. Are you under attack, and has Nomad been compromised?"

"First things first, and that was two questions," Gallagher said. "Contamination. Tell me how you got here."

"I landed in a field."

"Okay, I'll work with that. Which field?"

"I don't know, but it's full of cow shit." She lifted her boot. "See? Fresh."

"Anywhere else? Anywhere with crunchy dead crops underfoot?"

"No. I just walked out of the field and down a hill towards the lights."

"Fine, but we're going to need those boots off and tested. If you don't know exactly where you landed, you might have walked through contaminated land. Die-back."

"Damn. Okay. Give me a bag to put them in or something. But if I did traipse through infected vegetation, I've walked it all the way down here."

"Did you pass through any of the decontamination points?"

"I'd have noticed, I assume."

"They're arches over the road with a big trough of solvent to wash off tires and boots. Like a short carwash."

"No, I haven't seen one."

"Can we continue this somewhere else?" the other man asked. Ah, he was American. "If we stand in the middle of the road we'll have an audience before long." He opened the APC's rear hatch. "The Caracal's plenty big enough for you and your friend, ma'am."

He rummaged in the back and pulled out a sheet of plastic. She should have remembered all this. She eased off her boots and wrapped them in the sheet.

"Do I get these back?"

"Yes, ma'am. Get in. There's some rubber boots in the back that'll probably fit."

It was just a misunderstanding. It'd be ironed out sooner if she didn't get into a fight. "Come on, Fred," she said, beckoning to the teerik. "You can't blame them for being careful."

Fred hesitated. She wanted to reassure him that nobody was going to hurt him, but now she wasn't so sure herself. She thought he'd take off, but after a few seconds of bobbing his head like a confused parrot, he walked to the APC and managed to scramble in while the American watched with his rifle ready. She climbed in behind Fred and the rear hatch closed with a hiss of air. Now they were sealed in a dimlylit box, cut off from the driver's compartment by a locked panel. She found the promised wellies and tried them on, hoping she didn't have to walk far because they were way too big.

For a moment, she was distracted by a dog's chew toy on the deck, a plastic squirrel. It squeaked when she picked it up. Fred flinched.

"Just a toy," she said.

"Will they kill us?" Fred asked.

"No, they just want to make sure we are who we say we are." Ingram reached across and patted his wing, the first time she'd risked touching a teerik. He felt just like a very warm chicken. "I'd do the same if I was expecting an enemy incursion."

Ingram hoped she wasn't misleading him. Even if Marc and his anonymous comrade were part of the Nomad mission, there was no guarantee they'd see an intelligent alien as a harmless wonder. She hadn't, after all. She'd needed some proof that Fred's people weren't a threat. She still wasn't sure if she'd had it, and the line between a threat and a liability was a fine one.

But at least she knew what a decontamination point was now. The APC passed through one. A fine mist suddenly blurred the small windows and she felt the bump as the tyres went down into the trough. If die-back was that persistent, she doubted that disinfectant would stop it, but this was probably more to wash off any infected plant tissue.

The APC stopped. When Gallagher opened the hatch, the vehicle was backed up to a farm building's big double doors and his colleague was opening one side. Bright light spilled out. She squinted, expecting to see something unpleasant inside.

But it really was just an empty barn. There were a few hay bales stacked around the floor and a bright orange disc harrow half-covered with a tarpaulin. It looked and smelled the way farm outbuildings had when she was a child. Kill Line seemed untouched by the years. She sat down on a bale and waited.

With the lights on, she could take a proper look at her captors. Gallagher — yes, she'd have picked him out in a line-up as exactly what he was. It was difficult to define, and it wasn't even the fact that he looked like a hard case. It was a stillness that didn't seem calm. It was more like he was waiting for something to start so that he could finish it. The American with him looked like someone her mother would have called a nice young man, and he was watching Fred, who was hunched up with his wings folded tight against his sides. Gallagher was focused on her. He didn't seem distracted by an alien at all.

"I've checked the picture on your file, Captain, so I think you're probably who you say you are," Gallagher said. "And I know I'm not hallucinating Fred. But I do have questions."

"So do I, Marc."

He didn't blink at the familiarity. Ingram was worried that she'd lost her touch. "Me first, then," he said. "How did you get here?"

"A wormhole like the Ainatio one, but a few orders of magnitude bigger and better." Ingram tried to recall what people would have known before Erskine cut off the comms relay. Perhaps he hadn't been told about it at all. "You know about FTL communications, I assume."

"Yeah."

"Well, Fred's people are a considerable number of pages ahead of us in the manual."

"And this wormhole thing is where, exactly?"

"It's a portal. A Caisin gate. It's where I landed, in the cow field up the road."

"Of course it is."

"I detect a hint of disbelief."

Gallagher folded his arms and shifted his weight onto one leg. "You shouldn't be here. Fred *definitely* shouldn't be here. You should both be on Opis. Now, we all know Ainatio are the biggest con artists on the planet. Forty-odd years of telling the world *Cabot* was gone, but then they said they'd actually set up a base on Opis and you were all fine. So if they can lie that big, that long, and that convincingly once, they can probably do it again. It's easy to fake videos. What if the Opis base never existed and Nomad's a scam?"

It had never crossed Ingram's mind that they just wouldn't believe any of it. She was going to ask them where they thought Erskine had gone, but then she realised she didn't know how many of the Nomad fleet had launched at all, only that one ship had been attacked.

"Well, there's me," she said at last. "I'm still the age I was when *Cabot* launched. Otherwise I'd look in my eighties now. How do you think my crew felt waking up to find everyone they knew had been told they were dead, and that they weren't even allowed to contact them to explain?"

The American joined in. "You could have been in cryo here," he said, as if he was just making a helpful suggestion to jog her memory. "Like Alex Gorko. He said he did a couple of weeks as a test. I can't think what would make a forty-five-year stretch worth doing if you weren't going anywhere, but then I'm not a long-term kind of guy."

"Then what about Fred?" Ingram asked. "It seems to have escaped your notice that he's a *giant bird* totally unlike any terrestrial species. And he can hold a conversation."

"Bednarz built an AI who can do that."

"I know. Solomon's been to Opis. He spent years using a remote on the surface. You know that. Would he lie about it too?"

"Maybe," the American said. "He lied about you guys going down with your ship for forty-five years."

"Where is he? I'll talk to him."

"We're keeping locations undisclosed at the moment."

"Very well, what can I do to convince you?" Ingram looked from one man to the other, hoping they could at least read her frustration. "Opis is real. The gate system's real. We came here because Fred's monitoring probes picked up an explosion on an Ainatio ship. What proof do you need? Just tell me."

Perhaps Gallagher realised all those things and was simply doing a thorough interrogation, knowing there was an enemy force nearby. His American buddy might have been playing along with it, feeding in misinformation about Solomon to protect the AI. They were definitely in difficulties of some kind and the wrecked ship showed the scale of it, so it wasn't surprising that they didn't know who they could trust or believe. She wasn't sure herself. This was no time to try to pull rank on armed men, however indignant she was.

Gallagher ambled forward and squatted on his heels just in front of her. For a moment, she really didn't know what he was going to do next. She waited for the blow.

"Okay," he said, quiet and reasonable. "Money where your mouth is. Show me."

07

It's simple. We're a plague. We've brought die-back, famine, and disease on ourselves, and like any creature that exhausts its environment, we'll become extinct. That's how ecosystems balance themselves. As we seem unable to change our expansionist nature, the last thing we should be doing is exporting our sickness to other worlds. Dismantle the Martian and lunar bases now, and accept we've had our time in the sun. It's over.

Dr Maryan Kellard, founder of the Human Limitation Project (Mother Death movement) and prominent advocate for reprieving the AI known as Earthmother.

KILL LINE, EN ROUTE TO PORTAL EXIT POINT: 2240 EDT.

Most days, nothing would have shocked Chris, not one damn thing. He'd seen too much and forgotten far too little of it for his peace of mind.

As Marc retraced Ingram's steps in the Caracal, Chris looked for an otherworldly glow or some other sign of this alien technology. It was a gateway, Ingram said. You could just step through it from one point in the galaxy to another, no spacesuit or ship necessary, but you had to know in advance exactly where you wanted the door to open. Right now, though, it looked like this miracle of physics was easy to misplace.

Chris's mind raced, trying to cover all the angles. He decided it made more sense to believe the tawdry worst — that Nomad was another Ainatio scam — than to believe everything Ingram was saying. Perhaps he'd swallowed Erskine's revelations too easily, although he remembered not believing Trinder when he first showed him the footage from Opis. What did meeting an alien prove? Fred was amazing, a reasoning bird able to learn languages, but Ainatio had created another unique, impossibly clever thing with a mind of its own in the form of Solomon. Maybe Fred was one of Tad Bednarz's creations too. An astonishing feat of science didn't automatically mean hyperspace portals and aliens were real as well.

But then there was Solomon. If he knew the gate existed but hadn't told them, that changed everything. They'd put their lives in his hands. Even if he thought it was for their own good, even if he thought telling them about it would put them in danger — and Chris already had a growing list of uses for the gateway that a lot of people would kill for — then he'd hidden the fast lane to Opis when they desperately needed one. It would be impossible to forgive him for that.

Maybe he didn't know about it at all, though. Perhaps he didn't even realise the aliens were intelligent. That thought sobered Chris. He'd relegated aliens to a footnote because all he could think about was getting everyone out of here. Survival stripped away all the frills and wonders and left a guy with just the urgent core of existence.

Was Sol listening? Marc had switched off the radios until he was sure that Sol was on the level, because right then he didn't know if there were more bombshells about to drop like the *Cabot* lie. Chris couldn't even warn Trinder until they'd ruled that out because Sol was monitoring the Ainatio network. It wouldn't have been the first time Chris had found those he'd trusted most had put a knife in his back. He kept an open mind.

Marc had been silent since they set off, driving at a crawl to give Ingram time to look for landmarks in the dark. Chris knew from his previous existence that the silent routine was a good way to get some asshole to talk, because scared people tended to babble to fill a frightening void, but Ingram didn't take the bait whether Marc had intended to lay it or not.

"I can find my car with my screen," Marc said. "Bit of a design oversight if you can't remember where you parked your interstellar wormhole, isn't it?"

Ingram leaned forward between the Caracal's front seats. "*Left,*" she said firmly. She had an aristocratic English accent that sounded straight out of a movie, blonde hair pulled back in a regulation bun, and an aura of faint but expensive perfume. That fragrance must have mattered a lot to her if she'd bothered to take it to another star system and wore it in a crisis. "Up there. That turning."

It was the track to Cedar Hill Farm. Chris realised he should have made the connection right away.

"Fred, how did you pick the exit point?" he asked. *Holy shit, I'm talking to a giant bird.* "Did you try to intercept laser transmissions?"

"Not *intercept*." Fred's voice drifted from the back of the APC. "We traced the point of origin to contact Solomon. It was the obvious place to open the gateway."

"That's it, then. That's where the Lammergeier was laid up. Keep going, Marc. I know where it is."

Both Lammergeiers had moved onto the parking lot behind the brewery in the centre of town, leaving the field empty, but there'd be tyre marks and big depressions in the grass where the tilt-rotor's wheels had set down. It was just a matter of finding them in the dark.

"Marc, pull in over there. That's where the Lamm was. Look for the tyre marks." Chris leaned his head back to talk to Fred. "Fred, you must have some way to locate it. Or are you telling me you just jumped without any idea of how you were going to get home?"

"I know where it is," Fred said, sounding irritated. "Remembering and calculating precise locations is our job. Just let me show you."

"But this is where you arrived, yeah? Because if it is, you haven't been in contact with contaminated land. This is all inside the wire."

"Yes, this is the place," Fred said.

Marc parked the Caracal and let Ingram and Fred out of the rear hatch, then started walking slowly towards the spot where Chris had last seen the Lammergeier. Chris moved ahead carefully too. If the portal was real, he didn't want to blunder through it by accident.

"This gate must use a shitload of energy," Marc said. "That's got to be visible in some spectrum or other."

"A small gateway is effectively undetectable until the moment something comes through it," Fred said.

Marc glanced over his shoulder as if that was particularly interesting. "You've got it secured at the other end. Guarded. Protected."

"Yes."

"So whoever comes through would have to be one of yours or one of ours."

"Yes."

"I'm asking because this is how I'd launch an invasion, Fred. And I'd want to know how to shut it down at the other end without firing a nuke through it. But that's just me being hypothetical."

It was hard to tell if that was an oblique warning to Fred or just Marc wanting assurance that he knew the potential dangers of the technology, but Fred might not have understood it. He did seem to speak really good English, though. Chris tried to work out how he'd learned it.

"What does this gate look like?" Chris asked.

"A patch of heat haze or a greasy smear on your sunglasses," Ingram said. "But it's hard enough to see in daylight, let alone at night."

A portal that could fold space but was hard to find sounded even more dubious to Chris, so maybe she was playing for time and something else was going to happen here. He kept one hand close to his sidearm while he swept the grass with his flashlight. The Lamm took up a big space, eighteen yards by thirty, and Ingram seemed to be describing something the size of a door. Well, this was the right spot, or at least one of them. Both Lamms had been parked here together at one time and there were two areas of crushed grass and two sets of tyre marks.

"How accurate is this gate, Fred?" Marc asked. "What's the margin of error?"

"Very, very small. Look." Fred walked into the search area. "Here. It's right here."

Marc jogged back to the Caracal. Moments later, a bright searchlight beam sliced across the grass, throwing shadows that picked out the hummocks and depressions.

"Better?" Marc asked. "It's nice and stealthy, I'll give you that."

Chris tried looking from a few different angles before he noticed the faint oval of mist hanging in the air, distorting the field behind it like a dirty window. He'd never seen any weather conditions create a haze like that. Whatever it was, it was real.

"What's on the other side?" Marc asked.

Ingram put her hands on her hips as if she was going to square up to him. "The CIC of a prototype warship, crewed by Fred's comrades. They designed it. Trust me when I say it's complicated."

"I'll bet," Chris said. "Friendly?"

Fred interrupted. "We are *very* friendly to humans." It looked like he'd understood Marc's comment as a warning after all. "We aren't soldiers. We don't want to fight you."

Mark walked up to the patch of haze and studied it from a few feet away. "Captain, you have crew from APS states. Do they know about this, and do they have a way of contacting Earth?"

Ingram paused. "The short answer's no, and there's no access to Earth comms except the Caisin gate, which is in Fred's ship."

"And we would only allow those who have your permission to use it," Fred said.

"My point is the world's changed since you left, and the situation with APS here is volatile, to put it mildly," Marc said. "Loyalties are funny things."

Ingram bristled. "I trust my crew."

"Yeah, we'll tell you a story later about trusting the people you work with." Marc slipped his rifle off his shoulder. It was hard to tell if he now believed her or if he was just calling her bluff, but then good bluffers were like that. "I want to prove it's real. And I want to make sure Opis is what we've been told it is. I just step through this thing, right?"

"You're not going to step through anywhere until we're sure you're not contaminated," Ingram said. "If die-back reaches Opis and kills crops, we're dead."

Marc gave her a look that could have burned weeds off a path. "You knew about die-back before you decided to land here, even if you didn't know it was only a couple of fields away. So if I can't go to Opis, then neither can you or Fred. And I don't recall Erskine being told to forget sending follow-up missions because of the risk. Look, Captain, everyone here is screened all the time. Vehicles drive through de-con arches. The only people who've never been monitored or decontaminated are you and Fred. And what about you turning up in the first place? What alien lurgies have you brought with you that'll infect Earth and finish the job? We've had our shots, but the rest of the world hasn't."

He waited. Ingram was silent for a moment. Chris couldn't tell if she was speechless with anger or just realising how inconsistent the die-back precautions had already been.

"I'm sorry," she said stiffly. "But if I'd called ahead and APS answered, we'd have a different but equally serious problem."

"Take it from me, we're all clean. Insects spread it. Animals and infected plants can transfer it by contact. But if you really want to guarantee die-back never reaches Opis, you should deactivate that gate now and make sure nobody ever uses it again."

Chris cut in to stop the tussle. "It's worth remembering die-back only affects certain species," he said. He liked that fact. There was unspoken good news in it. "Wheat, rice, soy, maize. Humans do fine without eating any of them. Just not in large numbers. Because we were so dependent on them."

"And you'll have to blow up *Elcano*, too," Marc said. But he looked like he was just goading Ingram now because he'd won the point. "If you want to be sure, that is."

"Very well, I stand corrected." She had that carefully gracious tone that women put on when they were calculating how and when they were going to make you pay for whatever you didn't know you'd done wrong. "But I think I should go with you to smooth things over. Fred didn't get his boss's blessing to do this."

Fred's feathers fluffed up. The Caracal's searchlight caught a sheen of blue-green iridescence and a crest on his head that Chris hadn't noticed earlier.

"My commune mother is too ill to lead us and my daughter does *not* give me orders," Fred said. Chris warmed to him right away. "I do what needs to be done."

"I still need to warn Commander Bissey and CPO Aiken that Marc's coming. They're armed and they knew there was some kind of trouble here. But go ahead and poke your head in unannounced by all means."

Marc looked unmoved. "I'm with Fred. I've got top cover." But he gave her back her radio.

"Thank you, Sergeant."

Ingram held it so that they could all hear the conversation. "Ingram here, Peter. Fred's coming back through the gate with Sergeant Marc Gallagher. He's one of ours, so please cooperate with him. He's finding it a little hard to believe what's happening."

"As are we all, ma'am," Bissey said. "May I ask if Fred and Sergeant Gallagher need to be decontaminated?"

"I'm satisfied that the precautions here are adequate," Ingram said. Then she started explaining to Bissey what had happened. Chris pulled Marc aside for moment.

"I assume we're both thinking the same thing," he said.

"What, that we've got an instant ticket to Opis in the nick of time?"

"Are we going to take it?"

"We'd look bloody daft if we didn't after all the buggering around to try to launch *Shack* and begging the RAF for an airlift. But I want to take a good look at this gift horse's dental work. And we haven't told Ingram how awkward things are here."

"Yeah, but she knows we've lost a ship, so she must assume we're going to need a ride. We better level with her now so she understands we've got to move folks out fast. Absorbing a town's worth of evacuees is a lot to ask."

Marc spoke with his chin tucked in to his chest as if he was looking down at the ground. "What if we can complete the rail repairs in time? *Shackleton*'s still in one piece."

"But we can't be sure how long we've actually got before APS picks up again. This gate thing could be our earliest guaranteed ticket out, and as things stand right now that makes it the *only* one."

"The airlift might be earlier."

"Britain's still going to be within striking distance of APS eventually." Chris felt bad for saying it but he knew Marc was as pragmatic as he was. "And if die-back or some attack gets past your defences, we'll regret not taking this opportunity."

"If it's real."

"Goes without saying."

"And I'm just keeping all the options on the table because things here are changing too fast." Marc fished out his wallet and took a data card from it. "Just in case I don't come back, then, and you have to take Lawson's offer, the sat phone's in the Caracal with his direct number and my code programmed in. And here's the data Lawson wants. He'll have a secure link you can upload it to."

"I'll give it back when you return."

"If I don't, apologise to Howie for me, will you? Tell him I really was on my way to say goodnight."

There was no point in telling Marc not to be morbid. He was just accepting that anything could happen, and Chris understood why he worried about things left unsaid.

"Sure," Chris said. "But you'll be back."

Marc patted his shoulder like he was saying goodbye. If Ingram had overheard any of their conversation, she didn't look like it made any sense to her. She was still talking on the radio.

"Okay, after you, Fred," Marc said. "Captain, you stay with Chris. I'll come straight back so you know I've eyeballed the base."

He held his carbine to his chest and followed the alien. Then both of them just winked out of existence like a bad edit in a movie. One moment Chris was watching them walk away, realising Marc still had Ingram's sidearm shoved in the back of his belt, and the next they'd vanished.

"Well, shit." He could only shake his head. He recorded the gate's coordinates using Ainatio's comms tower as a reference point. "The damn thing's real."

"I take it you believe me now," Ingram said.

"Ma'am, I believe Marc just went somewhere. I'll believe the interstellar part if and when he comes back."

Ingram shoved her radio back in her shirt pocket. "He'd better. He's still got my pistol. It was my father's."

"And you're sure some galactic invasion won't pour through that thing in a few minutes."

Ingram tucked a stray strand of hair back into place. "I have every confidence in Sergeant Gallagher's ability to repel it single-handed before it gets the chance."

So she had a sense of humour after all. Chris waited, watching the smeared oval with his rifle held against his chest. He really hoped this was real. But it would probably be the first hurdle of many, and he couldn't gauge how Ingram would react when they asked her to take in nearly sixteen hundred people right away. She'd been working on the assumption that she'd have forty-five years to turn Nomad Base into a proper colony for civvies. Chris had spent too long dealing with the practical realities of moving people around and making sure they were sheltered, fed, and given medical care to underestimate the size of the task and the burden on Ingram's crew and resources. They'd be increasing the population of Nomad Base nine-fold overnight. It would put enormous pressure on food and shelter.

She probably wouldn't refuse, or at least he hoped she wouldn't. But if she said no, he and Marc might have to take the decision out of her hands. That wasn't going to be easy and it wouldn't solve the problems ahead.

"What are you thinking about?" Ingram asked.

"I'd be a liar if I said nothing." Chris was willing Marc to suddenly appear and say everything was great so that he could stop making depressing contingency plans. "Did Sol know about this?"

Ingram shook her head. "If he did, he didn't even tell us. When Erskine cut us off, we hadn't had any close contact with the teeriks, so we didn't know they were intelligent. And we didn't find out about the Caisin gate until today."

"So do you want to know how much shit we're in, ma'am? Because it's pretty deep."

"Let's sound the depths, shall we?"

"First thing you need to know is that we've got an APS informer on the Ainatio staff and we don't know who it is. They told APS that Sol was a banned AI and a lot of other stuff, so APS wrecked the launch rail and tried to cripple the ships. And they want to shut down Sol, obviously, but they've also demanded we hand over Marc and all the scientists. That's why we need to make sure nobody from Ainatio sees you."

"Ah," Ingram said. "Hence Marc's comment about trusting colleagues."

"And we've just carried out a cyberattack on APS and shut down their air force and some other stuff to give us time to evacuate."

"Was that Solomon's doing?"

"Yeah. Bednarz gave him a doomsday virus called a sabcode to use as a last resort. Anyway, we've also locked down the Ainatio site and trapped their personnel inside. Tim Pham, the APS sci-tech commissioner, is actually here in person. He's a former career spy, and we don't know how long we've got to get people out of here before APDU's on its feet again and comes to hand us our asses. Your government's willing to lay on an emergency airlift to take us to Britain, but that might not be far enough away when APS recovers."

"Do you have an estimate of how long you've got?"

"APDU could borrow a bomber or two from an ally at any time. That's all it would take to finish us off. Or they could be paralysed for weeks. We can't be sure."

"Let's roll this back to the beginning," Ingram said. "Are we at war with APS? The scrag end of a company battling a political bloc? How does that even happen?"

"They hit us and we hit them back. Look, this saga's going to take me all night, ma'am. Here's Major Trinder's report file. Very brief but thorough. His staff do good infographics."

Chris handed her his screen to read. Ingram scrolled through, making little tutting noises, and then the tutting was replaced by the occasional disapproving grunt. It didn't take her long to get the idea.

"Erskine left you here when APS threatened to bomb the site."

"Yes ma'am."

"And there's a new die-back variant that got out of the company labs."

"Apparently."

"Good grief. Does the British government know about the sabcode?"

"I think they guessed, but we're saying nothing at the moment."

Ingram sighed. "While I'd have appreciated a friendlier reception, I understand why you two were so suspicious. What an utter shambles. Where's Solomon now?"

"Around. He's staying away from radios in case the sabcode can worm its way back here, but... well, we cut him off until we knew whether this was another Ainatio stunt he kept to himself. I want to trust him, but right now we don't know what's real and what isn't."

"If Sol knew I was here, he'd want to brief me."

Chris ignored the proprietorial tone. "I think you're the one who'll need to brief him."

"So about this Tim Pham chap. Tell me more."

"Like I said, ex-spy, but maybe not so ex. He showed up to deal with the new die-back outbreak but he'd actually come for the FTL research, which we traded for free passage out of here. Then someone told him Ainatio was an even bigger can of worms. He's not a monster, just not on our side and not a nice guy. He might be conducting this unofficially and without wider APS knowledge, though, so APS states wouldn't know who hit them and why, not yet anyway. He's brought in two guys who look like special forces to find Solomon."

"Sol was a surprise to us all," Ingram said. "We came out of cryo to find we had an AI we'd never been told about. I had my initial concerns."

"But you're cool with him now."

"More than cool. The crew are fond of him. We need him back on Opis."

That was a handy lever to have, but Chris didn't know enough about Sol's relationship with Ingram yet to know if it could be pulled.

"The bottom line is we don't know how long we've got before APS is back in business," he said. "It's probably going to take weeks to fix the rail. As I said, Marc's done a deal with the Foreign Office if it looks like we can't launch *Shackleton* before APS comes after us."

"So you've still got an operational ship but no shuttle launch capability."

"Yes. And you realise where this conversation's going."

"I think I do. When can I speak to Sol?"

"When Marc comes back in one piece and says everything's okay."

"Of course." Ingram handed Chris his screen. "We've got a few issues at our end, too, but we can talk about that when everyone's here."

Chris stood watching the patch of greasy air, wishing he hadn't been so numbed by constant crises and shocks that it took conscious effort to feel any amazement at the things he'd seen tonight. Then Marc suddenly appeared again, not there one minute and there the next. It was a pretty uneventful entrance. A round trip of nearly five hundred trillion miles needed thunder and forked lightning.

"Game on," Marc said, looking pleased. "The gravity's a bit noticeable, but we'll acclimatise."

Chris was still waiting for reality to put a pin in the balloon. "So it's all real. And it looks like the videos."

"One hundred per cent."

"And it didn't hurt."

"No, I feel fine. No swirly tunnels or strange lights. My ears felt weird for a second, but that's it."

"Great. We'll get the guys together and work out where we go from here."

"Start without me. I'm stepping back for half an hour to check a few things." Marc looked at his watch. "Twenty-three fifty-nine. Be here to pick me up."

And then he was gone again. Ingram looked at Chris and shrugged. Chris shrugged back. It was burn-out on his part, not nonchalance.

"He doesn't hang around, does he?" Ingram said.

There was no way to approach this subtly. She'd worked out what was coming anyway.

"Captain, we need to get out of here, and you show up with an instant way to get to Opis," Chris said. "You can't blame us for thinking it's our lucky break. If you can't ship us out, we'll have to take your government's offer to resettle us, which probably means they'll take over Nomad. We can't hide Sol and what we know forever. You might be happy with that. But I've got to do what's best for a lot of civilians who didn't volunteer for any of this."

Ingram looked dubious. Chris didn't feel bad about upping the ante a little. The more he considered the possibility of APDU calling in favours from outside its borders, the more he realised how short a reprieve they might get.

"How many?" she asked. "The whole list Erskine sent me?"

"Fifteen hundred and seventy, or thereabouts. The rest decided to stay and go to APS states."

"Ah. Interesting choice."

Chris opened the Caracal's passenger door and ushered Ingram inside. "I'd better take you to the Brandts' farm. No prying eyes."

"And who are *the guys* Marc mentioned, exactly?"

"Dan Trinder and Alex Gorko. They're still in the facility. Oh, and Sol. I suppose we'd better include him now your story stacks up."

"So you thought he might have been keeping something from you instead of just not knowing about it," she said.

"Like I said, ma'am, he kept his mouth shut about *Cabot* all those years. And I owe my survival to a healthy dose of paranoia."

"We saw APDU troops at the gates on the probe feed. Was it Marc who went up to talk to them?"

"Yeah, young soldiers tend to do what he tells them," Chris said. "We could take them out in the time it takes to reload, but we want to keep the body bags to a minimum. Even if we're not here to face the backlash, some Ainatio staff will be, and APS is going to want serious payback. The next available target after that might be Britain."

Ingram said nothing, buckled up, and took out her own screen to study something. The Caracal ground all the way down the rutted track and was back on the road to Dogwood Farm before she said another word.

"Well, Opis is rather nice, and you've met Fred," Ingram said. "They call themselves teeriks. They're highly intelligent, sociable, and they design warships and weapons systems. Which they're sharing with us."

Chris could hear the catch coming. "That's handy. And generous. Why?"

"Food. We made nutrition bars for them."

Food was currency on Opis the same as on Earth, then. "You bought advanced alien technology with ration packs."

"Partly," Ingram said. "They were starving."

"This is where you cut to the bad news, isn't it?"

"You heard him say they're not fighters."

"I did."

"They're actually runaway servants. They stole a prototype warship they were working on as part of an uprising. Their overseers and their alien clients are looking for them."

Well, shit. Chris wanted his suspicious side to be wrong for once. "Y'know, that's not quite how I saw first contact panning out."

"You're a hard man to shock, aren't you?"

Even Chris was surprised how well he'd taken it, but it was shock fatigue. There came a point where his adrenaline ran dry and there really were no more fucks to give, just actions to be taken.

"No ma'am," he said. "I just deal with whatever comes and save the crying into my pillow for later. But it sounds like the whole Nomad project just changed. We'll have industrialised, expeditionary, armed, and potentially pissed-off neighbours. We could be shipping people into worse danger than they're already in."

"You're the one who asked me to ship them out."

"Captain, if you show up to check why our ships are under attack, and people ask for help to escape — people you already knew were due to come to Opis anyway — you don't get to claim you're just the taxi driver."

"I didn't say that," Ingram said. "But I want you to adjust your expectations. We're still debriefing Fred, but apparently Opis is off the beaten track and the ship's well hidden. And colonising space was never going to be easy or risk-free. Exploring Earth wasn't either."

Chris had lived the last ten years between frying pan and fire and it didn't look like that was going to change in space. The choice was never clear. Nobody could tell if Earth was beyond hope or not, so they could either ride it out in Britain and hope things improved, or at least didn't get any worse, or take a chance on a planet in a neighbourhood where everyone else was way ahead of them in the arms race.

But if Ingram had said Opis was a paradise without problems, he wouldn't have believed her anyway. She was being honest. He just felt bad for the people whose crisis he'd thought was solved and now maybe wasn't. He looked back at all the things he'd done to get to them to this point — extreme things, things he wouldn't want to remember in the years to come — and he wasn't ready to give up now and render all of those actions unnecessary and unjustifiable.

At least he felt something, though. He wasn't numb after all. He always had gut-wrenching anxiety when he thought he'd let people down by not protecting them well enough.

Aliens or not, the transit camp community would probably still want to leave. The Kill Liners and Ainatio staff had the British option. Perhaps this wasn't as crushing a blow as it looked, just an added complication. But was it safe to tell people the whole story and give them a choice? What happened if they changed their minds and wanted to stay, knowing about this Caisin gate?

He knew he couldn't trust Ainatio's staff. Maybe none of them needed to know the details until the last moment. The objective had always been Opis and how they got there was probably academic compared to what might be waiting for them on the other side

"You should have told Marc about the other aliens before he went back," Chris said.

Ingram looked unconcerned. "I think he'll shake it out of Peter Bissey or Fred by the time he leaves. If they don't tell him first."

"Okay, let's save this for the discussion with the others, so we all hear it at the same time."

"Very well."

The conversation lapsed into an embarrassed silence. Ingram turned her head and studied him. He could feel her eyes drilling a hole in his skull.

"You're the State Defence sergeant with an interesting history, aren't you?" she said. "I just remembered. Erskine sent me the personnel list."

Chris just knew Erskine would put a warning note next to his name, probably something like *psychopath* or *convicted felon* in bright red text. "Everyone in my team's interesting, ma'am. It's why we're here."

"I'm not knocking it." Ingram suddenly became brisk and breezy, like she'd worked out what she needed to do now and wanted to get on with it. "You're ideal Opis material. We need men who get things done."

"Yeah. We certainly do that."

"Major Trinder's report says Erskine offered your militia places in *Elcano*. But you stayed."

"And you'd have done the same. For the same reasons."

Ingram didn't answer. Chris pulled into Dogwood Farm and parked in front of the house, not sure what else she ought to know before he linked to Trinder and Alex for a discussion. He could see Howie keeping watch out of one of the living room windows, arms folded on the windowsill.

"That's Howie," Chris said. "He's waiting for Marc to say goodnight to him."

"His son?" Ingram asked.

"No, Howie came with my evacuee convoy. His family's dead, but that's pretty routine these days. He's kind of latched on to Marc lately, and Marc's fond of him." If Chris didn't say it now, he probably wouldn't say it in time, and Ingram needed to know. "You've probably decided you don't like Marc, but here's a heads-up for what it's worth. Both his sons were soldiers and they were killed in action within days of each other. That leaves a damn big hole in a man. I know he can be intimidating, and rank means zip to him these days, but cut him some slack. He's one of the good guys."

That was more than Chris intended to say. Ingram blinked a few times, then opened the passenger door. "Thank you for telling me, Chris. I'll keep that in mind."

Chris left it at that. He remembered sitting in the bar with Trinder, Jared, and the two Brits, trying to work out how things would fit together when they finally reached Opis decades in the future and had to work out their place in a world already shaped by a different uniformed culture and a new Opis-born generation. Now, if it happened, they'd have to make that culture themselves from the raw ingredients. They were back in that limbo of serving but not serving, either civilians in law but under laws that no longer existed, or a remnant still technically serving but with no chain of command to report to. Neither situation erased the oaths they'd taken. And here was Ingram, still in her navy working rig with the four gold captain's rings, no national insignia but still inextricably in her country's service. Chris appreciated her not trying to ram her seniority down their throats. Whether he'd like it if she thought she'd slot in automatically as his commanding officer was another matter.

"Let's go say hi to Mrs Brandt, then," he said. "She's the mayor's wife. Nice lady. Bakes awesome cakes. And you can talk to Sol again."

Ingram scuffed after him in her oversized rubber boots. Chris didn't get chance to knock on the door before it opened. Howie stood looking up at him expectantly.

"Hi Chris. Where's Marc?"

"He'll be along in a while," Chris said. "He had to go check out something. Don't worry, he said he hasn't forgotten and he'll see you later. Hey, there's someone I want you to meet. This is Captain

Bridget Ingram. She's a real sea captain. But keep that to yourself, okay?"

"Hi Captain Ingram." Howie held out his hand for shaking, then looked back up the passage. "Mrs Brandt, can Chris and his new friend come in?"

Joanne Brandt's voice drifted from the kitchen. "Come on in, Chris. Food and coffee in the usual place. I'll be right there."

Howie strode off. "I'll get some more plates."

Ingram watched him go and breathed a little *awww* sigh. "How adorable," she said sadly. "What a little gentleman."

"Yeah, he's a good kid. He deserves a better future."

The Brandts' living room had become a buffet in recent days with a table kept permanently covered with cakes, sandwiches, and other quick snacks. The room was the kind of place Chris would have retreated to for one beer too many and a snooze on the sofa. It was a haven of polished wood, sun-faded cushions that didn't match, and the muffled quiet that came from a lot of upholstery. Ingram helped herself to cake. Joanne walked in, dusting something off her shirt.

"Sorry, I was packing some food for the planning room. Doug just called me about the airlift. You guys have moved mountains. What can I do for you?"

"This is Captain Bridget Ingram," Chris said. "I'm sorry for stopping by this late, but I need to keep her under wraps for a few hours so nobody from Ainatio sees her."

Ingram turned on the charm. "It's lovely to meet you, Mrs Brandt," she said. "Thank you so much for your hospitality."

Joanne was all smiles. She was always cheerful, but now she seemed particularly pleased, probably because she thought everyone had been spared the prospect of a long overland evacuation to nowhere.

"Of course." She looked Ingram over. "Open house here. Are you organising the airlift? I thought your air force was doing it."

Ingram glanced at Chris. "Ah... no. I have another task."

Chris had to tell Joanne. He'd have to tell them all very soon, because he couldn't leave that kind of announcement to a stranger, and he needed the Kill Liners to trust him to tell them the truth. He didn't want Joanne wondering why he hadn't told her something that important when he had the chance.

And there was no way of grabbing the lifeline that Ingram had thrown to them without revealing who she was.

"Captain Ingram's the commanding officer of *Cabot,* Mrs Brandt," Chris said. "I realise this is going to sound crazy, but she's just come back from Opis. And we can't let Ainatio staff know she's here because one of them will go tell APS and we'll have even worse problems."

Joanne looked baffled. "I understand the secrecy, but I don't understand what you're saying about Opis."

"You know the instant comms wormhole?"

"Yes..."

"Well, Captain Ingram used a wormhole that can transport people and vehicles."

"Is this another one of Ainatio's secret projects they didn't tell us about?" Joanne asked.

"No, the technology belongs to aliens. They let her use it."

Joanne paused for a couple of seconds, eyes wide, then went on smiling as if she didn't dare stop.

"Aliens," she said. "Good Lord. Whatever next?"

"Do you believe me?"

"You're a plain-speaking man, Chris."

"I'll take that as a yes."

"It's just one shock after the next now. I don't know what I believe."

"Marc's been through the wormhole tonight," Chris said. "No ship. No cryo. You just walk through this portal gizmo and you're there."

Joanne looked ashen now. "I have to believe you," she said.

"I don't blame you for doubting it, Mrs Brandt. I wouldn't believe something until I saw it either."

Howie walked in with a tray of cups and plates. "What wouldn't you believe?"

"Ah, you'll see later, Howie," Ingram said, taking the tray. "Marc will tell you all about it when he gets back."

"I'd better get the food down to the town hall," Joanne said. She looked like she'd taken refuge in the nearest everyday thing she could find. "Do you want me to tell Doug you've got something important to discuss with him? I'll be discreet, obviously."

"That'd be good, Mrs Brandt," Chris said. "Thank you."

"Come on, Howie," she said. "You can help me."

Joanne was a born diplomat, even in a state of shock. The front door closed with a faint clunk, leaving the room so silent that Chris felt noisy just breathing. Ingram settled in the armchair in the corner and watched while he set up his screen on a chair in preparation for the meeting with Alex and Trinder. Trinder's icon was already highlighted in green, showing he was ready to start. Alex hadn't responded yet and remained red.

"Can you see that okay?" he asked.

"Yes."

"Good. Because Dan and Alex will definitely need to see you."

"Do you think it was wise to blurt all that out to that poor woman?" Ingram asked.

"About the aliens?" Chris nodded. "Yes, I do, ma'am. You heard what she said about Ainatio secrets. They've been lied to and kept in the dark for years. If we're going to build a new society on another world, I want it to start with the truth. The only reason we're not telling the Ainatio guys here and now is that we don't know which of them we can trust."

"Pham can't stop this, though."

"We don't know that. One strafing run from a friendly air force that's still flying for favours to be called in later and we're toast. And once he knows, he won't forget any of this exists. Earth's not my responsibility, but he's not going to think the gate's alien technology. He's going to assume it's human and that your guys had a hand in it. He already told Dan and Alex that Nomad is some kind of Brit plot."

"How did Marc contact the FCO, by the way? You were supposed to be cut off from the rest of the world."

It had taken her longer to pick up on that than Chris expected. "The same way he relayed a message to APS to ask them not to bomb us," he said. Maybe it was best to get all this sorted out now. It'd only fester if and when they reached Opis. "There's a special forces code or something that got him through to the Foreign Office on a sat phone. That thing must be fifty years old, at least."

"And if we use the portal to evacuate your people to Opis, he'll have to contact the FCO again to stand down the airlift, won't he?"

"Ah. I get it." No, Ingram definitely wasn't slow on the uptake. She was stealthy. That was okay. Chris could do dumb. "You want to talk to your government."

Ingram studied a pile of brownies on the table with a critical eye and reached for one. "Here's my dilemma. Now the adrenaline's ebbed, I'm thinking ahead. My crew haven't been allowed to call home. Everyone thinks they're dead, including surviving friends and relatives. Alex stopped it on security grounds. Now that APS knows about Nomad and has the FTL research, I can't see a reason to deny them that contact any longer."

"I can," Chris said. "Some of your crew are APS citizens. Nobody knows how they're going to react to us screwing their homelands. And even if they don't side with their countries, there'll be calls home and news is going to leak. First contact, culture shock, people going nuts. You get the idea."

"I thought you wanted honesty."

"After we're beyond Tim Pham's reach."

"He's locked up, you said."

"I never underestimate men like him. Look, I understand the need to maintain morale, but hold off a while."

Ingram ate the brownie in two bites. "Fair enough. We'll revisit this later. Has Marc given the FCO the research?"

"You'll need to talk to him about that. Just trust him. He'll do what's right."

Chris was glad he wasn't her. His only obligations were to people he looked in the eye on a daily basis, and that made his choices a lot less complicated. There were no competing duties to country and service to consider. When Ingram had left Earth, she'd never expected to return, and if she'd sent a message she'd probably have been dead and buried before the reply came back. Now everything could happen immediately and she had information that wouldn't just change how her crew saw their mission, but how mankind saw its place in the universe.

She also had access to technology that APS and everybody else would probably think was worth going to war to steal. If she didn't realise the obliging Fred had completely changed her mission, she wouldn't be much of a commanding officer. The Caisin gate was going to generate as many problems as it solved. But Chris still wanted to grab its lifeline and hang on as tight as he could, because the alternatives were even more uncertain.

Alex's screen suddenly changed from red to green. They could start the meeting now. Chris adjusted the angle of the device and pulled up a stool to sit next to Ingram.

"Okay, ready?"

"Ready," she said.

Chris pressed his earpiece. Solomon would be monitoring anyway so there was no need to get his attention. "Guys, cams on, please. I've got some news. It's kind of surprising."

"How surprising?" Alex asked. He was making coffee with his back to the camera. "Erskine's come back to rescue us kind of surprising?"

"There's someone here to see you. Forget the coffee and take a look at your monitor."

Alex turned. He obviously recognised Ingram right away because he went that unhealthy shade of bloodless grey that he often did. Trinder just sat there blinking, but he'd had plenty of practice from years of not reacting to Erskine.

Solomon's voice cut in. "Oh my. That's not possible. Captain? You're *here*?"

"Guys," Chris said, "Captain Bridget Ingram has the floor. Marc's gone to Opis but he'll be joining us later. Let the captain explain."

Ingram smiled serenely. "It's good to hear your voice again, Sol. We've missed you. And yes, I really have just arrived from Opis."

"I don't understand," Solomon said.

Alex dived straight in. "Oh. Sure. You took a cab." He was angry, not shocked. "Is this one of Bednarz's long-term surprises, or did Erskine's old man set this one up? This is like demining a frigging battlefield. Always something lurking to shit up your day."

"*Sit,*" Ingram said. "Please. This isn't another stunt like declaring *Cabot* lost. And good evening, Major Trinder. Chris let me have sight of your excellent reports, so I realise how serious your situation is. I'll give you a quick summary of why I'm here, and then I'm at your disposal." She took off her watch and held it between thumb and forefinger as if she was timing herself. "I arrived here earlier this evening — here being a field up the road — via an artificial wormhole called a Caisin gate. No ship necessary. You just walk through it. Sergeant Gallagher is on Opis now doing a recce and he'll be back shortly. I realise I'm dumping an awful lot of news on you at once, but we detected an attack on one of your ships and I came to see if we could help."

Trinder still looked expressionless. "Chris, is this true?"

"I watched Marc step through the wormhole and watched him step back again," Chris said. "He confirms it's Opis on the other side."

"Well, now it's your turn to shock *me*, Captain Ingram," Alex said. He'd had to break the news to *Cabot* that they were all officially dead. Maybe he thought Ingram was still mad at him. "There's only one thing we need right now and that's to get out of here and as far from APS as possible. You've got a walk-in wormhole, you say? Great. So how did you keep an eye on the ships in orbit here? Via the wormhole? Because we lost the FTL relay when Erskine abandoned us."

"I do realise this is hard to take in," Ingram said.

"I'm a quick study. Hit me."

"Very well. We found new allies on Opis. Intelligent aliens called teeriks, the black bird-like creatures you knew about already. It turns out they're highly advanced engineers and they detected the attack. But they're not the only intelligent aliens out there, they're in hiding because they're effectively valuable runaway slaves, they stole a prototype warship they designed, and they've ended up on Opis. Their overseers and the navy that owns the ship are looking for them. On the plus side, Opis is remote and well hidden."

Chris waited for the impact. If Ingram hadn't destroyed her target, she'd certainly caused some hull spalling. For a moment, Alex froze. Trinder actually blinked. Intelligent alien life wasn't so much of a shock, not after seeing the thriving plant and animal life on the live feed from Opis, but an assortment of arguing, thieving, warship-building aliens was a whole different matter.

Alex shuffled in his seat. "Shit."

"You did ask me to drop it on you," Ingram said.

"Is this payback for telling you you're dead and you can't phone home?"

"Oh, Mr Gorko, I'm *much* bigger than that. And more sadistically creative."

Alex rolled his eyes and looked up at the ceiling. "Okay, your government's offer of resettlement is now looking peachy. The weather's crap, but at least they don't have angry aliens coming to repo stolen warships. Look, we've got more than fifteen hundred people in need of urgent evacuation. For a few moments I thought we had a miracle rescue, but it's just another cesspit, isn't it? What an auspicious start as we take our place in the wider universe. Hanging out with the galaxy's most wanted. And they know where we live."

"Why didn't I see any signs of intelligence?" Solomon still sounded stunned. Chris felt sorry for him. He could hear the self-doubt creeping in. "Why were there no signs of civilisation on Opis?"

"Because the teeriks were hiding and it's not their homeworld, Sol," Ingram said. "Opis really is virgin territory. Don't blame yourself. We only realised when one of them tried to repair a radio."

Chris had been thinking in terms of the risk on Opis. Now he started to wonder about Fred's people being arrested, telling everyone where Earth was, and bringing the problem here. Maybe it was already too late to avoid trouble.

"We know we don't have a guaranteed safe option," Chris said. "Even if we reach Britain, we've still got APS and die-back to worry about. The situation on Opis sounds risky, but now some aliens know where Earth is, we won't stay a secret forever and we could get unwelcome visitors one day. But we can't afford to dick around. We have to decide."

"Let's see if using this gate is doable first," Trinder said. "Captain, could it move all our people, supplies, and equipment?"

"We haven't had a chance to discuss it, but the teeriks said it can, yes," Ingram said. "We'll have logistics issues about handling the influx on the Opis side, naturally, but if you want to evacuate now, I'll make it happen."

"I'm putting risks before feasibility," Alex said. "You haven't said how dangerous *you* think Opis is."

"Alex, if I thought we'd be taking civilians into a hostile environment, I'd have said so. The question isn't whether Opis is risk-free but whether it's a safer bet for you than Earth is now, and we can only go on the intel we have at the moment. It's incomplete, as intel always is. But the mission needs you all, and if you want to go to Nomad Base we'll get you there. It's your call, though."

"Does anyone else have this gate technology?" Solomon asked.

"Fred says FTL's widely used, but the Caisin gate's their own secret prototype," Ingram said. "Sorry, Sol — Fred's the teerik we deal with. Their device is something different. Precise and apparently capable of moving anything from a coffee cup to a lorry."

"Another prototype," Alex said. "So it's all experimental."

"Well, I made it here in one piece. And Marc Gallagher's used it three times now."

"Why did the teeriks head for Opis if it's that hard to find?" Trinder asked.

Alex spread his arms. "Who cares? We've got bigger problems. Would we be putting civilians in greater danger? Do we level with them and give them a choice? What happens if we do, and APS finds out about this Caisin technology?" He hadn't been placated. He'd just shifted the focus of his anger. He'd been forced to lie and smile for years and now he didn't have to do it any more. "Y'know, I liked this better when I thought it was a scam."

"You have options you didn't have twenty-four hours ago," Ingram said. "You'd have faced the same situation if APS hadn't shown up and you'd launched *Shackleton* as planned."

"No, we wouldn't. It'd be forty-five years later and your alien bird buddies would be in jail or dead."

"Possibly true, but the existence of aliens who might be a threat wouldn't have changed," Ingram said.

"We were going to Opis right up to the point where Pham screwed the launch rail," Chris said. "Okay, angry aliens wanting their ship back is bad news, but so is APS catching up with us sooner or later. They definitely won't forget they want to shut down Sol, for a start, and I don't think the fact we'd be on British soil would stop them."

"May we get back to the logistics for a moment so I can implement something as soon as you make a decision, please?" Solomon asked. "Speed will play a major part in the success of this evacuation. I need to work out how much traffic we can move in a given time. Unless anyone has any objections, my tasks will be to work with the teeriks and help you all plan the fastest transit. I'll also take care of the temporary accommodation in Nomad Base. So you can leave it to me, Captain, and focus on the security side."

Ingram looked genuinely emotional for a moment. "Damn, Sol, I'm so glad you're back."

"So you're voting to go, Sol?" Chris asked.

"My opinion doesn't count," Sol said. "But I still think it's the safer option, and my reason for existing is to keep you all safe, so that has to mean something."

"Marc needs a say in this too," Trinder said. "If he comes back in one piece and says it's doable, I'll think it's worth a shot. But I want to hear from him first."

"Marc left before we found out about the other aliens," Chris said.

Ingram glanced at him like he was suggesting she did it deliberately. He wasn't convinced she hadn't, although stalling seemed pointless. "I'm sure Commander Bissey will have briefed him by now," she said.

"Okay, if he's got all the facts, I'll trust his judgement, but it's not all on him. If we don't — or can't — give folks an informed choice, we're all responsible for this."

Trinder started tapping out something on his desk. "Assuming Marc gets back and the news is good, I'll put the detachment on alert for an immediate evacuation, tell them Opis is definitely on, and that they'll get a briefing of an... extraordinary nature."

"So who knows already?" Alex asked.

"Us and Joanne Brandt," Chris said. "I'm going to tell Doug when he gets back here."

"Who else?"

"Well, I'm going to tell my people the truth and I can't really stop Doug telling his. And yes, I do know that it becomes a risk to anyone who decides not to go, because they'll have information someone might try to beat out of them. The only folks we can't risk telling because it's a risk to *us* are Ainatio."

"This isn't going to help unite people in a new colony, Chris," Alex said.

"I know, but they're the guys with the asshole who dropped us in the shit and who'll probably do it again. I'm not going to risk it just to avoid hurting their feelings. If we find the traitor, I'll reconsider, but right now, no way."

Trinder shrugged. "Chris is right, Alex. We don't know enough about what Pham can and can't do to risk him finding out. This is massive technology. Every country's going to want it."

Alex moved on to Ingram. "Captain, are you or Marc going to tell your government about any of this?"

"I haven't even thought about it." Ingram rubbed her eyes as if she was tired. "Let's concentrate on an evacuation plan and how I can absorb a small town overnight without compromising my own crew's welfare."

Chris knew a lie when he heard one. Of course she'd thought about what to tell her government, even if she wasn't a serving officer any more. She had that same ingrained sense of tribal duty that Marc did. Chris knew how that felt and how powerful it was, and the only people he wanted to serve with were those who had it. But it wasn't always going to align with his.

"I'm not sure that was an answer, Captain," Chris said.

"My duty is to secure a colony on Opis and take in as many settlers as I can." Ingram was getting impatient now. Debate was another thing that nobody had time for in a real war. Chris suspected her officers didn't argue with her. "We signed up for Project Nomad, which is about preparing Opis for settlement — not first contact, not anthropology, not exoecology, or any other bloody kind of ology. We're claiming land for human colonists. And we *will* see it through. You'll have the gate option to return or pick up stragglers, but if you stay here, there might not be a gate, a ship, or even a colony to join if you change your mind in years to come. And whether Tim Pham or anyone else wants to pick your brains or bash them in regarding Solomon, wormholes, or aliens, that's all he'll get — brains. Because he can't reach any of it."

Chris gave her marks for brutal honesty. He liked her better in butcher mode. He watched her while the argument rolled back and forth about if and how much to tell people, how many of the remaining scientists would change their minds now they'd seen how Pham did business, and whether it was responsible to go at all when Britain was ready to take them. She looked composed rather than relaxed. But she had her hands in her lap, and while one rested casually on the other, the hand beneath was a tight fist. The woman was under pressure. There were too many options now because there were too many unknowns, and if she'd thrived in whatever war had earned her the butcher nickname, she probably missed the clarity of combat as much as Chris did. Sometimes it was better to pick the first purpose that made sense and live for it single-mindedly than dither between goals that couldn't all be achieved.

The clock ticked on. Chris was impatient to hear Marc's sitrep.

"It's nearly midnight, folks," he said. "I'm going to have to dip out for a few minutes to collect Marc. Captain, please don't go wandering outside. Stay out of sight and don't use the radio."

"Anything you say, Sergeant," Ingram said, absolutely deadpan.

"I'm serious." He'd have to leave his screen here and use his radio for comms. "Can I rely on you to stay put?"

She gave him a tight little smile. "I don't think Alex has finished with me yet, so I'm sure I'll still be here when you get back."

"Thanks." Chris knew Trinder would keep her talking if she looked restless. Sol would keep tabs on her too. "We don't know where Pham's special forces guys are. I'd hate for them to run into you. Especially when you don't have your weapon."

Chris grabbed one last sandwich, walked out to the Caracal, and headed back to Cedar Hill. He rated their chances of pulling this off at seventy-five per cent. That was good enough for him. He tried to decide if he was so worn down by years on the move that he just wanted somewhere to stop running, or if he really did think Earth was more dangerous than Opis. His old commander had always said that if you couldn't make up your mind between two options, then there probably wasn't enough of a difference between them to matter, but even picking the wrong one was safer than dithering.

Chris had picked Opis but he'd give his people a choice. They'd made a pledge. Where one went, they all went. It seemed dumb on first glance, but the comfort of being a community had mattered a lot more than places.

There was nobody about on the roads as he drove to the RV point, but the lights in the windows showed a lot of people were still up, probably making tough decisions on possessions to leave behind. Chris parked the APC facing the portal coordinates and left the headlights on low beam so he could keep an eye on the blurred oval. When he glanced in the rear-view mirror he caught his own reflection, tired and in need of a shave, and realised he wasn't the same man he'd been the last time he'd trimmed his beard, which was now more actual beard than carefully-maintained stubble. He'd seen a damn alien, an *intelligent* alien, a giant crow who could design wormholes and warships. He'd *talked* with it. The world would never be the same again and neither would he.

I'm human again. I felt it. Just for a moment, I was amazed.

But wonder took a back seat to practical reality again. He tapped the dashboard to open the Caracal's top hatch and deploy the machine gun, then climbed up into the gunner's seat. If anything he wasn't expecting came through that portal, he'd be ready. A six-hundred-round belt and two reloads — three minutes of continuous fire — would be useless against an advanced alien army or even a platoon with better weapons, but it was habit and it made him feel better. Yeah, first contact definitely wasn't working out how he'd imagined it at all.

He sighted up on the gun and adjusted the Caracal's lights. He was pondering Alex's argument about telling people what they really needed to know when Marc appeared in front of the vehicle, shielding his eyes against the headlights.

"Steady on, Chris," he said. "I come in peace. Take me to your leader."

"I didn't want to let any alien riff-raff in," Chris said. "No Fred?"

Marc brandished a blue metal cylinder the size of a large flashlight, then turned to point it at the portal. The patch vanished. "No, I left him explaining himself to a bunch of squawky teeriks. But I made sure we had our own key to the gate before we left."

"What did you just do? Where's it gone?"

Marc held up the blue gadget. "This thing sends a signal and tells the gate controls where to open this end of the wormhole. I don't know how it works out the size the aperture needs to be, but it does. And I've just told it to close."

"Cool. But can you open it again? Can Fred?"

"Point and press. Fred's end can place a gate anywhere, but apparently this gadget is what we need to make sure it opens where we need it. I'll show you when we send Ingram back. I'm hanging on to this with Fred's permission."

"You bypassed her."

"No, I'm just making sure we don't have a single point of failure." Marc actually looked happy for once. It must have been a productive visit. "Jeff Aiken took me for a quick drive around Nomad Base to pick an open site for the Opis end of the gateway, because you can't channel a convoy through a ship. And this one's *tiny.* I mean it's so cramped I kept hitting my head. Alien warlords must be short-arses." Marc flipped the portal flashlight over in his hand. "You know Jeff helped Fred learn English? Teeriks pick up languages just like that. He says they're living computers and they keep all those big complicated astrophysics numbers in their heads. I really want to go now. I don't mean I *have* to go, I mean I *want* to be there. I've been to another planet and seen aliens arguing and eating cereal bars. God, I wish I could tell my boys about it all."

Chris was still getting to know Marc but he felt he understood the core of the guy. Marc couldn't feel the good things in life without that regret creeping in. But he was happy at the moment. Chris was about to ruin his rare moment of elation and wished there was another way to break the news.

"I'm glad you talk about them," he said, shaping up for the reveal. "Not just because it's easier for me, either."

"What's the alternative? Pretend it never happened?"

"A guy told me the Japanese don't go in for grief counselling like Westerners do because they want to feel their loss or else they might forget the dead."

"Yeah. It's like that." Marc paused. "You want to tell me about someone?"

"You know about Jamie." Chris couldn't think of anyone else he missed. He held his breath for a moment and plunged in. "Marc, there's been a development since you left."

"Development. That's always ominous."

"Did Bissey or Jeff mention the other aliens? Fred's overseers?"

"What other bloody aliens?"

"Okay, sorry. Ingram dropped a bombshell. Fred's team stole that warship you were in. They're effectively slaves on the run from their overseers. And the navy that owns the ship."

Marc normally greeted bad news with a little creative cussing and got straight on with putting things right. This time he fell silent and stared down at the flashlight device for a long five seconds, then shrugged and got into the Caracal. Chris closed the top hatch and slid down into the driver's seat.

"So nobody mentioned it at the Nomad end," Chris said.

"Not a word."

"Maybe they thought Ingram told you."

"Nice try, Chris."

"Okay, I didn't want to make you any madder than you already are. It's done, and we bear in mind that we might not always get the whole truth from the *Cabot* guys."

"Did Ingram say what the chances are of these other aliens catching up with Fred?"

"Apparently Fred says Opis is a backwater. No passing traffic. But she hasn't got any other intel except Fred's viewpoint, and Fred stole a damn warship. That's bound to affect his version of the story."

"In an ideal world, we'd do a proper recce for a few months before we decided to ship out any civvies. But we don't have that luxury."

"So what happens if these teeriks open another gate to Earth and get pally with some other bunch of humans?"

"You're the bloke who doesn't plan too far ahead."

"Okay, I'm reeling a bit," Chris said. "I admit it. It's too much to take in even if it's not enough information to be useful."

"If it's any comfort, I know how you feel. We're entitled to some disorientation."

"Sol's scoping out the logistics for how long it'll take to evacuate via the gate."

"Oh, so you decided without me."

"No, the debate's still going on. I'm taking you back to Doug's place. They're probably still arguing over how much they can tell people in advance. Alex isn't happy about keeping Ainatio folks in the dark. He thinks it's divisive."

"So we're telling everyone else."

"I'm certainly telling my people. And I had to tell Joanne Brandt, and I'm going to tell Doug."

"Secrecy never bothered Alex before."

"I think he's just overcompensating for the whole Opis lie," Chris said. "The bottom line is I trust the Kill Liners and my own guys to keep it to themselves, but not Ainatio. So I'm all for lying to them."

"If Ainatio didn't employ treacherous shithouses, we wouldn't need to."

"But anyone who decides to stay after they're told the truth is going to be of interest to Pham, and he'll want to beat it out of them."

"Yeah, if he knows, he isn't going to give up on it just because there's a few hundred trillion miles in the way. Short of silencing Pham the ballistic way, I don't know what else we could do."

"It's a mess either way. But the one thing we know we can avoid is feeding the informer the intel in the first place." Chris took out the data card and handed it back to Marc before starting the Caracal. "Come on, I left Ingram on her own with my screen."

"That was bloody daft."

"It's locked. And she won't wander off. I told her Pham's ninja would get her if she went outside."

"I've still got her sidearm."

"It was her dad's. It might help workplace relations if you give it back."

"Yeah. It didn't slip my mind."

Marc was back to his normal self again, his burst of relative enthusiasm gone. Chris replayed the last few hours to work out what could have been done differently to spare the guy, but other than Ingram levelling with them from the start, he couldn't think of anything. When it all sank in, everyone was going to feel deflated by the speed at which their rescue turned into another potential crisis.

"Anyway, at least I got these," Marc said. He pulled something that looked like playing cards out of one of his packed vest pockets and held them up. "Fred helped me out with one of the probes he's got in Earth space. He took a look at something for me."

Chris glanced at the cards but couldn't see much in the dim light from the dashboard. "What are they?"

"Pictures of a house in Sydney," Marc said. "I made a promise and I wasn't sure I'd be able to keep it. Now I can."

He sounded like was preparing for an ending. Chris thought about what he'd said a few minutes ago and felt that cold, crawling sensation of dread, because he'd served with a guy who was in the best of moods on the day he finally gave up trying to live in an irreparable world.

But Chris realised he and Marc were both preparing for the same end — the last few days on Earth, leaving everything with meaning and familiarity, and tying up whatever loose ends they could. Somehow that seemed a bigger step than death itself. Chris hadn't realised he cared so much about an inanimate ball of rock. He had to ask the question again, the same one he'd asked Lennie Fonseca in what felt like a lifetime ago.

"It's over, isn't it?" he said. "Earth, I mean."

"It is for us, mate." Marc shook his head. "It's going to get a lot worse before it gets better, but we'll be dust before then. Might as well leave while we still can."

Chris made a point of taking each day he survived as a bonus in a world where so many had died. He didn't quit easily. He was ready to rebuild his America with his bare hands. But even he knew when it was time to call it a day.

"Just checking," he said.

* * *

AINATIO PARK RESEARCH CENTRE, SECURITY OFFICE: 0230 HOURS.

Trinder understood why guys broke down under all-night interrogations and would sign any random confession put in front of them just to shut their eyes for a while.

He'd tried to keep up with the ebb and flow of the arguments, but he couldn't think straight any more. At least he'd broken the news to Fonseca, though. She was watching the meeting, unperturbed, standing next to the wall screen map of Kill Line like a heavily armed TV weather forecaster and offering practical suggestions. The discussion had moved on to the practicalities of where to put the entrance to the Caisin gate and the fine detail of how to funnel people through it.

"Your best bet is the Becker dairy farm," Fonseca said, pointing to the appropriate spot on the map. "If you put the Caisin gate in the middle of the road, sure, it's easier to drive straight through, but like Chris just said, if a spy sat's watching or Pham's ninja has a micro-drone that wasn't networked when the sabcode hit, it's going to get attention. Becker is a jumble of agricultural buildings, so trucks disappearing there doesn't look anywhere near as obvious. I'd put the portal in front of the back wall of the milking shed. It hasn't been used in a few years and it's huge — big enough for sixteen-wheelers and buses. Any vehicle can just drive in and it's a good place to brief people discreetly if you plan to move them in batches."

"I still like the road version," Alex said. "One convoy."

"No, batches is the safest way to do it, because it's going to take hours to clear that many vehicles," Marc said. He was now sitting on a dining chair next to Ingram. With Chris sitting on her other side, it looked to Trinder like they were posing for a team photo of Kill Line Hard Bastards. "A line of autonomous vehicles can roll along at a uniform speed and distance and all slow down or speed up at the same time, but humans can't. They react to the vehicle in front, so there's always a delay, maybe just fractions of a second, but it ripples back down the line. We can't afford to have long tailbacks because we don't have enough troops to secure the queue."

"He's right," Chris said. "Convoys are organised in sections for a lot of good reasons. We only had a short convoy compared to this, and it wasn't easy with untrained drivers. Add livestock to this one, and we've got a lot of potential hold-ups."

"What livestock?" Fonseca asked. "Are we seriously moving animals too?"

"Any farmer who's got a cattle truck can take his animals," Chris said. "I told Doug. Trust them to be smart about it."

"This is crazy." Fonseca did her narrow-eyed look of disapproval. "They probably won't survive on Opis."

"Then we'll eat well for a while. And if they do survive, we've got fresh eggs and milk. Good for morale."

"Indeed," Ingram said. "I vote for eggs."

Trinder interrupted. "Anyway, back to batches, guys. It'll give the marshals at both ends of the gate some time to sort out ditherers and breakdowns and make sure the Nomad exit's clear. And we can brief each batch in the shed before they go through."

"That's a lot of briefings," Alex said.

"There's nowhere we can brief sixteen hundred people at the same time, even if it was a good idea."

"And why isn't it?"

"Human nature," Marc said. "People are going to be waiting around no matter how smoothly it goes. If we tell them everything in advance and say they can't change their minds, they'll be stewing over aliens and portals and imagining the worst for hours. Some are going to lose their nerve and bolt. And when we tell the boffins about intelligent aliens, which is probably the biggest science headline in history, some of them are going to want to share it with their mates who've stayed behind. We'll secure comms and movement as best we can but nothing's ever watertight. If anyone gets out of their vehicle and makes a run for it, we don't have enough people to spot them, let alone stop them. So that's why we'll do it in batches. Drive in, listen up, get back in your vehicles, drive at that fuzzy patch in front of you, and don't stop. Done. Welcome to Opis."

Ingram looked at Marc as if she was fascinated and had decided he wasn't a pain in the ass after all. "What he said. And Dan's right, we need time on the Nomad side at intervals to keep traffic clear of the exit gate, because drivers will slow down to follow parking instructions. Overall, this should make everything run more smoothly. And make sure you have a mix of cargo and passenger traffic in each batch, because if our lovely prototype gate has a glitch, we don't want people stranded at one end with their food at the other."

"We're already set up for that." Fonseca tolerated no helpful advice about her organisational skills. "I'm just modifying our existing evacuation plan."

"Remind me why we're sending the Ainatio buses through last," Alex said. "If we put them through first, we could forget about them."

"Because they're argumentative, so they're the most likely source of complications," Marc said. "If anything goes wrong, we want to know that the people best suited to settlement life are home and dry. And if your boffins arrive first and cause any hold-ups, our labour force and food providers are held up in a vulnerable position at this end."

"They're not all prima donnas."

"But enough of them are, Alex."

"Okay, so Doug's making sure we have somewhere in town to isolate and corral all the scientists," Chris said, cutting off the beginning of a spat. "Then we can — "

The phone rang on Trinder's desk. Everyone stopped dead. It was an actual phone, not a screen, the original wired internal system that had been kept running in case the network went down. Trinder could see Erskine's extension number on the small display.

"It's Pham," he said. "Mute your mikes and listen in." He put the call on the speaker and picked up. "Security. Trinder here."

"Ah, Major. If you'd stopped at sealing the building, we might have been able to part on relatively amicable terms." Pham sounded like he was trying hard to keep his temper. "But you let your AI do exactly what I said it would do. There'll be consequences. This is your last chance to release me and my personnel."

Trinder kept one eye on the Ainatio site map on the other wall and noted where the trackers were moving. "If you're worried about your team, Commissioner, we're providing hot food, water, and portable sanitation for those we can access without being shot at. We'll try to talk some sense into the hold-outs later. What can we get you?"

"I think I'll have Gallagher, all your scientists, and your illegal killer AI, please," Pham said.

"You forgot our conversation, Commissioner. They're not on the menu."

"And I think your AI's proven my point that it's a threat to human life."

"Has he killed anyone, then?"

"We have no comms or navigation." Pham had started his speech and he wasn't going to deviate from it. "And *Temujin* hasn't responded to missed radio checks and sent a helicopter to investigate, which tells me there's serious disruption over a much wider area. I can't confirm what's happening outside this redneck adventure park of yours, but I've done enough terrorist threat assessments in my time to know what happens when you knock different systems offline. Navigation, for a start. If your AI's disabled satellites, that'll hit our civilian population. I hold you responsible for death and injuries. And you *will* pay for it."

It was pointless to argue but Trinder did it anyway. "Oh please, spare me the outrage. You came here to loot Ainatio's intellectual property on the pretence of bombing us to save the world from a worse form of die-back. You marooned our civilians, knowing there'll be serious food shortages here and some of them won't survive on the road. You sabotaged our launch. And you attacked our ships, using ordnance you're banned from deploying in space. Don't try giving me moral lectures, Mr Pham."

Pham didn't miss a beat. "I'm guessing by your misplaced confidence that you know exactly how much damage the AI's done and you think we're helpless. How long do you think it'll take us to get aircraft here?"

"Have you managed to get any in the air?"

"If we haven't, nations that owe us favours will."

So far, Pham hadn't made any threat that Trinder and the others hadn't already considered. Aggressive swagger seemed pointless at this stage of the game, but he wasn't the type to do anything without a reason. He was trying to manoeuvre them into doing something that suited his plan, whatever that was.

"You've got access to a well-stocked kitchen in Erskine's suite, Commissioner," Trinder said. "But if you want room service, do call and let us know."

"Just remember the bombing run was delayed, not cancelled," Pham said. "And this problem needs more than sodium weapons to make sure there's no AI or die-back to trouble anyone in the future. Long overdue, I think."

Trinder hoped the technician who let slip that APS couldn't carry out its threat was right. "Then you'll all be vaporised along with us," he said.

"Is that why you've locked us in?" Pham asked. "Insurance against an attack on this site? If dying alongside you is the price of shutting down your AI, we'll pay it. Killing off die-back is a bonus."

Pham sounded completely sincere. He was on a crusade, and that made him far more dangerous than the average bribe-hungry politician.

"Okay, we'll try to remember to let you out some time," Trinder said. "Goodnight, Commissioner."

Trinder put the phone down and wondered why the hell he hadn't let the guy carry on to see where it went. He turned to Fonseca and Alex, looking for a reaction. "Okay, I blew that. Maybe I should have let him talk more."

"No, he said enough," Marc said. "Which I recorded for later use. He's probably done us a favour."

"If he hasn't got an actual nuclear strike force on the way. What's he up to?"

"He thinks he'll make us panic and run," Solomon said. "He knows I won't leave you, so when you withdraw from the campus, I have to transfer to a mobile frame. A definable target for his special operations people, no IT skills required. Exactly what Erskine tried to do."

"And for once we know something he doesn't," Alex said. "Or maybe he does know somehow that Britain's offered us an airlift. But we do have to run, one way or another."

Trinder could see Ingram glancing at her watch. "We can't be sure he's bluffing about bombs, though," she said. "He just might have a standalone backup designed to kick in if their networks are compromised. Some governments did have them."

Chris leaned forward, elbows on his knees, impatient. "It's not like we're waiting for anything. We pull everyone out now. We'll come and clear the gates at zero three-thirty hours. Everyone okay with that?"

Alex half-raised his hand. "Works for me."

"Okay, let's move." Marc stopped and looked down at his pocket screen as if he'd had a message, then carried on. "Dan, keep the squad frequency open and we'll flash you when we're back in range. You can move as soon as we've got the APDU guys calmed down and put to bed."

"Are you going to stand down the airlift now?" Fonseca asked.

"I'd rather wait until we've actually got people moving through the gate," Marc said. "Just in case."

"When you brief everyone, remind them that accommodation on the other side will be temporary and haphazard," Ingram said. "But my people are vacating their quarters and clearing non-essential buildings for accommodation until we sort out a more comfortable arrangement."

Solomon had been unusually quiet. Trinder wondered if he was still in shock in some AI kind of way because he hadn't realised the teeriks were intelligent. But Ingram's comment about accommodation got him going again.

"Captain, you'll be surprised at how much we'll be able to achieve overnight," he said. "Trust my calculations. And I'll make sure we send the emergency relief equipment through as soon as the gateway's established in its new position."

"Sol, I know you will," she said. There was a fond note in her voice for a change. "I'm heading back now. Do you want me to dust off your quadrubot?"

"Thank you, but no need," he said. "I'll bring my own."

"Any message for Fred?"

"I'll have to give that some consideration."

They were obviously pretty friendly. Trinder let a stray thought wander around his brain for a while about whose side Solomon would take in a spat between Ingram and his chosen people here, but he put it to one side.

"Okay, meeting over," he said. "See you when the gates open, guys."

The evacuation had begun and this time it would happen. Trinder was grateful for a long list of jobs to do and a tight deadline for completing them, because that pumped him up more than caffeine ever could. He turned to Fonseca to do a final check on a procedure they'd dusted off far too many times.

"Supplies?"

"Trucks on auto waiting to roll as soon as the gates open."

"Buses?"

"Five standing by, plus two cargo carriers for personal effects. Everyone was prepped for *Shackleton*, so they've already pared down their luggage."

"Support vehicles?"

"Mobile medical unit, field lab, utility vehicles, crop inspection pickup, water tanker, chemhaz fire truck, three excavators, two ammo trucks, and the truck-mounted guns. All the Caracals that aren't already on patrol are in the vehicle compound with the mobile artillery pieces, waiting for drivers, which will probably be Chris's militia after they've mopped up APDU. Oh, and I'll disable the gun and missile launcher on the roof. We probably won't have time to dismantle and move them."

"Time estimate?"

"Barring interruptions, we can have everyone plus supplies and vehicles safely in Kill Line and shut down here by noon."

"Remember to leave transport for staff and the APS personnel staying behind."

Fonseca looked up at nothing in particular as she did some mental calculations. "One bus and four minibuses," she said. "That should be enough. What did you have in mind?"

"Just something to get them to the coast if planes are grounded for longer than we expect," Trinder said. "*Temujin* has to have some small boats that haven't been compromised by the sabcode. They can ferry people from the shore, I expect."

"I get that some of our people are going to be dependent on APS's goodwill, Dan, but that does come second to getting the others away safely."

"I know, but I want to leave them with a functioning building, food, and some way of leaving if they have to make their own way somewhere."

"Do you think APS would do that for us if the situation was reversed?"

"Probably. They're not all like Pham."

"Tell me that when one of those armed kiddies shoots you. Being reasonable won't necessarily be reciprocated."

"I know. But it's worth trying."

Trinder knew that look on Fonseca's face. She wouldn't say it with Alex in the room, but he could read the words GROW A PAIR above her head in neon lights only he could see.

She moved across to the site plan and pointed out areas on the wall screen. "Okay. Most of the APS guys are here, here, here, and in the restaurant and club. If we're going to drive straight out and hand them the facility, though, we won't need to spend time herding them into more habitable sections by opening doors and bulkheads. So they can hang on for a few more hours."

"You're assuming no long-drawn-out firefights and stand-offs," Trinder said.

"Then they just have to wait longer for coffee and bathrooms."

"Don't provoke them, Lennie."

"All our soon-to-be ex-staff chose to go with APS *after* they were going to bomb us," Fonseca said. "When does our responsibility end? We're about to overwhelm a small outpost that's going to struggle to house us and doesn't have any supermarkets. Food supplies will be critical. And we're giving them away."

Some of the scientists on the resettlement list were people Trinder didn't like very much, and some of them he barely knew. They ranked higher than APS personnel on his guilt list, though, and even if he didn't care personally about the fate of Pham's team, he did care about being able to live with himself. He knew he couldn't do that if he abandoned anyone to possible starvation when they hadn't done anything to deserve it.

"There'll be fewer than two hundred people left here, so I think we can spare a couple of months' supplies for them," he said. "And we don't have the time to round up all the food that isn't already loaded. So they can have the contents of the restaurant and club cold stores. Anything else, Captain?"

"No, Major," Fonseca said stiffly. "Understood."

Trinder knew he might have cause to regret his generosity. He also knew she'd remind him of it if he did.

Alex looked up from his screen. "Right, I'm sending out an all-staff message now. Everyone, rail repair team included, will wait in their quarters until further notice and prepare for immediate evacuation, and if anyone's changed their mind, they have to notify me by oh-three-forty-five. And stand by for an announcement from you."

"It's going to be short," Trinder said. "I'm going to brief my guys now. Excuse me, folks."

He got on the secure net and summoned the entire detachment to the briefing room next door. They had to hear it from him. He did a head count as they reported in and wondered where to start, with aliens or interstellar portals.

"We've segregated APS and APDU from staff in the shared areas, sir," Schwaiger said. "The APS guys were getting jumpy when we left, though. I think clearing our people in a hurry made them think an attack was imminent."

"It is," Trinder said. "The militia's going to clear the blockade on the gates at zero-three-thirty. But I've got something important to tell you first, and it doesn't leave this room, okay? The staff can't be told yet. None of them."

Trinder looked around the room and just saw tired faces, not scared ones. They'd been ready to leave so many times now that it must have been hard to believe it was really going to happen, and he'd probably made it sound like he had bad news to give them.

"This is going to be a lot of information to assimilate," he said, "but we're back in touch with Nomad Base, they've got access to a wormhole that can move vehicles without the need for a ship, and it's been loaned to us by a race of intelligent aliens. We'll be evacuating everyone by convoy as planned, except we're going straight to Opis. I promise you this is real. Captain Ingram's been in Kill Line tonight."

There wasn't even a stunned silence. "Holy shit, sir," Luce said. "We had a sweepstake going, but none of us picked that one."

As Trinder recited the words he felt he'd already said a dozen times tonight, the list of unknowns and the hardship ahead and the chances of being caught in the middle of an alien dispute, he watched them all perk up. Sheri Ballam was smiling to herself while she shifted ammo from one pocket to another. Ray Marriott nodded happily.

"This is what I would have joined up for if I'd known it was coming, sir," Gerry Eaton said. "Guys would pay to be part of this."

There was a murmur of agreement. Trinder kept thinking he knew his people, and then they'd go and surprise him again. They weren't shocked by intelligent aliens and advanced technology and they didn't see the new risks on Opis as a problem to be tackled. They saw it as the exciting unknown where they could make a historic difference. They'd been waiting for something like this all their lives.

Trinder consulted his screen. "We've got two additions to the Opis list — Phil Berman and Ruth Chase. Other than that, the remainers and leavers are as shown on your screens, so we can start moving people to the buses as soon as the gates are secured. Everyone not involved in this initial phase, take up your positions to cover the entrance. We won't engage APDU personnel unless the transit camp militia requires it. Dismissed."

Fonseca nudged him as they went back to the office. "See? They're happy now. This is why people like post-apocalypse movies."

"Despite living in one for real?"

"Demolishing the old order's appealing. And it's not like we have a choice."

No, they didn't. And Trinder didn't either. He was leaving Earth for good, so he couldn't look for his family. The thought was entirely out of the blue. He hadn't even realised they were on his mind. But it wasn't true, because now there was technology that would let him look anywhere in the world and go there without worrying about long, dangerous journeys across the country. His excuses had been snatched from him.

He stopped before they reached the office door and turned to Fonseca. "Lennie, have you given any thought to what else the Caisin gate can do?"

"A few things have occurred to me, yes."

"Boon to mankind stuff? Or robbing banks?"

Fonseca shrugged. "Both, to be honest. But I settled for saving our asses when we thought we'd be living on nettles and roadkill this winter."

"Not enough traffic left to generate roadkill," Trinder said. "And we'd have done better than living on nettles in Britain."

"Yeah, but for how long?" Fonseca walked on. "Look at the map. A little stretch of water between them and feral Europe. I'd rather have a forty-light-year buffer zone, thanks, and never look back."

Trinder reassured himself that he couldn't do anything with the Caisin gate for a while, and maybe never. And he couldn't assume the gate was available for personal errands.

"Yeah," he said. "Looking back never helps."

When he opened the office door, Simonot was at the comms desk. He nodded towards the clock on the wall and gave Trinder a meaningful look.

"Are you going to make that announcement now, sir?"

"Okay, let's do it." Trinder sat down and muted his mike before switching it over to the broadcast system. "Is everyone in separate sections?"

"Yes, only our people can hear you." Simonot selected the communications overlay on the site map to display red icons in all the areas where APS staff were segregated and couldn't hear the broadcast system. "You can speak freely. Well, as freely as you can when you know the informer is out there somewhere."

Trinder knew he wasn't the kind of commander who could galvanise armies and stiffen anyone's sinews, but this was probably his last official announcement before he shut down. It wasn't just about purging networks and doing final housekeeping. This was the last Ainatio site, the final remnant of a global corporation, and no lawyers, accountants, or courts were left to dissolve the company. Trinder was an hour or two away from doing it simply by pulling the plug. It was a serious occasion that deserved a ceremony. But he had a feeling that Bednarz wouldn't have cared, because Ainatio had served its purpose. It had delivered Nomad. And that was all he'd built his business empire for.

Trinder took a breath to steady his voice and counted to three.

"Colleagues, this is Dan Trinder," he said. "We'll be starting the evacuation shortly after we've removed the APDU blockade on the gates. Those of you leaving tonight will board buses at your designated muster point and leave for Kill Line, and I'm pleased to say you *will* be going to Opis as planned. I repeat, we're going to Opis. Everyone else, those of you who've chosen to stay, you'll be left with transport, supplies, and facilities to tide you over until APS can retrieve you. We'd have preferred you to come with us, but we understand your reasons. So that's it. After one hundred and thirty-one years, Ainatio is now permanently ceasing all operations, locally and globally. We delivered on Tadeusz Bednarz's dream. We made Nomad happen, whether we realised it at the time or not. Goodbye, everyone. Safe journey, wherever it takes you."

He switched off his mike. Simonot was staring at him. So was Fonseca.

"Damn," Fonseca said. "That wasn't like you at all."

Trinder had meant every word. "Yeah, okay. But I did my best."

"I meant it nearly made me tear up."

"And that's not like you, either." Trinder put on his cap, slung his rifle, and checked his sidearm. "I'm going to do the rounds before we clear the gates. Call me if there's a problem."

He left through the side door of the security wing and unlocked the last quad bike left in the parking bay. The rest were now either loaded on a truck or in use elsewhere. He sat in the saddle for a few moments, listening to the sound of idling engines as the evacuation convoy formed up at the rear of the accommodation block, and tried to grasp the idea that he'd never see this place again. His memory of arriving sixteen years ago was vivid, although possibly distorted by time. He'd been excited about the extreme secrecy of the place and thought it was doing unimaginably clever things behind locked doors, which it was, except one of those clever things was lying on an epic scale. It was the year before die-back wiped out the US wheat harvest. It was also the last time he saw the outside world other than on a TV screen. This strange village had swallowed his best years. He'd thought he'd die here and end up with his ashes scattered in the carefully-tended gardens with the rest of the staff who'd lived on the site, unable to leave until old age or serious illness claimed them.

At least he could do a bit of travelling now.

He set off in the direction of the medical wing, following the dim green glow of safety markers dotted along the kerb. There were lights in most of the buildings, but there wasn't a soul about except for the technicians sleeping inside one of the APS decontamination tents on the lawn. They were piled around a small camping lamp on the floor. If Pham's other operator was still around, Trinder couldn't see him. He expected the guy to have found a way through the perimeter fence by now. Perhaps that should have worried him more, but Solomon was monitoring the area with a micro-drone, and if anyone was motivated to find those operators, it was their intended target.

Trinder rolled up to the exterior doors to Erskine's suite to find Zakko still standing guard outside, drinking something from a travel cup while insects whirled in the light above the doorway.

"Damn, Zakko, have you been here all the time?"

"On and off, just in case Pham gets ideas, sir," Zakko said. "Are you letting him out with the rest of them?"

"Sol's putting a three-day delay on the locks for this suite so we can lift the lockdown remotely for the others without worrying about him getting up to mischief. But he isn't going to starve."

"It's not him I'm worried about." Zakko took a long gulp of whatever was in the cup. It smelled like tomato soup. "What about Dr Kim? Will you let her out and give her a head start?"

Trinder had shelved Kim for later, but he wasn't comfortable leaving her to Pham, and it wasn't like she could do any damage to the mission now. "I don't know where she is."

"I do. She's on the top floor." Zakko stepped back from the doors and pointed up the side of the admin building. "I saw her pass that window a couple of hours ago. I know we can't take her with us, but we can help her get away. She managed to make it here from Korea without any proper transport, so she's capable of escaping again under her own steam."

"You saved her before, didn't you? When she first showed up in the county."

Zakko shuffled his feet and looked awkward. "I found her and she was in a bad way. I just got meds for her. Chris is the one who saved her."

He was unwaveringly loyal to Chris. No, it was Zakko who'd saved Annis Kim's life, and Chris had nearly taken a knife to him for stealing antibiotics for her from the transit camp supply. Chris said he regretted that now. Zakko had saved his life as well. Zakko just couldn't walk away from someone who needed help, even when it was a bad idea.

"Okay, what would she need to escape and survive?" Trinder asked. "She can't go home, not if APS intelligence is after her. She'll have to go into hiding. That's pretty easy over here, though."

"She needs a vehicle," Zakko said. "A gun and ammo. A radio and a screen, just in case some town out there is transmitting. Medical supplies. A survival kit. MREs and water."

"We'll have to see what we can spare."

"If Dr Kim hadn't shown up, we'd still be stranded in the camp. It was only Dr Kim giving Chris the coordinates that eventually made Erskine let us join the mission. So Dr Kim saved *us*."

Trinder recalled the arguments with Erskine over the transit camp people all too well. Kim had only been the catalyst. The people who'd fought to get Chris's refugees on the ship were everybody *but* Kim — himself, Solomon, and Alex, but not Kim. But this wasn't the time to present Zakko with a pointless argument for not saving the woman.

"We can leave a vehicle where she can find it," Trinder said. "But it's up to her to get to it. I'd have expected Pham to handcuff her to something solid, though, not let her wander around. He knows she's quite an escape artist."

"Once we've retaken the gate, I'll pin down which room she's in," Zakko said. "Maybe Sol can see a heat signature in the admin block."

"I'll certainly try," Solomon said.

Trinder hoped Kim hadn't decided to try to escape via the service passages like she had last time. He could see Zakko being delayed by the search and getting captured. Trinder wasn't prepared to lose him just for her, and he knew Chris wouldn't leave without him.

"Zakko, have you mentioned this to Chris?"

"Not yet."

"Clear it with him and I'll get Alex to put it all together."

"Thank you, sir."

"I'm surprised Pham hasn't shot her already," Trinder said. "Who's going to know? This place doesn't exist and she's already dead as far as the world's concerned. That was her cover story for getting here, remember?"

Zakko nodded. "I do. Which is why we have to help her."

"Okay." It crossed Trinder's mind that Pham had anticipated they might try to rescue her, and that he might have been using her as bait in some elaborate set-up, because that was Tim Pham. He sowed uncertainty. He let people's imagination, fear, and mistrust do his work for him. "But don't get shot. I know you like Dr Kim, but she's not worth dying for. Okay?"

Trinder left him to it and rode off. Perhaps Fonseca was right. They were going to a lot of trouble to placate an enemy, and even if it helped the folks left behind, it all boiled down to taking responsibility for people who'd chosen to sever that link. Trinder could have walked away. The APDU troops, guarding gates they couldn't even lock, could have been shot dead by now without ever knowing what had hit them. He could have picked easier options that would have made the evacuation a lot safer for the people he was supposed to look after.

But Pham could have made life easier for himself by shooting Ainatio staff, and nobody except his troops would have known or cared. Yet he hadn't.

Trinder's conscience and his rules of engagement — mostly the same thing, but not always — had been his handbook of right and wrong until the last few months. Now he couldn't tell the good guys from the bad by their actions. The only moral certainty left to him was the need to look after his tribe.

It was now 0325. He slowed to a crawl as he passed the training centre and stopped by the comms tower near the perimeter fence. From here, just east of the gates, he could see the APDU blockade sideways on, a very thin line.

The kids been there for more than twelve hours. Three of them were sitting in the cover of the front entrance, taking a break with their backs against the concrete pillars between the glass doors. Six more stood in a line across the width of the gates. Trinder wondered where the tenth one had gone, but then he emerged from the shadows zipping his fly and picked up a can of soda from the front steps before settling down in the doorway to drink it. For all Fonseca's disapproval of taking care of the enemy, she'd sent out a trolley bot loaded with sandwiches and drinks. Trinder hoped the troops would go home and tell their families that Americans were humane and hospitable even in a conflict, but he wasn't sure why that mattered to him.

Then the line of troops at the gate reacted as one man and aimed their rifles. Trinder could guess what they'd spotted. He parked the quad bike halfway down the path and began walking the rest of the way towards them, but all he got was quick glances from a couple of those closest to him before they turned back to face what they were really worried about.

Their focus was on the mass of vehicles rolling out of the darkness and assembling on the approach road in front of the facility. Even from this angle, it looked intimidating. Watching the small army approaching head-on — Caracals and gun trucks with their lights on full beam, armed men on the flatbeds of pickups — must have been worse. Trinder did a quick estimate and realised the force was too big to be just Chris's militia. The Kill Liners must have turned out as reinforcements. The vehicles slowed and assembled in a loose group that spanned about sixty yards, leaving a single Caracal to drive up to the gates.

It stopped ten yards out. Marc jumped down from the passenger side and walked slowly towards the gates with his arms held well away from his body, palms open. One of the troops barked "*Hold!*" at his comrades but they didn't lower their rifles far enough for Trinder's taste.

"Corporal Cho," Marc called. "Can we talk?"

He stopped right in front of the outer mesh gate, which was still partly open. The inner gate, separated from it by a few yards, was closed. Trinder knew Marc would have body armour under that heavily-loaded vest, but it was still a big risk to take.

The APDU kids were taking a risk too. They were staring down a mass of armed men and women who looked like an efficient but frightening vigilante mob. None of them were wearing Ainatio rig. They'd all reverted to their mix of civilian clothing and parts of old battered uniforms. If it was meant to psych out APDU, it was probably doing a good job, but it also sent a subliminal message that the company — and the scientists left behind — had nothing to do with this. Trinder appreciated the gesture.

Corporal Cho walked up to the inner gate like he was doing a changing of the guard, rifle held across his chest, and slid the mesh screen open. He stepped outside instead of letting Marc in. But their body language said they were at ease with each other, and they appeared to be chatting. Marc took something out his pocket and handed it to him. It must have been notes or something, because Cho studied them one by one, nodded as if he was thanking Marc, and put them in his pocket. Then Marc showed him something on his pocket screen. Cho watched it for a minute or two, then shrugged, and the two of them walked through the gate.

"Stand down," Cho said. That was all Trinder heard. Some of the troops didn't obey the order right away, possibly because they couldn't work out what was going on, and Cho had to shout the order again, but then they all gathered around him and Marc like they were getting a team briefing.

Trinder tried to approach as casually as he could, still not convinced that it wouldn't suddenly kick off and turn into a firefight. But the troops were listening to Marc, and that had to be a good sign. Trinder finally got close enough to hear the conversation.

"Ah, here's the boss now," Marc said, beckoning to Trinder. "Major, I was just telling these gentlemen that we'll agree not to put Commissioner Pham in front of a firing squad as long as they surrender their weapons and don't interfere with the evacuation. They don't want to harm unarmed civilians and we don't want to have to shoot them. You okay with that?"

Trinder tried to grasp what Marc had just said and did his best to improvise. "Yeah, I'm glad we agree that civilian safety comes first. None of us wanted this unfortunate situation." He hoped Marc could see he was floundering and needed a prompt. "You'll get your weapons back when we've left, but in the meantime, stack them on the steps over there. Then you can enter the building and have a meal and shower. We'll be gone by lunchtime. After that, the place is yours."

"What about Commissioner Pham?" one of the troops asked. "And the lieutenant? They're going to kill us for this."

"He's not here to make the call," Marc said. "Don't worry, we'll tell Pham he had a lucky escape. I was really looking forward to putting a round right between his eyes."

By now, Luce had come out with Fonseca, rifles ready. Trinder saw Chris walking towards him from the other side of the compound, as if he hadn't come in via the gate. His militia now popped up all around the entrance. It had the desired effect of making the APDU kids surrender their rifles and sidearms without having to be asked again. They didn't look happy or relieved, but they seemed to take Cho's authority seriously even if they thought they should have gone down fighting. Trinder wondered what he'd have done in their position. They didn't know what had happened to their families, and for all they knew they were passing up the chance to settle the score with the folks who were responsible. Trinder wouldn't have blamed them for opening fire. But the worst thing was knowing that some of them might be receiving bad news when communications were restored.

Luce, Marriott, and Fonseca escorted them into the building. Chris wandered up to Trinder and Marc.

"I love an anti-climax." He looked at Marc. "So did you really say it?"

"What, that we'd shoot Pham if they didn't surrender? There's no dishonour in surrendering to vastly superior forces when it saves the life of a much-loved senior politician."

"What was that bunch of papers you gave Cho?" Trinder asked.

"Photos of his home in Sydney to show him it hadn't been bombed and that his dad and sister were okay. Oh, and I played him the recording of Pham talking about nuking the site and saying it was worth them all dying to destroy Solomon. I don't think the commissioner mentioned that in his mission briefing."

"They'll be in deep shit when we leave," Chris said. "Cho isn't exactly the ranking officer here. He's just one corporal."

"What's Pham going to do, then, shoot them all?"

"If he really is doing this off the books, he's now got a lot of witnesses I don't think he wanted," Trinder said. "What else can he do to keep them quiet?"

"I don't think he has to do anything," Marc said. "I guarantee they'll never mention this outside their platoon. They're soldiers. I think most of it's come as a shock to them, but Pham wasn't expecting to find what he did, either."

"I hope you're not just telling yourself that because you don't want to see anything happen to them," Chris said.

"I wasn't joking about putting him down. I could make time to come back for a man-to-man chat if anything happens to those lads." Marc tapped something into his screen as if he was making a note to check later and make good on the promise. "Anyway, time to exfil. Our new planet awaits. Y'know, I think I've always wanted to say that."

He strode off. Trinder looked at Chris.

"He can be persuasive when he needs to be," Chris said. "But Cho set it up for him. Smart boy. Some things are worth dying for, but this isn't the day. Or the cause."

"So are we still putting Pham on a timer so he's locked up for a few more days?"

"Is this about giving Annis Kim a head start?" Chris asked.

"In a way," Trinder said. "But just in case we hit any delays, we don't want him charging out after us as soon as we release the rest of them."

"It's his ninjas you need to worry about. And they're in the wind already."

"No sign of them yet?"

"We've lost both of them," Chris said. "And I still haven't found a breach in the fence. I'll assume they're holed up in the worst possible position for us and plan accordingly."

Solomon joined in on the secure channel. "I've done the most thorough search I can outside the perimeter. It's a very large area to sift through. But I expect they'll come to us, or to *me* to be precise, so we won't have to look too hard."

"You're a massive flying death machine at the moment, Sol," Chris said. "I wouldn't worry too much. But I wouldn't put it past them to take hostages to force your hand. That's what I'd do, anyway."

"Thank you for that insight," Solomon said.

Trinder could hear engine noises and turned to look for headlights. The front gates began opening to full width, rattling and scraping, and then he saw the beams. Something was heading towards the facility. They walked up to the gates and stood behind the barriers by the empty guard house to watch a sixteen-wheeler rumble past to load a container of supplies. It was finally happening. He felt better already.

Chris leaned on the rail. "So we're giving Kim a getaway car, a survival kit, and supplies."

"And a weapon or two."

"She'll need them. She can't go home again. Where the hell is she going to go?"

"We can't take her with us."

"I wasn't asking. Anyway, this is for Zakko. I owe him. Any update on the informer?"

Trinder shook his head. It was the least of their problems now, but he wanted to be able to tell people so they could stop looking sideways at their colleagues and start life on Opis with a clean slate.

"Whoever they are, they'll be one of those staying behind," he said. "It's still a long list."

Chris took his screen out and scrolled through it. "I don't know half these people. And the ones I do know — well, it could be any of them. I've been surprised by nice folks who turned out to be assholes, but I wouldn't disbelieve it of anybody. Even someone who's coming with us."

"What, you think Pham said thanks for the intel, now beat it?"

"I wouldn't disbelieve that, either."

"Humans, huh?"

"Shitty little animals, aren't we? I don't know what Solomon sees in us."

"People like Zakko," Trinder said. "That's what he sees."

Trinder wondered whether to give Kim one of the old APCs, the ones that pre-dated the Caracal, but it would be conspicuous if she wanted to move around unnoticed. They'd have to find an old pickup instead, one with enough room for her to sleep in it. He couldn't do more than that.

"I'll go get her stuff together and pack her rucksack," Chris said. "Funny, this is where I came in. Bringing her here on a quad bike, through these gates."

"Right about there," Trinder said, pointing. "That's where I walked out and thought who the hell is this guy."

"When you find out, tell me."

It didn't seem like a few months ago. It felt like years. They had eight hours to evacuate this place but here they were, worrying about Annis Kim again and reminiscing. A truck rolled past them hauling a long trailer stacked with flat-packed tents and shelters, the kind that aid agencies shipped in after disasters.

"Yeah, we should all be more Zakko," Trinder said, and went off to see what he could find by way of a pickup.

* * *

ADMIN BUILDING: 0445 HOURS.

Annis mopped at the blood on her elbows and tried to remember when she'd last had a tetanus shot.

Did it matter? If she didn't get out of here soon, she might be dead before any bacteria got the chance to do the job. She'd tried crawling through the ventilation system, but it was blocked by a grille twenty feet into the duct and she didn't know where it came out anyway. All she had to show for hours of sweating, cursing, and struggling to back out of the shaft again was skinned elbows and pulled muscles in her neck.

She sat down against the wall and took a breather before turning her attention back to the door. The strip of metal gripper she'd pulled up from the edge of the carpet was too soft to dismantle a lock, even if she could work out how to bypass the security on the outer door, but the problem was the sealant. She could see it set in mid-ooze as it bulged out of the gap between door and door frame like some pale grey fungus. Even if she could tackle the lock, which was Ainatio's doing, she couldn't get the door itself open until she hacked out all that rock-hard industrial foam. It looked like the kind they used in ship repairs. Tim's operator had sealed her in from the outside, which was smart. They didn't have control of the locks, either to open or close them, and they knew she was as capable of escape as they were because she'd been trained the same way. But the sealant made sure she stayed put until Tim decided otherwise.

But Tim didn't look like he was planning to leave her here.

Whether she was going to live or die, he wouldn't abandon her and assume she was conveniently dead. He'd want confirmation, and, ruthless as he was, he wouldn't wall her up and leave her to a slow death. He'd shoot her. He was all about results, and making people suffer was a by-product of that, not his hobby. Maybe Ainatio would shut off all the power when they left and the doors would open automatically for safety reasons. That must have crossed Tim's mind, because unlocking doors wouldn't shift a sealant designed to hold ships together until they reached port, so she could work out what he'd planned. He had some further use for her. He'd made sure she'd still be locked up even if Ainatio released the doors, and then whatever Solomon had done to APS infrastructure had interrupted him. The sealant was meant to be removed at some point.

Yeah. With a power tool. And she didn't have one.

She stood up, took a breath, and leaned her shoulder against the door frame to get a little extra pressure as she sawed away with the metal gripper. It wasn't making much of an impression. She could only keep it up for a few minutes at a time before her fingers started aching, and then she had to take a break. Rather than just stare at the wall and think how screwed she was and how much her hands hurt, she stood at the window.

The office faced north. She kept seeing vehicle headlights in the distance on the west side of the site, which was probably the loading bay or the vehicle hangars at the rear of the staff club. She was in the admin building, somewhere above Erskine's offices. That meant the accommodation blocks were to her right, and the staff club and restaurant were to the right of those. Well, at least she was properly oriented now. The problem with the Ainatio campus was its sheer size, and all the interiors looked the same except for colour coding on different floors.

But the vehicle headlights had to be Ainatio on the move. They were evacuating already.

She'd heard what Trinder had to say when he broadcast from the restaurant, that Tim was cut off from APS and it didn't look like anyone was riding to his rescue. On one hand, that was good: there'd be no air raids for a while, so she wouldn't end up forgotten under tons of rubble. But her only allies had caused some catastrophic failure in APS's systems and now they were about to leave.

Maybe the window was still the answer. It wasn't the opening kind, though, and it was toughened glass, maybe even blast-proof. Her earlier attempts to break it had failed and all she'd achieved was a twisted shoulder from trying to use an office chair as a battering ram. So she'd take another look at the way the glass was set in the frame. If glass was put in, glass could be taken out.

If I had the tools...

She sat down again. She thought of all the equipment she didn't have and how all her useful stuff was in her rucksack in her quarters. Then her mind drifted to what she was going to do if and when she got out, because she couldn't go back to Melbourne and just live out her life as a spy who'd been fired. If she wanted to return to APS territory, she'd need to slip in with a new identity, and that meant never contacting family and friends in Australia and Korea again. It was like being dead without the peace and quiet. They probably thought she was dead anyway, but she knew *they* weren't, and that was what made it hard. How did you go home and apologise for being alive after staging your own disappearance as a cover story, anyway? But she still didn't want to spend the rest of her life worrying that some nosey neighbour would find out who she really was.

Japan was a possibility, but getting a job and blending in would be a problem. She might be able to disappear in Inner China, and they wouldn't turn her in to Seoul because they'd never forgiven Korea for leading Asia to break up Greater China into a collection of vassal states. But she'd be treated worse than a Westerner.

Sod it, she was an Aussie, regardless of her roots. She'd have been better off in Britain. She could have taken the spy's time-honoured path to the other side and done a walk-in to ask for political asylum. If she'd had the foresight, she'd have worked harder on cultivating Marc Gallagher's goodwill and contacts book.

A loud clunk from the door shook her out of her thoughts. It made a noise two or three times, then stopped, which meant someone was trying to release it remotely and hadn't managed to shift it. The sealant was holding fast. Annis jumped up and tried forcing the door, putting all her weight on the handle. It still wouldn't move.

"Dr Kim, we've located you."

Solomon's voice boomed out of the wall speaker. It scared the crap out of her but she'd never been so happy to be in a company that snooped on its staff twenty-four seven.

"Sol! Thank God." The security cameras must have been working. "Yeah, just like the last time. Locked in a room again. Still, it's a step up from the cupboard I was stashed in — "

But Solomon just carried on. "Dr Kim, I have to assume you can hear me. Unfortunately, I've had to disable signals from most of the campus for security reasons, so I won't be able to hear your response, and I can't view you via the security cameras. So I want you to listen carefully. We've tried to release the door, but the system's showing it's still shut. I want you to stand at the nearest window so someone can see you to confirm we have the right location."

Annis didn't need telling twice. She went to the window and waved. "Can you see me, Sol?" But he couldn't hear her. It just made her feel better to talk to him. "Over here, Sol. You got the right place."

She expected him to say that he could see her, but she heard nothing. The wait was almost unbearable. She pressed her nose to the window to see past her reflection and work out what was going on outside, then found herself staring at a disembodied eye right up against the glass on the other side.

It was a bloody micro-drone. The lens looked way too anatomical for her peace of mind.

"Gotcha," said another voice. "Hang on."

Hanging on was all she could do. The drone moved out of sight and she turned to the door, anticipating the noise of cutting tools or even scrapes and thuds as someone stuck a frame charge in place. But nothing happened. She was still staring at the door when someone rapped on the window.

Annis had a hood over her head when she was brought in here, but she was fairly sure from the view that she was on the top floor of the block. She was. And Zakko was somehow standing outside, tapping the glass. He beckoned to her, held up a drill, and pointed to the frame.

"Zakko will have you out of there soon, Dr Kim," Solomon said. "You have him to thank for this rescue. He insisted."

"Were you buggers going to leave me, then?" she asked, but he couldn't hear her. Of course they were. She was an enemy spy. Tim had made APS the enemy. What else did she expect? But there were still people she could count on to do the decent thing because she'd tried to do right by them. It was some comfort.

Zakko began drilling around the window frame. Annis decided the glass was probably going to fall into the room rather than outwards, so she moved away and sat behind one of the desks. While she watched him work, she realised she had a lot of questions she probably wasn't going to get answers to. If Tim had destroyed the launch rail and blown up one of the ships, presumably *Shackleton*, where were they going? Opis seemed to be off the agenda now no matter what Trinder thought. But there were plenty of countries who'd swing by and evacuate everyone in exchange for the FTL research. Marc Gallagher had called in a favour from his government once and he could probably do it again. Maybe she'd be able to disappear in Britain and claim political asylum after all.

"You're a diamond, Zakko," she said.

She'd miss him if everyone went their separate ways. She'd miss quite a few of the people here, in fact, and feeling that pang reminded her that she wasn't cut out for intelligence work. She had the tradecraft skills, and she'd proved she could survive anywhere, but the job required the kind of mindset she now accepted she didn't have or even want. She couldn't take the isolation, the need to keep her emotional distance from people. She didn't want to end up like Tim.

She'd always known he wasn't a nice guy. He'd always been a genuine patriot, though. He was as single-minded about protecting what mattered to him as Solomon was, but single-minded people could do terrible things for good causes even when they didn't plan to. Tim would do whatever it took to stop the wounded world — including other APS states — closing in on Australia. But he'd picked a fight with an entity that was learning unconventional warfare skirmish by skirmish, and Solomon could nurse a grudge like flesh and blood. The blackout had to be his handiwork.

Annis could join up the dots. Sol was the only one who could shut down enough APS systems to stop *Temujin* or anyone else sending help. If APS had been operating normally, there'd have been jets overhead by now. Tim would be even more obsessed with shutting Solomon down.

Zakko carried on drilling, as calm and methodical as if he was doing a spot of DIY around the house. A few minutes later, the window started to creak, then the glass slowly sagged away from the top edge, clinging on by a few stretched threads of some kind of plastic. It didn't so much crash to the floor as slide. Zakko switched off the drill and smiled at her.

"Zakko, you're a bloody hero," Annis said. "This is the second time you've saved me."

Zakko looked coy. "We could have blown the door, but Alex didn't want Pham to work out what we were up to just in case his operators could do something about it." He clambered in and picked up the glass to examine it. "Damn. I was hoping I could put this back in so they wouldn't spot an open window. Never mind. I'll sort it out later. Come on. Let's get you away from here."

"You're on a ladder, right?"

"No. A cherry picker."

"Five-star service. I like it."

Zakko held out his hand. "Come on. It's a really small platform, so it'll be a bit scary climbing out, but I won't let you fall."

He wasn't wrong. Annis wasn't troubled by heights but it was unnerving to climb out backwards and feel around with one foot to make sure she was stepping into the cage. Zakko pressed the controls and lowered the boom without saying a word. When she looked down, she could see Alex waiting in the pool of light from the cherry picker's headlights.

"My ex had a cat like you once," he said as the cage drew level with him. "Damn thing always climbed higher than it could cope with. I wanted to use the power hose to shift it, to be honest, because they always land on their feet, but you know what women are like."

"I'm pleased to see you too, Alex."

"Are you okay? No injuries?"

"Bruised pride and grazed elbows. I'll live. Thanks for getting me out. You two just keep saving me. So, next stop's Blighty, yeah? Good. I almost speak the language."

She really expected he'd tell her to hurry up because everyone was leaving and she had to get to the RV point. But Alex and Zakko just looked at each other, awkward and embarrassed, and Alex was the one who finally spoke.

"We're getting a vehicle for you and everything you'll need to get away before Pham's let loose," he said. "We did some planning ourselves in case we had to escape overland, so you'll have maps in the glovebox to help you find somewhere that won't be barbecued for a while. We're still moving vehicles and supplies, but we'll be done here and release most of the doors by lunchtime or early afternoon. Except Pham's, of course. He'll be stuck in Erskine's bunker for a few more days because we don't want him spoiling our party either."

Annis was gutted. "Oh. Thank you." She had no right to expect anything more, and she'd told everyone she was going back to Australia anyway, so there was no reason for them to think she wanted to come with them. But things had changed a lot in the last week.

"You don't look happy with that," Alex said.

"I'm fine," she lied. "But where are you actually going?"

"Opis, eventually. But not via Britain. It's complicated."

"Yeah. Okay."

"We can't take you with us. Sorry. But you didn't want to leave Earth anyway, did you?"

She hadn't, but she'd have been fine with it now. These were the only people she didn't have to fear or lie to.

"Can I ask you a few questions, though? I've been out of the loop and you guys look like you've been busy."

"Sure."

"What did you do to APS?"

"We made sure they couldn't send aircraft for a while if Pham called for backup. Just long enough for us to get away." Alex shuffled and brushed his hand over his beard as if he was tidying himself up. He always did that when he had something difficult to say. "But there might have been a few unintended consequences. Big outages. That kind of thing. We don't know the full extent because we're relying on foreign news, but Sydney seems okay, if that helps."

"Cyberattack?"

"Well, we didn't lob any hardware at Asia, so... yeah."

Annis's gut tied itself in knots but she had to keep going. "Where are the two heavies Tim shipped in?"

"We're looking for them."

"Did you find the informer?"

"Not yet."

"And all Pham's party are locked in."

"They are now. The troops who were trying to hold the gate surrendered a few hours ago, no shots fired, and they're safe inside the accommodation block. Food, showers, beds, movies. All very gentlemanly. When we're clear and sure we won't be sabotaged again, we'll open the doors for them. There won't be any comms or cameras because we're purging the security system, but everything else like the reactor, water supply, and all the housekeeping side will carry on. There's plenty of supplies so they can sit it out until APS comes for them, whenever that is. And we're leaving a few vehicles in case they need to drive to an RV point."

Annis realised she wasn't even a special case. Everyone, even that bastard Tim, got humane treatment. "That's pretty magnanimous."

"Yeah, we're the good guys," Alex said. "And a hundred of our staff are stuck here too. So now you're free, it's probably a good idea to find somewhere to hole up for a few hours without anyone spotting you until we can get your vehicle into position." Alex handed her a scrap of paper and pointed to a spot on a hand-drawn map. "We'll leave it *here,* outside the fence. Sorry, but I can't give you an exact time. There'll be a hole cut in the mesh so you can slip out and we'll mark the pickup with a repair sticker on one of the side windows so you can identify it. It'll be fuelled and charged for fifteen hundred miles, and you'll find food, water, rifle, sidearm, ammo, radio kit, meds, and the stuff Chris is retrieving from your quarters. You're good to go."

It was generous. She wasn't their problem to solve and she hadn't come to Ainatio to do them any favours. But being told she wasn't going with them still hurt.

"Thanks. Really, thank you. But can't I hide in Kill Line until it's time to go?"

"Sorry, no." Alex did the beard-brushing thing again. "Like I said, it's more complicated than it looks. We need to keep the town locked down until we ship out. Unknown informer. Walls have ears. Loose lips sink ships. That kind of shit."

"Okay. I understand. Thank you." But she didn't understand as much as she wanted to. She reached out to shake Alex's hand, then couldn't stop herself giving Zakko a hug and playing along with the Opis delusion. "I hope you reach Opis safely and it's everything Bednarz thought it would be."

"I think it's already exceeded his expectations," Alex said. "Good luck, Annis."

He got into the cherry picker's cab and they waved as Zakko drove away into the darkness. It was over too fast, and she hadn't said half the things she wanted or asked enough questions. But she was alive, free to leave, and Tim wasn't going to catch her.

"Bugger," she said to herself. "You're on your own now, girl. Again."

She hid in a doorway, studied the map in the dim light leaking out from the glass doors, and worked out how she was going to get from here to the vehicle without being spotted. She could do it. She'd managed to survive a journey halfway around the world by hitching, hot-wiring, stowing away, and walking, even if she'd picked up a few bugs and parasites along the way, so this was a stroll by comparison. She hadn't set the record straight for Grandma Park, but there was still plenty of time for that.

The sound of engines was now a lot louder. Everyone and everything was leaving, and by lunchtime the only people left here who wouldn't automatically regard her as a criminal were a bunch of scientists that included someone who'd betrayed their mates. She told herself she hadn't been rejected by her friends. She'd been set free, not just from that bloody cell of an office but from a job nobody could ever really leave.

At least the Ainatio guys didn't believe she was the mole who'd screwed up everything for them. All in all, it was the most that a spy who tried to be a decent human being could hope for.

08

It's magic. It's like being a ghost. It's the next best thing to omnipresence. That's why it needs to be kept out of the hands of people who'll use it as a weapon — at least until we know a lot more about our teerik buddies and whoever else is out there.

Marc Gallagher, on the many military applications of the Caisin gate.

FORGE WOOD, KILL LINE: EVACUATION DAY, 0615 EDT.

Marc heard the rustle and crack of twigs ten seconds before he picked any movement.

He lowered his rifle, disappointed that it was only a couple of Dieter's dogs. If it had been the APDU commandos he was sure were on the loose, his guess would have been vindicated and he'd have been able to take a crack at them. But so far APDU had done few of the things he expected, and that worried him. He might have overlooked something much worse.

Dieter's beloved springer spaniel and something that looked mostly pit bull trotted up to him, sniffed his legs, and cast around in the undergrowth for a few moments. Sal the springer carried on zigzagging from tree to bush, but the pit bull flopped down and looked at him with what could only be described as a daft grin.

"Well, at least you're happy." Marc patted the dog with suitable caution while he waited for Dieter to catch up. "Low expectations, mate. It's the key to inner peace."

Dieter emerged from the trees. He was a thickset, late-fifties to sixty-something who still looked like the cop he'd been, careful where he stepped and continually checking around him.

Marc nodded at the pit bull. "I thought all the dogs you rounded up were police or military. What's this bruiser, then? Undercover drugs squad?"

"I'll have you know you're addressing a *lady*," Dieter said. "This is Betsy. I found her locked in a pound all on her own. She's got a sketchy past, but she's turned out a good girl. Haven't you, sweetie?"

Betsy's grin widened and she heaved herself up to wander over to Dieter for a pat. Marc now saw the transit camp's dogs as a mirror of its humans, a functioning unit welded together from a motley assortment of the abandoned, the fiercely loyal, and the reinvented whose dodgy pasts qualified them perfectly to protect the pack. Betsy had a lot in common with Chris.

"So what's her job?" Marc asked. They walked back into town with Betsy on point. "Deterrence?"

"Pretty much. Plus sinking her teeth in and not letting go."

"Good girl," Marc said. "Just what we need."

The sky was clear, birds were squabbling in the branches above him, and the smell of damp soil and frying bacon scented the breeze. If things went to plan, this would be the last summer morning he'd see on Earth. He didn't feel ready for that, but he'd made his choice. How bad could it be? He could come back as easily as he'd stepped through the Caisin gate, as long as there was somewhere left to come back to. But he couldn't think about the portal without seeing more of its complications every time. Some of them would need facing sooner rather than later, and the one that loomed largest was who would have control of it. He didn't fancy being at the mercy of crows with high IQs and angry bosses.

"So, Opis," Dieter said. "Is it anything like that travelogue video that Alex showed us, or was that all bullshit?"

"It's nice countryside. But I've only seen the inside of a teerik ship and the immediate area around the camp."

"What does it feel like?"

"The gate? A bit weird, but only for a second." Marc made a point of doing risky stuff before he had too long to think about it, but he couldn't blame Dieter for wanting a few facts in advance. "It's not like a parachute jump. More confusing than anything. You'll be fine."

"I was thinking about the dogs."

"They'll be too busy exploring the kennels. Sol's put a lot of effort into the site plan. I'm amazed what he got the bots to set up overnight."

"Bless him. He cares. Maybe that's because he's used to having four legs now."

"Whatever you say to him, don't mention the D word. He sees himself as a cheetah."

"Yeah, he does move like one, I suppose. How about Ingram?"

"Nothing like a cheetah. More like a lava flow. Not in any hurry, but it'll ruin your day when it finally reaches you."

"I meant how is she going to feel about a dog pack on the site."

"As a small boy said to me, if we don't all get on, we can set up our own town nearby."

Marc kept thinking about that. Ingram was going to have a job on her hands to hold this unplanned community together, but it probably wasn't the newcomers who were going to be the problem. It was *Cabot* personnel who'd left Earth when things were generally chummy but who'd woken from cryo to find that even if their home nations weren't at war with each other, they certainly weren't getting on too well. So what came first, their national loyalties or Nomad? If it wasn't Nomad, everyone was in trouble.

"What's your take on her?" Dieter asked.

"Ingram? Absolutely charming and she'd kill you in a heartbeat. But she'd be terribly, *terribly* apologetic and send flowers. All very proper."

"I'll judge her by how she treats the dogs. Anyone who doesn't like dogs — "

" — is a wrong 'un. Yeah, I know. She'll be fine with them. She's a doggy sort of woman. She probably had gun dogs and foxhounds on her country estate."

Dieter was doing a bad job of stifling a smile. "I hope you phrase that better when you see her."

Yeah, Marc knew he needed to rewind quite a bit with Ingram. He wouldn't have handled things any differently if he had to do it all again, but it was time for some kind of peace offering. He needed a favour from her. He wanted Howie under her personal protection if anything went wrong. Chris's people would look after the kid like they'd been doing since they found him, but Marc wanted him to have a high-ranking guardian angel with the power to give him special treatment. She'd taken a shine to him, Chris said. Marc would make the most of that.

"I can handle her," Marc said. He didn't dislike her. He respected her, but she had to understand he wasn't a member of her crew. "I know what she wants."

Dieter just chuckled to himself. As they walked into the town square, dodging vehicles, it looked like everything with wheels had been hauled out, and that was at least a couple of hundred trucks, quad bikes, old family cars, cattle transporters, and tractors. Doug Brandt had told his people the truth, wormholes and aliens and all, but it didn't seem to have put them off going to Opis. Marc had to admit he was a bit offended that they thought it would be better than Britain. But Opis was a chance to start over in a clean world where they made the rules, aliens or no aliens. Britain was on borrowed time, and even if it wasn't, it lived on a permanent war footing to keep disease and marauding ferals out of the country.

"Life was better when all you had to do was dig a tunnel, cover the hole with a vaulting horse, and dispose of the soil in the exercise yard," he said.

Dieter chuckled again. "You're a hopeless romantic."

"The tourist trip of no return."

"They took the news well, all things considered."

"Well, they had the really big shock months ago," Marc said. "Once Alex told them about Opis, it wasn't such a stretch to add space-bending criminal crows on the run, I suppose. I just hope the news doesn't leak before we're out of here."

"Ah, come on, we're as secure as we can be. Scientists penned well away from the townsfolk. No network access to call their buddies back in the facility when they're told the wondrous news. No contact with anyone except our guys, Dan's, and Doug's carefully-selected council folk. And the Ainatio remainers can't open the doors to let their APS buddies out until Sol presses the button."

"Nothing's ever watertight," Marc said. "We're thin on the ground with half our troops in Nomad Base. And when it comes to Ainatio, stupidity's as efficient as malice."

"I know, but this is going to be *fast*. Speed seals a lot of leaks."

"Could you find Doug's missus and pick up my chicken, please? I need to go and see Chris."

"Chicken?"

"It's a long story. It'll be in a carrier. The sort you use to take the dog to the vet."

"Oh, a *live* one. You Brits and your primitive rituals. Okay, I'll meet you outside the town hall."

Marc knew where he'd find Chris. He walked up the gravel track to St Thomas's church and stood at the end of the path to the graveyard. The sound of digging carried on the air, a slow chug like a dying steam engine. The pace was too slow and irregular for a bot. He knew what he'd see in the cemetery.

"Chris, I told you we'd take care of that. Don't do this to yourself."

Chris was in a waist-deep, neatly edged hole, digging up Jamie Wickens' coffin. He'd tied a scarf over his nose and mouth, so he wasn't under any illusions about what he'd taken on. Kill Line didn't do embalming.

"Thanks," he said, voice muffled. He wiped his forehead with his arm. "I appreciate it, but you know why I've got to do this."

It was pointless lecturing Chris about kicking himself in the arse. Marc was back on that tightrope between knowing exactly why Chris was doing this — a sergeant's duty to his men, a promise to a friend — and finding it a bit morbid. But he'd have done the same. If his boys had had graves, he'd have moved them too.

"You're going to need a bot to help you lift it," he said.

"Yeah. I'll call one when I need it."

Chris resumed digging, carefully lobbing the soil to one side of the grave. Marc wished he'd tasked a bot to do the excavation while Chris had been busy, but there hadn't been much of a night left to do it in.

"Nothing moving out there," Marc said. "We just got back with the dogs. Are all your people as relaxed about bending space-time as everyone else?"

Chris heaved another lump of soil onto the grass. "They've reached their whatever point. Novelty fatigue. Nothing else is ever going to shock them. Everyone's seen it in the movies and thinks it's only a matter of time before it's invented."

He stabbed his shovel down into the soil again like he was finishing off a vampire, and the dull thud of metal on wood said he'd finally reached the coffin. Then he looked up at Marc. For a moment, Marc thought he'd relented and was going to accept some help, but Chris didn't say anything. He was just waiting. Marc took the hint.

"Okay, I'm going to pop over to Opis, then," he said. "I want to take Howie through myself and get Ingram to keep an eye on him. I need to know he's got top cover in case the shit hits the fan here. You okay with that?"

"Sure." Chris nodded, looking distracted for a moment. "He'll want to hang around and help, though."

"I know. Ingram can distract him."

"You're buddies now?"

"She'll be putty in my hands when I give her what she wants."

"Your balls for earrings?"

"A chicken."

"It's a different approach, I'll give you that."

"Sol says she's been waiting for a chick embryo to come out of cryo so she can have fresh eggs. Eventually. She likes eggs for breakfast."

"Good luck. So have you stood down the airlift?"

"Not yet."

"Leaving it a bit late, buddy."

Marc shook his head. "No, I want to see that line of vehicles out of here first. It minimises gossip time. Because the Foreign Office is going to wonder why we were in mortal danger and begging for help last night but we've miraculously solved the launch problem this morning. Kingdom sees all, remember. It can probably spot our vanishing convoy and the absence of a shuttle launch. And they can see what's going on in APS better than APS can. So I won't draw their attention to us until I have to."

"So you don't trust them."

"I don't trust *any* government not to employ stupid bastards who can't keep their traps shut. Plus I can't be sure APS hasn't got people on its payroll inside Whitehall. I don't know *any* of these people. We've got one chance to get this right, Chris, and I don't know what I should tell them anyway. Ainatio's research is going to keep them busy until we're gone and then we can all think about the implications of the other stuff when we're not on a deadline."

"They're not going to forget about it," Chris said. "Not when they think they've got a man on the inside and they don't know he's going to be trillions of miles away by tomorrow. They'll try to trace you."

Marc wasn't sure how to interpret the use of *think*. He decided it was confirmation that Chris saw him as one of his own instead of a foreigner with an intact country that should have had first call on his loyalties. That was nice, but it reminded Marc there was more than an oath anchoring him to Britain: there were comrades, distant relatives, and Sandra, even if he couldn't face going back. And then there was Tev, more or less behind enemy lines, and Marc had the power to ship him out with his family. There were some hard choices ahead.

"I'll dissuade them," he said. "See you later."

Marc went back to collect the limo and found Dieter sitting on the bench outside the town hall with a coffee, Sal at his feet. He had the dog carrier beside him.

"One Plymouth Rock hen," he said.

Marc peered inside. He'd been expecting a ginger chicken, but a black and white one would do. It looked unimpressed. It wasn't too hard to see it as a disgruntled miniature dinosaur.

"It's got stripes," he said.

"The word is *barred*, apparently."

"Ingram won't mind. Thanks, mate."

Marc put the carrier in the back of the limo and set off for Becker farm. It gave him a few minutes of leather-scented, soundproofed isolation for uninterrupted thinking. He hadn't been able to decide whether and what to tell the FCO about the Caisin gate because there wasn't a right answer, and whatever he did, and whoever he told or didn't tell, the gate would still exist. Like so many apparently wonderful things, its unintended consequences would happen sooner or later. There was no point in wondering if he should have left with Tev, because that didn't erase its existence either. He could leave it to Ingram to decide whether to tell the government about it because she outranked him, but in law they were both civvies now and that meant he was just sidestepping responsibility.

He could talk to her about it, though. They were in the same boat, neither of them under a real obligation to share the tech with any government, but both still immersed in a culture that put their country first. Chris said he'd warned her off letting her crew contact surviving friends on Earth, not just because it made the situation even more complicated but because so many of them were from APS countries. Maybe Ingram had already done it, but she seemed smarter than that. He'd find out when he told the FCO some half-truths.

That wasn't the only problem. If things got tough on Opis, everyone knew there was now an instant and easy way home, and some would feel they didn't have to try so hard to make a go of the colony. But going back wasn't an easy option either, even if nobody knew they'd left Earth at all. If they could keep their mouths shut — and that'd be tough even for him — the whole thing would still unravel if any of the *Cabot* crew returned. They'd look inexplicably young and there'd be difficult questions: where had they come from, why were they here, and where had they been? *Where was the ship if they'd made the journey back?* And then it would all start coming out, a word at a time, voluntarily or not, and every nation that could still get its shit together was going to want a piece of the technology. Half of them wouldn't even want it for space travel. It was too useful for all sorts of other violent and unsavoury stuff closer to home.

"I never used to be this negative, you know." Marc glanced in the rear-view mirror to address the chicken. "Turn problems to advantages, that's how they train us. But you've got to plan for the worst. I think you should, too."

He took one hand off the wheel and felt in the glove box for the bronze plaque that he'd looted from Erskine's office. If it belonged anywhere now, it deserved to be handed to the CO of *Cabot*. It was the kind of thing that would have ended up on the wall of the sergeants' mess as a general up-yours to the nation's enemies and an affirmation of survival, but he wasn't sure how Ingram would take it. Tev, generally a good judge of social propriety, had decided it was a bit tasteless to treat it as a joke. Marc slid it one-handed out of its plastic bag and took a quick look as he drove, wondering if he should have cleaned it first.

TO THE MEMORY OF THE SHIP'S COMPANY
OF SURVEY VESSEL CABOT
LOST WITH ALL HANDS
WE WALK IN THE UNCHARTED PLACES
AND ARE NOT AFRAID

No, it was fine as it was. The green patina looked nicely historic. But some of the crew might not find it funny, knowing the old friends and distant relatives they'd left behind still thought they were dead, and that others had already gone to their graves believing it. Marc wondered who'd thought up the memorial, and if the person responsible for the wording had known it was a massive, elaborate lie. It took a special breed of bastard to create a fake memorial to people who didn't know they were officially dead and erased.

The field next to the dairy farm was already full of Chris's people when Marc drove in, giving the assembly area the look of a music festival when the timetable had gone to rats and the audience was still waiting for the band to show up. They were standing around or sitting on tailgates with their boxes and rucksacks, something they were probably used to by now, and looking fairly relaxed for people who'd been told they were going to be on another planet within a couple of hours. Marsha, Jared's rather glamorous wife, had set up a refreshment wagon in the middle of the field and was handing out an impressive range of food and drinks with a couple of the other women and the astronomy kid. Marc walked up to the makeshift counter and admired the cakes. The wagon had the feel of a farewell party about it.

"It's just like the WRVS," he said. "Tea kept us going through four wars, you know."

"Couldn't waste the surplus perishables." Marsha leaned on the counter. "How did you acquire the limo?"

"Charming persuasion and an ability to hot-wire."

"What can I get you?"

"I'll have several seriously large black coffees when I get back," Marc said. "Got to see someone in Nomad first. Is Jared around?"

"I'll call him for you. And go steady on the caffeine if you're taking Mendoza's racehorse pills. They're not good for a growing boy."

Marsha put a coffee in front of him anyway, and he drank it. Jared appeared out of the crowd, radio in one hand and a clipboard in the other. He looked incredibly happy for a man who hadn't slept for thirty-six hours.

"He can't wait to see an alien planet," Marsha whispered. "He's ten years old again."

"I wish I was," Marc said. "My back wouldn't be giving me gyp."

"Hey Marc. We're all ready." Jared brandished his list. "*Cabot*'s environment guy says it'll take them a couple more hours to get all the latrines plumbed in, but they've got the first batch of emergency tents up and the marshals are ready to receive vehicles, so we can send our civvies now. There'll be enough room for them to put down a bed roll, at least temporarily."

The few trucks and buses that had come with Chris's evacuees to Hart County stood interspersed with borrowed Ainatio vehicles. They weren't leaving their old wrecks behind, then. Perhaps there were too many memories woven into them. Marc could understand that. And every bit of recoverable metal or composite they could take to Opis would come in useful sooner or later.

"Look, mate, can you do me a favour?" Marc asked. "I need to ask Ingram for something. Can I jump the queue and run a quick errand before you start sending traffic through? I'm going to take Howie just to make sure he's safe and settled. He worries that I'm going to get shot. It's okay, I cleared it with Chris."

"Sure. He's around somewhere." Jared scanned the field. He was a head taller than anyone else and he had the advantage. "There he is. *Howie!* Hey, Howie, over here, buddy."

Howie eventually emerged through the obstacle course of vehicles and adults, struggling under a huge rucksack that swamped him like a turtle's shell. Marc put a protective hand on his shoulder.

"You okay? You want a hand with that?"

Howie shook his head, wide-eyed and obviously scared. "No thanks. Are we going now?"

"Yeah. In fact, you and me, we're going through first. Think about it. You'll be the first kid in history to set foot on an extrasolar planet. It doesn't get much cooler than that."

"I suppose this the last time I'm going to see Earth, then."

"Is that what's worrying you?"

"It's kind of sad."

"Yeah, but you can probably come back and visit sometime." Marc regretted it the instant he said it, but it was what Howie needed to hear. "I bet you won't want to, though, not for a while."

It seemed to do the trick. Howie followed Marc to the limo. When Marc opened the passenger door for him, he paused to look back for a moment as if he was absorbing as much as he could of Earth to keep him going in a strange new place, then slid the rucksack off and put it in the back seat next to the dog carrier. He glanced at the chicken, which was trying to stick its head through the mesh, but said nothing.

"Okay, Howie." Marc started the engine. "Let's make history, eh?"

Jared waved Marc forward and guided him into the milking shed. It looked more like a giant warehouse with a lane the width of a small road between the milking stalls. It was perfect for swallowing a stream of vehicles. The high roof had ducts and pipes everywhere, and if Marc hadn't known what it was, he'd have thought the place was a chemical factory or something equally industrial. It certainly didn't look rural. He could see the oval of heat haze near the far end of the building, just in front of the breeze-block wall. Now it was almost as familiar as stepping into a lift. He drove slowly towards it, felt a split-second blip of pressure in his ears, and the concrete blocks dissolved into open grass and a warm but overcast day.

Howie gaped. "Wow... "

"You've just travelled two hundred and forty-six trillion miles," Marc said. "And we've still got a full tank of water."

"Are you sure?"

"Yeah. It's real. We don't have the budget for a movie set like this."

Opis lived up to Erskine's hard sell. Beyond the camp perimeter, it was clean and weird and wonderful, an unspoiled landscape with frilly purple trees and even mountains in the far distance. If a kid had to face the scary unknown, this was the best possible view of it. But the base itself had turned into a kind of urban chaos in the space of a few hours. This was Solomon's project. He was now foreman of a giant construction site that looked like it had quadrupled the camp's footprint, and there were more bots milling around than Marc had ever seen in one place. Most of the *Cabot* crew were out working on it too. That was their schedule stuffed for the next few months, then. Marc hoped they had a sense of humour.

"Okay, that's Commander Kokinos over there," Marc said, pointing him out to Howie. "He'll sort everything out. We need to find Captain Ingram."

Marc drove through a maze of barriers and chevron tape laid out on the grass like the passenger queueing system at an airport. Steve Kokinos, the officer in charge of the environment systems, was waiting at the exit. Marc lowered the limo's window and the sound rushed in like an explosion. It was the noisiest environment he'd been in for years, a continuous clamour of drills, cutting equipment, motors, and excavators, all underpinned by the rhythmic shudder of a pile driver somewhere on the site.

"Hi. Is the boss around? I wanted to see her before the floodgates open."

"I'll get her for you." Kokinos peered into the car. "You must be Howie. Welcome. And is that what I think it is in the pet carrier?"

"Yes," Marc said. "A bribe."

"Good. We accept those. I see you're going to fit in just fine."

Kokinos had a noticeable German accent but he wore an old Greek flag patch on his uniform, a symbol Marc could never look at without wondering why he'd let his boys go and fight in a country whose problems weren't theirs. But it was just a flag. He made an effort to separate it from a war that had happened after *Cabot* had left Earth. He parked the limo out of the way and sat on the rear bumper with Howie to wait for Ingram.

Opis didn't look that alien, all things considered, but everything else from the smell of the vegetation and the shift in the time of day to the drag of gravity said this was definitely *not* Earth. Howie seemed silenced by the enormity of it, but eventually said what was on his mind.

"Marc, are there wild animals and poisonous bugs here?"

"Yes, but they don't come into the camp. There's a barrier strip buried around the perimeter and it gives them a zap if they try to cross it."

"Even birds?"

"I don't know. We'll ask Fred. He's a bird of sorts."

"The alien, you mean."

"Yeah."

"And bots built all this before the ship arrived?"

"Everything. And they surveyed all the plants and bacteria, and worked out what drugs we'd need to live here without catching diseases, and treated the soil so we can grow the crops they developed at Ainatio."

Howie considered it for a few moments. "I suppose that's why it took so long and cost so much."

"Better than Mars."

"It doesn't look like another planet, though. Except the plants. But there's weirder plants on Earth."

"You're definitely on another planet."

"Okay. I believe you."

Marc had another twinge of doubt about his certainty given Ainatio's record on massive con tricks, but that was just fatigue grinding him down. Opis was real. He could feel the change in gravity each time he used the gate. He'd have given anything for a few hours' sleep right then, but he'd make do with just closing his eyes for a few minutes. He leaned forward to rest his elbows on his knees and put his head in his hands, certain he was still awake, but then loud, guffawing laughter jerked him out of the blissful semi-doze he'd drifted into without noticing.

Ingram was standing there laughing her head off with the back of her hand to her mouth, eyes streaming. She even started coughing. Marc hadn't seen anyone laugh that hard for a very long time, least of all at him. Kokinos was trailing her, looking like he needed to keep an eye on her.

"You absolute spiv," she said, wiping her eyes. "A *limousine*. It's still got its British diplomatic plates. Good grief, look at all those scrapes and dents. Did you steal it?"

"Of course I did. The ambassador owed me and Tev for saving his staff."

"I do so admire your complete disregard for the social order." She reached out to pat Howie on the shoulder, still trying to get her breath back. "Hello, Howie. How do you like our new world?"

"It's nice," Howie said in a very small voice.

Marc eased himself up off the bumper. "I brought you a few things you're going to need. But can I ask you a favour first? Would you look after Howie until I'm done at the other end? Personally, I mean."

Ingram didn't even blink. She just beamed at the kid. "Of course I will. Howie, Commander Kokinos is going to take you to the mess now and show you where you can eat. I'm sure we can find you a cabin. I'll come and see you later."

Kokinos took the childminding order like a man and even shouldered Howie's rucksack. Howie looked devastated. It wasn't hard to read him.

"I'll see you later today, mate," Marc said. "But everyone else is coming through in the next few hours, so you won't be alone. I'm not leaving you to fend for yourself. I just need to know you're in safe hands or else I won't be able to keep my mind on the job."

"Don't die," Howie said, like it was an order.

Marc gave him a salute. "No sir. No dying, definitely not."

Howie nodded and walked off with Kokinos, head down, not even a backward glance, as if he didn't want to look needy. Ingram did the kind of mock frown that was meant to disguise a real one and folded her arms.

"Are you expecting trouble, Marc?"

"Maybe. We still haven't found Pham's operator, or operators, because there's another one hanging around. If they went to that much trouble to stop us leaving, they're not likely to give up easily. They're after Sol. That seems to be top of their grievance list."

"And you're sure they're operators?"

"If they're not, they're some other closely related species of bastard. Anyway, this time tomorrow, it won't matter."

"We hope."

"So... do you want your bribe, then? Or peace offering. Whatever you prefer."

"I thought you'd never ask."

Marc opened the car door and took out the dog carrier. "You wanted a hen. I got you a striped one."

Her face lit up. "Gosh, and there was I expecting a dozen red roses. How did you know?"

"I hear all."

"You really are a gem. You have no idea what a fresh boiled egg means to me." Ingram opened the carrier, coaxed the chicken out, and held it in her arms like a pet. It flapped a bit before submitting with a single resigned cluck. "If she doesn't have a name already, she's Mildred. This saves me waiting for a chicken embryo. Thank you."

"You're welcome. One more thing." Marc was sure Ingram had a military sense of humour, as black as it came. If she didn't, though, he'd find out fast. "Erskine found this. It used to be on a wall outside Ainatio's gates. We thought you could put it behind the bar or something. Yours to do with as you wish."

He took the plaque out of the bag and handed it to her. She held Mildred under one arm while she studied it, frowning.

"Bloody hell." It came out in a nervous, humourless giggle and her flippant veneer peeled back for a moment. "They couldn't even be bothered to put our names on it."

"Engraving's expensive."

"I imagine so."

"Sorry. I thought you'd laugh, to be honest."

"I normally would. Must be the menopause approaching."

Her cheeks were flushed. Marc hadn't had her down for the easily embarrassed type and he wasn't sure what to make of it.

"I realise we didn't get off to the best start," he said. "Am I still *persona non grata*?"

"Oh, you were never *non grata* with me, Marc. I don't like yes-men anyway. Sorry — I never asked if you minded being on first name terms."

"Well, I'm not really a sergeant any more, and you're not really a naval captain," Marc said. It was tactless but not entirely unintentional. "So there's no rank issue. It's fine by me."

Ingram seemed to throw a switch and revert to posh bullshitter mode again. "Well, my little silent killing machine, would you like a cup of tea before you go? You do look weary."

"I wouldn't normally pass up a cuppa with the Butcher of Calais, but I'll take an IOU, if that's okay. We need to get a move on before APS realise we're tunnelling out."

"How very Colditz. I'll have the pot warmed and waiting. We have some serious talking to do, you and I."

"About the technology."

"We probably have the same concerns about how best to handle it. It's a different challenge for those of us who still have a nation to consider."

Marc nodded. "Yeah, as long as everyone's first loyalty is to Nomad. We won't survive here unless it is."

"Indeed. It has a lot in common with a ship."

He wasn't sure if she was putting him in his place and reminding him she did this for a living or just agreeing with him. "Anyway, thanks for taking Howie in," he said. "I'll be last out with Chris and Dan. You know, make sure the town's clear, that sort of thing. If our luck runs out, I want... well, you get it. Howie's had a tough time."

"Chris did warn me. And I imagine Howie's not the only one."

Marc tried not to blink. He wished he'd known what Chris had told her, but he could guess. "Okay, I'd better make a move. As soon as I get back, the convoy's going to start coming through. I'll see you later for that cuppa."

Ingram caught Marc's arm as he turned to walk away. She might have been the touchy-feely sort who clutched everybody, or liked to pretend she was, but there was real urgency in that grip.

"Marc, I expect you to walk through that gate later today and say job done. You're not going to die. You're all coming back here to reboot your lives. And we need you. So no boy-stood-on-the-burning-deck nonsense."

"Understood." Marc could feel his own embarrassed blush starting. He focused on the chicken. "Bye, Mildred. Get laying, girl."

Driving back between the barriers felt like a chauffeur's skill test that he was going to fail. For a moment, he wondered what would happen if a lorry was coming the other way through the portal and they met head on at the point where they swapped time and space. Would they crash, or somehow miss each other in some dimensional weirdness? He'd have to ask Dr Mangel. The bloke would probably enjoy a question like that. Marc couldn't ask Annis Kim because he'd never see her again.

He slowed the limo to a crawl and watched its piano-gloss black bonnet dissolve in front of him as it passed through the curtain of hazy air, and then he was back in the milking yard again with a cement block wall in the rear-view mirror and Trinder standing at the entrance with Alex. A queue of idling vehicles stretched out behind them.

Marc pulled over to one side when he reached the entrance. Trinder bent down to the open driver's window, clutching the blue flashlight gizmo as if he was worried he'd set it off and accidentally move the portal.

"Did you get what you wanted?" he asked.

"All sorted." Marc looked back down the line of vehicles queued up to cross. At its head was an autonomous Ainatio vehicle, and more were interspersed with the rest of the traffic. Bots wouldn't balk at the sight of the wall when programmed to drive on, so they'd keep the traffic flowing. "I hope this works, or else it's going to be a long day."

"You managed it okay," Trinder said.

Marc fished in his pockets for another Mendoza wake-up special. "Yeah, but I'm used to making myself do a lot worse. So are the transit camp drivers. They're military. They'll drive in pitch black without headlights and under fire. It's the Kill Liners I'm worried about."

"I'm betting on the glass floor principle," Alex said. "You *know* it's solid but you look down and you just can't step on it. But if keep your eyes up or look at someone already on the floor, you're okay. It'll work."

Marc forced a smile. "Yeah, if I had a sixteen-wheel robotic artic on my arse, I'd keep moving too."

They were asking drivers to accelerate into a wall, or at least that was how it looked from behind the steering wheel. It didn't matter what you *knew* was real. The primitive bits of the brain that kept you upright, afraid of fire, and quick to duck a punch also said that you'd smash into bricks or plunge to your death. There was no way of knowing how you'd react until it came to it.

"If it doesn't work, we can just pull the wobblers out of the line and take the wheel ourselves." Trinder tapped his screen. "Okay, ready?"

"Yeah." Marc thought about Ingram. "Commence Op Colditz."

Trinder waved the line forward. The Ainatio lorry didn't move. One of the transit camp's flatbed trucks rolled up slowly alongside it and cut in front, and then Marc realised what was happening. The traffic marshals along the line, some of Trinder's guys and some of Chris's, stood to attention and saluted.

Sod it, Jared. You could have told me.

The truck was carrying Jamie Wicken's flag-draped coffin. Zakko was at the wheel, all formal in a black parade jacket that the Ainatio detachment must have provided. Marc snapped to attention and looked straight ahead. Sometimes these things were too much for him, and this was one of those times. He'd kept Jamie waiting. Now he felt like a complete prick.

He counted until the steady whirr of the engine suddenly became silence and got as far as ten. "Resume," Trinder said.

The Ainatio lorry moved off, followed a couple of car lengths behind by Chuck Emerson at the wheel of a pockmarked but very clean gun truck packed with civvies. He followed it like he was boarding a car ferry. As the momentum kicked in, the trucks, pickups, and quad bikes moved smoothly through the milking shed at ten miles an hour, vanishing just in front of the breeze block wall.

Clearing the transit camp line didn't take long. There weren't many vehicles, and only fifty-two civvies — fifty-one now Zakko was fully badged — and half the militia were on the Nomad side doing reception and triage. Chris would be happier now his flock was mostly gathered safely in.

"See?" Alex looked at the rapidly dwindling queue, smug as shit. "And the cargo's interspersed, which should keep Ingram the Terrible pacified. We're awesome. Who needs Sol?"

"Don't upset him," Trinder said. "He's pretty fragile at the moment."

"What, because he's laid waste to more of Asia than Genghis Khan?"

"Tact, Alex. Sensitivity."

"I've heard of it."

They were now in a brief lull, waiting for the first tranche of Kill Liners. Alex kept checking his drone view of the approach road to the dairy, singing tunelessly under his breath. Marc considered punching him. Trinder still had a death-grip on the blue flashlight.

"What's Colditz?" Trinder asked.

Everything was forgotten eventually, and the last days of Kill Line would go the same way. Maybe even Earth would become a name that nobody recognised in the end. It was a shame. It needed to be remembered by someone other than Solomon, not just Earth the world, but Earth the people, all the individuals who'd moved mountains and given everything to save their small part of it.

"Just history, mate," Marc said. "Never mind."

* * *

NOMAD BASE, OPIS: 0855 EDT.

The new humans were arriving, looking more like visitors than conquerors. They were a very mixed population.

Hredt hadn't known what to expect, but Chief Jeff had told him there would be very old people and children among them. *Cabot's* crew didn't have any of those. Some of the crew had greying hair, but despite their variety of skin and features, they were all between early and middle adulthood. The elders among the new arrivals were visibly more frail and wrinkled. Hredt wondered how humans cared for their old ones at the end of their lives, and if they'd understand why he wasn't at Caisin's bedside now.

The evacuees' fleet of vehicles was equally mixed, some of them mechanicals able to drive themselves, many of them oddly shaped machines with attachments and trailers that moved more slowly, all with an escort of soldiers in the same plain black uniform that Chris wore. Chris seemed friendly. Marc appeared to scare the other humans, though, but he only wore parts of the same uniform, so perhaps he wasn't one of them. Dan Trinder seemed kind too, but Hredt wasn't sure which one of his names to use. There were a lot of new customs to come to terms with.

He watched the influx from the top of the irrigation control box next to the greenhouses. It felt discourteous not to greet the newcomers at the portal, but this wasn't his world any more than it was the humans', so he couldn't play the ambassador. And perhaps they'd need time to adjust to discovering they were far from alone in the galaxy. He'd wait.

I'm not hiding. It's just better for me to stay away from the ship until Turisu calms down. And I'm not hiding from the humans, either. I just need time to think. I'm not scared. I can make decisions. I can fly.

If talking to the inner self worked for humans, it would work for him. He had to see this through.

"Hredt?" A woman's voice called out from behind him. "Why don't you come down and say hi? Everyone wants to meet you."

It was Nina. She'd been working hard for the last few hours, helping put up the temporary shelters to house the new humans. She showed him how channels in the fabric were pumped full of water and expanded to become a building, and a substance in them reacted with the water to make the structure rigid. It was very clever. Humans were some way behind on physics, but they were very good at making new substances and living organisms.

Hredt turned, unsure whether to come down from the head-high box, or to stay where he was to speak down to her, which seemed disrespectful. But Nina solved the problem by climbing the access ladder to sit beside him.

"I'd only get in the way," he said. "You have a lot of people to bring in and not much time. I'll meet them when they feel more settled."

"As long as you don't feel you're not welcome."

He'd learned to shake his head from side to side. "No, not at all."

"You're not very happy, though." Nina had glossy dark hair that was cut level with her chin, but humans didn't seem to have any iridescence. "Your head's drooping. We do that too."

It was good that she noticed these things. "My daughter's angry with me," he said. "She thinks I'm a dangerous fool."

"She's just afraid. She doesn't mean it."

"She does."

"What did you argue about?"

"She said Learned Mother's dying and I should be with her, not involving myself in human politics and lying to everyone." Perhaps he was being too open with Nina. He'd never been in real danger before the commune fled, but he knew revealing weaknesses was a good way to guarantee they'd be exploited. "But I think this is all part of what Caisin wanted. We need allies. And as more humans come to the sector, we have to choose a side. I choose the civilised over the barbarian. Now my commune has to live with that choice."

"Hredt, I don't want to come between you and your daughter, but humans do this too," Nina said. "We say terrible things when we're losing a loved one because we're angry at the universe, not at our family. And no matter how much time you spend with Caisin, you'll never think it was enough. So you need to do what you think she'd want you to do."

"She wants to be left alone," Hredt said. "And she wants us to be free of Kugin foremen."

"If she's well enough to hear, tell her you did just that." Nina put her hand on his back, then jerked it away. "Sorry. Human habit."

"Ingram does this too. I know it's a gesture of comfort." If Hredt hadn't read all the entries in the encyclopaedia about human wars, he'd have thought they were just too kind and gentle to fight. There had to be some duality in their nature. "And thank you for learning to say my name. It's very thoughtful that you made the effort."

"I heard you speak another language," Nina said. "I didn't think you'd naturally make the sounds that we make by compressing our lips."

"That's because it's not our native language. We speak Kugal because we were born in Kugad."

"What's your original language like? Where did you come from?"

This was difficult. "I don't know. We've forgotten. All we know is that we're not from Kugad, and Velet probably isn't our homeworld. We're a species called ablun, but that doesn't help either."

Hredt watched her expression and knew exactly what she was thinking because he'd had those same thoughts himself. Teeriks didn't forget. Their phenomenal memories defined them and they passed on learned skills in their genes. It was impossible that they'd forget their origins, and yet they had.

"I'm sure you'll find out one day," she said. She was very tactful. "Solomon's looking for you, by the way. Are you ready to speak to him? I'll tell him you're here."

"I think I must," Hredt said. "I deceived him. I regret that."

Nina just smiled, got to her feet, and took a wrapped food bar from her pocket. "New flavour," she said, handing it to him. "Banana. Test it for me."

The ladder's rungs made pinging noises as she climbed down. Could Solomon's quadrubot climb? It didn't matter. It was Hredt's duty to go to Solomon after what he'd done. He swooped down to the grass and waited. A few minutes later, Solomon came loping towards him between the greenhouses, just the way he used to run when neither of them knew what the other really was.

"Hredt, I should have come to see you straight away," Solomon said. "I apologise. I've been rather busy in the last few hours."

Hredt needed someone who'd trust him and who he could trust. The relationship with Solomon needed a little repair to its foundations before it could begin.

"I'm sorry we misled you," he said. "We should have shown you we were intelligent. But we thought you were a mechanical. We didn't know you were an emanation until Chief Jeff told us."

"I admit I've evaded my enemies by pretending to be a bot," Solomon said. "And I don't blame you for being afraid."

"We're friends, then?"

"Yes. Of course." Solomon lifted his camera head to look towards the portal. "Those people arriving now are the transit camp evacuees. If you want to understand what humans can be, that community is a good example. They're all willing to put up with hardship while we build accommodation for them. They've endured a great deal worse."

"Are humans always like this?" Hredt realised he assumed Solomon was as much of an outsider as he was. Perhaps the emanation didn't see himself that way at all. "They're so quiet and disciplined. This must be a great shock for them. And the soldiers with them treat them kindly."

"Humans can be extremely unpleasant, Hredt," Solomon said. "But I chose these people for their qualities. That's my mission. My creator told me to decide what was best in humanity, and to find and protect those who embodied it. These people are the best, not because they're prodigies or geniuses, although some of them are, but because they embody the morality of taking care of each other. Loyal, courageous, hardworking, compassionate, and willing to die so that others can live. They're *special*. Not all humans are like that, and perhaps not even all the humans coming from the town and the research centre meet those ideals. You see those troops, though? They rescued the civilians from a war zone and were ready to carry them on their backs so nobody would be abandoned. People they'd never met before. They risk their lives for strangers."

Hredt hoped his new human friends were going to stick around, not throw their lives away in pursuit of virtue. But other teeriks had left his commune to fend for itself after their grand plans, and the thought of humans who wouldn't abandon others struck a chord with him.

"You're very fond of them," he said.

"They're why I exist. Don't you find selfless sacrifice remarkable?" Solomon stood up on his hind legs for a moment as if he couldn't quite see something in the distance. "We'll have hundreds more people arriving in the next few hours. It's going to be chaotic for a while. But this settlement will succeed. It'll be a model of what humans can achieve."

Hredt had expected a barrage of questions from Solomon but the emanation seemed more interested in watching the arrival. He was here with Hredt rather than working down at the gate, though, so he must have felt the conversation was important. Perhaps he found it hard to know what to say. He wasn't like any of the emanations Hredt had encountered in ships.

"My daughter thinks I've lost my mind," Hredt said. "I hope I'd realise if I had."

"People with new ideas are often seen as mad, Hredt."

Hredt wanted Turisu's approval. It was natural to care what your children thought of you. He wasn't going to get that approval, though, so all he could do was stand by his plan because there was no other option. "I still have faith in the Learned Mother's vision for the future. We can't always have been this helpless. Look at us. We have claws and beaks designed for tearing. We can digest meat. We can *fly*. Where did we come from? How did we end up serving alien warlords, unable to fend for ourselves?"

Solomon had a way of giving visible emotions to an expressionless bot. He turned the snakehead camera as if he was tilting his head in surprise.

"You have a very eloquent turn of phrase," he said. "You've progressed from no knowledge of English to remarkable fluency in weeks. I'd like to know where you came from as well. I'm certain your past was nothing like your present."

Hredt was embarrassed. He rarely mentioned these ideas to the others. He'd never planned to be a revolutionary and he hadn't wanted to join an uprising, but events had a life of their own, and now he'd brought a new intelligent species to the sector, one that would challenge the balance of power. A year ago, he'd have found it unthinkable.

"I should go back to the ship," he said. "I should be present when Caisin dies."

"It's a pity she can't see how well her portal's performing."

Hredt found himself nodding like a human. "Yes, it's a great achievement. But she'll never have the glory she deserves at home. She should at least be here to feel the importance of the moment."

"Bring her here, then," Solomon said.

"She's very close to death. She can't move."

"All the more reason. Can you set up another portal and place her here?"

Hredt thought about it. He could do it: he'd had to work out how to create a sidestream gateway to place a route between Earth and the open field here, like a spur road coming off the main one generated inside the ship, with a junction where it could be entered and exited.

"She might not want to," he said.

"You can ask. Is it going to make things any worse for you?"

There would never be another chance. He had to do it. "Where should I locate it so she has a good view without having strangers stare at her?"

"The roof of the main building," Solomon said. "I'll give you precise coordinates."

Solomon was encouraging him but Hredt didn't need much more persuasion. The thought of Caisin dying without watching her prototype performing in a real emergency was too painful to bear. He held out his screen to Solomon.

"Give me the coordinates," he said. "You'll know if I succeed."

The wind direction wasn't helping Hredt today. He exhausted himself flying back to the ship, and as soon as he entered the hatch, Turisu was waiting to pounce on him.

"You can't even be here for the Learned Mother," she said. Her feathers were raised. "You're fluttering around the humans like an idiot."

Hredt hissed angrily. "I've never told you to be silent, Turi, but I demand that you be quiet now." He could hardly believe he'd said that. He'd never chided her even as a fledgling. "We need the humans. They need us. How many times do I have to spell it out to you?"

Turisu showed no sign of backing down or even running out of anger. "You've given them control of the gate. When they learn how to use it, they'll take it, and they won't need us any longer."

"Turi, I've given them a locator, that's all. If they need to move their terminus to conceal it, then they can." All the locator did was transmit coordinates to the gate controls so the terminal end of the spacefold could be pinpointed exactly. "They're in a very dangerous situation, and the last thing we want is for their enemy to gain access. I trust them to use the system sensibly."

"You're a fool," Turisu rasped. "Why did you bother to come back?"

"To see the Learned Mother."

"Finally. How gracious of you."

"You think I'm callous, rescuing aliens while she dies, don't you?" Hredt said. "Well, it has to be done right now or it might not be possible at all. I want Caisin to know that her work has been vindicated and that it's helping achieve her aims. She'll understand why I did this. This alliance will save us."

"She'd never have agreed to an intervention on this scale."

"Really? We'll see."

Hredt pushed past her and headed for Caisin's cabin. Right then, he didn't even care about the egg. If the Learned Mother managed to lay it, the chances of the child surviving were slim anyway, given her age and health, and there was nothing he could do to help her. They were used to having medical assistance on call. Just as they'd never had to worry about being fed, they'd never had to dress a wound or diagnose their own complaints, however minor. If Caisin failed to produce the egg there was nothing they could do and it would die with her, taking her accumulated knowledge with it. But the only thing that mattered to him right now was giving Caisin the final comfort of seeing her handiwork fully tested before she died.

He wasn't going to get to see her without running the gauntlet of the rest of the commune. Maro was blocking the corridor. Pannit, Keejah, and Epliko looked less determined but they were between Hredt and Caisin's cabin too. There was no sign of Cosquimaden.

"How *dare* you come here," Maro whispered. "How could you do it at a time like this? How could you lie to us?"

It was a very quiet fight. They were trying not to disturb Caisin, but Hredt felt they'd reached the point where their anger had exhausted them and burned out. They were just recirculating the old arguments because they didn't know how else to fill the emptiness.

"I did what I had to," Hredt said. "And if you speak to me again like that, you'll feel my claws."

"You do crazy things without consulting us. You're going to get us killed."

"What will actually get us killed is doing nothing. You've never made an independent decision in your life, Maro, not one that really mattered. *None* of us has. Someone else always decided what we needed and wanted." Hredt no longer cared about approval. He wondered if he'd regret it tomorrow. "This is what it feels like to be free. It's not comfortable or easy. But it's better."

"But you *didn't discuss it with us.* You said you wouldn't get involved with the humans' world. Who gave you the right?"

"Hold a ballot, then. But first, get out of my way. I need to see the Learned Mother."

"It's too late."

"Is she dead?"

"No, but — "

"Step aside."

"You traded our only advantage for crumbs."

"And you were happy to eat them. Just as we traded our freedom for Kugin delicacies and never having to think for ourselves. We existed like *infants.* Now we have to be adults. You might not like it, but this is what Caisin intended. From the moment we took this ship, there was never any going back. And we can't go forward on our own."

It was the same argument they'd had before Hredt had left for some peace and quiet, and it was Maro doing the arguing while the other two stood looking like they wished they were somewhere else. Any moment now, Turisu would appear and he'd be trapped.

"I asked you to stand aside," Hredt said.

"You betrayed us."

"Maro, we're in a position to choose allies for the first time instead of doing what we're told to do for the advantage of savages. Now get out of my way."

Maro looked past him, back up the passage. "Turi, make him stop."

Turisu had come to join the argument. If this went on much longer, Caisin would be dead before he had the chance to do anything. "Father, what are you trying to do?"

"I'm going to show Caisin her gate doing what she intended it to do."

"This is insane. She's not even well enough to view it on a monitor."

"So you'd rather she be deprived of the comfort of being there to see her achievements in her final moments?"

"She's at the end of her life and you're coming to the end of yours. What about my sons' lives? What happens to them?"

"And they're my grandsons. Why do you think I'm doing any of this? It's all for *them*. It's *because* I'm getting old that I want to do this, while I still have the ability to give them a better future."

"We can't function without masters. Accept it. We've just exchanged Kugin foremen for human ones, except we're cut off from all other teeriks and that means our bloodline is finished."

Hredt saw no point in talking any longer. He stepped forward into Maro, chest to chest, and fluffed up his plumage. He hadn't fought since he was a child and that had just been a brief scuffle between young males, something they did without really knowing why. He was too old to take on Maro. But like most ablun, his son-in-law had never lashed out in his life and had no inclination to fight. They were a docile species. And that was the problem. Hredt could see it clearly now in a way he never had back in Deku. He wasn't sure where his own aggression had come from, but he knew he had to hang on to it.

Maro stepped back. "You're a madman," he said. "You're getting worse every day."

Hredt pushed past him and went into Caisin's cabin. The old mother was sitting on a cushion on the deck, breathing heavily, eyes closed. Hredt ducked his head down to speak to her.

"Learned Mother, forgive my intrusion, but there's something you must see."

She opened one eye. "I'm trying to die, Hredt. Must you fight outside my door?"

Hredt hated himself at that moment. He'd presumed he knew what would make her happy. He didn't.

"I won't let you leave this world without seeing your legacy," he said. "The system you created will free us. It's doing it now. I'm taking you to see it."

"Turi's right. You've lost your mind. I can't even stand."

"You don't need to." Hredt took out his portal locator. "I'm going to use the gate. I want you to see it working. It's doing great things. I can create multiple gateways now, sidestreams from the main generator that can be accessed at a point along their path. Look."

There was only one way he was going to be able to move her through the gate. He'd have to drag the floor cushion she was resting on. He hoped he had the strength. He pointed the locator at the deck as close to her as he could and the distorted patch of air formed.

"I know you mean well," she said. "But can't you let me die in peace? I can't even lay my egg."

Hredt locked his claws into the edge of the cushion. "You can at least see your engineering triumph, then."

She was heavier than expected. But he'd drag her through the portal if it killed him. He backed into it, confident that his feet would find a flat, solid surface on the other side, and heaved as hard as he could. The cushion slid towards him. Caisin's breathing was laboured gasps. For a moment, he thought he'd suddenly discovered strength he didn't know he had, but then he realised there was a mechanical gripper on the cushion, and something else had reached into the portal to pull it through.

He took a step back into the new location as Solomon hauled Caisin nearer the edge of the roof. Ingram was already there. From the top of the building, they could see the entire camp and the full extent of the evacuation. There were hundreds of humans down there now and even animals. Opis would never be the same again.

"Learned Mother, let me reassure you I'm not a mechanical," Solomon said. "I'm an emanation. My name's Solomon. You honour us with your presence."

"No English," she said.

"Fred, would you translate for me, please?" Ingram asked. She knelt down beside Caisin. "Learned Mother, we call that a Caisin gate. It'll always be called that. Your work saved our people. I promise you that we'll do everything in our power to help your commune and establish a safe homeland for teeriks. I have no idea yet what that'll entail, but we humans are very good at solving problems. Thank you, on behalf of everyone who'll make their home here."

Hredt translated into Kugal while Caisin cocked her head and watched the apparently endless stream of evacuees emerging from thin air. Even Hredt, who'd grown used to it, had to admit it looked impressive on this scale. They sat on the roof for a while — ten minutes by human reckoning — while Hredt pointed out the novelties to her, like the cattle on open-topped freight vehicles, and black and white dogs bred for herding that were darting around as if they were trying to round up the humans and restore some order to the area.

"Tell Ingram I think she means what she promises," Caisin said. "And that she needs to be prepared for a galaxy that'll see humans as easy targets."

Hredt almost lied to Ingram when he relayed the comment, but he didn't want any more deception to put their alliance at risk.

He translated word for word and braced for the response, because Ingram had proved to be a very direct woman even if she spoke a polite form of English.

"Tell the Learned Mother that we value her advice and that we'll be ready for whatever comes our way," Ingram said.

Caisin watched the arrivals for a few more moments, then turned to Hredt. "I think I must finish this now. Take me back, Hredt."

Solomon dragged the cushion back through the portal and left again with a brief nod. Hredt wasn't sure what to do next, but Turisu was waiting at the door and walked in as if she was going to continue her tirade but then thought better of it.

"Turi, I've seen the gate, and I've seen enough of the humans to know that Hredt has done the right thing," Caisin said. "No more arguments. Now leave me. Thank you all for your loyalty and skill. And don't mourn for me."

Hredt pulled a cover over her. "Get some rest," he said. "I'll be just outside the door."

Her voice was just a croak now. "I'm glad you insisted I see it. It's not so hard to die now I know you have allies, not foremen. It's a beginning. Never stop being a mad old man, Hredt."

Hredt wished he had some clever words to leave her with, but he didn't. He put his hand on her head for a moment, a son's parting gesture even though they weren't kin, then left.

The whole commune was waiting in the passage, even the boys, uncharacteristically silent. It was the done thing to sit with the dying but Caisin had sent them away. Now all they could do was wait there, cramped and anxious, and listen.

"I'm still angry with you, father," Turisu whispered.

"I'm sure you are," Hredt said. "But Caisin isn't."

Hredt made a conscious decision to switch to human time measurement from now on. Soon he'd establish an accurate mental clock and know exactly how much time had elapsed at any given moment without needing to look, which would probably amuse Chief Jeff. As he gazed at the unfinished conduit on the bulkhead, he realised he felt relieved, but it wasn't a happy kind of relief. It was more a sense of dreaded hurdles being cleared. There'd be many more to come.

Twenty minutes had now passed. Turisu suddenly looked up.

"I think Learned Mother has passed," she said. "We should check."

Turisu looked at the others, then stood up. "I'll do it."

Hredt had left his own parents as a child a little older than his grandsons, and he hadn't attended either of them at their death. He'd never seen them again. It wasn't the teerik way. For the first time, he wondered if there were any other cultures where children were expected to leave their families so early and never come back. He was still pondering his acceptance of the custom when Turisu came out of Caisin's cabin.

She was carrying something wrapped in a cloth. Everyone watched her, waiting for some announcement.

"The Learned Mother is gone," she said at last. "And I have her egg."

For a few moments, nobody spoke. They hadn't expected Caisin to be able to produce one. Now they had to do something about it and its chances of hatching were poor.

"All we can do is incubate it and hope for the best," Pannit said. "I'll set something up."

"But what do we do with *her*?" Turisu asked, cradling the egg. Her voice had become high and thin again, like a child's. "Where do we put her?"

The Kugin had always removed the bodies of the dead. Apart from a quiet gathering to recall their lives and achievements, there was no teerik ritual or memorial that a human would recognise. That had always seemed normal up to now, but without the foremen to deal with it, the question had suddenly become urgent, and it was no longer enough for teeriks to live on in the minds and skills of their children.

"Leave it to me," Hredt said. He had no more idea than Turisu did, but he knew he could work it out. "I'll take care of everything."

* * *

BECKER DAIRY FARM, KILL LINE: 0955 EDT.

"So how did you break it to your people, then?" Trinder asked.

Chris was leaning against the end wall of the milking shed, hands cupped around a mug of coffee, eyes shut. "I just said something like you know that wormhole we had, well, now we've got a proper one and we can go straight to Opis, and there's some friendly aliens there who are helping us out, and possibly unfriendly aliens who are looking for them, but it's probably a better bet than England because it'll only take one asshole rowing across the English Channel and not being shot on sight to infect the whole country. And if we end up there, we'll know stuff that someone might kill us to get hold of. We discussed it like we always do."

He made it sound so easy. But Chris and Jared were guys those people trusted with their lives, and they always told them the truth. That made shocks easier to deliver.

"And they just took it okay," Trinder said.

"They're fed up with wandering around. So am I." Chris opened his eyes. "They want to start over. This is their last evacuation. They said they'd rather stand their ground on Opis than keep going around in circles and end up in the same shit."

Trinder didn't pretend to understand the kind of bond that held the transit camp together. Shared danger and deprivation, a leader they believed in, and a group small enough to think like an extended family instead of a city made for a tight-knit tribe. But Kill Line hadn't really faced serious hardship yet and Trinder didn't know how they'd take it. Maybe they'd never have to.

"What are we going to do about *Elcano*?" Chris asked. "Leave her to chug along for forty-five years, or try to speed things up with teerik tech? That's a great brand name, by the way. We should set up a corporation."

"The question is how soon we want them revived," Trinder said. "Another thousand to feed and accommodate when we'll be struggling to care for the current population."

"One thousand and thirty-two."

"Now you sound like Sol."

"I was thinking we could move the ship to an orbit around Opis so we know where they are and can intervene if anything goes wrong," Chris said. "Then reviving everyone when we can feed and house them."

"Yeah, and move *Shackleton* too. Because if the portal goes down for any reason, including the teeriks changing their mind about us, those ships will be our only way off the planet."

Chris drained his mug. "See how easy this governance stuff is? Agreed course of action in two minutes."

"We've got to consult Marc yet. And Ingram. And Fred."

"If it's technically feasible, they'll go along with it. *Elcano* needs to be where we can keep an eye on her. If she's in orbit and something goes wrong, we can reach her and revive everyone without even using the gate."

It really did seem like all things were possible now. Trinder wondered if they were just looking for every reason not to burn out their lives wandering from crisis to crisis, and it was the military way to find the positive and build from it. But they did have sole access to game-changing technology. That was going to make a big difference to their lives, even if they hadn't worked it all out yet.

Chris shook his head. "This time yesterday, I didn't know any of this existed. Now I've arrested an alien, travelled between star systems six times, and covered... well, whatever six round trips is in miles. How many zeros in that?"

"A lot. It's four hundred and eighty light years. Where could you go if that was a single straight line?"

"I'll ask Nathan Marr." Chris actually smiled to himself, a proper smile that spread all the way. "The kid's going to love this."

The conversation was interrupted by the sound of engines approaching and a blip on the radio from the route marshal to tell them the first Kill Line group was on its way. The evacuation was a conveyor belt of humanity, a batch at a time. The drivers in each group would be briefed inside the milking shed to avoid possible surveillance, a video link to Nomad Base would monitor how fast traffic was clearing the portal and being dispersed across the camp, and traffic marshals all along the route from Kill Line to the milking shed would be keeping the convoys moving at the right time or manning roadblocks. With duties on the Nomad side and perimeter patrols around Kill Line on top of that, eighty-two troops and fourteen dogs were stretched thin.

Trinder consulted the view from the swarm of micro-drones criss-crossing the area. It wasn't comprehensive coverage, but they could see the main road to Ainatio, the most likely inbound path for any trouble, and they had an overview of the convoy route.

"Okay, I'm as ready as I'll ever be," Trinder said. "But Alex is going to be better at psyching them up."

"Just tell them straight," Chris pushed himself away from the wall and stared at the patch of mist that opened a road across star systems. "Isn't it weird that you can stand right behind this thing and still be on Earth?"

The first vehicles drove in, Doug and Joanne Brandt in the lead pickup. In a few minutes, the cavernous milking shed was full of drivers, some standing by their pickups, some having walked in from vehicles that had to line up outside. The place was silent except for the occasional click of an engine and a small child whispering anxious questions about the bathroom.

"Folks," Trinder said, pointing at the haze, "this is your exit for Opis."

"What is?" someone at the back asked.

"This."

"The mist thing or the wall?"

"The mist."

"Oh. It's not very big, is it? I was expecting... well, flashing lights. A big metal gantry. That kind of thing."

"Well, we're lucky it's low key and we can hide it in here, or we'd attract the wrong sort of attention," Trinder said. "You just walk or drive through. No swirly lights or anything. Our guys have been going back and forth all night to get the shelters set up, so I can promise you it works."

"Have you done this yourself?" Ingrid Morris asked, like it was a challenge. She was the town physician. "Has anyone looked at the longer-term effects?"

"I've done six round trips, and nothing's fallen off yet," Chris said. He could tell someone to zip it while looking angelically innocent. "Twice on foot. Nothing to it."

Trinder waited for questions about whether it hurt or other stuff he hadn't thought of, but all he got was silence, just the way it was when Alex first told them about *Cabot* and the existence of Nomad.

Please. Somebody say something. Anything.

Eventually Lance Webber spoke up. "Has it got edges we need to avoid? How does it know how wide to be? Or do we just drive at it?"

Trinder had to love these people. He imagined the long-vanished normal world dealing with the news they'd just received — politicians interrupting programmes to address the nation, media losing their shit, shares plummeting. But Kill Liners just shrugged and wanted a few more details in case they dented their fenders. Chris was right. Regular people subconsciously expected real science to eventually catch up with the aliens and galaxy-hopping the movies had fed them since childhood. When they said alien life, they didn't mean bacteria. They meant the likes of Fred. And now Fred was real, their new neighbour.

"You just drive at it," Trinder said. "As soon as you touch it, you're through. It works it out somehow. Don't forget we used a similar principle for instant comms, but ours couldn't handle much more than tiny objects and radio signals. This is the luxury version."

But he hadn't done it yet. He hadn't done it himself. He'd been too busy evacuating the facility and making sure the staff were kept well away from the townsfolk in case someone slipped up. He checked the video feed on his screen to make sure the other side was clear, then walked up to the patch of mist.

"Like this," he said, and stepped through.

Yes, his ears did feel odd for a second. And he was so excited to be on another planet that he just stood and stared and inhaled the air and marvelled at how bogged down his legs suddenly felt, unable to think of anything else for a few moments. Then he spotted Fonseca about thirty yards away with a group of guys in naval working rig, standing with her hands on her hips with her you're-holding-up-my-careful-plan expression.

"I'm just showing them how easy it is," he said, and turned around to retrace his half-dozen steps.

It was like changing the channel on the TV. He was straight back in the milking shed. He realised he'd be doing this for the sheer hell of it as often as he could until the novelty wore off or he was exhausted, whichever happened sooner.

"There. It's that simple." He got a polite ripple of nervous applause. "All you need to do is drive like you're going through the wall at the end. But you won't hit anything. You'll blink and you'll be on open ground in Nomad Base. You'll see the field marked out with lanes of tape to show you where to go and there'll be marshals directing you to parking and decontamination. Think of it as arriving for the county show and trying to get parked as quickly as you can."

Dr Morris was still watching Chris with her arms folded. Maybe she was waiting for him to start bleeding from the nose like they did in the movies. She gave Trinder a kind little smile, the sort she probably reserved for kids before administering unpleasant medicine.

"I was wondering what happens if we get a visit from the other aliens Doug mentioned," she said. "If things go wrong and Opis turns out to be too dangerous, can we come back or escape to somewhere else?"

There was only one answer Trinder could give if he wanted to get people moving. "If that happens," he said, "we always have a back door."

Damn, he shouldn't have said it. He knew how Marc felt about encouraging people to see Nomad as an extended adventure vacation. But Morris seemed satisfied. "Always helps to know," she said.

"We're doing this to save lives, folks," Chris said. "You're not here to storm beaches or build empires. And you're not expendable. We wouldn't be going if we didn't think it was safer there than here."

Trinder clapped his hands together. "Okay, mount up and start your engines. If there's an autonomous vehicle in front of you, just follow it and keep going because you're not going to crash into the wall. You'll be in the middle of Nomad Base right away. Look for the traffic marshals on the other side and follow their signals. We'll see you all later."

A couple of folks turned to glance behind them, the ones whose vehicles were already inside the milking shed. For a moment, Trinder thought they'd heard something that he hadn't. Then he realised they were searching for a window or a doorway to take one last look at the only home most of them had ever known. It was too late. If they could see anything beyond the press of bodies and vehicles, the only thing visible from the open end of the shed was the concrete yard. But, being Kill Liners, they got into their vehicles without complaint. The others trooped out to rejoin the trucks and cars parked outside.

Trinder checked his screen. It showed a live feed of Opis from a camera position at about head height next to the portal, looking towards the base that was now a building site full of bots. He'd be able to see how fast the traffic was clearing the exit and manage the speed of the line via the marshals. On the Opis side, another team of marshals was standing by to get vehicles clear of the portal and parked for the evacuees to be processed by *Cabot* crew or detachment and militia troops and eventually taken to temporary shelters.

It was a minor miracle to organise this much overnight.

But moving everyone out of Kill Line was the easy bit. Getting a roof over their heads and making sure they had food and water by the end of the day was another matter. Solomon was in command of his bot construction army once again, building a temporary Rome in a day.

Chris cocked his head to listen to something in his earpiece. "Fonseca says get on with it."

"I think we might have a recurring motif there," Trinder said.

Chris didn't take the bait. He walked over to Doug Brandt's pickup and leaned on the driver's side window. Joanne was in the passenger seat.

"You're going to be wrung out by the end of the day, Doug," Chris said. "Don't forget the gravity. You'll really feel it. Just go have a rest. You too, Mrs Brandt."

"We've got to be there to help process folks," Doug said. "We can't swan in when the hard work's been done. I'll come back when the last group's through and formally switch off the lights."

"You don't have to. We'll make sure the place is clear."

"But I'm the *mayor*," Doug said. "The last mayor of Kill Line. It's my duty."

He needed to do it to make leaving bearable. Trinder understood that even if he hadn't been that attached to anywhere.

"Okay." Chris said. "Just drive straight. I promise you won't hit the wall."

Doug took a deep breath and the pickup moved off. Trinder thought it was still quite something to watch a vehicle dissolve into thin air. The driver behind Doug thought so too, because he braked at the last moment, just enough of a dip in his speed to make the vehicle behind brake as well, but then the self-driving vehicles further back down the line nudged everybody on and the line started moving smoothly.

"It works." Trinder stepped back behind the safety barrier with Chris and watched the traffic stream past. It was sobering to realise how many vehicles he'd never seen before. "And at least we'll have plenty of spares."

"What a way to start a new world," Chris said. "A scrapyard, a cemetery, and waiting in line for food. I hope the teeriks don't think that's how we live."

"But it is," Trinder said. "That's exactly what Earth is now."

The next transits went smoothly. Implacable driverless vehicles and stoic farmers were a good mix for getting things done. Trinder and Chris polished their double act each time a group went through and maybe that confidence and ease percolated through to the evacuees, because people seemed more enthusiastic as the morning wore on. Maybe they were fed up with waiting, though, and just being on the move was a relief after so many false starts and near disasters.

Then a vehicle broke down in the shed and had to be towed clear. But Trinder checked and crunched numbers, and they were still ahead of schedule. When the next group arrived, Alex peeled from the line in Marc's stolen limo, looking pleased with himself. He lowered the window.

"It's okay, Marc knows I'm doing this," he said. "I promised him I'd make sure the car got to Opis while he's out in the Caracal."

"Don't get too attached to it," Trinder said.

Alex got out and looked over the Trident like he was thinking of buying it, then polished a dusty patch on the hood with his sleeve. "Most of the dents will buff out. And I don't mind all the dried blood and hair on the front bumper. Kind of adds character."

"Don't even think about it," Chris said. "It's British government property. He'll kneecap you."

"Ah, he won't need it on Opis. Ingram's going to drive him around in her scythed chariot." Alex buffed the hood again. "Anyway, time for me to relieve you. How's it going?"

"On schedule," Trinder said. "No Erin?"

"She'll be along in a minute. Any mutineers?"

"Of course not. They're Kill Liners. Dr Morris asked awkward questions about the long-term health effects of bending space-time, but Professor Montello here fielded that."

"Yeah, this is the easy crowd. Wait until it's the scientists. Oh hell, yes. Todd Mangel." Alex shook his head. "Get the incontinence pads ready. He'll wet himself with excitement when he sees the portal."

"Mind if I ask about Kim's transport?"

Alex took out his screen and fiddled with it. "It's taking a bit longer than we expected."

"How much longer?"

"I had second thoughts about Ainatio pickups. If we send her out in one of those, it'll be like painting a target on the roof. Even the really scruffy ones are too conspicuous and we can't fix that without spending ages on it. So we got hold of an old pickup from one of the farms and we're giving it a thorough service before we send it out."

"That's cutting it fine, Alex. She needs to be gone by the time we shut down the facility."

"I know. I'm on it."

Solomon popped up on their radios. "Gentlemen, I can confirm the site is now clear of all personnel, equipment, and supplies marked for Opis. I'm standing by to purge what's left of the security system, which is just the door controls now. As we agreed, I've put a three-day delay on the management wing's door system to give Commissioner Pham some time for quiet contemplation. When do you want me to proceed?"

Poor Sol: he sounded like he was joking, but he was doing the equivalent of burning his house down. He'd lived in that network for decades. It was both his home and, for most of the time, his body as well. Trinder felt sorry for him.

"Are you still in your bot?" Trinder asked.

"Yes, I'm still on the Opis side. I'd appreciate a decision so that I can terminate my connection with the facility network."

Chris checked his screen and then his watch. "At this rate, we'll have all the Kill Liners, vehicles, and most of the Ainatio fleet through the gate by fourteen hundred. The staff buses won't take long to push through."

"Are you saying you want to wait until the last vehicle's through before I remove the lockdown?"

"Does that give you any problems?"

"Not really. When do you think you'll get Dr Kim's vehicle loaded and in place? Because she needs a head start. And you still need to make a hole in the fence as arranged."

"We should have found somewhere to park her over here," Chris said.

Alex looked disappointed and for once it didn't seem he was joking. "It wouldn't have been as simple as that and you know it. We'd still be sorting out the getaway car but the convoy would be moving and she'd see or hear something and ask awkward questions. And one thing would lead to another, and now we'd be trying to keep a lid on more potential leaks. "

"Yeah, but now we're organising a shut-down to her timetable and dicking around over wire fencing."

"What happened to you? You used to be Max Grit, pitiless and granite-hearted. The sensible option would have been to leave her to Pham."

"Hey, I'm not the guy who got my ass handed to me trying to save her the last time."

Chris said it in that dry way he had when he was joking, but Trinder got the feeling he was genuinely worried about Kim's safety. Alex wasn't joking either: it wasn't like Chris to openly show regret or concern. But these were strange and stressful days.

"All right, if you two don't mind doing the briefings for longer, I'll go sort out her truck personally," Alex said. "I'll get Zakko to take care of the fence."

"Zakko stays on the Opis side. He's got a job to do." Chris said it quietly but Trinder could hear the finality in his voice. "I'll deal with the fence. Dan and Erin can do the gate briefings."

Marc's voice came over the secure channel. "Alpha Three here. "I'll do it now. I'm near the facility anyway."

Trinder wasn't sure if Chris was pissed at Alex for trying to commandeer one of his troops or if he didn't want Zakko to put himself at risk again because he knew the guy wouldn't give much thought to his safety. It was probably a bit of both. Alex wasn't one to back down even in the face of superior testosterone firepower, but he didn't argue with Chris. He walked away, talking on the radio with the mechanics.

"Sol, we'll make sure you're not waiting around for Kim," Trinder said. "Give Alex time to sort her out and then you can shut down when you think it's safe to do so."

The breakdown that had been towed out of the line now seemed to have been fixed. Its driver turned out to be one of Kill Line's mechanics. Everyone was laughing at the poor guy as he wiped his hands, red-faced.

"What can I say?" He spread his arms in an appeal to their better natures. "I was too busy getting everyone else's vehicle ready."

He joined the group waiting to transit. Trinder was preparing to brief them with Chris when Erin arrived.

"Time for your break, guys," she said. "Hasn't Alex shown up yet?"

"He's gone to sort out Annis Kim's truck," Trinder said, too smitten to think of the right thing to say to her. He opted for the functional approach. "It was getting urgent. I said we'd carry on for a while."

"I could do the next session with you," Erin said.

Chris just looked suitably expressionless. "Okay, that frees me up to go check on our restless scientists. Call me if you need me."

Trinder was now on his own with Erin. He was sure Chris really did have more urgent things to do, and so did Alex, but he almost felt he'd been set up for this. For a moment, he forgot about Kim. He tried hard not regress to a teenage boy when he looked Erin in the eye.

"Dan," Erin said. "A word before we start the briefing."

"Have I done something wrong?"

"No. It's nothing like that. You know how I always say we should tell people the important things before it's too late, because I never did and those are the biggest regrets of my life?"

"Yeah." She meant Jamie. She'd also lost a boyfriend or husband some years earlier, but Trinder didn't know the details and he hadn't dared ask. "I understand."

"Well, I can put up with Opis, but I don't think it'd ever feel like home unless you were with me. Can we stop tiptoeing around each other and do something about that?"

Trinder tried to think of some charmingly witty answer but he was fifteen and tongue-tied again. "Okay. I can't take you to dinner, but I've got a secret stash of moussaka MREs if that's okay."

"That'll do fine. I'll bring a bottle of vodka. See? That wasn't so hard, was it?"

No, it wasn't. He just hadn't been sure if he'd read her wrong, and he couldn't face a state of permanent, painful embarrassment because there'd be nowhere to avoid her in Nomad Base.

"Moussaka and vodkatinis," he said. "It's a date."

Trinder began to feel that life was turning the corner. He could catch up on all the time that being marooned in the Ainatio facility had taken from him because there was a new life on the other side of that small patch of disembodied mist, and he could re-shape it any way he pleased, all the baggage and restrictions of Earth cleared away. Fonseca was right; the post-apocalypse was appealing, at least in theory, because it threw away the rule book and everyone started over from the same level playing field. And now Trinder knew he wouldn't be starting over alone.

One of the cattle truck drivers leaned out of his side window while he waited. "You're looking pleased with yourself, Major."

"That's because it's all going to plan," Trinder said. "And that doesn't happen to me often."

The Kill Liners continued to roll through the gate. Some took it in their stride while others slowed down a little and looked like they were bracing to crash into the wall, but nobody lost their nerve. They all drove through.

"Maybe we worried over nothing," Erin said. "But it didn't hurt to plan for the worst. Hey, Marc's back."

Marc's Caracal drove into the yard and peeled off to park behind one of the barns. He emerged carrying a water bottle and paused to fill it from one of the taps.

"All done," he said, walking up to Trinder and Erin. "It's been years since I cut a hole in a fence. Very nostalgic."

"Did you see Kim?"

"No, and that's a good thing, because it means she's being careful. I hope she saw me."

"If she's got any sense, she'll exit now and go hide in the woods to watch for the vehicle," Erin said.

"She'll make it. She's nails." Marc checked his screen. "I put a micro-drone up to see if there was any activity before I moved in to the fence, but they've all gone to ground. No operators, no Kim, nothing. No movement on the road, either. I think I'll go and harass Alex about the pickup."

"I don't know what he's dicking around for," Trinder said. "It's not like we don't have any spare gear."

The radio interrupted. "Six Zero to Alpha Three, Echo Five. Unable to locate Dr Mangel, I'm starting a search, over."

Erin muttered to herself. Marc looked heavenward and shook his head.

"Echo Five here," Trinder said. "Alpha Three's returned from Ainatio and reports nobody about on the road. Say if you want us to search as well, over."

"If you can spare someone, yes," Chris said. "RV at the town hall. Six Zero out."

Marc let out a long sigh. "Didn't see that coming. Please don't let him be the informer. I thought he was a pretty decent bloke."

"The drone would have picked him up if he'd headed back to Ainatio," Trinder said.

"Only if he took the road. It's not hard to move through the woods without being spotted."

"Well, there's nothing more he can do to us now. If it's him."

"That depends where he went," Marc said. "Do we know his movements beforehand? How many people have we got to keep an eye on three hundred and fifty boffins?"

"So what could he see?"

"What we were worried about to start with. Lots of vehicles disappearing into a shed that couldn't possibly hold them all and not coming out."

"Would he necessarily think it was a wormhole, though?"

"Ainatio built one already. It just wasn't very big. But if anyone works it out, it'll be him."

Trinder didn't know Mangel well enough to know if he had a whole other side that would screw over his colleagues like that. If he'd had to bet real money, he'd have said not. But then he'd never have imagined any of them doing it at all.

Tad Bednarz, a futurologist whose record was now verging on prophecy, had told Solomon that colonising the galaxy would bring out the very best and the very worst in humanity. Trinder wondered if the man had ever thought that he'd find both among his own employees.

09

We got what we came for, but we're paying a heavy price for it. I want the roads out of Kill Line covered and eyes on the town. This is too coordinated and precise for a bunch of farmers and vagrants. I'm betting they've got outside support — a nation state — and I want to know what's so important that their ASD's shut us down while they get on with it. Work out what's going on, and remember you're here to destroy that thing. It'll be in a bot of some kind. You can manage that, can't you? There's two of you. Practically a battalion.

Commissioner Tim Pham, briefing his operators
on the second day of the Asian-Pacific CPS attack.

KILL LINE TOWN SQUARE: 1310 EDT.

Dieter already had the dogs out looking for Mangel by the time Chris got back to the muster point in the town square.

A murmuring, arms-folded huddle of Ainatio personnel stood in the shade of the trees outside the town hall, looking like a bunch of well-off tourists waiting for their bus to the next site of historic interest with a gift shop. The town hall's double doors were wide open. Chris could see a pile of luggage just inside the lobby, an assortment of pre-Ainatio bags in different colours and materials, Ainatio-manufactured red and black ripstop, and a lot of metal flight cases. The brainiacs were taking their work with them.

"He's got Todd's underwear," one of the women said. She caught Chris as he dismounted from the quad bike. "Your dog handler, I mean. He needed something to give the dogs a scent, so we opened Todd's bag."

"Dr Mangel can't have been planning to go far, then," Chris said. "Not if he didn't take his luggage."

There were other reasons to leave your luggage behind, of course. It was a great way to get a head start if you were planning to skip town and you already had your irreplaceable stuff in your pockets. And you wouldn't need luggage if you were planning to go meet your Maker. Chris knew nobody's personal radar was foolproof, but Mangel didn't fit either scenario. This was probably more a case of the rest of the staff getting panicky because the evacuation plan kept changing and Mangel was a loose cannon. And they still didn't know how they were getting to Opis.

Chris didn't want to play it down in case the guy was dead in a ditch, but he knew this was going to eat time he didn't have right now.

"He's a grown-up, he's smart, and he knows he's got to be back real soon or else he'll be stuck here," Chris said. "Or is there something else you're worried about? Who saw him last?"

"I had breakfast with him."

Chris had to look past the group — mostly women he couldn't put a name to — to see who'd spoken. Yeah, he thought he recognised that voice. It was Abbie Vincent. She didn't look so surly this morning, so maybe she'd finally given in and decided to make a go of it on Opis after all. At least she'd have the prospect of meeting new people. She just didn't realise how soon that would be.

"I guess you'd have told someone if he'd said anything that worried you," Chris said.

"He was a little down. Well, not down, more like wistful. Prematurely homesick."

"Homesick enough to want to stay?"

"I don't know. But he's probably okay. It's too soon to put his picture on milk cartons. He was reading a book on the brewery porch when I last saw him, and that was an hour ago." She looked at the luggage pile, walked into the town hall lobby, and bent down to pick up a rucksack and one of the flight cases. "I need to repack. Excuse me."

"Well, we'll find him." Chris decided it was time for a reminder. "Folks, it really matters that we know where you are until it's time to board the buses. I know you're used to everyone being able to find everyone else on the Ainatio site, but we can't track you here. If you wander off, you risk being left behind when your convoy unit has to leave. So stay put. After all we've been through, it's not long to wait."

There was a brief silence as if he hadn't made sense. One of the guys in the group — maybe thirty, dark, bearded, a face Chris half-recognised but now couldn't place — took a couple of paces forward, shoulders back, and gave him that look, the one that often ended with Chris swinging a punch. The guy was trying to be tough.

Chris didn't want to have to put him in his place, but the reflex was hard to batten down.

"I get why you haven't told us how we're getting to Opis, but it's got to be another country with a shuttle capability that can take us to *Shackleton*," the guy said. "So what is it, British navy? Air force? Or the Brazilians, maybe? And why the rush? I know it's urgent, but we bugged out of the research centre like it was on fire."

Chris couldn't stop himself taking a couple of steps forward as well. He realised he'd stopped blinking. *Don't push me, buddy. Not right now. Don't make me do it.* It was inevitable someone would ask sooner or later.

"Because the sooner we get clear of APS, the better," he said. "When they find out what's happened back home, they'll want payback, so we have to get out before they retaliate."

"Why? What else is going on? We can't get web access so we haven't seen any news."

Chris didn't know if these nice polite scientists would accept tough shit and collateral damage as a rationalisation for Solomon unleashing disaster on Asia. He'd have to lie a little if he was going to get these people out. But he knew he was just exporting a group of people who wouldn't understand what others had to do to save their asses and would never see him as a neighbour.

"I'm making an educated guess," Chris said. "If you lose comms and global positioning, you probably lose a lot of other things too. Big system outages always have a human cost."

"So this is bound to be on the news. Why can't we get a signal now?" The guy wasn't really worried about APS, then. He was indignant about not being allowed a data connection. "We know we're not cut off like APS because one of your guys must have been talking to Britain, or whoever's giving us a ride to *Shackleton*."

Okay, the guy wanted an answer. "You can't get a signal because we've blocked all comms," Chris said in his most neutral voice. "And you already know why. We're in this situation because one of your colleagues sold us out to APS. But we don't know who it was yet, so we're not taking any chances."

Chris thought he was just reminding them who'd started this and that some piping down was in order, but the way the bearded guy's shoulders dropped said it had come across as a warning. Sometimes Chris wasn't sure whether he'd headed off a confrontation or started it. One of the women in the group glanced sideways at her colleague, and for a few moments they all looked like they were sizing each other up as potential quislings.

"I'm going to see if the dogs have found Dr Mangel," he said. "I'll keep you posted."

As he walked away, Marc and Trinder arrived in the Caracal. Chris checked his messages while he waited for them to dismount.

"So what do we know?" Marc asked, nodding in the direction of Chris's screen.

"Descending order of shittiness, or ascending?"

"Random. It provides more mental stimulus."

"Dieter's got the dogs out looking for Mangel, I've just reminded the Ainatio folks that one of their buddies stabbed us all in the back so they don't get to demand answers, and Jared says they're having trouble getting some of the cattle on the trucks," Chris said. "How's your day going?"

"Well, I've just had a message from Ingram that Caisin's dead." Marc held out his screen as if Chris would need proof that he wasn't making it up. "Caisin as in Caisin gate Caisin."

"What, was she killed or something?"

"No, she was just old and ill. But apparently the teeriks don't know what to do because they leave disposal of the dead to their alien foremen. They don't know what happens to the body. Not even a funeral. So Sol's working something out. Oh, and Caisin's left an egg to hatch, if it survives, and Ingram says it's really important to them."

Chris could feel a twitch starting under his eye, a sure sign that he was running on empty. "Don't you just hate a slow news day?"

"Never mind, there's still time for something interesting and unusual to happen. I hope someone's kept Caisin's notes on the bloody portal. Jeff Aiken says they don't write anything down."

"And Kim's pickup still isn't in place yet," Trinder said.

Chris was getting fed up with this. "I could have done it myself by now. Twice."

"Okay, time to focus on Mangel," Marc said. "How likely is it that he's the informer?"

"Not very," Trinder said. "But who knows?"

Chris called Dieter on the radio. "Six Zero to Five Seven, sitrep please, over."

"Girlie and Sal are heading for Gorman's Peak. No deviation, straight route. Looks like he's just gone for a walk, over."

"On our way. Six Zero out." Chris could have done without the drama, but it was only Mangel being Mangel. Gorman's Peak was a big hill about fifteen minutes' walk outside the town. "Looks like he's gone to Gorman's Peak, guys."

"You can see most of the roads out of town from up there," Trinder said. "He'll wonder where the traffic's going. Or not going. Guess what happens next."

"Okay, if he does, we need to keep him apart from the others for a while."

Marc started walking back to the Caracal. "Let's pick him up. Then we can handcuff him to a radiator until the buses leave."

"I'll do another roll call here and make sure nobody else else is AWOL," Trinder said. "Have fun."

There was one road up to Gorman's Peak, just a dirt track that had been worn into the landscape, but with so few people left to climb the hill it had been mostly reclaimed by grass and bushes. The Caracal cut its own path through the growth, speeding up the steep slope with barely a rise in the engine pitch. When Marc reached the top, Chris could see Dieter and Mangel sunning themselves next to a quad bike with the two dogs, Sal and Girlie. It was a pretty good view from up here. He got out of the Caracal and checked what was visible.

"Yeah, you can see the northbound road that eventually joins the interstate," he said, pointing. "And the eastbound and westbound routes." The two-mile dead zone that had been burned off around the county as a die-back barrier made it even easier to see where traffic was going, or in this case where it wasn't. "He can't avoid noticing there's nothing moving."

"Well, he's not going back to Ainatio, and he's just one bloke," Marc said. "We'll deal with it."

"Better find out what Dieter's said to him, if anything."

Chris didn't think Mangel was capable of feeling embarrassed, but when he spotted the two of them heading his way, he actually got to his feet and looked sheepish.

"I'm sorry for causing a fuss," he said. "I just wanted one last look at this place, that's all. I've got my screen but I can't get a signal, or else I'd have called in."

"No problem," Chris said. Mangel didn't sound like he was lying, but good liars never did. Chris had his own lies ready, none the worse for being benign. "We just didn't want you to miss the convoy."

Dieter climbed on the quad. "Dr Mangel's got some questions I couldn't answer," he said. "We'll leave you to have a chat. Come on, ladies, mount up. We've still got a patrol to do."

So Dieter hadn't told him anything, which was helpful. The quad disappeared down the track. Mangel looked like he was working up to asking the obvious, turning his screen over in his hands.

"In all the years I've been at Ainatio, I've avoided coming up here. I never realised it was still so green beyond the burn-off zone." That didn't sound like the glib smartass Chris had first met. He suddenly looked years older, facial lines deeper, maybe close to tears. "You want to hear the real story? Nobody else has. Not anyone left here, anyway."

"Plenty of time," Marc said. "Go ahead."

"It's my wife." Mangel paused. "Before die-back broke out, she applied for a research post and we visited to see what it would be like to live here. She looked at the county from this spot and said it was so isolated that she wouldn't be able to stand it. She took a job in Florida instead and I followed her. But then she caught Variant J, and there I was, a widower at thirty-nine, no family down there, and I hadn't even had time to make friends. So I came back to Kill Line because I liked the idea of not having to see the outside world again. I thought it was odd that they wanted an astrophysicist when they'd abandoned space projects after *Cabot* was lost, but... well, you know the rest."

Chris felt his gut tighten, half embarrassment, half shame. He didn't look at Marc because he could guess the effect Mangel's revelation would have on him. It took a few seconds to find the right words.

"I'm sorry, Dr Mangel. I had no idea."

Mangel flapped his hand. "No, it's okay. I don't think even Alex knows, and he knows everything about everybody. I'm good at keeping secrets. I think that's why Ainatio liked me. And official records are chaotic or gone now, so we can reinvent ourselves in a more bearable form, can't we?"

Damn right: Chris had. He tried to imagine what it was like to never mention a dead wife's name, and if Mangel felt he had to do that to spare others' feelings rather than his own.

"Your bus isn't due to leave for a while," Chris said. "We'll collect you when it's time to go."

"Thanks, but I've wallowed long enough," Mangel said. "I've recorded what I need. I took a few shots of Kill Line first thing this morning, too. Here, take a look. There's something heartbreaking about an entire town being abandoned, whatever the reason. I just wanted an archive of the place in case nobody else had done it. You know, for Doug Brandt."

Chris browsed through images. It really was just pictures of a town turning into a ghost, not espionage for APS: pictures of the town hall, the brewery, the bar, the school, fields with crops still standing and longer shots of others in the distance, burned black to stop the die-back. Mangel seemed to have taken all of them without stepping outside the cordon Chris had imposed.

"Doug will really appreciate that," Chris said.

"You've moved a lot of vehicles out already, haven't you?"

"Yes. You always need to break big convoys into groups."

"Then where are they? I haven't seen a single vehicle heading out on any of the roads. Is there a route I don't know about?"

"Yeah, there is," Chris said, feeling like an utter asshole.

Marc had said nothing while Mangel was getting things off his chest, but he took the screen from Chris, looked at the images for a moment, and briefly turned into a different man just the way Mangel had.

"What was your wife's name?" he asked.

"Carol." Mangel smiled sadly. "I appreciate that you asked."

"You take as long as you like, Dr Mangel," Marc said. "I'll wait down there and when you're ready, I'll take you to the departure point."

Departure point was a weird phrase for Marc to use, but Chris guessed where he was going with this. Marc looked at Chris and cocked his head, looking for a response. Chris nodded. Marc almost smiled. Yeah, this was the best way to handle things.

Mangel dragged his gaze from the landscape and turned to look at Marc. "You don't have to do that, but thank you."

"No, I *do* need to do it," Marc said. "You and me, we know better than anyone that nothing's ever going to fix that broken part of us. But we've still got futures. I want to show you something. You need a real revelation to reset your view of the world, and I've got just the thing."

"Hell, Marc, did you find religion?"

"No, but I do have a big chunk of science. Get in the Caracal when you're ready. We'll pick up your bags."

Chris decided it was best if he didn't tag along for this. These were two bereaved guys who had stuff to say that was none of Chris's business. He started backing off to leave.

"I'm going to walk," he said. "I could do with some thinking time. I'll see you there."

"It's a long way," Marc said.

"I'll call Dan if I need a ride."

Chris made his way over the crest of the hill, but Marc came after him.

"You're okay with this, yeah?" Marc asked. "It's either lock him up for a few hours in case he gets the other boffins thinking and one of them finds a way to share the glad tidings, or I take him through the portal now and get Bissey to sit on him until we're done. Slim chance of leaks, I know, but we need it to be zero."

"Sure," Chris said. "And it's just coincidence that it'll also make a heartbroken guy unbelievably happy and take the sting out of whatever he recalled when he looked at that view."

"Yeah, well, after holding up Jamie's repatriation, it's the least I can do."

"Marc, don't even think that. It's all cool. Really." Chris had run out of words. This was why not using too many worked best for him. "We'll talk later."

He tapped his knuckles against Marc's vest, couldn't think of anything else coherent to say, and carried on down the hill before he made a fool of himself. All he could see for a few moments was the woman waiting on her doorstep in a wrecked and deserted suburb on the way to Baltimore, refusing to leave with Chris's rescue convoy because her husband was going to show up any minute, she said, although it looked like he never would.

Chris didn't regret the choices he'd made, and he couldn't have forced the woman to come with them anyway, but his ability to shut out what he couldn't go back and change had deserted him for the time being. Less than an hour ago, he'd looked at the Ainatio staff and thought there'd always be a gulf between his kind of people and theirs. But the divide was probably between those who'd lost loved ones and those who'd been untouched by that scale of destruction, cocooned in a nice peaceful town like Kill Line. Half the colony would be survivors of traumatic times. Rebuilding normality was going to be a bigger task than building homes.

It was harder coming down Gorman's Peak than climbing it. He slid down scree in some places and waded through small bushes in others, making a note to get back to hard training again. A Caracal was waiting where the dirt track flattened out into a level road. Aaron Luce was at the wheel.

"Taxi for Montello," he said.

"Marc called you, yeah?"

"Yeah, I'll bill him. It's turning into a hell of a day."

"Always does."

"Wormhole Central, then?"

"Drop me off in town and I'll pick up a bike. I think I'll do a round of the perimeter. For old time's sake."

Chris had gotten into the habit of walking the transit camp perimeter last thing at night, even when there was already a patrol operating, something that had started when the Baltimore convoy was on the road and had to camp in some angry, violent places. There were a dozen practical reasons for doing it, but mostly it made him feel better, and it seemed to make whoever he was looking after feel better too. He needed to do it one last time in the same way that Doug wanted to declare his town closed.

When Luce dropped him off, Matt McNally was in the square with his gun truck, talking to a guy he could actually put a name to. It was James Vincent, Abbie's father, as invisible a man as Chris had ever seen. Chris still didn't know what he did. Although he was leaning casually against the truck and looked like he'd been there for some time, he seemed agitated, but that wasn't unusual after what people had been through in the past couple of weeks. Matt looked up and half-raised his hand to indicate he needed Chris to come over.

"Hey boss. Mr Vincent's got a problem and I'm not sure I can help him."

Chris owed Debora Vincent for saving his leg, but he had a feeling that whatever this was about would be beyond his non-commissioned power to fix.

"Dr Vincent." It was easier to call them all Doctor and downgrade from there than skip a title and make their fur bristle. "How can I help?"

"Abbie's changed her mind," he said. "We've accepted she feels strongly and it's only making everyone unhappy trying to agree on something we don't."

"When you say change of mind, sir, you mean she wants to be resettled in an APS country, right?" Chris said. "I know that was on the table yesterday, but we'd need to ask them if they'll take her back now. And that's not going to be easy after what's happened.

"She's saying goodbye to her colleagues," James said. "She's going to walk over there and present herself at the gate. It's not as if they're going to shoot her."

"The place is still locked down."

"I don't think that's going to stop her. She'll just wait."

"And you and your wife still want to evacuate."

"We do. It's not the end of the world, though. It'll be a while before we board *Shackleton*, so we can talk to her or maybe visit before we go, can't we? Which country's helping us? That's the reason for all the secrecy, isn't it? A country with a space programme is letting us use their shuttles to embark. Because that's the only way we're going to get to Opis. I can appreciate they won't want APS to know they're helping us."

They all seemed to assume the big secret involved foreign powers and the risk of APS punishing any country that helped a mission that had basically declared war on it. Chris was starting to wonder if the universe was testing his moral fibre today to see what its breaking strain was. He couldn't nod and smile at that. He just couldn't. It wasn't fair on them.

"I think you need to assume you won't be able to see her again, actually."

"Sorry?"

How the hell did he tiptoe through this minefield? "Diplomatic relations will get pretty ugly after what's happened. I'm not going to lie to you. Say your goodbyes now, sir."

James looked a bit puzzled. "Oh. It's that bad, then."

"If you ever want to see Abbie again, I suggest you stay and go with her to APS."

"Seriously?"

"It's what I'd do. If you think you'll be happy letting her make her own choices but never seeing her again, though, come with us."

Once the Vincents went through that portal, they'd become security risks. They could never be allowed to return if their daughter was working for APS. Chris had always been able to make hard decisions but this stupid family row had messed up his resolve. He wasn't sure if he wanted to do the right thing for their sake, or for his own so he didn't have to have it on his conscience, or even if his motive mattered at all. Perhaps not adding more lies was enough in itself.

James stared at the ground for a while. Chris didn't ask where Debora was or if James was speaking for her as well. He hoped he hadn't steered the Vincents into staying on Earth just because they'd be a pain in the ass for Nomad.

"I don't know why, but Abbie's still insisting on going to Korea," James said. "I know she spoke to you once, Sergeant. She might actually listen to you if you explained to her what you've just told me. She wouldn't listen to us."

Okay, it was tough love time. Chris glanced at the personnel list on his screen to check Abbie's age.

"I can't force her to come back," he said. "I'm really sorry. I owe your wife, and I probably wouldn't be walking now if it hadn't been for her skills, but Abbie's a grown woman. It's not even borderline. She's twenty-seven. But I'll drive her over to Ainatio and make sure she arrives safely."

That obviously wasn't the answer James wanted. His face hardened. Chris could handle that reaction a lot better than watching a guy go through emotional hell about his kids. He was used to people not being happy with him.

"Very well," James said. "Debora and I have some thinking to do."

"I'll be here until the last bus has left if you decide you want to follow her over there." Chris could feel the sweat stinging his eyes. The first thing he was going to do on Opis was find a cold shower. "Or I can leave you a vehicle."

"Thank you, Sergeant."

James walked away. Matt looked at Chris.

"Wow, rather you than me," Matt said.

Chris shook his head as he watched James out of sight. "I'm going to Hell, aren't I?"

"I thought you did right by them."

"I hope they decide to stay with her. They're just going to be a permanent running sore on Opis if they part company. They'll be nagging to use the gate to go back and visit her."

"She won't want that."

"I'm going to give myself a cold blast in the Caracal. Let me know if she shows up."

"Sure."

Chris climbed into the crew compartment and maxed the aircon until he started to feel human again. While he was cooling down, he switched his radio to the squad net and listened in to see how the evacuation was progressing. He could hear Erin talking to one of the route marshals and telling him to clear space for Caracal Bravo Ten and let it through to the head of the line. But he couldn't hear Marc, so he must have muted his radio for a while. Whatever conversation was happening between him and Mangel must have been priceless. Chris wished he was there to see Mangel's face as he went through an interstellar portal in an APC.

Maybe he'd hear all the accounts of it later. He really hoped the guy was overjoyed and that it had taken the pain out of reminiscing about how much his wife had hated Hart County.

"Chris?" Matt stuck his head into the compartment. "Abbie Vincent's just been spotted walking down to the Ainatio road. With her luggage."

"On her own?"

"Yeah."

"Okay, I'll take the APC solo. If you come with me she'll think we're going to strong-arm her."

Matt stepped back with a hands-up-I-surrender gesture. "Fine by me. I'll go do something less hazardous, like infuriate a bear."

"Yeah. Thanks."

Abbie wouldn't get far in the time it took Chris to call Trinder, update him, and drive as sedately as he could to intercept her. He didn't want to come roaring up behind her like he was doing a traffic stop and make her even crankier. When he thought back to how he'd have handled the situation in his enforcer days, he wished he still had that dispassionate drive to get a situation fixed even if someone had to get hurt. What the hell had happened to him? Alex was right. He was going soft. No, he was just using soft skills because it was the most efficient way to avoid an angry, deceived, and bereft couple poisoning the fragile atmosphere of a new colony. He'd just made them think they'd thought of it themselves. He opened the secure net on his screen.

"Dan? I'm sorting out a minor domestic problem here. Abbie Vincent wants to stay and she's on her way back to Ainatio. So I'm going drive her over there."

"Can't say I'm sorry," Trinder said. "Parents too?"

"I've told them it's their last chance without telling them why. They might stay."

"Thank God this didn't happen at the gate."

"Yeah."

"Just dump her and run. The main gates will still be open."

"I don't want her wandering around for hours until it's time for Sol to purge the system and open the doors. She might run into Annis Kim, for a start."

"Is that a problem?"

"I don't know why, but it smells like one. Then we've got the two operators. They might pull some hostage stunt and we'll have the Vincents crying all over us, we'll say too bad, it'll delay the convoy, and Pham or APDU HQ get more time to do whatever they're going to do to hit back at us."

He had to put the Vincent soap opera to bed here and now. It wasn't for her benefit. It was so he could wash his hands of it and not have a loose end someone would ask him to tie up at the worst possible moment. He'd shove her in the gate and it was up to her parents whether they joined her. He'd told them enough of the truth for them to decide.

"Sol, are you listening to this?" Chris asked. "I need your help."

"Problem, Chris?"

"Yeah, the one called Abbie Vincent. She's started walking back to the facility. She wants to stay."

"I think we should let her."

"Yeah, but I want to make sure she gets there and hand her over to someone. I've told her parents I won't force her to go to Opis. Is there any selective way to release one of the saner APDU guys to check her in and keep her there? The Cho kid, maybe? He's smart and Marc did the hearts and minds thing on him."

"Why don't you just let her go?" Solomon asked. "She knows the situation and she's an adult. This is rather inconvenient."

"I wasn't asking you to let Pham out to welcome her."

"I suppose I could let Corporal Cho have access to the grounds. He and his platoon are back in their quarters. I could send a voice message to his room and open a few doors."

"Do it, please. If he's not there when we arrive, I'll wait."

"Annis Kim's vehicle is on its way, though."

"Great. Well, at least the APDU guys will be distracted by Abbie's arrival. That might be for the best."

"Don't rush. Give me time to get Cho moving. I'll tell him who's coming. There's no reason why I shouldn't, is there?"

"Only if he's met her."

"You're not normally bitchy, Chris."

"I'll be sweetness and light again as soon as I step into Nomad Base and the gate closes behind me."

Chris drove along the road linking the town to the research centre. Abbie had made it further than he'd expected. She was striding at a brisk pace, rucksack on her back, metal flight case in one hand and a tote over one shoulder. Fully loaded at that pace on a hot day, she'd be lucky to make it the two miles to the facility. Chris stopped the Caracal a few yards ahead of her and jumped out.

Abbie stopped dead, looking daggers, and put her flight case down to wipe her hand on her jeans. Chris aimed for maximum nice.

"I'm not here to drag you back," he said. "I'm going to drive you to Ainatio to make sure you get there in one piece, that's all."

"Really," she said. "Did Mom send you?"

"Abbie, I'm not interested in your family disputes. I'm just trying to minimise hassle."

He went to pick up the flight case but she dived in and snatched it back, purse-lipped like an indignant shrew. Okay, he should have expected that. She didn't need a man's help. He opened the rear hatch.

"Will you let me put the bags in the back, then? I can't break those."

"Thank you, Sergeant, but I've got this."

She took a moment to struggle out from under the backpack. After a lot of heaving and pretence of being able to handle the load, she dumped the two soft bags in the troop compartment and bundled the flight case into the passenger footwell.

Chris ignored the slight on his cargo handling and drove off. It was a four-minute drive at most, even if he took it slowly, so he didn't feel the need to make small talk. But Abbie seemed to take that as a challenge.

"My parents spoke to you, didn't they?"

Chris nodded, eyes fixed on the road. "I told them they'd probably never see you again if they came with us and you went to APS. The politics is going to be ugly, so I'd treat it as final."

He expected some grumbling response, but she seemed to brighten up a bit. "That's a fair assessment."

"Just be warned that Westerners might not be the most popular folks where you're heading. Not after what's happened in the last twenty-four hours."

"I know, but I feel I can achieve more results in Korea," she said. She sounded almost apologetic. "It's nothing personal."

And that was the end of the conversation. Chris slowed down and stopped well short of the Ainatio gates. They were still wide open and there was no sign of Cho.

"What are you waiting for?" Abbie asked.

"We called ahead to get someone from APS to meet you."

"Oh."

"It's better than wandering around until someone finds you. It'll be chaos in there for a while."

"Why didn't you ask one of the Ainatio staff?" Abbie asked. "They're not locked in."

"They're not the ones who decide if you get to go to Korea."

"Fair point."

She was a lot more human now, but she was probably just relieved to be getting away. They sat in silence until Chris saw Barry Cho jogging down to the gate. Chris realised letting an enemy soldier loose before the convoy was clear of Earth could go badly wrong if he'd misjudged the situation — and Cho — but the biggest threat was already out there. He kept one hand on his weapon while he watched for Pham's ninjas, and didn't get out of the Caracal until Cho reached the gates.

Chris walked towards him, hands held out to his sides to indicate he wasn't armed — a lie, but he hadn't come to start a fight — and raised his hand casually in acknowledgement. They stopped about six feet apart, Cho still inside the perimeter line, Chris just beyond it.

"Hi, I'm Chris Montello," he said. "Remember me?"

"I do." Cho nodded. "You want me to take delivery of a scientist, then."

Abbie was out of the Caracal by now, heaving her bags around. "This is Abigail Vincent," Chris said. "Plant geneticist. She was on your resettlement list to start with and she's decided she still wants to go to Korea. Her parents don't, but I have a feeling they're going to change their minds and come along later. They're okay. Her mom's a top biomed researcher. Her gadget rebuilt my leg. Be kind to them."

Cho looked Abbie over, then consulted something on his screen.

"Okay," he said. "I've got the original resettlement list and personnel files here. Just checking who's who. And I'll bear in mind what you said about Dr and Professor Vincent."

James Vincent had a title, then. Abbie allowed Chris to carry two of her bags to the gate and put them on the ground, but she still hung on tightly to her flight case. Now she was Cho's problem. Chris savoured his own guilty relief.

"Tell Marc Gallagher that Barry Cho said hi," Cho said, and gave Chris a nod.

"Will do. Thanks."

"Good luck."

Chris had parked the Caracal facing the gate, which wasn't tactical if he'd needed a quick getaway, but it did give him a few moments to observe what went on between Cho and Abbie while he started the engine. She leaned in and said something to Cho while he was looking down at his screen, and he paused for a split second before looking up. Then he picked up her rucksack and tote and they walked up the drive to the main building. Chris wished he'd had Solomon on board to lip-read what she'd said, but it didn't matter now. She was probably asking Cho to ignore Chris's request to be nice to her folks.

This wasn't about her passion to find a countermeasure for die-back, though. This was about being twenty-seven and never having been anywhere except the Ainatio campus. She wanted her own life away from Mom and Dad.

"Six Zero to Echo Five, Alpha Three — Abbie Vincent safely back at Ainatio, and Barry says hi, Alpha Three. On my way back. Out."

Chris turned the Caracal in a wide circle and headed back to Kill Line, content that he had one less problem to deal with. Lunchtime wasn't over yet. That meant the evacuation would be complete by 1500, patrols and all, provided there were no more last-minute dramas. His people and Trinder's had done a textbook job of moving a lot of people and cargo under difficult circumstances and he was proud of them. This was his tribe. It had excelled. There was no better feeling.

About two hundred yards down the road, he pulled over and got back on the radio to check where his key people were, then plugged his screen into the dashboard to clear his messages. Trinder sent him an update.

WE'VE GOT COWS LOOSE. BRIEF DELAY WHILE WE GET THEM MOVING.

GET DIETER'S DOGS ON THE CASE, Chris typed.

HE'S STILL TRYING TO ROUND UP THE PACK, Trinder replied. BETSY RAN OFF WITH A BORDER COLLIE FROM THE TOWN.

Chris finally had a clear shot at Trinder for teasing him about Fonseca. THEY SAID SHE WAS TOO GOOD FOR HIM. ROMANCE KNOWS NO BOUNDARIES, DAN.

MOUSSAKA, Trinder replied.

Chris didn't get the reference, but he found it funny anyway. He was still trying to work it out when he saw a pickup he didn't recognise approaching from the direction of the town. As it passed him, he saw Debora Vincent in the driving seat with James beside her. He did his best to wave goodbye in time, but if they'd noticed him — and how could they miss a damn APC on a deserted road? — they'd ignored him.

"Called it," he muttered. He rested his elbow on the open side window and savoured the light breeze with its scent of a summer that would soon be gone forever. "Done and done."

And he knew right away that he shouldn't have said it.

He heard the first explosion and held his breath. The second followed a few moments later. He thought it had come from the direction of the facility, but he jumped out to look around and listen to make sure. It wasn't particularly loud, but the day was as quiet as a grave so even a firearm discharging could be heard in the right conditions. But he still couldn't see any smoke.

Breaching charges. It had to be. He heard five more in quick succession.

Solomon came on the secure net. "Chris, I've detected doors not registering on the system, which means they've probably been bypassed. The management wing and the primary doors in the main accommodation block. Not my doing, of course."

"Pham's operators must be blowing them out," Chris said. APS had been flying in equipment every day and they could have brought in any amount of ordnance, especially if they expected to find locked doors when they started their rummage through the facility. Chris counted another five explosions at roughly regular intervals. "You have to purge the system and pull out now, Sol."

"I'm doing that right now," Sol said. "Why didn't they do it earlier if they had the explosives?"

"Who knows? Maybe this is a distraction and they already found a way to extract Pham. Or they realised some doors had been opened but his hadn't so they went for it. We already assumed they were on the loose anyway, so I'm not sure it makes things any worse."

"It's me they're after," Solomon said. "But that doesn't mean they won't target you to lure me out."

Marc interrupted. "Chris, get your arse back here, mate. We need to finish evacuating."

"Is Alex done with Kim's pickup?"

"He's out there now."

"Who's with him? He needs a second vehicle to get back."

"He took a dirt bike on the flatbed. Don't rush off to look after him. He's got this."

Chris took the rap over the knuckles as a painful truth — yeah, Marc knew exactly what he was thinking of doing — and drove off. He left the secure net open and listened to the clamour of overlapping voices as Solomon confirmed the Ainatio system was now shutting down.

"How many left to ship out?" Chris asked.

"The Dales' dairy herd and the Ainatio buses," Solomon said. "I thought it best to get the cattle moved first, given what happened with Liam last time."

Things weren't starting to go wrong, Chris told himself. The evacuation was a massive feat to pull off overnight at such short notice and there were bound to be minor problems.

But Dr Mangel had been found. The warring Vincents had done everyone a favour and withdrawn. Alex had finally managed to get a provisioned vehicle to the RV point for Kim. If those small hitches were the worst to overcome today, the most extraordinary exodus in history had gone like clockwork.

* * *

AINATIO RESEARCH CENTRE, VEHICLE AND MACHINERY DUMP: 1320 EDT.

"I believed you, didn't I?" Annis said to herself. "What a tosser. I knew it was too good to be true."

She lay on her back in the footwell of an old Ainatio truck, sweating in the stuffy cab as she tried to hotwire the vehicle. There was still no sign of the bloody ute that Alex had promised her. If she didn't make a run for it now she'd get caught. The series of explosions she'd just heard sounded controlled, more like a shots being fired, and unless Solomon had gone nuts and decided to blow up the campus, someone was probably trying to open doors. Zakko had mentioned using charges. Tim or his ninjas must have had the same idea. There was no telling what those guys had brought with them.

So how long did she have? She'd spent eight bloody miserable hours in a shed near the fence before she heard the wires make that shivering, twanging noise as someone cut through them. It took her a few minutes to find the gap, but she scrambled through right away and waited in the woods at the back of the junkyard until she started to suspect something had gone wrong and that she'd have to find her own transport. Now she was thirsty and exhausted. She didn't want to add dead or captured to the list.

Her watch said it was nearly one-thirty. If she'd known Alex was going to cut it this fine, she'd have left as soon as Zakko released her, hidden until nightfall, and sneaked into the abandoned town to forage for supplies and maybe even find a vehicle the Kill Liners hadn't taken with them. But, like a fool, she'd done as she was told and waited.

The icons on the dust-coated dashboard showed the hydro truck had a solar trickle charger, and the battery was still in place, so she should have been able to start the damn thing. She could top up the water tank from the river. There were other trucks around that looked in better condition, but they all needed some kind of charge or fuel that she probably wouldn't be able to find, so she had to get this wreck going. But whatever switch she flipped or wire she tried to reconnect, nothing happened.

She squirmed into a more comfortable position to relieve the ache from holding her hands up under the dashboard and stared at the cab's head lining, wondering if it was safe to pop her head up to check what was happening outside. Would she even hear the ute arrive? She thought she was in the right place, but the junkyard was bigger than she'd expected and she couldn't see all the vehicles without walking around. The up side was that it was such a maze it would be hard for Pham's heavies to spot her.

Okay, she knew she was being unfair on Alex. He'd saved her from being abducted last time and got in a fist fight for her, so he wasn't unreliable at all. And nobody was obliged to help her. She was just feeling sorry for herself. She needed to knock that on the head here and now.

She flexed her fingers, feeling the circulation return, and began again. As she tried to remember which combination of wire and switch she'd used the last time, someone tapped on the side window and made her jump. "About bloody time." She squeezed out from under the dashboard, expecting to see Alex, Trinder, or even Zakko. But she found herself face to face with a young APDU corporal. Her gut somersaulted. "*Fuck.*"

Annis didn't even have anything to use as a weapon. She couldn't see how she could get out of this. The corporal opened the driver's door.

"Go on, bloody well shoot me, then," Annis said. "Because you're not taking me back to Tim Pham. Go on. Finish it. Get it over with."

"If I shoot you, Dr Kim, you won't be any use to me." He was an Aussie, an Asian Aussie like her. "I just saw the ginger guy drop off a ute, which I suspect is for you, seeing as there's a window missing from where Pham's guys left you. I'll show you where it is, but can we do a deal first?"

"What?"

"I need you to do me a favour."

"Piss off."

"It's personal. If I let you leave, will you give something to Sergeant Gallagher for me? You know who I mean. And I bet you know where he is."

Annis hadn't expected that. "Seriously?"

"Can you get something to him or not?"

Annis had to think. Everyone would have assembled in Kill Line, but maybe the convoy had left by now. She didn't even know where it was going. If it had set off, she might not be able to follow it.

Alex had said there'd be a radio in the ute, though. She could try raising Marc on that, even if it wasn't one of the military ones.

"If he hasn't left yet, I'll do it. Because I don't know where they're headed." She started thinking suspicious thoughts. "Is this some trick to track them down? If it is, you can sod right off. I'd rather take the bullet."

"Dr Kim, he needs to know something. I'm Corporal Barry Cho. I owe him a favour and there's information he needs urgently. Will you do it or won't you?"

"And what if I won't?" Annis asked.

"You can still leave, but I'll know you're a selfish cow who wouldn't help her mates after all they've done for you."

"And apart from this manly debt of honour you owe Marc, whatever it is, you're okay with disobeying orders and even helping a traitor like me."

Cho pulled a don't-care face. "We were diverted here to support technicians dealing with die-back. Then I find we're attacking spaceships and harassing refugees instead, except we're not, because two black ops guys show up and we're told to stay out of it. So I wonder how official this is, what with no senior officers here and Tim Pham running this personally. Then I start wondering if we'll be allowed to go home again, knowing what we know. FTL. Killer AIs. A planet with all kinds of life. We all got to hear about it. So I don't know if my orders are lawful, if we're going to end up being held responsible for whatever Pham's done, or if we're becoming a liability he'd like to make disappear. All I care about is getting my platoon home safely and seeing my dad and sister again. Maybe that makes me a bad soldier. I don't care. Do you understand now?"

"Yeah," Annis said. She wasn't too far from that state of mind herself. "I think I do."

"Okay, take this and give it to Gallagher, please." Cho took a sealed envelope out of his pocket. It was Ainatio corporate stationery. "It's for his eyes only."

"How do I know it's not loaded with some virus to infect Opis?"

"I forgot to pack any bioweapons. Maybe your Ainatio chums can lend me some."

"You can't blame me for asking."

"Please, make sure he gets it. I mean it. Don't drive off and toss it out the window."

"Why do you think I'd do that?"

"Doing the right thing even if there's nothing in it for you is the difference between civilisation and the cesspit we're in today."

"That's not an answer."

"No, it's a reminder that the guys here had your back and your boss didn't. Maybe you don't know that's the most important thing in the world."

"I think I do."

"So you'll find Gallagher and give him this."

Annis took the envelope from him and put it inside her shirt. "I swear I will. If I can find him."

"He kept his word, Dr Kim, and he didn't need to. I thought he was fobbing me off. But he meant it. He checked to see that my folks in Sydney were okay after the outage."

It was starting to make some kind of sense. She didn't ask if this was part of the reason why the troops on the gate had surrendered. It didn't look like Pham had their loyalty, which surprised her, but he wasn't officially in their chain of command. Maybe that made a difference to how they saw their duty now.

"Yeah, Marc had two sons about your age serving in the army," Annis said. "They didn't make it home. So he cares about family."

Cho paused for a moment. "Okay, your ute's at the end of the next row." He pointed. "Plain white, grey roof and hardtop, not as dusty as the others, really old Virginia plates. Good luck. I take it you're not going home."

"I can't," she said. "But my family thinks I'm dead anyway."

Cho gave her a polite nod and walked away in the direction of the fence. She slid out of cab and ran at a crouch down the ragged row of parked vehicles, waiting for it all to go wrong and expecting a less helpful soldier waiting for her behind the ute, but she reached it and opened the door.

A quick check showed she'd been left with more than she expected. There was an old pocket screen in the glovebox as well and plenty of ammo. When she rummaged through her rucksack, everything was there, including the Ainatio multi-function bolt cutter that she'd looted and all her clothes.

"You're a bloody gent, Alex Gorko," she said to herself. "In fact, you're *all* bloody gents."

She started the ute and drove off slowly, trying not to rev the engine and make too much noise. There was a forest track north of the facility that eventually came out on one of the roads leading out of the town, so she'd find that and slip out. If she'd remembered right, she'd come out somewhere to the west and meet up with a proper road.

She followed a winding track just wide enough to squeeze between the trees. It brought her out on the dirt road north of Kill Line and when she stopped for a moment to consult the map, she realised she could hear engines. Great: the convoy hadn't left yet, so she could find Marc. Maybe he'd be grateful for whatever was in that envelope and Alex would relent and take her along with them, or at least drop her off in Britain — who else would be helping Americans now? — but she remembered what Barry Cho had said about civilisation.

She was only in this situation because she'd withheld information from Tim to protect the people she'd befriended. She wasn't a lost cause.

She almost opened the envelope. The old Annis would have done that, but she wasn't that woman any more. Grandma Park would have reminded her that honour came not from doing the right thing because people were watching, but from doing it even when they weren't and would never know.

Annis followed the track to the junction with the tarmacked road, then took a left, expecting a head-on with a thundering stream of trucks any second. But nothing was coming.

She hadn't been out here before. She'd never explored the little town. But she could see traditional-looking farm buildings in the distance and thought that it would have been a nice place to live if the rest of the state hadn't been a wilderness. She drove towards the sound of the engine.

Was she on the right road? The map showed a place called Becker Farm about half a mile south. When she passed that, she'd know she was in the right place.

* * *

BECKER DAIRY FARM, KILL LINE: 1405.

One day, Marc imagined he'd look back on the last few sleep-deprived weeks and still not be able to work out how he'd felt about it.

Maybe time would sift out the worst bits and all he'd be left with would be the memory of driving an APC through a space-time portal while his eminent astrophysicist passenger squealed in delight like a little girl. They'd laughed, but even that had been the borderline-hysteria laughter triggered by something grim and completely unfunny. Marc was starting to get that same perverse urge to laugh at the last of Liam Dale's uncooperative cows, still skittering around the milking yard and reluctant to try out interstellar travel after refusing to be loaded onto their truck. They were Liam's prize Jerseys, the ones he'd been prepared to die with, so suggesting he could portion them up as freezer packs and send them through with the supply truck wasn't going to go down well.

Alex came up and leaned on the safety rail next to Marc. He looked a bit dishevelled. "Been riding the rodeo long, cowboy?"

"Enjoy your trip?"

"I'm not cut out to be a biker."

"Has Kim found the pickup?"

"No idea, but I left it where we arranged. So Pham's out, then. How long have we got?"

"Dunno, but if he's going to try to stop this, he'd better get a move on." Pham and his mates were still too *not there* for Marc to drop his guard. "You know how much sabotage I can do in ten minutes with the right kit?"

"You're so rugged." Alex took off his glasses and wiped them on the hem of his T-shirt. It was his anxious tic. "Have you told your Foreign Office about the gate?"

"What sort of tosser do think I am? We can't tell anyone until we know what we're dealing with. And that's a long way off." A resonating clang stopped the debate for a second as a cow slammed into the metal barrier. Marc hadn't seen it coming and jumped back. "All we can do is make sure we don't hand anyone a loaded gun before we understand what the gun can do."

"We can't keep the lid on it forever."

Marc hadn't stood down the airlift yet, but he couldn't leave it any longer. The evacuation was almost complete. If Pham and his operators turned up, he could hold them off with Chris long enough to get the last buses through.

"But we *can* keep a lid on it long enough to work out more implications," Marc said. "I'm going to call the FCO now and tell them we don't need the airlift. You can listen in if you like, so you don't think I'm nipping off to tell them everything and launch an invasion."

"I didn't say you were. Look, I helped Erskine plan her evacuation so the staff we left behind didn't storm the shuttle, so I think my moral high ground's under ten feet of water. But I know it must be hard not to do the patriotic thing."

Marc wished Alex hadn't reminded him. "They're going to go through the spy sat imaging and wonder where we went. It's not like they won't keep an eye on the situation if they can."

"They'll still be watching the APS show."

"Actually, it's a network with global coverage. Still, they'll be distracted by the goodies I'm uploading. And now I've told you I'm afraid I'm going to have to kill you."

"Make it quick."

"I promise you won't feel a thing."

Marc walked around the side door of the milking shed and found some shade to have what was going to be a short and interesting tap-dance on eggshells. In the normal world, the one that had already mostly disappeared before he was born, he'd have passed the intel up the line and let his superiors work it out because that was the government's job. It would have been planned, investigated, and argued over by global experts for years before anyone was allowed to even say hello to the teeriks. But the majority of people involved in this evacuation weren't British citizens and they didn't even have a functioning government. The buck now stopped with him and three other amateurs, and at that moment he knew more about teeriks and their technology than anyone in Whitehall, even if that amounted to sod all. The supreme teerik expert was a former Royal Navy CPO. If Marc cared about his country, sloping shoulders and saying it was above his pay grade was a cop-out. He'd be handing some chinless Tarquin in the MoD a ticking bomb, knowing full well that he'd poke a screwdriver in it and set it off.

Who had a claim on Opis anyway? No government had ever been involved with Nomad. A corporation had made it happen, and now that corporation was gone, unless he counted Erskine, and he didn't feel the need to.

Well, too bad. The experts had made a piss-poor job of Earth and it was time for the peasants to have a crack at changing the course of history. Maybe that was why he was here. He'd missed making a real difference but he was definitely making one now. Any information he withheld from the British government could be shared when he knew the size of the problem, and the situation did now look like more of a problem than a gift. Ingram had agreed an alliance with a bunch of alien boffins who were on the run with a state of the art warship and an instant go-anywhere, bomb-anywhere precision portal. And then there was the challenge of explaining that Sol didn't always go around devastating continents.

Yeah, when Marc looked at it like that, a period of quiet reflection seemed his best bet.

He routed his call to the FCO via the Lamm 1 comms hub and watched it connect on his screen. It was after office hours in London, but Lawson would pick up his direct line wherever he was.

"Mr Lawson, it's Marc Gallagher," he said. "Change of plan. Ainatio's decided it's still worth trying to get to Opis while APS is temporarily inconvenienced, so we're withdrawing to another location. No evacuation required. But thank you."

"You've found another launch facility, then."

"Something like that. Complicated boffin stuff." Marc knew Lawson would have surveillance images from Kingdom on his desk that showed no operational launch sites in North America at all, but they both knew they weren't being completely honest with each other. "Just trust me to do my job the way I always have and with British interests in mind."

"I do. Will we be speaking again?"

That was a tough one. "I think I'll be in radio range for a while longer," Marc said, leaving the door open for a change of mind. "In the meantime, stand by to receive the data I mentioned. Use it wisely."

"Thank you, Sergeant. The country will always be grateful."

"I'll bet. A statue would be nice. Okay, stand by for data." Marc tapped the file icon. It was odd how Lawson addressed him by rank, like he was saying he didn't regard Marc as a common private contractor. "I'll update you if and when I can."

"All I can do is wish you a safe journey," Lawson said. Perhaps he thought Marc's survival chances were zero and he wasn't sure how to address someone on his way to die. "You're a courageous man."

"I'll send you a postcard. On second thoughts, scrub the statue and do me a favour. There's a young APDU corporal here who's been a peacemaker and saved his mates from getting into a fight they wouldn't have survived. He's worried about his dad and disabled sister in Sydney. I'd hate to think of them being punished because he's helped us. Anything you can do for them?"

Lawson went *hmmm* and sounded like he was thinking. "If they're at risk, I'm sure we could help if they walked into the British embassy and asked for asylum," he said. "Give me the details and I'll have someone make contact with them."

"Tell them their son's okay and that's he's a smart, brave kid," Marc said, uploading the names and address. "Corporal Barry Cho. Thanks, Mr Lawson."

There, it was done and dusted. The FCO had what they wanted, he'd done all he could for Cho, and he hadn't let anything slip to compromise the Caisin gate or drop Ingram in the shit. Lawson hadn't asked anything else about the APS situation, so he probably knew more about what was happening than anyone here did. Now Marc didn't have to worry about it again until the inevitable disagreements among Ingram's people about how to use the gate.

It had to happen. However enthusiastic they were about the mission, that crew had given up a lot to be there, and their emotions about the countries they'd come from were probably not just fresh but raw. Finding out what had happened to home while they were in cryo must have been painful for many of them.

He thought it over as he walked back into the milking yard. Ingram had to make Nomad everyone's primary tribal loyalty or the colony wouldn't survive. Opis wasn't a weekend cottage in the Cotswolds. It was a commitment for generations, maybe even the key to the long-term survival of mankind. Ingram really did have to make it a nation in its own right because if she didn't, someone else would.

In the yard, Liam had resorted to bribery to get the last of his lorryphobic cows through the gate. He was rattling a yellow bucket at the last two holdouts, cooing "Come on, girls, dinner!" with a big fake smile on his face. Alex and Jared watched like it was a cabaret. Two border collies crouched at the entrance to the yard, barring any escape.

"What is it?" Jared asked.

Liam held the bucket out for him to take a look. "Cattle nuts. Dry food pellets. Want one?"

"Time was when I'd have said yes." Jared took a pellet and studied it. "Don't tell me what's in it."

"Grain, molasses, vitamins, protein. They love it."

Liam walked backwards towards the Caisin gate, still shaking the pellets. He couldn't see where he was going, and Marc was sure he'd shut his eyes anyway, but he backed all the way up the milking shed and into the haze until all that was left of him was an arm with a rattling bucket on the end and his head dipping in and out. The cows stared. Then they relented and ambled forward to melt into the mist. Marc was convinced that the animals followed Liam out of morbid curiosity.

"He's a nutter. Imagine if the portal had gone down while he was halfway through." Marc glanced at Jared, who was tossing the cattle nut in his palm. "Would you really have eaten those things?"

Jared broke the pellet in two and chewed a piece thoughtfully. "Says a man who's never literally starved."

"Snare, bait, knife. Dinner."

"In the city?"

"Yeah. A nice pigeon. You must be a picky eater. What's it like, then?"

"Kind of like old dried-out bread dough," Jared said, offering Marc a chunk. "Not sweet, though. Can't really taste the molasses."

Marc tried it. It wasn't as bad as he expected, but it made him cough. "Ingram would love this. Ship's biscuits. She could pretend she was Nelson."

Jared burst out laughing. "Okay, let's move these barriers back. Five buses and a few Caracals to go, and we're out of here."

Marc paused for a moment to listen and noticed the town was even quieter now — no engines, no machinery, and no distant voices. Alex was killing time passing his hand through the gate's haze. Chris was sitting on his Caracal's tailgate. He gestured with the gate locator like a security guard with a flashlight.

"Go on, Jared, go join Marsha," he said. "We can handle the rest."

"You sure? Scientists are harder to herd than cows."

"We'll use cattle prods. Off you go. Your alien adventure awaits."

Jared laughed, pushed his sleeves back, and strode up to the gateway. "Look at me, Ma, I'm a damn spaceman." And then he was gone. Chris smiled to himself and stood up. Alex wandered back down to the doorway.

"Okay, shall we move the Lammergeiers now, before the buses? I hope you're ready for Pham if he shows up." He put his forefinger to the middle of his forehead, indicating a shot. "Lamm One's all we've got left of Ainatio's data now, so it outranks most of the scientists."

"Yeah, the Lamms can taxi through," Marc said. "They can sort out how to actually fly them in different gravity and all that later."

"This is the scary bit, then." Chris pointed with the locator. "I switch this off, point it at an open space where the Lamms can land, and switch it on again, right?"

Solomon's voice cut in on the secure channel. "Correct, Chris. But we're still clearing this side of the gate. Give us two minutes, please."

"Copy that. Ready when you are."

"Y'know, we could do with a few more magic flashlights," Marc said. "One for everybody."

"Do you really mean everybody?"

No, Marc didn't. He realised he meant himself, Chris, Trinder, Ingram, and a few trustworthy sidekicks, plus a DNA lock to make sure only authorised people could activate the gadgets. It wasn't an egalitarian start to the new world, but every time he stopped to think about the Caisin gate, he came up with another worrying use for it.

When did I get so paranoid?

When I first saw nice people do bloody awful things.

"Just being colloquial," he said. "I meant the chosen few."

"Handy, isn't it?" Chris said. Either he was getting to know Marc's thought processes a lot better or Marc's caution showed on his face. "Too handy by half."

"It's bad enough if someone gets hold of this, opens a gate to Opis, and shoves something nasty through it," Marc said. "Die-back. An army. But now Fred's got that spur route thing worked out, maybe it means someone could open a gate halfway along the main pathway and exit somewhere we can't see them."

"Or enter."

"Yeah."

"But Fred's crew controls the point of origin," Chris said. "So they can throw the off switch any time."

"And that's another issue we've got to look at. In case we ever have a falling-out with them."

Chris peered at the end of the device. "I'm not sure even Fred knows all the things the gate can do yet. We keep forgetting it's a prototype."

Alex looked at both of them as if he wasn't sure if he was included in the everybody category. "If Fred's clients were pissed at losing a warship, imagine how they'll react when they realise what the teeriks were building on the side. Earth politics might be the least of our problems compared to the alien variety."

"There's no avoiding it now. We're involved in it no matter where we go. We can't *unknow* what we know and neither can the teeriks. And they know where we live."

"OPSEC, lads," Marc said. "This is where everyone learns the value of keeping it zipped."

"Chris, you can send the Lamms through now," Solomon said.

It was the first time Marc had ever seen Chris look the slightest bit nervous. Chris held the locator out in front of him, blinked a few times, and switched it off. The haze at the end of the shed vanished.

"This thing better come on again," he said, and headed for the field.

Marc checked his watch as he followed him. Dieter and his dogs were still out doing last-minute sweeps and there were five teams watching the roads. He scanned an empty sky. APDU's air force didn't seem to be back on its feet yet, and neither did any of those allies that Pham thought owed APS some favours, so if he was planning anything, he was running out of options. The only aircraft Marc could hear were the Lammergeiers.

The two red tilt rotors appeared over the roof of the milking shed and swept low over the farm, rotors horizontal, to land a couple of lengths apart. Marc always found it a comfort to see a helo even if he didn't need one. Chris pointed at a spot and must have had a thumbs-up from one of the pilots because he nodded and turned around to aim the locator. Marc held his breath just in case the thing didn't work this time.

But the hazy oval materialised in the air just like the last time. The first Lamm rolled towards it and vanished, followed a minute later by the second. That gate was going to put aircraft carriers out of business one day.

Chris came jogging back, looking at the end of the locator like he was surprised it worked. "Awesome," he said, pressing his earpiece. "Dan, we're re-opening the gate in the milking shed. Get the buses rolling. We'll be ready for you."

He seemed on edge as they walked back towards the shed. Perhaps he wasn't worrying about Pham, though. He might just have been thinking the same as Marc right then, that this was probably the last he'd ever see of Earth. He re-opened the portal at the back wall of the milking parlour and wandered back to stand with Marc and Alex in the open doorway, admiring the afternoon sun.

"So who's going to break the news to the first Ainatio group?" he asked. "That'll be one for the photo album."

"You do it," Alex said. "They're scared of you. Anyone want a coffee? I rescued the dispenser before Marsha left."

"Yeah, and three sugars, please," Marc said.

Chris nodded. "Me too. Thanks."

Alex wandered off. Chris folded his arms. In a cap, tactical vest, and sunglasses, he looked intimidating. Marc could easily see him showing up on some dodgy businessman's doorstep in a well-cut suit and knuckledusters with a final demand for payment plus interest. Then Chris took off his sunglasses and right away he was every mum's ideal son again. It was his guileless blue eyes.

"You ever done a bus tour, Marc?" he asked. "You know, where the tour guide stands at the front and points out all the interesting things you're passing? Maybe we should just do it like that."

"You mean, 'We're now passing through a fold in space-time and if you look to your left, you'll see Nomad Base a lot sooner than you expected'?"

"They'll crap themselves."

"Or they'll squeal like Todd Mangel." Marc had to smile to himself. It was good to know there were things in the universe that could bury pain and grief, even if the euphoria didn't last. "I haven't seen a grown man that excited since we beat you lot six-nil in the World Cup final."

He could hear the buses coming now. It was a short drive from the centre of the town and the glossy red roofs of the vehicles were already visible above the hedges lining the road. Marc was about to comment when Dieter came on the radio for Chris.

"Five Seven to Six Zero, my drone's spotted a grey pickup moving south towards you. No ID on the driver yet and no radio contact, over."

Chris looked at Marc. "Six Zero here, how close?"

"Nearly at your position, over."

"Understood. Six Zero out."

"I bet it's the Meikles," Marc said. "The husband wanted to leave, really. The wife didn't."

"Well, if they're here, they're here. We shove them through with the buses."

They looked towards the gates to the milking yard. Marc could see the lead bus at the point where it had to slow to a crawl and swing wide to make the left turn into the yard. But he could hear another engine noise — a higher pitch, a vehicle approaching at speed — coming from the other direction. Shit, it was going to be a head-on. That was all they bloody needed now.

Or maybe it was Pham's operators.

He'd taken his eye off the ball. He should have known they'd time it like this.

"Shit. Is it Pham's guys?"

Marc swung his rifle off his back and aimed. So did Chris. Alex wasn't around. The lead bus lurched to a halt halfway into its turn through the gates and a scruffy pickup swung around and shaved between the gatepost and the bus before squealing into the yard and slamming on its brakes.

It wasn't Pham's ninjas or even Seb Meikle. Annis Kim was at the wheel. It was just as well Chris reacted first and slapped his hand on Marc's shoulder just before he opened fire.

"Whoa, whoa, *whoa*. It's Annis. Take it easy."

"Give me strength." Marc could have done without the drama. "Why is everything a three-ring circus with her?"

"We should have ID'd the pickup," Chris said.

"You said Kim's would be *white*." Dieter sounded irritable. "But it's grey."

"That's just the roof. Okay, sorry. My bad."

Kim pulled up to the open shed doors and got out with a flounce as if she was storming in to have an argument. Then she paused, looked at the line of traffic, and seemed to realise where it was heading. Marc braced. Without a queue of vehicles, you could see right past the pickup to the end of the milking shed. The portal was always hard to spot, but if anyone could see it at the worst possible time, it was her.

"Let's hear her out," Chris said.

"You're always pleased to see me, aren't you?" Kim looked rattled but indignant at the near-miss. She planted herself in front of them as if she thought she'd get one chance to spit it all out. "Marc, I've got a message from Barry Cho. He said it was urgent." She thrust an envelope at him. "Just read it and tell me if there's anything I should know before I leave."

Chris nudged Marc. "Go on, I'll sort out the buses. We're nearly done."

"Okay, mate. Thanks."

Marc tossed a mental coin between playing this out in full view of a bus full of Ainatio staff and stepping into the barn for some privacy. He opted for privacy and steered Kim inside the shed, positioning himself so she'd have her back to the end wall, and opened the envelope.

"How do I know this is really from Cho?" he asked.

"Marc, try going one minute without looking for the catch." She sounded genuinely tired of it all. "And it's not booby-trapped. Read it. Then I'll be on my way."

Cho had very small, neat writing. Marc had seen Kim's undisciplined scribble once and the note didn't look like she'd forged it, but he wasn't sure why she'd want to. She was right: he was paranoid now. He read the note twice.

'Sergeant Gallagher, your informer is Abigail Vincent. Your mate dropped her at the main gate earlier and she asked for Pham. I said he was still locked up so she couldn't see him, and she thought I was stalling. She said she'd done her bit to warn him about Solomon and everything else and now he could keep his side of the bargain and make sure she got to Korea. Thanks for being a good bloke. Drinks on me if we ever meet again. Yours respectfully, B. H. Cho.'

"Bugger," Marc said.

Kim glared up at him. "What is it? Come on, I could be halfway out of the state by now if I hadn't agreed to do this."

"He named the informer." Marc felt suddenly deflated. He had to tell Kim the truth and hope it passed for an apology. "Abbie Vincent. She's back at Ainatio, luckily for her."

Kim looked furious. "I swore I'd swing for the bastard who made me the company leper. And trashed the rest of my life."

"Yeah, well, I apologise for suspecting you. In my defence, I changed my mind before I saw this."

"It's okay." Kim raked her fingers through her hair and looked away from him as if she was either going to eff and blind at the random unfairness of the world or burst into tears. Marc felt bad for her. "Well, I can't go home anyway, so I'm heading back the way I came. I should have kissed your arse when I had a chance to get a trip to England, shouldn't I?"

Marc winced. "I didn't think Botany Bay was a return ticket."

For a brief moment, the relationship thawed. Kim seemed to see the joke. Marc racked his brains for some amends he could make very fast and with minimum disruption. Then movement caught his eye.

Behind Kim, two border collies trotted down the length of the milking shed from the direction of the portal. She turned around to see what he was looking at.

"Cute," she said.

Shit. Marc held his breath. It was just the farm dogs tooling back and forth, and no traffic was due back through the portal, so all he had to do was steer Annis out and get her to move the pickup so the buses could get through. The boffins were probably huffing and demanding answers by now, or at least wishing they'd used the toilet before they boarded. But fate was determined to stuff up his day right to the last second. While Kim was watching the collies, they sniffed around, looked disappointed, and loped back to the portal. Then they disappeared in front of her.

"Ah... " she said. "Hang on, what happened there?"

Marc clung to the knowledge that people saw things but didn't take them in if it didn't fit what they expected. He acted like he'd seen nothing.

"Dogs," he said. "They're getting impatient."

It could have worked, but Kim's gaze was now fixed on the end wall. If he'd hauled her away, it would only have intrigued her more, so he waited a few moments for her to give up. And that was long enough for very bad luck to shove a Caracal through the gate with Erin driving.

Erin just raised a forefinger from the steering wheel in acknowledgement as she drove out of the shed, giving Kim a glance that said she hadn't expected her to be coming along as well. She probably thought Marc had decided to let her tag along after all.

"Oh my God. What have I just seen?" Kim's voice wavered. "I didn't imagine that. Don't tell me I did."

There was only one thing Marc could say. "You're the PhD physicist. You tell me."

"What the hell's going on?"

"Okay, whether you like it or not, you're going to Opis."

"What?"

"You've seen it, so you've got two choices. Walk through it and start a new life on Opis, or — well, sorry, love, but I'll have to shoot you. You can't go back anywhere now. You can make all the promises you like about keeping it to yourself, but you and I know what'll happen. Make your mind up now. But you can't walk out of here."

Marc never drew a weapon unless he was ready to use it. He hoped she didn't think it was a threat. Well, it was, obviously, in the sense that he was telling her bad things would happen if she didn't make the right decision, but he hadn't aimed his sidearm at her to force her to pick that option. For a second, the subtle distinction fascinated him. He had no idea why it mattered.

"Come on, don't make me shoot you," he said. "I bloody hate all the paperwork."

"Ainatio couldn't create this," Kim said. She seemed oblivious to his pistol. "They just couldn't. So whose is it?"

"Prof, you don't know the half of it," Marc said. "But you will."

10

Technology reveals our true selves, with all the good and evil laid bare. The more it enables us to do, the more godlike our powers become, and the more we see who we really are when the natural constraints of our physical bodies are removed.

Reverend Martin Berry, minister of the
Church of St Thomas, Kill Line.

Chris could hear Kim from halfway across the yard. The buses had powered down to wait for the pickup to move and the place was quiet enough for raised voices to carry.

"You are *shitting* me," Kim was saying. "It can't happen. And if your IQ was in integers you'd know that."

Chris swore under his breath. Rich came jogging through the yard.

"What's the holdup, Chris?"

"Annis Kim's here and she's seen the gate." Chris spotted people standing up in the buses, craning their necks to see what was going on. "Keep everyone on their bus. Nobody gets off, okay?"

But the doors of the first bus hissed open before Rich could move. Phil Berman stepped down onto the concrete.

"Chris, what's happening?" he asked. "Was that Dr Kim? She nearly rammed us."

"Long story, Phil. Just get back on board. We're going to ask you to do something that sounds crazy, but I swear it's real, and you'll be fine. We've just got to move the pickup." More people had started to drain out of the bus, probably just to stretch their legs. They'd been waiting around in the town and now here, and the buses were crammed. Chris waved them back. "Folks, get back on the bus, please. Right now. Get on and shut the doors. You'll be moving any minute."

More traffic marshals showed up, followed by Alex minus the coffee. He took one look at the pickup and swore.

"I should have known," he said.

"She's seen it."

"Shit."

"They're all watching. We'll have to push them through fast and explain later." Chris handed Alex the locator. "Don't lose this, okay?"

By the time Chris turned his attention back to the lead bus, Phil was standing in front of it and staring into the milking shed. Marc noticed he now had an audience and steered Kim away from the doors.

"What are those two fighting about?" Phil asked. "I thought we were having a route briefing."

"Wait one. I'll be straight back." Chris took Rich aside. "Rich, stand the guys by to take over the driving. We'll have to rush the buses through the gate without the usual courtesies."

He went back into the shed and found Marc and Kim in front of the portal, head to head. Marc had Sal's squeaky squirrel toy and was gesturing with it. This was a weird, weird day. Chris prayed they'd have the luxury of looking back on all this and seeing the funny side.

"*Look,*" Marc said to her. "Don't take your eyes off the squirrel. Calm down and *watch.*"

He tossed the squeaky squirrel through the haze and it vanished in mid-air. Kim just stared.

"I've just thrown a dog toy two hundred and forty-six trillion miles and it's landed on Opis," Marc said. "I thought you liked that kind of stuff."

Kim wouldn't listen to him. "Look, I've seen the FTL data and Ainatio wasn't even close to building a full-size portal. If they had, and Erskine kept that secret too, she wouldn't have needed *Elcano.* She wouldn't have needed to leave anyone behind. She wouldn't have needed to maintain or prep the ships, either. And there's no way any of *you* lot developed this after she left. So tell me the bloody truth right now or I'm not going anywhere."

Chris couldn't tell if she'd seen the portal by accident and had to be dealt with, or if Marc had softened for some reason and offered her an escape route. He was surprised Marc hadn't just bundled her through it like he'd have done in a hostage rescue.

But then Marc did exactly that. "Okay, I'm bored, you're noisy, and we're going." He picked her up bodily, ignoring the cursing and kicks, and spoke to someone on the radio at the Nomad end. "Alpha Three to Cab Two, coming through with a pedestrian. Not voluntary, so we need someone to receive and process her immediately, over."

Kim's impressive range of swear words was cut off as Marc stepped through the portal. Chris hoped the shock of finding herself on Opis would quiet things down. He went back to Phil to try to reassure him, but he must have heard some of the row. Rich herded the stray scientists back on board and stood in front of the doors while Chris did his best to play things down.

"What was she going on about?" Phil asked. "What *truth?*"

"Phil, I'm going to drive you through," Chris said. "You're going to see something weird, but it's perfectly safe."

"The shed's empty." Phil was a solid guy who always kept his head, one of the few Ainatio staff Chris would have trusted, but he looked like he was losing his nerve. "Where are all the vehicles going? What the hell's in there?

Chris steered him back up the steps onto the bus. With the research centre now open, there was no telling who'd show up next. Chris had to get the buses moving. Phil slid into the driver's seat.

"Move over," Chris said. "I'm doing this."

"Hell no." Phil started the bus like he'd learned at the last minute from a manual, which he probably had. "I want my hands on this damn wheel. What about the briefing?"

Chris let him have it straight. "There's an interstellar gateway set up in there. The patch of haze. We're going to drive through it and we won't hit the wall."

"What?"

"Phil, move aside. *Now.*"

Phil wasn't a soft touch but he was smart enough to concede. He got out of the driver's seat and stood in the aisle, clutching a rail.

"What's happening?" someone called from the back of the packed bus.

"You're going to Nomad Base," Chris said, and slipped the brake. "Right now, in fact."

He thought he'd at least hear some shrieks as he drove the bus at the wall, but there was dead silence followed by a few incoherent noises and then a shout of "Whoa, what the hell?" as the bus nosed through the haze and he felt the gravity shift. He kept going across the grass towards the far side of the parking zone packed with vehicles in carefully-organised rows. Then the clamour started up behind him. The penny had dropped. The scientists had realised where they were.

Phil leaned over him. "How in the name of God did we do *that?*"

"You'll have to ask a physicist, Phil," Chris said. "Sorry to scare you. It didn't quite go as planned, but we did it. Blame Dr Kim for dropping in unannounced."

One of the marshals waved him into the parking space. As he cut the engine, he decided to try to smooth the scientists over and stood up at the front of the bus to address them. They were already on their feet trying to get a better look at the base.

"Yes, it's Opis," Chris said, as loudly as he could without shouting. He hated raising his voice. "This is Nomad Base. And no, the gateway isn't ours. It's alien. You can have chat with the builders later if you like. They're here."

"You never warned us." It was Lianne Maybury's husband, one of the die-back team. He looked furious. "You never told us a damn thing. What the hell are you playing at?"

Chris held on to his temper. It was harder than usual. "How many times do I have to say this? One of your colleagues sold us out. That's why we didn't tell you anything. We only found out about gateways and aliens sixteen hours ago, but during the night we still built you somewhere to eat, sleep, and crap, and yeah, now you're on Opis, just like we promised you would be. You're welcome. Don't mention it. It's your touching gratitude that makes the job worthwhile."

Chris always got silence in the end. He still hadn't had to shout. Maybe, just for once, he looked as angry as he felt. He was about to turn and step down off the bus when Fonseca came up behind him.

"I'll take it from here, Sergeant," she said. She stepped into the aisle. "Ladies and gentlemen, I know I can count on your patience while we process you. You're scientists, so you know this is going to be tedious and full of decontamination and record-keeping. But it beats Tim Pham hauling you back to Asia for a show trial, right? Excuse me — back in a moment. Please stay on the bus until I return."

She stepped outside again. Phil glanced at Chris, raised his eyebrows, and slumped back in the driver's seat as if he was going to take a nap. Chris followed Fonseca. Sometimes it was reassuring to see her in harpy mode.

"Why did Marc bring Annis Kim?" she demanded.

"I don't think he had a choice." Chris looked at the long walk back to the gate. "Anyway, we found out our informer was Abbie Vincent. She's back at Ainatio and so are her parents. So we don't have to stare suspiciously at everyone now. You know, like the way you're staring at me."

"Are you going back to Kill Line?"

"Of course I am. We're clearing up. One last sweep."

Fonseca withered him with a glance. "You make damn sure you come back here."

"Why does everybody think we're planning some heroic last stand? We're just checking for stragglers and bugging out."

"Because you're you, that's why. Go on, do what you have to and come straight back."

He took that as a normal-for-Lennie show of concern. If she wanted to show how relieved she was when he returned, she knew where to find him.

Chris trudged back through the one-way system of bollards and passed the rest of the Ainatio buses, now lined up in a neat row. The scientists were staring open-mouthed as they filed out of the vehicles, apparently not as balky as the bunch on Phil's bus. When he got nearer the gate, Chris could see Alex and the remainder of the traffic marshals arriving on foot. Alex made a beer gesture at him.

Chris gave him a thumbs-up. Yeah, he was going to get totally wasted at the earliest opportunity. He could almost taste that beer now.

Alex slowed as he passed him. "That was fun," he said. "Let's never do it again, huh?"

"Who's got the locator?"

"I handed it to Britzilla. I thought it was for the best."

"Wise man. See you later."

Chris carried on and walked through the haze, realising he was no longer sure how many times he'd done this and how many air miles he'd clocked up. The noise level dropped dramatically, he felt the gravity change, and he was back in the yard with Marc and Trinder, inhaling the scent of grass and cow shit.

Now it was just the three of them plus Dieter and his dogs left to finish up and close the gate on Kill Line. Trinder held up his screen.

"We checked them all out," he said. "Everyone's accounted for. And I just knew Kim would find a way to come with us."

"You think she staged all that?" Marc examined the locator like he was working out where the batteries went. "You should have seen her face when Erin drove through the portal. When I hauled her through it, she kicked me in the nuts. And she meant it."

"Whatever happened to all the nice girls?" Chris asked.

"And before you start on the irony of me shanghaiing her in Nomad after I nearly put a hole in Ben Tusa for trying to do the same... just don't."

"At least Zakko's going to be happy. He was worried about her."

"She's a survivor," Marc said. "When the last atom winks out of existence at the end of the life of this universe, she'll still be there complaining about it."

"You said *this* universe. She's been talking dirty to you about cosmology, hasn't she?"

"I didn't understand a word of it."

"So no Pham and no ninjas." Trinder sounded disappointed. "After all that."

Marc was cooling off, flapping the collar of his polo shirt to get some air circulating. "So far. Don't tempt fate, Dan. You know what happens."

"I suppose we're telling everyone about Abbie Vincent, yeah?"

"I've already made a start," Chris said.

"What a bitch." Trinder shook his head. "Who'd have thought it?"

Now that the immediate crisis was averted, Chris allowed himself to mull that over, and he felt robbed. It was the only way to describe it. He'd given Abbie a ride and even thought he was being the bad guy. If he'd known she was the traitor all along, and that maybe she'd already sold them out when he first ran into her near the shuttle runway — okay, what *would* he have done about it?

He would have been obliged to make an example of her so everyone felt justice was done, and there was no way to live with a traitor, so that example would have needed to be extreme. It was just as well her parents had decided to stay as well. Nomad didn't need to start with baggage like that. Innocent or not, they'd be pariahs, and a grievance magnet for everyone with a beef.

"Fifteen hundred and whatever down, four to go," Trinder said. "Plus mutts."

"End of an era, kind of." Chris got on the squad radio. Dieter was driving the last Caracal, so he could get here fast once he'd crammed fourteen excited dogs into the troop compartment. That was going to be fun to clean out afterwards. It was just as well they had bots to do those jobs.

"Six Zero to Five Seven, position check, over," Chris said.

Dieter took a moment to respond. "Five Seven here. I've hit a delay." Chris could hear yaps and barks in the background. "I'm looking for Betsy and Girlie. I'm giving the Kill Line perimeter one more go and then working back in. I'll be in and out of range. Give me fifteen minutes, over."

"RV at the milking shed. Six Zero out."

The dogs would show up. It wasn't like them not to come when called, but it had been a hectic day and maybe they'd reacted to all that anxiety reeking out of people. It must have thrown up some fascinating smells they wanted to check out.

"You know he won't leave them behind," Trinder said.

"Yeah, don't worry."

"Are you going be pissed at me if I start fretting about what Pham's up to? The guy doesn't shrug and say win some, lose some. He'll be trying to pull off some counterattack or something."

"He'll have to come to us to do it," Chris said. "There's nothing else left for him to wreck. Sol's in Nomad Base."

Marc twirled the locator. "And this won't be any use to him. Fred can lock him out."

"He doesn't know that."

"Then he'll find out fast."

Trinder wandered around the yard, stopping from time to time to just stare into the hazy afternoon sun. Maybe he was going to miss the place. It was home, after all.

"Where's your gear, Marc?" Chris asked.

"Sent it through hours ago." He was still wearing his heavily-laden vest, every pocket stuffed with destruction. He patted one. "I've got everything I need on me if I get stuck here."

"You're as bad as Fonseca. We're not going to get stuck anywhere."

Marc walked down to the farm gates and stood looking across the field on the other side of the road. Chris took out his water bottle and drained it, then listened to the sounds of the countryside for a few minutes, enjoying the quiet. That beer would have hit the spot right now.

"Oh, look, the prodigal returns," Marc said suddenly. "Well, one of them, anyway."

He pointed across the field. Betsy the pit bull was trotting through the long grass towards the farm, carrying something in her mouth. Those wide jaws made her look pleased as Punch about whatever she'd picked up. Chris couldn't work out what she was carrying, but he assumed it was edible, and probably a rabbit.

He was getting ready to give her a scratch behind the ears and tell her what a clever girl she was when he realised she wasn't carrying it but dragging it, and it was putting up a fight, writhing every few seconds. Marc noticed too.

"I hope she's not going to kill it in front of us," Marc said. "I didn't think dogs did that."

"Maybe she's going to give you live prey to teach you to hunt."

"That's meerkats."

"Yeah, and lots of other animals."

They were debating how carnivores taught their young when Betsy crossed the road and finally got close enough for Chris to see what she was hauling. It wasn't a rabbit. It was far too big, and it wasn't an animal at all. It was a matt black python bot with an Ainatio logo, a segmented snake-like thing used for squeezing into tight spaces like drains — or climbing comms towers. Chris didn't dismiss them as obsolete junk any more, not after Erskine used them to trash Ainatio's tower and lock Solomon out of the network. There were different configurations, but they all recorded data and did small survey and repair jobs in spaces too small for humans and where remote guidance signals couldn't reach. They could free themselves if they got stuck, too, but this one didn't seem to be having much luck escaping Betsy's jaws.

"Bloody hell, she's caught a python. How did she find of one of those? Looks like she managed to switch it on." Marc went up to her as she came into the yard and held out his hand. "Drop it, Betsy. Give it to me, hun. Good girl."

The dog stood with her feet planted and the bot still firmly clamped in her mouth. Then the python convulsed again and a laser beam sliced out across the grass growing alongside the concrete, shaving a few inches into hay. Marc jumped back and cursed.

"Bloody thing. I should have known."

It was probably trying to cut itself free the same way it would have done in a collapsed building, and whoever had last programmed it hadn't added Dog to the list of objects it had to leave intact. Betsy seemed to have the upper hand for the time being, though. She was smart enough to put a bite on it just behind the head end joint so it couldn't bend far enough to squirm around and cut her. Chris hoped she didn't get tired or bored and drop it.

"So how do we power it off without decapitating her?" Marc squatted, staying carefully behind her as he pulled his knife out of his belt. "Is there a switch? You can't bash these things on the head. They're probably crushproof."

"Marc, you're going to lose a body part if you get too close," Chris said. "Pin it down. Tail first, then grab the head by the neck joint."

"Gosh, Christopher, I'd never have worked that out for myself. Thank you so much."

Marc took a breath and lunged to grab the python by its tail. It started struggling, probably because its sensors told it that it was now jammed in something else.

"Bugger me, it's strong."

Trinder moved in and reached cautiously for the head, working his hand up the length of the body until his grip was touching Betsy's jaw. The python shot out its laser again.

Trinder held on tight. "I think I'm going to need a change of boxers."

"Okay, when she lets go, we just slam it on the ground. Ready?" Marc put his hand on her back. "Betsy, we've got it. Drop it, Betsy." She stared back at him like she wasn't convinced he had what it took to do this. "Come on, let go. Drop it. Leave." Betsy finally opened her mouth and they wrestled the python flat on the ground. "Good girl. Now for a bit of dissection."

Chris rummaged in the pickup for tools and found Kim's rucksack. "We've got some bolt cutters. Wait one."

"Why did you pack bolt cutters for her?"

"I didn't. They were already in her rucksack when I collected her stuff."

"Yeah, that'd be right."

Chris placed the bolt cutters in Marc's reach. They were red with an Ainatio logo. At least Kim pilfered useful things. "Be nicer to her when you see her again," he said. "Most women just carry nail files. Do you want me to cut while you two hold it?"

"No, we're good," Trinder said. His knuckles were white with the strain. "Neck joint?"

"Yeah, got to be." Marc poked his blade between the segments and the python started its weird rhythmic writhing again. "That'll disconnect the laser if nothing else."

Betsy looked pleased with herself. Chris made a fuss of her and got on the radio. "Six Zero to Five Seven, we've got Betsy here. She's found us, over."

Chris waited, watching Marc and Trinder as they probed for potential weak points in the bot's tough casing. Dieter's fifteen minutes were up and he still wasn't here.

"Six Zero to Five Seven, over."

There was no answer. Chris didn't want to distract the others when they were disarming the python, but he was going to have go look for Dieter. Now the Ainatio network was shut down, he couldn't locate the Caracal's transponder. But the guy must have been outside the five-hundred meter radio range.

Marc let out a long *ahhhhh* like he'd just downed a beer. "*There* we go," he said. "I've got the hands of a surgeon."

Chris looked around. The python was lying in an S shape on the grass while Trinder prodded it with a pocket screwdriver. Betsy watched like a smiling mom who was pleased to see her kids learning to do things for themselves.

"So they do have a switch," Trinder said. "But you've got to release this small plate to get at it, which means Betsy didn't set it off. They're not networked. They're programmed in advance about where to go and what to do. Someone tasked this. It's got to be APS."

Marc held his hand out for the screwdriver and started trying to get into its mid section. "There's always a chance that Betsy interrupted it while it was going about its honest business, but I'm going to assume the worst. She found it while it was spying on Kill Line." He pulled off the head covering and examined the severed connection. "All the time we were looking up for ninjas and drones, we weren't looking down for python cams, were we?"

"That's desperation on Pham's part," Trinder said. "They're not much use if they can't transmit live images."

"No, but they move fast and they could have been lurking for hours, shuttling back and forth to unload data."

"He's still left it too late, then. We're out of here as soon as Dieter shows."

"Unless Pham's got some last-minute op planned and it's timed for when we think we've made it and our guard's down. Oldest trick in the book. I must be losing my touch."

"Maybe Dieter's run into another python and he's trying to deal with it," Chris said. "But that doesn't explain why he's not responding to radio checks."

Trinder straightened up. "I'm going to jump straight to a conclusion and consult Sol. He can check this for stored data and tell us how many more we might have to hunt for. If they've recorded the portal activity, we've got to round them up before they report back, if they haven't already."

"Maybe it doesn't matter if they've seen it," Chris said. "Pham can't get hold of the technology."

"No, but his first thought isn't going to be aliens," Marc said. "It'll be nation states. APS has just been stuffed by a massive CPS attack, he'll think someone's already got better FTL than he has, and he'll probably assume it's Britain because that explains why I'm here. I don't want to leave my country in the shit if I can do something about Pham now."

"Yeah, and we've just built a whole evacuation around keeping the portal under wraps," Trinder said. He took the disabled python away from Marc. "We did all that for good reasons. So we hand the bot to Sol. If it's too late, it's too late, but we need to know."

"Okay, but keep Sol Nomad side," Chris said. "If he comes back here — well, if it can go wrong, it'll go wrong now."

The comms link routed through the portal was still active. It wouldn't take long for Trinder to call Solomon to the threshold and step through to hand the python over while Chris looked for Dieter.

"Six Zero to Five Seven, position check, over."

There was still no answer. Chris wished he hadn't been in a hurry to move the Lammergeiers. One of them could have covered the whole area in minutes flying on AI alone. Chris muted the radio for a moment.

"Dan, see if we can get a Lamm back for recon." But Trinder had already stepped through the gate, and then someone responded to Chris's position check.

"Well, hello, Six Zero. You must be the repentant hitman."

It made Chris start. He knew it wasn't Dieter but he still felt a blip of relief at getting a response before realisation dawned. The squad radios had unique hardware keys and there was no way APS had gotten the Ainatio net up and running again. If this guy was talking to Chris right now, he had Dieter's personal radio. The rest were accounted for.

Chris gestured to Marc, indicating *listen.* "Six Zero to unknown callsign, identify yourself, over."

"Let's talk about Five Seven," said the voice. "I'm not here to monologue. I'm here to negotiate, *here* being the junction of the northbound road out of Kill Line and the forest track to the research centre. Bring your psycho Pom mate, too. And resist the urge to call in an airstrike. Five Seven's still got a pulse."

Chris hadn't heard much of the guy's voice before because he'd never been summoned to answer his questions. But he was pretty sure he was now dealing with Tim Pham.

* * *

CAISIN GATE ENTRY POINT, NOMAD BASE: 1530.

Trinder held up the python in two hands by its tail like a record-breaking catch. It was a lot heavier than it looked.

"I don't have much time, Sol." he said. "We're guessing the dog found it in the town. Has it recorded anything?"

"I'll check." Solomon snaked his head around as he looked it over. He'd shut down a continent with a few lines of code, but primitive sewer bots whose design hadn't changed much in a couple of centuries were beyond his digital reach. "I try not to think of these things as my nemesis."

"How many did we have? I can't check records now."

"Six. The shuttle technicians were the only people who kept them. But I know the APS technicians took some."

"Can we get an armed drone or one of the Lamms back to do a search? And before you ask, you've got to stay here."

"I could save you a lot of time."

"Sol, APS are gunning for you. They'll want the gate technology — if they know about it — but they're not going to give up on you either way. Especially after the sabcode. They know you did it."

"They'd think I did even if I hadn't."

"All the more reason to stay here, then."

"Very well, I could programme Lamm Two to look specifically for this type of bot and destroy it. Five to ten minutes to turn a Lamm around. Twenty to thirty to unpack a drone in this chaos and arm it."

"What if Pham's already extracted data from the pythons, though?" Trinder asked.

"I can't tell. APS is still blacked out, so the most effective action to be sure we've stopped them relaying information would be to obliterate the Ainatio campus completely before they're back online. But I don't believe the information is damaging enough to justify killing Ainatio staff and those conscripts — and yourselves, of course.

You're only two miles from the target and it would be a substantial blast radius. If I haven't made myself clear, I think you should abandon the search for the pythons and evacuate immediately."

"Pham's going to think the technology's British," Trinder said. "You know how APS will react."

"I'm aware of the politics, Major, and I'd feel dreadful for Marc. But as Chris says, you can't save the whole world. Nor can you predict or control how governments are going behave. My task is specific. The intel now presents no threat to Nomad. Once you're all safely here and the gate is closed, APS can do nothing."

It was true, but Trinder wasn't sure he could nod to that and still look Marc in the eye. If he found another excuse to avoid taking action in the same way he told himself he couldn't do anything about finding his family, he wasn't sure he could live with himself either.

"Okay, I've got to go. Just put a Lamm on standby, and if we get into difficulties I'll call for support."

Once the urgency of getting people through the portal had overtaken the amazement factor, Trinder had been stepping back and forth through the portal without worrying what was on the other side. But now he had no idea what he'd be walking into. He took a breath and raised his rifle.

When he emerged from the milking shed, the world looked the same as he'd left it. But Chris was talking to someone on the radio and Marc was almost back to back with him, scoping through as if he was giving him cover. Trinder heard Chris replying in that flat-calm way he had when everything was falling apart.

"He'd better be there when I show up."

Chris switched off his radio at the handset and turned around. For once, he wasn't difficult to read. The distracted look had gone and his face had set hard.

"Stay off the squad net from now on," he said.

"What's happened?"

"That was Tim Pham on Dieter's radio. He's got him and he wants to talk terms. You two better go back to Opis. There's no sense in adding to the hostage count."

"Give it a rest, Chris," Marc said. "I've been doing this shit a lot longer than you and I'm not walking away from it. Not even for Howie. Anyway, Pham's invited me. Bring your *psycho Pom*, he said, didn't he?"

Trinder's heart was already hammering. "What Psycho Pom said. I'm not going anywhere either."

"Okay, we need to get a drone in the air, see the location, do the numbers, and check whether Dieter's there." Chris shook his head. "Why didn't I see this coming? Pham sat back and let us show our hand before deciding the best place to apply the pressure. He doesn't need an army to do it, either. Just a couple of guys in the right spot."

"Location?" Trinder asked.

"There's a right turn to Ainatio off this road, just a dirt track. We used to patrol it to about a mile from the campus." Chris gestured vaguely to the road that passed the dairy farm and took out his pocket screen. "Sol? Sol, this is Chris. We've got a hostage situation. Pham's holding Dieter. I need drones for a recon immediately, nothing big and obvious though. Can we route a secure channel another way? The squad net's been compromised."

"Do you know where Dieter is?" Solomon asked. "We can put a gate anywhere and extract him."

"Please, leave the extraction to us," Chris said. "We know what we're doing. It only takes a fraction of a second to go wrong and Dieter ends up dead. And we don't know if we can use the gate without being spotted. Just help us out with the comms."

"Very well," Sol said. "What happened to the squad net?"

"Pham's got Dieter's radio. But I want to shut down the gate in case one of Pham's guys finds it, so does that mean we lose all comms?"

Solomon paused for a moment. It sounded as if Fred was there talking him through it.

"The probes are instant comms relays in their own right," he said. "That's how they transmit images and sound back to the teerik ship. So they don't need the gate. Leave it to us — Fred and I can re-route signals through them to create a secure channel for you via your Ainatio network radios, you'll be able to talk with Ingram's team, and we'll give you a feed from the probe on your screens for aerial surveillance."

"Are APS comms and navigation still down?"

"I'd tell you immediately if they weren't. A probe's going to be at your location in a few minutes and shared control will be transferred to your screens. You can move it around yourselves."

"Thanks Sol. We'll let you know if we need extra support when we've found out what we're dealing with."

"Very well. Stand by."

Marc tapped the blue flashlight in his top pocket. "Lucky for us we've got a gadget that's perfect for hostage extraction. If we can get close enough to Dieter, we open the portal right there and he's out."

"In front of Pham and his buddies. I've just had to remind Sol about that."

"I know. But we might have to live with it."

"So you're saying forget the bigger security implications of revealing the gate's existence to grab Dieter."

"Well, yeah. That's exactly what I'm saying."

"Just checking. A few minutes ago, you were worried about Pham assuming it's British technology."

"Yeah, and I haven't changed my mind, Chris, but we're not going to abandon Dieter and we've got no control over Pham's imagination. I could show him a sworn statement from Fred saying yes, this is definitely our weird crow-alien technology, don't blame the monkeys, and it wouldn't change a thing."

Trinder lobbed in Solomon's casting vote to settle it. "If a python's already taken evidence of the gate back to Pham, the only way to guarantee the news doesn't get out is to vaporise the facility to make sure nobody survives, and Sol says he won't do it," he said. "Too much collateral damage, including us. So work on the assumption that Pham's seen some glimpse of the gate in action. He still won't know how it works. And he'll find something else to pin on Britain anyway."

"Okay, subject closed." Chris studied his screen. "Sol, should I be able to see anything from the drone yet?"

"*Probe.* Not yet. Wait."

It felt like forever. Trinder watched Chris redistributing his magazines from pocket to webbing to pocket again, the only outward sign of how agitated he was. Then Chris took his knife from his belt and slid it carefully down his ankle into his boot, as if he was rehearsing with every weapon he wanted to use on Tim Pham.

Marc took the cue and rummaged through the pouches and pockets on his own vest. "Anyone need a stun grenade? I've got four. Dan?"

"I've never used one in earnest," Trinder said. "I'm more likely to deafen myself."

"Yeah, it does that anyway. Bike chain?"

"Sorry?"

"If you want it, I've got one."

Trinder couldn't work out if Marc was joking to relieve the tension. Maybe the chain was for real, though, and that was what he'd heard rattling in his pocket a few days ago. A few days? Two, three, this morning? His sense of time had gone haywire.

"I'll pass, thanks," he said.

Solomon finally came back to them. "Gentlemen, you should have an image on your screens now. You all have control to move the probe around, but one at a time, please."

Trinder's screen showed an aerial view of the three of them, the pickup, and Betsy mooching around the yard.

"Thanks, Sol. Controls?"

"Direction, higher or lower, stop, and so on. Just like a virtual tour. And I've set it to detect human body temperature."

Trinder took a moment to spot the probe, a speck in the sky not much bigger than the micro-drones he was used to. He watched it track northeast as Chris dragged his finger across his screen.

"Good work, Sol," Chris said. "Thank Fred for me. I think we've found Pham."

Trinder nodded, eyes now on his screen. "There he is."

Pham was exactly where he said he'd be, in a clearing close to the road where the dirt track ended and widened into a space big enough for a Caracal and one of Ainatio's landscape maintenance trucks. Trinder could only see three people: Pham leaning against the Caracal, a man who looked like one of the operators tinkering with a python, and Dieter, identifiable by his grey hair and the black Ainatio-issue pants that the militia guys had taken a liking to. He was sitting propped up against the front wheel of the APC, head bowed, not moving. At first Trinder thought the dark patches on his shirt were just shadow, but then he realised it was something else entirely. It was blood.

"Sol?" Chris didn't even raise his voice, let alone cuss. "Get the medics standing by. We've got eyes on Dieter. He's injured."

"And the other guy's going to be around somewhere." Marc pointed the flashlight at the gate and pressed his earpiece. "Alpha Three to Cab Zero and Echo One Four, shutting gate temporarily. Wait out."

Chris put Betsy into the back seat and started the pickup. "I'm going to loop around through the woods. Maybe Pham's expecting that, but I never like using the front door. Anyone got a better idea?"

Marc studied his screen. "Let me look for the other guy first, because he's got to be out there. They're not going to let us walk in armed without some precautions."

"Just those two operators, then?"

Marc took the probe higher. "There he is. In the undergrowth on the south side of the clearing. So he can pick us off any time he likes. The guy with Pham looks like the younger bloke, so this one's the older guy in the zipper jacket. The first one I saw."

Trinder's heart was pounding so hard now that he was sure it was making his voice shake. But he was weirdly happy to be that scared and still able to function. "Does Pham know I'm still around?"

Chris shrugged. "Maybe not. He asked for Marc. But that might be because he doesn't trust him and wants to keep an eye on him."

"Okay, if he thinks I'm tactically insignificant or he's forgotten me completely, drop me off in the woods," Trinder said. "I'll come up behind Zipper Guy and keep him busy."

"I've got a better idea," Marc said. "Chris drops *me* off in the woods and takes you instead. Pham knows I'll be getting up to mischief elsewhere, so he sends one or even both of his blokes after me, and then you've got less to deal with. Meanwhile, Dan, what with you being so nice and non-threatening, you can sneak up to Dieter like you're checking his pulse or something, open the portal right next to the APC, and haul him through."

"Now you're talking," Chris said.

Trinder thought about it and decided the extraction itself might be as dangerous as trying to take on Zipper Guy. He could still look Marc in the eye and not feel it was something to keep him busy while the other two did the serious work.

"If I get close enough, and I can place the portal accurately, I can just roll Dieter across rather than lift and carry him," he said. "By the time Pham notices, we're gone."

"And then you stay gone," Chris said. "Don't come back. We'll be fine. So that's the plan, then. Marc peels off and keeps Zipper Guy busy, I get Pham and Python Man focusing on me, and while they're distracted you get Dieter through the portal. Marc, you've got first call on the probe. You're going to need it more than us."

Chris drove off, scraped through a gap in the fence, and cut across the road to climb a shallow bank into the woods. It was a bumpy ride with the three of them crammed together in the front bench seat. Chris was trying to speed and the woods weren't going to let him.

"He's certain you won't leave a man behind," Marc said. "Exploit that."

"He's right. I won't."

"But he sees that as weakness. So while he's worrying what I'm up to, he's convinced you'll give him anything he wants to save Dieter. But what he thinks is a sheep in wolf's clothing turns out to be a wolf after all." He passed Trinder the locator. "You're a wolf at heart, Dan. Tev thought so. Go and sink your fangs in."

Trinder wasn't expecting that. Marc could have been humouring him or psyching him up, but it helped all the same. "Thanks," he said. "I'll have to live up to that for him."

Chris stopped the pickup a quarter mile from the RV point and let Marc out. He gave him a nod and there was a short, awkward silence. Trinder could hear birds singing their hearts out. It just didn't fit the moment.

"See you later, buddy," Chris said. "Wherever."

"Yeah. Don't worry. Dieter's going to make it."

Trinder wanted to say something in case he never got another chance, but all he could do was raise his hand briefly to Marc as Chris drove off.

They were winding and bouncing between trees again. Trinder's racing pulse had given way to noticing every sound, every smell, every movement around him in almost overwhelming detail. The pickup was a vivid slice of the moment: the smell of musty fabric and sunbaked plastic, Betsy making lip-licking sounds, the suspension creaking, Chris exhaling every so often as if he was trying not to sigh.

"Tev told me Marc didn't plan on going home because he wanted to keep doing the job until it finished him," Trinder said, and then wished he hadn't mentioned it. "I hope that's not what he's doing."

Chris looked straight ahead. "No. No, he wouldn't let Howie down, whatever he said." Roots and bushes crunched under the pickup's tyres. There was an occasional bang as it caught a branch that sprang back and hit the bodywork. "Dan, I had a few years where every single day was like this. I still don't plan beyond the next meal break if I don't have to because I got used to not knowing if I'd live to see it. So if we all make it back to Nomad tonight, we promise each other we're going to live like normal men for a change. Wives, kids, digging the garden, painting fences. Beer and barbecues. That's what being human is. This isn't."

For all Trinder knew, he wasn't going to make that trip, but he'd been there once before with the nukes that never came and it had left him with a clarity he hadn't experienced before. He knew he was alive and what that really meant. For once, he thought Chris was wrong. Being human wasn't living a comfortable, fairly predictable life. It was this state he was in now, surviving minute to minute with no guarantee the next one would come.

Eventually Chris stopped the pickup and switched off the engine. Trinder checked the probe feed to see what Marc was monitoring. The view took in a big sweep of the woods, and he could see Marc moving towards the dirt track east of the clearing, with Zipper Guy still in position south of it. There was also a live comms icon. Sol had now re-routed the signals via the probe. They could use their Ainatio radios to talk securely again, and that gave them a much longer range.

"Okay, time to walk." Chris patted his vest like he was checking he had everything. "Pham knows we're coming, but I'll keep the pickup out of his reach, just in case."

Trinder turned to the back seat. "Stay, Betsy. We'll come and get you later. Then we can all go home."

"Got everything you need?"

"Not really, but I've got what I know how to use."

Chris patted his shoulder. "Dan, you've got this. I'm just jumpy because Dieter's losing blood and this is taking way too long for me."

Trinder secured the portal flashlight on his webbing next to his water bottle for quick access. "Does it look like a weapon? If I try to conceal it, it'll just draw their attention."

"To be honest, it looks like one of those tacky flashlights with storage inside the grip for survival gadgets," Chris said. "The kind they sell to weekend campers who don't know how to use them and never will. Hell, it's blue as well. It'll just make you look clueless. No threat at all."

"Gee, thanks, Chris."

"Looking harmless is a tactical advantage. I've got some experience there."

Trinder followed Chris with his rifle slung muzzle down across his back, trying to look like he had no plans to use it, but mentally rehearsing how he'd swing it into a firing position when he had to. It was going to be hard enough operating the flashlight and trying to move Dieter at the same time. This was the moment he realised he didn't know enough about the device. How near to someone could he safely open the gate? If he was too close, would he end up tearing them apart? If Dieter had a gunshot wound to the chest or abdomen, time wasn't on his side, so it was a risk he'd have to take.

Now the clearing was right in front of them. "Here we go," Chris said.

The Caracal was parked with its aircon still humming as if the driver had just jumped out to take a leak. Pham was leaning against it, looking bored. Python Man walked towards them with his rifle aimed and stopped a couple of yards back.

"Put your weapons on the ground," he said. "All of them."

For a moment Trinder thought Chris was going to go for his pistol, but he slipped his rifle off his shoulder and laid it down with his sidearm. Trinder followed suit. Python Man didn't seem to recognise the flashlight for what it was because he just picked up the weapons and withdrew. Trinder kept an eye on where he stashed them.

Pham straightened up, pistol in one hand and a wound dressing on the other. He didn't look very statesmanlike. He did look like what he'd once been, though, a full-on spook. He studied them with a slight frown.

"Where's Gallagher?" he asked.

"I don't know," Chris said. "What did you do to Dieter?"

"No offence to Major Trinder, but I really wanted to see Gallagher." Pham jerked his head in the vague direction of the woods. "Never mind. We'll find him."

"I asked what you did to Dieter. Let me see him."

Trinder assumed Pham's nod was a silent order to Zipper Guy, because the one who'd been working on the python stayed put. It also meant that Zipper Guy was close enough to see Pham and hear him without a radio. Marc would be able to see him moving on his screen. Trinder was tempted to look for himself, but reaching into his pocket was probably asking for trouble.

"Dieter's still got some time," Pham said. "But we've got things to discuss first."

Chris looked across to Dieter and called to him. "Dieter, it's Chris. You're going to be fine. We're here to get you out. Hang on."

"Chris, let me get to the point and tell you what I want," Pham said. "Give me the AI so we can shut it down safely — because you *know* you can't trust those things — and let's come to an agreement on the technology."

Chris didn't waver. "Dieter first."

"I really did come here for the FTL." Pham went on as if he wasn't listening. "I wasn't too fussed about die-back, to be honest, even if the agriculture minister was having hysterics. It's not going to reach us anytime soon. But then I heard that you still had an ASD AI. Now that really was naughty, so I had to bring in some help to pull a few plugs. We need to shut your AI down, preferably before we let him loose on another planet. Which brings me to the main event of the day. Is that wormhole thing you've been sneaking through his invention, or did a human being do it? Damn, it's funny how the whole comms blackout suddenly falls into place."

"I need to take a look at Dieter right now." The only clue that Chris was longing to rip Pham's head off was how completely emotionless he sounded. "The longer you dick me around, the less chance you have of finding out."

Pham indicated Dieter with sweep of his hand. "Okay, knock yourself out."

"Let me check him over." Trinder swung into his role. "I've had first responder training."

That sounded suitably petty and bureaucratic, and therefore harmless enough to be overlooked. He barely remembered his last first aid training refresher, but all he needed to do was look useless and self-important. He squatted next to Dieter with Chris and started checking for a point to open the portal where he could just roll Dieter through.

The guy wasn't going to be moving by himself. He did *not* look good. His breathing was ragged and Trinder could see the pain on his face. There wasn't as much blood around as he'd expected for a man who was barely conscious, though. Trinder tried to recall his half-day of training and realised the guy was probably bleeding internally.

"Hey Dieter. We've got medics standing by." Chris went to unbutton his shirt to take a look but Dieter tried to bat his hand away. "Where's the entry wound?"

"Can't breathe," Dieter said. "Knife. Get Girlie."

Knife? "Let me take a look," Trinder said, now taking the first aid role more seriously. "Where does it hurt?

"Shoulder. Please, get Girlie."

Dieter wasn't making sense but it didn't matter. All Trinder had to do was get him out fast. Pham wandered over.

"I'd advise doing a deal if you want to get him to a medic in time," Pham said.

Chris stood up and turned slowly to face him. "How about I *don't* tell our AI to level Sydney if you just go fuck yourself?"

He said it calmly. Trinder stopped worrying about where Dieter's wound was and what had made it and started getting ready to place the wormhole. He watched Chris and Pham intently, waiting for the moment when one of them expected the other to snap and shut out everything else around them.

"Come on, Chris, if all I wanted to do was kill him, I'd have shot him." Pham had a smug kind of smile that must have tempted Chris to punch it off his face. "But I know what I'm doing. I wanted to give you enough time to consider the offer." He looked at his bandaged hand. "His husky went for me. But at least it made him stop and get out of the APC."

Chris suddenly looked like pure frozen hatred. His expression hadn't changed, but his eyes somehow looked much darker. "You calculated where to stick a knife in him so he'd take longer to bleed out," he said. "You really did that, yeah?"

"It's down to you now," Pham said. "If you're sensible, we can all come out of this with what we want. I take a strategic and tactical weapon away for safe keeping, Dieter gets medical help in time, and you get money, mansions, cars, women, ice pops, whatever you want. But I want the *real* wormhole technology, not the monkey model that Annis tried to palm me off with. Come on. We know you never leave a man behind."

Chris had stopped blinking. This wasn't part of the act. Trinder had to do it right now. Pham's attention was firmly on Chris, and Python Man began closing the gap, probably expecting Chris to go apeshit. He was right next to Trinder now, standing way too close. Trinder's only space to open the gate was right behind him. He didn't know if he could move a big, solid guy like Dieter fast enough.

Now.

"Dieter, I'm going to move you," he whispered. "You want some water?"

It was easy to reach for the water bottle and take out the gate locator instead. Nobody was looking at him. Chris took a step towards Pham, Python Man moved in, and Trinder stretched his arm back to make sure the gate would open close behind him, clear of both himself and Dieter.

"I'm going to sit you up, buddy." He hooked his left arm under Dieter's armpit, his right hand still clutching the locator behind his back. "It'll hurt, but hang on."

Trinder took a deep breath to ready himself for an all-out effort. He could do this. It was just an explosive lift from a squat and a few steps backwards, as hard and as fast as he could. He pressed the locator's button. Static brushed the back of his head and he knew the portal had opened, silent and barely visible. All he had to do was hook his right arm under Dieter's, still holding the flashlight, and he could grip him with both arms.

One, two — *three.*

He lifted with his legs in one big upward thrust and staggered a few paces backwards, falling through the haze with Dieter roaring in pain, then he hit the ground, pressed the switch, and the portal was closed again.

Now he was on his side, struggling to get up. He was aware of people around him and someone shouting, "We've got him, Dan, it's okay, we've got him." But then he realised he was looking at Python Man looking back at him, shocked and disoriented for a moment, flat on the ground like he'd fallen through the same way Trinder had.

Trinder's arm drew back before he could even pull a rational thought together. It was automatic. He smashed the flashlight as hard as he could into Python Guy's face, one, two, three times, and the guy landed a punch that Trinder didn't really feel. That was when the voice said *grab anything, grab the pistol,* and Trinder let it take his hand to the guy's holster and put the weapon to his head.

The shot made his ears ring. It jolted him back to being the Dan Trinder who knew where he was and realised what he'd just done. It was like slamming on the brakes and watching everything on the passenger seat fly into the footwell, except he was looking at a dead man instead of the contents of his rucksack.

"Oh *shit,*" he said.

Bissey put his hand on his shoulder. "Nothing wrong with your reflexes, eh?"

It struck Trinder as an odd thing to say. He'd killed a man and it shocked him to his core, not because he felt guilty about taking a life but because it was so quick and so irreversible. He knew it had changed him. It was already the watershed between the self he knew and a new Dan Trinder. Behind him, Jared was cussing out some guy and telling him if he didn't have a clear shot then it was his job to move his ass and make sure he did.

"I've got to go back." Trinder realised he'd dropped the locator to go for the pistol and got to his feet to search for it in the grass. The order to go and stay gone didn't count now and Chris couldn't give him orders anyway. "I've still got the locator. Pham's going to kill Chris and I'm not leaving Marc even if he wants to go that way."

"It's okay, we've got a fix on both of them," Bissey said kindly, like he was talking to an elderly relative. "We're monitoring. We'll get them out. Are you okay?"

Trinder tried not to look at the dead guy. He still couldn't believe he'd done that. The more he tried to stop the image embedding itself in his memory, the more it set solid and threatened to become the only thing he'd be able to see when he shut his eyes.

"What am I going to do about him?"

"We'll take care of the body," Bissey said. "Go through de-con and see Surgeon Commander Haine. He'll sort you out."

Trinder didn't want to be sorted out. He wanted to carry on fighting because it wasn't over yet and he couldn't sit on his ass. He found the locator and realised Fred had to open a gate for him to get back to Kill Line.

"I don't want to see a medic," he said, feeling in his vest for his screen. "I need to see what's happening."

Then someone called out his name, just *Dan*. He looked around to see Erin jogging towards him. She slowed to a purposeful march and walked straight up to him as if she was breaking up an argument with Bissey.

"I'll see he's okay, Commander," she said. "Come on, Dan, let's go."

Erin tried to steer him away. The screen was focused on Zipper Guy. He couldn't see Chris or Pham.

"I'm not going to waste the doctor's time," he said. "I don't need medication. I just need to get Chris and Marc out."

"No."

"I'm not leaving them."

"Dan, it's someone else's job now. All you'll be doing is adding another man we have to extract." Erin held her vest open so he could see a hip flask. "How about an appointment with Dr C-Two-Aitch-Six-O? He's always cured me."

Trinder looked at the liquor and knew that wouldn't help either. "You know what I've just done?"

"Look, if there was anything useful you could do by going back now, I'd say so and go back with you. Sometimes you just have to sit things out."

"Is that medical advice?" Trinder asked.

Erin took out the hip flask, shook it, and held it to her ear.

"I do believe it is," she said.

If Trinder could have opened the gate there and then, he'd have even defied Erin. But he couldn't. He was dependent on Fred.

He put it at the top of his list of things that needed to change.

* * *

FORGE WOOD, NORTHWEST OF AINATIO PARK RESEARCH CENTRE: 1620 EDT.

"Davis? *Davis!*"

So Python Man's name was Davis. Pham looked around and walked a few paces back up the track, pistol held ready.

"Davis, are you there?"

Chris wondered if he believed the wormhole was real or not. If Python Man's disappearance wasn't down to Marc creeping up to garrotte him with piano wire or whatever guys like him did, there was only one place he could have gone, and Chris had missed it.

Trinder had done it. He'd pulled Dieter through the portal, which was no mean feat. But Davis must have gone through the portal with him.

Pham wheeled around and strode back towards Chris, his pistol now aimed. Chris had always thought a quick death would be a bonus because he'd seen the alternative, but now wasn't a good time. He couldn't forfeit his chance to make Pham pay for what he'd done to Dieter. Even trained cops missed most of the shots they took, though, so with any luck Pham was no different. But he stopped a couple of paces away. He wasn't going to miss from that distance.

"Here's a wild assumption," he said. "Your wormhole's one of Ainatio's military projects, and shipping the bogans out to the promised land is just off-label use. Or a cover story, even, because why would you need spaceships if you've got that?"

He'd almost worked it out, except he was too rational to make the leap to aliens being involved. Chris braced for instant oblivion. But Pham hit him so hard in the side of his face with the pistol that his knees buckled and he heard something crunch inside his head. He wasn't going to give the bastard the satisfaction of going down. He staggered a couple of steps and managed to stay on his feet.

And that was a mistake. If he'd had the sense to fall, he could have reached for the knife in his boot and been ready to drive it home the instant he got up. Well, fine. If Pham was going to try beating answers out of him, he'd need to move in close to do it, and when he did Chris could take him.

"There's a logical explanation," Chris said. His head stopped ringing but his left cheekbone had gone numb and it was hard to speak, like he'd been to the dentist. "But you'll just beat the shit out of me anyway, so why should I bother?"

"Who did Ainatio develop it for?" Pham asked. "Britain? Is that why Gallagher's here and Ainatio's been running a facility in a dead country? I have to hand it to them. Perfect place to hide."

Chris was ashamed he hadn't punched Pham out right away and rammed his pistol up his ass, but the guy who kept his temper would come out ahead. He just wasn't sure it would be him.

He owed Marc, though. "It's nothing to do with the Brits," he said. "They don't even know about it."

"Where does it lead to?"

"An alien planet."

"Who built it?"

"Aliens. See? I knew you'd look at me like that."

"Open it."

"I can't. Trinder closed it behind him."

"Sure he did. Never mind, I can wait. He'll be back for you and Gallagher."

"Don't count on it."

"Oh, I think I can. Especially if Trinder knows you're wounded. You can act the tough guy if I kneecap you, but he's the one who'll cave in to stop me doing your other leg."

"Maybe, but he can't see me now."

"If you bastards are smart enough to build something like this, you're smart enough to monitor what's happening."

"And now you're brave enough to do it without your buddies to hold me down, are you? I'm not Dieter. I'm not an old guy you can safely torture all by yourself, you frigging coward."

Pham just needed a few more prods. Everyone had a button waiting to be pushed, even someone as used to keeping their nerve as him. He was a bad-tempered bastard. Chris could see it in the way he'd pressed his lips into a thin line so often that it looked permanent. He'd work on that.

"A lot of your mates would be dead by now if I'd been willing to send in teenage conscripts and lose most of them," Pham said. "So I don't need morality lessons from a bloody murderer. Least of all one protecting an ASD AI that's killed civilians." Pham took a step closer. He was still holding his gun like he planned to use it. "And you know where that thing is."

Chris shrugged. "Yeah, well out of your reach."

"You know what he's done to Asia, don't you? Of course you do. You know more than I do. You must have some pretty sophisticated tech. The old sat phone call to me was a great gimmick, though."

Chris was relying on Pham going for fists or a knife if he lost his shit and then the gun would just become a blunt object. But maybe he was the type who could hit pause, take a deep breath, and aim properly. Chris kept goading him anyway.

"There's no point in telling you the truth," Chris said. "I want to, just to see your face, but you won't believe it."

Pham kept looking around, a slow sweep from side to side, like he was waiting for the gate to reappear. "No wonder Erskine trashed the FTL gear. You all knew you were giving APS obsolete research and that you had something way better than that."

Chris didn't have a good solution to this. If the python bots had images of the gate operating, or he didn't manage to kill Pham to shut him up, then the secret was out, and if that wasn't a problem now then it would be in the future.

"It's not our technology," Chris said. "The aliens let us borrow it."

"I really should shoot you, but you're my bait."

"Aliens."

"Maybe I'll just slice open an artery."

"Really. Actual aliens."

"Okay, so you're saying you've done a deal with aliens far more advanced than us. So they now have an easy way to get to Earth. Is that your best shot?" Pham was still scanning the area, stalling, waiting for the gate to open again. "May I say that however amateurish that lie is, it'd be typical of the fucking irresponsible way you cowboys play fast and loose with technology."

Chris really needed Pham to make a lunge for him. He was harder to rile than he expected. "If you'd left well alone," Chris said, "we could all have got what we wanted and gone home."

"No, this technology is exactly what we *didn't* want you to have. Look at die-back. It's not that you want to destroy the world, it's that you're so bloody careless about letting psycho ideologues get hold of these things." Pham still had a textbook grip on his gun. He did that half-turn away that usually meant a guy was about to swing a punch, but then he just looked at Chris as if he felt sorry for him. "You know my problem? I always try to explain to the garbage why I've got to dispose of it. You think you're the good guys. You can't see yourself as anything but heroes and champions of freedom. Every terrorist thinks they're a hero too and so do the lighthuggers. You're all the bloody same. Yeah, go on, go and play wagon trains on your little planet until your AI decides you need culling after all. Leave Earth in peace."

"At least we agree on something."

Chris started the mental rehearsal for pulling his knife. The swelling under his eye made it hard to see straight. His face was numb but he probably wouldn't have felt the pain anyway because he was still pumped up on adrenaline.

And now he couldn't wait any longer.

He'd count down from three. He'd drop down, pull the knife, and cannon into Pham as low as he could to knock him off balance and pin him to the ground. It wasn't easy to put a knife in someone while you were on top of them because they'd curl up automatically to protect themselves, but he'd have to make the best of it. He started to count.

Three, two —

He never finished. He saw a flash of something dark that thudded onto the ground a few yards away. For a moment he thought one of the dogs had found a way out of the Caracal.

But it was Davis's body. Chris froze and so did Pham. He could see the hole in Davis's head and it put the brakes on everything for a second or two.

"If that's how you want to play it," Pham said, "I'm game."

Chris went for his knife but something grabbed him and yanked him backwards. He thought he'd been hit or hadn't heard an explosion because it was still in the process of killing him. It didn't just knock him over; it lifted him off his feet. He ended up flat on his back in short grass.

But now he was looking up at the underside of a quadrubot's head, the grey weatherproof gaiter that covered its long neck. He wasn't in Kill Line any more. He was at the exit end of the Caisin gate.

Solomon's camera head peered into his face. "I'll call a medic. Have you any other injuries?"

Chris scrambled to his feet. He was pumped up on adrenaline and vengeance and he wasn't ready to come down. The most he could manage was to try to sound calm and rational. He failed.

"Sol, send me back *now*."

"You literally took a knife to a gun fight," Solomon said. "We had to get you out."

"Pham's still there. He knows about the gate. *Send me back*."

"And he can stay there, Chris. You could have been killed. Dieter's having surgery, Dan's got a few bruises, and I'm about to recover Marc. The evacuation's almost complete. Please let it go."

"*Send me back*. I'm not done yet."

Chris took out his screen to check if the probe was still transmitting. It was, but Marc had control of it. The view was darting around the clearing, showing Pham still in the clearing, scanning the trees like he was expecting an attack.

"This is for your own good, Chris," Solomon said.

When Chris looked around, Ingram was watching with Zakko, Fred, and another teerik with a red crest.

"We took your coordinates from the probe," she said. "We thought your number was up. It probably was."

"You told Sol to pull me out."

"No, I made the call," Solomon said. "Would you excuse me for a moment, please?"

He paused, absolutely still for a second, and then turned away to rear up on his hind legs. The portal haze appeared again and he seemed to step through it and reappear almost immediately. He'd hauled Marc through by his collar. Marc was dumped unceremoniously on the grass but he jumped to his feet right away, still clutching his rifle.

He was damn angry. He rounded on Sol. "I didn't call for extraction. Why the fuck did you do that?"

"You needed it."

"You don't get to make operational decisions for me. Got it? Don't ever do that again." He looked at Chris, then cast around. "Where's Trinder? What's happened to Dieter?"

"Dieter's in surgery," Chris said. "Pham and his guys put a knife in his gut to get answers out of us. Come on, I'm going back."

"I should have dropped the tosser the minute I saw him," Marc said, more to himself than anything. "Forget that poxy knife, Chris. Zakko, can he borrow your rifle, please? And where's that flashlight gadget? Dan had it. We need it pronto."

"I'm sorry," Solomon said. "You're both too valuable to lose. Pham and his associates are of no relevance now to Nomad. They're not worth your lives."

"That's what we *do*, Sol," Marc said. "That's why you think we're so bloody fantastic, because we're ready to die to get the job done. The downside of that is sometimes we actually *do*. Now stop interfering and let us do our jobs. I'm not asking you for your opinion, I'm telling you what I want you to do."

Chris turned to Fred. He was the one with real control, even if he didn't know it. The portal was the teeriks' device and they could stop humans using it any time they liked.

"Fred, we've still got to retrieve Dieter's dogs," Chris said. "One's in the pickup and the rest are in the Caracal. They're his comrades, so they're *our* comrades. Do it. You'd want us to go back for you, wouldn't you?"

"Very well, I'll do as you ask," Fred said.

Marc held his hand out to Zakko for his rifle and passed it to Chris. "How did they manage to jump Dieter?"

"I think they took Girlie."

"What, we need to get her back from Pham? I'll do it."

"No, I'm guessing from what Pham said that they killed her."

"Shit. Okay, I'll check that out." Marc loomed over Solomon. "Sol, I'll probably apologise to you later for losing my rag, but right now, you're top of my bugger-about list. Don't do it again."

"And why did you dump Davis back in the clearing?" Chris asked. "I could have finished Pham if you hadn't pulled that stunt."

"Oh, that was me." Ingram said it with a kind of fake embarrassment, as if someone had asked her who'd painted the lovely picture they were looking at. "I didn't know if he was booby-trapped. Been there, done that, dropped the infected bugger over the side."

Marc looked at her, wary. "Yeah, I remember that bit in class."

"Fred, put me back in my last position," Chris said. He could hear his own voice, same as always, brisk but not panicky, but he was fit to swing for Sol right then. "In the clearing, please, next to the APC's left-hand door if you can."

Marc showed Fred the pickup's location on the aerial images. "And put me back *there*."

"You're risking your life for a dead dog," Ingram said.

Marc shrugged. "I used to do it for a lot less."

If Chris saw Pham, he'd shoot him on sight. No: no, he wouldn't. He'd want to do it so badly that it'd keep him awake at night if he didn't see the bastard go down, but the voice that talked sense to him and told him to keep a lid on things was now saying it wasn't the time for personal vengeance because there was urgent work to do and evacuees to settle. It could wait. The gate could put him right in Pham's face any time he wanted.

Chris ignored the voice. He had to end this now.

He waited for the portal haze to reappear, got comfortable with the rifle, and stepped through. Now he was exactly where he'd asked Fred to put him next to the Caracal. He scoped through as far as he could see on that side of the vehicle without moving out of cover, then looked away for a moment to check the probe feed on his screen, but there was no sign of Pham or Zipper Guy in the immediate area. The Ainatio truck had gone as well.

He'd really expected Pham to still be there. The guy knew him well enough to realise he'd do whatever it took to free Dieter, and he obviously knew Dieter lived for his dogs, so he should have expected Chris to come back.

Perhaps Chris couldn't see Pham or Zipper Guy because they were in the Caracal, though.

He stood back to the side of the door and eased it open, ready to fire, but all that emerged was the smell of dogs and crazed barking from behind the sliding mesh barrier. Now that the adrenaline was ebbing, he had a throbbing headache, he couldn't see so well, his mouth wouldn't do what he wanted it to, and he was dying for a drink, not even a beer, just ice-cold water. He was all in. He got into the driver's seat and slid back the grille in the bulkhead.

"Hey, you're going home," he said. "Your dad's going to be okay. Calm down."

It took some willpower to turn the Caracal around and head straight back into the haze. He wasn't going to forget about Pham. The missed moment would just simmer for years, like the way he felt about his ex-boss and his ex-girlfriend, but it wouldn't be uppermost in his mind all the time. He'd remember it when he needed to.

But Pham didn't seem the type to give up any more than he was. If Pham ran away, it would only be to get a bigger stick and come back to finish the job. APS had the FTL data. They'd make it work for ships, and then they'd be able to reach Opis. It was probably going to happen sooner than anyone wanted to think.

When the APC pushed through the portal, the exit point now emerged at a site just behind the main building. More people had gathered to see what was going on. Bissey was talking to Fred and Zakko. There was no sign of Ingram or any teeriks.

"Hey Zakko." Chris handed back the rifle. He was still furious about Sol and Pham but he wished he hadn't lost it in front of everybody. Still, a guy who never showed his temper was all the more likely to be heeded when he did. "Thanks, buddy. I didn't need to use it after all."

"Do you want me to take the dogs?" Zakko asked.

"Yeah, thanks. I want to wait for Marc."

"Jared says you have to see a medic right away. You look pretty bad."

Chris hated this phase because he knew he'd be wrecked for the rest of the day. There was no point in toughing it out. He'd be no use tomorrow if he didn't get himself sorted out now.

"I still need to wait for Marc," he said.

"He might be hours."

"Then I'll wait for hours." Chris consulted the real-time Nomad site map. It had already changed since he'd looked at it a few hours ago. More structures were in place. "I'll go find my ruck later."

"Jared's still got it."

"So apart from Dieter, everything's going okay."

"It's been kind of hectic, but yeah." Zakko opened the Caracal's door. "But here we are. Somewhere clean and safe at last. You did it, Chris. It's not where any of us thought we'd end up, but it's kind of nice. And thanks for giving me a chance."

"You earned it," Chris said.

If Zakko hadn't driven off then, Chris knew he'd have made an asshole of himself by tearing up. He sat down on the grass, following Marc's progress via his screen, and wished he'd refilled his water bottle. It was the first time he'd ever neglected it. Bissey wandered over and sat down with him.

"Sorry about dumping the body on you," he said. "But we didn't know if he was a plague mule."

"I didn't understand what Ingram meant."

"Before your time, and not your war. A kind of suicide bomber, but infected with a lethal disease instead of explosives or chemicals. Quite a good way to wreck a country. Or an isolated colony." Bissey sounded as if it was an occupational hazard where he'd come from. "We had a spate of them. We couldn't let even one slip through, and Ingram didn't. Ram the boats, blow 'em out of the water, whatever it took. One nearly managed to board the ship and Ingram just leaned over the side and shot him. That's our captain." He smiled. "So we were jumpy about APS slipping die-back in. If you can't shut down the portal, you can just kill off the colony."

Chris thought about that for a while. The uncomfortable feeling that he'd missed something about Pham started to resolve itself.

"Maybe that's what Pham was planning," he said. "If so, I think we stopped him."

"Yes, Dan Trinder's quite the brawler, isn't he?"

"Sorry?"

"He battered Pham's henchman with the locator before he shot him." Bissey said. "He seemed such a quiet chap."

Chris struggled with the idea of Trinder battering anybody. He knew the guy would take a shot when he needed to, but that wasn't the same. "Is he okay?"

"Just a black eye, I think. He went off with your sniper. I understand she had a bottle of vodka for him, so I imagine they had a stiff painkiller or two."

Erin was probably picking up the pieces. As far as Chris knew, it was the first time Trinder had killed anyone, and that was a particularly traumatic way to do it.

"Yeah, Dan's not afraid to get stuck in," Chris said, happy to build Trinder's reputation as a badass. "I'll go see him later."

Chris started wondering about Pham and contamination warfare.

"We're still screening for die-back, yeah?" he asked.

"Absolutely," Bissey said. "Every time a bot passes you. All vehicles sniffed on entry, too. We even tested Trinder again. Marc looks like the last one we'll have to do."

Chris suspected that was wishful thinking. The portal was a massive temptation to make bad decisions and he'd already been seduced by it. He knew he could find Pham any time with the teeriks' probes and reach him wherever he was, and that was just the start of it. Pham was right to see it as a dangerous weapon.

Chris went back to his screen and watched Marc wandering along the dirt track, probably seeing if Betsy could find a trail, but there was still no sign of Pham or Zipper Guy. Bissey sat there in silence, saying nothing. Chris wasn't sure if the guy was keeping him company or if he was keeping an eye on him. He was relieved when Howie turned up. The kid handed him a lunch bag.

"Captain Fonseca says you have to eat this."

Chris studied the contents. There was a bottle of orange soda, a bar of chocolate, and a longlife tuna sandwich from an MRE pack. It had to be from *Cabot*'s supplies. Chris hadn't had tuna for years and he didn't care that it was older than he was.

"Is Marc all right?" Howie asked.

"Sure." Chris gulped down the soda and started on the tuna. Damn, it was good. "I'm watching him right now. Look."

They sat following Marc on the probe feed. It was early evening in Kill Line, but Chris had lost track of Opis's day again. He'd settle for dividing the day into light and dark and rely on his screen's adjusted clock until he got used to it. It was the first time it had sunk in that his Guard-issue wind-up watch would need adapting.

Eventually Marc came to a halt and looked like he'd found something. He went back to the truck and came back with a piece of tarpaulin. Chris distracted Howie because whatever Marc retrieved wasn't going to be pretty.

"Hey, Howie," Chris said, turning the screen face-down for a few minutes. "Marc's going to be on his way back soon. What do you want for dinner tonight? They do pizza here."

Howie looked like he was considering it, but he did glance at the screen as if he knew what Chris was up to. "That'd be nice," he said.

"And fries."

"Yeah. I'd like that."

Chris picked up the screen again and took a look. Marc was moving around the back of the truck like the job was done and there was a dog-sized lump on the flatbed, wrapped in the tarp. Chris wondered if Fred would leave the probe in place for a while so he could use it to check on the situation at Ainatio, but it reminded him why he didn't look back at things he couldn't change and never looked too far ahead.

It was all so deceptively easy. There was no anxious wait for Marc to reach an extraction point or worries that a helo sent to pick him up would be brought down by ground fire. He just sent a request for the portal to be opened at his location and drove the pickup forward like he was adjusting his parking position.

The vehicle nosed through the haze at the exit point as Chris watched. Marc got out to open the offside rear door for Betsy, who jumped down and shadowed him like he needed close protection. Chris and Bissey wandered over to look in the back of the truck. Howie stayed where he was and watched from a distance, so Chris hadn't fooled him one bit.

"It's Girlie," Marc said.

The husky's tail was poking out of the tarp wrapping. Chris was glad Dieter wasn't here to see this.

"So Ingram wasn't joking when she said you went back for a dead dog," Bissey said.

He probably didn't mean it the wrong way, but Chris was still generally riled with the world and didn't want to get deeper into conversations that were only going to remind him how mad he was.

"No, we went back for Dieter's partner," Chris said. "We treat her like any other fallen cop."

"I'll leave you to it, then," Bissey said. Again, it was hard to tell if he was giving Chris some space with Marc or if he'd just been keeping an eye on them for Ingram and now felt the crisis was over. He started walking back towards the admin office. "But call me if you need any assistance."

Marc had that resigned look that said *don't ask.* "Dieter's bound to want to see her, so I'll clean her up as best I can," he said. "But not today. I'll get Mendoza to put her in the infirmary's cold store and I'll do it in the morning."

Chris resisted his reflex reaction to say he'd do it. "I'll help you," he said.

"Medic first." Marc gestured in the direction of the infirmary, a small unit tacked on to the lab block. "I'm getting nag messages from Jared. You look like death warmed up, mate."

"Yeah, okay."

"Get in, then."

Howie went up to Marc and stood in his path. "You could have died."

"But I didn't, did I? Because I promised you I wouldn't."

"Major Trinder bashed a guy and shot him dead. Right at the gate. It can happen to anyone."

Howie didn't seem shocked. Chris didn't want to imagine what a kid must have seen to be able to shrug that off. He'd always assumed that Howie's trauma had been losing his family, but maybe the neighbourhood had turned ugly long before that. Marc gave Chris a look that said he'd deal with this. It was weird to have someone who stepped in and took over the difficult stuff when Chris had always been the one expected to do it.

"Did you see it, then?" Marc asked.

Howie shook his head. "No, but everyone's talking about it."

"He had to do it to stop the bad guys getting in," Chris said. "It's probably upset him a lot, so be nice to him when you see him."

"Yeah, I will," Howie said. "It's not his fault he has to do bad things to save us."

"Now there's some moral philosophy." Marc beamed at him. "So where are we billeted? Is Captain Ingram looking after you okay?"

Howie bent down to make a fuss of Betsy. "She's been busy, so I haven't seen her much, but she says we can have her cabin as long as you play chess with her later, and you can help yourself to her drinks cabinet. But I don't think she's got one. I looked."

"Blimey, I'm getting VIP treatment." Marc consulted his map. "Okay, I'll see you up there. I won't be long. I've got to go through de-con and see the docs. Take Betsy with you. Ingram won't mind."

Chris still had the chocolate bar Fonseca had put in the lunch bag. "Hey, Howie, take this. Don't tell Fonseca I didn't eat it, though."

"Okay. Thanks."

Howie wandered off with the pit bull, examining the chocolate as he went. Chris waited for him to be out of earshot.

"Have you seen Dan yet?" Marc asked.

"No. Apparently Erin marched him off with a bottle of vodka."

"That's probably better therapy than a shrink. Not that we've got one."

"I did my best to be all 'That's Dan for you, he's lethal,' but wow, that's a hard intro to soldiering."

"Tev called it. He said he was harder than he looked." Marc only had to drive sixty yards to the medical unit but they were back on a crowded construction site again. "Y'know, I ought to find out how he's doing."

"Here we go."

"What?"

"It's always going to be there," Chris said. "The gate. Earth's a step away. We're not going to be able to ignore it."

Marc turned the truck and backed up to the doors. "I didn't say I was going to pop over to Fiji for tea and cakes, mate. But FTL comms aren't a secret now. APS has it, we have it, and that's just the start."

"Yeah, but if you call someone, they'll want to know where you are. Explain that."

"I know. I said *find out*. I'm not an idiot."

"Okay. Sorry. Bad day."

"Looks like it. You're going to have to pretty yourself up before Fonseca sees you."

Chris put himself through de-con again with Marc and the truck before Marc unloaded Girlie and carried her through the rear doors. Nobody would dare try to stop him taking a dog into the medical centre, so Chris left him to it and went to find someone to examine his injury.

The centre was a small unit that probably hadn't expected to be this busy so soon. Chris headed for the first face he recognised, which turned out to be Dr Morris. She was talking to one of *Cabot's* officers, a surgeon commander, but she stopped dead when she saw him.

"Oh dear, Chris, that does look painful." She sat him down on a stool at one of the benches. "Commander, I think we're going to need a scan here."

The *Cabot* guy joined in the examination. His name tab said HAINE and Chris estimated he was probably only in his forties, but he looked like he'd spent most of those years drinking, playing some kind of contact sport, and having a lot more fun than Ingrid Morris.

"What happened, Chris?" she asked.

Chris slipped back into Nice Boy mode and submitted to being mauled. "The APS Commissioner for Science and Technology hit me in the face with his sidearm, ma'am. It's kind of numb in places, I can't see or talk properly, and I've got the mother of all headaches."

"Now there's a patient history you don't get every day," Haine said. "And I thought I was just going to be checking stool specimens for the next few years before being replaced by bots."

He ran a scanner over Chris's skull and studied the image on the wall display with Morris before pointing out the detail to him. There was no fracture or eye damage, just a lot of bruising and swelling.

"We'll zap you with the machine to speed up healing," Haine said. "That should improve your vision by the morning, but the loss of sensation will probably take a couple of weeks to resolve. So take extra care when shaving, eating hot foods, and having fisticuffs with armed politicians."

"I'll try, sir."

"You're the chap Jake Mendoza grew a new knee and femur for, aren't you?"

"I am, sir." Chris thought it was nice to be identified as a medical curiosity instead of an ex-con for a change. "When Dieter's out of surgery, can I sit with him?"

"I can't see any reason why not," Haine said. "We're under Nomad sickbay rules now, and I make those up as I go along. You have my permission."

Chris was content to have a few drugs pumped into him and submit to a claustrophobic treatment hood over his head for an hour if it meant being on hand to keep an eye on Dieter. There was nothing he could do for the man, but being there made him feel less helpless. This unit wasn't a hospital and it didn't have a waiting area, though, so when Morris let him leave he sat on the steps outside and counted how many hours he had to kill. He wasn't going to make good decisions at the moment. It was probably better to stay out of everyone's way until he was himself again.

He filled his water bottle from the medical unit's supply, drank his fill, and settled down on the steps again to read his screen. The Earth probe was still active after all. Maybe it was an oversight, or perhaps Ingram or Sol wanted to keep an eye on what was happening within APS, but whatever it was he had to ignore it and try thinking more about a future beyond the next meal and settling scores with Pham.

"Damn, you got to learn to duck," said a voice.

"Hey Jared. Yeah, the asshole got me."

Jared settled down next to him. "You going to sit out here all night?"

"No, when Dieter's out of surgery, I'm going to go sit in his room and wait for him to wake up."

"Mind if I join you?"

"I insist. Damn, I feel like we haven't seen each other for weeks."

"Yeah, we've got a backlog of dumb movies and hot sauce to clear. Make a start in a couple of days, yeah? Those movies aren't going to trash themselves." Jared handed him a bottle of beer beaded with condensation. It was the Kill Line brew. "Now put that damn water down and have a man's drink. You kept your promise to everybody. We're home."

The bottle felt like cold heaven. Chris held it against his forehead for a moment, luxuriating in the almost painful intensity, then touched it to his black eye but it felt too weird. He opened the seal and took a long gulp.

"Oh man, that's good. Thanks. But *we* kept our promise. We did it together. And so did the folks who came with us."

"Okay, here's another promise. Dan says you swore you'd live like normal guys if you made it back alive today."

"I'm already planning a picket fence," Chris said.

Chris hadn't kept his promise to Jamie, but he hadn't abandoned him either. When Dieter was on the mend and Jamie was reburied, maybe life could gradually become the kind of normal most of them had never known. The test would be whether they could look back at Earth and not feel they had to worry about it or wonder what the hell was going on.

Chris was going to try. He just wasn't sure if painting fences could ever stop him imagining Tim Pham in his crosshairs.

PART TWO

11

Yesterday you took the courageous step of venturing into an unknown world with strangers to begin a new life. Today, you'll be asking what happens next, and how we go about turning an emergency evacuation into the pursuit of a happier, safer future.

These are our immediate priorities: adequate food, water, shelter, and medical care for everyone, and the safety and security of our base — our home. These are the tried and tested procedures those of us in uniform have been trained for and have carried out before. There will be endless queues, there will be bots everywhere, there will be constant, annoying noise, and there will be long periods when nobody tells you what's happening and you feel frustrated. Different people clutching screens will keep asking you the same questions about yourselves. Things will go wrong because the meticulous plans first made forty light years away and a century ago have been overtaken by events.

But I ask you to bear with our rules and procedures, not because those of us in uniform follow orders without thinking, but because we know and trust our proven methods.

When you look up at the roof of your tent, or queue to use communal facilities, and wonder if it was really worth leaving your home for this, remember this is where humans were destined to be. We've always had the drive to explore, to find out what's around the corner, to go further each time. We couldn't see over the horizon when we first ventured out from caves, and we couldn't see the far shore of the ocean when we set out in small, fragile boats, but we did it, because this is who we are: explorers who want to see and understand and experience everything the universe can offer us.

Opis will become a human stronghold, the first of many. You're making history. Whatever happens to Earth, if mankind survives, it'll be because you dared to venture out here.

And you're survivors. You're already well organised, strong communities prepared for any eventuality. When this temporary disruption passes, we can begin forging Nomad into the world we want it to be. And while we work towards that goal, my new friends and neighbours — welcome home.

> Message to all personnel and new arrivals in
> Nomad Base, from Captain Bridget Ingram,
> CO *Cabot.*

MAIN BUILDING, NOMAD BASE: 0645 OPIS TIME, THE MORNING AFTER THE EVACUATION.

The best place to start the day in Nomad was the roof of the main building, and never more so than today.

Ingram surveyed her realm with a mug of tea in her hand and geared herself up for the day ahead. Aerial imaging and the real-time map provided more information than human eyes ever could, but some things needed to be seen the old-fashioned way to be fully appreciated.

There was a lot more Nomad than there'd been this time yesterday. A *lot* more.

The base had ballooned from a small outpost to a town. The arc-lit disaster movie scene of the previous night looked more orderly in the less dramatic light of early morning, somewhere between a refugee camp and a building site. Ingram counted more than fifty shelters and facility trailers to the north of the original cluster of base buildings. Between the tent city, some empty cargo containers, and crew giving up their quarters, everybody now had some form of shelter, even if it wasn't much like home.

Nomad had coped. Ingram was pleased. Cramming people into shelters wouldn't have been her choice, but faced with the alternative of abandoning them to their fate, she didn't have another one.

"Bloody excellent effort, the lot of you," she said to herself. "Bravo Zulu, *Cabot.*"

Permanent housing was already being built. On the east side, a construction bot like a giant scrap metal mantis rolled along at a glacial pace in the wake of a floorlaying machine, spray-printing homes. Ingram took a slurp of tea and consulted the real-time map. Data from all Nomad's monitors — bots, satellites, drones, sensor telemetry, direct reports from personnel — merged into a continuously updating picture of the base, and since last night's influx, the map had come into its own. There was too much happening for flesh and blood alone to keep track of it all. This was a job for Solomon, or at least for the AIs he managed.

Ingram was slowly warming to the new houses. They were all slightly different, with wide pitched roofs that looked oddly Tyrolean, a marked contrast to the domes and cubes of the base buildings. When she dragged the timeline slider back and forth, the map showed an overlay of the work scheduled for the coming weeks or reversed what had already been completed. Gardens with fences appeared as features to be added. As she rolled it back, the map showed the previous plan and the notes told her the layout of the original Kill Line had been preserved as far as possible so that neighbours remained neighbours.

Had anyone asked them if they wanted that? It was probably Solomon's decision, and perhaps it was for the best. Familiarity made the huge adjustment easier. People could always move later if they wanted a change.

"Sol, are you around?" Ingram tapped through the overnight reports while she listened for a reply. "Anything iffy, awkward, or embuggering to report?"

"Good morning, Captain. No, there's nothing I can add to Commander Bissey's summary. Unloading cargo fell a little behind schedule, but we caught up."

"I'm glad to see the houses progressing. Did you think up the ground plan?"

"In a way. After Mr Brandt couldn't return to formally declare the town abandoned, I said we'd simply transplanted Kill Line so no closure was necessary. He seemed happy with that. I think it reduces everybody's sense of dislocation."

Solomon could be remarkably sensitive. Sometimes Ingram regretted never knowing Tad Bednarz, because the tools he'd created were possibly even more remarkable than the mission itself. This base, this carefully altered environment, was the bots' world. They'd spent seventy-three years creating it. They'd built and rebuilt themselves, evolved, mined, manufactured, surveyed, analysed pathogens and dangerous life forms, filtered the water, altered the soil, modified native plants, and developed drugs. They'd had their original programming and continuing direction from Ainatio once an FTL comms link was established, but they'd also learned and worked out things for themselves. Ingram wasn't sure whether to worry about that or accept it as a technological miracle.

Either way, she no longer knew about everything going on in her domain and she'd know even less as the settlement expanded. Even on the human front, it wasn't really her domain any longer. Chris and Marc had left her in no doubt about that. She adjusted her binoculars to watch the area allocated to Chris's people.

"I see the transit camp's taking care of itself," she said.

The shelters were the same emergency relief types as everyone else had, tents turned into rigid shelters by water pumped into reactive foam channels. But the residents had set up their own communal cooking and laundry facilities, and now some of the men were fencing off a play area for the children, levelling it carefully with their own tools. She could see a couple of American flags draped over doorways, despite the absence of America. It looked like an army camp.

"They always have, Captain," Solomon said. "If you're worried about people retreating into separate ghettoes here, none of them mixed back on Earth, either. Ainatio, the town, and the camp were three separate populations until Jamie Wickens was killed."

People brought with them whatever they would miss most and gave them comfort and continuity. That was exactly what *Cabot's* crew had done. But the conventions Ingram had expected to honour were long gone. There was no America and no Ainatio, not in any legal sense, and the only rules that counted were the ones that would be made here, right now. Her brief was to hand over control of Nomad to the first civilian settlers, but she'd thought she'd have forty years to prepare for that, not forty hours. She also expected there'd be a colonial administration structure back on Earth to answer to one day.

Their new world was in free fall. The Caisin gate just made it more complicated.

"The anti-aircraft guns parked next to the crop tunnels," she said carefully. "Whose are they?"

"Ainatio's, Captain. Major Trinder brought them."

"I see. And most of the transit camp and Kill Line is either armed, trained to use arms, or both."

"You were aware of that. I think you expressed approval."

"I did."

"If you're nervous, Captain, these are all people with considerable self-discipline and a strong sense of community. You have *Cabot*'s missile launch codes. I don't think you need fear a violent coup."

"I don't. They're not obliged to take orders from me, though. It's a mess, Sol. The company doesn't really exist, I don't have authority over Chris, and I certainly don't have it over the Kill Liners. Other than my responsibility to my crew and a broader duty to protect the civilians here, I don't know who I'm accountable to any longer. And I don't want to use force, even if I could, especially as there are more of them than there are of us." Ingram had to pause and think for a moment whether she meant that. Yes, she did. Her objective was to establish and secure a colony, and she didn't need to be a dictator to achieve that. "We're rescuing allies, not accepting an enemy surrender and disarming them. I'm just looking for voluntary cooperation. By the way, you have the missile codes as well."

Marc Gallagher had summed it up. If they were going to survive, they had to forget where the battle lines were drawn on Earth and make Nomad their nationality. As far as Ingram was concerned, it wasn't about erasing identities or imposing some single bland utopian culture that rode roughshod over deeply-rooted values. It was about pragmatism. She didn't care if people hated each other's guts as long as they didn't get into spats that would sap everyone's resources and morale.

"I think that's eminently practical, Captain," Solomon said. "Committees do have their uses."

Ingram finished her tea and shook out the last drops from the mug. "I could hand over to Doug Brandt now, seeing as he's the only democratically elected civvy here, but that means dumping the hardest military and political decisions on him before he's even unpacked his toothbrush."

"Committee it is, then."

"I prefer *joint command*," Ingram said. "More action, fewer biscuits. Are you moving the teerik ship today?"

"That's the plan. You said you wanted everything inside the perimeter so you could keep an eye on it. I've earmarked a location on the south side and I've made construction of teerik quarters a priority. They can't live in the ship indefinitely. You've seen it for yourself."

Ingram couldn't remember if she'd suggested it or if Jeff had, but the teeriks needed protection and food, and Ingram needed the ship where she could see it. She didn't want to wake up one morning to find an empty parking space and a thank-you note for the food bars.

"Are they happy about that?" she asked. "I haven't seen Fred since last night. Do they get a vote too?"

"Jeff says they're keen to move out of the ship. Nina Curtis's team is devising more interesting meals for them as well. The lure's there."

"Good. Enough to use the portal to bring *Elcano* and the other ships here?"

"Possibly. But not reviving the personnel. We can't feed an extra thousand mouths at the moment."

"I know," Ingram said. "We leave them in cryo until we can. Dan Trinder raised it and I think that's a good plan. We have all personnel where we can protect them, even if they're still on ice, three extra vessels of our own if we have to move everyone without teerik assistance, and, as we pacifists say, a shitload of missiles and other kit if we ever need to ruin someone's day."

"I can't fault Major Trinder's logic. Let's pick the right moment to overcome Turisu's objections."

"She's a stroppy madam. What's her problem?"

"According to Jeff, she's worried that repeated spacefolding is going to show up on someone's sensors."

"Well, we can't tell if she's right, so let's be guided by Fred. Where *are* you, by the way? Network or quadrubot?"

"Network, but I'll be going mobile soon. Captain, are you worried about APS going after our ships?"

"I wouldn't rule it out," Ingram said. "Better safe than sorry."

"Are you monitoring the news from Earth?"

"Haven't had a chance, Sol. You'll keep me posted, I'm sure."

"Do you intend to allow everyone here to have access to the news?"

"I'm still not sure if having a one-way mirror to Earth will do more harm than good, but I don't think censoring what people watch is going to help either." Ingram also wasn't sure it was going to be good for her, or that she'd be good for Earth if she did what her gut was telling her to do. "I agree with Chris on one thing, though. We won't understand the consequences of calling home if we don't know what the risks out here are."

"I'll ask the teeriks to leave the probe relay in place for the time being, then," Solomon said. "But enough people know what I did to APS for news to get around anyway, Earth feed or no Earth feed."

"Are you worried some people are going to find it hard to work with you?" Ingram asked. "Because I'm making it damn clear that if you hadn't taken action, we'd have lost the AI running the mission and left nearly sixteen hundred civilians in the lurch."

"Have you had a meeting I'm not aware of, Captain?"

"I haven't had time for meetings either, Sol."

"I meant that you seem to have consulted Chris and Major Trinder."

"It was just a chance conversation. I'd have included Marc and Doug Brandt, too, but I didn't happen to run into them."

Solomon didn't say anything for a moment. Ingram waited for him to express some misgivings about failing to stamp her authority on the newcomers right away.

"Am I allowed to say I'm glad you've turned out the way I anticipated, Captain?" he said at last.

"Maybe." She hadn't expected that. "Is this going to make me cringe?"

"I was of the opinion that however much you relished your authority in a warship, you were more motivated by outcomes than status and would do whatever seemed most productive, because your sense of innate superiority made you immune to the opinions others held of you."

"Well, thank you, Sol. And I didn't even know you existed, let alone that you were passing sentence on me."

"I'm seldom wrong about humans," Solomon said. "Except Erskine."

"So I've gone from being the undisputed warrior queen to asking for a show of hands because I don't feel threatened by the little people," Ingram said. "I'm glad we had this chat."

"Captain, what's the situation you'd *least* like to find yourself in right now?"

Ingram didn't need to think too hard about that. "Having Erskine walk in and try to run the show. She could make a delicate situation much worse."

"It's going to take at least a year before food production can take the strain. Andy Braithwaite might disagree on the timing, but he'll err on the side of much more caution."

"Is that true, or are we just clearing our yardarm?"

"It's true."

"And for that I'm grateful."

"But I agree that it's best for everyone else if Erskine wakes to a fait accompli, rather than reviving her while you're still trying to work out a stable form of governance."

"We've just carved up control of Nomad between us, haven't we?" Ingram was fascinated by how fast it happened once a suitable emergency appeared to justify it. "Backroom deals."

"Pragmatism," Solomon said. "By the way, your Joint Command colleagues might like to join you to watch the teerik ship take off. It'll be quite a spectacle. And a handy opportunity for a private conversation with them to share your suggestions without firing up the rumour mill."

"Good idea, Sol," Ingram said. "Send them an RPC."

Her earpiece made a soft click — Solomon's equivalent of closing the door behind him to indicate the end of the conversation — and he was gone. She climbed down the ladder and went back to the admin office to make a fresh cup of tea and finish reading the overnights. The whole building seemed to be deserted, at least the parts where people weren't dozing on kip mats or in sleeping bags. All those who were on duty were moving equipment and supplies.

At some point today, she'd have to visit the various camps and be seen to be around and approachable, but in the meantime she'd send out her message. In historical terms, this was an important day for mankind, even if its pioneers were still queueing to use the toilets. She looked through her message to the evacuees again and wondered if it would be better if she delivered it as a speech. But nobody wanted to struggle to hear what a loudspeaker was saying when it was finally their turn to use the lavatory. The text version would do fine. She hit send and went back to reading the overnight reports, struck by the lack of crises beyond a temporary problem with fencing the cattle.

Ten minutes into a fascinating diversion about how the cows were reacting to slightly higher gravity, Logan Haine walked in.

"Bridgers, there's a man asleep in your bunk with a pit bull curled up next to him, a small boy cleaning your cabin, and a chicken on the bookshelf." Haine pulled up a chair and lowered his voice in mock tact. "I'm your doctor. And your friend. If you ever want to talk, I won't judge."

"I'm glad you're in a good mood," she said. "Have you slept yet?"

"No. I'm fine. More to the point, we have a live patient."

"I know. Good work. First real test passed."

"It tested our transfusion capacity, too. We had donor blood, but we used a fair bit of the SanSynth supply as well, so we need to brew up some more soon."

"Is he conscious?"

"Conscious enough to be devastated about his dog, but don't think about asking him questions yet. Chris and Jared sat with him like he was on suicide watch. I treated Chris yesterday, by the way. No fractures."

Haine looked absolutely worn out and also ecstatically happy. He had an instant tribe now, fellow medics from Kill Line, Ainatio, and the transit camp, and they'd saved their first casualty on the table. That was their day made. Ingram could hardly begrudge them the few hours they'd spent huddled together bonding and organising. It had paid off.

"I see you've already formed a scab-lifters' union before the rest of us have even unpacked," she said.

"Well, somebody's got to work out how much to bill you and where the golf course should be," Haine said. "We've got specialists now, you know. Actual *consultants*. We need a golf course to retreat to for the day when we've finished botching your surgery. And a bar, of course, so we can discuss your symptoms in callous and disparaging jargon." Haine got up and prodded the coffee machine into action. "Now tell me about your unorthodox domestic arrangements."

Ingram knew Haine was coming down off a high of hairy-arsed emergency medicine after tedious weeks of treating upset stomachs and insomnia. He missed what he called *proper doctoring*, his case list of gruesome engineering accidents, combat injuries, and alcoholic poisoning. Now he'd seen some action again. He liked it.

"Well, Doc, it's like this," she said. "Mildred likes the sunny spot on the bookcase. Howie likes to help people, but he's only got my cabin to keep him busy because Marc told him not to wander off. Marc... Marc Gallagher deserves better than having to sleep in a warehouse. And I slept on the floor of the dry lab. My back's killing me now, so I expect medical miracles from you, for which you will *not* bill me."

"Oh, I'll do a discount for you. I'm disappointed about Gallagher, though. I hoped you'd snared a proper alpha male, as befits your Boadicean status."

"Howie thinks I'm a retired pirate queen. Marc's been telling him about Calais again. Don't disillusion him." It still felt uncomfortable to be a historic figure from Marc's schooldays. If time travel ever became available, she'd give it a miss. "So what do we have at our disposal now we've annexed Ainatio HQ and Kill Line?"

"Excellent diagnostic and surgical kit and a general family practitioner unit," Haine said. "Plus experienced nurses, a physiotherapist, three general surgeons, one trauma surgeon, lots of biomed types, and two dentists. That's what we need now we've got a normal mixed population. Oh, and there's Kill Line's veterinary practice. They'll come in handy for something, I'm sure. A body's a body."

"No shrinks?" Ingram asked.

"Apparently Bednarz said people didn't need counselling, they needed friends. So there aren't any, not now, at least." Haine pushed a packet of flapjacks across the desk to her. "That was a splendid pep talk you sent around, by the way. Very positive. Uniting, even."

"I'm rather good, aren't I?"

"You are, Bridgers. I'm going to do my rounds now and get to know a few more neighbours. I assume you will too."

"Of course. What kind of host would I be if I didn't pester people when they're queueing for the heads?"

It was a start. If all the interest groups around Nomad meshed as fast as the medics, life would be simple. Ingram cleared the overnights and collected a quad bike to ride over to the tent camp, dodging bots before they had to dodge her. She threaded her way through the Kill Line section and stuck to her meet and greet objective, pausing to introduce herself to any civilian she spotted, and checked the length of queues for meals and showers. They were longer than she'd hoped, but humans didn't operate at the predictable speeds of bots. She'd see about setting up extra facilities.

Just beyond the main path through the tents, someone had set up an open-air classroom to keep the younger children occupied, but there was no point in expecting them to concentrate on a routine class. Ingram watched the noisy excitement as two of the teachers tried to corral the kids into some semblance of attention and get them to watch the display screen they'd unrolled and hung from the side of a tent.

But these children had just landed on an alien world. It was so thrilling and overwhelming that if they couldn't get out and explore it yet, they wanted to know everything about it, all at once, and right *now*. Ingram was debating whether to slide away and leave the staff to it, but once the kids spotted her uniform, they jumped up and crowded around her, asking questions she couldn't answer: were there wild animals, where did the aliens live, and how were people going to put thirteen hours on a clock face? She was caught in a pincer movement by seventy small enemy troops, pinned down and in need of extraction.

Solomon's voice cut through the chatter. "Let me show you." He trotted into the centre of the group. Ingram had to concede that the friendly talking dogbot act always broke the ice. "Would you like to see what the rest of the planet looks like? I can show you everything the satellites can see on the ground. Mrs Alvarez, would you like to connect to the network and watch the screen? You have a link to the sat feed console." He showed her how to zoom in and switch feeds without interfering with the routine survey work. Suddenly the screen was full of alien forests and exotic rock formations, and the kids fell silent, mesmerised.

"You're fantastic," Alvarez said, and patted Solomon on his head. "Thank you."

"I can do even better than that." Solomon was partly addressing the children, who'd met him before, but apparently that was during a night of terror in a bomb shelter. He seemed to have made them forget that association. "In about an hour, you'll be able to see a real alien spaceship fly overhead and land to the right of that light tower." He stood on his hind legs and pointed. Ingram kept forgetting he could do that. It went down a storm with his audience. "It belongs to the teeriks. They're the clever bird aliens we found here. I've never seen it before. So it's going to be very exciting."

The class was satisfied. They sat down in front of the screen to gaze at random images of landscapes around Opis that were as varied as Earth's, and that so far only satellites had explored. Ingram was tempted to stay and watch. Seeing children transfixed by alien snowfields and dense jungles of extraordinary plants turned Project Nomad from a tough mission she was determined to complete into something that put a little more meaning into life. She had a glimpse of mankind's future. It wasn't one she ever thought she'd see.

"Thanks, Sol," she whispered. "That was inspired. You're a natural."

"No, I'm learning. The last time I tried to deal with children, I wasn't very good at it."

"You'll always have a job in the education department."

"Captain, I came out to find you because you should be going to watch the prenu lift off. You've been glad-handing evacuees all morning, which is commendable, but the sooner we have the ship and the Caisin gate generation system on our turf, the better. Time to go. Everyone else is waiting in the rover."

Ingram followed him to the vehicle, feeling like a sixteen-year-old who'd been scolded for staying out too late. Bissey was sitting at the wheel, drumming his fingers on it like a keyboard. Chris, Trinder, and Marc were crammed in the open rear section. Marc was eating something that smelled like a heavenly bacon sandwich. Ingram climbed into the passenger seat and looked back at them.

"Good grief, Chris, that's matured somewhat overnight."

His black eye had ripened spectacularly. There wasn't as much swelling, but the bruise extended halfway up his left temple and down his cheekbone as well. Pham must have put some force behind the blow.

"Accelerated healing," Chris mumbled. "I'm fine."

Solomon managed to squeeze in the back. Marc put his sandwich on the quadrubot's back while he took out a notebook. "You make a good picnic table, Sol. So we're going to watch this thing dig itself out, are we?"

"I understand there'll be a lot of soil displaced," Solomon said. "We need to park well clear."

Bissey drove off out of the base and across the open grassland towards the teerik camp. "Perhaps we should put up the weather roof. Or stand even further back."

"Why does it need to dig in when they've got all that camouflage tech?" Trinder asked.

"Apparently the ship was designed for use against a species that can detect solid objects even if they've got anechoic stealth measures," Bissey said.

"Please don't tell me there are bat aliens now."

"If form follows function, then I imagine they're out there somewhere, Major."

Fred was already waiting to direct them to a safe observation point when they reached the site. His feathers looked ruffled, quite literally, and Ingram guessed that there'd been more arguments with his daughter.

"Everything okay, Fred?" she asked.

"The commune's nervous, that's all," he said. "We haven't carried out these extractions on our own before. And never in real operational circumstances."

"But you know which button to press."

"Of course. Excuse me. I have checks to make."

Fred scuttled away through the scrubby bushes and disappeared. Ingram turned in her seat and draped her arm over the back as casually as she could.

"I think we'll all be happier once they've moved in next door," she said. "And we need to see what this thing can do in combat."

Marc opened his pocket notebook and held it out to her so she could see what he'd written. He'd put a line through it.

"First item crossed off my shopping list," he said. "Stop the teeriks doing a runner and keep an eye on the assets."

Chris salvaged a scrap of bacon from Marc's sandwich. "Good place for a meeting," he said. "Nobody sees us in a huddle and thinks there's some drama going on. We should have more meetings at picnics."

Chris said things so innocently that Ingram found it hard to tell whether he was being sarcastic or genuine. He was harder to read than Marc. Trinder was somewhere between them on the transparency scale. He seemed to have had a rapid metamorphosis from corporate security to keeping pace with special forces, so perhaps he wasn't sure himself who the real Trinder was.

"Can I get something icky out of the way first?" Trinder asked. "We know zip about teerik biology except what the reverse-engineered rations told us. Is anyone going to do an autopsy on Caisin? The more we know, the more we can take better care of them. And the more we know their vulnerabilities."

"Gents." Ingram knew they were right but this wasn't the time. "I have no intention of getting into such a sensitive area with the teeriks at this stage of the game. You all know how we'd react if someone suggested we dissect our gran because she might as well be some use. There'll be other opportunities to learn."

"If we cremate her, who'll know?"

"I will. And so will the scab-lifter who does the PM, and things never remain a secret forever. But we're interring the body, so that's a non-starter anyway."

"Okay." Trinder didn't look chastened. "Sorry I asked."

Ingram hadn't planned to lay down the law like that when she was about to negotiate a tricky agreement. "Okay, I wanted to discuss how we're going to operate so we get off on the right foot. Cultural minefields apart, I'm not going to try to impose my rules on you. You've got your own way of doing things and I don't think it's dissimilar to ours. Let's look at how we can best work jointly when we need to. I also wanted to talk about *Elcano*."

"I've got a list too," Chris said.

"I thought you might."

Ingram thought he was just picking bits from Marc's snack in the jokey way people did when they were winding up a friend, but he really was salvaging it like a hungry man who'd learned not to waste crumbs. "You're not going to revive the passengers yet, are you?"

"You know we can't," Ingram said. "Food situation."

"Erskine situation, too."

"Yes, I thought about that."

"So we're going to ask Fred to move all the ships."

"Yes."

Chris pressed on with his shopping list. "Do you think the teeriks could upgrade them as well? We're kind of vulnerable if everyone else can outrun us."

Bissey looked around. "That was my worry, too, ma'am, if you recall. We *really* don't know what's out there now."

"Well, we know some of them can afford to have teeriks designing warships," Chris said. "And that Fred hasn't told us anything tactically useful about his previous employers. Which might mean he's still loyal to them, or at least too scared, or just that it's his teerik habit of not telling anyone his trade secrets. Which means he won't tell anyone else about ours."

"That sounds like a plan," Ingram said. "I'll see Fred as soon as he's available."

"We do need to get some answers out of him, though," Marc said. "I know it's only been a couple of days since we found out about the

Caisin gate, but Jeff and others have been talking to the teeriks for weeks and the lack of intel worries me. If they want protection, we need to know what we're protecting them from."

Trinder was studying his palms as if he'd blistered his hands putting up tents. He still had that same faraway look on his face that he'd had after he shot Pham's henchman. "And the gate location device," he said. "Fred seems to be developing new ways to open and route gateways, and we don't need to be able to do the big math to know those flashlights are probably going to become critical in securing the system. We need more of them, but with limited access. Senior uniform personnel only."

Marc glanced at Bissey, who still had his back to him. "No offence, Commander, but we'd be a bit nervous about giving one to anybody in your crew who's come from an APS state."

That was a step too far onto Ingram's turf. "I like to think I can trust my team."

"Okay, reverse the situation," Marc said. "If you heard that APS had nuked everywhere south of Watford, and you had the wherewithal to pay them an unfriendly visit, how would you react? I know what I'd do. And don't say you're better than that."

Ingram bristled. "How about Dr Kim, then? We weren't expecting to find an APS spy in your luggage. Should we confine her?"

"No, she's got every reason to avoid APS." Marc took it as a straight question, possibly to deny her the satisfaction of scoring a point. "She lied to her boss for us. She copped the flak from Pham when Abbie Vincent sold us out."

"Anything else on your list, then?"

"News and comms access," Chris said. "Total minefield."

"Okay, I'd like to say no media until everyone's comfortably settled and past the stage where depressing or enraging news starts a fight," Ingram said. "But we need something to keep people occupied, and I can't keep a lid on it forever. If I lie and it all comes out, you know what effect that has on trust and morale. But direct comms... yes, that needs to remain restricted while we work things out."

"Well, your crew, your call," Chris said. "But I don't think it'll help matters. It also means restricting access to the flashlights. Locators. Whatever we're going to call them. So can we answer that question now? It got lost earlier. Who gets one?"

"Assuming Fred can make more, let's say you three plus me and our Two-ICs. Which makes six in all, as Marc doesn't have a deputy." It was a good opportunity for Ingram to jump to the main point of the discussion. "While we're on the topic, how do we manage shared command? Let's agree we share security duties but I can't give your people orders and you can't give orders to mine. Apparently yours wouldn't take any notice of me anyway. And if we have any problems, we get them sorted in a joint meeting."

Marc nodded. "Sounds fair. Although I prefer dispute resolution by arm-wrestling. But there's no definition of areas of responsibility. The high water mark doesn't help us much here."

"If you substitute air or space for sea, it does."

"Fair enough. You cover anything not on dry ground or under it." Marc looked amused. "See? We could have negotiated the surrender of Scotland in no time."

"Doug still runs Kill Line," Chris said, clearly determined to stick to business. "He's the only elected guy here. So he's in the loop too, if it's not just us talking military shop."

"Do they still want to call it Kill Line?" Ingram asked. "I was hoping for something less *noir*. Herdsman's Brook. Fox Hill. Dun Runnin'."

"I think the *noir*'s stuck," Trinder said. "We like *noir*."

"Doug gets a seat on the board. Yes?" Chris just wasn't giving up. "There has to be a civilian voice from the start or else we'll get too comfortable running the place."

"Okay, deal," Ingram said. "And for what it's worth, I would have stuck to the plan to have the civvies take over right away if it hadn't meant dumping some hard decisions on them."

"Like what we do about the gate in the longer term," Trinder said.

"Among other things."

"And if we deliberately delay reviving the families in *Elcano* just to keep Erskine out of the way," Marc said. "All those kids."

"Then we'd better get our act together on governance and make sure everything's immune to disruption before it's time to wake them up, hadn't we?" Ingram said. "And you know it's as much about the food situation as it is the effect of Erskine's presence."

"I'll leave you to take a sounding from Alex on that."

"Where does Alex fit in?" Chris asked. "He's the only voice the Ainatio civilians have."

Ingram had forgotten about him. "Fine, Alex has a seat too."

"And the teeriks?"

"I think you'll find they believe we were here first," Ingram said. "So I don't know if they expect to be formally involved in decision-making."

"If what Fred's told us is true, they've never been allowed to make decisions about anything," Marc said. "But they own the transport system. So we might as well play nice."

"Very well, seven seats," Ingram said. "Which makes them heavily over-represented."

"But enough to be worth having sandwiches at the meetings, and an odd number for a casting vote if need be. Done."

If that was their meeting, it appeared to be over. Marc smiled to himself and fished another packet out his pocket to hand to Chris. When Chris peeled it open, it looked like a soft sponge cake of some kind. He really was having trouble chewing anything harder. Ingram felt sorry for him.

"Don't fall for it, Captain," Marc said. "I saw that look."

Ingram ignored him. "Chris, come and eat in the mess. We can get you a proper meal. Risotto, or fish and mashed potatoes or something. You can't live on cake."

"Thank you, ma'am," Chris said. "That's very kind."

Marc shook his head. "You're a soft touch, Captain."

"Obviously," Ingram said. "Or I wouldn't have let you put a pit bull in my bunk."

For a moment, there was almost a spark of comradeship, the kind of wardroom banter Ingram was used to. But then they lapsed into silence and went back to waiting. None of them were the type for small talk, at least not in front of her.

Solomon stood completely motionless like a gun dog, probably listening to voice traffic and monitoring frequencies. Ingram was on the point of nodding off after a mostly sleepless night when she felt a faint vibration rising under her seat. She opened her eyes and looked towards the scrubby area of bushes and small trees where she'd first followed the trail through the undergrowth to get to the ship's access shaft.

Nobody said a word. They all slid slowly out of the rover and stood a little way apart, scanning the ground for a clue to where the ship would emerge.

The vibration was as distinctive as an earthquake, a sensation Ingram would never confuse with anything else. Now she thought she could hear it. It was more a feeling in the back of her throat, a very low frequency, but then it reached the threshold of her hearing.

"I think this is it, chaps," she said. "Buckle up."

The ship hadn't been where she estimated at all. She'd guessed how big it was and how far it had embedded itself by counting her paces. Much further to the right, small plants began to shiver, leaves rustling. The ground domed. Her eyes followed the shallow curve and she finally worked out where the ship would break the surface. A spray of soil shot into the air, not a huge amount, but whatever mechanism lifted the frigate was now either digging up through the layer of dirt or forcing itself out with the downward thrust of its drive.

When the hull broke through, the spray of soil became a waterfall of particles draining off the curves. Everyone took a few steps back. Then the noise ramped up. Prenu Nar P12 lifted clear of the ground and revealed her full form.

She was gunmetal grey and all featureless curves, her hatches and openings flush with the surface and almost invisible. There were no identification marks at all. The ship reminded Ingram of an ancient car, one giant central teardrop flanked by two smaller ones like tightly-folded wings, a stylised swallow frozen in mid-dive.

"Holy *shit*." Trinder was wide-eyed. "You couldn't make it up."

Whatever he said after that was lost in the roar of the drive. Nar P12 shrugged off a small hill of soil, raining it on the ground below. Now that Ingram could see the ship's underbelly, she noticed grooves radiating from the waist and wondered if they were part of the mechanism that dug the vessel into the ground. She could imagine the ship working her way into the soil like a flatfish burying itself in a sandy seabed. Nar P12 hung fifty feet in the air for a few moments before slowly edging forward and accelerating towards the base, peppering the rover with soil and small stones as she passed almost overhead.

Ingram knew they all had one thought. They had to get to grips with the prenu, examine her, and work out how they could make the interior a better fit for a human and teerik crew. The ship was too good to treat as a camper.

The sound faded as Nar P12 vanished. Ingram hoped the Kill Line kids had looked up at the right moment.

"A flying land submarine," Marc said. "What a time to be alive."

Ingram wondered when she'd reach revelation overload and see these things as normal for Opis. That time wasn't yet. She was going back to the base to crack a bottle of Andy Braithwaite's finest vintage Neuron Annihilator and drink a toast to teerik engineering.

"Imagine a fleet of those," she said.

Ingram hadn't known it until now, but this was what she'd been waiting for all her life, and for all the wrong reasons.

* * *

NOMAD BASE CEMETERY, TEERIK COMPOUND: 0945, LOCAL HUMAN TIME, SIX DAYS AFTER THE GREAT ARRIVAL.

The humans gave Caisin a very good *send-off.*

That was what Chief Jeff called it, and while Hredt knew it was slang, it spoke of wonderful journeys and exploring interesting new places, so much more uplifting than *funeral* and *farewell*. It sounded magnificently free.

On a warm, sunny morning in the fresh air, standing in open grassland that had been marked as Nomad Base's burial ground, it didn't seem so sad. Ingram gave a moving speech about Caisin's genius, and how mankind was indebted to her because her invention had saved lives and given generations to come a future beyond Earth. The captain always seemed to have the right words that made people listen. Caisin received the rites reserved for the leader of a nation, with *Cabot's* crew in formal uniform bearing the coffin, and a grave marked by an engraved block with a simple and mostly honest inscription:

CAISIN, LEARNED MOTHER OF THE ANSITU COMMUNE
INVENTOR OF THE CAISIN GATE
FRIEND AND ALLY.

"I don't think she saw herself as the humans' ally," Cosqui said. "And Ingram hardly knew her. But at least it's more dignified than a Kugin eulogy listing the casualty numbers inflicted on the enemy."

Jeff, looking smart in a proper dark blue cap, jacket, and trousers, hadn't picked up a word of Kugal and seemed to be worried that the incomprehensible conversation meant something was wrong.

"Would Caisin have approved of all this, Fred?" he asked.

"Yes, but she'd make a show of grumbling about it."

Hredt looked around to see who else had arrived. There was Dan Trinder and Alex Gorko, and Chris Montello carrying a ceramic jar, but he couldn't see Marc, the first human he'd brought back through the portal. That was a shame. Marc was the only person who'd ever silenced Turisu, and he hadn't had to say a word. He just *looked*.

Hredt could also see Solomon in his red quadrubot form, talking to the holy man with the white collar. "And now we have another ceremony."

"You don't have to stay for it," Jeff said.

"But we must. As you do for us, we do for you."

"Okay, just ignore any tense moments. Funerals bring out the worst in people."

Hredt was grateful for what he'd learned to call the *heads-up*. Jeff nodded in the direction of the large gathering of scientists and technicians Ingram referred to as Ainatio, as if they were a single colonial organism. On the other side was a mixed group of *Cabot*'s crew, the soldiers in black, and the townspeople. The Ainatio group looked uncomfortable, shooting glances at a woman standing on her own on the edge of the crowd.

"This is a memorial for one of the engineers who designed *Cabot*," Jeff whispered. "They're scattering his ashes. That's why Chris has the funeral urn."

Chris walked out of the group of soldiers, looking equally uncomfortable. He turned to face the crowd and hesitated for a moment.

"I promised someone I'd bring Derek Levine's ashes to Opis," he said. "He was one of the engineers who designed *Cabot*. He spent forty-five years believing his team made a mistake that cost the crew their lives, but when he was dying, Solomon defied the company edict and showed him the secret video feed from Nomad." Chris stopped. Hredt thought he was finding it too emotional and had paused to compose himself. "Actually, I didn't know the guy," he said. "I think it's better if the person who asked me to do this and stayed at his bedside in his final days is the proper person to scatter them. Dr Kim, would you mind? I think he'd have liked you to do the honours."

"Oh boy... " Jeff murmured.

The woman who'd been standing apart seemed surprised and took a moment to step forward. Chris stood in that very upright posture the soldiers here adopted when the flags were raised at the base and handed her the ceramic jar. She checked the wind direction discreetly with her hand, then faced the gathering. Hredt was fascinated.

"Derek Levine was a truly great engineer and he deserved better than having so much of his life blighted by a big lie," she said. "He deserved to come on the mission, too, and we're here because he did his job right. So whatever you believe in, even if it's nothing, science says Derek Levine is part of Opis now, and always will be."

She opened the jar and shook the ashes into the air. The breeze took the fine pale dust and carried the plume a respectable distance before the rest was swept up into the sky.

"You did it, Derek," she said. "Rest in peace, sir."

Hredt was enthralled. He thought it was an even more wonderful way to be commemorated than Caisin's funeral, and he wished he'd asked for cremation instead. He hadn't realised how much like flying it would be. She would have enjoyed that.

Dr Kim walked away with the empty urn and nodded at Chris as she passed. The Ainatio people seemed more embarrassed than hostile, looking down or shuffling their feet, and then everyone began drifting away and heading back to the base.

"Are they angry with her?" Hredt asked. "Did Chris do something wrong?"

Jeff shrugged. "If they're angry, it's because she reminded them Levine was one of their own, but she was the one who was there for him when it mattered."

"Who is she?" Hredt asked.

"Dr Annis Kim. She's a propulsion expert. And an APS agent. An enemy spy."

"Oh my. You treat her very kindly for an enemy."

"That's because you can trust her more than some of the people on your own side," Jeff said, and didn't explain. He checked his screen. "The next ceremony isn't until this afternoon, but you're welcome to attend that too. They're reburying one of Chris's troops who was killed recently. They didn't want to leave him in a cemetery that was being abandoned." Jeff lowered his voice. He was looking at the departing crowd, which had now separated enough for them to see the holy man with the white collar talking to Chris, nodding and patting his shoulder as if they'd agreed on something. "Chris never leaves anyone behind, ever, and some folks treat it as a bit of a joke

— not in a nasty way, but they don't understand how important it is to people like us. We bring our comrades home, dead or alive. It's a kind of faith. It keeps us going."

"Oh, we understand that," Hredt said. "We know how it feels to be abandoned by other teeriks. We have a duty to our own."

"Exactly. Well, now that you're living on the base, you'll hear all kinds of things, because humans gossip. You know Chris and Marc took a risk and went back for Dieter's dead dog. That's because the dog was his comrade. It worked with him and faced the same dangers. So even a dog gets repatriated."

"Why is refusing to abandon the dog a joke? It's very sad."

"Humans can be weird, Fred. Come on, let's head back."

Hredt looked around to call the others to join them in the rover, but they were already walking back to the compound. It was the first time they'd been able to wander freely in the open air without worrying what might be lying in wait for them since before they'd left Deku. He'd let them enjoy it. He hopped onto the back of the vehicle.

"So you're having a chat with the Captain now," Jeff said as he drove off. "You know why things are moving so fast? No bureaucrats. If Earth had an instant link, they'd have a dozen committees now that'd sit for years and we wouldn't be allowed to talk to you because the experts would take over. We'd never get anything done."

"But you *are* the experts now." Hredt imagined human bureaucrats as Jattan clients, always thinking they could improve a design themselves and then complaining when their tinkering didn't work. "And even if they could contact you, what could they do about it if you ignored them?"

"You're a rebel, Fred. I like that."

"Look how well we understand each other, how we cooperate. No scientist could do any better."

"I'm an ordinary bloke," Jeff said. "Not an officer. No fancy education, no money, no connections. It's pure luck that human and teerik paths crossed and I happened to be there when they did. I'm glad I got the chance."

"Chief Jeff, we're doers and makers, you and I. We understand the same things. Bureaucrats never could."

Jeff winked at him and parked by the flagpoles to let him jump off. "Good luck with the boss."

Hredt walked into the building feeling like an emperor. Everything he did now was his decision, a new lease of life for him and for the commune too. They needed the purpose that the alliance with the humans could give them. They'd been lost and terrified for the first time in their lives when they landed here — scared of what the Kugin would do if they caught them, scared of not having the Kugin around to tell them what to do, scared of trying to survive without even knowing how to find their own food — but now they could learn to think for themselves and do something they found meaningful, whatever that turned out to be. It was the Kugin who needed to worry. Without teerik technology to wage war and keep control of their colonies, they'd have struggled. History would have been very different. Caisin could have brought them down if the rest of the communes had kept their word simply by giving other empires the technological edge that the Kugin kept to themselves. But the opportunity had passed.

It wasn't too late to turn the humans into a power that could keep the Kugin in line, though.

Ingram came down to the lobby to meet him. She'd changed into her usual blue shirt and darker blue trousers, a softer and more crumpled material than the formal uniform. Clothes changed humans into different people. Hredt wondered which was the real Ingram, the captain in her gold-decorated uniform, an icon of authority who expected obedience, or the woman he was with now, relaxed and treating him like an old friend.

"Fred, thanks for coming," she said. "I hope everything was okay today."

"We appreciated it very much, Captain." He followed her up the stairs and along a corridor. The building was so crowded that every room he passed had cushions or sleeping mats on the floor, even the small laboratory. "It was comforting. Thank you. It was very generous of all of you to put so much effort into the ceremony when you're already working hard."

"You're welcome. These things matter."

"We wouldn't want to take resources from the new arrivals. It must be hard for them."

"We're running at maximum capacity, but we can keep that up for a while," Ingram said. "We could do with more bots, but that means we have to take some offline to build more of themselves, so there's no easy solution."

She led him into the room with her name on the door. If this was her office, it was very small for a warship's captain. A Kugin commander would have refused to work in such a humble space. "But we're not starving, and that's what matters," she said. "Nina Curtis is bringing her team's latest creations for you in a moment. You've got a personal chef. Even I don't have one of those."

Ingram smiled, so she was joking. Jokes were still an uncertain area for Hredt. He settled down on a floor cushion — humans were thoughtful — and wondered whether to tell her what he could do for Nomad or wait for her to ask him.

"How's Caisin's egg?" she asked. "Forgive me if I'm being rude. I don't know what's considered polite."

Hredt couldn't recall ever being offended by a question. "We've seen movement through the shell," he said. "We didn't expect the chick to develop. Caisin was very ill."

Ingram had that same look on her face that Hredt had often seen on Jeff's. It said she didn't understand something but didn't know how to ask, or perhaps whether to ask at all. Hredt tried to guess.

"It's common to produce an egg near the end of life," he said. "Although many don't survive."

There was no sign of comprehension on Ingram's face. "Oh. Can we help? We don't know much about you, except what you can eat, but we have doctors who treat nonhuman species. They're willing to learn."

That wasn't the unspoken question, then. Hredt wanted to help. "The child's important to us. It'll preserve much of Caisin's knowledge."

Ingram looked puzzled. "Do you mean that you have genetic memory?"

"Yes."

"What kind of things do you remember?"

"How to find places and do things. Locations. Language. Skills. Not all the small detail, but general ability and understanding. Detail would be a problem, I think. If you had all your ancestors' exact memories, how would you cope? How would you know who you were? How would your mind find room for it all? Our brains seem to filter what they need to keep in the new generation."

"I've always wondered that." Ingram was alert and interested. Perhaps that was what she'd wanted to ask. "We don't have that kind of memory, just instinct. But I see it in movies and I wonder how it could work when the child would inherit memory from both parents, and both their parents, and... well, all the way back."

"This is true," Hredt said. "Caisin's child will only have her accumulated memories. There was no other parent."

Ingram opened her mouth slightly and did a slow nod. "Parthenogenesis."

Hredt had to stop and consult the new database Jeff had given him. He hadn't had time to look at all of it. "Yes," he said. "Yes, that's exactly it. It happens to old teerik mothers."

"We have species on Earth that can do that. Not us, though."

"That was what you really wanted to ask. I can tell."

Ingram's face flushed. Between their gestures, movements, and the way they changed colour, humans didn't seem able to disguise their intent very well.

"Actually, yes," she said. "But asking who fathered a child is regarded as extremely rude by most humans."

"Kugin would ask."

"Would we like the Kugin, Fred?"

"I don't think so."

"You say very little about them, although I haven't formed a good impression of them so far."

"They're barbarians. No rules or graces. Loud and violent."

"Fred, if we ever had problems with the Kugin, would you tell us what we needed to know to defend ourselves?"

"Oh yes." Sometimes Hredt thought he knew humans well because he'd learned their language, and then he'd realise he didn't. "We're used to revealing very little. That's how we protect ourselves. I'll try to be more helpful. You're the first allies we've ever had and it'll take us time to get used to that."

"Understood." Ingram smiled. Sometimes the smile went all the way up to her eyes and sometimes it didn't, like now. "Are you happy with your new home? I know it's still quite basic, but we'll make it more cosy later. If you like cosy, that is."

"Oh, thank you, it's very good," Hredt said. "We like the extra space. We won't argue so much now. The prenu made life hard."

"The ship's on my list of things to discuss, actually. You know we'd like to learn to operate her. Some of my crew are experienced pilots."

"Chief Jeff did mention that. Commander Searle."

"Yes, Brad's very keen."

"You can fight and we can't. It makes sense for us to help you make use of... *her.*"

"May I ask you another favour, Fred?"

Being asked for favours was a new experience. Hredt was used to demands. He'd stopped worrying that humans might be too gentle to survive in this sector after seeing Chris, Marc, and Major Trinder keen to do violence to their enemies, but human courtesy still set them apart from other species. They let enemy spies live. Working out when he'd gone too far was going to be a challenge.

"Of course," he said.

"We still have three ships out there. *Elcano* has more than one thousand people in cryosuspension, including two hundred and forty-nine children. All three ships are armed with nuclear missiles and other weapons that we need." Ingram took a breath as if she was moving on to something sensitive. "We can't revive anyone until our food production's stable, but we do need to move the ship closer so we can access it quickly if there are any problems. And we can never be sure that our enemies on Earth wouldn't be able to attack the remaining ships, even now. Is there any way you could use the gate to bring them all here? We'd be very grateful."

Hredt couldn't see any problem. "We know exactly where *Shackleton* and *Eriksson* are, and if Solomon can provide coordinates for *Elcano*, we can do it. Do you want it to happen now?"

Ingram leaned forward in her chair, elbows on her knees, hands folded loosely together. "This really is very generous of you. Thank you. If you could do it soon — if it won't cause you any problems — we'd all feel a lot safer."

"What's good for you is good for us," he said. "And you came to our aid. We remember who our friends are. And so will our children. We'll do it right away."

"Thank you. We won't let you down, Fred. We *will* protect you, with all the means at our disposal."

Hredt believed that. These last few days, he'd seen how humans refused to abandon anyone, even a dead animal, and now they wanted to retrieve their comrades in *Elcano*. He was sure they'd do the same for teeriks.

"We need to do this from the ship, so if Commander Searle would like to come with me, he can explore the prenu," Hredt said. "He can also tell us what needs to be upgraded in your ships. You need spacefolding vessels out here, even if you only intend to use them as defensive weapons platforms, and you need camouflage right away. We should also see if we can improve your personal weapons."

Ingram didn't seem to be expecting that. "That's incredibly generous, Fred. Thank you."

"This is what we do. We make good ships. Well, we make them with the assistance of mechanicals and craftsmen, but we design the best warships and weapons in this sector. Now we'll do it for people who *deserve* them."

It had turned into a strange day of contrasts. Only hours ago, Hredt had been preoccupied with the fate of the dead. Now he was changing the future for the living. He was helping to build a human empire, even if the humans hadn't thought that far ahead yet, and while Caisin had dreamed of complete independence, helping humans didn't make teeriks their servants. He'd learn from them. He'd learn how to be as fearless and free-spirited as they were, ready to cross the galaxy in woefully underpowered little ships and tackle the unknown.

It was just a pity that he'd only learned to fly and take risks in the final years of his life. Sometimes that thought saddened him. But he could make up for it in the time he had left.

Brad Searle was waiting outside the building with one of the rovers. Nina sat in the back with a large white box on her lap, and Hredt could already smell what was in it.

"Have you got time to test some new food for me, Hredt?" She rattled the box. "I've got enough for the whole commune to try."

Hredt peered inside. It looked like small pies and smelled interesting. This was another thing teeriks needed to learn from humans. They had to be able to feed themselves.

"That smells wonderful," he said. "Are you coming to visit the commune? My grandsons will be excited."

Nina handed him one of the pies. "I'd love to. And the invitation still stands to come and look around our laboratory."

Hredt pecked at the pastry. It wasn't like the bars at all. It was salty and oily, much closer to roast meat. "This is very good. We must seem completely helpless to you. We can't even feed ourselves."

"Hredt, you'd be surprised how many humans can't cook a meal and don't know where their food comes from."

"I lived on takeout pizza for years," Searle said. "Never did me any harm."

It wasn't easy to eat in the back of a moving vehicle, but Hredt couldn't wait. Humans were even better cooks than the Kugin.

"You do eat meat, don't you?" Nina asked.

"Yes, we enjoy it when we're given it," Hredt said. "I don't miss the Kugin, but I miss their roasts."

"I've been going through the bio surveys the bots did years ago. From the biochemical analysis, there seem to be some native species here that you could eat. Animal species, I mean."

"I think you might be more advanced in some sciences than we are, Nina."

"That's fine. You do the spacefolding and we'll make dinner. Everybody's happy."

Searle drove around the perimeter of the base to avoid the construction work. "Fred, if you design ships and systems, you know a lot about everyone else's offensive capability and weak points, including the Kugin and Jattans. If I were them, I'd be more worried about the all the intel you've got than losing a ship."

Hredt hadn't seen it that way before. Intelligence was simply another set of data like the tensile strength of a metal, something he had to factor into his calculations, and the teerik way of keeping everything to themselves was about their own survival, not anyone else's.

"Intelligence ages fast." Hredt finished the pastry and hoped there'd be some left for him after the commune got their claws on the box. "We were always getting updates on enemy technology and having to change specifications."

"The Kugin have spies, then."

"*Everybody* has spies. We could have brought the Kugin down, I suppose. But we only thought of denying them our skills. And we wouldn't have known who to pass the information to."

"I hope I haven't taught you bad habits," Searle said. "Did you *want* to topple the Kugin empire?"

"We just wanted to escape. But removing the Kugin would be good. Although some other empire would take their place, I suppose."

"Yeah, regime change isn't all it's cracked up to be."

Turisu and the boys were outside the new house, examining the churned ground with Cosqui and still looking a little lost. The ship hadn't buried itself yet and it dominated the compound. It threw a shadow across the house. It was hard to believe such a large hull felt so cramped inside. Searle parked the rover and stared up at the ship with a smile on his face as if he'd seen an old friend.

Turisu met Hredt with an accusing stare. Hredt put his faith in food to distract everyone and nudged Nina forward so she could waft the fragrance of those lovely pies.

"We're going to do some work in the command centre," he announced, gesturing towards the ship. If he said it firmly enough, Turisu would accept it, especially if he didn't tell her exactly what the work was. "Turisu, this is Commander Searle, who understands ship systems, and this is Nina, who develops the special foods for us. Look what she's brought today. Nina, Commander Searle — this is my daughter, Turisu, and she speaks English. These are her sons, my grandsons. Demli and Runal."

Hredt thought he'd cornered Turisu rather well. She raised her red crest as an involuntary warning to Nina, but it didn't have any effect on a human. Nina just smiled and tilted the box so the boys could see the contents. They made the decision for their mother. By now, Cosqui and the others had come to see what was happening.

"We like your food," Runal said. "Can we try it now? Please?"

"Yes, and I want to hear exactly what you think of it." Nina put the box down for a moment and wrapped some slices. "Hredt, take this with you. Now, who'd like to practice their English as well?"

Hredt gestured to Cosqui and they slipped away to the ship. Searle was already examining the underside of the hull, exposed above soil for the first time in months.

"I can't wait to see it dig itself in," he said. "I've been trying to visualise how that works. Where's Sol?"

"Here." The quadrubot emerged from between the landing struts. "I'm not really equipped for ladders. Is there a level route to get to the command centre? It's probably easier for me to enter your network. I'll have to input the data for you anyway."

Hredt avoided Cosqui's dubious look. If an emanation like Solomon wanted to find a way into the system, he'd have done so by now. The damage he'd inflicted on Earth in the last few days was proof. This time, though, he was asking permission as diplomatically as he could. Hredt held his screen up for Solomon to capture the schematic images.

"Let's investigate it," he said.

Solomon cocked his head. "Well, if you can get obsolete Ainatio screen devices like that to download from your network, we shouldn't have any problem."

Yes, Solomon could have walked in. Hredt couldn't tell whether the AI had pointed that out as a warning or to prove he meant well. Hredt took note, though.

"Follow me," he said. "I'll show you the way."

Hredt guided him through the access hatch and led them through the passages to the command centre. Cosqui activated the assay probes' display with their current view of Earth from within its atmosphere.

"We have the previous locations of your ships from the time of the explosion," she said. Hredt noted how her English had suddenly improved. She'd either been studying hard in the last few days or she'd been feigning a lack of fluency for some advantage. "We can start there and follow the trajectories."

"Just as well you were keeping an eye on us, wasn't it?" Searle leaned on the rail to watch Cosqui gesturing to the control panel. It was dangerously low for a tall human. "If you designed this for the Jattans, I guess they don't like switches and buttons. I'm not a gestures man myself."

It was fascinating to hear humans reasoning aloud and see what grabbed their attention. "Yes, I find this interface very hard to use," Hredt said. "But we knew we'd never fight a battle for ourselves, so we didn't modify it. I think those choices will fall to you."

"We're ready, Hredt," Cosqui said. "Orbital data, please."

"My apologies. I ramble."

"You do, Hredt. Commander, the simplest method is to place the portal in the ships' paths so they just fly through it. I have the exit points calculated already from *Cabot*'s position and Solomon can establish a link and adjust the orbits as necessary."

"I can't contact *Elcano*, though," he said. "I'm locked out of her network."

"If you can locate her, we can place you inside the ship with the gate, and you can do what you need to from within. Would that work?"

"It would," Solomon said. "I can interface with her AI. And if you allow me to send data to your computer, this is my last estimate of the positions of all three vessels."

Cosqui gestured at Hredt. "Send it to Hredt's screen and I can read the data there."

"Very well."

Hredt watched the numbers appear on his screen, then passed it to Cosqui. She could do the calculations without resorting to the ship's computers. But Hredt got the feeling this was more about not wanting Solomon to interface with the prenu's system than showing off her mathematical skills. Solomon would probably think she didn't trust him, but the commune had seen what the emanation had done to Ainatio's enemies in the last two days, and it was sobering. They'd monitored some locations in the region called Asia-Pacific, partly at Marc's request, and even Hredt felt briefly uneasy when he saw the destruction. It was a strange realisation. Teeriks needed strong allies, but that kind of strength could easily be turned on anybody, including them.

He had to stop thinking those thoughts. This was all about trust, about the humans giving their word. It was going to take some time to learn what trust really felt like and how much it required of both sides.

"The abandoned ships, then," Cosqui said, studying the screen. "We move them first, in case we fail. This hasn't been tested yet. I don't want to kill your comrades."

"Neither ship should have deviated far from the projected orbit," Solomon said. "They require corrections at intervals, but they won't have strayed far."

Cosqui gestured at one of the displays to enhance the image. "There's a heat signature coming from that one."

"I left some maintenance systems operating," Solomon said.

"And here... this one is inert."

Two images of identical ships, white with Ainatio's red A logo on the hulls, now hung in the air in the centre of the chamber. "Yes, that one's *Shackleton.*" Solomon could distinguish between them but they still looked the same to Hredt. "And that's *Eriksson.*"

Cosqui fluffed up her neck plumage, pleased with herself. "Now we place a portal *here* and let them move into it, *Eriksson* first... and..." She paused for a count of three, then gestured with a flourish and another display appeared, little different from the previous one. "Yes, *Eriksson* is in this system now. You can make contact now and adjust her trajectory to bring her back to an Opis orbit."

Solomon stood motionless for a few moments. "Done," he said.

"Now we move the gateway into *Shackleton*'s path. There... it's aligned... and it's *here*."

Solomon froze again. "Orbit set. The onboard AIs can now do corrections and bring both ships into stable orbits. I think that went well for a trial run."

"Now for *Elcano*," Cosqui said. "Send me the numbers, Solomon." She studied the figures on the display, then closed her eyes and calculated. "Are you ready? When the probes locate the ship, I'll place you there before I attempt to move it."

"I'll be ready," Solomon said.

Now she had *Elcano*'s projected course, Cosqui could move a probe. She sent one on a short superluminal hop across the system to close the gap with *Elcano* and then set it to locate the ship. While she waited for the probe to sweep a corridor along the projected course, Hredt handed her his carefully-wrapped treat from Nina.

"Thank you for your support, Cosqui," he said. "You earned this."

"Yes, I did," Cosqui said, but she broke the pie in half and shared it with him. It was soft and crumbly, and dissolved in his mouth. Like the lemon flavour that had so enthralled him when he was living on half-rations, the taste was like nothing he'd ever eaten. It was as pleasantly rich and salty as the last one, but somehow *fruity* as well.

Cosqui pecked at the last few crumbs on her sleeve. "What do the ships' names mean?"

"They're all great explorers from Earth history," Searle said. "Brave men who set out in ships we'd regard as unsafe today."

"Braver than you, then?"

"Very possibly."

"But you risked coming here in your slow little ship and you knew nothing about Opis. You didn't even know if you'd wake up from hibernation again."

"That was part of the appeal," Searle said. "We never achieve anything by playing safe. Are you going to name this ship properly, by the way? "

"What should we call it?"

"I don't know. Caisin?"

"Not a human name?"

"Caisin changed the world we'll be living in. That's worth commemorating."

"We'll think about it," Cosqui said. "I'll show you around after we retrieve *Elcano*. May you kill many Kugin with it."

Searle raised an eyebrow. "Is that your equivalent of 'May God bless her and all who sail in her'?"

"I don't know what that means," Cosqui said. "But I do hope you kill lots of Kugin."

It was good to see Cosqui getting on with the humans so well now. An appreciative client was a rare treat. Hredt hoped the humans stayed that way when they grew more familiar with the technology.

Solomon was still watching the display, as still as if he'd switched off the quadrubot. Cosqui gave the image an occasional glance while she dusted herself down and folded the food wrapping.

"There she is," Solomon said. "Still on course."

Elcano, white and anonymous like her sister ships, appeared on the display. Searle stepped forward for a closer look, leaning on the rail. If he leaned any further, he'd fall off the dais.

"Can you give me a view from the other side, please, Cosqui?" he said. "I need to check for damage."

"I can scan the whole hull for you if you like."

"Wonderful. Thank you." Searle turned to Solomon. "Ready? And no tapping on Erskine's inspection plate and saying neener-neener."

Solomon watched as the image of *Elcano* became a stream of close-ups as the probe skimmed up and down the length of the hull. "I wouldn't dream of it."

"Is Erskine very important?" Hredt asked.

"She was," Solomon said.

Cosqui activated a display for Searle and showed him how to interpret the results of the inspection. Then she opened the Caisin gate on the deck below.

"Walk through, Solomon. If the data you gave me is correct, you should exit on the bridge."

"It's correct." Solomon's quadrubot trotted down to the deck and paused for a moment at the threshold. "As long as you calculated correctly and I don't emerge outside the hull. I don't have thrusters."

"If that happens, which it will *not*, I have your position and I can retrieve you and reposition you. There's no need to worry."

Solomon disappeared. Searle looked happy. "No sliding down ropes or scrambling up ladders to board enemy ships now, huh?" he said. "We can place a boarding party anywhere we want. Did Caisin realise what a game-changer the gate was going to be?"

"Of course she did," Hredt said. "That was why she kept it to herself. Imagine it in the hands of the Kugin."

"Is it why you decided to escape when you did, that your foremen were close to finding out?"

"Unfortunately, yes." Hredt didn't want to sully Caisin's memory by criticism. The poorly prepared escape was nobody's fault. "We had to leave before we were truly ready. Unlike you, we've never had a crisis to test loyalties. But we aren't naive enough to think all teeriks would stick together. I confess that a safe life and a full stomach carry more weight than an ideology. If we hadn't been afraid of the gate being discovered, I think we might have postponed our rebellion, and then I suspect it would never have happened."

"The others never knew about the gate, though."

"Caisin didn't know who to trust. It was dangerous enough planning a mass escape. You know from your own experience with a treacherous comrade that it counts for nothing if someone sees an advantage to be gained."

"So you left at the right time, found out who you couldn't rely on, and survived to tell the tale," Searle said. "It might not have gone to plan, but you got a worthwhile outcome."

"Yes. Yes, I do believe we did." Seeing the debacle through Searle's eyes turned it into an intelligent decision. Hredt felt better. "Thank you for being positive, Commander. We only saw it as a terrible mistake."

"You're welcome. Shouldn't we have heard from Solomon by now, by the way?"

"I'll call him," Cosqui said. "Solomon, what are you doing?"

Solomon took longer to respond than Hredt expected. "I've overridden the onboard AI and started deceleration," he said. "When I can pinpoint where she emerges, I can adjust her course to bring her back into the right orbit. Now I've re-established the link with her AI, I don't need to be on board when she transits. I've checked the cryo logs and everyone's alive and well. The comms have been tampered with, though. So I want to come back now."

"There's nothing to fear."

"I'm *not* afraid," Solomon said, but he didn't sound convincing. "If anything goes wrong with the gate, though, I'll have to use a conventional signal to return instead of the FTL link, and it'll take my transmitted consciousness forty years to reach you."

"No FTL on board?" Searle asked.

"It seems Erskine sabotaged this end of the system as well, Commander."

"Wow. She really wasn't taking any chances, pal."

Hredt thought it best not to remind Searle that every time they used the portal for a different task, it was an experiment. They could now safely move living creatures, they could establish multiple gates, they could create points of exit and entry away from the generation point in the ship, and now they could scoop up fast-moving vessels and place them where they needed to be. The reality had matched their calculations precisely, and teeriks didn't make mistakes.

But Hredt avoided overconfidence. Cosqui radiated calm, so perhaps Searle didn't notice, but Solomon seemed to be fully aware of the risks. He was right to be slightly irritable.

"Cosqui, the exit point... it's still in the command centre, isn't it?"

"It is, Solomon. Just step through."

They waited. It was so quick and silently uneventful that sometimes it was hard to believe the gate was working, even for Hredt. Then Solomon emerged from the haze and climbed the shallow steps up to the dais to stand close to Searle as if he needed reassurance. Being in a physical body made him vulnerable and the threat of isolation must have distressed him. Hredt had never come across any other emanation or mechanical with such complex emotions, or much by way of emotions at all. It was a testament to an extraordinary design. There was nobody in this part of the galaxy who could rival it.

"It's okay, Sol," Searle said quietly. "You don't have to worry about her again. She won't have access to everything like she used to."

Hredt realised Erskine had shut Solomon out of the ship's systems in the same way she'd cut off *Cabot*, but in the light of the emanation's virus attack it had all started to look very different. The woman must have been afraid of him.

"Is Erskine going to be a problem?" Hredt asked.

"No," Searle said firmly. "She's one woman. And she'll see the situation very differently when she's revived."

"I've disabled automatic revival so that everyone remains in cryo until we activate it manually," Solomon said. "And that was unsettling. I was suddenly aware how far I was from home."

"You're turning into a meatbag, Sol. Welcome to the neurotics' club." Searle smiled charmingly at Cosqui. "That was magnificent engineering. I'm in awe. Are you going to give me the guided tour now?"

"It's nice to be appreciated," Cosqui said. "You're so unlike Kugin."

Hredt took the opportunity to leave Cosqui to her new devotee. "I'm going home," he said. He'd have to tell the others what he and Cosqui had done, but he'd pick his moment. "I need to see how Nina's getting on with Turisu."

The house the humans had built so quickly for them was exactly what he'd asked for, a single level with multiple chambers off a big central room, wide passages to accommodate wings, and a more spacious lavatory arrangement closer to the ground. The only furnishings were the sparse cushions and covers they'd removed from the ship, but they had food to eat and screens to read, and sleeping platforms at the right height. That was enough.

Nina was in one of the side chambers, helping Keejah and Pannit with their English, explaining how to work out which words could be shortened when spoken. Hredt watched from the doorway for a while, struck by how much she seemed to be enjoying their company. Her enthusiasm was infectious. He felt more confident about the future just watching her.

Runal tugged at his sleeve. "What did you do in the prenu, Grandfather?"

"We retrieved the other human ships," Hredt said. "There will be three in a stable orbit around Opis soon. That makes four with *Cabot*."

He pretended he didn't notice Turisu had come up behind him until she let out a long, exasperated rattle. He was ready.

"You used the gate for *that*?" Her crest rose. "Why didn't you discuss this with us? Here you go again. You have no right to do this."

"And what's the alternative, Turi? I've heard nothing from you except what I should *not* do. Tell me what I should."

"If that caused a detectable spike, we'll all be in danger, including the humans."

"Then it's just as well all three ships carry substantial weapons. One also has a thousand human settlers waiting to be revived."

Turisu let out an angry rasp and scuttled out. Hredt was determined not to be ignored and called after her.

"And I've told Captain Ingram we'll upgrade their ships and weapons, and train their pilots to fly the prenu as well. So it's done. We have *allies*. We'll work with them."

There, he'd asserted himself. With Caisin gone, somebody had to lead. But she'd only been laid to rest this morning, and here he was congratulating himself for replacing her and arguing with his daughter in front of the boys. What was it Jeff had said? Funerals brought out the worst in people. Perhaps they brought out the worst in teeriks too, and that was why the foremen took the task away from them.

Runal got up and went after his mother. Hredt picked up the screen that had entertained and educated him for the last few weeks and took refuge in it. There was a great deal more he could access with it now that he could connect to the humans' library, and he had some time to look through what was available. The scale of the information delighted him. Maro wandered in as he was poring over marvellous images of public buildings. Hredt braced for the argument with Turisu to continue by proxy.

"This is an invasion," Maro said. "More humans are coming."

"How can it be?" Hredt asked. "This isn't our planet, so if anyone invaded, it was us. The humans were here first. And they would have come here anyway."

"What if millions of them come here? *Billions*? Turisu told me what you've promised them. You're handing them too much power."

Hredt thought a few million humans was far too few. It would take at least a few billion to make the Kugin realise they weren't free to do as they pleased any more.

"How could we hand them any power when we had none?" he said. "We never did have. All we have is our talents. Do we have a better plan? Are we capable of surviving on our own? No. So we help the humans and the humans help us. They'll eventually change the balance of power here whether we help them or not, but for once in history we have the chance to choose allies. They're our *equals*. Not our masters."

"It's happening too fast," Maro said. "We can't control it. That's not an alliance, it's a takeover."

He walked out before Hredt could say that the speed of the transformation was a separate debate from whether it should happen at all, and that neither they nor the humans were in control. Events had a life of their own. Perhaps he'd corner Maro tomorrow and say it anyway so that Turisu would have to hear it.

He pulled his cushion across to the alcove by the window and settled down to watch Caisin's egg, wrapped in her favourite blanket on a low table close to the heating vent. Now that the light was behind it, he could see movement through the shell. It was surviving against the odds. And so would the commune. If the egg hatched, he'd need Nina's advice on what to feed the fledgling, because they'd never thought they'd need to look after a baby when they fled. There was no infant food in their rations.

"Poor little orphan," he said to the egg. "But at least you'll hatch in a world where teeriks decide their own fate."

There was a knock on the open door. It had to be Nina coming to say she was going back to the base. Only humans tapped doors, especially ones that were already open. He looked around.

"I'm off now, Hredt," she said. "That was fun. Thank you for letting me meet your family."

"Thank you for feeding and amusing them," he said. "Please, come and look at Caisin's child before you go."

Nina knelt next to the table and sat back on her heels to study it. As eggs went, it was fairly average, perhaps with more red speckling, but it was a normal size, narrow and tapered at one end, the length of a large human hand. Nina watched it for a long time, smiling when she saw movement.

"How long before it hatches?"

"Four weeks, normally."

"How do the boys feel about having a younger brother or sister?"

"The commune isn't really a family." It was time to explain teerik life to her. "It's unusual to have three related generations in one commune. Runal and Demli are only with us because we left before they were apprenticed, and Turisu stayed with me because we have complementary skills. I thought she would be happy to know she wouldn't lose her sons."

"Oh." That was enough to take Nina's attention away from the egg. "Is that really why you left?"

"I didn't think so at the time. I thought we were joining an uprising. Then I thought we were escaping before the Kugin found out we'd created the gate. But perhaps the thought of losing the children played a bigger part than I realised."

"So the rest of the commune isn't related either?"

"No, they were introduced for skills."

"I don't understand."

"You need the right range of skills in a commune. Kugin pay a great deal to obtain the ideal mix."

Nina frowned. "It doesn't sound like you had any choice."

"We don't. But it's the way things have always worked. We leave our families and don't look back. And we know our children will do the same. Except us — we broke the custom, because our respective skills combined well and the foremen wanted to keep that. Seeing how we argue these days, I wonder if the custom was based on experience."

"Perhaps you'll remember your origins one day," Nina said."

"I hope so. But it must have been a very long time ago for us not to have any memory of it."

Nina folded her arms on a low table and rested her chin on them while she watched the egg. Then she began singing to it. Hredt knew humans sang and he'd listened to the range of their voices in passages from the encyclopaedia, but hers was particularly soft, and even though the words made no sense to him it all seemed very comforting.

"It's a French lullaby," she said. "We learned it at school and it's the only one I know. I don't know anything about ablun development, but the child can probably hear through the shell."

She was the only human who used the name for their species. Jeff said she was a biologist and details like that were important to her.

"Yes," Hredt said. "I shouldn't have argued where it could hear us. It might have distressed it."

"It's okay. The lullaby put that right."

"Will you help us to feed it, Nina? We have no infant food."

"Of course. We'll work something out." Nina looked at her screen. "I have to go now, Hredt, but I'll come back tomorrow with some more test recipes. If you like, I'll sing to the egg again, just in case you've had another argument."

She smiled, but it didn't sound entirely like a joke.

"Thank you," he said. "Caisin's child needs as much help as we can give it now. You're a very kind person."

She put her hand on his wing. Humans did that to each other a lot. "When I was a child, I used to dream of having alien friends on other planets," she said. "Then I grew up and studied science, and I realised that it was impossible. Yet here we are, talking, being friends. Isn't life fantastic? We never know what's in store for us."

Yes, it was. It all depended on how you chose to look at it. Hredt decided to choose to see the fantastic view of a joint human and teerik future that made Nina so happy.

* * *

NOMAD BASE, OPIS, MORNING BRIEFING, CO'S OFFICE: 0745, ONE WEEK LATER.

"The frozen stay frozen until it's safe to thaw them out," Ingram said. "I'm sorry, I realise this is upsetting their friends, but we've got the walking and metabolising demographic to worry about first. I'll say it again. We'll revive everyone in *Elcano* when there's adequate food and shelter to do so. If there's a genuine emergency, we'll have to take the risk, but until then we stick with the plan. Right, Sol?"

Solomon's voice drifted from the speaker near the ceiling. "Right, Captain."

Jeff preferred the boss when she was her old self, irreverent and imperious. She'd been much too conciliatory lately. It was all very well trying to be democratic, but tough decisions had to be taken and those didn't happen in committees.

Steve Kokinos smiled. "I think food regulations require us to describe them as cook-chill rather than frozen, ma'am."

"What if we'd left *Elcano* where she was?" Ingram was into the indignant rhetorical questions now, which she usually didn't bother with once she'd made up her mind. "They'd be griping that we hadn't used the technology to retrieve them."

"I'm only passing on the question," Alex said. "And this is what happens when they don't have anything to occupy them. The sooner we have a lab for them to play in, the better."

There was nowhere to hold the morning briefing in an overcrowded camp now except Ingram's office, which was the size of a budget hotel room, a claustrophobically tight fit for eleven. Jeff looked on the bright side. Only essential personnel could squeeze in there and everyone kept it short and to the point so they could get out as fast as possible. Jeff was pressed shoulder to shoulder with Bissey, Searle, Haine, Kokinos, Andy Braithwaite — civvy, alcohol baron, and emperor of all things edible — and Alex Gorko. Marc, Chris, and Trinder were jammed in there as well, somehow occupying their own corner, and they didn't look like it was their idea of a fun start to the day. Chris's black eye was now more of a yellow patch but he still held his head slightly to one side like he was trying to protect the injury. The three of them had the air of men who had arses to kick elsewhere and wanted to get on with it.

"Ainatio scientists are supposed to be highly intelligent," Ingram said. "Can't they do the maths?"

"Yeah, I've explained the supplies safety margin to them," Alex said. "And I suspect a few of them want their buddies revived just so that they can settle old grudges with a shiv, but it *is* kind of creepy to stroll around down here knowing most of the staff and their kids are stuck up there somewhere, completely oblivious. I get why reviving the children means thawing their parents and then we might as well revive the lot. But let's not rule out unpacking those with skills we could do with right now."

"I don't want any piecemeal revivals just for convenience, Alex, because managing the resentment and all the why-him-and-not-her isn't worth the time and aggravation," Ingram said. "Andy, am I being overcautious? This is your realm."

"No, it's pretty simple," Andy said. "We have enough food, but only if nothing goes wrong, and I can hear Fate giggling as I say that. Two failed harvests' worth of surplus for the full population is what *I'd* call enough, and we won't have that this year, and possibly not next year either. Reduced rations is a last resort. So if we don't absolutely need more mouths to feed, we shouldn't do it. I'm meeting Doug Brandt and the Kill Line farmers after this, so I'll have more accurate projections for you later, but it won't be that much different from the last estimate. Crops have to grow, even fast-maturing ones. And if we fall back on the nutritional carbs we can extract from processing local vegetation, that still requires time and resources. There's no immediate need to make this any harder than it is."

Ingram started tapping at her screen. "How's the livestock doing?"

"Surviving. They're on the experimental pasture at the moment, but we're going to try them on carb pellets from adapted vegetation so we can keep the regular dried feed in reserve. People ask me why we're bothering, so I do my usual sermon on cultured meat using resources without contributing fertiliser, milk, glue, leather, and all the other stuff you only get from a complete animal, but if you can all stay on message about that, I'd appreciate the reinforcement. Remind the moaners that technology can fail. If animals malfunction, you can at least eat or reuse every bit of them."

"Testify, brother," Chris muttered.

"Yeah, we heard about you and the sack of flour, Chris," Andy said. "You should have eaten the insects. Terrible waste of protein."

Ingram kept looking at the clock with its twenty-six hour display. It was still hard to glance at the time without consciously having to work it out, and maybe she was just doing that rather than getting impatient. But she looked like she wanted them to get on with it so she could move on to what was really on her mind. Jeff still didn't know what he was doing here. It was good to hear all this discussion, but he had nothing to contribute except a nod and a joke now and then to show he was listening.

"So, moving on. Refits." Ingram pushed herself away from her windowsill perch and swung her arms as far as she could in the space. "Sol, have we got enough bots embarked in the ships to carry out the work? I realise we'll be guessing until Fred tells us what needs to be done and the materials required, but we're not going to be able to release bots from the base for some time."

"*Shackleton* has a full repair complement, as does *Elcano*," Solomon said. "But I robbed *Eriksson* to achieve that. So however quickly Fred says the jobs can be done, we probably can't keep up with that schedule. He's used to shipyards where employees have everything they need to follow instructions. But we can work that out. As long as we make installing camouflage a priority, the rest can follow as and when we can resource it. The stealth system is hull-mounted, so all we need to do is produce what he instructs us to make, and the *Shackleton* bots can fit it on all four ships."

"Brad, you said you wanted to extend surveys for another couple of weeks," Ingram said. "So you're obviously comfortable with the timescales."

"We can only go as fast as we can, but spending extra time on the task is useful in more ways than one," Searle said. "Cosqui's more forthcoming with intel than Fred. When we check a piece of equipment together or I explain a system to her, she'll say that won't work against the Kugin because of this or that, whereas when I'm doing an inspection with Fred, he'll just say we need to update it to standard x or y. So I'm getting a better picture of what kind of potential adversary we might be dealing with. I'd like to carry on."

"But you haven't got much out of her so far," Ingram said.

Searle had his earnest face on. Jeff quite liked him. He always got to the point and didn't bugger around.

"Ma'am, we need to make up our minds," Searle said. "Do we sit the teeriks down and interrogate them thoroughly now because we want answers and we don't know them well enough yet to really trust them? Or do we let them tell us things at their own pace? We're going to be stuck here together for a long time. They saved a lot of our people, and to do that they risked giving us access to something that could get them killed. They didn't have to do it at all. We'd never have guessed the Caisin gate existed. And they've just buried their leader. I say we take the softly-softly approach, and I'm being practical, not sentimental. We might make them clam up if we're too demanding."

"I'm totally persuaded, Commander," Ingram said. "But we've been able to communicate with the teeriks for six weeks. If we write off the first three weeks as making sure we're both speaking the same King's English, then they've had three more weeks to tell us more about the other aliens who can probably give us a serious spanking and have good reason to. But we still don't have enough actionable intelligence to be confident of protecting ourselves."

"Dai can confirm this, because he was there, ma'am, but yesterday Cosqui seemed to suggest the Kugin area of influence was nine star systems, one of which is further from here than we are from Earth. So we already know they can reach home."

Hiyashi nodded. "Yes, I can confirm that. But we can work out a lot from what we see, too. We know the Kugin have warships at least as good as the prenu — the original, anyway, before the teeriks did their upgrade — because nobody hands their allies hardware that's better than their own. We know that optical camouflage works against them, or Fred wouldn't keep going on about adding it. But we don't know much about the Jattans, except they prefer gesture-activated controls."

Ingram looked sympathetic. "Yes, we can guess a lot. But that's not the point. We need to be told. For all kinds of reasons, not least of which is trust."

"Let's not forget it works both ways," Hiyashi said. "Teeriks have access to intel as part of their design work, and they don't forget. They memorise everything, they don't write things down, and apparently their offspring are born with some of that knowledge. They know the strengths and weaknesses of everyone's armed forces, friend and enemy, because they need it to do their jobs. If they have access to our ships and systems to upgrade them, they acquire all *our* sensitive information too. And so do their children. And as we keep saying, they really do know where we live, and they probably always will."

"Let's discuss that later," Ingram said.

Jeff tried to recall how he'd felt not knowing about intelligent aliens. This had all happened in six weeks: that used to be his total annual leave period, no time at all. But expectations changed quickly when people got used to things. Just establishing the most basic communication with aliens was incredible in its own right, but here they were, worrying about the grey areas and why the teeriks hadn't handed over everything they knew about their old bosses. Jeff tried to keep a baseline in mind. Back on Earth, nobody had evidence that higher alien life forms existed, let alone intelligent ones. The Nomad mission had come from blissful ignorance to dissatisfaction by way of astonishing new technology in less than two months. That wasn't enough time to form an accurate overview and yet they had to have answers.

"I bet they're having a similar meeting about us," he said.

"Yes, but if they're not telling us everything for the same reason we're not telling them... okay, perhaps I underestimate how much of a culture shock freedom can be."

"So you're okay with me hanging out with Cosqui and taking the subtle approach," Searle said.

"You'll be working on those ships for months," Ingram said. "I'm sure you'll make progress on the intel."

"Cosqui's taken a shine to you," Jeff said. "Make the most of it."

Ingram looked across at Marc, Chris, and Trinder, who'd become a kind of three-headed hell-hound in Jeff's eyes, a single defensive entity. He understood why Ingram had made a concession to their autonomy, but he still felt it was a mistake.

"You're very quiet, gentlemen," Ingram said.

"Our intel needs are more basic." Chris unfolded one arm to count on his fingers. "We need to know where the Kugin keep their vital organs, the kind of round it'll take to put an unpluggable hole in them, and what they'll be using on the ground against us."

"It would be nice to know what they look like, too," Marc said. "In case we end up shooting the wrong aliens one day."

"I'll keep asking Cosqui," Searle said. "Her idea of wishing us luck is saying she hopes we kill many Kugin. So she's probably got some tips."

The conversation lapsed. Ingram looked at the clock again. "Anything else? No? Good." She straightened up. "Thank you, gentlemen. Everyone involved in the next meeting, stay, including Sol if he's still listening." Jeff was nearest the door, so he got up first. "Not you, Chief. I've got tasks for you."

Jeff reversed and the room half-emptied. He was left with Bissey, Alex, Trinder, Chris, and Marc. It was hard to guess where this was going, but he caught a whiff of politics. Ingram pulled her desk out into the vacated space to squeeze into the chair behind it.

"Gents, when we finally revive the *Elcano* party, we know we'll have some challenges," she said. "I realise there's some ill-feeling towards Erskine over the way she handled the initial evacuation, and it's too raw and recent for some people to shrug it off. We need time to get the colony in shape psychologically before we re-ignite simmering feuds. The food and housing situation is genuine, but I'm glad it's there to give us time to take stock. Which I think you all know anyway."

"Seconded," Alex said. "And she did try to destroy Sol."

"Even if I can move on, Erskine might not," Solomon said.

"And can you move on, Sol?"

"I believe the phrase is hell no, Alex. But I'll try."

"I think I might have some issues with her, too," Ingram said. "She's always been pleasant to me, but she might expect to run Nomad."

"Told you." Marc nudged Chris and gave Ingram a nod. "Sorry, we had a discussion before Erskine left, about what would happen when she arrived with people who were used to her being in charge, and Nomad had been chugging along for years with its own system and had a second and even third generation."

"Plans have to adapt," Ingram said cryptically.

"No objections here. Adapt away."

"Maybe we should see how Erskine feels about it," Chris said. "She might just say great, the buck doesn't stop here any more and I can see out my time drinking Braithwaite's bootleg gin and playing bridge. And Kill Line would want an election. The way things line up at the moment, Erskine wouldn't get a majority and Doug would win. The question is whether everyone would accept the vote, and what role we'd have as a military or police force in responding to that."

"You really did think quite hard about this, didn't you?" Ingram said.

Chris shrugged. "Camp life's dull. We had to make our own entertainment."

"Either way, gentlemen, I just don't relish the idea of Erskine descending from Olympus to guide us when life here hasn't settled down and we're still working out how we run this colony together."

Ingram looked to them all for some nod of agreement. Jeff kept his head down. "Even if we have a glut of crops and Food Fair Express opens a branch here, I don't want to revive Erskine until this settlement is stable, even if we need to wake up everyone else."

"We could pop back to Earth and pick up supplies now we've got the portal," Jeff said. "But I know that's for weaklings, because Marc's giving me the hairy eyeball."

At least that made them laugh. But Jeff was now in a position he didn't like. He'd served under Ingram for a long time and in tight spots that forged strong loyalties, and she always wanted him to speak his mind. But he didn't do politics, not even parish pump stuff, and running Nomad was politics.

"Chief, you've been awfully patient," Ingram said. "And baffled, I think. I wanted you here so we can look at other security matters. Teeriks. You're the teerik whisperer. We have a teerik issue."

"I think Nina Curtis is doing more whispering now than I am, ma'am. And she's got the advantage of food parcels."

Ingram meshed her fingers. "She's terribly fond of them, and she's a dear, sweet girl. But she's a scientist, and security isn't hardwired in her the same way it is in us."

"Has there been a breach?"

"No, but Dai made a good point. Teeriks know everything about everybody in defence terms, including us."

"We're handcuffed to them forever now," Trinder said. "If they fall into enemy hands, we're screwed. So we'd better take good care of them."

Ingram narrowed her eyes. "Dan, you ruined my punchline. Okay, what he said. There's no walking away from them once we let them into our ships, and we can't erase their memories."

Marc did his *huh* laugh. "Well, we can, but only once."

"You jest, Marc, but that's something we need to face. If the Kugin or the owners of the prenu show up, we can't let the teeriks be captured."

"You can't bring yourself to say it, can you?" Marc said.

"Let me try. If capture looks inevitable, our last resort will be to shoot them. There. I said it. Don't tell me you weren't all thinking it."

Jeff wasn't, and the idea upset him. It upset him more because he knew she was right. "It's going to be hard to look Fred in the eye now, ma'am. But what do you want me to do?"

"Visit the ships with Fred and let me know the lie of the land."

"You want me to spy on them."

"No, I want you to keep your eyes and ears open. They've bolted once and they might do it again. This is as much to protect the teeriks as it is to protect us. We probably won't need to worry about this in our lifetimes, but we're here to plan for the worst and make sure we're ready for it."

"I'd tell you if there was a problem anyway, ma'am," Jeff said.

"I know you would."

"Are they going to let Sol into their network?" Marc asked. "If he can get in, at least we can see whatever's recorded. Just because they don't write stuff down, it doesn't mean data doesn't end up in their computer. Interaction with engineering bots and that kind of stuff. I'd imagine Earth's location and detail about ships' enhanced defences will leave some kind of audit trail."

"I still don't get how that works," Chris said. "They've got to have a way to produce plans for shipyards. So they do write stuff down. How does that protect their trade secrets?"

"There's a big difference between saying 'cut a piece like this from metal that's made exactly to that spec and weld it like that' and understanding the principles and the maths well enough to invent your own FTL drive," Marc said. "And defence depends on continuous improvement. You've always got to stay one step ahead of the enemy. I think that's the teeriks' USP. They work out better ways to do things."

"Are you their agent?" Bissey asked.

"I know we've been preoccupied with saving our arses, Commander, but now the heat's off for a while, think about their commercial value. Wars are fought over far less."

"So do we have a designated teerik slayer in the event of an emergency?"

"Since you put it like that," Chris said, "we all are. Because any one of us could be with a teerik when it's the only option left."

"And you're okay with that."

"Yes, because I'd want a buddy to shoot me if I was going to fall into enemy hands and that enemy didn't have a rep for treating prisoners kindly."

Nobody asked Jeff if he thought he could do it, and he really wasn't sure that he could. He said nothing and Ingram didn't press him. She'd probably catch him privately later. The meeting had fallen silent. If they'd all agreed to slot teeriks if the worst happened, then it had been a silent nod and it would never be recorded.

"Anything else to discuss?" Ingram said. "Okay, I think we've all earned breakfast now. Thank you, gentlemen."

Jeff went back to his cabin to sort out his admin and think about his new task. It needed doing and he wasn't comfortable with it, a contradiction he was used to, and Ingram had a point. Someone close to Fred with security sense needed to keep an eye on things. Searle seemed to be Cosquimaden's favourite human now, and she was as good a barometer of what the commune was thinking as anybody, but maybe Ingram thought Searle was too new to teerik wrangling to spot when things weren't quite right.

Bissey's detailed schedule for the week landed on Jeff's screen within half an hour. Fred would work out temporary stealth shielding for all four vessels, Solomon would get the hardware built and installed, and then Bissey and Hiyashi would do weapons surveys with Cosqui with the aim of upgrading armaments. Fred thought the stealth fit would take two to three weeks, but the rest was anyone's guess.

"Interesting times," Jeff muttered, stowing his bedding and leaving the cabin tidy for whoever wanted to use it while he was out. The most interesting thing was that everyone seemed relaxed about the need for all these defensive measures. It was either a sign that they'd defaulted to what they knew best, or they'd accepted that anything this sector had to throw at them was better than staying on Earth so they would stay and fight if they had to.

The shuttle to *Elcano* was almost full when they took off for the inspection two hours later. Fred had to flatten himself on the deck for takeoff and lock his claws around the bars holding the seats on the deck because there was no way for a large bird to buckle up. There was also no pressure suit for him. Jeff thought he would have needed one in the prenu for emergencies, but perhaps teeriks went out on trials so rarely that the Kugin didn't think they needed them. He'd have to do something about that if they were going to be shuttling back and forth for months.

There were a few nervous moments as the onboard AI manoeuvred the shuttle alongside an airlock and sealed a connecting ring against the hull. Searle put his helmet on.

"I'm not going to knock," he said. "Because if someone knocks back, I'll crap myself."

Elcano was a big, heavily-armed taxi, nothing much beyond cryo berths, cargo, weapons sections and a small bridge with an equally small mess deck. Once they were clear of the shuttle and into the rotating cryo section, there was gravity and they could walk normally.

Solomon had opted to accompany them in the quadrubot instead of taking the easy route by just transferring to the ship's systems, which seemed odd until Jeff thought about what had happened to Sol the last time he'd encountered Erskine. It made no logical sense, but it looked like the AI wasn't taking any chances. Solomon trotted along behind Fred, stopping occasionally to poke his probes into ports in the bulkheads. Eventually Jeff couldn't hear his motors any more and turned to see him some way behind, busy with an open panel. Jeff wandered back to see what was happening.

"There," Solomon said. "Nothing untoward so far."

"She hasn't dug her way out of the box of Transylvanian soil, if that's what's worrying you, mate," Jeff said. "Fetch your stake and we'll sort her out."

"I wish I could cultivate a sense of humour about it," Sol said.

"Stick with the navy. You will."

Fred was fascinated by the cryo berths. Nobody needed cryo out here, not with FTL generally available, so *Elcano* must have been like a trip to a science museum for him. The cryo bays were scruffy garages and the whole place was like the back room of a funeral home. Jeff had never seen one, but his imagination filled the gaps and he felt uncomfortable wandering around between the berths knowing there was a human being in nearly all of them, not dead but not really fully alive either.

Bloody stupid. I spent forty-five years in one of those things and saw loads of them when they revived me. I'm going soft.

Mendoza and Haine were having a poke around the status panels and doing a quick visual check through the transparent sections of the lids.

"...and anyway, we can safely maintain this state for decades, and everyone went under expecting to wake and find everyone on Opis a lot older," Mendoza was saying. "But it's not like they had enough interaction with them before they were chilled down to feel they knew their younger versions. They ought to adjust quickly to finding their colleagues here haven't aged. It's going to be a surprise, but one that's easier to manage."

Haine peered into an empty sarcophagus. "Not a full house, then."

"Some people who were allocated berths chose not to go," Mendoza said. "They wanted to stay with their friends and family because they thought they were all going to die when APS paid us a visit."

"What an excellent psychological test," Haine said. "So we know who the noble ones are. It's going to be quite the soap opera when everyone's revived and catching up on old times, isn't it?"

"And with all those grievances still lovely and fresh," Mendoza said. "But to be fair to Erskine, she was short of options."

Haine smiled. "I'm sure everyone will shake hands and forget all about it. That's my experience of people. Understanding. Magnanimous. No grudge-bearing at all."

Mendoza was still straight-faced, but it didn't last long. He burst out laughing. Haine started laughing too. Sometimes Jeff envied doctors that matter-of-fact cheerful indifference that came from seeing too many bodies in various states of disrepair. He scuffed his boots on the gantry to remind them he was there.

"Do you need anything, Commander?" he asked.

Haine looked up. "Beer. You'd think they'd have filled the empty berths with something potable."

"I think they were out of Dom Perignon, sir."

"Tragic. Okay, cryo's fine. You can worry about the health of the nukes now."

Fred peered into the berth and reached in cautiously with his hand. Jeff prayed for Haine to keep his mouth shut and not make a crack about frozen turkeys. He could almost see it forming on Haine's lips and had to look away before it started him off as well.

"This is very strange," Fred said, fluffing his feathers as if he'd caught a gust of chilled air. "I wouldn't want to be unconscious for all those years with no idea of what was going on around me. Is this how you arrived here?"

"Yep," Jeff said.

Fred trotted after him. "And you remember nothing of it."

"Nothing at all."

"And you're now very old, technically speaking."

"Eighty-three, I suppose."

"But you started ageing normally when you were revived and you'll live another forty years, perhaps."

"Technically speaking."

Jeff realised he had no idea how long teeriks lived. Now he wanted to ask but didn't feel comfortable about it. But he could approach the topic from a different angle.

"Do you mind if I ask how old Caisin was?"

"By the human calendar, one hundred and five," Fred said.

Jeff was happier to know that teeriks had a decent lifespan. "Beats us," he said. "On average, humans are lucky to reach seventy now. Life expectancy's been declining for years. For most people, anyway. But I'm new old stock, so to speak."

"You'll reach double that," Fred said. "We'll make sure of it."

Solomon was still trotting along behind them, investigating terminals as he went. They ended up in one of the missile bays and Jeff sat back on a locker while Sol got on with the survey with Fred, who looked like he was enjoying himself. Teeriks bounced a couple of times on both feet when they were enthusiastic, almost like they were about to take off. Fred darted around with his screen, taking notes and making a little burbling sound in his throat. It was hard not to see it as a human whistling to himself while he worked.

"Here are the plans, Chief Jeff," he said. "Look. And I've written out the full formulas. It's strange to break the habit. But Solomon needs to understand the concepts, not just follow my instructions."

Fred showed Jeff a beautifully drawn, intricate image of one of the missile launchers that was almost a blueprint, superimposed on Ainatio's bog-standard schematic. Jeff wanted to ask when teeriks developed technical drawing skills like that if they didn't write anything down, but he was worried Fred would think he was being suspicious rather than honestly curious.

"It's a work of art, Fred," he said. "It really is."

Fred's neck feathers fluffed up and he rocked his head a little. "I'm enjoying this. I like to be busy."

Jeff took Solomon aside while Fred was examining the missile launchers. "You're going to play fair with them, aren't you, Sol?"

"Of course. I'm not tricking them into anything."

"They're writing stuff down. They said they never do that. It means they trust us so much that they're willing to take the risk. Make sure we deserve that trust."

"But I have to communicate instructions to bots," Solomon said. "And teeriks have to instruct shipyards and engineering works back home, so they obviously don't keep *everything* in their heads, do they? I don't think that means what we think it does. We're still only copying them, though, not suddenly becoming able to calculate and invent as they do. We're not exploiting them."

"Okay," Jeff said. He thought of production lines for classified devices, and how workers didn't necessarily understand the complete object they were making a component for. And bots probably had no wider understanding at all. He was willing to bet the important detail of the Caisin gate wasn't written down at all, though. "Okay."

He kept a closer eye on Fred the next day, but for Fred's benefit, not to assess him as a flight risk. *Shackleton* was still in her prelaunch state and in good shape as far as Jeff could see. *Eriksson* hadn't fared so well, though. When they boarded her the following day, the poor old girl looked threadbare, with whole compartments gutted. Jeff put his hand on the bulkhead and patted it.

"We'll put you back the way you were, sweetheart," he said. "Don't you worry. You'll be gorgeous again."

The ship had become the Hangar Annie to be cannibalised for spares and materials, but she still had all her armaments, and the only things that Fred didn't regard as interesting antiques were the nuclear missiles. He'd struck up a good working relationship with Dai Hiyashi, the weapons engineer officer now responsible for them.

"These are very effective," Fred said, reading the technical data Solomon had given him. "You seem to be able to achieve much higher yields. This is a very different kind of warfare for us."

"Don't the Kugin use nukes?" Hiyashi asked.

"They prefer to preserve as much of their target as possible," Fred said. "If you want to seize a country and its resources, it's no use if it's reduced to a radioactive wasteland. This is why the bulk of our projects are anti-personnel devices and weapons, and the means to deliver the troops to use them. We live in a sector where conquest and exploitation is the order of the day, not erasing the enemy."

"You can't pay taxes when you're dead, eh?"

"Or mine rare metals."

"I'm a surface warfare man myself," Hiyashi said. "I've never fought in space."

"I have," Solomon said. "It's very slow."

"Oh yes. I forgot. Solomon the Satellite Slayer."

"Someone who's good at croquet and math would be feared across the galaxy."

"So what's the best deterrent use we can put these missiles to, Fred?"

"Direct strikes on key buildings and infrastructure."

"Are you seriously telling me that's a novel approach to war here?"

"Unless you want to take over the Kugin or Jattan empires with minimal damage, yes. You would be feared. It'll seem very unpredictable to them. Destruction for its own sake."

"Bloody hell, we'll be the berserkers of the galaxy," Jeff said.

Hiyashi smiled. "Until the Kugin copy us, and then we'll be the charcoal briquettes."

"Deterrence, sir." Jeff tapped his head. "This is where the war's fought."

"If you make an example of a city, and look as if you could do the same to all of them if you were sufficiently offended, you could well be right." Fred sounded completely confident. "So after we improve your ability to conceal your settlements, repel attacks on the ground, and conceal your ships, we can enhance your destructive capability. The next step will be to install spacefolding drives. And what you can't do, we can help you automate."

"I like this," Solomon said.

Jeff was seeing another side of Fred. He wasn't sure if he was up for nuking a city as a warning shot, but humans were the new kids on the block and obviously had a lot to learn about the psychology of their various alien neighbours.

By the time they surveyed *Cabot* two days later and gave the duty maintenance crew some respite from a tedious week, Fred and Sol had worked out that the refit programme would take longer than they wanted, but bot labour was limited. The exciting upgrades would have to come later, perhaps much later, and the shortfall wasn't down to the teeriks' capacity. It was Nomad's. They didn't have the manpower, bot or human, to divert from the housebuilding programme yet to produce raw materials or manufacture parts.

But Fred was sure they could get the essentials in place and make a start on FTL drives by the first quarter of next year, going by the Earth calendar. Jeff found it hard to be disappointed at a delay in something he hadn't even imagined possible only a few months ago. It was too easy to get miracle fatigue out here.

Jeff went to look for Ingram to let her know he'd been a good little spy. He found her sitting at one of the tables behind the labs, staring at a plate of sandwiches and a chessboard with all the pieces set up.

"Are you locked in a grudge match with yourself, ma'am?" Jeff asked, sitting opposite her.

"No, I'm waiting for Marc Gallagher," she said. "He promised me a game."

"You've seen Commander Searle's report."

"Yes. Good refit schedule. I agree with Fred. The priority is making sure we aren't noticed so that nobody decides to pay us a visit, and if they do, we're able to barbecue them. By the time that phase is completed, housing construction's going to be over and we can release more bots."

"And we're going to need a foreign policy, ma'am."

"Oh. Yes. Vaporise a small city to say keep clear of Opis and we won't do this again. It's going to be a challenge. But it's still all theory, Chief. They might never find us."

"Do it to them before they do it to us."

"Words to live by," Ingram said.

"Anyway, Fred's very enthusiastic about it all." Jeff wanted to get that over with. "Likes Hiyashi a lot, too. No signs at all of cold feet. He's a very happy teerik."

"Good. Nina says the rest of the commune are bored senseless and want to get on with some work."

"Oh. Yeah, she's still helping them learn English, is she?"

"Hearts and minds, Chief. And stomachs. Turisu's husband's started to cave. You know — 'We're stuck here, so we might as well help the humans because it's our safety as well, and can we have more pies please.' We get there in the end."

"It's a shame Fred's daughter is such a misery. Ah, she'll come around."

"Do you feel you're being displaced by Nina, Chief?"

"That's pretty direct, ma'am."

"Do you?"

"In a way, yeah."

"Explain."

"Well, I'm an ordinary bloke who got a chance in a million to do extraordinary things. And I liked it. But now the people with the letters after their names have moved in and I'm just an informer. Petty, I know, but you did ask."

Ingram fidgeted with the chess board, picking up each pawn in order and rotating it three-sixty degrees. "Chief, you have a unique relationship with Fred. You were the first person to make a breakthrough and have an actual conversation with him. You taught him English. If circumstances were different, you'd be back on Earth on the lecture circuit and overwhelmed by awards and interviews. Nobody's going to displace you, so whatever Nina does, you're still the teerik professor here."

"Okay, ma'am." Jeff wished he hadn't said it. "I'm going to the mess, then, to bond with our new comrades. See you later."

Sometimes it really didn't help to speak your mind. He felt stupid for admitting it mattered to him. He wasn't a scientist and he should never have expected anything more than to solve a problem on the day and then leave the real work to the pros. If anyone had the right to Fred's time, it was probably Todd Mangel. He could have a proper conversation about FTL on Fred's level. Dr Kim probably could too.

Jeff carried on to the mess, another piece of territory he felt he'd lost. It was just an unused office in the main building with all the welcome of a dentist's waiting room, but it had become a general social club for the Ainatio contingent and a few of the militia. Chris's mate Jared was helping out behind the trestle table bar, and Jared made very good beer. It was a nice change from Andy's bathtub gin and it gave Jared instant baron status on the base. Jeff accepted a pint from him and got the impression that Jared really wanted to run a pub. He was another guy who'd found something unexpected that he'd have liked to do for a living but probably never would.

"Where's Chris?" Jeff asked.

"He sits with Dieter most evenings. We take turns."

"How's Dieter doing?"

"A lot better." Jared lowered his voice. "Chris asked Reverend Berry to let Dieter bury Girlie in the cemetery. That'll help. We'll do something appropriate when Dieter's well enough to cope with a little ceremony."

"That's good of the vicar."

"Yeah, the Reverend's a nice guy." Jared paused and looked up. "Hey Dan. Beer or paint stripper?"

"Beer please." Trinder slid onto the seat next to Jeff and sat staring at his palms. "I just finished digging a trench. Look at that blister. I need to wear gloves, but if Marc sees them he'll question my masculinity really loudly."

"He won't notice," Jeff said. "He's playing chess with Ingram."

"Oh. *Oh*. Really? I thought that was just a rumour."

"It's just chess."

"Sure."

"Okay, we're planning a Redcoat coup. Keep an eye on it."

"Hah."

Jeff had revised his snap judgement on Trinder from competent and mild-mannered to closet bastard after the incident with Pham's guy. Trinder seemed to be as surprised by it as anyone else. He was back to mild manners today, though, and looked a bit dazed.

"What mission day is it?" he asked. "It feels like we've been here a year."

"You're not wrong there. So were you and Erskine chummy?"

"She'll want to court-martial me when she wakes up. The last time we met, I was busy disobeying her orders."

"Nothing she can do about it here, mate." Jeff studied his beer to work up some proper appreciation for it. "It's like the Foreign Legion. We put our pasts behind us and forget."

"Ah, *La Légion*. All long gone now."

"They won't mind us muscling in on the concept, then."

Jeff didn't actually want to forget anything. He thought Chris and Marc did, though, and Trinder had all the marks of it as well. Opis was a blank canvas. He couldn't blame anyone for wanting to make a fresh start on it.

"Ingram," Trinder said. "She must have been young to make captain, what with her age now and the time she must have spent training for Nomad."

Jeff shrugged, waiting for the awkward question. "Not unusual, really. Lots of smaller ships for coastal defence, so lots of commands available and younger COs with a lot of balls and experience going through the system faster."

"Why did she leave, then? She doesn't strike me as the type to think her work's done. There must be large parts of the European coastline she didn't get around to pulverising."

And there it was. Trinder was neither daft nor mild-mannered. Jeff would be loyal to Ingram to the last and he didn't want anyone thinking ill of her. They always seemed to think she'd blotted her copybook somehow and had to leave.

"I think she felt like I did," Jeff said. "That we'd lost the battle for civilisation on Earth, even if we were hanging on, and it was time to find somewhere we could regroup and rebuild while we still could."

"Makes sense," Trinder said. "I'm starting to like it here. Just knowing there's nobody else waiting to drop their crap on me feels pretty good."

"Apart from armed aliens."

"That wouldn't feel so bad somehow. It's other humans who piss me off."

Jeff waited for Trinder to ask if Ingram was thinking of other uses for the Caisin gate that might involve sorting out unfinished business on Earth, but he didn't. It must have crossed his mind, though. It had certainly crossed Jeff's.

"This is great beer, Jared." Trinder slid the glass towards him for a refill. "You and Marsha could open a restaurant here. Or a proper bar. We need one. That's the kind of thing that makes a community."

"Y'know, I'd never really thought beyond the army," Jared said. "For longevity reasons. But there's no real estate trade here for Marsha, so maybe her fancy cakes are the way ahead."

"I'm in," Jeff said. He had one eye on the door, just curious to see who regarded this as their local now. Erin Piller walked in and wandered over to Trinder to drape her arm over his shoulder.

"You promised me moussaka."

"You promised me vodka," Trinder said.

"Well then."

"Okay." Trinder gulped down his beer and stood up to go. "Excuse me, comrades. Haute cuisine MREs beckon."

Everyone seemed to be getting themselves *allocated*, as Bissey put it. Jared chuckled as he watched them leave.

"They make a nice couple," Jeff said.

"Yeah, Erin could do with a change of luck. She's lost too many people."

Jeff had to remember that he'd slept through the worst of Earth's decline and the US had been hit the hardest. Everyone from Ainatio and the transit camp had lost everything and everybody, even if it didn't look that bad from the outside. He tried to remember that when he dealt with them. He was about to ask Jared how he'd ended up on a convoy out of some hellhole with Chris when his screen chirped and he pulled it out, expecting some minor problem he was being asked to fix.

But it was actually a social message. It came from Fred.

Caisin's egg is hatching, it said. *Please come. I want you to be there.*

"Well, bugger." Jeff jumped up. "Sorry, Jared, I've got a birth to attend. The egg's hatching. I think it's early."

"Damn, you're teerik royalty now, buddy. They ought to name it after you."

Jeff found a quad bike and headed south across the base to the teerik compound. He hadn't been to the new house before, so he just rapped on the door and went in, waiting to be intercepted and taken to the right room.

Nobody came out to see him. But he worked out where to go. All he had to do was follow the noise.

The chick was sitting on a small cushion on a coffee table, and Nina was kneeling there, talking baby talk to it. The teeriks watched, huddled in a group, but it didn't look like joyous wonder at the new arrival. Fred turned to Jeff and did that little head bob that could have been anxiety or relief.

"I'm glad you came, Chief Jeff," he said. "He hatched very fast."

The chick was ugly, like all baby birds, and he was loud. He didn't so much squawk as scrape nails down a blackboard. He was about the size of a blackbird and had a recognisable tuft of a tail, but no feathers had emerged yet, just the bumpy beginnings of quills. And he was red, totally and completely red — a brilliant scarlet everywhere except his black legs and yellow eyes. Even his beak was red, and that beak looked even more formidable than Fred's.

Nina was enchanted. She cooed to him and he waddled unsteadily towards her with his beak wide open.

"I think you've got a friend for life," Jeff said. "He's very cute, Fred."

Fred edged forward for a closer look at the chick, but it squawked at him, head lowered, bony little chicken wings spread, and he drew back.

"He's going to look pretty snazzy with scarlet plumage." Jeff tried the accepted lie that their baby was beautiful. "I think he wants his dinner. Have you decided on a name for him yet?"

"No, no, there's something wrong," Fred said. Teeriks didn't seem to have facial expressions, but this time Jeff could see Fred's eyes had widened in something that looked like horror. "Something's very wrong."

Jeff couldn't see anything wrong with the chick, just the strikingly different colour. If they let others bury their dead — or whatever happened to them — and didn't have a clue about that, then maybe they never saw their chicks until they reached the cute fluffy stage.

"He looks healthy enough to me," Jeff said.

"You don't understand." Fred sounded both heartbroken and confused, like he'd had news so bad he couldn't believe it. "That isn't a teerik. It isn't an ablun at all."

12

AIs changed who we sent into space. We outsourced the planning, the foresight, the precision, the risk, and even the protection of missions to them, all the skills military personnel used to provide. That meant we could send humans with softer, kinder skills — less disciplined, less resilient. But the problem is that space hasn't changed and never will. It's still hard and unforgiving out there. And military personnel — problem-solving, objective-focused, tenacious, ready to take big personal risks for the survival of the group — will always be the right people for the job.

Tad Bednarz, on the necessity to recruit military
personnel for Project Nomad.

NOMAD BASE: LATE AUGUST.

Trinder finally realised why nobody minded his troops taking over the bot hangar.

The building was prime real estate in a crowded base, with a small kitchen area and a bathroom that had never been used. Self-maintaining bots didn't need a john. But whenever Trinder woke up in the darkness, unsure what had disturbed him — a body still on Earth time, unfamiliar noises, a nightmare, even someone else's nightmare — he understood the catch.

In the dark, the hangar was a graveyard with motionless bots for headstones. They were eerily quiet and almost impossible to see until a disembodied light started moving, like it was doing right now, just a soft whirring sound and the ghost of an outline. The strange private world they'd inhabited for more than fifty years was an unnerving place for a human to be. Trinder was the interloper. It was hard not to imagine they were somehow aware of that.

He felt under his pillow for his screen to check the time and realised it wasn't midday. It was just after nine in the morning and he'd only managed four hours' sleep. Adjusting to a longer day was going to be a challenge, with or without medical help, but night duties weren't helping. He stowed his sleeping bag and showered, trying not to wake everyone else.

With no real hazards, security consisted of rounding up small children who'd wandered off or fixing jammed toilet doors in the communal bathroom trailers. Marc had started rifle and handgun training for everyone to keep their skills sharp and adapt their aim to the gravity, and there was still perimeter patrol with Chris's guys, but life had lost something. Trinder had gotten used to extreme stress fast and now he didn't so much miss it as notice the gaping hole it had left in him. He needed something to plug it.

But the question he'd debated back on Earth about his team's role had been answered. They were cops now, not soldiers. If the last few weeks were any guide, their task would be whatever problems were left when the engineers, medics, and agriculturalists had sorted out theirs. He reheated the mug of coffee he'd left last night, reluctant to waste any now, and studied the live Nomad map to see what had changed while he was asleep.

There were more houses. There were foundations for a school. There was also a new icon he hadn't been expecting.

A little graphic of Earth was rotating in the upper right corner. What did that mean? A comms link, news channels, the feed from the teerik probes? Who else had it? Only two people could have made it available: Solomon and Ingram. Trinder didn't want news from home when it wasn't home any more, but that little blue sphere kept dragging his eyes back. The choice was now imagining the worst or facing reality.

Reality won. But the menu that opened when he tapped the globe wasn't what he expected. Suddenly he had a choice of news channels, movies, sport, education, and something called Nomad TV. For a moment he was pissed that he hadn't been consulted, but it seemed so damn *trivial* after everything that had happened that he couldn't stay irked for long.

He opted for Indian news because Solomon had said they had people on the ground in APS. But their top ten news stories turned out to be a political leadership challenge, a cricket bribes scandal, and some pop star's lavish wedding, featuring a dress so heavily embroidered with real gold thread that she could only walk a few yards in it. Despite Earth's problems, there were still places where life seemed to go on almost like nothing had happened.

APS's woes had been relegated to the news-in-brief section already — road crews still clearing abandoned cars, salvage teams trying to raise a cargo jet that had crashed in Hong Kong's Victoria Harbour, and studio guests yelling in a heated debate about overdependence on driverless transport. Trinder tried to recall the last time he'd flown anywhere or even driven long-distance. He carried on watching for a while, just for a glimpse of the world he'd lost.

There was a news conference from Seoul, though, and it had been first broadcast twenty hours ago, so APS had either managed to launch a replacement satellite themselves or some ally was helping them out. The APS president was talking bland Statementese, going on about the need to work together and help the victims and learn lessons, no fingerpointing at all beyond speculation about amateur hackers. Trinder couldn't find any mention of Tim Pham. But Pham could hardly stand up in public and accuse anyone of having a ASD AI on the rampage without inviting very awkward questions.

There was no mention of Kill Line or even America, but he'd expected that. If an obscure corner of country that no longer existed had been scoured with sodium bombs, nobody else knew, and if they did, they didn't care.

Trinder put the screen in his pocket and followed the dim path of emergency floor lights to the exit. He inched the side door open just enough to squeeze through without letting the sunlight crash in, and made it a few paces down the path before the door opened behind him again. Jon Simonot was right on his heels. The kid had missed his calling as a ninja.

"Sir, have you seen the Earth link? Alex Gorko got it all online overnight. Movies and everything."

"I've seen the news, what there was of it."

"I just wanted to know if Pham nuked Kill Line in the end. Doug Brandt hasn't asked, but I know it's on everyone's mind."

Trinder shook his head. "I don't know. We're last week's drama, if they knew we existed at all."

Simonot nodded. "Okay, sir. I bet Sol knows, though."

Trinder wasn't sure if that was his way of saying that if Sol knew, Trinder knew too, or a hint that he thought the AI was keeping secrets. But Sol always had. He'd known the truth about Nomad and *Cabot* from the start.

"I suppose that means the *Cabot* crew have news access too," Trinder said.

"Well, it's only been live for a few hours, but I don't think civil war's broken out yet. Not while they've got Brazilian soccer and new movies, anyway."

Trinder had put his imaginary money on news from home generating some upset and anger before everyone moved on. Marc thought people would get homesick because it wasn't just easy to *see* Earth, it was also easy to go back, in theory at least. Perhaps they were both wrong. Maybe *Cabot*'s crew didn't want to look back at all. They'd left Earth expecting to be completely cut off, and even if that felt like only a few months ago, they'd already been prepared for the world to change out of all recognition by the time they were revived. For everyone else, though, the Earth they could see had been home just weeks ago. It still had its pull.

Trinder took a Caracal and drove around the perimeter to look at the overnight construction, as good a way as any to remind himself why he was here. Leaving Earth was always going to be hard. Memory would erase the unpleasant stuff, and people would develop a rosier view as time went on, so news reports would be a reminder that they hadn't abandoned a paradise. That was no bad thing.

Nomad Base wasn't quite paradise itself yet, but it was getting there. The housing zone had started to look more like a town and the first tranche of homes was ready for the first one hundred and fifty families to move in. Trinder knew these were big milestones, historic stuff, but for the first time in his adult life there was no immediate crisis driving him — no epidemics, no die-back, no economic collapse, no terrorism, no small wars, and no secrets to keep. The problems here were modest. They were *domestic*. Surviving on an alien world would have its challenges, but he didn't feel an axe was hanging over him, and that made him restless. He kept looking for it.

"Good morning, Major." Solomon sounded almost chirpy. "I take it you've seen our new entertainment network."

"I have, Sol. Was that your idea or Alex's?"

"The credit goes to Alex. All I had to do was identify the entertainment sources on his shopping list and access them."

"So we're stealing satellite TV. On a galactic scale."

"I'm sure we'd be happy to pay the subscription if there was still a means to do so."

"And what's Nomad TV?"

"Just a more reassuring way of disseminating information. More digestible for civilians than memos and audio messages."

"I hope Alex isn't going to video everything."

"Major, everything you do in a public space here is picked up by one sensor or another," Solomon said. "Security cams. And all the bots. They have to monitor their surroundings to do their work, so we can get them to monitor other things as well and use that data for other purposes. That's how we have a real-time map. That's how I can locate and identify people around the site. So we might as well share relevant parts of that data with everyone living here so that they know what's going on. People like to feel they're being told everything."

It was no different from the surveillance they'd had at Ainatio, just with a wider audience. Trinder still didn't like it and he knew he wouldn't be alone.

"And who decides what's relevant? Build consent and anonymity into this or I'll get it suspended." The old Trinder would never have thrown his weight around like that. He knew he should have done. "Okay, so the teerik probes are still in place, or you wouldn't have an Earth link. Did Pham deploy the bombs in the end? There's nothing about it on the news."

"It doesn't appear that he has," Solomon said. "Not yet, anyway. From what I can overhear, I gather APS and APDU personnel were only evacuated last night."

"How did you pick that up?"

"Russia gave some APS agencies bandwidth on their comms satellites. Their security isn't a barrier to me."

"Isn't sharing sats a risk for them? And you?"

"The sabcode burned itself out, as Bednarz said it would."

"You sure?"

"Yes, or I wouldn't be attempting to access them. There's been no report of further disruption for days. Anyway, the staff we left behind appear to be on their way to APS countries as arranged. I haven't picked up any mention of Pham at all, which isn't surprising, but I did catch something on Dr Mendoza's patients. Mikel Lask passed away a few days ago. The remaining four are still in the hospice in Sydney."

Ainatio's infirmary usually had a few sick and elderly employees seeing out their last days because there was nowhere else for them to go. This time, though, the last of them had been evacuated to

Australia as soon as Pham landed, a generous gesture that had given Trinder entirely the wrong idea about the guy. The terminal patients had decided they'd prefer to die on Earth. Trinder thought it was a lonely choice with all their buddies leaving, but they wanted to stay with each other. Their tribe had probably become those who knew what facing the end felt like. It was a shame that they never knew about the Caisin gate, but maybe those things were irrelevant when you were on the brink of a much more significant journey.

"I still think you're taking a risk hacking into those comms," Trinder said. "Even if the sabcode's dead."

"But I had to know if the outages had harmed our patients. I'd never have forgiven myself for that."

"It's okay, Sol. I understand." Trinder decided to change the subject. "Is the teerik chick eating yet?"

"I'm afraid not. But chickens don't need to eat for a few days after hatching because they absorb the yolk sac, so perhaps that's what we're seeing. The child does appear to be abnormal, though. I accept what Fred says about the unusual colouring and slow behaviour."

"It's a baby. What do they expect, differential calculus?"

"Some attempt to mimic sounds, apparently. And he has spurs on his legs that they don't have."

"Is that like having a sixth finger or something? No, don't tell me. They don't know."

"I imagine its abnormalities are the result of having an elderly and sick mother," Solomon said. "They named him Rikayl, by the way."

"Is that significant?"

"Only if you have a conversation with Fred and want to be courteous."

"Okay. Right."

"Nina's been trying various food formulas and Rikayl flings them aside. He seems very hungry, but he won't eat. One of the Kill Line veterinarians attempted to force-feed him with a syringe. Let's just say it didn't go well. The man needed sutures in his hand."

"Anything else I need to address?"

"Dr Mangel's asked if he and Dr Kim can work with Fred on the new drives."

It was kind of Mangel to get Kim involved. She wasn't quite an outcast, but she still wasn't accepted as one of the Ainatio tribe either, except by Alex. "Do astrophysicists do that stuff?" Trinder asked.

"I think he wants to understand the physics rather than get involved in drive design. He's still very excited about it. It'll be a test of how open our teerik allies are to sharing information."

"Can't we just reverse engineer it?"

"Probably not. As Marc said, it's one thing to give a shipyard a set of plans and specifications for materials, and another to be able to work out why the item needs to be that shape or made out of that particular substance to start with. Fred's people have quite an edge intellectually and they use it."

"Well, if Fred says yes, I'm all for our guys getting a better understanding of what we've sold our souls for," Trinder said. "It sounds like we're being told more than the teeriks' previous clients, though. I'll sleep better when we're not wholly dependent."

"Do you sleep well now, Dan?"

Solomon never normally called him Dan. "What, you mean the damn bots waking me up?"

"No, I meant your traumatic experience." Sol was tiptoeing around Trinder killing Pham's operator. "I think it would unsettle anyone."

"If I'm having nightmares, I don't remember them," Trinder said. "Don't worry. I'll see the doc if I need to."

No, he wouldn't bother the doctors at all. The incident was still too raw not to be on his mind all the time, but he was among men and women who'd had to deal with the same thing, including Erin. He'd get through it the same way they did. He just wasn't sure they'd defaulted to the same level of savagery. Killing someone, even an enemy, wasn't meant to be something that slipped your mind like picking up your dry cleaning. Being preoccupied by it seemed a reasonable reaction. It was the way he'd gone from standing up to Erskine to battering a guy's head in within weeks that worried him. The shooting was a split second decision that could have gone either way depending on who grabbed the gun, but reaching for the nearest blunt object first and using it in the most primal way was a different kind of violence. Trinder wasn't sure that was normal.

"I'm glad you realise there's no shame in asking for help," Solomon said.

"Yeah, I'll be okay." Sometimes it wasn't easy to steer Solomon off a topic. "I'm going to take a walk around the crop tunnels now. See what's growing."

"Dr Maybury's in there. She's rather down in the dumps. Perhaps you can cheer her up."

"I'll see what I can do."

Other people's problems were always a useful distraction from Trinder's own. He wasn't on casual chat terms with Lianne Maybury, but she was harmless, and he really did want to see what they'd managed to grow.

The crop tunnels ran in neat rows across the shallow incline to the east of the base, transparent cylinders gridded by irrigation pipes and solar collector lines. As Trinder drove towards them, the skyline could have been any rural county in America before die-back took hold. But if he looked behind him towards the distant mountains, he could see the stark line between the familiar terrestrial vegetation around the base and the reds and dusty greens of the Opis wilderness. Nomad was an island of terraformed land, a micro-environment, as separate from the world around it as Hart County had been. It was also a breach of international law. But Bednarz hadn't given a rat's ass about preserving pristine ecosystems any more than he cared about building illegal AIs, and there was nobody around to enforce the law now.

Trinder stepped through the decontamination airlock at the main entrance to the tunnels and paddled his boots in a big tray that looked like a soggy deep-pile doormat while the system sniffed him. When it decided he wasn't contaminated, it opened the inner door.

The still air inside smelled of damp soil and fresh green things. Gravel crunched under his boots. For a moment he was ten again, trailing around after his grandfather at the garden centre. As he wandered between the stacked beds and tower planters of spinach and peppers, he tried to see himself doing some farming — just vegetables, nothing with horns and hooves — and it didn't seem impossible.

An occasional flash at head height caught his eye as he explored, but he didn't see what it was until he stood still and waited for it to pass him again. He hadn't seen a single insect or any other native creature other than some bird-sized things high in the sky and small animals well outside the perimeter defences. But in the tunnels, even self-pollinating crops needed a bit of help from pollinators.

Eventually the insect tracked back again and settled on the retaining rail around one of the spinach beds. Trinder edged closer for a look, but now he could see it wasn't organic at all. It was a bot the size of a hornet, bee-like in structure but made of opaque grey composite. Being a machine, it wasn't scared and it didn't fly off. He studied it until he heard someone crunching along the gravel path behind him.

"Bee bots," Lianne Maybury said.

Trinder studied it. "We had a stash of these in Ainatio when I joined, but I don't know what happened to them. No imported bees, then?"

"I don't think we've got real bees in the cryo store, but I suppose we could always pop back to Earth and collect some. They might be rather confused here, though."

Lianne had been in charge of die-back research for at least ten years, but Trinder had rarely spoken to her. Ainatio had its own castes and cliques. Now she was in the same boat as him, trying to work out whether her old skills would fit into a new world or whether she'd have to learn another way to be useful.

"These plants look really healthy," Trinder said. "Must be nice not to have to worry about die-back."

"Who said I wasn't? I'm still wondering what I missed."

"It's not your fault."

"Of course it's my fault, Dan. It was my department. Honestly, I've gone over it a hundred times and I still can't see how it got out."

"Well, there's no die-back here, and the real damage was done a long time before you even started working on it."

"Yes, but there was something wrong with our procedure. And until we work out what it was, it's a mistake we could make again. For all I know, there's a pathogen here waiting to attack crops. I need to know I'm competent to deal with it."

Lianne stopped for a moment. She wanted to talk. Solomon had obviously worked that out. Trinder couldn't tell if she'd kept her anxiety to herself and couldn't hold it in any longer, or if she'd driven her colleagues nuts about it and there was nobody willing to listen any more except him.

"I wasn't expecting APS to let me go," she said. "I really thought they were either going to accuse me of bioterrorism and drag me off to stand trial, or make me continue the research for them at gunpoint. I don't understand them."

At least Trinder could answer that one. "It was Tim Pham," he said. "He told Chris he didn't believe the Ainatio strain was going to reach Asia. He didn't care about it."

Lianne's permanent frown vanished for a moment because she'd raised her eyebrows so far. "Seriously? After they were going to nuke us for it?"

"It was the agriculture minister who was panicking, not Pham," Trinder said. "Pham was the one who decided to postpone the bombing. Damn, I sound like I'm making excuses for him, don't I? I'm just saying he had a different agenda."

"Was that before or after Abbie stabbed us in the back?" Lianne shook her head. "That's another thing I didn't see until it was too late."

Trinder had finally found someone who kicked themselves in their own ass harder than he did. "Nobody else suspected her, either," he said.

"Do you know why she did it?"

"No, other than she didn't want to come here."

"But I thought they already approved her for resettlement. "She knew she didn't have to leave Earth."

Trinder shrugged. The bee bot lifted off in a straight vertical, more like a Lammergeier than an insect. "I heard she wanted to carry on her die-back research. Something about her work on pollinators."

"But she never worked on pollinators," Lianne said. "Not directly. She was actually working on a counter-virus to infect die-back and neutralise it that way."

"I didn't know viruses did that to each other."

"Some can. But we never got anywhere with it. I don't imagine she told Tim Pham that, though."

"So she wanted to get away from her family that badly," Trinder said.

"I know she wasn't very likeable, Dan, but I felt sorry for her. Imagine living your entire life in a research centre. She was born there and she probably thought she'd die there. I think she just wanted to be absolutely sure that she got away from her folks, and let's face it, doing a big favour for Tim Pham guaranteed they couldn't drag her to Opis. She wanted her own life."

Trinder found it hard to pity Abbie. There were plenty of less destructive ways to run away from home. "What did she think about Nomad?"

"What do you mean?"

"Well, when Erskine came clean about the project, a lot of staff were pissed at her for all the lies, but some just didn't want to go into space."

Lianne slipped back into her perma-frown. "Abbie thought it was a waste of time and said we'd mess up Opis like we messed up Earth. Quite a few people thought the same. But we all wanted to stay and carry on with die-back research because we were damned if we'd surrender to the thing. But I did, didn't I? I decided we'd lost the battle and I retreated."

"Would Abbie have tried to sabotage the mission, though?" Trinder wanted to ask about the others who thought like Abbie, and if any of them were here now, but this wasn't the time to cross-examine Lianne. He'd let her talk and circle back to that later. "Did she rat us out to stop Nomad?"

"Why would she?" Lianne shrugged. "She didn't want to go, and in the end she didn't have to. She wanted to get on with her research."

It didn't matter now. Abbie couldn't do any more damage, except for destroying people's trust in their neighbours when they realised they didn't know each other very well after all. Nomad had been spared a disruptive influence, and Trinder would never had to worry about her again. He watched the bee bot making its orderly way along each row of tomatoes, and warmed to the idea of a house with a garden so he could grow things. His grandad would have been pleased.

"Would you like to see something awesome?" Lianne asked.

Trinder wasn't due to relieve Fonseca until midday. He had time to kill. "Yeah, I could do with some awe right now."

"Follow me, then."

The crop tunnels were interconnected on a grid pattern like a warren for obsessively tidy rabbits, and most of them were already full of regular salad crops, herbs, and greens. But there were also potatoes with purple striped foliage and a perennial rice that was a cut-and-come-again crop. Trinder admired the potatoes' eggplant-coloured leaves and wondered if that meant the spuds were the same shade.

"Awesome indeed," he said. "Fries and jambalaya."

"There's something even more awesome than that," Lianne said. "Look in here."

A door slid open and a strong floral perfume hit Trinder like he'd accidentally walked into the women's bathroom. It was intense and exotic, a lot like jasmine. Maybe it was. The tunnel was full of glossy green bushes four or five feet high, smothered with thousands of white star-shaped blooms that had already started to fall. Trinder inhaled and took a guess.

"Some kind of jasmine? Gardenia? Weird citrus hybrid?"

"Coffee, Dan. *Coffee.* Coffea arabica Pascoe Four-One-Nine. Developed specially for the mission."

The world was suddenly a better place. Trinder went over to the bushes and drank in the scent. Maybe there was a hint of coffee in that perfume after all.

"Okay, I'm officially awed," he said. "But this didn't happen in the last few months."

"No, these were grown from the seed store the unmanned ships brought. They're mature. Bednarz thought of everything, or his team did, but whoever it was, I salute them."

Morale lived or died with the small things. It really had brightened Trinder's day, not only because he'd now have plenty of proper coffee, but because someone had cared enough about the quality of future strangers' lives to make sure they had a few small luxuries.

He picked up a fallen flower and sniffed it. "Between you and Andy Braithwaite, you've got the leisure beverages market sewn up. You'll have a great time here."

"That's what Paul tells me," Lianne said. They walked on and emerged in another tunnel full of beefsteak tomatoes. She picked one with the colouring of an apricot, pale orange dappled with deep red at its stem end, and handed it to him. "Don't look back, he says. But husbands always tell you what you want to hear. That was my life's work. I'm forty-five. Logic isn't going to stop me feeling that it was all wasted."

Maybe that was what really bothered her, not the disasters that had happened on her watch. "But it isn't," Trinder said. "That's the research your team's taking to APS. Maybe Seb and Abbie are going to make a breakthrough based on that. Look how many old drugs are dusted off to treat new diseases. No knowledge is wasted."

Lianne just looked at him. He knew he was on the knife edge between a pep talk and a lecture on the finer points of egg-sucking.

"Now who's going to make *you* feel better, Dan?"

"I'm fine," he said.

"Come on, my grandad was Navy. I know the look of someone who isn't ready to hang up their uniform."

"Lianne, I was a glorified security guard for years and then I had a few weeks of excitement and, I admit, pants-wetting terror." The last thing Trinder wanted was sympathy. It made him think everyone except him could see there was something wrong. "I'll go back to filling in forms and it'll be like none of it ever happened. I shall now go and savour this fine tomato. Thank you."

Trinder did feel better, though. He'd pointed out positive things that hadn't occurred to him before. It was one of those rituals like making yourself smile until you believed you had a reason to. Did he really mean he'd go back to being a desk jockey? The hell he did. There were still potential dangers out there, probably worse ones than APS or die-back, and even the best automated security couldn't replace trained, committed people who wanted to defend their community. Uniforms would not be hung up anytime soon.

He continued his drive around the perimeter with his perfect tomato perched on the dashboard like a still life study and stopped off at the livestock compound.

Liam's cattle seemed to be doing okay. They were sharing a field with some sheep, and most of them were lying down, which Trinder's grandad had always said was a sign of rain on the way. Trinder thought they were probably just taking it easy. He also hated himself just a little for looking at the sheep and thinking that he could wow Erin soon by cooking her a moussaka from scratch. The allure of his MREs would only last so long. Steve Kokinos made a thing of his Greek ancestry, so maybe he was the guy to ask for a masterclass.

"Hey Dan." Joanne Brandt came over to him and they leaned on the fence together like a couple of proper farmers. "Can we put up a statue to Alex Gorko? I love my grandchildren, but it's bliss to be able to park them with a cartoon channel and get on with some work."

"Yeah, Alex has a knack of knowing how to keep people happy," Trinder said. He'd still kick his ass about the base news later. "Ingram can probably give him an honorary knighthood. It's not like anyone's going to stop her."

"It's the little things."

"Are those Bill Dawud's sheep, by the way?"

"They're Marty Laurenson's now. Bill gave him a few ewes to start another flock."

"Really? That's terrific. I still feel bad that he put his animals down."

"Nobody could have guessed how things were going to pan out, Dan. It's just good that he's ready to start over."

"This is all going to work out, isn't it?"

"I do believe it will. It's certainly working out for the chickens. We have an egg glut. We're storing and preserving a lot, but nothing beats fresh-laid. Would you like some?"

"Sure." Trinder now had visions of whipping up a special tomato omelette for Erin. He'd never cared much about cooking, but it scored points with her and suddenly it mattered. "Why so many eggs?"

"More hours of sunlight, I suppose. That's what makes hens lay. Give them enough light and their hormones react by producing eggs. And that's every day for most of the breeds we've got here."

"I didn't know that. Damn, every day's a school day."

"So I'll get you some eggs. I'll be back in a moment."

Trinder was still working out how to cook them in the hangar's tiny multi range when Joanne came back carrying a mesh box rattling with an assortment of eggs in white, brown, and a tasteful pale blue. One of the hens trailed after her like it wanted its eggs back.

"That's Mildred," Joanne said. "She's quite the explorer. I thought she'd be good for Ingram because she prefers hanging out with people rather than hens, which is weird for a chicken, but she wanders back here quite often. She's a tad eccentric."

Mildred inspected Trinder's boots and then settled on the Caracal's step to sunbathe. He was going to have to move her to climb into the cab.

"I'll give her a ride back to the office," he said. "It seems rude not to."

"I really do think she's asking."

Trinder had never handled poultry except to carve it. He picked up Mildred like a cat, scooping her with both hands. She tolerated his amateur technique and let him place her on the passenger seat next to the box of eggs.

"Come on, Mildred," he said. "Let's go see your mom."

He dodged ruts to avoid bouncing Mildred off the seat and stuck to the paved road to the centre of the base. It really needed a proper name now. It was time for streets and avenues and squares. There were people and places to be commemorated, like Mikel Lask and Derek Levine, and maybe even Annis Kim's great-grandma and Caisin. Not looking back didn't mean forgetting where you'd come from and erasing your history. It was about sifting out the good parts for continued use and leaving the worst visible as a reminder not to do it again, because folks had to know how they got here. This was part of the teeriks' problem. They had no past. They didn't know where they came from, and if you didn't have anything to cherish that defined you, even an idea, you just fell. There was nothing to hold on to.

Trinder had to think about what he clung to. He was pretty sure it was his grandparents and their place in Vermont. If anything summed up what Earth had lost, it was that.

"I'm getting maudlin," he said to the chicken. "Hey, look, it's Jeff Aiken. Scooch up, Mildred. Let's give him a ride."

Jeff was striding along the road with the purposeful gait of a man who had to get something done before he changed his mind. Trinder overtook him, slowed to a halt, and opened the passenger door. Jeff broke into a jog to catch up.

"You're a lifesaver, sir." Jeff squeezed into the front seat, avoiding the treasure trove of eggs and a slightly indignant Mildred. "Are you going near the medical centre?"

"Are you okay?"

"I'm fine, I just need to get to the veterinary office." Jeff sat Mildred on his lap like a child who needed holding onto. "Nina's taken Rikayl to get a scan done. I'm expecting blood and tears. The vet's, probably. But I promised Fred I'd keep an eye on things."

"Yeah, Solomon updated me," Trinder said. "So they're still working on the ships. Not at Rikayl's bedside or wherever."

"It probably takes their minds off it, sir."

"I like to think I'd stay with my kid if he was sick."

Jeff looked like he was shaping up to say something but couldn't pin it down. He rocked his head slightly and frowned.

"Y'know, I think they're so used to their foremen thinking for them that they've got no instincts left. And all they care about is work. People get that way too."

"What are we scanning for if we haven't found out much about teerik biology yet?"

"Well, if he's not eating because he's got an obstruction in his gullet or something, we can certainly spot that."

"Sol says chickens live off their yolk sac for a while after they hatch."

"Yeah, but teeriks aren't birds, are they?"

"But they do lay eggs, and an egg is basically a bomb shelter with its own independent food supply. So, you know, form follows function. They might operate the same way."

Jeff lowered his head to whisper to the chicken. "That sounded really clever, Mildred, so it must be true." Then he pointed to the dashboard. "Anyway, I see you've got a special tomato. Officers only, eh?"

"Dr Maybury gave it to me because I'm so nice."

"Never accept salad ingredients from strange women, sir. They're only after one thing."

"She might be testing it on me."

"If it's poisonous and you don't make it, can I have your snazzy carbine?"

"Yeah, it's what I'd want. Every time you smoke a Kugin, Chief, think of me."

Jeff poked the tomato with his forefinger. "If we ever find out what they look like, I will."

Nowhere in Nomad was more than a few minutes' drive away yet, not even taking it slowly for Mildred and the eggs. Trinder pulled into the parking bay at the back of the medical centre and looked for the separate huddle of cube buildings marked VETERINARY CLINIC. He hoped teeriks weren't easily offended.

Jeff got out, clutching Mildred. Trinder went to open the clinic door but it was ajar, and that was odd. Everyone secured doors here, because *Cabot*'s crew were either used to warships or spacecraft, where lives depended on keeping the outside out. Someone was going to get their ass kicked. Trinder hoped it wasn't one of his guys. He walked in and looked around the small lobby.

"Anyone home?"

There was no answer. Jeff was behind him, though, and he'd seen something Trinder hadn't.

"They're all out here, sir. Oh dear. A non-compliant patient."

He put Mildred down and pointed up in the air. Trinder joined him to take a look. There was a comms mast at the back of the buildings, about sixty feet high, and it took Trinder a few moments to spot what Jeff was pointing at. Halfway up the protective mesh that enclosed the lower half of the structure, there was something bright red, climbing like a bat by hooking its claws into the wire grid. Trinder hadn't actually seen Rikayl before. For a starving chick, he was making impressive progress. He looked like a spiky oven-ready chicken that had way too much paprika in the rub.

Jeff swore to himself and trotted off in the direction of the mast. Trinder followed. They found Nina, two of the vets, and Bissey standing at the base of the mast, calling to the teerik and trying to coax him down. Both of the vets were wearing big protective gloves. They'd obviously learned their lesson. A small crowd of onlookers had gathered to make helpful suggestions.

"Dare I ask what happened?" Jeff said.

Nina looked desperate. "He just went crazy when he saw the scanner. Considering that he can't fly, I'm amazed he got away from us."

"Always close the hatch."

"But we did. We shut the doors. He scrambled up the wall and out the window, and it wasn't even open that far."

Trinder watched, waiting for the chick to decide he'd climbed high enough. They still had that instinct to get aloft, then, just like Fred wanting to fly. The only problem was Rikayl had no flight feathers yet.

"He's going to break his neck," Trinder said.

Nina let out a little sigh of annoyance. But she did look scared. Nobody wanted a dead teerik on their watch, especially her. "Do you have a suggestion for getting him to come down?"

"Food isn't going to work, so we either wait for him to get bored or we go up and get him," Trinder said. "It's a shame we don't have any python bots left. Maybe we can find a suitable drone."

"I can do it. You don't need a bot." It was Chris, right behind him. "Have we got any nets? Sol, are you getting this?"

"You mean a safety net?" Trinder asked.

"No, something to throw over him. If I get up there and try to grab him, he's going to panic and fall."

"No, he'll to try to take your arm off," one of the vets said.

"Well, he can't fly off, so he's stuck." Chris took off his jacket and handed it to Trinder. "If we wait, he might be too exhausted to hang on and he'll fall anyway. Can someone get me a safety line? Carabiner at both ends, please."

"I ought to do it," Jeff said. "Fred left the kid with us and I don't want him coming back to a corpse."

Trinder wondered if that was a dig at Nina. But Chris was taking charge of the rescue, and while he was debating the method with Jeff, Zakko arrived clutching a safety line, a harness, and a sheet of agricultural netting formed into a rough bucket shape by clips. No, it didn't look like that was going to work. They abandoned the net idea and the vet handed Chris his bite-proof gloves. Chris shielded his eyes against the sun and took another look at where Rikayl had gotten to.

"I hope he's got an instinctive fear of falling," Chris muttered. "But he's avian, so maybe not. Ah, shit, what's he doing now?"

Rikayl had reached a flat section of rail. He'd been climbing with his face to the mast up to that point, but now he'd stopped and taken a grip on the rail with his feet, facing outward. Maybe he'd suddenly realised how high he was and that climbing down was going to be hard. For a moment or two, he glanced around as if he'd noticed the terrific view of the base, and then he lowered his head and seemed to fix on a point below. He was staring at the ground.

"Get your excuses ready, folks," Chris said. "I don't think he's going to hang on."

Nina looked distraught. "He can't fly."

"Neither can I." Chris said it in his usual unemotional, inoffensive way, but Trinder could tell when he was irritated. "So I'm going to climb as fast as I can and hope he's still perched when I get up there. Then I'll grab him by his neck and work out how to subdue him while I bring him down."

Chris started climbing the ladder. There was no ladder cage, so he was depending on that safety line, and he hadn't hooked it on to anything yet.

Trinder could see Rikayl wasn't taking any notice of Chris, even though he could probably see him. He was still looking down at the ground, apparently not scared at all. If anything, he seemed perfectly calm. He shifted his weight a little, head still lowered.

And then he just pushed off from the rail.

Nina gasped. Everyone else froze. All Trinder saw was a red streak as Rikayl stretched out his featherless wings and didn't even flap, probably because he couldn't. He didn't plummet, though. Maybe there was enough lift for him to glide a little, but he was going to hit the ground hard enough to kill himself. It happened so fast that nobody had even reacted by the time Trinder heard a loud squawk.

Rikayl must have hit the ground in the parking area. Trinder started running. When he rounded the corner of the building, he couldn't see a body, but there were a lot of feathers, black and white ones. It took him a moment to piece things together.

The teerik chick was sitting on the top rail of a barrier a few yards away, Mildred's lifeless body clutched in his claws while he ripped raw chunks out of her.

"Oh *shit*." Trinder knew teeriks had the natural equipment to be raptors, but it was still a shock to see the chick beak-deep in another creature's guts. "You little bastard."

Jeff caught up with him. A blizzard of small feathers was drifting around now and folks who'd been watching the aborted rescue had come to stare. There wasn't much else they could do.

"Bloody hell," Jeff said. "Well, at least we know what he wants to eat."

Trinder had to look away. It was like watching a puppy savaging your gran. Chris appeared, clutching his jacket, and watched the spectacle for a few moments with no expression at all. Nina pushed past the knot of onlookers and walked up to the feasting Rikayl.

"You wanted meat?" she asked. Rikayl certainly trusted her. He made no attempt to defend his lunch or haul it away when she got close to him. "Is that it? Raw meat?"

"Should have worked that out," Trinder said. "We know teeriks like roast meat."

"Yeah, but there's a big difference between enjoying a plate of barbecued wings and ripping the entrails out of a live chicken," Chris said, folding his arms to watch. "And we've got farmers and livestock here. If our featherless cherub here gets as big as Fred, how do we keep him away from the animals? How are the farmers going to react? Because I might be able to wrestle him now, but that isn't going to last long."

Bissey sidled up to them. "I've got a few concerns too."

One problem had been solved. Rikayl wasn't going to starve, not unless chicken meat turned out to be toxic for him. But now there were questions about exactly what he was, a teerik who'd been born damaged or just normal for the species and they were all like him underneath.

"I don't really know them any more," Jeff said.

"We never knew to start with, Chief." Chris picked up a few feathers. They'd have to clean up the mess before Ingram saw it. "And I don't think they know themselves, either. Who's going to break the news to Fred?"

* * *

RECREATION AREA, GENERALLY KNOWN AS THE BEER GARDEN, NOMAD BASE: 1815 HOURS, EIGHT DAYS LATER.

"Are you sure you don't want another one?" Marc asked.

He studied the chess board. Chess was like golf, a way to do discreet business without attracting attention, but it bored the arse off him. So did golf.

Ingram shook her head. "It's kind of you, but I don't think fate wanted me to keep chickens."

"Okay. At least you can still get fresh eggs."

"Doug Brandt was very nice about it, but he made it clear that Fred's going to have to manage Rikayl. No sheep-worrying. It'll reach the stage where the dogs go for him, he'll kill one, and it'll escalate from there."

Ingram had taken Mildred's grisly end far better than Marc expected. She was always calm and gracious on the surface, even when she wanted to punch the shit out of someone, but he felt he knew her well enough now to know when she was keeping a lid on it. She just seemed sad about it. But if she wasn't war-gaming the worst scenario, she wasn't Ingram.

"And there we were, worrying about your APS crew wanting to avenge their countrymen," Marc said. "Who'd have thought it'd be farmers versus aliens?"

Ingram shook her head again. "Poor old Mildred."

"My job's doing stuff we can't be seen to do. Say the word and I will."

"Marc, we can't go around assassinating the inconvenient offspring of our allies."

"Sorry, I wasn't aware the policy had changed."

"Come on. Promise me."

"All right. Scout's honour."

Marc studied the chessboard, chin resting on his hand, beer within easy reach. He could feel Betsy leaning against his leg under the table and getting heavier, slumping as she dozed off. She'd latched onto him. She was a very protective dog, but it was hard to tell if she was guarding Howie or if she thought Marc needed looking after as well.

"Anyway, we've got other issues," Ingram said. "What do we do about Earth?"

They'd kicked this around for a while and it wasn't getting any easier, just more defined. "We don't know enough to do *anything* yet," Marc said. "We could make matters a lot worse."

"Marc, I don't think you can walk away and let the homeworld rot any more than I can."

"I'm with the Mother Death nutters now," he said. "Wipe out humans and let the cockroaches take over."

"You don't mean that."

"Do."

"I know what keeps you awake at night."

"You do, do you?"

"Yes. Tev. And probably a lot of friends and relatives you'd like to save before the cockroaches move in."

Okay, Ingram knew him at least as well as he knew her. Marc did worry about Tev, and plenty of others as well. Tev had made his choice before anyone knew how easy it would be to get to Opis. Nothing else had changed, though. Marc still didn't know if Tev's family would want a one-way trip or how bad Earth would have to get before they decided to abandon it.

"Yeah, I worry," he said. "And you and me, we still have loyalties and moral obligations to a functioning country, which is something the Americans don't have to worry about. So no matter how often I say we've got to make Nomad our nationality, my gut keeps reminding me I'm English."

Ingram leaned forward, arms folded on the table. There was nobody eating nearby. The two of them created their own exclusion zone, and that was the point of meeting over a game of chess. Nobody would start worrying about secret Brits-only intel meetings because they were sitting there in plain view and looked like they had a thing going. But she still kept her voice to a whisper.

"Some days," she said, "I don't feel I have the right to keep the gate secret, and I should contact One-SL and hand it all over to her. If I hadn't left the service, the decision would have been easy."

"*Him,*" Marc said. "The First Sea Lord's a bloke now. And if you were still serving, you wouldn't be here now. And you were going to say *but.*"

"Oh. Yes. But... doing it by the book feels like cowardice. Because I know there'll be consequences if and when the gate becomes common knowledge, and some of them will be ugly, so I'd just be passing the buck to someone else to start a war."

Marc nodded. "Been there, thought the same thing. But we're overlooking one fact. The technology's not ours. It's the teeriks'.

And the Kugin are going to say it's theirs when they find out about it because the teeriks work for them."

"That doesn't absolve me from passing on intelligence," Ingram said. "If anything, it makes it more urgent."

"I know, but it makes the consequences clearer. Anyone with two brain cells will see that grabbing the technology is going to end in tears. Although that never stopped anyone before."

"Marc, I'm just saying I don't know what to do. Which is a first for me. I'm decisive. I don't always make the right decisions, but I make them. Indecision's fatal in our game."

Our game. Just a couple of months ago, neither of them had known gate technology existed or that there were intelligent aliens. It was an impossibly short time to adjust to that kind of culture shock so he hadn't even bothered to try. He kept his focus on things he could do something about, which meant looking after the people here.

"I don't know the answer either," he said. "I just want to help Tev and everyone else I'm afraid for. So I try to break the problem into chunks. If I call the FCO and tell Lawson about our new toy, things are going to happen, and you know this as well as I do. He'll have to pass it up the line. Then someone's going to want to pay us a visit. Then it'll leak inside Whitehall, because it always does, and then someone else will want the technology for urgent local problems, not future space colonies, and by local problems I mean taking on APS or fighting whichever warlords are apocalypsing Europe now. At that point, too many gobshites know, word gets out, other countries decide they need it too, and trying to acquire it gets people killed. So I ask myself if I want to report to the Pearly Gates and tell St Peter, 'Yeah, sorry, mate, that war was down to me.'"

When Marc said it out loud like that, it sounded calmly analytical and he wondered why he'd thought there was a dilemma at all. Like Ingram, he'd probably feel different tomorrow. But he'd cleaned up enough shit caused by politicians to know he was pretty close to predicting the future of Caisin's technology.

Ingram stared at the chess pieces, looking like she was going to make a move, but he could see from her defocus that she was just thinking with her head down. He studied the parting in her hair. She always wore it pulled back into a neat bun or a ponytail. There were no dark roots and he didn't know why he found that noteworthy.

"We're only postponing the inevitable," she said.

Marc frowned half-serious disapproval at her. "That's like saying murder's okay because we're all going to die in the end. But you're right, nothing stays secret forever, at least not without a bloody big sacrifice by someone."

"You gave the FCO the Ainatio data, though."

"Yeah, and I admit it doesn't feel like enough."

"What would happen if we provided blueprints of actual FTL drives? Like the ones the teeriks are fitting for us?"

"I've thought about that, too."

"And?"

"Most of the same problems. If we give HM Gov FTL drives or gate access, and they do the decent thing and to use it to evacuate people rather than invade China, where do they go?" Marc asked. "What happens if forty-one million people want to come here? We can't even handle an extra thousand at the moment. Whether they step out in Nomad or find other sites, or even other planets, they're starting from scratch and most of them won't survive. And even if we could magically absorb an entire country here overnight, who's on the passenger list? We're a screened population, we've been scanned for die-back, and we've had all our Opis shots. We'll probably be importing some scum — criminals, perverts, terrorists, enemy agents, even some unlucky buggers with infectious diseases — but also someone else's government and armed forces."

"Ours," Ingram said. "*Our* government and armed forces."

"Yeah, and we'll *still* lose control of the situation, and we won't be able to protect the people already here, the ones we look in the eye every day and came close to dying with. Well, you didn't, but I did. And the other problem is we don't know the first thing about this part of space, only that there's probably some nasty alien buggers out here, and we're soft, edible things who've hooked up with fugitives who stole a bloody warship and invented a gadget everyone's going to kill to get hold of."

Marc had thought this through every night, and it never got any better. Ingram must have done the same. She'd just edged up to it a question at a time, probably testing his position. He felt a lot better for getting his doubts off his chest. Maybe it wouldn't keep him awake now.

"Got to agree on every point," Ingram said at last. "There's no clean heroic option. I was just hoping you saw a brilliant angle I'd missed."

"Nah. We're buggered."

"I got as far as wondering if Britain has the industrial capacity to build FTL ships, let alone enough of them to move millions. Then I wondered about *our* ability to visit Earth and sort out a few international problems to give the government a few years' breathing space."

"See? QED." Marc leaned back and spread his arms. "In the end, the Caisin gate makes bad choices easy. Personally, I'm up for putting a few enemies in their box, but if we didn't literally wipe them off the map for good we'd fuel another war for the future that we might not win. And how do we explain this surprise visit? We're going to be packing alien weapons, right? Because if you're relying on our own kit, it's a bunch of rifles, a few gun trucks, and nukes. Limited options. All or nothing."

"It's just a thought," she said. "Which I've immediately shelved on account of your open contempt for it."

"Here's my personal prediction, Captain. The government won't use the portal to save the people I care about. They'll be the last in the lifeboat, if they get a place at all. So it's like Quinn Worley and the rest of the mega-rich tossers pissing off in their personal spaceships and leaving the plebs to sink."

"I don't think Opis is an attractive prospect for oligarchs," Ingram said. "It's too wild a frontier at the moment."

"But they won't believe that. So we watch and wait. Which also gives us time to work out how we break the news about aliens. Remember them? Huge culture shock when humanity finds it's not alone?"

"Funny how you get used to them." Ingram gave him a slightly sad smile. "And that actually sounds like a plan to me."

"I was just thinking out loud," Marc said. "Things always sound clearer when you tell someone else."

"And what about Tev?"

"Same. Watching brief. If it gets bad, I'll work out how to extract him and his family. Easier said than done, though, until we have more reliable intel about the situation in this neck of the woods."

Ingram reached across the table and put her hand on his as if she was reassuring him. He thought she was doing it to feed the rumour that they were an item, because that made sure nobody interrupted them or got too close. But then he noticed her cheeks had flushed and he realised it was genuine.

"Thank you," she said. "I actually do feel better when we discuss this."

"Why aren't you having this conversation with your First Officer?" Marc asked. "Or have you?"

"I didn't want to burden Peter with a moral choice that's my responsibility."

"Yeah. Right."

"Oh, very well, I think he might disapprove of all this, but you're like me. An extreme risk-taker. And you've seen dirty politics at very close quarters."

"Assassinating enemies so we don't have to waste thousands of lives on removing them the polite legal way, is that what you mean?"

"The Royal Navy doesn't do black ops. We turn up in a big grey ship with loud guns and missiles and blow shit up conspicuously. We drop off chaps like you to do the quiet things we don't ask questions about."

Marc never thought he'd warm to Ingram when he first met her, but they'd reached an understanding, and he was starting to think the kindness and consideration wasn't an act. She'd admitted being unable to make a decision, too. Perhaps she felt she couldn't say that to her officers. She was the Butcher of Calais, undefeated, hard as nails, another pitiless, death-dealing female everybody feared. She didn't have doubts, except when she did.

"Yeah, I'm not a gentleman," Marc said. "But at least I play chess with you. Nobody else will."

"Well, they will, but they don't try to win," she said. "They're afraid of upsetting me."

"Bad loser? Keelhauled the last one who beat you?"

She tapped her left shoulder board. "Fear of the stripes. But it's win or die with chaps like you, and I say that in a fond and admiring way. You go for my jugular and delight in grinding me to dust. I like a proper fight."

"No point playing if you don't give your opponent the courtesy of taking it seriously."

"Where did you learn? I associate it with the bespectacled and underweight rather than meat-eating rugby types like yourself."

"Warlords. It's a good way to get to know the local gangsters in the assorted shitholes I've visited on His Majesty's business. They think chess makes them look like Machiavelli instead of primitive thugs."

"Harsh judgement, Sergeant."

"Accurate assessment, Captain. Step off the boat some time."

"Marc, I know you think I'm a posh cow who sees you as an amusing tradesman, but I do actually care what you think. You never defer to me. I hold no fear for you, so I can trust every word you say. And I rather like you for it."

"Well, you just started another round of rumours by patting my hand."

Ingram looked a little awkward and fiddled with her beer. "I can be a terribly convincing actress."

Marc realised he was disappointed it was just a cover story. Maybe he hadn't given up being alive after all.

"Ahh, you're okay," he said, realising he might well have given the wrong answer. "I know I'm a surly sod, but I do respect your honesty."

Betsy woke up and pottered around under the table, then put her front paws on Ingram's bench as if she was going to jump up. Ingram gave her a wary look. Betsy's prizefighter looks didn't do her any favours.

"She won't bite," Marc said. "She's just grateful for people being kind to her now."

Ingram stroked Betsy's head with the caution of a woman who wasn't convinced. Betsy basked in the attention and grinned.

"I didn't think you were a dog person," Ingram said.

"I'm not, not really. But military dogs saved my arse a few times, so I'm repaying the debt."

"How's Dieter doing?"

"Healthwise, good. Mentally... could be better. He turns up at the range for training, though. About time you did, by the way. You might be a crack shot on Earth, but you need to adjust for Opis."

"I know. I'll show up."

"Then there's fieldcraft. I'll be starting sessions for everyone next week."

"Is this necessity or boredom?"

"Both. Oh, and rugby. I've finally found enough manly men to form two seven-a-side teams. One of them's Alex, but it's a start."

"Oh, please don't let anything painful happen to him."

"Yeah, he's incredibly brave and absolutely inept. Dangerous combo. Don't worry, I'll look after him."

"Nobody's going to risk tackling you. You know that, don't you?"

"That's why I need Tev back." Marc tried to lighten the mood. Ingram really did seem a bit down. It must have hurt to have the ultimate transport system and the best new weapon since gunpowder was invented and not be able to use it. "He always knocked me flat. Like being hit by a lorry."

"Let's stick to chess, then," Ingram said.

They finished the game and she beat him fair and square, although she gave him a look that said she thought he'd backed off. There'd be no convincing her now.

"Can you cook?" he asked, gathering up the plates and glasses before they left.

"It's not quite my forte."

"Okay, I'll make you a curry some time. Because I do an absolute belter and I've still got a stash of spices."

"That'd be lovely," she said. "Thank you."

Marc could have just apologised and asked if he'd said the wrong thing. But apologies usually unravelled into explanations, and he'd end up going too far the other way. He'd just make an effort to be kinder to her next time.

On his way back to the shipping container he'd made his home, he looked up and tried to imagine where *Elcano* was, but he had no idea where to start. Betsy gazed up into the sky with him, frowning like she was searching for enemy bombers. He wasn't even sure if the ship had established a final orbit yet. Sol said it wasn't just a matter of slamming on the brakes and that he'd had to do complicated maths with Cosquimaden to gradually loop *Elcano* back towards Opis when she shot out of the gate. Marc wasn't looking forward to Erskine being back on the scene, but he did worry about all those kids stuck up there with her.

"Come on, Betsy," he said. "No Heinkels up there today."

The long route home was a brisk walk to cover the shortfall in mileage while he worked up to his normal daily run. If he paced himself and put in some leg time at the makeshift gym Zakko had set up, his knees would adjust. The gravity was just enough to make itself felt and he was taking longer to acclimatise than he'd expected. Today's walk took him around the back of the central buildings and up through part of the tent city, through the transit camp sector, and then across Kill Line. Some days he extended it and did a loop through the Ainatio overspill zone, where Sol had parked all the boffins and techies who couldn't find a space in the base buildings. But he'd take it easy tonight.

This time it was enjoyable instead of a necessity. He could hear people watching movies or talking about the news as he passed doorways, and kids were playing ball games wherever there was an open space big enough. Cooking smells drifted on the air. Somebody was laughing. He knew so many people by sight now that he could wave or nod acknowledgement and get a "Hi, Marc" back. Nomad was now a town, even before all the houses were built.

Betsy trotted at his side through the camp, then peeled off down a side path, looked back over her shoulder at him as if she wanted him to catch up, and trotted on. She was probably looking for Dieter.

"Okay," Marc said. "Let's visit your dad."

He found Dieter sitting in the dog compound with Sapper, the German shepherd who'd been Girlie's buddy. Nobody could tell Marc animals didn't grieve. Sapper was visibly miserable, ears drooping, head down, and he looked up expectantly when Marc approached, but his disappointment was obvious and he settled back into that forlorn pose. It was disturbing because Marc had been through the same reaction himself, that split second when the front door opened and he expected Greg or John to walk in when he knew they were never coming home again.

Marc bent down to make a fuss of the dog. "Is he eating?"

Dieter shook his head. "Not much."

"You coming down the range in the morning?"

"Sure."

"Want to sink a few beers tomorrow night?"

"Yeah. Yeah, I'd like that."

Marc wanted to tell him not to dwell on what had happened, but he knew he'd have reacted the same. It wasn't about being stabbed and nearly dying. It was about the poor sod slamming on the Caracal's brakes when he saw Girlie lying in the road, paws hacked off, and not being able to stop seeing it. Marc had tidied up the body with one of the vets and he couldn't stop seeing it either, not even after all the shit he'd seen in his life and put out of his mind. He hadn't even told Chris about it. It didn't look like Dieter had either. If he had, Chris would have been twisting Fred's wing up his back to make him open a gate to wherever Pham was so he could do the same to him.

"You know you can call me any time, don't you, mate?" Marc said. "I'll be straight round."

Dieter nodded. "I owe you."

"Nah. Least I can do."

It was funny who you struck up friendships with. Marc didn't know much about Dieter, but he knew the kind of bloke he was and that was enough. They sat in silence in the compound for a while, just patting the dogs when they came over to socialise, then Marc got up to leave and Betsy followed him.

"She's decided you need protection," Dieter said. "I think she was confiscated from a drugs dealer. Interesting that she defaults to that job instead of fighting."

Even dogs could decide to turn their lives around, or maybe Betsy was saying that Marc looked like a criminal and she was comfortable with what she knew. She escorted him all the way home, and he didn't want to admit it, but he was pleased. She settled down in the alcove between the partitions that separated Marc's closet-sized room from Howie's and rested her chin on her paws, watching the front door. Howie was still out with Nathan Marr and his parents, doing some early evening stargazing.

Life was getting so *normal.*

Marc had started walking the dog and picking up Howie from after-school activities and fetching laundry and doing odd jobs around the house, all the dad stuff he used to do and that now made old scars ache like fresh wounds. And he'd had to come to an abnormal world, another planet, to do it. He wasn't sure if he was creating a fake life to fill the void or if it was happening naturally and a real one was forming around him. Solomon kept nagging him to pick a plot on the housing map to speed up the resettlement process, but that meant deciding whose tribe he identified with. Marc didn't know. Maybe there wasn't a tribe for him any more.

He'd leave it to Howie or toss a coin. For the time being, the container would do fine.

Every morning for the rest of the week, Marc had a full house for the rugby session. Another hopeful had joined each day, which wasn't bad going considering the 0700 start. Hiyashi and Bissey had played before, most of the Brits knew roughly how the game worked even if they hadn't, and the Americans didn't, but they did know how to handle the ball. And the idea of two seven-minute halves made it sound easy until they actually tried. But nobody had dropped out yet.

But what gave Marc most hope for the crushproof nature of the human spirit was Alex giving it all he'd got. The bloke must have been pushing forty from one side or the other, and he was carrying a few extra pounds, but he kept up with the training even though it turned him a worrying shade of beetroot.

"Come on, you lazy buggers, this is a schoolgirls' game," Marc yelled, keeping up with the play. "Real men play eighty minutes in fifteen-man teams."

"It only takes a second to break someone's leg, though," Bissey said, limping after Hiyashi, who was actually pretty good.

Marc gave him a shove to get back on the imaginary playing field, which was neither level nor marked. "It's just a scratch. Crack on."

It was another bit of normal that Marc hadn't experienced for years, as near to a good laugh as he'd had in a long time. He resisted the urge to push everyone to excel. It didn't matter if they were useless or world-class as long as they were enjoying themselves, getting fitter, and forming bonds. Fourteen minutes' play plus a bit of circuit training was plenty for blokes adjusting to exercise in higher gravity, even the fitter ones. Marc took pity on Alex and called it a day.

"Are you on a fitness binge?" he asked. "You've lost weight."

Alex braced his hands on his knees while he got his breath back. "I'm fed up being the ginger bespectacled kid who's no good at sport."

"New woman? That's usually what gets a bloke into the gym."

"It's easy for you." Alex deflected the question. Marc would have to find out by some other means. "I bet you were always on the first team."

"I'm coming down the other side of the hill, mate. Age. Everything hurts and nothing heals like it used to."

Alex straightened up. "So, you and Ingram, then. Two apex predators. Cute."

Marc didn't blink. "Nothing going on at all."

"Yeah."

The more Marc denied it, the better cover it became. "Wrong class. She thinks I'm the gardener. And we're just comparing body counts."

"Uh-huh." Alex took a long drink from his water bottle and wiped his mouth on his sleeve. "So that's why you haven't picked a housing plot yet. Waiting for a four-bedroom mansion in the executive suburb."

"Bloody hell, is Sol telling everyone?"

"It's a small town, Marc. You're a celeb, or what passes for one here. People are interested."

"No, they're not," Marc said. "Sol's doing some social engineering."

"He does that with everyone. Because that's actually his main objective, if you think about it. Chris calls it his thoroughbred breeding programme."

Marc took it at face value but Alex's expression froze for a moment before he looked away. Marc was used to that reaction. Alex thought he'd touched on the unmentionable subject: happy families, kids — sons. Marc needed to dismantle that barrier for everyone else's sake.

"Count me out, mate," he said. "Just think what the likes of me and Ingram would spawn. The universe isn't ready."

He hoped he'd defused the tension. He didn't want Alex feeling he had to negotiate thin ice every time he opened his mouth.

"Sol still wants you to move, though."

"Okay." Marc gathered up the rugby balls. They only had three and one of them was an American football. "I'll give it some thought."

Solomon cornered Marc just before lunch. He did it literally this time because he'd decamped to the quadrubot again, and Marc found him waiting outside the container when he went back to pick up his laundry. Betsy stood in the doorway like a nightclub bouncer who'd decided Sol's name wasn't on the list. The dogs still seemed wary of a metal version of themselves that talked like a human.

"I have to move you, Marc," Solomon said. "We need to clear this section. You're the last occupant still here."

"I know," Marc said. "That's why I like it."

"I chose a house for you."

"Great. Tell you what, I'll get a tent and camp out."

"Marc, that's not fair on Howie."

"Ingram's always got room for him." Marc didn't really mean that. "They get on well."

"But I had the bots build it somewhere you wouldn't find too social," Solomon said.

"What's that supposed to mean?"

"You value your privacy. I didn't think you'd want neighbours right next door. And we do have an empty planet to choose from."

Marc didn't think he was that solitary. He kept himself to himself, that was all, because he was a tourist in the land of the living.

"Is this prime location in the same hemisphere?"

"Check your map," Solomon said.

"Y'know, Marsha was an estate agent. She could give you some tips about selling houses."

"Don't you want a nice bathroom and a proper kitchen?"

Marc took out his screen. "Okay, I surrender. Where is it?"

"D Seven Four."

A red dot popped up on a spur off the main road that led into the zone allocated to Kill Line. It was almost part of the town, but not quite.

"Not the transit camp, then," Marc said.

"You expressed no preference. Make up your mind."

"Don't give up the day job, Sol."

"If you prefer to be closer to Chris's community, I'll ask. I'm sure they'll welcome you."

"No, it's okay. You've built the place so I'll take a look."

"Do you want me to come with you?"

"Are you going to point out all the desirable features?"

"Not really."

Marc realised he was well on the way to giving in without knowing why he was resisting in the first place. Yeah, he'd look at the house. He wouldn't mention it to Howie yet in case it didn't work out.

"Okay, I'll drop in later," he said. "No need to accompany me."

"Thank you."

"Are you nagging Chris and Dan like this?"

"Not yet."

Marc had to go through with it now. What did he expect? He wanted to merge into the background, and he couldn't do that by making a fuss about a bloody shipping container. It was a matter of where he fitted in. In the Ainatio accommodation block back on Earth, there'd been no garden fences to chat over and nobody's windows faced his. Once he shut the door, he was in his own world. But he couldn't hide any longer. If Solomon relented and built him an isolated cabin halfway up a mountain, he'd just look like he was making a big show of rejecting the community he'd fought so hard to bring here.

He sat down on his camp bed and thought about how much extra stuff he'd need in a new house, like a table and a sofa. Betsy hung around, watching. She was a dog. She wasn't going to judge him when he took his framed photo of John and Greg off the storage crate that doubled as his bedside table and stuck it in his inside pocket.

"Come on, Betsy," he said. "Let's go for a walk."

There were only bots around when he arrived at the house. All the occupied homes in Kill Line were on the other side of the site, so he didn't have an audience when he stood on the doorstep and looked around like a burglar to see if anyone was watching. Betsy planted herself outside the door. She was definitely keeping watch, something she must have been taught by her dealer owner.

The interior of the printed house was the same set of colours as outside, muted greys and greens, and it was just a shell with nothing to soften it — no curtains, no rugs, and no upholstery. The windows had shutter blinds and the flooring looked like loop pile carpet even though it was just a textured polymer. There was a small kitchen with basic embedded appliances, a pretty good bathroom with a bath and shower, and a fenced garden at the back. It also had three bedrooms, not one as he'd expected.

It wasn't a solitary male's habitat. Sol didn't make that kind of mistake, so he'd taken some decisions for Marc and assumed he'd assemble some kind of family around him.

"Subtle, Sol. Very subtle. Not."

He took out the photo of John and Greg. They'd just won a pairs race and were still in the bright red kayak, wearing helmets and looking elated. He stood it on one of the windowsills and adjusted it, not so he could see it but so that the picture had a good view. Yeah, he knew full well how daft that was. But even the sanest blokes talked to photographs when it was all they had left.

"Well, should I?" he said. "What do you think?"

How long had it been since he'd been able to ask them anything?

Marc realised he'd lost count. For more than eight years, he'd known to the day and the estimated hour how long it had been since they'd died. He'd held those two ticking clocks in his head all that time and he could read them at any given moment. Now he'd lost them. He could sit down and work it out again, but the elapsed time was no longer hanging in front of him like a display that only he could see. He could manage the years, and after a second or two the months, but the days took some effort, and the hours were a hard slog.

It's the length of the days here. It's the different seasons. I've lost my sense of time. I haven't forgotten them.

That mental clock had been a memorial and now it had stopped. Marc was mortified. He went out and sat on the front step, trying to look like he was just taking a break so that nobody passing by would ask him if he was okay, because he couldn't pull himself together to stand. Betsy wandered over and shoved her snout in his face to give him a reassuring lick. When he'd finished wondering why being able to recite the elapsed time was so important, he went back into the house, picked up the photo, and carefully removed the slip of paper between the image and the UV cover.

To the right of the slip was John's date of death, and to the left, Greg's. It didn't matter any more. Marc didn't know why he'd clung to those dates instead of any other event in the calendar. It made more sense to focus on their birthdays or the day the photo was taken, but all he was doing by counting the days since he'd lost them was recording how long ago he'd withdrawn from life.

He tucked the slip of paper into his wallet and took out another piece to tear it into a narrow strip roughly the same size, then wrote on it in steady capitals. The inscription probably wouldn't make sense to the casual observer, but it meant everything to him. He took his time to make the letters perfect.

JOHN AND GREG. ALWAYS HERE.

He studied his handiwork for a moment, making sure the lettering was fit for a memorial, then positioned it at the bottom of the photo before sliding the frame and cover together again. He was still looking at it when someone rapped on the open door and walked in.

"Hey Marc." It was Chris. Annis Kim was with him, carrying a small crate of beer. "We'll beat it if you're busy."

They were the last two people Marc expected to team up for a social call. He hadn't seen Annis to speak to since he'd shanghaied her here.

"It's okay, I'm just working out where to hang the Vermeer," Marc said. "That wall, I think. Next to the Rembrandt."

Kim put the beers on the kitchen worktop. "Not quite a housewarming, but they'll keep the fridge company while you move in. Give me a shout if you need any girly stuff done like soft furnishings. I'm crap at that kind of thing but I'll give it a go."

Marc knew it was time to clear his slate. "I'm sorry I was an arsehole to you, Annis. It's a bad habit."

"Yeah, you're a bit of a dick, but it turned out you were right," she said. "And it beat being suicided by APS intelligence, so no worries."

She gave him a thumbs-up and left. Chris hung around for a moment.

"You okay, Marc?"

"I'm good. Really." Marc still had the photo frame in his hand. "This'll do for me. I'm here now and there's no point pretending I'm just passing through."

Chris just nodded. He must have seen the photo, but he didn't comment. All he did was pat Marc's shoulder. He was one of those blokes who said a lot less when he had a lot he wanted to say.

"Welcome back," he said.

Yeah, Chris understood better than Marc had ever realised.

* * *

NOMAD BASE: EIGHT WEEKS AFTER THE KILL LINE EVACUATION.

This was a job for a sniper, but Chris knew the duty was his.

He didn't want Erin to carry the can. He sighted up as casually as he could, shoulder braced against the corner of a wall, and watched. There it was: a bright red, noisy ball of feathers that couldn't be trusted. Rikayl was perched on pipework that ran between two of the biomanufacturing sheds, watching the kids playing in the empty construction compound.

Rikayl had grown fast. He was now the size of a large falcon, probably thanks to all the meat and raw eggs Nina was feeding him, and his spiky quills had grown into lipstick-red plumage. If Chris had spotted him for the first time on a hike, he'd have thought what an amazing sight he was. Now all he could see was a predator he knew too little about.

And how much bigger was he going to get?

That worried Chris. Adult teeriks were five feet tall or more when they stood fully upright. If they were built like Earth raptors, they'd weigh at least thirty pounds, and if thirty pounds hit someone at top falcon speed — a hundred miles an hour or more — it'd do a lot of damage even if it didn't plan to. Rikayl could fly now, not low-level flight like Fred but occasional climbs to a decent altitude. A high-speed dive wasn't beyond him.

Chris made an effort to look relaxed as he scoped through. Folks here were used to troops using their rifle optics like binoculars, and as long as he didn't look too focused, nobody would think he was waiting to open fire. He wasn't. He was just ready to. He'd been out here a few times to make sure Rikayl kept his distance, and Ingram must have seen him, but she hadn't said a word. Diplomacy was a miserable tightrope to walk. Chris was glad he'd always had alternative means of persuasion.

"Steady on, Chris." Logan Haine sidled up to him, keeping clear of his arc. "Can't hunt the natives for sport these days. Polite society frowns on that sort of thing."

Chris didn't take his eyes off Rikayl. "If your kid was out there, Commander, would you trust him?"

"Not really. But he hasn't killed anything since Mildred's demise. I don't think humans look like prey to him. Let's face it, I was up for casseroling her myself. Did he finish eating her, by the way?"

"Yeah. He cleared his plate."

"Good. I hate to think of her going to waste."

"You're a doctor. Does he look like a genetic abnormality to you?"

"To be fair, Chris, so few of my patients have feathers and beaks that I'd hesitate to offer an opinion."

"I think he's a throwback."

"Interesting theory."

"And?"

"A few crunched genes wouldn't do that, assuming theirs work like ours."

Chris sighted up again. "There's nothing wrong with him if you think of him as a bird. Then he's actually pretty smart."

"Well, the colour looks like a bigger physical change than it is. One or two genes can make huge differences to appearance. So focus on his behaviour. I'd put my money on Caisin's age and health resulting in some intellectual impairment."

Haine usually put things more colourfully than that. Chris thought Rikayl's intellect was doing just fine if he'd worked out how he could plummet from a considerable height minus functioning flight feathers and take out a hen without killing himself. It might have been sheer luck, but Chris doubted it.

The teerik was still watching the children intently, head cocked to one side as if he was trying to make sense of them. Maybe he was. He didn't have a mom, he knew he didn't look like anybody else, and he spent most of the day trailing after Nina, a familiar voice he'd heard even before he'd hatched. Perhaps he was trying to work out what he really was. If Chris hadn't been worried about the kids, he'd have felt genuinely sorry for him.

Haine watched for a while, arms folded. "By the way, you didn't come back for your checkup. How are you doing? I'm only asking because I've got forms to fill in. I don't care, not really, not unless you pay for the premium package. If you opt for the lifetime special rate, I can even feign sympathy and a degree of friendliness."

"Ah, it's just weird electric shock sensations now and again," Chris said. "No numbness. I don't bite my cheek any more."

"Okay, form filled," Haine said, looking up at the clouds. "I'll be off, then. It's going to pour down in a minute. Try not to shoot our allies, there's a good lad."

He wandered off. Chris got the feeling that Ingram had sent him to relay the warning in a way that wouldn't feel like scolding. It was hard to take offence at Haine. And he was right about the weather.

The wind rose from nowhere. Then the rain started, and the kids abandoned their games and ran for shelter. Canvas flapped like sails and the flags outside the main building came alive, cracking and rattling their halyards.

Rikayl didn't move. Chris pressed close against the wall where the covered walkway between the buildings gave him some shelter and waited to see what he did next.

The teerik stretched his head back and stared up into the sky like he was wondering where the water was coming from. As the shower became a torrential downpour, puddles started to form where the churned ground hadn't been levelled yet. Rikayl glided down to flap around in the shallow water, shaking himself and ducking his head like he was in a birdbath. It was more a case of covering himself in mud than bathing, but he seemed to be having fun like a toddler jumping in puddles.

Eventually he backed out of the water, flapped his way back to the pipe, and sat preening his feathers as the rain washed him clean again. He looked bedraggled but happy. He was just a kid.

Chris slung his rifle, waited for the rain to ease a little, then sprinted back to the tents. While he dried himself off at the entrance to the shelter, he wondered if he'd take that shot now he'd seen Rikayl as a baffled, lonely child having fun with mundane things.

Yes, he would.

It was sad, but a threat was a threat, and he'd been shot at by women and children too many times for that to make him hesitate. But Haine had a point. Rikayl hadn't attacked anything since Mildred, so he'd realised humans were off limits, too big, or not meant to be edible. Or perhaps he just wasn't hungry any more.

Chris stood in the doorway with a mug of coffee and let the day sink in. The worst thing happening today was a rainstorm, a blissful contrast to the routine nightmare of hunger, shit, and death back home. But the novelty of small concerns wasn't enough to stop the feeling that he'd reached the edge of a cliff again. He was the go-to guy for the dirty, desperate jobs, at his best in crises and extremes, and Nomad would soon become an orderly place for long-term planners and people who worried about public transport and waste management. The bots had already done the pioneering and he'd completed his rescue mission.

But a guy always had a choice. He could either accept he was surplus to requirements, or he could find out what kind of Chris he could have been if he'd lived a different, more normal life. Maybe he'd like it.

The downpour ended in a thunderstorm, followed by a perfect rainbow and air so still and clear that he could taste how clean it was. The only sounds in the camp were water dripping off a roof and a vehicle idling somewhere. The background murmur of conversations, songs, and movie soundtracks was gone. Nearly everyone from the old transit camp had moved into their purpose-built homes, and Chris would be the last man out at the end of the week. He had no chores left here beyond packing his few possessions. Now he needed something to do. He'd go check in with the admin office.

He didn't expect to find Fonseca there, but she was on her own when he went in, which was a relief. The last thing he needed was an audience placing bets on his progress with her.

"Hey Lennie," he said. "I've got some downtime. Any jobs that need doing?"

"Well howdy, stranger." She looked him over. "Have you been avoiding me?"

Yes, he had. He only wanted her to see him at his best, not nursing a black eye after letting Pham slap him around like a bitch. He was still ashamed he hadn't killed the bastard. He was going soft.

"I didn't think you were looking for me," he said.

"Touché."

"Are you pissed at me?"

There was a housing allocation map on the wall display. Fonseca kept clicking it on and off with her handset. "No, but if you shoot Rikayl, other people will be."

"Come on, I'm not going to shoot him. But I don't want to have to explain to some mom that her toddler's in surgery because we wanted to be nice to a predator."

"At least hold off until we can operate all their gadgets without their cooperation," Fonseca said.

"Wow. And I thought I was the callous one. Look, I'm just ready to intervene if he goes for someone."

Fonseca shrugged and did her fake coy look, the one that left him wondering whether he had a chance or if she was just yanking his chain. "Actually, I *am* pissed at you," she said. "I told you not to make a heroic last stand, but you did."

"You've had weeks to tell me that."

"I know. I just wanted to be sure I was still mad at you. Please tell me you're not working out how to get back to Earth to whack Tim Pham."

Chris was used to people not knowing what he really thought, but Fonseca could read him like a floodlit billboard. He'd perfected the art of looking like everything was under control even when he was screaming inside, but maybe she'd caught a glimpse of his temper when Sol interrupted his attempt to stick a blade in Pham.

"I don't need to waste my time on him," Chris said. He actually had a pressing need to do it and he was more than happy to make the time, but this was never going to be an honest conversation. "He knows what he's lost. It's going to eat at him for the rest of his life. So, is there any work that needs doing?"

"Everyone who isn't on base duties is working on house interiors, mostly their own," Fonseca said. "Are you good with cushions?"

"I'm more of a carpentry guy. I learned in prison. Who brought cushions?"

"The bacteria farm makes yarn from the local vegetation, apparently. You want drapes? Pick a colour."

"Awesome. Okay, if nobody wants me, I'll go look at rocks."

"Rocks. Oh."

"I like rocks. I was doing a geology degree before they shut down the college. I must have told you that."

"Nope. Never had you down for a geologist."

Chris took a silent breath and tried to be casual. "Well, I'm going to take a day off soon and go look at cliffs. The coast's only a few miles away. Let me know if you want to come."

It only worked if he walked away now with his dignity intact. So he did. Fonseca called after him.

"A couple of the *Cabot* guys are geologists. They used to be Army engineers."

"They don't need me to show them the cliffs, then," Chris said, and left the ball in her court.

He really did want to see the coastline, but a proper recon was long overdue as well. Satellites and drones had been mapping the planet for years, and maybe folks thought that was enough until Nomad settled into a normal routine, but the ocean just over the horizon and the mountains in the other direction were a constant reminder of everything they didn't know and hadn't seen. He needed to assess the place himself.

Rikayl stayed away for the next few days. He might have gotten bored with watching humans, but he could have been smart enough to realise Chris would do something if he stepped out of line. He didn't need to know anything about humans if one of them was watching him without communicating. That seemed to signal hostility in any species.

Whatever his concerns about Rikayl, though, Chris's sense of wonder had found a breathing space to surface for a while. He was living alongside aliens he could talk to and work with, the kind he imagined as a kid, and that was pretty amazing. As far as Earth was concerned, life on other planets was still moss and amoebas. When Nomad finally decided to make contact, the conversation was going to be one hell of a sitrep.

The teeriks had taken to walking around the base in the morning before they went off to work on the ship refits. Chris could tell the females from the males because of the red crest, but he relied on identifying individuals by their jackets. He always recognised Fred, though. Fred was now heading straight for him with a crow-like swagger that made him look like he'd ridden into town for a gunfight.

"Hi Fred. How's it going?"

Fred looked up at him. "We've made progress," he said. "It's much harder having to rely on mechanicals to rebuild components, and materials are slow to process, but I believe *Elcano* can have a spacefold drive before the end of the cold season."

Chris let the vessel slip his mind more often now, and it worried him. He needed to keep reminding himself there were hundreds of helpless people stuck up there. "But the stealth measures work and the improved armaments are on line, yeah?"

"Oh yes. Let me reassure you." Fred bobbed his head in a nod. "All four ships are invisible to sensors, and a Kugin patrol would have to be right on top of them before they could detect them by eye. And *Elcano* and *Shackleton* both have better pursuit guidance systems in their missiles now. If you ever deploy those in earnest, your reputation as a formidable foe will be greatly enhanced."

"Thanks, Fred. We're grateful. You're clever guys."

"We're grateful too." Fred shuffled from foot to foot for a moment, looking at the ground. He used human body language as if he'd learned it as part and parcel of the spoken one. "Chris, I came to apologise. I'm sorry Rikayl alarms you. We'll make sure he stays in the compound."

Well, that was awkward. Chris had gotten the kid put under house arrest. He also noted that someone in Nomad had ratted him out. He had his money on Jeff via Ingram.

"Fred, you can't lock him up forever," he said. "It's not good for him or you. Okay, I was scared for the kids, but I think he understands they're not dinner. If he wants to come here, I'm fine with that."

Chris was fine with it because he knew he could get a shot off in a under a second. If Ingram felt differently, she could tell Fred to ground Rikayl herself. She hadn't. She'd made it his decision.

"You're always very kind," Fred said. "We don't know what to do for him. Without help from you all, I think he would have died. Thank you."

Chris had been called a few things in his time, but kind wasn't one of them. It would have been nice to delude himself that it was a hidden quality.

"You're welcome, Fred," he said. "You saved us, we save you. That's the deal."

Maybe he was better at diplomacy than he'd thought, though. He'd almost let guilt get the better of him, but he'd made Fred feel better and he was ready to deal with the worst if it happened, so that was probably the best compromise for now. He carried on with his to-do list, the top of which was seeing Jim Faber to get hold of the Opis surveys.

The survey section had been temporarily rehoused in a tiny back office, a closet with some uncomfortable chairs crammed between screens displaying real-time weather and geological data from sites around Opis and images from the satellite network. Its scope made Chris think of all the places he'd never visited on Earth.

"Knock yourself out," said Jim. He'd made it onto Chris's radar because he was trying to get a baseball league going, but it turned out he was a military geologist with some heavyweight qualifications. "I didn't think you were a sapper."

Chris shook his head. "Infantry. Fourth Eastern State Defence. Hey, this is really great. Thank you."

"Any time. I've given you network access as well so you can browse somewhere with cushions."

Everybody seemed fixated with cushions. It was probably down to the unyielding composite Ainatio had used to form seating.

"I was going to head out to the coast." Chris indicated the area on a chart. "Anything I should know?"

Jim called up the maps and pointed out some areas. "There's been some big rock falls there in the last couple of years, so stand from under, as they say."

"How accurate are the sensors?"

"Enough to pick up tremors from the teerik ship digging its way out and pinpoint its position." Jim scrolled through a few screens and pointed to graphs and diagrams for the day's recordings. "That exciting squiggly line there. Imagine what a proper quake would look like. So trust us if we say we're not sitting on a snoozing volcano."

"This is great." Chris logged in and checked that he understood how to read the data. "Beats the sports channels."

"You're a sick man, you know that?"

"They do say. Thanks, Jim."

"Can I ask you something?"

"Is it about Fonseca? If so, no."

"Earth."

"Okay. Ask."

"How bad did things get? We've more or less caught up with forty-five years of highlights, but I want to hear it from someone who was out there, not tucked up safely in Fortress Ainatio."

"How long have you got?" Chris asked. "Here's my headline. Seriously frigging bad."

"So we did the right thing."

"Jim, if you knew what we'd had to do, you wouldn't have any second thoughts about whatever you left behind."

Jim nodded a few times like he was making himself believe it. "It's just that the world looks more or less okay on the news channels now. Well, not Asia so much, not yet, but I haven't seen anything like the apocalypse."

"That's because they're not based in Europe or America," Chris said.

"You understand why I'm asking."

"Because you're not sure Ainatio told you the truth? Yeah, they lied a lot, but they didn't lie about that. If nothing else, remember that we just carried out a mass evacuation. You don't ship kids and old folks to another planet on a whim."

Chris considered telling him he knew what it was like to have to pop antidiarrhoeal tablets like candy because the water was usually contaminated, or drive through human roadblocks because if you stopped you were dead. But Jim seemed sufficiently convinced that Earth really was as deep in the shit as he'd been told.

"Thanks," he said. "Enjoy your rocks."

Chris was looking forward to a dull evening at home with a few beers and the contents of the survey, all seventy-odd years of it. *Home.* That was going to take some getting used to — a permanent house with an indoor bathroom. He'd moved in two days ago and he still found himself opening the bathroom door and leaning against the door frame just to admire the modest miracle of a truly private space.

The novelty of not having to go outside to visit a latrine or a shower block would never get old. He could take as long as he liked to shave. He could leave his shampoo in the shower or doze in the tub. It was his territory. The house had less stuff in it than his prison cell, but this sterile box of a place made him oddly happy. Perhaps he really could be Normal Chris. When a guy didn't let himself think about what he couldn't have, he forgot what he really wanted. The last real house he'd lived in was reduced in his memory to walking through a pool of yellow light from the front door as he came down the steps, trying to keep his balance because the cops had cuffed his hands behind his back.

This place needed some soft furnishings, though. Chris now fully understood other folks' obsession with cushions. He propped himself up in bed with his screen — yeah, he definitely needed more fabrics in here — and studied the seismic trace left by the teerik ship digging itself out of the ground. An enemy with some kind of ground monitoring system would detect it coming or going, although if it was fully armed, knowing about it wouldn't help them much. But whoever it was going to be used against, Fred had said they used echolocation.

"Damn." He took another look at the sheets and felt the fabric. They were the good quality linen from Ainatio's infirmary, the ones he'd coveted for the transit camp. "I got my wish."

Rikayl was back the next day. Chris was on his way to the mess with Jared to grab lunch when he saw the teerik riding on Nina's shoulder. He was too big to sit there comfortably now and he was hanging on with his claws dug into her jacket, squawking at everyone she passed. It was hard to tell if it was a greeting or a warning. He made Nina look like a pirate who hadn't got the memo about the regulation bird to wear on her shoulder. But she was beaming like a proud mom.

Jared slowed down to watch the spectacle. "Damn, she's crazy. But hey, people pet tigers and wonder why they get their arms chewed off."

"She's the food lady," Chris said. "He knows which side his bread's buttered. Or his chicken."

"So what happens to all Caisin's knowledge? Does it deteriorate if it's in a brain that can't use it?"

Chris shrugged. "Maybe it's like stashing a secret formula in your dog's name tag. He's got it, but he doesn't know what it is or what to do with it."

"Sure, but you can take the tag back and extract the data," Jared said. "Junior's knowledge is locked in his brain."

"Does it worry you how weird our conversations are these days?"

"Only when you mention it." Jared burst out laughing. "Who'd have thought it a year ago, huh?"

Rikayl suddenly turned his head, looked towards them, and took off right away. Nina ducked to avoid his thrashing wings and spun around as if she was going to call him back. But he was gone, and then she spotted Chris.

She'd always seemed a bit too sweet and naive to be real, but she didn't look sweet now. She made a beeline for him, lips pursed in sour anger.

"Happy now?" A couple of the *Cabot* guys passing by stopped to watch. "He's scared of you. He knows you were going to shoot him. Why do you even need to carry a rifle on the base? Is everything a threat to you?"

"Until proven otherwise, yes," Chris said. "And if he was scared of me, he sure hung around playing in the rain a long time."

"He's not dangerous. He's calming down."

"Look, I get that first contact is a really big deal," Chris said. "But he's got a prey instinct and even the other teeriks don't know what he's going to do. I'm being cautious."

"He's not a wild animal, Chris. He's sentient."

"So was everyone who ever killed their neighbour."

Nina was getting red in the face. "Not everything you don't understand is dangerous."

On Chris's scale of angry people, she hadn't even shifted the needle, but this was Nina, Little Miss Nice, so it was her equivalent of spitting fury. Chris was pissed off too. He'd taken enough dumb-grunt insults in his time.

"Noted, ma'am," he said, expressionless. "I'll keep studying him with the optical assistance of my ML-Forty until I do. Is that okay?"

Nina paused for a second while that sank in, then stalked off.

"Damn, she's been around military personnel long enough to understand," Jared said. "I don't like to think the worst of people either, but it saves time."

"You should have said that to her to see if she'd laugh."

"We've taken a hell of a lot on trust with the teeriks."

"Yeah, more than two months in and Brad's still piecing together intel from Cosqui."

"They're still scared. Wouldn't you be if your masters could show up at any minute?"

"Sure, but they said they'd be killed if they got caught," Chris said. "In which case, I'd tell my new armed friends everything about the Kugin including their shoes sizes and favourite movies."

"Maybe they've worked out that *we'll* kill them if they get caught." Jared shrugged. "When your life depends on keeping your mouth shut, it's hard to break the habit."

They joined the line in the mess hall, which didn't seem to have gotten any shorter even though most people had moved out into permanent housing and could cook for themselves. Nearly all the food wagons around the base had been shut down and the bots were busy delivering rations to homes like a grocery service. But the Ainatio people were used to having a canteen. Maybe they liked it better, too. It was somewhere to socialise and run into people you wouldn't otherwise see.

"I need meat," Chris said, trying to read the menu behind the servery. The line wasn't moving. He was duty security officer until nineteen hundred and he needed to be out and about. "I haven't had a burger for ages."

"Salad." Jared patted his belly. "Guess who cleared up too many leftovers from Marsha's bake sessions. I've got to get fit again."

Chris was ten places from the front of the line and hoping they wouldn't be out of burgers by the time he got served when Solomon's voice whispered in his earpiece.

"Chris, I'm sorry to interrupt your meal break, but we appear to have lost Rikayl."

Here we go. "I know, I watched him fly off," Chris said. "He'll come back when he's hungry."

"I meant that he's left the base."

"Okay, we'll find him. I'll go ask Joanne Brandt for a hen to use as bait. Which way did he go?"

"The cameras on the construction site picked him up heading northeast. I've launched some drones, but it's difficult to locate a single organic object flying at thirty miles an hour."

"Well, let's hope he's got a bird's eyesight and sense of direction." Chris would have to take one of the rovers out. If Rikayl saw an armoured Caracal after him, he might not come back at all. "I'll drive around with a chicken. He might forget that I'm the guy with the rifle."

"Nina Curtis wants to look for him. I don't want unarmed personnel to go off site alone, but I know she'll try."

"Oh. You want me to drive her."

"It's the easiest way, Chris. He'll come to her."

Jared was watching the one-sided conversation. He could fill in the gaps. "Chris, I can do it," he said.

"It's okay, it won't take long. Just grab me a burger, please. Sol's trying to get me and Nina to kiss and make up, aren't you, Sol?"

"You're duty security officer, Chris," Solomon said. "As well as a competent marksman if she's misjudged Rikayl's tractability."

Chris didn't see that coming. "And you're a pragmatist, Sol. Well done."

This was going to keep happening because Rikayl was a damn bird, and birds flew wherever they liked. If Nina was going to go rushing after him every time he wanted to stretch his wings, he'd be a full-time job.

Chris decided it was quicker and more tactful to ask Joanne for a chicken carcass rather than get her to sacrifice another live hen. She obliged.

"You can always clip his flight feathers when you catch him," she said.

"Yeah, I won't miss my fingers. It's not like I play the piano." Chris took the plucked carcass and imagined it quartered and smothered in hot sauce on a barbecue. But at least Rikayl wouldn't waste any. "I doubt any of the vets will volunteer to do the clipping."

Joanne smiled. "Good hunting, Chris."

He secured the chicken to the cargo bed of the rover with repair tape so Rikayl couldn't snatch it and fly off again, then drove to the food lab to pick up Nina, wondering how he always got stuck with chauffeuring women who didn't like him. It just kept happening. She'd gripe about him being armed. He knew it.

"Alpha Three to Six Zero, if you need a hand, I'm out here anyway, over."

Marc always knew when he was needed. It was like telepathy. "Thanks, Alpha Three. Spotters appreciated. Out."

Chris switched on the rover's dashboard screen to follow Marc's radio tracker and tried not to antagonise Nina by having an opinion on anything. Silence worked pretty well. She didn't say a word about the rifle this time. She glanced at the chicken carcass, then busied herself looking around as Chris drove along the flight path Sol had projected. Maybe Rikayl was considerate enough to fly straight.

He could have been miles away by now, though. Chris hadn't driven this far out of the base before and if he kept going, he'd end up at the coast, so maybe the day wouldn't be entirely wasted.

"Do you know where you're going?" Nina asked.

"No, but I studied this terrain on the planetary survey last night, so I know roughly what's out here," Chris said. He'd been driving for ten minutes. "Eventually we'll hit limestone cliffs along the coast. Maybe with fossils. That'd be cool."

In all the years the bots had been surveying the area, they'd never found a large predator, so Rikayl probably wasn't going to run into anything big enough to see him as lunch. Chris didn't think he was remotely scared, either. Rikayl was a kid who could fly. He was bored. The countryside beyond the camp, especially the parts with trees and rock formations that sheltered small, edible prey, would be much more interesting.

"I'm sorry for being rude earlier." Nina blurted it out without warning, still looking up at the sky. "I imagine you've seen too many people like me who thought they knew best. I didn't mean to put anyone at risk."

The apology caught Chris unawares. "No problem." He attempted to mend fences and talk about her favourite topic. "So is Rikayl a throwback? That's my crazy theory. Commander Haine says no."

Nina did a doubtful *hmmm*. "I'd say no as well. It's not just a few differences. That's a lot of genetic characteristics to reset. However many human genes go wrong, we don't revert to early hominids or apes. But it's odd, I admit. I can't imagine why he's the way he is. It might be connected to parthenogenesis rather than Caisin's age and health."

It was a normal conversation, not a lecture. She seemed to have revised her view that Chris was a trigger-happy knuckle-dragger, so at least that would make the job less fraught. Now, how he could get Rikayl's attention at a distance if he couldn't see the chicken? Maybe the teerik sense of smell was acute enough to make it worth whirling the carcass around on a line, because if they reacted to flavours, they probably had the anatomy to pick up scents. Then Marc called in on the rover's radio and interrupted Chris's disturbing mental image of being hit in the face by a badly-swung chicken.

"Alpha Three to Six Zero, on me. I've got eyes on Squawker and I'm following, over."

Chris heard Nina sigh and mutter a thank you under her breath. "Roger that, Alpha Three," he said. "I have your position, out."

"*Squawker*," Nina said.

Chris shrugged. "If you haven't got a nickname in the army, you're nobody."

"What do they call you?" Nina asked.

"Chris," he said automatically.

She burst out laughing. She thought he was joking. She was still laughing when they caught up with Marc, who'd come to a halt and was parked fifty yards away, sitting on a quad bike with his arms folded.

Chris saw him point to the trees. "Alpha Three to Six Zero, Squawker keeps circling and going back to the tree, over."

"Alpha Three, I'll try to lure him with dinner. Wait out."

Rikayl was perched on a branch, a splash of scarlet in the dark green foliage. Camouflage wasn't his strong suit. He didn't seem to be watching Marc, though, or even looking in Nina's direction. He was scrutinising something on the ground.

"Sol, this is Chris. Stand down. We've found him."

"Yes, I know, I can hear you," Solomon said. "I've got a drone overhead now. If he flies off, I can track him."

"Don't let it get too close. You might spook him."

But Rikayl either hadn't noticed the drone or didn't care. He was far more interested in whatever was happening on the ground. Chris assumed it was a small creature that looked like an interesting snack.

Chris slid out of the rover to tie a line on the chicken. If he dragged it along casually and looked like the nice man with a free dinner instead of the nasty man with a gun, Rikayl might decide that it was a better deal than whatever he was stalking.

Nina jumped down from the rover. "Maybe I should take the chicken. I'll get in his line of sight."

Chris was as sure as he could be that Rikayl wouldn't harm her, and he had forty or fifty yards' grace to take the shot if he was wrong, so he let her. Nina wound the end of the line around her hand and headed in the direction of whatever had grabbed Rikayl's attention. In a year of bizarre events, watching a respectable scientist taking a dead chicken for walk was pretty near the top of Chris's Weird List. He hoped he didn't start laughing.

Nina was now twenty yards out. Rikayl glanced her way once and returned to his observation duties.

"If it's better than a chicken, it must be interesting," Chris said.

Solomon interrupted. "Chris, the drone's picking up an unusual formation on the ground."

"There's nothing there, Sol," Chris said. The ground wasn't flat, but he could see there was only vegetation. "Maybe a small animal."

"There's a slight distortion. It looks convex."

Chris's mind went straight to volcanoes. "Do you mean ground deformation?" But he knew there were no volcanoes around here. "What can you see, Sol?"

Nina wasn't wearing an earpiece. Chris wasn't even sure that she had a radio on her, although everyone was supposed to have one for emergency location if they went outside the wire. He started the long walk after her just in case he needed to pull her back.

"Oh." Solomon said suddenly. "It's a teerik. Where did he come from? Good grief."

Chris thought he meant one of Fred's commune had followed them. But one had stepped out of nowhere, literally nowhere, about five or six yards from Nina. Chris couldn't work out where it had come from and he didn't know who it was, only that it was a male — no red crest — and instead of a jinbei jacket it wore a mesh of dark green belts woven together. It was also clutching something in its bony hand, a curved, matt-grey metal tube that looked like the handle of an umbrella. Teeriks didn't fight, but Chris's rule on any handheld object he didn't recognise was to treat it as a weapon until he knew better.

He slipped his rifle off his shoulder. The teerik paused and stared at Nina, head slightly on one side. She stopped in her tracks.

"Hi," she said. "I'm Nina."

Chris was sure he'd never seen this teerik before. The creature said something unintelligible to Nina, and she spread her hands, shaking her head like she was telling him she didn't understand. Chris started to press his earpiece to call in Fred to interpret. Then everything went horrifically wrong.

It only took a split second. The teerik swept the umbrella-handle object left, right, left, like someone rehearsing a table tennis move. Chris didn't see a blade, or a laser, or even blood. He just watched something slice through Nina and cut her in pieces. Through his filter of adrenaline, she looked like coats dropping from a rail, suspended for a heartbeat before she collapsed in sections like a statue being dismantled.

Everything outside Chris's visual tunnel was now blurred and irrelevant. He squeezed off a burst of fire and he knew he hit the teerik because he saw feathers go flying. But the creature turned and ran, a weird loping stride on its little claw hands and back feet until it reverted to running upright and started flapping to get some height. Rikayl swooped in, shrieking. Chris thought he was going after the teerik, but he skimmed past and landed by Nina.

There was nothing any medic could do for her. But her head turned slightly. She was still conscious. A voice in Chris's head said *don't look, don't look, you can't save her,* but he knelt to grab her hand, because he couldn't let her spend her last seconds alone in uncomprehending agony. There was no time to say anything to her. She'd already survived far too long in the state she was in. He felt himself reach for his sidearm without thinking to end it for her, but then she was gone.

Chris had seen bad shit before. Some things he could forget and some he could bury, but he didn't know how he'd ever shut his eyes again and not see what he was looking at now.

He'd only stopped for a few seconds and he'd lost track of the teerik already. Marc obviously hadn't, though. Chris could hear the rattle of automatic fire. Rikayl was still shrieking his head off, wings spread as he stared at Nina.

"Got him. He's still moving. Going in." That was Marc on the radio. "Sol, anyone else out here we should know about?"

"Nothing on the sensors. However did I miss this?"

Chris, numb and on autopilot, ran to give Marc cover while he moved in on the downed teerik. It was floundering on the ground, still clutching its weapon. Marc put three shots in its head while it was fumbling with the device.

"Fuck. *Fuck.*" Marc pushed the weapon out of its reach with his boot, but the teerik was definitely dead. "Sol, get the Lamms in the air. See if there's anyone else around."

"Already done," Solomon said. "I've put the base on alert and Major Trinder's deploying the Lammergeiers. There'll be a patrol on the ground in five minutes. And I've tasked a bot team to retrieve Nina."

Marc picked up the teerik's weapon. "Can we check for transmissions? This tosser came from somewhere and he had to have a ship. And a ship means he's got mates and a comms system for him to call it in."

"I haven't detected any radio signals," Sol said, "but I'm looking for other indicators."

"Maybe the teeriks picked up something. They've got better sensors than we have."

"You think they knew about this?"

"Squawker here takes off from the base and the next thing we know, he's found a teerik who fights and carves up Nina like a fucking joint. So yeah, I'll assume the worst and work from there."

Chris was still scanning the tree line for other teeriks. He was okay as long as he was pumped up like this. It was coming down later that was going to be hard. "Sol, I'll take care of Nina."

"No, Chris, you'll do as I ask for once," Solomon said. "Leave this to me."

Marc cut in. "Where did it come from? Have they got a portal too?"

Chris could hear the Lammergeiers approaching. Rikayl still stood guard over Nina, making little hiccuping noises, but when Chris approached he started shrieking again, wings spread and head down.

"Sorry, buddy." Chris took off his jacket and edged forward cautiously to cover the body. Rikayl backed off but resumed his vigil the moment Chris stepped back. "I should have made her stay behind."

Marc grabbed his shoulder hard enough to hurt. "Pack it in, Chris. No bloody guilt. Shit happens. It's the default state of the universe. Not another word, okay?"

It had been a very long time since Chris had been around anyone more battle-hardened than himself to shake some sense into him. He retraced his steps, looking for the telltale haze of a portal, trying different angles, ready to fire. One of the Lammergeiers flew over and circled back.

"Locate the deformation again for me, Sol," Chris said. "Can you put a drone over it?"

Chris waited for the drone to move into position overhead. From where he was standing, there was still nothing below. He moved forward a step at a time, looking for the familiar patch of blurred air, but it really was empty space. Maybe a gate had already opened and closed. If others already had portal technology and they knew Fred's commune was here, things were going to go downhill fast. How the hell had it happened? Fred had questions to answer.

But then Chris spotted it, and it wasn't a portal at all.

About ten yards away, an outline suddenly emerged, like a soap bubble in the shape of a small vessel viewed from the side.

He took aim and walked forward. It wasn't going to help if it really was a ship and it turned its guns on him, but he'd do as much damage as he could. As he got closer, the bubble seemed to solidify and darken, and then it drained away like thawing ice. He was now looking at a matt ochre ship with its hatches closed, about seventy feet long with no visible gun ports. If that was the stealth bolt-on the Ainatio ships now had, it was very effective.

"Sol, bring the drone down to my eye level at this position and send Fred an image of *this*," Chris said. "Ask him how we get into it and keep it grounded. It's got to be technology his guys use."

Marc backed up to Chris, still checking around them for the teerik's buddies.

"Send him a picture of the teerik, too," Marc said. "Ask if he knows him. No, on second thoughts, get him here. Because I've got a shitload of questions for him."

13

Ex agricolis et viri fortissimi et milites strenuissimi gignuntur.

(Both the bravest men and the most vigorous soldiers are produced from farmers.)

Cato the Elder.

INCIDENT SITE, EIGHT MILES NORTHEAST OF NOMAD BASE: 15 MINUTES LATER.

Marc lowered his head to look Fred in the eye at point-blank range, nose to beak.

"Simple question," he said, pointing to the body on the rover's flatbed. "Who's that bastard there?"

He was aware of Jeff Aiken to his right, just in his peripheral vision, leaning against one of the Caracals like he was going to push away from it at any moment and intervene. Fred was his mate, and Fred was upset about Nina. Marc understood that. But humans came first, and Opis had suddenly become a very different world for all of them.

"I don't know him," Fred said.

"Take a closer look."

Fred inched up to the rover, sideways on just like a crow, as if he didn't want to look too closely. He wasn't used to seeing bodies. Marc hoped that was the reason, anyway.

Fred tilted his head to stare. "I don't recognise him. Did Chris shoot him?"

"No. I did. Is that body armour he's wearing or something else?"

"I don't know. We can test it."

"So it's not teerik kit."

"No."

"Fred, how about not making me drag information out of you every time?"

"I think it's Jattan. I haven't seen it before, but they have a certain style of manufacturing, and that resembles it." Fred seemed to pass

551

through the squeamish stage and into morbid curiosity. He studied the body more closely but still didn't touch it. "Did you intend to kill him, Marc?"

"No, I wanted him alive so I could get some information out of him. I shot the bastard because he was going for his weapon."

"What weapon?"

Marc opened the gun locker behind the driver's seat. "That one."

Fred peered in. "It's not a weapon."

"Well, it does a bloody good impression of one."

"It's a tool. It's an energy-bladed cutting tool."

"With a six-foot range?"

"Yes. And further."

Marc wondered if this had been a monumental balls-up instead of a deliberate attack. He took a breath. "Okay, let's try this. Teerik shows up to join the revolution, peace-loving kind of bloke, sees weird aliens, panics, whips out his toolbox in self-defence, and kills one. Is that feasible?"

"But how would he know where we were?" Fred asked. He sounded genuinely baffled. "Opis isn't where we agreed to meet the others. You *know* that. Once we realised they weren't coming, we had to hide somewhere they wouldn't think of going in case one of them betrayed us."

"See, that's what's bothering me," Marc said. "You said Opis was a backwater. Too far off the beaten track for anyone to end up here by accident. So how come they're here?"

"No, this has nothing to do with us." Fred straightened up. "We're not involved. We're as worried as you are."

"Do you think they detected spikes when we were operating the gate?" Marc asked.

"No, I don't see how they could," Fred said. "I checked. None of the gateways was large enough. I would have seen the readings right away. I think Caisin achieved a far more efficient device than any of us realised."

"Are you done, Sergeant Gallagher?" Jeff growled.

"No, Chief Petty Officer Aiken, I'm *not* done." Marc looked around to give Jeff a sod-off-before-I-make-you-sod-off look and spotted Ingram approaching from the direction of another parked Caracal. She stopped dead for a second, probably because she was close enough now to see the camouflaged ship. Marc carried on. "Fred, we need to get inside that ship. How do we open the hatches? Failing that, do you know the layout of the thing so I can portal my way in? And can we deactivate that camouflage?"

"The ship looks Jattan, but I've never worked on one like it," Fred said. "I'd need to check."

"Good. I'll cover you."

"It might have a handprint security system."

Marc moved a couple of spare magazines into his top pocket for easier access and gestured to the dead teerik with his rifle. "If we need one, this tosser's not going to need his hands again. I'll take one of his."

Fred jerked his head back. Marc didn't need to look at Jeff to know he was seething. He walked Fred the few yards to the ship, giving him cover like a bodyguard in case one of the hatches burst open and they came under fire. This was mental. He should have been using Fred as a shield, not lining up to take a bullet for him. But Nomad probably needed Fred in one piece more than it needed him.

"Marc, I have micro-drones ready if you need to inspect the ship's interior first," Solomon said. "None of our sensors can penetrate the hull."

"Thanks, Sol. Let's do that."

Marc worked his way along the side of the ship to what looked like the main hatch. Its lower edge was about chest height.

"Which way does it open?" he asked.

Fred inspected it. "I can't tell yet."

"Okay, get behind me as soon as it starts opening."

"Do you plan to shoot?"

"Depends. You just concentrate on not getting shot."

How many times had he done this, waiting to kick down a door and not knowing if he'd still be alive in ten minutes? North Africa, France, Turkey... extrasolar space. They were all the same in the end. But it wouldn't have been any safer doing a gate entry, not without some idea of the deck plan.

Fred touched the hull. "This is expensive military-grade optical camouflage," he said. "We wouldn't install this on a freight vessel, especially one this age. Do you see the inset channels?" He drew his claw along one of the debossed lines that ran the length of the hull. "This has been — retrofitted, is that the right term? — to look like a decorative finish. Expert work."

"Why would a teerik be in a Jattan ship?" Marc asked. "I thought you were all stuck in trade communes and never went out on your own."

"Unless we're taking part in trials, no, we don't. So why was he with this particular ship? It's for short-range freight or worker transport. Like resupplying orbitals. Hardly the type to require full trials after refitting."

"Ah. The good old white van." Marc tried not to jump to conclusions, but he could see where this was heading. "So... someone with a lot of resources who wants to keep a low profile. Terrorist. Smuggler. Special forces. Law enforcement."

Fred pointed to a barely visible rectangle at the bottom of the hatch, like the filler cap on a car's water tank. "All are possible. So I hope this isn't booby-trapped."

It was a good point. The dead teerik had come out of a concealed ship and made a run for it when he could have sat tight and nobody would have been any the wiser, so maybe he'd rigged a self-destruct device. That was human thinking, though. The teerik was a bird, more or less, so perhaps he'd been trying to lead them away from the ship the way some birds pretended to be injured to draw a predator away from their eggs.

They'd find out soon enough.

Fred teased the cover open with his claws and looked inside. "This opens the hatch manually. I can activate it, but I don't know what might happen next."

"Open it, then," Marc said.

He turned for a moment to make sure nobody had wandered up behind them to watch, but Ingram was busy taking a look at Nina's body. If the ship blew up, he didn't want any more casualties today.

Except me. I'd be dead. Funny how I forget that.

He was ready to move when the hatch did and open fire if necessary. He'd have lobbed in a grenade, but he didn't know yet if that would end up destroying the intel they needed, so he waited for the micro-drone. It descended to hover next to his head.

"Stand by, Sol." He prodded Fred. "Okay, Fred, now."

Fred was too short to get a head-on view of whatever he was doing and seemed to be feeling his way around. It didn't bode well. Then the hatch made a grinding sound and opened with a pop and a hiss just like in the movies, sliding to one side and away from Marc.

"Send it in, Sol."

The golfball-sized drone entered the hatch and disappeared. "I've lost the signal," Solomon said. "It's that hull again."

"Okay, I'm going in. Have I got control of it now?"

"You have."

Marc slung his rifle across his back and lifted himself on board, a few vulnerable seconds when somebody could have popped up and shot him, or worse. He felt better when he had the weapon back in both hands. The first thing that struck him was the smell — stale biscuits or wet dog, a sort of unwashed mustiness — followed by the faint hum of what he hoped was a generator and not an explosive device charging up. The air felt a bit damp, like a greenhouse.

When his eyes adjusted to the dim yellow light, he recognised the style of the interior. It was like the teeriks' stolen ship, with no switches or buttons and a lot of space around the consoles, presumably for all that Jattan hand-waving that went on. And the deckhead was just as low. Even if Marc didn't know exactly what Jattans looked like, he knew they were short.

He checked his screen. The feed from the drone showed it mapping the ship at the moment, bouncing its laser off every surface, but there was no sign of a crew. Given the size of the ship, it wouldn't have been a large crew even if it was fully manned. The vessel was a single main deck divided into compartments, with a level below that turned out to be more like a crawl space with a cargo area, tanks that could have been water or liquid fuel, and something that looked like a small engine compartment. Marc dragged his finger around the screen and sent the drone further into the compartment to search.

He looked for personal stuff for a clue to who the dead teerik was and if there'd been anyone else on board, but he wasn't sure he'd recognise it if he saw it. What did teeriks normally stick on their cabin bulkheads when they weren't hijacking warships? Did they have the equivalent of coffee cups and dirty plates to leave lying around? He was expecting to find an abandoned meal, the source of that musty smell, but there was nothing. He made his way back to the hatch and stuck his head out.

"All clear, Fred. Want to come in and take a look?"

Fred fluttered into the opening and peered around. He had the advantage over Marc. He'd spent a lot of time squeezing himself into Jattan-sized spaces and he knew which controls to avoid waving at. Marc gave him his screen to check what the drone had recorded.

"I'll extract their data first," Fred said. "This console here is probably the navigation system. Weapons are likely to be stored in this locker *here*." He cocked his head for a moment. "You can smell something. You're inhaling."

"Yeah. We'd say wet dog. And it's not the teerik, because you don't smell like that."

"It's Jattan."

Marc ran through the possibilities in his head. Some were worse than others. "A Jattan's been here recently, you mean."

"It might be an old scent left behind by poor cleaning," Fred said. "But Jattans need high humidity, and this ship feels humid to me, which also means you can smell them more easily. And they don't like bright light. Hence the dim illumination here. So I suspect we have a live Jattan here as well. I know you'll want to consider the worst possibility."

Marc did. He tapped the screen to indicate the consoles. "Okay, get all the data you can, immobilise the ship, disable the stealth, and make sure the comms can't be used again."

"Why remove the camouflage? It might attract others here."

"So *we* can see it without sitting right on it," Marc said. "Because we need to see it to shoot it down if it tries to take off. I'm going to get Dieter in to search with the dogs. If I can smell Jattans, it'll be like a homing beacon to them. What do Jattans look like?"

"They walk on two legs like us, but they have multiple arms. I find it hard to compare their faces to any Earth species. Eels, perhaps."

"No pictures?"

"No. I know you don't believe me, but none of us make a habit of recording personal images. Not us, not Kugin, not Jattans. *Taking snaps* is a very human thing, I think."

"Okay, draw me one later. Right now, how do we stop one? Where's their equivalent of heart and lungs? Or brain?"

"Their major organs are in their central core, which is well protected by their ribs," Fred said. "Their arms can regrow. They have multiple pairs, as I said, but only two pairs function the way yours do. The rest are vestigial. They had aquatic ancestors and that's how they propelled themselves through water, by rippling all these smaller limbs located down the length of their flanks. And, yes, before you ask, that's not dissimilar to how the prenu and other ships we designed for them bury themselves in soil."

The world had started to fit a pattern Marc could recognise. "And the echolocation. They see with sonar. Because they evolved from sea creatures."

"Yes. They do have eyes, but they're not as efficient as their natural sonar."

"You could have told us all this sooner."

"I'm sorry. It's hard to know what you consider relevant."

"Hang on... if you designed that burrowing mechanism to evade species that echolocate, does that mean the prenu was meant to be used against other Jattans?"

"Yes. Actually, other nations of the same species. Jattan is a nationality, marbidar is the species. Like English are human."

"So they're as tribal as we are." That might have been good news or bad. A species with its own internal wars would have less blood and treasure to devote to chasing aliens. On the other hand, maybe the arrival of a pushy new species that ganged up with teeriks who stole their ship would unite warring Jattans against a common enemy. "Can you manage to tell me about their weapons and defences, or do I have to wait another couple of months for that episode?"

Fred carried on, but he'd balled his little fists against his sides. Marc was ready. He could only interpret that as an effort not to react. Maybe it was a submissive gesture instead. He'd know for sure if the next thing he felt was talons ripping into him.

"Their armour is also exceptionally effective," Fred said meekly. "You would need something that could penetrate a patrol vehicle. Your RPGs might be suitable."

"You sound like you've designed weapons to use against them," Marc said.

"Not personally, but I'm very familiar with them. The Kugin don't trust even their closest allies, and as you've worked out already, the Protectorate buys equipment to police or attack its fellow Jattans and other marbidar. Do you intend to kill or capture this one?"

Marc noticed some marks on the bulkhead that could have been lettering or just scrapes in the paint. He realised how little he knew out here. "We can't say no hard feelings and send them on their way," he said. "Once they know, they know. Normally we'd worry about the political implications of shooting someone else's citizens, but we're aiding and abetting hijackers and making use of a stolen warship, so I think we're past the apologies stage."

"Our fates are definitely locked together now," Fred said.

Marc knew a *gotcha* when he heard one. It was all the more sobering to hear it coming from an alien, and one who'd apparently only been capable of broken pidgin English a few months ago.

"Is there any point taking it prisoner?" Marc asked. "You give the impression that Kugin wouldn't do a deal to rescue a Jattan. It's their technology that's at stake, plus your expertise. I'd say you were worth more."

"It's not the custom with most military powers to take prisoners at all unless they have some immediate use," Fred said. "But the Jattans have Kugin protection, so it rarely happens to them anyway."

"Simple, then. I'll do whatever stops them informing on you and bringing their mates here. Do you have a problem with assassinations?"

Fred did a bit of headcocking like he was thinking profound thoughts. "None at all. I was worried that you might not realise how savage warfare is out here. Nobody spares dangerous enemies. I know humans have moral rules and want to be good people, but the Kugin will laugh at you before they kill you."

"We had enemies like that too," Marc said. "But we got real in the end."

"This is as it should be. You have to be serious about protecting your people. If you think there are limits to how far you should go to ensure their survival, you're playing a game. And it saves nobody."

At least Fred wasn't squeamish. He didn't kid himself that he wasn't responsible for what his weapons and ships got up to, either. Marc turned around in the small space, trying not to accidentally wave at controls he didn't recognise, and started to edge his way out.

"I'll get someone to give you a hand," he said. "But when we're finished here, you're going to sit down and tell me everything you haven't mentioned about Kugin, Jattans, and everyone else we don't know about. We can't defend ourselves if we don't know what we're up against, and as you so rightly pointed out, if we fall, you go down with us."

Fred bobbed his head a few times, but it didn't look like he was agreeing. "I know that. You ask, I shall answer."

"No, you volunteer *everything* we need to know about to evade them, repel attacks, and kill them if necessary. We don't know what we don't know, so I want to hear *the lot*. You're not some illiterate peasant I'm bribing to tip me off about vehicle movements. You design their most advanced ships and weapons. Do *not* fuck me around on this, Fred."

It was a conversation Ingram should have had with Fred from the start. Nobody told their allies everything, but you didn't stand by and let them guess their way out of a crisis, especially if you relied on them for survival.

"You swear a lot now," Fred said.

"That's because I'm fucking angry. One of yours killed one of mine. And it was a terrible way to go."

"Marc, may I ask you something personal?"

"Yeah. Go ahead."

"I'm very upset about Nina too. She was my friend. But do humans really cease to exist when they die?"

Marc thought he was asking about an afterlife. "You'd need to ask Reverend Berry about that. The holy man with the white collar."

"I meant whether there was a possibility of preserving brain patterns, or regenerating them from tissue," Fred said.

"Oh. Well, the boffins tried all that in the past, and it doesn't work."

"That's very sad."

"Yeah. It is. The best we can do is not forget them."

"We forget nothing," Fred said. "And because we pass the strongest memories to our children, Ansitu teeriks will never forget Nina."

It was all getting a bit too close to home for Marc. "Thank you. She'd have been touched by that." He barely knew her. "I'm going to go and find Chris. See you later."

Marc knew that could have gone better, and maybe he should have told Fred he also wanted to know how to get on the right side of the Kugin. But he already knew the answer to that, and he wasn't going to do it.

And it wasn't going to bring Nina back. Her death was going to have a big impact on the base, not because she was some towering personality but because this was the first harsh reminder that they were a bloody long way from home and there were dangers out here they couldn't even imagine yet.

His radio came back to life as soon as he jumped down from the hatch. He could hear the change in the silence.

"Sol, you didn't hear any of that, did you?"

"No, I'm afraid the ship's a dead spot," Solomon said. "Which is probably connected to the reason we failed to detect it in the first place."

"Okay. Here's the bad news. We might have Jattans on the loose. I'm getting Dieter in. It won't be hard for the dogs to pick up their scent. Even I can smell them."

"Wait one." Solomon went quiet for a few seconds, probably doing a lot of other jobs simultaneously. "I've notified everyone now. Major Trinder's putting the base on high alert, and he's asked Turisu to ensure the prenu is fully buried again to protect the gateway. I've tasked satellites to search for transmissions, but it might be too late. This ship could have been here for some time."

"Yeah, that's my worry as well." Marc tapped out messages to Dieter, Trinder, and Chris. "Fred's trying to extract the ship's data. Can we get someone to give him a hand?"

"And keep an eye on him?" Solomon asked.

"Yeah, since you ask."

"I'll do it. I'll transfer into the bot."

"Okay, I'm going to catch up with Chris. Back later."

Chris had taken the quad bike. Marc headed back to the rover, but to get to it he had to walk past Jeff Aiken, who looked like he was waiting for him. Sod it, he liked Jeff. He just wished he'd accept that however nice Fred was, he still hadn't told them much and it was now obvious they knew even less about teeriks than they'd thought. That question was top of Marc's list for a serious conversation once the immediate crisis was under control.

He carried on walking in a straight line. He didn't do stepping aside.

"You finished now?" Jeff asked.

"Yes, Chief, I do believe I am," Marc said. "And if you've got a problem with me, let's have it out now. Otherwise we'll be too busy fighting aliens and I'd hate to miss this valuable exchange of ideas."

"I think you're out of line with Fred," Jeff said.

"Bit hard on him, was I?"

"Something like that. He's got as much to lose as we have. Probably more. And we need his help."

Marc didn't like dealing low blows and he liked justifying himself even less, but it saved time. "If you'd been here an hour ago and seen what a teerik did to Nina Curtis, you'd understand," he said. "You want to know why I'm pissed off? A medic once told me there's two minutes of oxygen in the blood stuck in your brain with an injury like that, so she was probably conscious long enough to know what was happening to her. *And a teerik did it*, after Fred told us they can't fight. You're navy, Chief. I know you had a hard war. But you haven't had to serve alongside troops you're told to treat as allies, the bastards who smile at you one minute and shoot you in the back the next. You never know them well enough. *Never.*"

Marc hadn't told Jeff the medical stuff to shock him or score points. But he wanted him to understand what they were dealing with, and what might happen to everyone if they got this wrong.

Jeff looked down at the ground, hands in his pockets, lips clamped in a tight line.

"Yeah, I get it," he said, and walked off.

Marc hoped he'd think it over and they could have a beer and shake hands later. Nomad was too small to afford the luxury of nursing grudges.

The teerik's body was gone when he looked in the back of the rover. It hadn't joined the undead, so someone must have taken it back to the base for the medics to play with. At least they'd have a specimen to dissect now and they could give up trying to work out teerik physiology one blood test at a time. He checked in the weapons locker behind the seat to make sure the cutting tool was still there, and wished he'd asked Fred for a five-minute lesson in using it, but maybe he could work it out for himself.

"Don't worry, we took the body." Ingram walked up behind him. "The more we know about teerik biology the better, and with any luck that's the only dead one Haine's going to get his hands on for the foreseeable future."

"Yeah, I guessed as much." Marc closed the locker's lid. "Stop me if Sol's briefed you, but I asked Dieter to get the dogs on the case, and Fred's pulling out the data with Sol and immobilising the vessel. Let's hope that there's no mothership waiting for a radio check."

Ingram pushed a lock of hair back into her pony tail. She was capable of doing up her hair securely so it was either a tic or an affectation. "Just as well we've got missiles on the ships."

"But we don't have enough ordnance to take on a fleet," Marc said. "And while we're doing the maths stuff and waiting for the missile to arrive on target, Alien Warlord pops out of a wormhole in his death-galleon and zaps the base from orbit."

"True, but it all hinges on whether the teerik got a message out to say he'd found Fred's commune. If he didn't, we can keep a lid on this."

"Yeah."

"Is there a problem between you and Jeff?"

Marc closed the gun locker. "Chief Petty Officer Aiken doesn't care for the way I handle Fred. Which is tough shit. Green on blue attacks happen, and getting intel out of Fred is like drawing teeth. I'm just focusing Fred's attention on the worst scenario."

"Carry on with my blessing," Ingram said. "You're asking the questions I want answered. I've got to be seen to be the nice policeman, but you can scare Fred as much as you like. It makes my job easier."

There was a world of difference between agreeing to that tag team approach beforehand and finding out you were the blunt object afterwards. "I suppose I've got to admire someone devious telling me how devious they are."

"So was the one you shot a combatant?"

Marc took a swig from his water bottle. "Fred says the cutter's a tool, not a weapon. But I had to use a bread knife on a target once and it didn't make me a baker. So if you're asking me if I could have avoided killing the teerik, no, I couldn't. It was going for that cutter. But I can believe it wasn't designed to be a weapon. Imagine using that thing in a confined space or at close quarters. You'd slice through everything and everybody else in range."

Ingram nodded. "But he knew how to use it aggressively. You're certain it couldn't have been unintentional."

"Ask Chris. You don't carve someone into chunks by mistake."

"Marc, I'm not worried about rules of engagement," Ingram said. "I'm trying to work out what the average teerik is capable of."

"So am I. They're obviously not as helpless as they claim."

"Absolutely." Ingram rubbed her eyes wearily. "I'm heading back now. I'm sure we're doing this first contact thing all wrong, but it's too late for diplomacy. I'm going to reassure everyone as best I can and look at Plan B, just in case. We need to be ready to decide when it's too dangerous for civilians to stay here. I'll stay, and I know the crew will too, but I can't ask that of civilians."

"What about Fred's commune?" Marc asked. "They'd have to go too, unless we shoot them. We've discussed this. We're handcuffed to them for the foreseeable future, and the unforeseeable one as well, whatever we do."

"But your FCO contact would jump at the chance to make it happen," Ingram said quietly. "It's not as if we'd have to beg for sanctuary. It'd be a terrible waste to shoot them if we can just evacuate them."

"And we're still so blasé about hobnobbing with intelligent aliens that we haven't factored in the massive culture shock yet."

"I doubt the FCO's going to hold a news conference to announce the wondrous discovery."

"Yeah, but you know bloody well it won't stay secret for long. Okay, if the time comes, I'll call Lawson. But don't assume you can just ship people out again. What are you going to do if they say sod you, missus, we've had a gutful of running away, Earth's still a cesspit, so we're staying put? Who's going to force them through the gateway at gunpoint? Not me, not Chris, and not Dan. We couldn't force people to come and we can't force them to go."

"I'll have to respect their wishes," Ingram said. "And they'll have to accept that they're taking their chances. But this is purely making sure we're prepared, not planning for it with an expectation it'll happen. We're not even two hours into the incident."

"I know that, but if it does go to rats, we can't go home and pretend the last couple of months haven't happened. The galaxy's changed around us. Aliens know we exist and we won't be able to hide from them forever."

"Yes. I know. I want another Caisin gate generator built inside the base, in a fortified bunker that we control. The one in the prenu's too vulnerable, especially as we're going to need that ship to fight one day."

"Oh good."

"What?"

"You're back. I thought you'd gone managerial on me when we need you to be the Butcher of Calais."

"It's not the politically responsible thing to do, but all aliens need to learn they can't kill our people and get away with it."

"That's more like it," Marc said. "I'll see what I can do."

It was business as usual, a choice between bad, worse, and worst options. Scientists would be outraged in years to come that laymen had trampled over Opis and killed extraterrestrials, but this wasn't a science mission. It was a last resort to save people whose survival chances on Earth had been shrinking by the day.

Marc started the rover and drove off to follow the tracker on the quad bike. This was the furthest he'd been off-camp. The lush, vivid landscape was pretty, but he was looking for vehicle tracks and signs of a second alien moving away from the ship. Without knowing how long it had been there, he couldn't even begin to guess when the Jattan — or Jattans — had left the vessel.

Perhaps the teerik had been on his own all along, and the Jattan was a myth. But they wouldn't be that lucky.

He found Chris parked just a mile away, sitting in the saddle and checking something on his screen. He didn't look up. Marc stood behind him and looked over his shoulder.

"You all right, mate?"

"I'm fine. Not the first, won't be the last." Chris seemed okay, but he always did, whatever was going on under the lid. There wasn't any way to unsee what he'd seen. "You remember the teerik warship shaking the ground when it dug itself out?"

"Yeah. What am I looking at?"

Chris pointed to the graph on his screen. "Seismic data for the last six months."

"Found something?"

"The recording gear here is incredibly sensitive. It picked up the warship like a small earthquake. Now look at this trace here."

"Chris, I haven't a clue, mate. Cut to the punchline."

"Okay, the prenu caused *this* bit," Chris said, pointing at a sequence of vertical zigzags. His finger then moved back along what looked like a flat line to Marc. "If I zoom in earlier on this trace, though, there's this even smaller blip, which is from before the evacuation. What if that was the camouflaged ship making a hard landing? The date would have been before the Caisin gate opened. And it means the teerik and his buddies, if he brought any, could have been here for a few months already."

"A lot of assumptions there, but I'm listening," Marc said. "So that would make Fred right, that the Jattan ship didn't come because they noticed spikes. But it's bad news if the prenu was tracked here."

"Not if you consider that nobody's turned up with a battleship to seize the ship yet. They might not have reported in yet. They might not even know where it is."

"But they've come here, and Fred said this was the back of beyond," Marc said. "And if they've been here a couple of months, did they miss the ship moving out of the teerik camp? Or are they still waiting for something, like reinforcements? I've spent months laid up doing observation before the shooting or bombing starts."

"They might have been searching somewhere else entirely," Chris said. "And it wasn't airborne for long. But yeah, the fact they've turned up here doesn't seem like coincidence. They might be gathering intel on *us*."

Trying to extrapolate always ran the risk of imagining something totally wrong and acting on it. All they really knew for sure was that a lone teerik shouldn't have been here, and that he had a Jattan ship that had contained Jattans at some time. There were plenty of ways to interpret that, most of them worrying.

"So what are you going to do now?" Marc asked. "Dieter's getting the dogs out."

Solomon cut in on the radio. "Marc, Dieter's already here. Chris, do you want to accompany him?"

"On my way, Sol." Chris started the bike. "Tell him to hang on. Did you hear what I said about the seismograph?"

"I did," Solomon said. "Now we have even more questions."

"Anything in the ship's logs?"

"The data has Jattan military encryption, so we're taking the hardware back to the prenu to use its computer," Solomon said. "We should be able to access it."

Marc had his doubts. "Sol, if the Jattans have any sense, they'll have changed all their encryption as soon as they knew the prenu had been hijacked. So if this landing is a military mission, they'll have the latest encryption, and Fred's decryption won't work."

"Probably, but teeriks designed the encryption system too. They can work it out."

No wonder everyone was after Fred and his commune. Marc had never thought about their codebreaking abilities before. They were the ultimate number crunchers. It made perfect sense.

Now he was still buzzing with adrenaline that needed to be used. He could drive around for hours looking for a Jattan or two that might not exist, and just duplicate what everyone else was doing, or he could work out what Jattans would do next if they'd spent months on Opis in radio silence.

"Sol," Marc said, "can you ask Fred a question for me?"

"Certainly, Marc."

"Ask him what the Jattan government would do if they knew where their prenu was. Whether they'd wait and see, or charge in mob-handed."

"Wait one," Sol said.

Marc hoped Solomon was better at getting intel out of Fred than he was. It didn't take long.

"Marc, Fred says they'd come for it as soon as they knew and they'd probably bring Kugin with them for support," Solomon said. "The Kugin would want to make an example of the thieves, which would include us. So if you're thinking through the significance of the seismic data, assuming Chris is right, then yes, the delay is uncharacteristic. But as the prenu is highly classified and the theft of it is a national humiliation for Kugin and Jattan alike, this might be an attempt to recover it quietly."

"Thanks, Sol. Am I needed anywhere else right now?"

"If I see anyone who requires help, I'll call you."

"Okay, I'm going to head back and check out the teerik compound. If someone's looking for the prenu, they'll head for the teeriks sooner or later. I can devise some traps."

Marc drove back to the base, wondering how the teeriks would feel about him when they realised he'd killed one of their own. Then he started thinking how he'd feel if a teerik told him they'd killed Tim Pham. Would he buy them a beer, or feel human honour had been insulted, even if Pham had it coming? He'd never thought about species loyalty much before. The only people he'd come across who didn't put their own kind first were the Mother Death nutters who wanted a human-free Earth. Some of them really did want complete extinction, and tried to make it happen, but they had some self-hating mental issues going on. Others were a bit more selective. When they wanted humans to stop breeding — or breathing — they meant everyone else, not them. At least the death wish kind were willing to swallow their own poison. It still didn't make them any less dangerous, though.

As Marc drove across the Nomad perimeter, he glanced up at a constellation of drones patrolling just above the base. At ground level, he passed armed sentinel bots, there were fewer people out and about than usual, and when he detoured past the housing area that had now become Kill Line by default, he spotted some of Chris's militia guys on foot patrol. It all had the feel of Britain's streets when he first joined the army.

Jackson Allitt was standing on a street corner nursing his rifle. Marc pulled up next to him.

"Okay, it isn't going to stop an alien fleet," Jackson said, indicating his weapon. "But it makes me feel better. Is it true about the woman scientist?"

"Yeah." Marc nodded. "Afraid so."

"Tell me it's nothing to do with our teeriks."

Marc did his best. "As far as I can tell, no, it isn't. Did you get the update on how to spot a Jattan?"

"Ugly asshole with lots of arms. Hard to take out so use an expanding shotgun slug or an RPG. Yup. Got it."

"Spot on. How are people taking the news?"

"Part shock, part here-we-go-again," Jackson said.

Marc felt better for seeing how nothing fazed Chris's people. They were utterly nails. "We won't know whether we've got other aliens to worry about until Fred and Sol crack the ship's data," he said. "But it's safe to assume they've come for the prenu and see what defences and booby traps we can rig around the teerik compound."

"Marc, could I ask you to do something else first?"

"Yeah, sure, mate."

"Go see Howie. He's really upset."

"About the scientist."

"No, about you. He thinks you're going to get killed."

Marc should have anticipated Howie's reaction. The kid was entitled to fret after what he'd been through, and if Marc was honest with himself, there was a good statistical chance that he'd be right one day.

"Will do," Marc said. "Where is he?"

"At the clinic with Chuck Emerson. Haine and Mendoza have put all the medics on standby and he wanted to help out."

That sounded grim. "Okay. I'll do it now."

Marc carried on to the centre of the base and turned into the parking area behind the lab block. Betsy was sitting outside the entrance when he rolled up. She got up to greet him, then wandered off like she'd handed over to her relief. He found Howie in a prep room with Chuck, patiently making up first aid kits from piles of meds, wipes, and dressings.

"It's a damn bad business, Marc," Chuck said, shaking his head. "I'm going to get something to eat. Back later."

Chuck withdrew tactfully and left them to it. Marc pulled up a chair, switched his radio to receive-only, and dusted off his dad skills again.

"Well, here I am," he said. "They told you what happened, did they?"

Howie nodded. "Nina's dead. A teerik killed her. And you killed the teerik."

"Yeah, that's about the size of it."

"I don't want you to die as well."

"I won't. I promise."

"You *can't* promise."

"Okay. But there's stuff I've got to do because it's my job." Marc wasn't sure this was helping. All kids went through a stage of being scared about losing people, but Howie had a good reason. He hadn't even told Chris any detail, though. Maybe it was time to tackle it. "Howie, you've been through some bad stuff. You don't have to keep it bottled up. If you want to tell me things, you can. I know it hurts to remember, but sometimes that's what it takes to make it all stop."

"You always remember your sons and it still hurts you."

"Yeah. You're right. Sorry."

"Am I a bad person because I want to stop remembering?"

"No. Not at all. Have you ever talked to *anyone* about it?"

"No."

Marc waited. Howie packed more kits, frowning. He was working up to it. At that moment, nothing was more important than letting this kid have his time. The Jattans could wait. Marc could slot them later.

"Marc, how do you know someone's dead for sure?"

This was going to be a tough listen. Marc braced himself. There was such a sense of bereaved comradeship when so many people had lost loved ones that nobody needed to explain what it felt like, but the unspoken details were different for everyone.

"After a while, you can see it," Marc said. "Do you want to tell me why?"

"I had to leave Mom and my sister. Laura. Dad died a long time ago. It was just us."

"It's okay," Marc said. "You did everything you could."

"We were the last people left in our street. Everyone else was gone. Mom and Laura both got sick and I tried to look after them and get a doctor, but they got worse and wouldn't wake up. It was really hard to tell when they were dead. Now I keep thinking maybe they weren't, but they couldn't speak or move and they thought I just left them."

Oh God. Marc's heart broke. But a kid could confess something like that. Adults glossed over it with assurances that the loved one hadn't suffered, agreeing to lie and be lied to because the truth wouldn't change the past and they had to find a way to put it behind them. Marc prepared to tell Howie a lie just like that, the kind of lie he hadn't been willing to tell Jeff Aiken.

"Did you touch them?" he asked. "How did they feel?"

"They were cold and kind of set hard. Like dolls. I tried to put Mom's arm under the blanket but I couldn't."

Marc had been ready to pronounce them dead no matter what Howie had said, but he was glad he didn't have to lie to the kid. Howie would have worked it out one day and probably never trusted him again.

"Then they were definitely dead, Howie. You don't have to worry about that any more."

"I didn't know what to do with them. I tried digging a grave in the garden, but the ground was too hard and I wasn't strong enough. I covered them with our best quilts and put flowers on top. Not real ones, just plastic. But they were nice. Then I started walking to the city because I thought I'd find a police officer or someone in charge and I knew I had to tell someone they were dead. Chris's patrol found me. He said he'd never leave me behind."

Yeah, Chris took the pledge of no man left behind to a whole new level. Howie went quiet and started assembling another first aid kit. There was no way a kid could go through the end of his world and not be broken in some way, but he'd learned to bury it. It explained his permanent cheerfulness and his need to look after the old ladies in the transit camp. Howie wasn't going to give in to the horror. He was in a permanent state of whistling in the dark.

Marc leaned forward, arms folded on the table, and lowered his head to Howie's eyeline. "Howie, you're ten years old, mate. Nobody expects you to do what a grown man should do."

"I'm eleven on November twentieth."

Marc did the maths. He wasn't sure about the exact timing, but Chris's convoy had arrived in Hart County a couple of years ago, so Howie couldn't have been more than eight when he lost his family. It was hard to imagine how kids that age could cope with all that misery, and yet they did. Marc felt his eyes sting and blinked away tears before they got a chance to escape. That was the last thing Howie needed to see.

"Howie, you did more than most grown-ups could." Marc tried not to think too much about what the kid had to see and do to care for two dying people. That would have been the worst of it. "Just remember that your mum and your sister knew you took care of them to the end. They were really proud of you and they knew how much you loved them. I can promise you that."

"Your turn." Howie shut the discussion down abruptly. Marc had probably gone too far for this session. The kid needed time to think it over. "Tell me about your sons."

Marc let himself slip into autopilot. It was almost like he couldn't hear himself. "John and Greg," he said. "Twenty-one and nineteen. They were killed four days apart, eight years ago. They volunteered for the army when they didn't have to and fought alongside the Russians on the old Greek border. That's about it, really."

It came out in a monotone as if he was relaying a message. It never got any easier to think about it, but he'd managed to find a way of saying it without engaging his brain, like singing a foreign song without understanding the lyrics, just mimicking the sounds.

But I'm still alive. And I don't have to be. I've got to stop being a ghost.

"I don't know what to say," Howie said. He was such an old man sometimes that Marc took it the way an adult would say it, but Howie was being a literal child for once. "I think your story's sadder than mine. Which one died first? Because, you know, I'd want to get even for my brother. I bet he did."

Marc had thought this over time after time. What state had John been in for those last days, knowing Greg was gone? Had it made him do something daft, something reckless that got him killed as well? Or had they been separated somehow and he never found out? There were so many gaps in the official report.

"Greg was first," Marc said, and defaulted to what he'd hoped. "Yeah, John probably took some of them with him for that."

"Do you feel better telling me?"

"Not sure. But at least you know what makes me the way I am."

"Yeah. And you know the same about me."

This was the kind of conversation you could only have with a drunken pal or a child, someone free of adult inhibitions. After eight years of every opportunity to put his pistol in his mouth, and a few chances to go back and kill as many Ottoman troops as he liked, Marc had done neither. He'd carried on doing his job. Habit filled the void. He wasn't afraid of dying because he'd got so used to the idea that each mission might be his last that he was ready for it rather than indifferent to it. Now he worried that it would be one bereavement too many for Howie and break the kid.

"Why me, Howie?" he asked. "I'm not nice. I offend people. Why do you care about me?"

"Because I really like you. And you don't want to be grumpy. I can tell. You want to be like you used to be and have a family to love, but then you feel bad because if you did, they'd have to be different people, because you can't go back in time."

That was pretty perceptive for a kid. Howie had probably spent a long time feeling guilty for wanting a mum and a dad and a sister again. It was like blaming the dead for dying and making you have to go out and buy replacements.

"Yeah, that's it," Marc said.

"I'm okay now about leaving Mom and Laura. And it's not wrong to want to find other people you can love. It just hurts."

"Yeah. It does. Look, I've got to check out the security in the teerik compound. Want to come?"

"Okay. I won't get in the way."

"Howie, you never get in the way. Think of it as training." Marc could either roll with it or do the usual and shut it all out just to get the mechanical workaday shit done. No, he'd let it carry on hurting and see how far he got. "We can watch a movie later. I might even try making a pizza. How's that sound?"

"You're going to be looking for Jattans."

"We've still got to eat."

"Okay."

Betsy was waiting outside again when they left the clinic, sitting in the rover like she knew what Marc was going to do all along. Dogs really could read people. Marc understood Dieter's devotion to his pack a lot better now.

Before he started the engine, a faint sound made him stop to listen. It was an odd noise, a long falling note that sounded like a singer trying to hit the right pitch over and over again. Every so often there was a pause followed by a brief shriek, and he realised it was Rikayl. Marc could only interpret it one way. The teerik was grieving. He was either calling for his adopted mum or crying over her.

"Poor Rikayl," Howie said. "He's lost both his moms now."

This was getting too much for Marc. He started the rover and backed out of the parking bay. Perhaps this was how all new colonies started, struggling for a foothold and fending off hostile locals, and they lost people, but in the end the majority made it — except when they didn't. But the unlucky colonies never had an interstellar portal to get them out of a tight spot.

He winced at the thought. He'd decided the Ainatio brainiacs wouldn't take survival seriously enough because they had a galactic fire exit, and here he was rattling that very door. Ingram had gone for the option even before he had. The only saving grace was that they both planned to stay and evacuate everyone else.

Howie looked into his face. "You're smiling."

"Just gas," Marc said, and Howie laughed.

Trinder had already put patrols in and around the teerik compound. Ray Marriott and Darryl Finch were on the gates, armed and ready, and when Marc drove in, he could see a couple of Caracals at opposite ends of the grounds, gun hatches open. There was no sign of the prenu but there was a sea of freshly churned soil that looked like the worst mole infestation in history. The prenu had dug itself in.

"Real aliens." Howie looked around the compound. Fred's grandsons were playing some kind of game with small stones outside the entrance to the house, sitting flat against the wall, probably their compromise between being told to stay at home and wanting to be out having adventures. "Isn't it cool? You said it would be."

"There," Marc said. "I told you I keep my promises."

"Marc, we've been waiting for you," said Solomon's voice in his earpiece.

"I've only been gone half an hour. You could have called me. Where are you?"

"In the prenu with Fred. I didn't want to interrupt you."

That was decent of him. "Okay. I'm going to crack on with laying some traps for whoever might turn up here."

"I need to tell you something first, Marc. We've decrypted the first batch of logs."

"That was quick."

"We appear to have a Jattan arms dealer called Gan-Pamas at large. The dogs lost the trail twenty yards from the ship, and there were track marks heading northwest before we lost them on rocky ground. So he has personal transport, possibly the equivalent of a quad bike."

"And the teerik?"

"His name was Lirrel, but we don't know how he ended up with Gan-Pamas. Fred's never heard of a lone teerik able to desert their commune like that. But I don't think Gan-Pamas is in a hurry to alert the Kugin or the Jattan navy about the prenu."

"Who's he working for, then?" Marc asked. "Dissidents?"

"I forgot you'd played this game before," Solomon said.

"I've even got the T-shirt, Sol. And *you* never forget anything."

"Anyway... from the comms log, Gan-Pamas appears to have been paid to find the prenu by an exiled Jattan politician. The ship was supposed to be top secret but evidently it wasn't secret enough."

It was reassuring to know aliens behaved just like humans, no matter how many arms they had. "So the exiled Jattan's planning a coup and he needs to tool up," Marc said.

"Correct. The opposition is probably arming for a civil war."

Marc had imagined the worst part of establishing a colony would be tedious, exhausting routine, water from recycled urine, and blight in the tomato tunnels. Alien revolutions hadn't made the list. But coups and civil wars were things he understood very well, alien or not.

"Destabilising governments," he said. "My comfort zone. Dodgy arms dealers, bent engineers, a prototype warship, and a civil war. And that's *before* they know about the Caisin gate. Just as well I cleared my diary."

"I'm glad you can see the amusing side of all this," Solomon said stiffly.

"No, I can't," Marc said. "But right now it's a case of laugh at it or cry my bloody eyes out."

It wasn't the problem they'd expected, and there was a Jattan out there armed with — well, what, exactly? But if Gan-Pamas was hiding from the Jattan government, so were they. They needn't have been enemies. It all depended on whether the Jattans really would see humans as implicated in the teeriks' theft of the prenu.

But that would mean throwing the teeriks under the bus, and while Marc would do whatever it took to save people here, that wasn't it. Teeriks were valuable assets, they knew too much about Earth, and they were *allies.* That had to mean something.

In an ideal world, Ingram should have been sitting down with a Jattan leader and opening diplomatic relations. But however hospitable Opis was, the world wasn't ideal. It was probably already too late to talk.

* * *

TEERIK COMPOUND: 1450 HOURS.

"I warned you this would happen," Turisu said. She was pacing around the room, twitchy and scared. "I told you they'd detect the spike. Now they're coming for us. *You put humans first.* You study their library, you talk like them, and now you think like them. It's going to be the death of us all. We need to leave."

Hredt didn't know which was more embarrassing, that she was speaking Kugal in front of a human who didn't understand it, or that she was berating her father in front of everyone. Marc sat at the table looking completely unperturbed, waiting to continue what he called the *debriefing*. From time to time, he looked bored and picked up parts from the dismantled rifle spread out on the table. Hredt teetered on the edge of losing his temper.

"It's *not* detectable spikes," he said. "There were none that significant. I don't know what brought the Jattan here, but *that* is the question that should worry us. And where else would we go? This world was our best option."

But Turisu wasn't giving up. "If we leave now, we have enough food to survive in the ship while we work that out. We could try Bhinu. The Esmos Convocation would welcome us. Having their own teeriks is worth more than a Kugin reward for handing us over. We should take our chances with them."

"Be quiet — just *shut up!*" Hredt hadn't meant to shout, but it burst out of him. He didn't shriek or rattle a warning note. He yelled words as loudly as he could, like a human. He'd never done that before. "Nina's *dead.* Doesn't that mean anything to you at all? She made the food that saved us from starvation. She befriended us. She looked after Rikayl when we didn't know what to do. She was kind and patient and she cared about us as *people*, not as useful tools. But she thought all teeriks were like us, and it cost her her *life*. Can't you feel some shame? Have you no respect for the dead?"

Maro stepped in. "Don't talk to my wife like that."

"You mind your place," Hredt snapped. "I promised to help the humans and I'll keep my word. If you don't like it, take the prenu and leave. See how far you get. We'll have betrayed the humans and taken their only means of escape. If I were them, I'd tell the Kugin about the prenu and the gate as revenge. The Kugin *will* find you and kill you, the portal *will* lead to war, and all your plans for a quiet, obedient, safe little life will be *ashes*."

"The humans have enough ships to evacuate all their people," Maro said.

"But we haven't completed their spacefold drives yet. They can't even outrun Esmos's warships, let alone Kugin or Jattan ones."

"So we wait to die."

"No, Maro, we wait to *fight*."

"We don't fight," Turisu said. "We *can't* fight."

Hredt spun around to look at her. "But we *can*. If there's one thing we can learn from today, it's that teeriks can be aggressors. The instrument that killed Nina wasn't designed to be a weapon, but that's irrelevant. It was used as such by one of us."

"There's no great revelation there, father," Turisu said. "If we were attacked, we'd lash out too. It proves nothing."

Hredt was appalled. "Nina wouldn't provoke anyone, let alone attack them."

"We only have the humans' word for what happened."

Turisu believed what she needed to believe, and perhaps Hredt did too. But he knew Nina. "Why would Chris lie?" he asked. "Why would Marc lie? However terrible Nina's death was, what happened to her shows that we aren't as helpless as we think. It's just a tragedy that she had to forfeit her life for us to see it."

Hredt realised he'd said *Marc* and *Chris*. Marc would recognise his own name in the jumble of meaningless sounds. Hredt would have to apologise to him.

"I hope you don't express that bizarre logic to the humans," Turisu said. "Telling them their comrade's death was a useful lesson won't be appreciated or understood."

Marc looked up from the component he was turning over in his hands. Turisu stopped. The sudden silence was heavy.

"Turisu, don't take it out on your dad." Marc sounded weary and disappointed. "Using the gate didn't bring Gan-Pamas here, so yeah, maybe you should be worrying about who or what did. For the record, I had no choice with Lirrel. If he'd surrendered and hadn't gone for his cutter, I'd have taken him prisoner. And I know your English is good enough to understand what I just said."

Turisu fluffed up her neck feathers. Hredt had no idea that Marc understood any Kugal. It was painfully embarrassing.

"I'll accept your account of what happened," Turisu said. It sounded grudging, but Hredt knew she was nervous of Marc and wouldn't dare call him a liar. "It was unfortunate."

"It certainly was," Marc said. "I never got the chance to interrogate him. Because I'd love to know why he came here and how he found the place. So, Fred, shall we continue? Time's against us."

Hredt resumed his examination of the rifle. "Turi, leave me to my work, please."

She swaggered out with Maro in tow. Keejah and Epliko looked unsure whether to leave or not, and Cosquimaden had already disappeared. Pannit was in his room, because he was the sensible one who valued his peace and quiet. Hredt didn't mind the others staying, but they tiptoed out anyway. Marc had a way of clearing a room.

"We'll go and keep an eye on the boys," Keejah said. "They're trying to coax Rikayl down from the communications mast. He's just sitting there staring across the camp."

Now Hredt was alone with Marc. He studied the rifle parts, trying to regain the momentum that had let him reveal details he wouldn't even have muttered in his sleep. Marc fidgeted on the pile of cushions he'd tried to assemble into a seat deep enough for a human.

"Okay, Fred, tell me more about Jattans."

"The thing to remember is that they always think they know best," Hredt said. "So they're overconfident in combat and make mistakes. If they didn't have Kugin support, they'd probably have been invaded by now or wiped out. The Kugin protect them because the Jatta Protectorate controls most of the rare mineral production on Dal Mantir. There are many other nations on their homeworld, but none are spacefaring in their own right, so the Jattans are what you would call a superpower. They like to feel they're... *big boys* in the wider galaxy, so the Kugin humour them with the honour of fighting alongside them. Even though the Esmos Convocation produces better troops."

Marc took notes. "So they're not as super a superpower as Kugad is. Big fish in a small pond. But Kugad needs their goodwill to maintain access to minerals."

"Yes, *big fish*. I like that phrase. Although it's not goodwill that the Kugin want, it's a stable Jattan government keeping the mines operating. They don't care if that's driven by admiration or fear."

"And Jattan tactics?"

"The Kugin prefer them as fleet escorts, and avoid deploying them as ground forces except as artillery," Hredt said. "Jattans have less experience in close quarters combat so they often overstretch themselves. Inexperience doesn't make them hesitant. Quite the opposite."

Marc leaned forward and folded his arms on the table, probably because it was more comfortable than trying to sit upright. "I thought teeriks just crunched numbers and designed clever stuff, no politics," he said. "But you talk like a strategic analyst."

"Marc, to build clever things, we must take account of the limitations of the client's ability."

"I bet they love your presentations at pitch meetings."

"We try to compensate for their shortcomings in the design. So we have to understand why they do what they do, and why they fail."

"We call that idiot-proofing." Marc raised an eyebrow. "Have you compensated for anything with the prenu?"

"In places."

"Which places?"

"Safety measures, mostly. The weapons system won't fire if it predicts it's going to hit an ally. We have friendly fire incidents just as you do. The Kugin are wary of careless Jattan enthusiasm."

"So does that mean we can't defend ourselves against a Kugin ship if we're using the prenu?" Marc asked.

"We disabled the fail-safe before we took the ship," Hredt said. "We aren't fools."

Marc smiled but still looked sad. He always did. Hredt wondered if other humans noticed. "So what did the Jattans want from the prenu, apart from the ability to attack other Jattans? It's not big enough to land a regiment or pack a large weapons payload, but it's overkill for policing."

"They wanted it to do everything, as all clients do," Hredt said. "When the project began, it was intended for long-range rapid reaction strikes to protect their planetary colonies, but then they wanted it to cover security tasks on Dal Mantir itself. The combination was challenging."

"It makes sense," Marc said. "Great special forces vessel. Stealthy, fast, and you can insert operators anywhere with the gate. Shove a bomb right into the enemy's living room while you're miles away from anti-aircraft defences. Except the Caisin gate wasn't in the original spec."

"You've seen the prenu fly, though," Hredt said. "It's not just a space vessel. It can adapt to almost any atmosphere to operate as an aircraft as well. It can do many things. That's what they wanted."

"But can it do any one of them better than anyone else's hardware?"

"It was some way short of Kugin ships, naturally, because you never make your customers stronger than you are. So when we decided we weren't going to deliver it to the Jattans, we planned a few enhancements. It's much faster now and can generate more power for weapons than we documented in the reports. That's what kept us occupied in the period before *Cabot* arrived. We worked. Fortunately, that work didn't require a shipyard."

"Crafty little buggers, aren't you?"

"In our position, Marc, you would do the same."

"Of course I would. So did you draw me a Jattan?"

Nobody saved personal images. Humans seemed to find it hard to accept that. Hredt had done his best sketches and hoped they would suffice.

"I'm not a skilled *depicter*," he said, handing Marc his screen. "But this is an approximation of a Jattan and a typical male Kugin."

Marc frowned as he studied the drawings. "Are the females any better looking?"

"They look similar enough for recognition. Better is a relative term. You would probably notice the differences between male and female, but even if you didn't, you could still tell which species was which."

"Knowing you, this is pretty accurate."

"Accurate enough."

"The Jattan looks like an armoured bipedal newt that's been half-eaten by an octopus. It's those bendy arms. They look like tentacles."

"I'll note the likeness."

"I see what you mean about the head being protected. You'd have to shoot from an angle and aim down into the body to do them any serious damage." Marc gave it some visible thought. "Just as well we're taller than them."

"As I said before, their armour's very good. But you might slow them down by hitting enough limbs."

"I thought you said they weren't good at close quarters."

"They're not, but that doesn't mean they won't attempt to do you harm and succeed."

"And the Kugin." Marc seemed amused. "They're lookers too. Gorgeous. Best looking spider-eyed hippo I've seen in years. How tall are they?"

"Nearer to your height."

"Why does nobody out here have necks?"

"In the case of Kugin, gravity, probably."

"Ah. I keep forgetting that. The Kugin world has higher gravity, yeah? You must find it easier to fly here."

"I do. And the Kugin planet is called Velet."

"Can you give Sol these pictures so he can circulate them, please? And are there any species out here that *won't* want to kill us?"

Hredt considered it. "The bidaren. The Esmos Convocation, mostly. They always seem to look for a compromise. But the Kugin won't kill you if you surrender."

"You said nobody takes prisoners."

"That's true, but if a nation surrenders and poses no threat, the Kugin will just declare it a province of the republic, tell the government how much tax or goods in kind they require, and let them run their own affairs. There's no value in having an empire if you kill everybody in it."

"*Parcere subjectos et debellare superbis.* Very Roman of them." Ingram's voice made Hredt jump. Even Marc looked startled. She tapped on the door frame with the knuckle of her forefinger despite the fact that Hredt could already see she was there, the same show of politeness that Nina had used. "Hello Fred. Can we come in? We need to discuss a few things."

"Yes. Of course."

We turned out to be Chris, Major Trinder, and Commander Bissey. Ingram leaned over the low table and looked at the dismantled rifle, then studied the sketches. "So this is a Jattan, is it? Not hard to spot, then. Gosh, the Kugin look like bad boys. Sorry. I interrupted your analysis."

"I was trying to sum up the capabilities of those most likely to pursue us," Hredt said. "I'll give you specifications for all the equipment known to this commune, but you have more immediate needs. We can make these rifles more accurate by linking the optics to a guidance system, which will take time, but we can begin right away. I've read about your shotguns, too. Those might be *very* suitable for dealing with Kugin. Few spacefaring civilisations here are used to facing ballistic weapons. But all these devices are relatively short range. I'd prefer you to be able to engage them at a safer distance."

"Gan-Pamas is our priority," Ingram said. "If he hasn't told anyone you're here yet, we've got time to arm properly. If we're too late, then I'd rather we took out ships before anyone gets close enough to us to experience a shotgun slug. Although I suspect it would take a lot more ordnance than we have now to stop a fleet."

Hredt had thought it over. Once humans fired on Kugin or Jattan troops, they would be at war. It didn't matter if they did that in space or here in Nomad Base. They had to be ready for the consequences.

"Then we have to make you the enemy nobody wants to take on," Hredt said.

Ingram smiled. "That's everyone's defence policy."

"I'm being specific. They should be too scared to land on Opis for fear of the terrible things humans will do to them. They should fear for their ships if they approach too close. They should also fear your retribution against their homeworld if they transgress. You need to be monsters."

"*Appear* to be monsters, or act the role?"

"You'll be tested as soon contact occurs, Captain. You need to show real aggression. They don't know anything about humans, which is your advantage for the time being, so if you used a nuclear device against a minor target — *overkill*, that's the word you use, isn't it? — they won't know you don't have thousands like it or even more powerful ones. Nor do they know you don't have a spacefolding fleet waiting to invade. They don't know how you arrived here. This makes you look a great deal more menacing than you might think."

"Oh. I see." Ingram didn't seem convinced. "Fred, humans are primates. Our instinctive animal reaction to a threat is to warn it off and escalate by stages until it goes away. If it doesn't, that's when we either attack or run. So deploying nuclear weapons as a first resort will seem extreme to people here."

Bissey stood with his arms folded, looking unhappy. "We've got about eighty missiles in all, Fred, not enough to lay waste to a whole planet, and your ex-bosses might call our bluff."

"Then you could surrender, hand us over, and pay your taxes," Hredt said. He wanted to see their reaction to that. "Although you said yourselves that harbouring us would seal your own fate."

Ingram ignored Bissey's comment. "Fred, if the very worst happens, we'll evacuate and take you with us. I promised you we'd protect you and I stand by that."

Hredt thought Earth had always looked rather nice, despite the stories of plague, war, and famine. "How will your government react?"

"I don't know," Ingram said. "But you'd be safe, and welcome, however tedious and bureaucratic they were about it."

"But evacuation is a last resort, like nuclear weapons."

"It is. I plan to stay, as most of the military personnel will, unless it's clear Nomad's going to be wiped off the map. But that's a very long way from where we are now. I'm just making sure we're ready if everything goes wrong."

"If you stayed here, though, who would speak for us on Earth?" Hredt asked.

"Chief Jeff, Alex Gorko, and Dr Mangel." She used Hredt's own name for Jeff Aiken. "Jeff won't want to leave, but he understands that you're our priority."

Hredt was going to ask what would happen to Rikayl, and what the government would do with the ships and the Caisin gate, but if the situation was that bad, politics would be the least of his problems. They'd take whatever chance of survival they had. But he was sure the humans could fend off attacks until they were better armed.

It wasn't even about numbers. They could detonate a nuclear weapon inside the national assembly in Deku without leaving Nomad. This was the potential of the Caisin gate. They just had to find that pre-emptive violence in themselves.

"Opis is your world," Hredt said. "We'll be guided by your decision."

"Let me put a scenario to you," Ingram said. "Assuming only one ship's landed, with just Gan-Pamas and Lirrel, he's now stuck here without transport because you've disabled his ship. So he has to call someone to get a lift home. How would he send that signal without the ship's comms system? Would he have a long-range personal link?"

"He might," Hredt said. "But I don't know. His living depends on secrecy. He isn't procuring mass-produced weapons. He's looking for a unique ship. If word got out and he was beaten to it by another dealer, it would be a major disaster and the Kugin would pursue him. And he may well support the opposition — he'd certainly have to be trusted by them to be given this task, so he'd involve as few associates as possible. He probably hasn't even told his client where he's going in case he's cheated. Perhaps the only person he could trust was Lirrel. A teerik deserter has as much to lose as he has."

"You follow Jattan politics."

"No, but we have to understand the world in which the client has to operate, as I've been telling Marc. And we're not fools. Teeriks have seen many powerful generals rise and fall, and we don't forget them."

Ingram knelt at the table and rolled a bullet back and forth on the surface with her palm. "If he's sure the ship's here, though, when would he tell the client that he's found it? What's the Jattan politician's name, by the way?"

"Nir-Tenbiku." Hredt couldn't see how Gan-Pamas expected to recover the prenu on his own now. "Even if he thought he'd only be dealing with teeriks and wouldn't meet any resistance, he should know he can't pilot a ship like that single-handed. But he's a Jattan, and they're blind to their limitations."

"I like an enemy who makes mistakes," Ingram said. "Although I'm reluctant to write off the Jattans until I know more about them."

Dan Trinder made a little noise in his throat. "Perhaps there's a possibility of negotiation. Fred, will the Jattans go away if you let Gan-Pamas have the ship? Minus the portal, of course."

"No, they won't," Hredt said. "Gan-Pamas would also want to take possession of *us*, you'd become an enemy supporting the Jattan insurgency, the Kugin and the Jattan navy would still want to punish us, and we'd be minus a valuable asset. There's no positive side to it."

"So back to Plan A," Ingram said. "We find him. We silence him. Then we prepare to defend ourselves, perhaps next week, perhaps in ten years, but the day *will* come."

Chris finally spoke. "So are we all willing to do what it takes? Because if I've understood Fred right, there aren't any rules of engagement out here. No lawyers. No interplanetary cops. Nothing. Win, surrender, or die. Is that right, Fred?"

"A fair summary," Hredt said. "Yes."

Chris seemed to be aiming his comments at Ingram. "Okay, I agree with Fred. If we're serious about staying here, we need to be so ruthless and brutal that nobody wants to piss us off. If we can't face what that entails, we won't make it."

"And what *does* that entail, then?" Bissey asked. It didn't sound like a question to Hredt, more an objection. "Dirty tricks? Double-crossing? War crimes?"

"Here's an example, Commander," Chris said, quiet and polite. Hredt was fascinated to see how he made a weapon out of restraint. "On my first day in prison, I was beaten up by the alpha con, the guy who ruled the joint, because that's how they check what you're made of and teach you your place in inmate society. So I considered my position. I paid him a visit a couple of hours later. I cut off his ear and fed it to him, then I kicked the shit out of him, and then I kicked the shit out of his buddy who came to help him. Sure, I got a month in solitary for it, but nobody ever messed with me again. The ear made an impact on them because they'd thought I was some nice white-collar boy who couldn't do that kind of stuff, but then they decided I was a psychopath and they didn't know how far I'd go if they pushed me. The moral of the story is you do whatever it takes to make people too scared to be a problem to you, even if it means doing things that you'd rather forget you were capable of. I hope that answers your question."

"Unfortunately, it does," Bissey said. "How do we know the opposition aren't the good guys by our standards? How do we know that we're not planning to eliminate the Jattan equivalent of Gandhi? We should at least attempt a dialogue. I'm sure Fred could interpret for us."

Ingram interrupted. "Gentlemen, let's agree that the overall principle of deterrence is sound — we need to show strength. But first we have to find Gan-Pamas and silence him. If we get it wrong, we won't get another chance to get it right. After that, we'll work on becoming the resident psychopaths of whatever this sector's called."

"*Mastan*," Hredt said. "The Kugin call their area of influence *Mastan*. It means *our neighbourhood*. And to give them their due, they do maintain order."

Marc just raised an eyebrow at him. "Do they make the trains run on time too?" Hredt didn't understand that. "As long as they don't try to run our railway, fine."

"We're taking risks with civilian lives to show how tough we are," Bissey said. "And there's a real danger of aliens calling our bluff."

Chris looked at him, unblinking. "How about we ask the civvies what *they* want to do?"

"We'll talk about this later." Ingram headed off further argument. "We've got a Jattan to find. Fred, Jeff's bringing some food over later, but we'll leave you and Marc to talk. Solomon can keep you up to speed with the search."

The day was finally sinking in. Nina was gone. Hredt couldn't stop thinking about how much the world around him had changed just from knowing he'd never talk to her again. He would have to visit her friends in the laboratory and give them his condolences the way humans did. He'd known that taking the prenu would have serious consequences, but he could never have imagined how events would have turned out, none of it, not the existence of humans, not Caisin's strange child, not the instant town or the reburied dead or the friendships or the ocean of knowledge and language he'd been given. And even if some of his human friends snapped at him and got impatient, it was a measure of their civilisation that they hadn't turned on the commune and slaughtered every teerik for what Lirrel had done.

The Kugin would have. Anyone rash enough to kill a Kugin condemned his whole community, so it rarely happened.

"Marc, when we find Gan-Pamas, I'd like to speak with him and find out how he located Opis," Hredt said. "You can understand why we worry."

"We all want to know the answer to that, Fred," Marc said. "But he might not give us the chance. Is he likely to surrender if he's cornered?"

"Are you asking if he'd rather die than be taken prisoner?"

"Yeah. Because if he does know you're here, he knows we won't let him go home. He'll probably assume we'll act like everyone else out here and put a round through his skull, or whatever equivalent he's got. I don't blame him."

"Yes, it would be a huge effort for him to believe humans won't abuse or kill prisoners," Hredt said. "And he can't be sure you're not going to turn him in to the Jattan security services, no matter what you promise him."

"In a way, I hope he decides to go down fighting, even if the intel's worth having. Because I don't know what we'll do with a live prisoner who knows too much."

"You disapprove of shooting prisoners."

"I've never actually shot an unarmed *prisoner*," Marc said. "But I'll shoot an unarmed *target* when I get the chance, because I'm not fighting a duel for my honour, I'm removing a threat. Armed — well, by definition, that's always a threat. And I'm glad that I shot some people, because they needed shooting. Does that make it any clearer? Probably not. In the end, if I can look at my orders and think, yeah, that's going to save innocent lives, I don't lose too much sleep."

"So why do you want Gan-Pamas to fight?" Hredt asked.

"Because if he doesn't, and one of my less insensitive colleagues shoots him, they'll feel guilty, and that bends people out of shape," Marc said. "Look at Dan. He does what he has to, but he feels bad about it."

"Chris won't be troubled," Hredt said. "Nor will Captain Ingram. Commander Bissey already seems to have doubts, though. Doubts about the consequences of starting what you might not be able to finish are understandable. Moral doubts about pre-emptive aggression are failing to understand that your ethical standards mean nothing here."

Marc nodded but didn't comment. They went back to discussing the politics and military capabilities of the spacefaring civilisations that might cross their path, with Hredt filling in the technical data, and the more he revealed, the less stressful it became. It felt more like unburdening himself than revealing the trade secrets that had been the teeriks' shield. He forwarded what recorded data he had to the humans' network and recited other details as they occurred to him.

"I might omit some things," he said. "It's not deliberate."

Marc leaned back on his cushions and rearranged his legs to cross them. He was obviously uncomfortable at a low table. "Don't worry. If someone asked me to tell them what I knew about terrorists, it'd take days and it wouldn't be in any particular order."

"Will you remember all this?" The humans here seemed far more intelligent than the average Kugin or Jattan and yet they were technologically backward by comparison. "I can record it all if you like."

"I'm just getting an overview, Fred. When something strikes me as really important, I can always ask you again."

The door opened and Cosquimaden came in, followed by the boys and Rikayl. Cosqui peered at the parts on the table.

"I was going to check the prenu," she said in English, "but there are too many humans guarding the access tunnel."

Marc looked up. "It's just in case Gan-Pamas manages to get to it and ends up killing one of you. It's safer in here. Leave the Jattan to us."

Rikayl waddled up to Marc, looked into his face, and put his head in his lap, which was completely unlike him. Marc had never shown any sign of fear before but he certainly seemed wary of Rikayl now. Then he put his hand on the child's head and stroked it carefully like Hredt had seen him do to the dog that followed him around. He bent forward a little to speak.

"Sorry, mate," he said. "I know you're upset. I should have shot him on sight. But at least he didn't get away with it."

Rikayl didn't move. After a couple of minutes, though, he raised his head, looked up at Marc again, and opened his beak.

"*Neeenah*," he said.

Hredt knew he wasn't imagining it. Rikayl had managed to speak. It should have been a cause for celebration, but instead it was heartbreaking.

"Yeah, Nina's gone, mate." To Marc's credit, he treated Rikayl like the bewildered child he was. "But you'll get through it. Grow up big and strong for her, eh?"

Rikayl acted as if he understood he was being given sympathy. Hredt looked at Cosqui and the boys. They were staring, mesmerised. After a while, Rikayl stood up and wandered off, head down, and Demli followed him into the hallway. Marc seemed to have caught Rikayl's mood.

"I know he doesn't understand everything that goes on," Marc said. "But he was there when it happened, and he went to her. It's bound to traumatise him, Fred."

Then Marc paused, looked away, and put his finger to his ear. He was receiving a message. It occurred to Hredt that Solomon was probably monitoring the conversation via Marc's radio, and might even have been prompting him about the conversation in Kugal. He didn't know if the AI could already analyse languages, but it wouldn't have surprised him.

"Okay... yeah... we're locked down," Marc said. Hredt couldn't tell who he was talking to now. "Yeah... look, I understand, it's not exactly my first date... okay, get one of the lads to drop off a shotgun and some ammo, will you? Thanks."

He stood up and checked his pistol. "Fred, I want you all to stay in here, preferably in this room. Because it's easier to protect you if you're all in one place. Just a precaution."

"What's happened?" Cosqui asked.

"Someone's approached the freighter, presumably Gan-Pamas," Marc said. "He set the dogs off. But we still don't have a visual on him. The drones can't see anything. I'm betting the dogs can hear him."

"Do you think he was trying to escape?" Hredt asked.

Marc shook his head. "I'm not sure if he even knows his teerik's dead. He could have been away from the ship all day and just came back to find it surrounded by aliens with guns. We didn't see him leave while we were there, and the site's been crawling with our people ever since, so this is probably the first time he's been back to it."

"If he hasn't tried to contact anyone already, he definitely will now," Hredt said. "The question is whether he observed your activities and was ready to risk being shot to get back to his ship."

"I'm assuming that arms dealers out here need to be as tough and resourceful as they are on Earth. And he's got a lot of good reasons for seeing this through. If that was me — well, even if I wasn't planning to escape yet, I'd take the risk and go back to my transport to either recover something important or use its comms."

"The ship would have been good bait, but he knows you're there now."

"How come we can't track him, though?" Marc asked. "We've got drones, satellites, sensors, dogs, competent men and women with night vision, infrared, lidar, every bloody system you can get. Plus Solomon collating it all."

"He might have a stealth suit," Hredt said.

"Like the system that hid the ship, you mean?"

"Very similar. You wouldn't see a thermal signature, either."

"Yeah, but what about ground transport? You can't completely hide heat from an engine. Oh. Maybe *you* can."

"There are some very efficient coolants available."

"Well, the dogs can't pick up a scent, but they've got phenomenal hearing," Marc said. "And he can't stop the things he treads on making a noise. So at least we'll know when he's nearby."

"This is going to end at very close quarters," Hredt said.

Marc took a few moments to answer. "Yeah, for one of us, it will. But don't worry, I won't let him take you. Or the prenu."

Hredt went to the window and looked out. It would get dark in two hours. He was checking to see that Demli and Runal weren't still outside, but he noticed some of Trinder's troops standing on the site of the prenu's burrow as if that alone would stop the Jattan navy if it happened to show up.

This dreadful day was still far from over. But Hredt could at least trust the humans to do everything in their power to protect his commune. For all the potential danger, he felt safer right then than he'd ever felt in his life.

* * *

INCIDENT SITE, NORTHEAST OF NOMAD BASE: 1605 HOURS.

"Damn," Jared said. He took out his earpiece for a moment to scratch his ear. "That's got to be hard on Marc."

Chris watched Dieter taking a slow walk around the edge of the cordon with Griff on a long leash. The Labrador kept pausing to sniff and listen, and if Gan-Pamas was anywhere nearby, the dog would know first. Chris sniffed the air occasionally as well. He was pretty sure he'd be able to smell the Jattan even though his hearing fell a long way short of Griff's. He just wasn't certain he could aim accurately at a near-invisible soap bubble.

"She should have called me," Chris said. "You can't ask a guy who's lost his own sons to stand by to kill someone else's."

"Didn't she say you had to be ready to shoot the teeriks, and you told her we *all* had to be ready because we didn't know who'd be with them if and when the shit hit the fan?"

"Yeah. Something like that."

"Exactly. And it just happened to be Marc. She didn't single him out."

Chris couldn't believe Ingram hadn't thought through the consequences. "She could have called me. I don't care how tough Marc is, that's going to wreck him. Ah, fuck it, when we're done here, I'm going back to the compound to relieve him."

Jared kept checking his watch, "He won't thank you for it, Chris."

"He's got ten teeriks in there. Think how one guy's going to work through all of them without a lot of blood and panic as soon as the first shot's fired."

"Yeah, but it won't be any different if you're that one guy," Jared said. "Look, she trusts Marc. She likes him. Hell, I think she *more* than likes him. But business is business."

"Sure, but you don't ask a guy with his baggage to do that if there's an alternative."

Chris rarely let himself get like this. He either acted or he didn't act, but he didn't spend ages talking about it. He'd have gone down to the teerik compound, suggested to Marc that he did something else, and sat with the teeriks until Gan-Pamas was captured or killed, or everything went wrong and he dispatched the teeriks himself. He realised it was all about Marc being the devoted father, and devoted fathers deserved special treatment because Chris hadn't had one.

No, Marc wouldn't thank him. He'd feel insulted because it was a necessary part of his job, a tough profession where even good soldiers struggled to make the grade, and Chris was implying that he was too old, tragic, or unstable to be allowed to carry on doing it. That didn't stop Chris from feeling that he had to take the burden off him.

"Where's this transporter, Sol?" Jared asked. "We could blow up this ship, you know. One missile. The Jattan still doesn't get away or call home."

"But it'll be useful one day," Solomon said. "And we have a Jattan ship we can reverse engineer ourselves. We can't very well dismantle the prenu."

"If he saw his ship go up in flames, he'd have to show himself eventually. And it's one more thing we have to guard. It ties up resources."

Chris was all for blowing it up for convenience's sake, but he saw Solomon's point. He could also think of a dozen ways to use it for undercover work, as long as it wasn't on some galactic BOLO list. Those few days thinking he could become Normal Chris and that a private john and a vegetable patch would change his life were over before they'd started.

"So much for the vow to be normal guys with wives and kids and stop doing this shit once we dealt with Pham," he said.

Jared gave him a look. "There'll always be a Tim Pham, even if it's an alien, and you'll always go after him. Anyway, how do we know this Jattan's one of the bad guys? He just wants something we've got that we shouldn't have but don't want to give back."

Chris thought about that for a while. Jared knew he wouldn't cross the road to avoid trouble even when he could let it pass by and never have to see it again. Maybe this situation wasn't even trouble. They didn't know the Jattans. The only species that had harmed humans so far was teerik, or ablun, or whatever this Lirrel liked to call himself. And now all he could see was Lirrel with that metal cutter.

Stop. Stop thinking about it. Think about something else.

"Here it comes," Jared said.

Chris concentrated on the noise of the approaching transporter to try to shut the image of Nina out of his mind. If he crammed his brain with as many irrelevant thoughts about the vehicle as he could, there'd be no room for recalling the last few hours. The giant breakdown vehicle came from the direction of the base, its folded flatbed jangling as it bounced over the uneven terrain, part autonomous vehicle and part crane. Chris didn't know if it had been shipped in complete or if was another machine built here by bots, refashioned from other equipment or created from ore mined on Opis itself. It might even have been recycled from the components of the original unmanned mission ships that first landed bots and launched satellites here seventy-three years ago.

Chris kept thinking about Bednarz's unfathomably complex feat of creating two robotic AI universes, one on Earth and one on Opis, purely for the preservation of humans who, for the most part, had no idea how they worked. He wondered if Bednarz thought he was normal and everyone else was dumb, or if he saw himself as a god above even the really smart people. The only person left who'd actually known the guy was Solomon, but Chris wasn't sure the opinion of a virtual son was a reliable account. Sol said surprisingly little about Bednarz anyway.

Then the half-formed mental images of Bednarz and bots dismantling their comrades collapsed, and his memory crashed back in with a replay of the teerik swinging at Nina, vivid and detailed and refusing to go away. He couldn't stop himself screwing his eyes shut like a kid. Even when he could look away from the mental video loop, he could actually *feel* it there waiting to start again.

"You okay?" Jared asked.

"Yeah. I'm fine."

The transporter spent ten minutes unfolding a platform and sliding it under the Jattan freighter segment by segment, lifting it clear of the ground. Then it manoeuvred itself in stops and starts and eventually swung in a wide U-turn to face Nomad Base, mowing down a small tree in the process. After more creaking and groaning, it headed south, towing the ship on the platform behind it like it was pulling a sleigh.

Griff was still wandering around the site, sniffing and listening. Gan-Pamas didn't seem to be around. He'd know his ship was gone sooner or later, though, and then he might come into the base to try to recover it.

Chris waved to Dieter to stand down. "Let's go."

"You *sure* you're okay?" Jared asked.

"I will be."

Chris drove back, trying to think like a Jattan. Alien mind or not, some things had to work the same way for everyone. The guy had probably made a big effort to find Opis, he had a heavyweight client expecting results, he had to confirm the prenu was here, and, if he didn't realise Lirrel was dead and not just missing or captured, he'd try to retrieve him. Nobody would walk away and leave a valuable asset like a teerik.

Maybe the guy wouldn't abandon a friend, either.

"You think we might be thwarting heroes like Bissey said?" Chris asked.

"Fred isn't likely to see *any* Jattan as a good guy," Jared said. "Jattans are happy to buy Kugin ships made with teerik slave labour. So how can we know?"

"What if the best thing for humans is an alliance with Jattans?"

"Well, we're here to survive. We didn't come here to be martyrs for anyone else's cause."

"Yeah."

"You've had a rough day and it's not the first," Jared said. "Don't do anything dumb and heroic without a damn good reason."

"It doesn't change a thing. This isn't about Jattans versus teeriks in some morality war. It's about hiding the portal, the teeriks, and Earth."

"And even that's a tad too selfless and ideological, buddy. Nomad first."

Chris nodded. "Yeah. You're right."

"Look, he was expecting to find teeriks here with a ship, but he wasn't expecting to find us," Jared said. "And that has to look kind of worrying. We just show up and we're in cahoots with teerik hijackers. And yeah, it could even look like it's our plan, not Fred's. We're muscling in on Gan-Pamas's business."

"What if he already knows about the Caisin gate?" Chris asked. "What does he do next?"

"Would you try to tackle unknown aliens and seize something that major on your own?"

Chris shook his head. "No. I'd sneak off the planet and return with some backup, no matter how badly I wanted the reward for finding it."

"But he's still here," Jared said. "So unless he's a one-man army, or thinks he is, he's going to go to ground and wait."

"Yeah. And if we're totally wrong and he's escaped in a second ship because we had no idea he came with backup, we're screwed."

"When did we ever know everything that was going on before we got into a situation?"

"That'd be never."

"So we'll know what to do when we see it needs doing," Jared said.

The only people Chris saw as he drove into Nomad were security patrols and a few Kill Liners at work in the fields. Livestock couldn't wait for aliens to sort themselves out. Cows needed milking and feeding and their shit had to go somewhere. A temporary slurry lagoon had been excavated next to Liam Dale's farm, and manure and everything contaminated with it from straw to water was dumped into the pit every day, not just from his herd but from all the other livestock. He was out with a mini earth mover, shoving the waste into the channel that fed the lagoon. Chris tried to hold his breath as he caught a lungful of the stench on the breeze and decided farmers were the toughest folks in the world. Liam waved to him, apparently unaware of the smell.

Chris pulled over to chat. "Hi Liam. We still can't find the Jattan. I realise some jobs won't wait, but go home as soon as you can. We don't know how dangerous he is. Let's err on the side of caution."

Liam stood there in his shit-caked rubber boots with a large wrench in one hand. "Is it true he's got some camouflage suit and we can't see him?"

"Apparently. But the dogs can hear him even if they don't seem to be able to pick up his scent, so if your dogs start barking, call us and get indoors."

"Okay. Go careful."

Chris carried on towards the teerik compound. "There's always a job worse than yours," Jared said.

"Amen."

If Gan-Pamas really had been doing recons, he wouldn't have had any trouble working out where to start. The teerik compound looked like a small garrison in its own right. Chris dropped Jared off at the main building, picked up a shotgun from the armoury, and doubled back to the compound to sort out Marc.

Trinder was waiting outside the house with Aaron Luce when Chris arrived. They both gave him a you-too-huh look. It was good to realise your comrades had exactly the same thoughts and had made exactly the same decision.

"You want to toss a coin for it?" Trinder asked. "Otherwise I'm pulling rank and replacing him."

Chris shook his head. "I've got this."

"We're going to have to stand watches if this runs into tomorrow," Aaron said. "You want me to do the next one, Dan?"

"Yeah. Thanks. The three of us can cover this."

"Is Ingram around?" Chris asked.

"She went off with Lee and Hiyashi to move the gun trucks into position," Trinder said. "It's not her you need to have the argument with, though. It's Marc."

"Yeah, I know he won't like me interfering." Chris took a breath and pushed the door. "I'm right, aren't I?"

"I'll pull you out of there at twenty-five-fifty-nine," Aaron said. "I'm off to get a few hours' sleep first."

Chris braced for an argument. Marc wouldn't like being nannied. He'd managed to survive eight unhappy years without coming unravelled, but Tev Josepha had felt the need to keep an eye on him as well, so maybe he and Chris were both projecting how unhinged they'd be if they were in his situation. But Chris saw the archetypal good father every time Marc was with Howie, or even when he was talking to the younger personnel. There were too few good guys like that in this life. Chris would do whatever he could to look out for them.

Marc was working at the table with Fred when Chris walked in. There was no sign of the other teeriks, but it sounded as if they were at the far end of the house, squabbling and arguing. Chris would have to make sure he knew exactly where they were at any moment in case he had to do the worst. Fred was hunched over a shotgun, adjusting a small tube attached to its rail.

"What is it?" Chris asked.

"A rather primitive targeting device," Fred said. "Gan-Pamas has expensive stealth measures fitted to his ship, and his personal protection seems equally efficient if the dogs can't follow his scent. And as Solomon hasn't located him, it means we can't rely on thermal or optical signatures, or even sonar. We could detect exhaled gases, but by then he'd be within striking distance of you. So this is something simple and inescapable to highlight him. Liquid pigment. An opaque coating. Unless he already has gate technology and can step out of this world, he's a permanently solid object we can find. And if he had gate technology, he wouldn't need the prenu. So you fire it and it coats him so that you can aim more accurately."

Marc looked at Chris, expressionless. "In other words, we're going to paintball him to death."

"But aiming a paint pellet at a target you can't see is as hard as using conventional ammo." Chris would have to put his faith in his hearing and a shotgun. "But if he's got some ballistic protection, we'll stand a better chance of seeing the pellet deflected."

"It's not a pellet, it's a spray, a reactive coating," Fred said. "It has a hundred-yard range and it'll disperse itself over anything in its path. You can sweep it across a small area once you have an approximate idea of where he is, which is where your dogs can be helpful. They identify the general direction and you move in with weapons equipped with the spray."

"And you just cooked up that chemical."

"It's a coating used on ships' hulls. There was a container stored in the prenu. We diluted it to make it spread further." Fred held a pellet between his thumb and index claws. The object was the size of a sausage link. "It's under pressure, and when it's released, it spreads as a fine mist. It can be dosed so that it's attracted to a particular material, but as we don't know exactly what Gan-Pamas is using, we'll rely on its general coating ability and use the colour and opacity to outline him."

"And by then he's squeezed off a few rounds and half of us are dead before we can see him," Chris said. "But one of us will get him. Can this be deployed from a Lammergeier?"

Fred cocked his head, thinking. "Yes. But how vulnerable are they to ground fire? We don't know what weapons he has. In his profession, he'll have access to equipment even teeriks might not be familiar with."

"Which have to be stealth-coated too, right?" Marc seemed relaxed, given the kind of day he was having and how much worse it might get. "Or else we'll see a disembodied ray gun drifting along like a bad remake of *The Invisible Man*."

"Possibly, but his personal protection could be loose enough to conceal quite large weapons."

"Ground to air missile?" Chris wasn't joking. If teeriks had microprobes that could operate across a galaxy and a portal that could fit into a small ship, anything could be miniaturised. "Ground scanner?"

"He's a Jattan," Fred said. "He's smaller than I am. If he's not in a vehicle, he'd struggle to carry that many items."

"Okay, so if he's got a rifle or something, we'll see part of it emerge, and that's a second or two of advance warning. And once he's discharged it, we have a bearing on him." Chris examined the pellet. He didn't want to use the dogs to get up close. That was their job, but it was going to be hard to face Dieter if any more of them got killed. "And we can still hear him because he has to tread on stuff and his clothes have to move when he does. So he isn't as undetectable as he thinks. What about the teerik metal cutter? Can I use that? Can you show me how to use it?"

"I'd advise against it," Fred said.

"Why?"

"Think of it as a very long blade you can't actually see until it connects with a solid object."

"That's pretty much what a bullet is. I'm good with bullets."

Fred didn't look like he was going to give way. "You might do yourself more harm than you do him."

"He just wants to get into that prenu and lift off," Marc said. "He'll avoid a fight if he can. It's about the money. Or his cause. Or both. He needs the ship more than his manly tentacled pride."

Fred took back the pellet and slid it into the tube attached to the rail. "He'll struggle to fly it single-handed. Cosqui's disabled the extraction mechanism anyway. And he's got to get into the access tunnel first."

"What if he's got some code or AI that he can inject into its system, override Cosqui's settings, and autopilot it?" Chris asked. "We're primitive monkeys by comparison and even we could manage that. And if he's got a mole inside the Jattan procurement department, he's got a head start about the specifications."

Fred moved on to the Marquis on the table and examined its muzzle. "I don't know. But I can add more lock-outs to the system. And, as I said, he has to get into the ship first, which means using our access from inside this house or digging a hole himself."

Chris wasn't going to get any further with this. But he had the rest of the evening and it was time to send Marc away.

"Okay." Chris tried to look like this was all routine. "Off you go, Marc. I'll call you if anything happens."

Marc stared at him for a few moments. Chris didn't flinch.

"Ingram sent you to relieve me, did she?"

"No, I just decided you'd had a long day. Now go eat, feed Betsy, reassure Howie, and get some sleep. We need you fresh for the big stuff."

Chris waited for a blunt put-down. Then Marc nodded like he'd just realised something he'd forgotten and bumped his fist against Chris's shoulder, just a light tap.

"You're all right, Chris," he said. "Don't let anyone tell you you're not. See you later, Fred."

Chris hadn't expected that reaction at all, but it proved he'd made the right call. He settled down at the table to watch Fred working, fascinated by the way he could use his claws.

"I had a girlfriend who did that," he said.

"She modified weapons?"

"No, she used her nails like tools. She had these really long, lacquered fingernails. She'd use them to pry things open and press buttons. It used to make me wince because it looked painful."

"Oh, I see," Fred said.

Chris really wasn't cut out for small talk. He gave up and just watched for a few minutes, then decided to familiarise himself with the layout.

"I'm going to walk around the house and check everything's secure," he said. "I'll do that every half hour, just to be on the safe side. Is that okay with you?"

"Thank you," Fred said. "Yes, please do."

Chris really did have to do rounds, and he needed to memorise the layout of the teerik house. But he was also doing the recon he hoped he wouldn't have to use for real, working out where all the teeriks were and visualising the route he'd have to take to make sure he could shoot all of them cleanly. If he could get them all in one room, that might solve some problems, but it would also make it easier to defend the commune if the house was breached. He kept telling himself that it could go either way and that he wasn't just working out how to kill them. He almost made himself believe it.

He checked the windows a few times. They were integrated into the wall material, not separate frames, so if Gan-Pamas tried to get inside he couldn't enter without breaching the wall itself. The doors were guarded from outside and the sounds of the struggle to open them would alert Chris immediately, so that was another unlikely point of entry. Chris also had feeds on his screen from the drones and all the cameras around the base, so he could see almost as much as if he'd been out patrolling.

So what would he do if he was Gan-Pamas?

If he'd located the prenu, he'd either dig a long tunnel from outside the compound, which would probably take days, or he'd hole up somewhere and wait for everyone to get bored with being on constant alert and start making dumb security errors. But he was still just one guy, armed or not, so he'd rely on sneaking around rather than staging a frontal assault. Fred said Jattans were headstrong, but they couldn't be dumb enough to believe they could charge a couple of hundred armed humans singlehanded.

Chris carried on building his mental map of the house. He peered around doors, trying to be diplomatic and not scare anyone. Four of the teeriks were watching a video which sounded like a cop show, and didn't even look up when he checked on them. The two boys were in another room, still playing that dice game or whatever it was. Rikayl was nestled on a cushion in the corner, head almost under one wing, but he had one eye open. He watched Chris, then hissed like an angry goose without raising his head. The boys looked around.

"Are you sad about Nina?" one of them asked.

"Yes, I'm very sad," Chris said. It didn't quite cover what he felt, which was that he was afraid to shut his eyes because there was only one image in his head, but it would do for the kids. "We all are."

There were only two teeriks he hadn't clocked yet, Turisu and Maro, but he could hear them at the end of the passage. Their door was shut and they sounded like they were having a fight. He looked back from the end of the corridor and worked out the distance he'd need to cover if he had to take action in three rooms, none of them adjacent, plus the front room where Fred was working. It'd be hard. He'd definitely have to round them up at some point. There'd be arguments, but it was better than not being able to defend them properly.

Or shoot them.

Chris had learned to switch off a long time ago. It had always worked. But it wasn't working today.

"Sol?" he whispered. "Has Marc briefed you about the spray?"

"Yes, Chris. Actually, he keeps his mike open so that I can hear the sound in the room. It would be helpful if you could do that too."

Chris took the polite rebuke. "Okay, my bad. Why haven't you analysed their language and translated it?"

"I'm trying," Solomon said. "But they rarely speak anything other than English in the areas I can monitor, which is gracious of them, but it doesn't help me learn. Ideally, I need them to speak Kugal and inject English terms so I can use them as reference points. If they use an English technical term, for example, I can narrow down the meaning of the words they use around it and build from there."

"You could have asked them for lessons."

"You missed the point. Although Marc might have spoiled that."

"Oh. Yeah."

The teeriks hadn't been open about critically important stuff before they needed to be. If they didn't think humans understood Kugal or Jattan, they might speak more frankly in those languages. Now they thought Marc understood Kugal. Chris wasn't sure if he did or not.

He went back to the front room and sat down with Fred again to watch his progress with the paint launcher.

"This is just aim and fire, yeah?"

"Yes." Fred indicated a pressure switch behind the tube. "Press this to load the liquid. Then fire the weapon as you usually do. It's separate. Very basic, as I said, but you don't have to learn to use a gun differently in a difficult situation. I thought that was important."

"Good thinking," Chris said.

"I have enough material here to make fifteen more tubes. Then I'll need more items from the ship. If you hand me your weapon, I'll fit one for you."

"I didn't realise you could make things yourself."

"We don't physically build ships, but we can do small things."

"We could print components if you give us a three-D spec."

"Thank you. That might be quicker."

Chris passed him the shotgun. If a breaching round or three didn't at least slow the Jattan down long enough to drop a grenade into the top of his armour — if Fred had drawn Jattans accurately — he'd be surprised, and not in a good way. He wanted to get close enough to put a hole through Gan-Pamas the first time.

"How many sprays have I got?" he asked.

"Five. I'll give you an extra pellet to practice with."

"Any weapons I should be especially worried about?"

"That depends how close you intend to get, although you might not be able to control that."

Chris knew he was being optimistic. "Fifteen, twenty feet?"

"Anything he's likely to use will kill you."

"Okay. I'm glad we sorted that out."

That wouldn't stop Chris, because there were plenty of things that should have killed him by now but hadn't. The Jattan knew as little about humans as humans knew about him, maybe less, because at least Nomad had a teerik informer. Chris picked up the modified gun, hefted it, and didn't notice much difference.

"Awesome," he said. "Thanks, Fred. Mind if I ask you a dumb human question?"

"I'm sure it'll be anything but dumb, Chris." Fred's command of English was statesmanlike now. He really was a remarkable creature. "Please ask."

"Are the Jattan opposition the good guys?"

Fred picked up another length of cut tube and peered down it. "Not if they know where your homeworld is."

Yeah, Fred wasn't a poor naive serf. Chris nodded. "Thanks. I just don't want to start a war with the wrong folks."

He'd done enough talking today. It had drained everything out of him. He did his regular rounds, heated up a meal for Fred, took a couple of Mendoza's racehorse pills, and kept an eye on the drone feeds. There was a lot of activity in the base, but nothing seemed to be happening.

Trinder arrived to relieve him ten minutes early. The two teerik kids rushed out to see who'd arrived, studied Trinder for a moment, and went back to their room. Chris showed him his modified shotgun and waited for his reaction.

"Seeing as I've got this and most people haven't, I'm going to patrol," he said. "See you whenever."

Trinder examined the gun. "Fred, can I have one of those, please?"

All Fred needed was a pair of wire spectacles on the end of his beak and he'd have looked like a fairy-tale watchmaker. He kept his eyes on the tube mechanism.

"Anyone would think there were no other troops but yourselves," he said. "Why do you take on every duty?"

"Because I can't ask my people to do what I wouldn't do myself," Trinder said. "And I hate sitting on my ass."

Chris left them to it and walked around the compound wall, listening and inhaling every few yards. There was no barking, no rustling, and no smells except the crushed grass where he'd trodden and the faint spiciness that always hung on the Opis air. Somewhere out there was a mass of plants with scented blooms or leaves. If and when things calmed down, he'd drive out to find them and just fill his lungs with the fragrance.

He walked the long way back to the centre of the base, looping around to where he thought a Jattan might have to start digging a long tunnel. There was nothing he could see that the assortment of land-based and aerial sensors couldn't pick up as temperature changes or shifts in soil density, but he did it anyway. They'd missed the Jattan ship the first time and they might well miss Gan-Pamas sneaking in.

Maybe they should have let Rikayl out. He seemed to be able to find the ship easily enough. Funny: Chris hadn't thought about it until now, but the kid had flown off as if he was going somewhere rather than just trying to get away. If it was a coincidence that he'd found the ship, it was a pretty big one. What had he detected? If something had grabbed his attention, it wasn't the ship landing, because it had probably arrived months ago.

Chris was still working through the possibilities when he walked past the main entrance and ran into Ingram. She was sitting outside on one of the low barriers that had been put up in case a construction bot overshot its track, studying her screen.

Chris gestured with his shotgun. "Fred's kindly fitted this with a paint sprayer. Can't beat old tech."

"You'll have to get awfully close," she said.

"I'm planning to."

"And I didn't realise you'd relieved Marc."

There was no hint in Ingram's tone that she was angry, but she was raising the issue, so she must have been irked. Well, it was going to happen sooner or later. Now was fine.

"I didn't want a man who lost two sons to have to shoot two kids, ma'am," he said. "Three, I suppose. We've got the teerik watches covered."

Ingram didn't blink. "Is this going to be an issue between us, Sergeant?"

"Only if you do it again, ma'am."

"I realise I'm not your CO, but next time, tell me."

"Next time, maybe ask *me* to do it," Chris said. "I'm an asshole who used to hurt people for money. Just because Marc's competent to do it doesn't mean he should."

"He happened to be there, so he wasn't chosen to do it. And I wouldn't try to give him special treatment, because he wouldn't accept it. But yes, I agree he's the most competent man here for the difficult jobs."

Ingram might have been defensive, or just telling Chris that he wasn't half the man Marc was. That was probably true and it didn't hurt. The worst thing was that she didn't rip him a new one, and that wasn't because she had no command authority over him. It was because she was so confident of her place in the world that he didn't really matter to her.

"I'd save him for the really difficult tasks, then," Chris said. "Not easy assassinations that any thug could do for you. Goodnight, ma'am."

Chris walked on. "Goodnight, Sergeant," she said.

Nomad was too small and too dangerous a place to have feuds. Chris knew he'd pushed the boundary of necessary military discipline and he'd have to make his peace with her later, but he didn't feel like doing it right now. She was probably the most experienced officer here, though, and that meant she should have thought about it harder.

Perhaps she had but she didn't care, even if she seemed to be keen on Marc. Maybe she was like Fonseca, all smiles and sympathy but ready to sell a guy's kidneys if she saw a great pair of shoes her pay check wouldn't stretch to. And Gina — she was another one, all tears and I'll-wait-forever when Chris was jailed but stepping out with his ex-boss within weeks. He never learned. He accepted he either had bad luck or bad judgement whenever it came to women.

Screw it, if he ever met a woman who was just kind, he'd marry her, no matter what else she didn't have going for her. Niceness was seriously underrated. Even Annis Kim was surprisingly kind, considering she was a spy, so he wasn't asking for the impossible.

"I think you did the right thing, Chris," Solomon said.

"I left my mike open, didn't I?"

"You did. Ingram will have forgotten about this by tomorrow."

"Fine." Chris doubted it. "Has Dieter turned in for the night?"

"Marc sent him home. Check your screen. Marc's out tracking with Betsy and some of the other dogs. I think it's Betsy who's managing them, to be honest. He has no idea, but they do come back to him when he calls."

"Always pays to have a good Two-IC," Chris said. "Where's Howie?"

"Marc dropped him off at Jared's place. Don't worry, everyone you're concerned about is safe and well."

"Okay. I'm going to walk the perimeter. I'll see you later."

The sentry sensors recognised him as he approached the invisible barrier and shut down a section of the field to let him pass without making his hair stand on end. He was now in what passed for wild Opis, outside the protection of the base, and it was one of the few times he felt more comfortable using night vision. Opis's moon wasn't visible tonight and it was truly dark out here even with Nomad's lights behind him. For a moment, he lifted his visor and looked up. He thought he'd seen clear night skies before, but Opis's atmosphere was completely untainted in a way Earth's had never been in his lifetime. The stars looked an arm's length away, impossible numbers of them.

He could have reflected on the beauty of it, or the wonder of being so far from home, but at that moment all he could do was worry who else was out there. He'd wondered that before he ever knew real honest-to-God aliens existed, but it hadn't made him feel like he did now. He was a speck of nothing, further from Earth than anyone had ever been, with nobody left from his old life, his pre-Guard life, to tell about it.

He didn't know if he was overwhelmed because he finally had a concept of how vast space was, or because he was scared to think how hostile it could be. But he had an inkling of how his father felt when he looked at a frightening world he couldn't handle and just wanted to pretend the monsters weren't there, until one day he decided his own son was a monster too.

Did I get him all wrong? Have I been unfair on him?

It had been eighteen or nineteen years since Chris had decided to make monsters afraid of *him*. He'd reinvented himself as the guy people crossed the road to avoid, not the one who did the avoiding the way his dad did. Tonight he was out looking for a monster again with a weapon in his hand, not shutting his eyes and hoping the creature would pass him by. But maybe he was just locked into the habit of needing a monster to defeat, and this one wasn't a monster after all.

The Jattan was just in the wrong place at the wrong time. Chris still had to do it. He aimed the shotgun into the wilderness, felt for the switch with his left thumb, and fired the paint spray.

It was kind of weird. It ballooned out in a teardrop shape and seemed to be expanding forever. Then it dropped. He could see the bushes picked out in it like a Christmas tree sprayed with fake snow. Something small skittered through the grass, probably trying to escape this lunatic who was flinging paint everywhere. But Chris was satisfied with the result. If Gan-Pamas was in range and he could get a rough bearing on him, he could deposit that spray close enough to reveal the guy's outline.

He'd lost track of the time. When he checked his screen, he realised he'd been out here for an hour, and he hadn't done much patrolling. There was still the rest of the perimeter to check out. As he retraced his steps, Solomon radioed him.

"Chris, we might have a contact," he said.

"Where?"

"I haven't pinned it down, but it's the old Earth relay satellite. The original one that was launched from the first unmanned vessel, not the FTL link. Someone attempted to route a transmission but it didn't accept the inbound signal."

"From here?"

"I have an approximate location four miles northwest. It has to be Gan-Pamas."

If the Jattan was trying to route a message using that sat, it meant he had no other comms. He'd probably realised he'd run out of options. Chris hoped that was the reason, anyway, because the alternative was that he had some other means of sending a signal and was just staging a diversion.

"He'll be long gone by the time we get there," Chris said. "But his trail might not be. Make sure the compound's watertight and let's go find him."

* * *

LOCATION OF SIGNAL ORIGIN, THREE MILES NORTHWEST OF NOMAD BASE: 0620, FIVE HOURS LATER.

"Abso-frigging-lutely *nothing*," Dieter said, rubbing his hands as if he was cold.

He joined the huddle by the Caracal with his dogs, looking tired and fed up. All Trinder could do was offer him the last of his coffee. It had been a long night for everybody, just like the previous one, and it probably wasn't going to be the last.

"What do you mean by nothing?" Trinder asked.

"Sapper can smell crushed vegetation, but none of it leads anywhere," Dieter said. "Sal's trying to find Gan-Pamas's specific scent, but she hasn't picked up anything at all. She had a good sniff around the ship, so she knows what she's looking for."

Chris rubbed Sapper's head. "There's got to be a good reason why they can't smell him." Sapper and Sal looked up at him as if they were grateful for his defence of their skills. "It's telling us something."

"Yeah, that he was never here," Trinder said. "Sol, are you sure about this position?"

"The *satellite's* sure." Solomon was in an armed quadrubot today, distinguishable from his usual frame by the bulges in the backplate. It looked like he planned to do the dirty work himself if he thought his humans were losing their nerve. "I'd have to conclude that he used a drone, stealth-coated or too small to detect."

No scent, no vehicle tracks, nothing; Gan-Pamas had vanished. Trinder had thought the signal was their lucky break, but they'd combed the entire area and it just kept raising more questions. Maybe the Jattan had managed to cloak whatever transport he had and even make himself silent. But he couldn't disguise the effects of gravity. Anything soft that he trod or drove on would show depressions, and they'd already found tracks, even though they'd ended abruptly. Presumably the Jattan would also disturb air and create a draught if he moved at speed.

But that didn't help one damn bit, because he'd be too close by then. There was, as Dieter said, nothing.

"I saw the ship when I got close enough," Chris said. "I don't know how we get close to Gan-Pamas other than waiting for him to get close to us, but I think the paint spray is still our best chance of getting a fix on him."

"According to Marc, he likes dimmer light and more humidity," Trinder said. "Fred told him."

"Yeah, but it rained overnight, so that could mean anywhere."

"How about the river? He'll need water, and he can find somewhere shallow enough to wade for a distance and come out on the other bank."

"And then what?" Chris asked. "Even if he's a survival expert, he's here to do a job. He'll still end up back at the base."

There was one thing worse than Jattans discovering humans and teeriks camped here with something that belonged to them, and that was Jattans getting into the prenu and finding the Caisin gate. Keeping Gan-Pamas out of Nomad was a priority.

"Okay, let's call off the search, pull everyone back, and wait," Trinder said. "They can beef up the perimeter patrols instead, in case he doesn't blip the boundary sensors."

Both dogs jerked their heads up, ears pricked. Dieter looked around too. "It's Marc," he said.

Marc rolled up in one of the rovers and got out with an armful of insulated foil packs. "Here, have a bacon sandwich," he said. "A proper one. Sorry, Sol, I didn't get you anything."

Trinder had slept six hours in the last forty-five and he'd reached the permanently hungry stage of fatigue. He'd have eaten whatever came out of that pack, even if it crawled out. Nothing beat hot, greasy, salty food for a quick boost. Dieter broke one of his sandwiches into pieces and fed the dogs first.

"Sod all, then?" Marc asked.

"Zip," Chris said. He checked his live map while he ate. "And it looks like Bissey's been in Ingram's office a long time. Either that or they've left their radios behind."

"I think they're having a robust discussion," Solomon said.

Marc munched contentedly. "Eavesdropper."

"No, Marc, I'm not listening in. But the outcome of that conversation will be clear to us very shortly."

"Is this Bissey wanting to make contact with the Jattan because he might be a good guy after all?"

"I would imagine so."

"Fred won't like that," Chris said.

Marc sighed. "Yeah, well, nice as it would be to invite Mr Gan-Pamas for a cup of tea and a chat, I don't think we're going to get the opportunity."

"It'd be just our luck if he's already managed to get off Opis," Dieter said.

Chris paused and gestured to his screen with his sandwich, oblivious of Sapper following its movements with an expectant expression. "Better put some dogs at the key sites, too, Dieter. If I was trying to infiltrate, I'd distract you by sabotaging your utilities and trashing your crops."

"What is he, a bloody one-man army now?" Marc muttered.

"No, but I don't want to be left in the dark with no food. I'd go protect the larder and the lights."

Trinder had a random sleep-deprived thought. "Maybe it's only teeriks and humans who can smell Jattans. You know, like only some people can taste certain chemicals. It's genetic."

"Are you volunteering?"

"I've done dumber things, Chris."

Solomon was still staring out across the long grass. The lack of visible eyes in his snake-cam head made him look inscrutable, as if he was seeing what mere flesh and blood couldn't, which he probably was.

"We're treating Gan-Pamas as if he's special forces," he said. "For all we know, he's not used to wilderness environments at all and he's already struggling."

Marc chewed thoughtfully. "We don't actually know what a Jattan arms dealer is, either. We think of some smarmy git in a silk suit brokering deals from his Rio penthouse or an unshaven heavy with a gold tooth and crates of guns in the back of a truck. Maybe this one's something else entirely. All we've got is Fred's opinion that this guy's dangerous. I mean, he is, in terms of our need to hide certain things from aliens, but maybe he's a reasonable bloke."

"You think Fred's unreliable, then?" Solomon asked.

"We're all unreliable, Sol. We all see the world our own way. Anyway, one man's gunrunner is another man's civil servant in charge of defence procurement. Or patriot."

"But you'll still terminate him."

"Oh, yeah. It's not about who he is. It's about what he knows. But the longer this drags on, the more time Bissey has to nag Ingram into talking to him."

"I didn't think she was an easy woman to browbeat," Chris said.

"She isn't. But she's on her own now. No Admiralty to back her up, no government, nothing. So it's like the middle of a battle. She's got to hold that crew together with the force of her personality and her people skills. Crew who came from APS states are probably having doubts after seeing what Sol did. And you've got to know your first officer has your back. If he gives the crew the impression she's making a big mistake, it erodes her authority, and that's not good for any of us."

"Is he doing that, then?" Chris asked.

Marc went quiet as if he was thinking, but he didn't answer the question. "As long as we pretend we've got rules, we have rules. But none of us have any command to answer to and we aren't even legally serving members of any armed forces. We just brought the habit and structure with us because it works and we like it. But the only real objective authority is weapons. Superior strength."

"Do you think Bissey's getting mutinous?" Trinder asked.

"No. Just diverging."

"I'd rehearse this speech if I were you," Trinder said. "Because you know you're going to have to go through it all again with Bissey."

"And I shouldn't have to. Ingram said shoot or capture. You either follow orders or quit. But she's been with Bissey through a lot of battles, she trusts him, she listens to his arguments, and I admit he actually has a reasonable point. If we get this wrong, the consequences could be disastrous for humanity, not just us." Marc folded the foil bags and looked like he was done. "On the other hand, that applies equally to what happens if we *don't* shoot Gan-Pamas and the Jattans turn out to be as bad as Fred says."

"I'm not crazy about shooting aliens we haven't even met," Chris said. "But if we don't silence him, and the Jattans take the teeriks and the prenu, they might realise Earth's ripe for a visit and we won't get a second chance."

"Exactly. Come on, Dieter. Load the dogs and we'll drive you back to base. You too, Sol."

"I still want to mooch around," Chris said. "I'll see you later."

"Go ahead, Marc." Trinder just wanted a break. "I'll wait for Chris."

Trinder and Chris sat in the Caracal and finished their breakfast. They were out of coffee now as well as luck.

"If these camo suits made troops and equipment completely undetectable, the Jattans would run the galaxy," Chris said. "But they don't. So there's a vulnerability. There's one in everything."

Trinder nodded. "Fred thinks it's the Jattans' own prototype, or at least something the Kugin don't know about. It's way more effective than the official gear they've got now, apparently."

"So we're all doing it, then."

"Yeah, maybe Lirrel did what Caisin did," Trinder said. "A little upgrade project on the side that the boss doesn't know about, then he skips town."

"Maybe teeriks go AWOL with company property more often than we think," Chris said. "Beats stealing paper clips."

"Would Fred know, though? They lead cloistered lives."

"Probably not." Chris had that preoccupied look. "We need that suit in one piece for Fred to reverse-engineer it and make versions for us. Imagine that combined with the Caisin gate."

"I'm trying not to, Chris."

"Or maybe we'll find it's not fantastic tech and we're just not as good at tracking people as we think."

The suit, whatever it turned out to be, had become one more technology to commandeer and then try to keep from falling into the wrong hands on Earth — or out here. Trinder could see Nomad's commanders sliding accidentally into an arms-control role for which they were both unqualified and unelected. They'd already made a decision on who shouldn't have Caisin's technology, a morality call if they were honest with themselves, and even if they'd just shelved it while they assessed the gate's implications, the policing habit was now taking root. They'd add more gear to the list. Sure, there was technology he was glad some folks didn't have, but doing something about it took them down a path they hadn't thought through and had never intended.

Trinder drove back to the base, thinking of all the things he could have happily misused the Jattan suit for back on Earth. Chris stared out of the window. Then the radio blipped and Liam Dale's voice drifted out of the dashboard speaker.

"Sergeant Montello, it's Liam Dale here," the voice said. "I can see you're on your way back from your radio tracker, so can you come and sort out this damn bird before I shoot him?"

That was one way to get Chris's attention. "Hi Liam. Do you mean Rikayl?"

"Yeah. He's been flying over the cows and scaring them, and now he's taking an interest in the slurry lagoon. If he tries to use it as a bird bath, he won't last long."

"He shouldn't even be out, Liam," Chris said. "I'm on my way. Don't let him see your shotgun, or he'll fly off-camp and it'll take forever to find him."

"Okay."

Chris looked at Trinder. "Come on. Let's get it over with."

Trinder turned the Caracal around and took the track between the crop tunnels to Liam's farm. The slurry pit was on the far side of the pasture, probably not at regulation distancing, but Liam knew what he was doing. He'd fenced it off and signposted it as a hazard. It was just a temporary, open pit a few feet deep to collect waste and run-off water while the bots built a proper lined pit with biogas extraction further away, but everyone dumped their animal waste and dirty water there now and it was already filling up. Trinder had done his homework on storing manure when he thought they'd have to shelter livestock in Ainatio's underground bunkers for a few weeks and he'd found it was way too dangerous. A guy wouldn't even smell some of the gases at lethal concentrations. That was if the methane content didn't ignite and explode first, of course.

"He picks his moments, that kid," Trinder said.

"You can stay in the vehicle. I'll do the bird scaring."

Rikayl was perched on top of the locked gates when Trinder pulled up, the highest vantage point on what would be a fairly big farm before long. Liam wasn't around. That was just as well given how unpredictable Rikayl could be and Liam's tendency to do as he pleased. Chris opened the door and the smell wafted in as he got out. He called up to the teerik.

"Rikayl, that's dangerous stuff, buddy. Off you go." He clapped his hands together a few times. "Go on. You shouldn't even be out. Shoo. Beat it. Go home."

Rikayl glared at him for a moment, then opened his beak and let out a loud, angry rasp before flying off, skimming so low over Chris that he almost clipped him. Chris ducked and didn't look amused.

Trinder had to laugh. "You've got a way with animals."

"Little bastard." Chris climbed back into his seat and got on the radio. "Hey Liam, Rikayl's gone home. We'll have a word with Fred and work out how to keep the kid away."

"He'll be back," Liam said.

"Then I'll come back and move him on again. See you later." Chris closed the channel and rubbed his eyes. "I don't want to have to fish a body out of a pond full of shit. Fred's got to lock him in."

"We've stopped wondering about him, haven't we?"

"What, why he's not like the others?"

"Yeah."

"I haven't stopped wondering at all," Chris said.

Trinder carried on to the teerik compound. The other teeriks were still in the house, heavily guarded, with Aaron Luce on coup de grâce duty today. He nodded at Trinder with a knowing look as he walked in.

"Missing any teeriks?" Trinder asked.

"Not as far as I know. I'll check."

"Good, because Rikayl got out."

Luce's face fell. "Oh shit. Sorry, boss."

"We have to lock him in. He was hanging around Liam's farm."

"I'll work out how he got away and put a stop to it. I should have checked. It's not like he's easy to overlook. Sorry. It won't happen again."

It was no big deal from the wider security perspective. Whatever technical knowledge was stored in Rikayl's memory was locked in there, so he couldn't tell the Jattans anything. But losing him would upset the commune, and they needed to be kept calm.

Fred was in the main room with Ingram and Bissey, looking as if they were having a heavy meeting.

"Morning," Trinder said. "Are we interrupting?"

"Not necessarily." Ingram smiled but it didn't look like she meant it. "Is there a problem?"

"Not yet. Rikayl was hanging around the slurry lagoon on the Dales' farm and scaring the herd. Chris drove him off, but we wanted to speak to Fred about keeping him away for his own safety. Manure chucks up some dangerous gases."

Fred drooped his shoulders wearily. "I do my best. I didn't even notice he'd gone. It could only have been a few minutes ago. The boys were supposed to be keeping an eye on him."

"Remember he likes splashing in puddles," Chris said. "If the slurry looks like water to him, that might make it irresistible. Maybe we need to make him a pool. There's no other open water on the base."

Ingram eased forward gradually to the edge of her seat. Trinder wasn't sure if she was working up to a sensitive subject or just uncomfortable on cushions designed for teerik asses.

"While you're here, we'd like to bounce an idea off you," she said. "We've been discussing how to send a message to Gan-Pamas. Literally. With a loudhailer."

Chris's poker face almost failed him. Trinder saw the corner of his mouth twitch. "As in, 'Lay down your weapon and come out with all your hands up'?"

"Yes, that's exactly what I mean," Ingram said. "Only a little more nuanced."

"I'm willing to do it, Chris," Fred said. "It can't do any harm. I can record the message. I won't be in any danger."

Chris looked like he was considering it. "Yeah, it might even lure him in."

"That wasn't what we meant," Bissey said. "This is about communicating with him."

"But what if he actually surrenders?" Trinder asked. "What are we going to do with him? Say 'Sorry, buddy, you can't go home, but you're welcome to help yourself to coffee and use the TV lounge'?"

"That depends on what he has to say," Bissey said.

Chris seemed to be as calm as ever, but Trinder knew he wanted to be back in a world where men nodded meaningfully at each other and knew what had to be done, and didn't have endless debates about things that weren't any easier when they were dissected.

"Okay, why not?" Chris said. "It might flush him out and we might get some useful intel. But we all know how this is going to end, yeah? He becomes a liability. We have no choice."

"And we'll be making the biggest mistake in human history," Bissey said. "We're planning to kill an intelligent alien before we even attempt to communicate with him."

"Commander, we've already killed a *really* intelligent alien, because he killed Nina Curtis. I'll give anything my best shot, but we're betting Earth's safety on a coin toss that the Jattans will want to talk and not add the Solar System to their conquest bucket list. And that's before the Kugin find out. *And* before they hear about the gate."

"We're postponing the inevitable," Bissey said. "We can't hide from other intelligent species forever. This is our chance to manage the encounter. One Jattan, not an army. A Jattan who might be on the right side of the next government if the coup theory's correct."

Chris's faint smile hadn't lasted long. "And if you're wrong about Jattans and they just want conquest, we don't get a second chance, Commander. But even if you're right, if we end up best buds with the opposition and the Jattan government hands them their asses, we've harboured rebels and backed the wrong horse. I think that's going to set the tone for Kugin-Jattan-human relations for the foreseeable future. Which will be very short for us, because they'll wipe us out."

Ingram was silent but Trinder was used to that by now. She'd let an argument swirl around for a while and pitch in at the end. He wasn't sure if she let guys air their opinions to make them feel like they'd been consulted, or if she just waited to see who the winner was before making a decision, because she sure as shit wasn't afraid to intervene.

Bissey plodded on patiently. "Yes, there'll be difficulties and setbacks, but that doesn't mean we avoid it. You're saying we should never risk interaction with aliens, just in case."

"Well, I risked interaction with Fred," Chris said. "But I'm saying we don't know enough yet to make any irreversible decisions about Jattans. Fred worked out Earth's position without our help. Anyone with a teerik probably could. Just because Gan-Pamas knows we're here, it doesn't mean we have to tell the whole damn galaxy."

"I see your point, but we don't know their intentions yet."

Chris frowned slightly for the first time. "Which part of they've already killed Nina Curtis do you not understand?"

"But Gan-Pamas didn't do that," Bissey said. "He might be panicking and working out how he can talk his way out of this."

"Then he could have made contact by now."

"After we killed his teerik and seized his ship? Sergeant, I understand why you feel the need to stand your ground, but we're in an unprecedented situation and sometimes we need to risk making the first move."

Chris was really good at feigning patience. "I took an oath to protect the civilians in my community," he said. "They're not here to make sacrifices. We are. I'm sure you took an oath a lot like mine, Commander. If necessary, we die so that the nation lives. Yeah, we'll have to face the Jattans one day, and they might be great guys once we get to know them, but that time is not now, because we have to act before we know enough. I say again — if we gamble on Jattans being willing to talk and it turns out that we're wrong, there's no second chance."

Bissey put his hands on his hips. "You're going to shoot him on sight, then."

"Are you going to stop me?" Chris asked.

Marc walked in. "And how can we tell if he goes for his gun if he's invisible and his gun's invisible too? You've got to give us the benefit of the doubt, Peter."

"Oh, the Gang of Three's complete." Bissey didn't sound like he was joking. "Are you the only troops we've got, or is killing this chap some kind of management perk? Thank you for taking this so seriously, Marc."

Trinder decided to intervene. "We're used to this type of operation, and you're not, Commander." He said it so that Chris didn't. He could see the Montello-Bissey grudge match happening right here and now if he didn't step in. "If this was taking place at sea, we'd call you and take instruction."

Ingram finally spoke up. "Gentlemen, we'll broadcast a message," she said. "And if Gan-Pamas shows the slightest hostility or violence, we'll respond robustly."

"How about the bit in the middle, though?" Marc asked. "Y'know, the part where he waves a white flag? Are we going to hold him indefinitely? Because that makes him a hostage, and you know what'll happen next."

"Fred, refresh my memory about the Jattan rules of engagement regarding prisoners, please," Ingram said.

"Jattans don't take prisoners, Captain, and neither do Kugin, unless they're of immediate use."

"Very well, if Gan-Pamas *is* of immediate use, we take him prisoner, get what we can, and then revisit the situation," she said. "If he isn't, then we shoot him. But if this escalates, the absolute priority is *not* to become an invasion gateway to Earth."

Marc puffed in annoyance. "And that's 'revisit,' pronounced 'I don't know.' I'm not hearing a clear order in there."

Ingram hovered on the edge of a smile. "There isn't one. I'm not your commanding officer."

There was a lot to unpick in those few words. Trinder glanced at Fred, who was looking increasingly miserable. "Come on, Fred. I'll help you write your message."

"What are we going to say?" Bissey asked.

Fred fluffed his feathers. "That Gan-Pamas has entered human space without permission and his teerik has killed an unarmed female of high status, so he must surrender and explain himself, because humans are a warlike species with codes of honour and they expect courtesies. He'll understand that. He'll think he can negotiate and pay blood money."

"That wouldn't get me to put my hands up and walk in," Bissey said.

"Nor would telling a Jattan that you don't blame him for his servant's behaviour and that we can forgive and forget," Fred said. "Because that'll make him suspicious. The fact that you mean it won't be understood. He will, however, understand being called to explain himself and make recompense."

"That's dishonest," Bissey said.

"It stands a better chance of getting him to come forward and talk, Commander, which is what you want."

"You're luring him out to shoot him."

"No, I'm protecting this colony. You *and* us. I'm portraying you as formidable enemies rather than weaklings who tolerate their comrades being murdered, because that marks you for conquest. Start as you mean to go on. That's what you say, isn't it?"

"We do," Chris said. "So if I see him first, I drop him. If you see him first, Commander, he's your problem. But he doesn't leave this planet and he doesn't get his one phone call to his attorney."

Chris nodded politely to everyone and walked out. Marc gave Ingram a look, shrugged, and followed him. Trinder hung around, partly because he'd offered to help Fred compose his message, but mostly because he didn't want to leave him alone with Bissey and

Ingram to be persuaded to word things differently. He could sit this out as long as it took.

The silence was punctuated by squabbling and squawking from a room somewhere down the corridor, no doubt the two boys arguing over whose fault it was that Rikayl had escaped. Eventually Bissey stood up to leave, looking uncomfortable.

"So every vehicle on perimeter patrol broadcasts the message via external speakers," he said. "For how long? Hours, days, weeks?"

"I have absolutely no idea," Trinder said. "Until we get a result, probably. Maybe we do it every fifteen minutes or half-hour to start with and then reduce the frequency as we go. We'll send bots outside the wire to test how far the sound carries."

Bissey almost said something but Ingram got to her feet and cut him off. "I'm glad we've sorted that out. I'll see you later, Major. I'll put out an alert to residents to let them know they'll hear some odd things later."

Fred waited for them to leave and even went out into the passage to check they were really gone. Solomon trotted in as Ingram left, and Fred came back looking downcast. It was all body language rather than facial expressions, but Trinder could read it clearly now.

"I like Captain Ingram very much," Fred said. "But I don't understand her sometimes. Why does she think the response to Gan-Pamas has been *sorted out*? I saw no agreement there whatsoever."

"That's humans for you," Trinder said. "She feels she's sticking to her rules, and everyone else feels they're sticking to theirs."

But of course it *had* been sorted out. Ingram had reminded Marc she wasn't his commanding officer. She'd signalled to him — and to Trinder and Chris as well — that she wouldn't interfere if they ignored her rules or anyone else's to get the job done, while still sticking to her own, in Bissey's eyes at least. Trinder was certain she never ran her ship that way. But she wasn't on her own bridge giving orders now. She was relying on cooperation from people she had no control over and trying to avoid alienating her own crew, some of whom might be wondering whose side they were on after the CPS attack on Asia, and that meant using a kind of psychology that looked very much like politics. Trinder wasn't sure whether to feel sorry for her because it made her look sneaky and manipulative or to admire her restraint. On the other hand, maybe he'd believed the history book version of a straight-talking, reckless buccaneer when she was actually a much more subtle operator.

Fred settled down on his cushion. "I keep telling you your rules mean nothing here. You have to understand that to survive."

"I think this is more about surviving each other, to be honest, Fred. I'm betting that most folks will do whatever's necessary when it comes to it."

Fred cocked his head. "Except Commander Bissey. A very nice man, a very *moral* man, but he runs the risk of being a very dead man. Is he one of those who believes in surviving after his death? If he's afraid his conduct in this life will affect the next one, I understand him. If not, I don't."

Fred picked up his screen and studied it. He was making notes. That looked like a big change in habits to Trinder.

"You said you never wrote anything down," Trinder said.

Fred passed the screen to him. "This is for your records, not mine. This is what I think we should say to Gan-Pamas."

It was exactly what Fred had made up earlier on the spur of the moment, word for word. Trinder thought it was a fair summary of their position, but it omitted the awkward specifics.

"Fred, aren't you going to say he'll be treated fairly if he surrenders?"

"But he won't," Fred said. "He'll be shot, but perhaps that's fair from some perspectives. And he won't believe it anyway."

Trinder would have felt better adding an explanation to Gan-Pamas about there being nothing personal in this, but that he knew too much and they couldn't reasonably expect him not to tell anyone they were here. He didn't know if that made him moral or not. It certainly wouldn't make any difference to Gan-Pamas.

"Sol, can you record this, please?" Trinder said. "When Fred's happy, we can distribute the file."

"I'm ready when Fred is," Solomon said.

The AI still wasn't saying much, but Trinder could work out at least a little of what was going on in his head. He now had English text with a Jattan translation, and that would help him unpick Jattan without openly asking for lessons. Fred wasn't dumb, though. He must have realised what Solomon would use it for. It was getting harder to understand his motives.

"Quiet while I read, please," Fred said.

Trinder listened to him recording the warning. The rhythm reminded him of Asian languages like Malay, except for the clicks and split-second breaks like an intermittent audio signal.

"I'm finished," Fred said.

"What are the silent bits?" Trinder asked.

"What silent bits?"

"The breaks. Like you switched off the sound for a second."

"Probably high frequencies. You can't hear them. But your dogs would."

Trinder was now wondering if it would achieve anything, but it was more about Ingram humouring Bissey than actually saying anything meaningful to Gan-Pamas.

"Okay, let's distribute this and get going," he said.

On his walk back to the main building, he met Jeff Aiken coming the other way with a crate that smelled like teerik breakfast. Like everyone else, he seemed subdued, probably preoccupied by Nina's death and shattered assumptions about teeriks. Trinder nodded at him and went to get in the Caracal, but Jeff stepped in his path.

"Sir, if the worst happens, I won't let the Kugin take Fred or the others," he said quietly. "I know what you have to do. But I'll make sure nobody needs to."

Trinder felt like an utter bastard. "I promise it'll be an absolute last resort, and by the time things get that bad, we might have to save a few rounds for ourselves. So don't worry. We all want the same outcome."

"I hope so."

"We do. Look, we're going to dig a pool for Rikayl. He's hanging around the Dales' place and Chris thinks it might stop him getting too interested in their slurry pit."

"I'll start digging, then," Jeff said, and carried on.

Trinder drove off and headed for the admin office to check what he'd missed overnight. Erin was sitting in front of Fonseca's desk, chatting with her like they were old buddies. Few things were more anxiety-inducing for Trinder than finding his ex and his current girlfriend swapping stories.

"Hey Dan," Erin said. "You think that message is going to work?"

The news hadn't taken long to escape. "Depends what you mean by work," he said.

Fonseca leaned back in her chair, twiddling her pen. "I wouldn't trust us if I heard that. Especially as it's his teerik who killed Curtis. Why didn't Bissey write something himself? You know — we come in peace and all that."

"I think it has something to do with the whole thing being a lie from start to finish," Trinder said. "We're executing the Jattan for being in the wrong place at the wrong time. It's not even directly about Nina. I feel sorry for Ingram. She's got a crew that's partly APS and looking over its shoulder at Sol, an XO who's trying to talk her out of the inevitable, and all she's got to hold it together is her dad's pistol and her charisma."

"She'll manage," Fonseca muttered. "Chris or Marc will do as they please and shoot the Jattan, and she can shrug and say she couldn't stop them. Lack of a single formal authority works both ways."

"Damn." Trinder shook his head. "You women all scheme the same way, don't you?"

"I don't," Erin said. "Anyway, how do we know the Jattan didn't leave the teerik with orders to kill any aliens who approached his ship? That would make it a very different situation. And it would explain why the teerik did it out of the blue."

It was a good question, or perhaps it just sounded like one to a man who wanted clarity in a situation where it wouldn't be available until it was too late. War was full of tragedies where friendly forces or civilians were sacrificed to protect some critical secret. Trinder had always thought it took the worst kind of bastard to go along with a plan like that, but now he knew all it needed was regular guys in a desperate situation, and he was one of them.

He nodded. "It would explain everything, wouldn't it?"

"I'm going to find a position on the roof," Erin said. "See you later."

Trinder looked at Fonseca and she looked right back.

"Don't give me that look, Dan," she said. "We went through the selfsame debate when Jamie Wickens got killed, only faster. Erin wanted to go after the guys who'd shot him, and I told her we'd do it by the book, and she said where were the prisons and judges to deal with them if we arrested them. That really stayed with me. I mean, what's *the book* if it's just there to make us feel the consequences aren't our fault and that we're in the clear because we followed a procedure? Everyone talks about sticking to moral principles, foundation of civilisation, ends don't justify means, yadda yadda yadda, but what if your high-mindedness gets a lot of other people killed? What's the principle worth then?"

"I'm tired, but I think I agree with you," Trinder said. "Can I go now?"

Fonseca sighed and opened the desk drawer. She took out a candy bar in a plain wrapper that looked like the chocolate Ainatio used to produce on-site.

"Would you do me a favour, please?" she asked. "Give this to Chris. He's avoiding me and it's my fault. Just give him the candy. He'll understand."

"You need to make your mind up about that guy," Trinder said. "Okay, sure. Any message, seeing as you've time-warped back to high school?"

"No message," Fonseca said. "And no looking inside the wrapper."

There'd be a message in there, then. "Wouldn't dream of it."

Trinder picked up his overnights, which had already been dealt with by Luce and Fonseca, and went back to the Caracal to clear out the debris of cups and takeout containers. He should have left it to a bot and gone to bed. But he'd reached the stage where he'd have a twitchy, restless sleep and keep waking himself up with dreams of falling. The only thing he could do was slog on until he was so completely drained that he was on the brink of falling over. Then he could count on oblivion for a few hours.

It took another thirty minutes before it hit him. He made his way to the barracks, one of the temporary buildings that had been converted when evacuees moved out, and flopped down on his bunk. He wanted a shower but he couldn't move now. He managed to kick off his boots, left his radio on so people could locate him, and then the world was gone.

He woke with someone shaking his shoulder. He knew where he was, but the day escaped him for a moment. It was still daylight but that didn't tell him much. Solomon's camera head peered into his face and he remembered he still had Chris's chocolate bar somewhere. He fumbled around and found it shoved in his shirt pocket, remoulded into a curve by his body heat.

"She's going to kill me," he said.

"Major, you didn't answer your radio." Solomon didn't apologise. "I thought you might be ill."

"I'm fine. What time is it? What day, come to that?"

"Your radio tracker shows you came in here at oh-eight-forty-five and it's now fourteen-fifty."

"I could have done with eight hours. Any sign of Gan-Pamas?"

"No. I'd have woken you."

"You just did."

Trinder realised he could hear the broadcast messages now. He got to his feet and opened the vent in the window a little wider. It sounded like an election campaign going on. Then it stopped.

"Captain Ingram asked for the message to be played at longer intervals," Solomon said. "She thinks it might be counterproductive to bombard the Jattan with noise because he might think it's a tactic to demoralise him."

"I thought it was."

"She's just going through the motions, Major, because Commander Bissey is..."

"Being a pain in the ass?"

"Your words, not mine."

"Wants to do it by the book?"

"I prefer that."

"Yeah, he knows the outcome's going to be the same, but he just wants to tell himself he did the right thing." Trinder was glad he'd had that chat with Fonseca. It crystallised everything for him. "Covering your ass with your conscience is the worst delusion."

He knew that all too well. He knew as soon as he said it that he wasn't talking about Bissey, either, even though it was true. He was talking about his own good, honest, dutiful reasons for not searching for his family.

"Anyway, we've only managed to add paint round adapters to one hundred and forty weapons so far, but there are at least twelve rounds for everybody now," Solomon said. "That's probably more than enough. We're as ready as we can be."

"Yeah, that should be plenty," Trinder said.

Trinder hoped Chris, Marc, or even Erin saw the Jattan first. He hoped the alien wouldn't accept the invitation to surrender. He hoped that anyone dumb enough to accept that surrender thought hard about how long they were locking Gan-Pamas up for and that he could never contact anyone again. And he hoped they'd realise that shooting him would have been the kinder option, and didn't then start talking about "someone" needing to put the poor creature out of its lonely misery. Trinder thought about Erin's theory that the teerik had been left to guard the freighter with instructions to kill intruders and clung to that.

He took a long shower and felt better for it. Would Erin still be on the roof? He checked the chocolate bar again and tried to decide if it looked misshapen enough to send entirely the wrong message to Chris. There was nothing he could do to straighten it now, and the textured pattern would have melted into smears as well. Maybe the deformed chocolate was fate giving Chris a friendly warning that Fonseca was a lost cause.

When Trinder went to check the roof, Erin was still there in her favourite sniper position, watching the base below with field glasses while she lay prone on a couple of sleeping bags bunched into a mattress. She had a regular little camp site going there.

"Did you have a nice nap?" she asked.

"I did, thanks. Sol woke me."

"I told him not to."

The broadcasts started up again. Trinder listened for a while. Hearing the same message firing off from all directions at slightly different times made it sound like some kind of weird feedback.

Erin scoped through with her rifle. "We used to do curfew patrols with a loudspeaker. Go back to your homes. Anyone on the street after nineteen-hundred will be detained. Stop looting the store or we open fire. That kind of thing. It didn't last long, though. The authorities gave up. You still need some social order before people feel they have to comply, but there wasn't any left."

"You don't talk about it much," Trinder said.

"I don't want to remember much."

"Sorry."

"I don't mind you asking questions," she said. "I meant I don't want to harp on about it all the time and make it all I am. It hurt too much. I really need this clean slate."

"There's a lot of broken people here, Erin."

"We're *all* broken. Everyone had to leave something or someone behind. But broken stuff can be made into something better. Cheesecake crusts. Mosaics. Roads to amazing places. Food for swans. We can build something fantastic. I wasn't crazy about coming here, but damn, I'm glad I did, even now. And I'm going to fight for it."

"Me too. But there aren't any swans. Just a chicken-eating teerik."

"Do you see yourself as broken, Dan?"

Trinder still thought about the APS guy he'd killed, but he didn't feel disturbed about it today. It was like he'd been officially told he was a long way down the psycho league and killing someone who would have killed him was nothing compared to a teerik who'd hacked an unarmed woman to death. That made him feel uneasy, though. He didn't want to think that Nina's death had done him some good.

"Not as much as I did," he said.

"Good." Erin smiled her sunshine smile. "Dan, we're sheepdogs. We guard the flock and we take out the wolf. It's not personal. Any other time, we'd look at the wolf and say wow, that's a beautiful animal. But not when the flock's vulnerable."

The message broadcasts stopped again, dropping off one by one like a choir singing in the round and finally reaching the end of the song with one single, pure voice followed by ringing silence. Trinder wondered what Gan-Pamas made of it, if he'd heard it at all.

"How do we know what Fred's actually saying?" Erin asked.

"We don't. Solomon will, eventually. I don't think Fred would lie, though. He knows his life depends on it."

"So does ours." Erin passed Trinder a packet of cookies from her stash of food tucked away under the sleeping bags. "I just want to get it over with. I've nearly finished decorating the house. I made drapes. That's a first for me."

"Can I come and see it?"

"Damn, Dan, I'm expecting you to move in with me. Don't play hard to get. I've even got chores lined up for you. I need a vegetable patch dug and I don't want a bot to do it."

"Wow, full-on frontierswoman," Trinder said. "You'll be canning pole beans next. Okay. Consider it dug."

"I'll take that as a yes."

"You know it is."

"Got any moussaka MREs left for your dowry?"

"Sorry, we've eaten the lot. Will my charm and good looks suffice?"

"Well, you're not moussaka, but you'll have to do. Are you at a loose end, or checking up on me?"

Trinder shrugged. "Loose end. And I was missing you."

"That's what happens when you don't follow your own orders," she said. "You make everyone else take rest periods but you just carry on, and then you end up wrecked and no use to man or beast."

"You care, really."

"I do."

Trinder took out his screen to see who was where on the map and texted Luce a reminder to check where Rikayl was. He hadn't seen the teerik since he'd strafed Chris. Luce sent a reply right away.

PLAYING CARDS WITH CPO AIKEN.

That didn't sound like a joke. SAY AGAIN, Trinder typed.

JEFF'S TEACHING HIM TO PLAY PATIENCE. SOLITAIRE.

Rikayl was definitely smarter than everyone thought. Teeriks had good memories and were naturally good at numbers, so card games were probably a great way to keep the kid busy. With Nina gone, Jeff had stepped straight back into the role of liaison, and he seemed pretty damn good at it.

OKAY, Trinder typed. BUT LOCK THE DOOR.

He looked around at Erin. Her attention had moved to the south of the base. She was watching something with her field glasses.

"Jeff's teaching Rikayl to play cards," Trinder said.

"That's nice. Don't get into any poker games with him, though. Did you know there are little animals like guinea pigs with long legs out there?"

"I've seen the small ratty things like mini kangaroos. How long?"

"As tall as a cat. But little bodies."

Trinder understood why Ingram liked coming up to the roof. It gave him a sense of being in control of the situation, able to see most of Nomad, and with all non-essential personnel staying indoors it was a lot quieter than normal. Sound carried a long way. He could hear engines running, the occasional bark of a dog, and one of Joanne Brandt's cockerels who'd taken to crowing after lunch.

"Isn't he supposed to do that in the morning?" Trinder asked.

"Maybe he pulled an all-nighter too," Erin said.

The barking started to pick up. More dogs joined in. Trinder could hear a swell of sound from the direction of Kill Line, but he could also hear it from the other side of the base, where some of Dieter's dogs were patrolling with the militia guys. He couldn't remember exactly how many dogs the Kill Liners had, but it was at least seventy, more than enough to make themselves heard for miles.

"They don't like the noise either," Erin said. She sighted up and scanned the base again, sweeping right to left. After a while she paused. The barking was constant now, but the message broadcasts had stopped. "Dan, I can see Liam's land from here. Look. Look at his sheepdogs."

Trinder took out his monocular. Liam had a couple of border collies and they were standing in the field with the cows, looking through the fence to the east. The farm was only a house and three fields at the moment, plus a makeshift milking parlour, a barn, and some other outbuildings still under construction. The cows were all on the west side of the field, huddled together with the dogs facing away from them as if they were shielding them. And the collies were barking. Whatever had gotten their attention, they weren't taking their eyes off it. They kept up that constant, steady bark.

Trinder didn't know much about dogs but Dieter kept trying to correct that. Lesson number one-hundred-and-whatever: when collies weren't herding, they were watchdogs, not attack dogs. They generally wouldn't go for an intruder, but they'd warn you when something wasn't quite right.

"You're wrong, honey," he said to Erin. "Sheepdogs don't take out the wolf. But they do tell you he's coming." He got on the radio. "Sol, we need to check out Liam Dale's farm *now*. Get a drone over it and see what his dogs are watching. I'm going down there."

Erin started moving her sleeping bags to a new position. "I can take the shot if I have it, yeah?"

"If you're certain, yes."

"Be careful, then. Remember what I said."

Trinder ran downstairs, alerting Ingram on the way, and grabbed the first quad bike he found. By the time he reached Liam's farm, Liam was out front with Chris, who looked like he'd just stepped out of the Caracal parked nearby. Liam was carrying his shotgun. Chris had his rifle and a shotgun as well. He didn't look like a man who'd come to take a surrender.

"My cows were spooked by something and then the dogs went out and stood in the field," Liam said. "Is Rikayl out again?"

Chris shook his head. "No, I just checked. He's accounted for. You stay here. I'll take a look."

"I'll come with you," Liam said. "You two aren't used to livestock."

Trinder wasn't going to argue with him. The three of them piled into the Caracal and drove the short distance to the field, approaching the dogs from behind to try to work out what they were looking at.

Trinder couldn't see anything and the collies probably couldn't, either. They kept jerking their heads back and forth like they were watching tennis, ears pricked. But they could hear something and they knew the direction it was coming from. From time to time they'd focus on a point and bark at it.

"He's here," Chris said.

"How could we have missed him?"

"Easily. Don't ask me how he got past the perimeter defences, but he did."

Trinder looked up to check if Solomon had the drone in position. "Maybe he's been here all along. Sol, can you confirm where the drone is?"

"Right above you, Major. I'm concentrating the search where the dogs are looking."

Trinder called Fonseca on the radio. "Echo Five to Echo One Four, we need the Dales' farm sealed off, tight cordon, dog patrols. Possible sighting of Gan-Pamas, out."

If the Jattan had been here all along, it explained a few things, and also meant they'd wasted two days. But if he'd been on the farm, the dogs would have reacted sooner, and why would he be here anyway? It was a relatively convenient base to watch for teeriks, but Trinder wasn't sure why it was a better place to hide than the cemetery or anywhere else relatively deserted.

Chris stepped back and opened the Caracal's door. A few moments later, Fred's recorded message boomed out across the field. The dogs flinched at the sudden noise but went back to staring and barking.

"Nobody can say he didn't get the message now," Chris said.

He played it twice. The dogs suddenly shot forward and stopped at the electrified wire fence, barking frantically. Gan-Pamas must have moved, and he must have been on the other side of the fence to start with, because he couldn't have cleared it without Trinder seeing some movement in the grass or the fence wire flexing. Trinder jogged after Chris as he headed for the fence. He could hear the sound of vehicles approaching. Everyone was converging on the farm.

"Chris, that's the rear of the slurry pit," Trinder said. "He can't get out without climbing over the security fence or cutting through it, and that's going to be visible."

Chris ran to the nearest stile and scrambled over the electrified wire. "Ah, hell. Please tell me he's not in there."

"It's damp," Trinder said, trying to shut out the image of submerging in the stuff. "And nobody goes there. Even if they did, they wouldn't smell him with all that manure around. There's a logic to it."

"You think he's in the actual shit. You're serious."

"Why not?"

"He's an oxygen breather, according to Fred. Why haven't the gases killed him? Why hasn't he drowned?"

Trinder's screen showed more tracker icons converging on the farm and crowding around the boundary. "Who knows? He's an alien. We don't know much about his anatomy."

Liam came up behind them. "Watch your step. There's an open slurry channel into the pit from the milking shed and it's not fully planked yet. I've just shut it at the other end in case something tries to use it as an escape route."

"How liquid is that stuff?" Chris asked.

Liam pulled his calculating face, rocking his head slightly. "There's been a lot of rain, so I'd say like canned beans in sauce. Can I remind you guys this is dangerous? Let me fetch the tractor so we can do whatever needs doing at a safer distance. We need to be ready to pump it out."

"Okay. How deep is it?"

"About six feet. Officially, you should wear full breathing apparatus."

"We'll lose him if we don't get down there now. Anyway, it's not a confined space, there's a strong breeze, and it hasn't been cooking for long."

"Look, I'll get a rope and you don't make a move without that safety line tied to my vehicle," Liam said. "Not that it'll save you from a pocket of hydrogen sulphide."

"I understand the risks," Chris said.

"I hope you do."

"Six Zero, this is Two Two." It was Jared on the radio. "I've got eyes on via the drone feed. Tell us where you need us, over."

"Two Two, we think he's in the slurry compound, so cover as much of the security fence as you can. He's got to climb out or cut through. Liam's going to drive his tractor through in case we need to pump out the pit, so when the gates open, make sure nothing gets out, over."

"Copy that. Paint rounds ready. Two Two out."

"I can see bubbles," Solomon said.

Trinder stopped to check his screen again. "That could just be gases escaping."

"But the surface was swirling around. Again, that could be natural activity as materials decompose. But it could also have been from someone sliding into the liquid to avoid splashing."

They were making a lot of assumptions. Trinder hoped they weren't chasing an animal that had found a way past the perimeter barrier. He was now right behind Chris, moving along the side of the slurry channel and flanked by wire fencing. The compound itself opened out into what looked like a scruffy back yard with a filthy swimming pool about thirty feet by forty. On the far side, Jared and thirty or so guys from Chris's militia and Trinder's own detachment were lined up facing the gate. More were spread further back along the boundary. Jared waved. Chris acknowledged him.

"If I fire into that pit," Chris said, "am I going to ignite any gases?"

Trinder tried to recall science class again. His recent research into storing manure hadn't addressed using ballistic weapons against aliens submerged in it. "Depends on the exact ratio of gas to air and how hot your muzzle flash is," he said. "If we were indoors, I'd say don't risk it. Out here — probably okay. But I could be wrong."

"Sol, can you hear us?" Chris said.

"I can, Chris, and the answer is that while the drone can't detect much methane now, there's no way of knowing what'll happen if the slurry's disturbed."

"I admit I didn't think this through," Chris said. "But once I can target him by sight, everyone else can make a run for it."

The edges of the pool were marked by an uneven stripe of lumpy pale grey foam, the only part of the spray-on pit lining that was visible above the muck, and there was no long grass or other compressible material around that might show footsteps or disturbance if Gan-Pamas was still on solid ground. If he had the same kind of stealth device that hid the ship, they would have to get closer to see the broken outline.

The smell was unpleasant but not overwhelming from this distance. While they waited for Liam to reappear on the other side of the compound, Chris kept his rifle aimed at the surface of the slurry. Trinder loaded a few paint rounds and watched for heat-haze effects. If the Jattan was moving, there was a chance there'd be distortions caused by the device adapting to the different background, but that was another big guess on his part. There'd been different methods of cloaking on Earth, but he had no idea what Jattan technology was capable of beyond the camouflage that had hidden the freighter.

Every glint of sun on a pebble and every faint sound made him hold his breath in case it was Gan-Pamas. Eventually he heard heavy tyres rumbling closer and Liam's bright yellow tractor appeared. It had a long boom attachment and a tanker trailer hooked to the back. Trinder wondered how he'd even get it all in the compound, but the troops formed a tight line behind him and Liam unlocked the gates to inch through, uncoupling and manoeuvring the machinery back and forth until he got it where he wanted it. The boom turned out to be a pump with a mixer, like a giant food blender crossed with a wet-vac cleaner.

"Safety first," Liam said, hitching a rope to the tractor and gesturing to Chris with the other end. "If you lose consciousness, I'll drag you straight out, okay?"

Chris rarely let any emotion except a distracted faraway look show on his face, but he did blink a few times.

"I'll pass, thanks," he said. "I'm more at risk if I can't chase a target than if I fall in."

"Okay." Liam shook his head. "Your choice."

The dogs had stopped barking. It was the first time Trinder had noticed. It was so quiet now that he was sure he could even hear the manure bubbling. When he glanced at the cordon of troops outside the fence, he spotted Ingram and Bissey behind the front rank, watching with their arms folded like referees scrutinising a game.

"What now?" Liam asked.

"We wait," Chris said.

"How about I just start pumping the slurry out and see what happens? I can clear that lot in twenty minutes, even with a small pump like this."

"Okay," Chris said. "But if he's in there, don't purée him with that thing."

"He'd have to be right underneath it. And very small."

"If he's in there, he's got to have some air supply."

"Maybe he doesn't need it," Liam said. He always seemed unmoved by the extraordinary times he now lived in. "Stand back as far as you can. Once I start stirring it up, you know what happens."

"I get it," Chris said.

It was a whole new world for Trinder, even though he'd spent years living next door to a farming community, and now a lot of the strange vehicles and machinery he'd watched drive through the Caisin gate made sense. Liam put on a pair of heavy gloves and started coupling pipes and drive shafts, connecting the pump and the tank to the tractor engine. Then he got back in the tractor cab and backed up a few feet to lower the boom into the pit. It rattled into life before settling down to steady chugging. Gas began bubbling up. After a while the engine note changed and Liam went over to the tanker to check the gauges.

Chris squatted at one end of the pit and dipped his head a little like a golfer studying the green before playing a shot.

"What is it?" Trinder asked.

"I'm looking for a breather tube breaking the surface," Chris said. "Sol, can you see anything?"

"Nothing visible, Chris. The thermal imaging isn't showing anything unusual either."

There was so much solid waste in the pit that it was hard to work out what was emerging as the level of the slurry dropped. It wasn't just straw and unbroken lumps of manure but small branches and other debris as well. For a moment Trinder thought he could see the outline of a back, someone crouching with their head down, but the slurry moved and the convex shape revealed itself as a curled sheet of bark as it flipped over.

One thing was certain, though. If Gan-Pamas was in there, his cloaking would be useless. He'd be coated in enough crap to pick out his general shape. Could his weapon cope with immersion like that? They'd find out.

The drone hovered overhead. Trinder didn't dare take his eyes off the pit. Another large lump moved, he felt his gut knot, and then the object turned into the anticlimax of a sodden paper sack inflated by trapped gas.

"He's not in there," Trinder said. "It's down to a couple of feet deep. You've seen the interior of the prenu, so you can imagine how tall he'd be. We'd have seen something by now."

"I could hide in that," Chris said. "If I really had to."

Chris walked around the edge of the pit like he was working out how to jump in. The contents now reminded Trinder of metallic paint with different shades forming swirls where the separate components hadn't been thoroughly mixed.

"What's that?" Chris said, pointing. "Liam, stop the pump."

Liam got down from the tractor cab and handed Chris a long metal dipstick, a substantial thing more like a pole. Chris knelt at the side of the pit to poke around. Trinder wished he'd accepted the safety line, even if there wasn't much manure left in there now.

He'd also hoped for a more clearcut sequence of events, one where Gan-Pamas was suddenly spotted at a distance, shots were exchanged, and the Jattan went down, all noble, manly stuff. Prodding the debris in a pool of shit to find a fugitive who'd gone to ground wasn't the spirited defence by outgunned underdogs that he'd had in mind.

Chris probed the slurry slowly and hesitantly, but Trinder didn't think he was afraid. It looked more like he was trying not to do too much damage. That didn't fit his executioner mode at all. Then something moved.

Chris pulled back. "Got him."

It didn't seem possible that there was an actual person in that shallow layer, but gradually a shape unfurled, a kind of inverted cone with the illusion of transparency where the shit hadn't stuck. It was hard to pick out a head, but whatever shape the suit had given the Jattan within it, it looked like a bipedal creature. The shape shook off more manure and straightened up a little. Trinder couldn't see any weapons.

Then it lifted what looked like two thick arms and Gan-Pamas released his helmet.

Yes, it was a Jattan. It looked just like Fred's drawing, but it was tiny, the size of a twelve-year-old kid. Gan-Pamas was clearly exhausted, slumped and panting. There were at least thirty or forty people watching and there wasn't a sound beyond the breeze and distant calls of animals Trinder had never seen. Nobody looked ready to open fire.

"Sol," Chris said. "Get Fred on the radio. I need an interpreter."

"Is that wise, Chris?"

"Get him now, please."

Fred had nothing more urgent to do. Chris waited, squatting on his heels, just watching the Jattan with an unreadable expression on his face that might have been disappointment, regret, or even shock. Eventually Fred came on the channel and Chris disconnected his earpiece to use his radio handset. Fred's voice boomed out of the small speaker.

"I'm ready Chris."

"Okay. Ask Gan-Pamas why Lirrel killed Nina. Those *exact* words, please."

There was a pause before Fred came out with a string of incomprehensible sounds. Gan-Pamas reacted instantly. He said something, his body turned towards Chris, and he kept repeating the same sound. Without being able to see the Jattan's eyes, it was hard for Trinder to be sure he was actually talking to Chris, but Chris was acting as if they were having a conversation.

"What's he saying, Fred?" Chris asked.

This wasn't good. The longer this went on, the harder it became to finish off Gan-Pamas, and the worse it would be for the guy who had to do it. There was something terrible about a big group of armed men and women surrounding a small creature like that and working out the best point at which to kill it. It was a sentimental reaction based on equating size with weakness and childlike innocence, and it didn't change the reality of needing to keep Nomad hidden, and it didn't make it any easier. Adrenaline was starting to ebb.

Trinder edged forward, rifle ready. Now that the Jattan had removed his helmet, he had a chance to aim a burst down into the top of the head and get this over with. Bissey could call him a monster later.

Chris tapped his radio impatiently. "Fred, I need to know what he said."

Gan-Pamas said it again, whatever it was. Trinder was sure he heard the word *teerik*. What was he saying about Lirrel?

"He says he couldn't trust the teerik," Fred said at last. "He says he's sorry."

Chris hung his head for a second as if he was thinking hard about what came next. Then Fred said something in Jattan.

Whatever it was, it sparked a strong reaction from Gan-Pamas. He tried to sit upright and started gabbling away, really agitated, looking up into the sky and then back at Chris. Trinder was ready to fire now. It looked like things had tipped over from a tense conversation to a row, but nobody except Fred knew what it was about.

"Fred — " Chris said, but that was as far as he got.

Trinder didn't even see Gan-Pamas raise a weapon. The next thing he knew, something punched him in the chest and lit up every nerve in his body. He went down like someone had pulled a plug. He hit the compacted ground hard and couldn't move, but he could see his arm outstretched and his fingers twitching. This was how he'd imagined an electroshock round would feel. He struggled to get up, but his body just wouldn't respond. All he could do was lie there on his side and watch. Chris jumped down into the pit — Trinder couldn't work out why — and Liam swung his shotgun off his shoulder and opened fire. Trinder thought he counted four shots. He was sure it was about to erupt into a firefight.

The next thing he knew, Jared was trying to turn him onto his back and tapping his cheek, asking him if he was okay. Then it was Ingram looming over him, and Chuck the corpsman, and finally Chris, absolutely covered in shit and hay. Seeing that and feeling queasy was the first thing that told Trinder he wasn't dying.

"He's just winded, I think," Jared said. He sat Trinder up and Chuck checked him over. "It was some kind of shock weapon."

"Dan, when you can stand up, I'll take you to see Dr Mendoza," Chuck said. "You're going to feel weird."

"Oh yeah. Weird as hell."

Normal feeling was starting to return to Trinder's limbs. He felt disoriented and bruised, but that might have been from falling on concrete. Chris stood over him.

"I thought you were dead," he said.

Trinder's mind was racing all over the place. "What did Fred say? What the hell's going on?" He put his hands behind him and eased himself into a sitting position. "Is Gan-Pamas dead?"

"Yeah, Liam killed him. And I'm done. I'm going back to the farm to hose myself down. What a clusterfuck."

Chris just walked off. Jared looked up as if he was debating whether to stay with Trinder or go after Chris, but in the end he just shook his head and waited while Chuck went to fetch a vehicle.

"Sol, what did Fred say?" Trinder asked. "Tell me. What kicked all that off?"

"Fred says he asked him if he'd told anyone what he'd found here," Solomon said. "He says Gan-Pamas told him he was a traitor."

"He said a lot of words for a short conversation." Trinder made himself stand up. He hated looking like the makeweight against Chris and Marc. "What was the rest about?"

"Apparently he just kept apologising for Lirrel and said he couldn't trust him."

"Okay. But it's over now, yeah?"

"I have to assume it is," Solomon said. "I'll replay the exchange and use it to improve my knowledge of Jattan."

Trinder had learned to read between the lines with Solomon. The AI was going to analyse that conversation until it was threadbare. It looked like Jattans were the trigger-happy types that Fred had said they were, but there was always room for misunderstanding. Maybe Fred had exercised his new-found freedom to tell the client what he really thought of him.

"Dan, Chris is seriously pissed," Jared said quietly. "And I've never seen him hesitate like that. I'm going to go check he's okay but... hell, they're so *small*. They're like kids. We're going to have to get our heads around that one day."

Trinder wondered what Bissey thought now that it had all blown up and it was a civilian who'd shot the Jattan. He dusted himself off and realised there were flecks of shit on his shirt. Then he took a closer look, peeled open his vest pocket, and felt soft, melted chocolate inside. Fonseca's peace offering hadn't survived the shock weapon. There was no giving it to Chris now. He'd have to tell her.

Chuck came up to him. "You okay to walk?"

"Yeah, I can get to the Caracal," Trinder said.

It wasn't supposed to be this way, any of it. If they were lucky, nobody would find out what had happened to Gan-Pamas and Lirrel, and if the time was ever right, humans could pretend they'd never met a Jattan before.

Ingram was there giving orders when he reached the APC, gesturing in the direction of the slurry pit. "Pump the rest out, then," she was saying. "We've got plenty of time now. But I want that suit and every bit of kit removed and analysed down to the last molecule. And the Jattan. We'll learn from this. The next time, it won't be one man and an unstable teerik. It'll be an army." Then she noticed Trinder. "Oh, Dan — how are you? Damn, that was close. I'll come and see you later. Look after him, Chuck."

Trinder was about to tell her she was wrong, but he thought better of it. The conflict wasn't going to be one day in the future. It had started a few minutes ago.

This was the day war had come to Opis, less than six months after humans had first set foot on it.

14

There'll be plenty of luxuries in space, but if and when we encounter other civilisations, normative moral relativity won't be one of them.

> Tad Bednarz, discussing the potential problems for future human colonies with Solomon.

MAIN BUILDING, NOMAD BASE: NEXT MORNING.

It was like being back home, not just Earth but home, *her* home, her family's house in Somerset, surrounded by woodland and pasture with the smell of freshly-manured fields on the breeze.

Ingram wanted to be there so badly that the longing hurt as if something was lodged in her throat. When she opened her eyes, she was still on the roof of the main building, contemplating the world with a mug of tea as she did every morning. Nomad was now more a garrison town than a remote base. Homes that looked like proper houses outnumbered the original print-built domes, and most of the vehicles she'd see during the day were military or agricultural. Gradually, one building at a time, the detachable, collapsible, and temporary had tipped over into permanence.

Brad Searle pushed himself back from the safety rail he'd been leaning on at the edge of the roof. "We're never going to get rid of that smell."

"That's the perfume of life and fertility, City Boy."

"So you really come up here every morning."

"Rain or shine. So what's your verdict on all this? What brought Gan-Pamas here?"

"We can rule out the power spikes theory," Searle said. "Not just because I'm persuaded by the seismic data and I believe Fred, but because I'd have expected it to get the attention of a state navy, not a sketchy arms dealer. We'd have had a joint Kugin-Jattan task force in our face. If Gan-Pamas had seen a spike, he wouldn't have known what it was and he wouldn't have been looking for it anyway because he only knew whatever Jattan procurement knew about the prenu.

That didn't include Caisin technology. That was a retrofit, and it must have been done late in the process, or the Jattans might have spotted something weird during inspections."

"Agreed," Ingram said. "So how do we end up with teeriks stumbling across this supposed backwater, and then Gan-Pamas? I can only think of deeply worrying explanations."

"Me too, ma'am," Searle said. "I'm thinking it's either a leak in Fred's commune or Opis is on Galactic Main Street. If there's another explanation, I can't think of one yet."

Everyone whose opinion Ingram took seriously had said the same thing now. They really needed to know what brought people to Opis. According to Fred, it wasn't even the only terrestrial-type planet within easy spacefolding distance. There were quite a few and it seemed more than half of them had no advanced species to claim them. The sector was perfect for human colonisation. But when things seemed too good to be true, they usually were.

"Maybe it's us, Brad," she said. "Maybe we've become visible without realising it. Either way, we have to let the civilians know we're prepared for every eventuality. I'm going to address a town meeting today to sound out the Kill Liners' views."

"On what?"

"On where we stand right now. I think I'm obliged to listen to them if they feel it's not what they signed up for. Dan said they were told that there might be unfriendly aliens, but we've lost a crew member in the worst possible way."

"We should stay," Searle said flatly. He had no home to return to. Ingram did. She could see that thought on his face. "We've come too far and it's insane to abandon this now. If humanity wants to spread out into the galaxy, it has to face the uglier side of alien civilisations. They won't be entities of pure light who've evolved beyond greed and violence. Most of them will be meatbags like us or worse, no matter what they breathe. Fred's right. We need to be the nastiest assholes on the street and *act* like it."

Well, Ingram had asked him to speak freely, and he had. She wondered if her willingness to evacuate civilians who hadn't volunteered for the pioneer life was actually her own homesickness. Once she'd let that single weak thought loose in her mind, it had raced around throwing all the other sensible, duty-bound brain cells into a panic. Or maybe it was just that she'd never been responsible for the welfare of civilians on a permanent basis before. It didn't feel the same as having a crew of fighting men and women who could take care of themselves in a crisis and knew what the ultimate risk looked like.

"Heads on spikes, you mean," she said.

"If that's what the locals understand best, yeah."

Ingram stared into her tea. "Well, that's one consensus that's emerging."

"If you hint at a chance of going back to Earth, you're committing to handing the gate over to a government. If you'd thought that was a good idea, you'd have done it by now."

"I intended to find out what we were really dealing with, in case I was doing the equivalent of giving a child a chainsaw," Ingram said.

"And you still should."

"Thanks."

"Anything else, ma'am?"

"The prenu. That's your priority now. We really need that ship operational and under our control, especially as it's going to be months before our own FTL's ready for trials. And get a name sorted out. Ships need identities. Nar P-twelve doesn't inspire anyone to give their all."

"Yes ma'am. Preferences?"

"That's up to the teeriks. Preferably something that doesn't advertise what the ship is, in case our comms are ever compromised."

Ingram had never been in doubt about her authority. Once she was on the bridge of her ship, she was the law. There'd been no state or statute that Britain recognised on the other side of the Channel, and no international criminal court to argue about its actions, so she did as she pleased in the pursuit of her orders: to defend the country from attack, invasion, and contamination by any means necessary.

She used those means fully. She liked those rules. It was easy, but Nomad wasn't, and the longer she didn't tell the government what was really happening, the harder it became to imagine telling them at all.

She really needed to talk with Marc about all this. But after Chris had read her the riot act in his politely lethal way, she wasn't sure if Marc would want to listen. Every time she thought about him having to consider killing teerik children, her stomach knotted. How could she not have realised? But their lives had fitted them with very different filters. Where she saw aliens whose safety came second to the survival of her own species, he saw someone's sons, even if it didn't stop him doing his job. She should have known. All she could do was apologise when she caught up with him today. She had to lance the boil sooner or later.

What day was it? Saturday. Ingram knew the date but the actual days had blurred into one continuous Monday. It was time for Captain's Rounds, which had become checking how the civilians were coping rather than running her finger along surfaces to seek out undusted corners of the junior rates' mess. It wasn't quite as easy now that most people had moved into permanent housing. It felt like years since she'd been able to ride a quad bike through the muddy alleys of the tent city and see lots of people who wanted to talk to her because they had nothing to fill their time or there was something that needed fixing. Now, just months later, she felt like a door-to-door salesman hoping to find somebody at home.

The Kill Line neighbourhood didn't look like the original faux-historic town, but it certainly felt like it. Solomon said he'd tinkered with the layout to create a town square because people needed a place to gather, somewhere to see as the heart of their tribe. This morning it looked like life was going on as it always had, despite the interruption of trillions of miles. The supplies committee was out in the square, unloading food and assembling household ration boxes for distribution. They organised themselves the way they always had and they didn't need Solomon or a team of officers from *Cabot* to do it for them. She was worrying unnecessarily about the resilience of civilians.

She parked the quad bike and watched for a few moments. This was what Bednarz had wanted. It might not have been on the scale he'd envisioned, not yet, but civilians were already making their own decisions about how the colony was run. She knew she'd see the same thing when she rode through the transit camp sector. This was a small American town that didn't even need America to exist to be confident of its identity. Perhaps Nomad was already dividing itself into nations. It wasn't necessarily a bad thing.

"Captain." Doug Brandt waved to her. He shouldn't have been shifting heavy loads at his age. "How are you today?"

"I'm always fine," Ingram said. "But how are you? Individually and collectively, that is."

"My hip's playing up, but the town's running smoothly and everyone's fed, housed, and unharmed. So all's well."

"All set up for the town meeting this afternoon?"

"Yes, you'll have a full house."

"I hope I can put everyone's mind at rest."

"People always feel better if they're given all the facts, Captain, even if it's not good news. Oh, and Martin Berry would like to talk to you about Nina Curtis's funeral arrangements."

Ingram still had difficult conversations ahead. "I'll be honest, Doug, I still need to consult her friends. I have to offer them the option to decide the details, when they feel up to it."

"Of course, whenever they're ready to discuss it, he's available," Doug said. He leaned in a little, the kindly grandad now rather than the mayor. "You know, folks here really appreciate that you're not always trying to be the commanding officer."

Ingram was halfway down the road to the transit camp quarter before the comment sank in. What did Doug mean, that she'd failed to show leadership, that they didn't want her in charge and were glad she knew her place, or that they were relieved she hadn't declared a military dictatorship and brought back hanging? She knew Nomad didn't need the kind of command she exercised at sea, and Kill Liners had a leader they'd elected, but she didn't know if she'd notice when her diplomatic restraint crossed the line into sloping shoulders and not doing what was required of her.

The transit camp was also running things its own way. There was a vehicle checkpoint and visible security in the form of foot patrols. Ingram wondered who the checkpoint was intended to keep out, because she couldn't imagine Jattans rolling up in an APC, but the most significant thing was the security detail. Marty, the sheep farmer from Kill Line, was patrolling with Zakko, walking slowly along the street with one of his border collies at his heel. She wasn't surprised that Chris's militia had turned out to patrol Kill Line for Doug Brandt, because that had been their arrangement on Earth, but she hadn't expected to see Kill Liners with rifles alongside the militia here. The boundary between the two communities was blurring. Ingram stopped to chat and make a fuss of the collie.

"How are you chaps doing?" she asked.

"We're good, thanks, ma'am," Zakko said. "Are you looking for Chris?"

"No, I'm just being a mother hen." Ingram could see from Chris's radio trace that he was with Trinder and Marc in the main building, probably having a meeting to which she wasn't invited. "I'm doing a Q and A session in the community centre later to bring everyone up to speed, so could you remind people here that they're welcome too? If there's no standing room, I can do another session here afterwards. I assume you'd hold it in the bar."

"Sure, ma'am." Zakko smiled his angelic smile. He really was a very sweet lad. "Chris briefed us last night, but I'm sure everyone would welcome an update from you. The beers are on us."

Of course Chris had already briefed them. He'd made time to address his adoring public after hunting down aliens and before thinking of himself. He was an act she couldn't follow and she wasn't going to try. She rode off to finish her rounds and detoured via the bar, modelled after the original in the transit camp. It was a community centre with alcohol, a place to eat, drink, hold meetings, run school classes, and leave messages. People were chatting outside the doors and wandering in and out. Like Kill Line's square, it was a hub, and having proper houses for the first time in years didn't seem to have changed the residents' need to congregate outside. Perhaps it was a hard habit to break, and living behind closed doors felt a lot like being cut off from the world.

Ingram strolled in and did her best hearts and minds routine, shaking hands and asking if they needed anything, but she wondered if she'd ever understand just how bad things had been on Earth for people to feel that living on the road or in wooden huts they'd had to build themselves was a better life than staying put in the cities. The crew of *Cabot* had been spared all that. Ingram made a mental note that her benchmark of what was intolerable for a civilian didn't apply to many of Nomad's citizens.

It finally dawned on her that the benign divisions between the different groups that made up Nomad weren't entirely driven by a need to hang on to the past. It was because the transit camp and Kill Line people had ready-made lives and a physical focus that wasn't the centre of the base. Nomad itself, the original core of offices, labs, warehousing, and crew accommodation, had nothing they needed to visit on a regular basis except the medical facilities, and getting there meant a fairly long walk or a drive. Nomad's residents — *Cabot*'s crew and the Ainatio staff, the qualified and white-collar types — had no reason to venture socially outside their territory either.

"Shops and buses," Ingram said to herself on the way back. There'd been a monorail in the original Nomad plan to link the different zones, but that had been based on a lot more people and more varied facilities. "All this whizz-bang bloody science and it boils down to having a bus service to the supermarket."

If the three groups didn't start mixing now, they probably never would. Ingram wasn't sure where to draw the line between social engineering and just making sure people got on, and was considering calling Solomon to discuss it when he radioed her.

"You must be psychic," she said. "I was just going to call you."

"I see you're on your way back, Captain."

"I am. Problem?"

"Possibly, and more than one."

"Go ahead."

"Commander Bissey's asked to see you. He says it's a private matter and he'll wait for you. Alex also wants to talk to you, and as that involves information that I've input, I can tell you that it's about the situation on Earth."

"I admit I took my eye off that ball. More sabcode fallout?"

"No, APS appears to be recovering its capabilities. I mention problems with a caveat, because I was spying, and I don't have a complete picture. There's a lot of activity and voice traffic between Seoul and Canberra about restricting flights and imports. Borders are being closed."

Ingram felt the shudder of a door slamming forty light years away. "Human epidemic or agricultural?"

"My guess would be that Korea has a confirmed outbreak of die-back, possibly more than one."

"Bugger. Oh, *bugger.*"

"You said it was only a matter of time, Captain."

Ingram thought of the last-resort escape route. "Please tell me Britain's still clear. No, wait until I get there. Five minutes."

It was bad timing, but there probably wasn't a good time for news like that. Even if Britain managed to maintain its quarantine cordon, the ripples from Asia would reach it in some form sooner or later when more people started trying to enter the country as one of the last disease-free havens. The psychological effect of APS countries finally succumbing to the virus was going to have a knock-on as well. An unstable world would become even more unstable. Ingram told herself not to pole-vault to conclusions. A single outbreak might be contained, and APS wasn't squeamish about sealing towns and shooting people trying to break quarantine.

She was still telling herself that when she parked the bike and ran up the stairs to her office. Bissey was sitting on a chair in the corridor, looking grim.

"Sorry, Peter, I'll catch up with you as soon as I can," she said. "I need to talk to Sol first."

"It's okay, ma'am," Bissey said. "They told me."

"I'll brief you as soon as I know more myself."

Alex was waiting in her office, leaning back in a chair with his hands clasped behind his head. Despite that, he didn't look relaxed at all. His eyes were fixed on the ceiling and it took him a moment to react to her.

She pulled up a seat next to him. Sitting behind the desk felt like too much imperial distance. "Are you all right, Alex?"

"I'm fine, Captain. The crop genetics team isn't doing so well, though. They got pretty close to Nina." He sat upright and gestured to the wall. "How could you bear to leave a place like that?"

It was her picture of the Ingram estate, the view from the lodge, which took in the big house and the avenue of cone-trimmed yew trees on a sunny day, a textbook idyll.

"All things come to an end," she said. "I passed it to my cousin. He had children and I didn't. And I knew he wouldn't turn it into a conference venue or a fat farm and ruin the interior."

That wasn't the half of it, but it would do for now. The good thing about post-*Cabot* Americans was that they'd lived in an age of very high mortality and social collapse, and never asked anyone what had happened to the rest of their family. They always assumed they were dead or missing.

"Erskine said we didn't need to bring the art and glories of Earth with us because we'd create our own original culture on Opis," Alex said. "But I have to say, like quite a few other things, she got it all wrong. Anyway, Captain, I'll cut to the chase. It looks like Asia's got its first die-back outbreak. It's probably not brand new, but we weren't really watching because we took the don't-look-back thing to heart. Sol spotted some unusual air traffic patterns while he was guilt-tripping over the sabcode and we've taken a closer look."

"Sol, how far back did you go?" Ingram asked.

Solomon's voice emerged from the wall panel next to her desk. "Six weeks. It's more about what's not happening than what is. After the sabcode took out the APS networks, regional air traffic ceased for three days, then resumed at much lower volumes, mostly inbound to the worst-affected areas, probably aid flights. A week ago, though, outbound Korean flights to Australia stopped and haven't resumed."

"Just Australia?" Ingram asked.

"I can't be sure," Solomon said. "I've only hacked into the Australian government network, and I don't have complete access yet. I did it initially to monitor our staff in hospice care, but I've now compared data from various government departments and moved a teerik probe to observe. Australia's closed its border to all flights and maritime traffic from Korea and China, although it's still operating normally with New Zealand, Japan, and Malaysia. A number of government agricultural scientists have been seconded to Korea and there was an aid flight carrying rice a couple of days ago, so it certainly doesn't look like a trade boycott, especially following a national disaster. There's some kind of pathogen they're investigating. No actual mention of die-back, but looking at the traffic patterns in Korea, a large area in the southwest of the country appears to be cut off. That's one of their rice-growing areas, and I might be reading too much into it, but if die-back is present in their rice crop, that's disastrous. It's still their main domestic crop and they import a lot too."

"It's not the only agricultural disease, of course," Ingram said. "It could be a livestock virus. They didn't disappear just because die-back arrived."

Alex took off his glasses and polished them. Ingram had already worked out it was his bad-news tell. "But if it *is* die-back," he said, "you're looking at a completely destabilised Korea in a very short time. The dominant political and economic power in APS won't be able to feed itself. *We've* been through that cycle, and now there's no America. There'll be huge refugee movements, official and otherwise, civil unrest, and a high chance that it'll spread to China and the rest of the Asian mainland, and possibly India and Russia too. Islands like Australia and Japan might be able to keep it out, but APS as we know it will be finished and I can't see that *not* having a knock-on effect on what's left of the rest of the world."

Ingram didn't even need to look at the map. Alex was right about population movements. They'd flow west, and that would put more pressure on Europe, and that would translate into pressure on Britain.

"Very well, there's no point in hoping it's swine fever or that APS has some miracle cure," Ingram said. "All we can do is hope that we won't be in a position where we have to abandon Opis."

"You really do plan for the absolute worst, don't you?" Alex said.

"Don't you? You should."

"If this is confirmed as die-back, things would have to be exceptionally bad here before it was worth leaving."

"I'll keep looking," Solomon said. "If it is, we have to rule out returning to Earth in an emergency. Bednarz predicted the need to leave Earth to preserve the human species, and this is exactly the kind of scenario he anticipated."

"Being under attack from eel-headed aliens?" Alex asked. "Not that we were."

"Opis is a lifeboat, but like all lifeboats, it'll be uncomfortable until we make landfall," Solomon said. "If Earth is off limits, though, we need to identify other worlds in the longer term. As you said, Captain, we plan for the very worst, even if we're fairly sure it won't be necessary."

"I'll borrow that line, if I may," Ingram said. Now she caught herself thinking it would be better if it really was die-back, because the choices would be much clearer. "At least that gives me a clear topic when I address Kill Line. Otherwise I'll just have a rambling list of assumptions and don't-knows to reel off to them."

"I suggest Sol streams the meeting to everyone else as well," Alex said. "Because the die-back thing is really going to make a difference. God, I hope the Meikles have a miracle lined up in the nice new lab Seb's bound to have."

"Do you want to go back to Earth, Alex?"

"No, I was just thinking about our people who stayed behind. And Tev Josepha."

It was too easy for Ingram to forget them. Now she definitely needed to see Marc regardless of whether he'd decided he hated her guts or not. He'd want to help Tev.

Ingram felt her chronological years had suddenly caught up with her. "If we open a gate for them and they're in quarantined territory, Alex, we won't be able to do any more for them either way," she said.

Alex got up to leave. "I don't think Marc Gallagher's going to see it that way."

No, he wouldn't. Ingram knew that already.

She now had a couple of hours to get her thoughts together for the meeting. While she searched for neutral terms to stop her own homesickness colouring the talk, she kept trying to compose a voice memo to the food research team to ask if they wanted her to make the arrangements for Nina's funeral or if they'd prefer to do it. She pondered on Doug's comment about how nice it was that she didn't behave like a CO. Did it sound like she was putting pressure on them, or was she being weak and indecisive by not assuming the responsibility right away? She was the captain, and Nina had been a member of her crew. It was her duty. She sent the message anyway.

Damn, she hadn't had a quiet chat with Haine yet, either. Medics weren't invulnerable. Dealing with Nina's body would have difficult and she should have paid the medical team a visit sooner. She'd make it her priority when she finished the meeting.

There was a tap at the door. "Ma'am?"

Bissey. She'd forgotten Bissey. *Damn.* "Sorry, Peter. Come in. Has Sol briefed you fully on the die-back situation?"

"He has."

"Take a seat. What's on your mind?"

Bissey looked embarrassed and didn't say anything, and he'd never been hesitant before. As Solomon had said it was personal, Ingram wondered if Bissey had done something socially awkward, like getting some woman pregnant. Well, she wasn't going to discipline a man for fraternisation when increasing the number of humans was one of the aims of the mission. She didn't know why it was so urgent, but needing to talk to her before the Kill Line meeting gave her an awful idea.

"Peter, please tell me you haven't knocked up a Kill Liner's wife," she said.

"Good God, no." He looked indignant. "Whatever made you think that?"

"It's urgent and awkward, yes?"

"I think so. But it's not that."

Ingram stopped prompting him. He could spit it out. "Go ahead."

"Captain, I'm not sure I can do this any more," he said, then lapsed into silence.

Sooner or later, everybody had a breaking point. Some people never looked as if they'd reached theirs even when they had. Others still had a way to go. But nobody was bulletproof.

"It's okay be overwhelmed by what's happened," she said. "This isn't the English Channel. It's not a war like the kind we understand, and we're not sure from one day to the next who we answer to. And you've done some high mileage in ugly situations. Do you want to talk? I've always got time."

"It's not that at all," Bissey said. "Or maybe it is."

"Tell me."

"Ma'am, I just can't support what you're doing any longer."

"Oh."

"Yes. Sorry, but I can't."

She'd let him talk. He'd get to what was really bothering him. "What do I do that makes you feel that way?"

Maybe he expected a stronger reaction. He frowned briefly as if he thought he'd misheard her. "Do you remember those lectures at Dartmouth about the Law of Armed Conflict? I do. I know there's no court to try us and no politicians around, but that doesn't change how I see it. What happened yesterday was *wrong*. Going along with Chris and Fred on this policy of being the new monsters in town is *wrong*. We had an opportunity and an obligation to try to talk to the Jattan if nothing else."

Ingram resisted the urge to argue with him because that did no good with someone who was on the edge. He thought what he thought, and that was that.

"Okay," she said. "But Chris did try to talk to him. You have to give him that. He listened to you."

"Did it change the outcome? No."

"Peter, I know you're under a lot of stress. I want to be helpful, not pick a fight."

"Is that what you think, that I'm having some breakdown?"

"You tell me."

"You couldn't possibly be wrong, could you? I have to be unhinged."

Bissey seemed disappointed, not defensive. It dawned on Ingram that she'd misread him. He wasn't crumbling under the stress at all. He'd finally drawn a line that he wasn't going to cross.

"So this is a protest, is it?" she asked.

"No, ma'am. A protest is action designed to change someone's mind. I don't think I can change yours or influence the prevailing culture that's emerging. This is me saying I can't accept the team responsibility any longer."

"If you're going to cite military law, remember that the same legal system regards us as civilians now," Ingram said. "We might be going through the motions of being a navy, but we're not. We've been making up the rules as we've gone along since before we left Earth. The situations we're facing have never happened to humans before."

"Captain, our humanity depends on our willingness to abide by *ethical* rules, and those rules aren't for easy choices but for the *hard* ones," Bissey said, emphasising the words as if she was a little slow on the uptake. "It doesn't matter whether we're civilians or not. It's about right and wrong."

"You're talking as if we've committed crimes."

"Yes. I am."

Ingram admired his honesty, but he should have ironed this out with his conscience when he was a midshipman. "The key word's *mutual*," she said. "If your enemy operates by a different set of rules, or none at all, upholding laws and prevailing ethics doesn't mean you're morally superior, it means you're *dead*, and you've failed to do everything you could to protect those who rely on you to defend them."

"And that's how it becomes a race to the bottom," Bissey said.

"We treat our enemies properly in the hope that they'll treat us the same way, and it hasn't always worked that well."

"Have you no regrets?" Bissey asked, frowning. "Is there nothing you've done that you've looked back at and wondered if you went too far?"

"I don't regret one single action I've taken, Peter. I look at all the people who weren't poisoned, who weren't bombed, and who weren't shot, and I thank God I did it."

"I'm not a savage," Bissey said. "If I forget the basics of decency, I have no right to call myself a man."

Ingram knew she should just tell him his objections had been noted and ask if he wanted to be reassigned or discharged. That would have covered the situation whether he was driven by moral outrage or mental health issues. But she found herself arguing when she should have been listening, feeling a fool for thinking he was asking for help, and hating herself for turning on him after all they'd been through together.

"Do you feel you have a problem?" She tried to get back to the mentor and counsellor role, which had never been her strong suit. "Do you feel under stress? I'm asking because this has suddenly become about me, and it really should be about you and how I can help."

"No, I feel under less stress now, actually." Bissey sat back in the chair. "It *is* about you. And I understand it better now the world around us is stripped down to basics and there's no other authority muddying the waters."

"Peter, our job can be ugly. We do the killing and the dirty work so others don't have to. We take the guilt and the nightmares and the regrets to protect lives and our way of life."

"So the ends justify the means," Bissey said.

"Yes, Peter. Yes, they *do*."

"You know where that thinking ends."

"Yes. *We survive.* If you have rules at the expense of outcomes, you're not fighting for your life or anyone else's. I know you never approved of what I did in the war, but you didn't resign, either. Why? Because the government sanctioned it and gave you top cover. They made it moral for you. Now there's no government to tell us what we're allowed to do. We can't hide behind them. But that doesn't change a thing for me. I still do what I think is right."

"I think it's unlawful, and so I can't serve under you," Bissey said. He ignored the point about Calais and the defence of the Channel. "You need to reassign or discharge me. Not send me to Logan for some pills and a pep talk."

It broke Ingram's heart. Bissey had strong moral views, and so did she, but she drew the line in a very different place.

"I respect your choice, Peter," she said. "But we're going to face a battle for our existence at some point, returning to Earth is looking even less like an option, and I need to know that my First Officer won't hesitate to do what I ask. So with regret, I accept your resignation."

"And I think you're wrong about not handing Caisin technology over to the government, too," Bissey said.

"It's not our technology, Peter. We'd have to take it from the teeriks. I really didn't want this to degenerate into point-scoring, but it seems you're squeamish about killing aliens in certain ways, but fine with killing them with government approval, stealing from them, and exploiting them."

"Shall we draw a line under this before we wreck an old friendship?" Bissey said.

"Yes, let's. You're relieved of duty, then, and I'll appoint someone to your post as soon as possible. Alex Gorko will discuss an alternative non-defence role for you when the current emergency's over."

Jeff Aiken was going to be furious, both with Bissey for losing his nerve — or regaining it, maybe — and with Ingram for removing him. He always said the two of them had held the Channel fleet together. The sad thing was that neither of them was wrong, but they'd still never find common ground. Bissey gave Ingram a polite nod and left her sitting at her desk.

It wasn't the first what-have-I-just-done moment she'd had in her life, but she hadn't actually done anything except remind Bissey what he already knew about her, and listen to him while he told her what she already knew about him. It was still going to cause ructions in a small community like this, though.

This wasn't one of her better days. And now she had to face Kill Line with her composure in shreds.

"Solomon, I hope you heard all that," she said.

"I can't really avoid it, Captain."

"Do you disapprove?"

"I don't think you had any choice," Solomon said. "I'd have done the same. If I felt you were losing your way, I'd have told you. This is a moral argument, not a legal one, as you said."

Ingram would have to replace Bissey fast. Her first thought was Searle, but there'd be a hiatus. "Well, I need a First Officer right now, so I'm appointing you as acting Number One. You're doing a lot of the job now anyway."

"I won't let you down, Captain."

"I'm thinking of Searle as a replacement. We see eye to eye, and he's American, like the majority of our citizens, so that might act as a social adhesive. That's pretty important right now."

"Not Marc Gallagher?"

"Sol, I think he'd eat broken glass rather than take an order from me."

"That's one way of putting it. Time for you to get to your meeting, I think. I've arranged the streaming and sent out reminders to all personnel and residents."

Ingram tried to be upbeat. She even forced a smile to convince herself. "See? You're the Jimmy already, aren't you?"

She made an effort to keep the half-smile nailed in place all the way to Kill Line. The assembly room wasn't completely packed, but

Ingram didn't take that as lack of interest. Every home had a TV wall and could switch to the interactive channel to watch events and ask live questions. When she addressed her ship's company via the vessel's broadcast system it was one-way, even though the technology could have handled a dialogue. The interactive screen was a reminder to her that she wasn't giving orders today.

She leaned on the makeshift lectern. "We can't ignore what's happened in the last few days," she said. "So I'll start by telling you what we know and don't know. We know the Jattan and the teerik who landed here were looking for Fred's ship on behalf of a rebel Jattan politician, and the likely use is to aid a coup or a civil war. We don't know why they decided to look for it on Opis. We don't know if the Jattan informed anyone of his whereabouts, our presence here, or the existence of the ship, or if and when his absence will be noticed. We do know, sadly, that aliens will kill humans if challenged. We don't know if the Jattan would have harmed us if we hadn't reacted to the killing of Nina Curtis, but as we don't intend to hand over the ship or Fred's commune, we have to assume we'll be treated as hostile in any future encounters. I also have an update on Earth, which reached me in the last hour. We think die-back might have reached Korea."

She heard the murmur in the audience and paused for a moment. She almost expected questions to start, but everyone sat there in silence waiting for her to go on.

"Anyway, I'd stress that none of this is in the public domain yet, and it's come from Solomon's observations of flight patterns and comms traffic. Die-back's *not* been mentioned by name. But all traffic and trade from the Asian mainland have been stopped, and Solomon's identified an area of Korea that appears to have been quarantined. We'll update you when we hear more. That kind of detailed intel isn't normally shared outside the ops room, but we want you to know everything that's going on. The ease with which we can move using the Caisin gate did make returning to Earth an option in the event of a major emergency that the colony was unable to handle, but that option is looking increasingly unlikely. Now I'm open to your questions, and I'll answer them as fully as I can."

"Should the alien situation worry us enough to think about going back to Earth?" Doug asked. "You seem to have everything under control. What happened to Nina was terrible, and people are upset and nervous, but our troops dealt with the problem quickly and we have a period of grace to prepare better defences." Doug sounded like the mayor that he was. His use of *our troops* was interesting. "Our worry was always that even if there were safe havens on Earth, we didn't know if they'd still be there for our grandchildren. It now looks like they won't, but we always suspected that would be the case, which is one of the reasons we're here."

Ingram couldn't argue with a syllable of that. "We're all in the same boat," she said. "My expertise is no greater than anyone else's when it comes to die-back. But I think your summary is a pretty fair one."

One of the teachers raised her hand to ask a question. "We're all willing to serve to defend the colony, even if we never imagined carrying a rifle," she said. "We had the chance to train when we were back on Earth, but I didn't take it up. Can we get that training now?"

"I'll certainly ask Marc Gallagher," Ingram said. "I'll let you know."

Solomon whispered in her earpiece. "He says tell them yes. He was talking to Dan and Chris about it earlier."

Ingram indicated her earpiece. "I've just been told that Marc will be happy to do that and he's organising it already."

Kill Liners asked direct, practical questions about what was required from them. It was always easy to answer those. They didn't ask many, because they didn't seem to expect anyone else to do things for them if they could do it themselves, like the security patrols and managing rations. Then one of the beef farmers, Mike Hodges, looked like he'd finally steeled himself to ask something awkward.

"Ma'am, I have to ask. Can we trust the teeriks?"

It was probably the first thing most people wanted to ask but didn't feel they could.

"I trust Fred and his commune," Ingram said. "And they've put a lot of trust in us. Whether we can trust all teeriks is another matter."

"So if we see one we don't know, do we open fire? Because we don't see enough of our teeriks to be sure of telling them apart, so it'd be real helpful if ours wore something we could recognise."

It was a very practical question. It was also the one that had lost Ingram her First Officer.

"I'll ask them to wear some Nomad ID," she said. "If you do encounter one you don't know, it's best to alert security, because we don't know what other weapons they might have and it would be useful if we could question one. By all means defend yourselves if you don't have that option, though. Your safety comes first."

That was a cop-out and she knew it. So did Mike Hodges.

"But all other aliens are easy to spot, right?" he said. "They don't look teerik and they don't look like us. So we can drop them."

"Actually, I'd like to take them prisoner and get some answers out of them as well," Ingram said. "But not at the expense of a human life, or our own teeriks' safety. If you feel your life's threatened, you open fire."

She thought that was honest as well as being clear. It still put the onus on civilians to make the call, though. Liam Dale had. She couldn't argue with that or blame him for it now.

"I should add that I'll take responsibility for any mistaken shootings," she said. "I can't put that burden on you and then blame you if you get it wrong."

Ingram felt she'd been completely straight with the Kill Liners and they seemed as satisfied as they could be. The session looked like it had come to a natural end. Doug got up from the front row of chairs.

"Thank you, Captain, that was helpful," he said. "We were going to vote later on whether we felt it was safe to stay here after what happened to Nina. That was when going back to Earth was a possibility. Now that it isn't, we'll still go ahead with it. Think of it as a vote of confidence. It's how we always do things, so this is no different. Just to put it on the record that we've considered the situation and consulted our residents."

"Understood," Ingram said. Votes of confidence always sounded ominous. If Kill Liners didn't feel safe here now and they couldn't leave either, she still had to respond with some kind of action plan that would reassure them. "Thank you for your time."

If anyone watching the session from one of the other groups had questions, they hadn't asked any. Ingram expected to be cornered by Ainatio staff when she got back to the main building, and they'd have very different concerns, she was sure of that. She made a point of walking around the labs and offices for a while to draw their fire, but apart from questions about Nina's funeral, she wasn't put on the spot, and nobody mentioned Bissey, so he obviously hadn't said anything. If he had, the gossip would have flown around the base in minutes. She went back to her office and left the door wide open in case anyone felt she was hiding.

"That's the most any leader could do, Captain," Solomon said. "You've been seen to go to the population and consult them, even if there's not much anyone can do except sit tight. And you've kept them informed. Apparently that's always been a significant factor in how satisfied humans are with those who govern them."

"But I *don't* govern them," she said. "They have an elected leader. Even the transit camp people have agreed on who they want to speak for them. I just command a ship. Not even that now, I suppose. Forty-five years of preparing for civilian rule has just collapsed on itself like a dwarf star."

"They'll still look to you as the one responsible for keeping aliens at bay."

"But they did that for themselves as well. Liam dealt with a problem that I tried to manage rather than solve."

"I wouldn't take Commander Bissey's resignation too hard, Captain. That's what all this is about, isn't it?"

"Sol, we fought a war together. I'll take it hard, thanks." It was more than losing a trusted officer and a friend. Ingram felt she'd been judged. "I suppose I'd better formally announce Peter's departure now."

"All done," Solomon said. "Everyone knows. Memo in your inbox, extended morning meeting for senior officers scheduled for tomorrow."

"I should have done that right away."

"No, you've kept people informed and you're giving them time to think through the ramifications."

"I said that, did I?" Ingram checked her mail. "Gosh. *'If any of you have the same misgivings about a deterrent approach, I would appreciate your sharing them at the meeting.'* I try not to use gerunds, Sol, so they'll know I didn't write this. But that's more or less what I would have said. And it does sound like I mean obey or quit."

"But you do."

Sometimes Solomon knew her better than she knew herself.

The rest of the day was unnaturally quiet. There were fewer people walking around outside, and fewer small, annoying issues reaching her inbox. It felt as if everyone had decided their petty problems were embarrassingly small in the light of one of their shipmates losing her life, and that whatever it was could wait. Bissey's departure might have struck a chill or two as well, but nobody knocked on her door demanding answers, not even Aiken or Haine. That was more worrying than anything. Were they secretly glad to see the back of Bissey, too scared of her, or more worried about aliens showing up? She wondered when to visit the teeriks to see how they were doing, but when she checked the radio locations on the site map, Jeff was already in the teerik compound with Dai and Brad, probably getting down to the small detail of upgrading base defences. So that was what had taken priority. She was reassured. She'd wait.

"Captain," Solomon said. "I'm monitoring the news channels, and they're reporting that the Korean president's going to address the country later today. Not APS, the Korean government. This is speculation on my part, but I think it'll be about die-back."

"What are the media saying?"

"They're guessing. They're linking it to the post-outage recovery. There's been criticism of the government for not sending aid to some regions quickly enough."

Ingram glanced at her watch, the one that had belonged to her grandmother and would never show Opis time. She had no plans to have the face and the mechanism changed. But no matter how much of her past she thought she'd brought with her, most of it was still anchored trillions of miles away. It would take years to loosen those ties, not months, and she wasn't the only one.

"There's one thing nobody's asked yet," she said.

"What would that be, Captain?"

"If die-back really has started to spread again, do we have a wider responsibility to people stuck on Earth?"

"Why would we?"

"Ask Marc. Do you think he'll shrug and say too bad, I'll forget about Tev?"

"Are we just talking about evacuating Tev and his family?"

"Actually, I think we need to ask what happens if it looks like we'll end up as the last surviving remnant of humanity. That's very long term and very pessimistic, but we have to consider it."

Solomon went quiet for a while. "We can't even revive our colleagues in *Elcano* at the moment. What can we possibly do for billions of others?"

Ingram had debated the political implications of the Caisin gate with Marc more than once, but this was the first time the choice seemed as stark as asking whether Nomad Base should turn its back on Earth's problems forever.

"I know what we can do, Sol," she said. "We can ask that very question. Maybe the answer is nothing at all. We certainly can't do anything for the foreseeable future. But we have to think about it."

"I think we're talking very long term indeed," Solomon said.

"Fine. Project Nomad is about the survival of mankind. You can't get much more long-term than that."

"Actually, Bednarz's vision was the survival of the best of humanity, not all of it. Given our circumstances, I think the debate's going to be an unnecessary distraction, but if it's crossed your mind, it'll occur to others, so perhaps you're right." Solomon sounded taken aback. No, it probably wasn't in Bednarz's plan, or his, but neither was die-back or warring aliens or Caisin gates. "I'll think about it. If you'll excuse me, I have checks to run."

Ingram knew she'd rattled him. She needed her sounding board, and there was only Marc she could count on now to tell her the tough truth. She tapped the comms on her desk. She'd have to face him before she had her apology adequately polished.

"Hi Marc," she said. "We need to talk about where we go from here if die-back's spreading again."

"Oh good," he said. "I've been thinking about that, and I've got a plan to run past you."

Ingram picked her words carefully. "Is it something you and I need to discuss before the next command meeting?"

"Yeah. Just so I don't embarrass you. You might even talk me out of it."

Ingram checked the map for his radio tracker. "Probably best to meet at your place."

"Okay. Fifteen minutes?"

"Look, Marc, I want to apologise for asking you to terminate the commune if it all went wrong. I wasn't thinking. It was crass of me. I should have asked someone else. I saw security risks, not sons."

"No big deal. I hadn't noticed."

"Your comrades did."

Marc sounded relaxed about it. "Don't be hard on Chris. For all the ear-carving and back-alley justice, he's very protective of... well, everyone whose ears aren't fair game. Even gives dodgy aliens a chance. Decent bloke."

Ingram wasn't convinced Marc hadn't noticed, but if he could be bothered to lie to protect her feelings, she was still in his good books. That was a relief.

"You're very gracious," she said.

"Can I have that on my headstone?"

"One day in the very distant future, yes."

"Okay, I'll see you soon."

"I hope it's a good plan, Marc, because mine won't endear me to people."

"Well, mine might not endear me to you," Marc said. "But it might be the best we can manage while still protecting Nomad."

That was her purpose and duty, Nomad and the welfare of one thousand, seven hundred and forty-four souls — two thousand, seven hundred and seventy-six if she included *Elcano*. She'd already lost one of them. She didn't plan to lose any more before their time.

* * *

NOMAD BASE STAFF CLUB: THREE HOURS LATER.

This place was all flags.

They were pinned to the walls, draped on the edges of shelves, or suspended from the ceiling above the heads of the patrons, which was probably in contravention of some fire regulation. But nobody was going to take theirs down anytime soon.

Annis had thought that the *Cabot* crew had already steeled themselves to forget Earth before the ship launched, but the latest news from Earth seemed to have put paid to that for many of them.

She looked around the crowded club, more of a staff room than a bar, and tried to guess who'd want to go home and save their old homeland if they could, and who'd want to leave it to its fate. Everybody seemed to be having intense conversations in low voices. It hadn't been a happy week and it showed no signs of getting better.

Once people began moving into permanent housing, the assorted drinking dens around the tent city and in the base itself had disappeared almost as quickly as they'd sprung up. All that was left in the main base was this oasis used almost exclusively by *Cabot*'s crew, the *Ainatio* scientists, and a few of Dan Trinder's troops.

In a way, it was also used by the dead. There were a couple of photos on the wall behind the bar, one of Derek Levine and one of Nina Curtis. Both were neatly framed in black with test tubes secured to the wall below them, makeshift vases for single sprigs of a plant with small white blossoms. Someone had taken the time to find a plant in bloom in a place that didn't yet have gardens.

Annis knew the bars in Kill Line and the transit camp would be doing the same thing tonight, talking about die-back and wondering how long Earth had left. If it really was die-back, she was willing to bet the virus wouldn't stop at the Korean border, and even if it did, nobody would believe it wasn't heading their way. Fear and panic would do the job even if the virus didn't.

She checked the flags again and ticked the countries off a mental list. She could see Brazil, the United States, assorted European countries that had also ceased to exist while *Cabot* was in transit, a Union Jack alongside a Royal Navy white ensign, and an assortment of APS states — Singapore, Korea, Japan, the Philippines, Australia, New Zealand, and Taiwan. The reality was that most of *Cabot's* crew were British or American, with a sizeable European minority. The APS contingent was fifteen individuals, and as far as she could see, only four were in this club.

Phil Berman hadn't taken his eyes off the news channel on the big screen for half an hour. He kept reaching for his beer, totally distracted and never quite connecting with it. His burger was getting cold, too. Annis took a few chips from his plate.

"Don't waste food," she said, munching.

Phil looked away from the screen for a moment and picked up the burger obediently in both hands. "You must still have a lot of friends in Seoul," he said. "I'm really sorry. And none of those Korean troops and technicians deserved to go home to this. Poor bastards. They seemed like nice folks."

"What if it's not die-back?" Annis asked. "What if it's Mad Soybean Disease?"

"What? Is that a thing?"

"Listen to you all. You've decided it's die-back and the world's ending. Again."

"It might be, and it would be."

"Okay, fair enough. Haven't we had enough pessimism and misery this week? Anyway, yes, I have friends in Seoul, but I think we saw each other as colleagues rather than mates." It wasn't strictly true, but there was nothing Annis could do for them if the worst had happened. "It was hard to have close friendships with the kind of job I went into."

"Physicist?"

"Spy."

"Oh... yes. Even so, we know what comes next because we lived it in America. I feel terrible for the Meikles. They thought their kid would be safer in APS than here."

"Ask me again if it hits Melbourne," Annis said. "I've still got family there."

She didn't need to say they weren't close. But they'd stayed in touch, and there were no feuds, problems, or unhappy memories, and she wondered why she'd ever put herself in a position where she had to let them think she was dead. She'd made a rational sacrifice for honour and country — family honour — but now she couldn't believe she'd been so stupid.

Had she always planned it that way? She could never have foreseen she'd end up on another planet, so she'd probably reassured herself that she could go home when her mission was done and tell her family the truth, all the noble patriotic stuff, and they'd eventually forgive her for putting them through hell. It was difficult to remember exactly what she'd felt back then, though. Time made a liar of everyone. Breaking it to them that she wasn't decomposing in a ditch would have been hard enough no matter when she did it. But events had now made it unthinkable.

"Do you think we're obliged to do anything?" she asked.

Phil shrugged. "I don't think there's anything we can do now."

"I bet you Ingram's thinking about it."

"Annis, I spent the last decade working at having no discernible opinion on my boss. It's a hard habit to break. All I'll say is that I'm glad Ruth and I changed our minds, even if we do have vertically-challenged tentacled gangsters for neighbours."

Annis would have put a bet on Erskine pulling the ladder up and saying it was really sad about APS but everyone knew it was only a matter of time. She had form for it. Ingram was the damn-the-torpedoes type, though, despite the harmless Lady Bountiful act. If Tim hadn't been such a tosser and tried to sabotage the Nomad mission, she might have helped him, but there was zero chance of that now. Britain was another matter. If Ingram still needed to cling to a navy she'd left years ago, Annis suspected she'd find it hard to resist offering her country a helping hand too. Marc already had.

"I wish there was an obvious answer," Annis said.

"Yeah, I remember those. They were great. Haven't seen one for years, though." Phil turned to look past her at the door. He was waiting for Ruth, but his expression said it wasn't her who'd come in. "Here's Dan."

"Are you going to volunteer?" Annis asked. "I hear everyone in Kill Line who isn't already tooled up and firearms-trained is putting their name down for a carbine and Marc's training sessions. Even the old ladies."

"I never imagined I'd have to, but I suppose I must."

Annis stood up to go to the bar. "Do you want another beer, then?"

"Might as well," Phil said. "I think Ruth's forgotten about me."

The bar ran on an honesty system. Nomad had no currency, but it did have an economy that allocated resources. Getting Phil a beer meant Annis had to record what she'd taken from the bar and who it was for, to keep people within their allowance. It was rationing by another name, but like everyone else, she was fine with that because she knew they didn't have the luxury of a food surplus. If they wanted more out of the system, then they had to put more in by doing some extra work or helping someone out, someone who didn't want their beer allocation.

Annis dispensed a half-pint from the pump and decided they might still look back on this period as Opis's halcyon days despite the tragedy: no money, no complaining about the conditions yet, and everyone with a common goal, ready to defend the colony. She wondered how long it would last when the population started to grow and the crises were over.

She was pouring a beer for herself when her attention drifted to a conversation at the far end of the counter. It was getting a little tense. Jenny Park was having an argument with Sara McDowd about die-back.

"And why now? Why, after all these years, is it spreading *now*? First Solomon trashes Asian infrastructure, with God knows how many dead, and now this, just as people are starting to get their lives back. Call me paranoid, but that sounds like what we used to call a war."

Jenny was one of the civilian food technologists. Annis knew she came from somewhere in Honam in southwest Korea, so her home town was probably in or near the area Solomon said had been quarantined. She was almost nose to nose with Sara, who was one of Trinder's troops and not a woman Annis would have voluntarily picked a fight with.

"Perhaps you should ask the APS technology commissioner," Sara said, mock-polite and helpful. "The one who blows up ships and leaves civilians marooned. And tortures old men. And mutilates dogs. I'm sure he'd be able to give you an answer."

This was Annis's turf. Even so, she should have stayed out of it, but a sense of ownership and the previous beer told her to dive right in.

"I agree, it really is shitty timing," she said. "But if we're going to talk about coincidences, the last time I saw Tim Pham, he had his people trampling all over contaminated land and bagging samples. And he was going to shoot me, but that's neither here nor there. I mean, that's where I'd start looking. He said he didn't think die-back would ever reach Asia. After all that's happened, it'd be a bloody riot if he walked the virus in on his boots. And... Dieter's not an old man, not really, but I think Sara's general point stands. Take it from someone who knows Tim really, *really* well."

Jenny looked baffled for a moment, then her eyes widened in angry disbelief. "You think this is a *joke*? Whose side are you on? This is your country that's being destroyed. Your people."

"I'm Australian," Annis said. "And Nomad's our country now. And nobody's waging war on anyone. Someone's ballsed up. If die-back carries on spreading, as it will, nobody's spared. Everyone's got a vested interest in *not* spreading it."

"But you lie for a living. Why the hell should I listen to you just because you were Tim Pham's tart?"

"Well, I've got a bottle in my hand, for starters."

"Ladies..." Trinder stepped in. "That's not how we do things around here. Let's play nice."

Jenny turned around. "Patronising shit," she said, and stalked out.

Trinder looked at Annis, straight-faced. "Okay, about your application for the diplomatic service, Dr Kim. I'm sorry, but you weren't the successful candidate this time."

"I can't stand conspiracy theorists, that's all," Annis said. "And Sara was right. Besides, if Jenny thinks some foreign government's using die-back as a bioweapon, you can bet the elected pond life back on Earth are thinking the same. Which bodes ill for some innocent countries."

"Yeah, that's crossed my mind before, unfortunately," Trinder said. "And Marc's. Ruth just collected Phil, by the way, so you might as well have his beer. Maybe it'll inspire you to start a galactic war."

Someone turned up the screen's volume. Conversation faded as everyone paused to watch the Indian network they seemed to like best. The anchorwoman had her disaster face on.

"Tonight's top story — in grim news from Seoul, Korea has confirmed that die-back virus has been found in rice crops. The Steel Border isolation policy that kept APS free of the disease for more than fifteen years has finally yielded to its relentless spread around the world. As panic buying began in the cities, with some food stores drafting in armed security guards to hold back frightened shoppers, the country's Prime Minister appealed for calm. An outbreak in Gyeonggi is thought to have originated from infected plant material in Russian aid shipments following the terrorist attack on power grids across the APS region. But the Russian agriculture minister denies there've been any cases in his country, and he's asked for Russian scientists to be given access to samples for independent testing. Meanwhile, thirty more cases of the virus have been confirmed in... "

"It's okay, they're blaming the Russians," Sara said. "That'll end well."

Lev Noskov, one of the engineers, made a vague gesture at the screen with his glass. "Ungrateful jerks. We sent them aid."

"I'd never say so to Jenny, but it *is* unusual timing," Sara whispered.

Annis shook her head and drained her beer. "Not really. APS relied on tight border security for its quarantine. When Solomon fried its systems, it was an open door for smugglers and illegals waiting to get in. And here we are."

"So it's Sol's fault."

"No, it's the fault of whichever wanker thought a virus like that was a good idea in the first place."

Trinder helped Annis out with the spare beer. She poured half a glass into a disposable cup for him.

"You okay now, Dan?"

"Yeah. Fine."

"Gan-Pamas could have fried you."

"But he didn't." Trinder raised his cup. "Cheers. I actually came to find you. I need to ask you a favour. Private stuff. Can we talk somewhere quieter?"

Normally, she'd have ribbed Trinder about it and loudly mentioned embarrassing rashes. But she couldn't bring herself to be cheerful with Nina gone, even if she'd rarely spoken to the woman. Good manners cost nothing. She followed Trinder and expected him to pause on the steps outside the entrance, but he kept walking.

"Oh, this is *really* private stuff, then?" she said.

Trinder fell back to walking beside her. "We need your expertise, Annis. We can ask the teeriks, but we need a human propulsion expert on this, and you've got unique knowledge."

"Who's *we*?"

"Marc, Ingram, and Chris. And me."

They were on the path to the main building now. "You're worried that the teeriks have got a security leak, aren't you?" Annis said.

"That's not what this is about." Trinder ushered her through the doors. "Ingram's office. Up you go."

Annis couldn't imagine what they needed from her, but she'd know in a few moments so it wasn't worth speculating. Ingram was leaning back at her desk, arms folded, and Marc was parked with his backside on the window sill. Chris budged up on the bench seat to make room for Trinder and Annis.

"Take a seat, Dr Kim," Ingram said. "We've had an idea. We want to run it past you for feasibility."

"Why me?" she asked.

"Because you have both the expertise and the most current contacts in Earth's technical and academic community," Ingram said. "And you're rather trustworthy for an enemy spy."

Annis sat down next to Chris. "Okay. I'm a sucker for flattery. What do you need?"

"I've been arguing *against* what I'm about to suggest for the last few weeks," Marc said. "The captain's been a bit less hard-line about it. But with what's happening on Earth, the game's changed. There's still nothing we can do right now, but I think there's some help we *can* give Earth in the longer term."

"And what's that, Marc?"

"How would we go about giving the right people on Earth the plans to build an FTL drive, with a list of planets they might like to visit? And by the right people, I mean the sort that'll use a ship to evacuate ordinary people to another planet, not use it to transport their dinner party chums and their art collection. Or start a war."

"Bloody hell," Annis said. "You nicked my lines, you thieving Pom."

"Yeah, now I've said it, I feel like a prat. It's not going to work, is it?"

"It'll work *eventually*. The question is how long it'll take and if you'll like the kind of worlds it creates." Annis was surprised. She never had Marc down for an idealist, or even Ingram come to that. "What didn't you like about the idea before you changed your mind?"

"Sharing our technology with Earth?" Marc said. "Well, it's hard to turn your back on your country when you've spent your adult life serving it, and I didn't think Britain could hold out indefinitely. I'd given the FCO Ainatio's stuff, seeing as APS had it, and part of me wanted to give them Caisin access too. But the other part of me — the sane bit — said it wouldn't be used to evacuate members of the public. It'd be political, and some other country would get hold of it, and it'd generally make matters worse. APS is going to be too busy fighting die-back to attack anybody, but Britain's going to cop the fallout from Asia falling apart. If we can give the right people the de-enriched spec, in other words no Caisin, just a guide to how to build a really fast spaceship, we can save a lot of lives. But definitely not Caisin. It's a can of worms and we don't know the half of it yet."

"Is it just Britain, or does everybody get a piece of this?" Annis asked. "Or just countries with no die-back?"

"If it's everybody, nobody's got a tactical advantage, so it might head off any wars over it," Marc said. "This is why *who* we give this stuff to really matters. I mean, this could all go horribly wrong, but Earth's going to rat-shit whether we intervene or not. And if we can leave an infected area without bringing die-back with us, so can they. We're not talking about any time soon. It's going to take years. I'm just saying now's the time to think about it."

Chris looked weary. "This is crazy. What are you, amnesiacs? A few months ago we busted our asses to slam the door on Tim Pham. Sol said it didn't matter what he knew because he couldn't reach us. I thought he would, eventually, but we'd have years to prepare for the backlash. And now we're talking about giving *everyone* ready-made FTL. If we let APS have the plans along with everyone else, what do you think Pham's going to do with them? This is going to be his first port of call, with a frigging army."

"It's not the fault of APS citizens that they've got an unelected dickhead for a tech commissioner," Annis said.

"But he knows about Opis. He worked out the Caisin gate, more or less, and I told him nobody would believe him. So when oven-ready FTL lands in his department's inbox, it's going to make his portal theory look totally credible. And he isn't going to let this drop."

Ingram rubbed her brow. "You know, I'm beginning to wish I'd just handed this to the First Sea Lord without telling anyone, and enabled Britain to become a merciless galactic power."

"You still can," Marc said. "And now we've kicked the idea around, I'm not sure you'd be wrong. Chris is right about Pham. But this won't happen overnight, so we've got time to work something out."

"I can work it out right now," Chris said. "I go back and finish him off. How many other people is he likely to have told about the portal?"

"There's guessing and there's knowing," Annis said. "It's the precision, immediacy, and scalability of the Caisin gate that makes it so dangerous. If Tim had come to me with that theory and said teerik blueprints proved it existed, I'd have told him there was a big difference between the FTL tech needed to do that and the kind that reduced a thousand-year journey to a few weeks."

"Yeah, you told me that, too, really loudly," Marc said. "Look, let's work on the assumption that even if we hand over the plans to a secret chosen few, he'll get to hear about it anyway and we're going to turn Caisin into the Holy Grail or the Loch Ness monster. Some nutter will want to hunt for it. But the only real grounds for doing nothing is if sharing FTL threatens the existence of this colony. Let's focus on that."

Annis had her ups and downs with Marc, but sometimes he surprised her. "Can I play devil's advocate for a moment? What if we drop this tech in their laps and they don't believe it's real?"

"Depending on who *they* is, they've chosen their own fate," Ingram said. "We can't do more than that."

"Okay, assuming we can identify public-spirited people who can deliver on the technology as well, where do we expect them to go when they build the ships, if not Opis?" Annis asked. "It has to be other worlds. If we can't cope with an influx via the gate, we won't be able to cope with ships. It's not just food and housing. It's stuff like the meds and immunisation we've had to take to survive the native bacteria and other pathogens here. They won't have had any of that. And die-back — we've been tight on biosecurity, but we can't rely on others to be that thorough, and if it reaches Opis we're finished.

And then there's just the general worry about undesirables, which is anyone from an invading army to the local pervert. No security checks. They can't come here."

"You sound like Marc," Ingram said. "That was one of our first arguments, almost word for word. Look, this is going to sound feeble, but we'll give them alternative locations. They exist. Fred can help with that. I don't know how a colony this size is going to stop anyone landing on Opis when there's a whole planet to choose from, though. But we'll try. Divert, then warn off, then repel."

"You just can't see it, can you?" Chris said. "Like we don't have enough potential alien enemies out there. So let's create some extra human ones as well."

Ingram looked at him like he was an argumentative teenager. "Whatever we do, Chris, APS knows Opis exists and that it's a viable environment, so even if they show up in fifty years instead of five weeks, they'll come, and we can't lock down a whole planet."

"Yeah, I didn't say it was an easy option," Marc said. "But if the choice is help Earth or ignore it, then this is what helping looks like. Nomad comes first because we dragged people out here and it's our job to keep them safe. Okay, there'll be some difficult decisions. But like I said, this isn't going to happen overnight. It's long term. Ten years minimum, probably more. We've got time to work things out."

Annis never thought she'd have this conversation. Her nightmare journey from Seoul to Kill Line had been all about seizing Ainatio's FTL. Now they were giving a much better version away for free.

"Have you mentioned this to Fred?" she asked.

"Not yet," Trinder said. "It's just us at the moment."

"But how about Sol?"

Solomon's voice drifted out of the speaker panel. "I have misgivings. This isn't what Bednarz intended or wanted. He didn't want mankind exporting its failings, as he put it. And you're not taking die-back risks seriously enough. Even if they land on another planet and infect that somehow, we'd still need to enforce a planetary quarantine here, and we can't do it."

"How was Bednarz planning to stop people leaving Earth, then?" Chris asked. "Did he say you had to kill everyone who wasn't as lovable as us?"

"Opis was intended to be *different.*" Solomon's voice was always controlled and calm, but he sounded a little terse now, and it wasn't the finely-timed pauses he normally used to convey mood. Annis could definitely hear a change of tone. "He said he believed populating the galaxy would bring out the very best and the very worst in humanity, and he wanted me to seek out the best and protect it."

"Yeah, but if those were his exact words — "

"They were."

" — then he obviously accepted the assholes were going to leave Earth and screw the galaxy, so he wanted a breeding colony of saints on Opis. Correct?"

"I can't argue with your logic. Those are the implications of his words."

"Well, all we have to do is sit back and concentrate our efforts on making Opis a no-go zone. Which we've got to do anyway on account of the neighbours. Your mission's intact, Sol."

"You mock the idea, Chris, but here you are, discussing how to save a world of complete strangers, many of whom don't deserve to be saved, when you could and *should* focus on your own welfare, because we have serious challenges here," Solomon said. "Making sacrifices for strangers is one of the reasons you represent the best of humanity. This is why I chose you. But I find it extremely frustrating that what makes you the best is also what makes you want to put yourselves in harm's way for the worst."

Chris nodded. "Yeah, there's that. There's also the fact that it's a lot less work to give Earth the kind of FTL that everyone else here already has than to put effort into hiding it. And they won't even be looking for anything like the Caisin gate, because regular FTL explains very short journey times."

"Just bear in mind that once people on Earth know there's a way out, there'll be rows and riots over who goes and when," Annis said. "It's not a simple lifebelt where you grab it and your troubles are over."

"We realise that," Ingram said. "But we also have to weigh it against doing nothing. Nothing is frequently the right response. It just requires you to hold your nerve in the face of vague demands to act."

"Are there enough companies left who can still manufacture this kind of thing?" Trinder asked. "I don't know if we're talking about a garage workshop or the most advanced factory in the world."

"Well, Fred's upgrading our drives with a team of bots, in situ," Annis said. "So it's doable, but on what kind of scale, I don't know. And getting a ship ready is only part of the battle. Finding a new planet and establishing habitation is a big task. Look how long it took to build Nomad. Seventy-three years. Forty-five just to get the first ships here."

Marc turned around and looked out of the window, hands in his pockets. "So is it worth spending a bit of time scoping this out?"

"It's flawed, but yes, I think it is."

"Can you come up with a list of the right people?"

"Probably some."

Ingram took out her screen and started scribbling notes. "I'm going to do a reassuring talk to everyone on why we can't use the greatest instant transport system in the galaxy to bring refugees here," she said. "Because even clever people who understand the risks and logistics are going to succumb to the urge to act rather than think when they see upsetting things on the news."

"Yeah, like me," Marc said.

"Inadequate food and resources... *Elcano*'s at the front of the queue... might be bringing people into a war zone... can't bring everyone, so there'll be fights over who gets to come... risk of introducing die-back... can't provide immunisation etcetera for millions... have I left anything out?"

"Perverts and general vermin," Chris said. "Lack of security checks and a small vulnerable population."

"I think that's ample to make the point." Ingram frowned at her screen. "I'll add that it takes at least a couple of years for food shortages to bite, and we'll use the time to come up with better ideas. When we know whether we're able to go ahead with sharing technology, then we announce what a terrific idea we've had."

"You don't look happy about it, Chris," Marc said.

"No, I'm not. Apart from completely reversing our position on Pham, we just made a decision for a whole world without a single vote. Two worlds, if you count Opis. We're changing the course of history. Just five meatbags and an AI."

"I didn't make any decision," Solomon said. "I strongly advise against this."

Annis hoped this wasn't going to get too philosophical. "I'm not sure I did, either."

"Everything everybody does every day changes history," Ingram said. "That's causality. We just can't see it as clearly as a handful of people taking a single yes-no decision. And as someone who's already been judged by history at least once, I can tell you that the consequences of your actions are almost always too complex to predict, so you might as well make the choices that seem clear and urgent."

"Unfortunately, we're wired to feel bad about doing nothing when other people are suffering," Trinder said. "It's really about making ourselves feel better, and it's the root of some very bad decisions."

"Is that a no?" Ingram asked.

"It's an abstention. But I'm hoping that we'll get more facts to work with in the time it's going to take us to set this up. Because this isn't just a matter of creating a distribution list and hitting send, is it?"

"More like cold-selling insurance and teaching everyone quantum physics," Annis said. "So no."

Ingram put her screen down as if she'd finished her list of plausible reasons. "I think that's probably where I am, too. If something happens to convince us it's a bad idea, we can put it on hold. But we still have to go through the same process. Dr Kim comes up with a list of people and organisations we can safely give the blueprints to. Or whatever the format is."

Annis was fascinated by people who didn't even think about the commercial side of off-the-shelf FTL. They just wanted to do their jobs, and that seemed to boil down to vague, oddly innocent stuff about saving lives. If they'd thought about how rich it could make them, they were ignoring the fact, yet none of them was naive or remotely innocent. Maybe Solomon had a point about the best of humanity. It was admirable, but sometimes it ended up cutting its own throat.

"You know how much this tech's going to be worth?" Annis asked. "However saintly the list of recipients is, it'll be traded. It'll be sold. It'll be used for other purposes. It'll fuel a massive bribe economy when people try to get seats on the ships. It'll price out the poorest. You're not responsible for humans being vile, but if you're calculating the net benefit, factor that in."

"What do we say when someone asks where the FTL came from?" Chris asked. "When do we tell them it's alien tech? Or do we lie and say it was in Mad Tad Bednarz's secret vault or something?"

"Can of bloody worms," Ingram muttered. "Well, if life was simple, the world would never have needed the likes of us. We'll work on that."

"Look at it another way," Trinder said. "If it's too complex to work out what'll happen if we do it, what happens if we don't?"

"Some people die and some people live," Annis said. "And if human civilisation doesn't wipe itself out in the next few years, someone develops FTL drives independently from Ainatio's research, and our species ventures out into the cosmos. And if nobody cracks it, it doesn't."

"And nobody knows or remembers we were the people who could have made mankind a spacefaring civilisation but didn't," Chris said. "Or maybe Nomad's that civilisation already. Any thoughts, Sol?"

Sol wasn't saying much. It could have been a hissy fit because he didn't want the wrong kind of people moving into his personal simulation game, or he might have decided it was a decision for humans to take.

"Either decision will have enormous consequences," Solomon said at last. "All I care about is that the community here survives and grows. Whatever you decide, I'll always be here to defend it. I'll only give you my opinion when you want it. But you know how I feel and I hope you'll take my concerns seriously. I did *not* bring you all here to sacrifice yourselves to maintain humanity's lowest standards."

"Well, while you philosophers slug it out, I'm going to do some homework on my contacts book and try brewing my own hooch," Annis said. "This conversation never took place, either. I'll let you know when I've worked something out."

Ingram gave her a thumbs-up. "Thank you, Dr Kim. I realise this is a difficult situation for you."

Annis got up and opened the door. "Don't thank me. I'm pretty sure that if APS survives in any kind of shape and you help it build an FTL fleet, one of the first things it'll do is invade Opis. Don't be too quick to stop Chris going back to slot Tim Pham."

She went back to her quarters and raided the fridge for something she could ferment with the wine yeast Andy Braithwaite had given her. The overripe tomatoes were worth a shot. As she weighed them and worked out the ratios for the other ingredients — damn, it'd only make two bottles — she digested the conversation and decided Chris was right. This was a massive decision whichever choice they made, and they were just five random meatbags, only one of which had any training for the mission, and the mission bore little resemblance now to the one Ingram had been trained for.

And Solomon wasn't happy about his good humans doing good deeds for bad people. That was a situation to keep an eye on.

It also struck her that she hadn't asked any of them what was in it for her. This bloody daft altruism was catching, and it was no way to stay alive in uncertain times. She put the tomatoes aside and took out her screen to call Ingram.

Annis had a price. It was a relatively modest fee, but it was the main reason she'd finally ended up here with everyone back home thinking she was dead.

"Captain Ingram," she said. "I have a request. In exchange for helping you plunge Earth into even more chaos, I'd really like it if we committed to naming some significant feature in this town after my great-grandmother and putting her contribution to Ainatio's research on the record. You think we can make that happen? Names matter. It's our immortality."

"I think that might be eminently doable," Ingram said. "And should we need to gloss over the existence of aliens, how about we explain the FTL as your great-grandmother's work?"

Annis paused. She'd balked at lies before. She was a physicist first and foremost, searching for the most fundamental truths of the universe. Anything built on bad data eventually collapsed. It didn't feel right. Grandma Park would have disapproved.

"If it's really necessary at the time to avoid more misery and conflict, I might agree to it," she said. "But it's a lie, and she wouldn't want that. For the time being, a road and a school would be fine."

"I'll make it happen," Ingram said. "Thank you."

Annis might have been a ghost, but she was a spectre with some influence now. And perhaps, if she got to grips with the teeriks' technology, she might improve on it using Grandma Park's work. Then her ancestor could rightly take her place in history.

It was good to have a real goal again.

* * *

CEMETERY, CHURCH OF ST THOMAS IN OPIS: 0930 HOURS, NEXT DAY.

The cemetery next to Nomad's brand new church was doing more trade than the maternity wing. It was a grim start for a new colony.

The graveyard already had five residents, three of them human, with a sixth to come, if Chris counted the memorials to Derek Levine and Mikel Lask and overlooked the fact that their remains were elsewhere. The maternity unit had yet to score.

"What do you think of the church, then? They're making it look like the one in Kill Line." Chris squatted on his heels next to Jamie's grave, nodding in the direction of the building that was taking shape on the other side of the field. There were always volunteers working alongside the bots whenever he passed. "Tim Pham still hasn't nuked the old place. You know what? He didn't save APS after all. They've just had their first case of die-back. And we've gone crazy, because we're seriously thinking of giving them FTL to help. Anyway, Kill Line had a vote on whether they think it's too dangerous here. I can't see them wanting to run away, though. They're tough. You'd have liked them a lot. They did you proud, buddy."

This was Chris's regular visit to the grave. If he was passing by any other time, he'd still drop in because not acknowledging Jamie was like ignoring him in the street. He understood exactly why Marc took that photo with him when he went to look at his new house. You could either join the dead or bring them into your world. It wasn't crazy. It was coping.

Sometimes, though, you had to shut them out. Chris had tried to forget what he'd seen happen to Nina and it wasn't working. He also couldn't shut out Gan-Pamas. He'd have to try harder.

He patted Jamie's headstone and went on his way. When he reached the gate, he turned to look back at the small cluster of headstones and decided that was what Marc needed — a memorial for his sons, somewhere to come and get things off his chest, or leave flowers, whatever made him feel better. Chris would mention it to him when the time was right. Nina's funeral would probably make it a natural topic of conversation.

Chris didn't have to be anywhere else until noon, so he took a leisurely walk back home. *Home.* Damn, that took some getting used to. It was a pleasant stroll, he didn't notice the gravity any more, and if he rode the quad bike everywhere, he didn't get to talk to people or pick up the general mood around the place. Solomon kept him informed, but that wasn't the same. Everyone saw the world through their own personal lens and he needed to assess Nomad his own way.

His filter was still set to paranoid. It had never failed him in the past, and he took his favourite Marcus Aurelius quote to heart; the skills he used to deal with problems today would be the same ones he could rely on to fix things tomorrow. He didn't worry too much about the future anyway, partly because street patrols in a collapsing society had taught him his own future could end in the next few seconds, but he was still worried about giving FTL to Earth. It had kept him awake last night, and that didn't happen often. What had been a general doubt at the meeting yesterday had turned into a full-on hell-no by this morning.

What made Marc think it was a good idea? Ingram must have been out of her mind as well. They were two tough, smart, pragmatic people who'd seen and done serious shit in real wars. This was the wrong time to discover their caring side. Chris could understand if they'd wanted to give their own country an edge, and he wouldn't have minded that so much because there was no America now and Britain was a kind of almost-America to him. It would probably have pissed off every other nationality in the *Cabot* crew that their country wasn't getting the technology, but those who'd woken up to find their nation had been reduced to an ungoverned space ruled by thugs and warlords knew it was a bad idea to give garbage the ability to reach Nomad.

Maybe giving Earth the teerik manual wouldn't be enough. Maybe nobody would have the capacity to actually build a ship or get hold of the raw materials to do it. There were rare metals and all kinds of stuff that had come from countries that weren't functioning any longer. That was why so much technology had failed. It was hard to manufacture spares. But if they could source all that stuff, either now or in the future, it was only a matter of time before Earth's problems moved out here.

What a frigging mess.

Don't do it. Not yet, anyway. Get more intel. Think more. A lot of people are going to die whatever we do, and we can't change that, but we can *change what happens to the folks here. Like Ingram says, the best answer to 'We have to do something' is often 'No, we don't.' So she needs to listen to herself.*

They'd see the point before too long, though. They weren't fools, and asking Kim to list the sane adults on Earth who could be trusted to do the right thing with the data was an admission that Ingram already had her doubts.

Whose decision was it, anyway?

Chris carried on walking and tried to focus on the moment in the way he used to. His mental chart of the colony was changing almost as fast as the live map on his screen. First it was just Nomad Base, a hub of concentric rings of buildings with agricultural areas on the northern and western edges of the wheel. Then the tent cities and the teerik compound pushed the perimeter further south and east, and the housing zones extended it to the north and northeast.

The housing areas were the tipping point, not just for him but for everyone. The plots allocated to Kill Liners had inevitably become known collectively as Kill Line, and whether Ingram called it a suburb, a neighbourhood, or a zone, it was now a town in its own right again, separate and definable, with a street plan almost identical to the original on Earth. The transit camp had gone the same way at breakneck speed.

He'd expected that. People stuck together, not because they were afraid of change but because having a neighbour you knew and could rely on counted for something. Only the farms had shifted position, because the terrain was different here. So was Nomad a town, or a collection of villages? Chris decided it was the latter.

It was probably time to stop calling it Nomad, too. Yeah, Chris knew Bednarz believed humans were inherently nomadic, never satisfied and always on the move because the greener grass was never quite green enough. But it sounded more like an unimaginative name for a line of motorhomes. Ingram would have to come up with something better if everyone intended to stay. So would the transit camp. Unless they'd all changed their minds and wanted to move on, they weren't nomadic or in transit any longer. This was home.

Chris was walking up the track between the Ainatio housing on his left and the teerik compound on his right when something made him look up. Above him, at about seventy feet, Fred and Rikayl were flying in big slow loops. It was quite something. Fred was getting more height now and Rikayl looked like a kid out with his grandad, sticking at his side as if he thought the old man was going to run into trouble and might need help. Chris was glad he hadn't had to shoot him.

Eventually Fred spotted Chris watching and spiralled down to land a few yards away. Rikayl followed suit and stood a little behind Fred, watching Chris sideways with a suspicious eye. Maybe Nina had been right and Chris really had scared him. It was an uncomfortable thought. Chris held his vest open with one hand, a gesture that would have started trouble anywhere else, but maybe Rikayl would get the point.

"I'm not going to shoot you, buddy," Chris said. "Look. Holstered." He gestured to his shoulder, then held his hands clear. "Rifle's slung. Okay?"

Rikayl didn't look convinced. Fred turned to glare at him.

"Chris is our friend, Rikayl," he said. "He protects us. He's not going to hurt you."

"*Wankaaaah*," Rikayl rasped.

It took a moment to dawn on Chris that Rikayl was repeating what he'd heard. Given who had most contact with the teeriks and the word itself, Chris could guess the rest. It was actually pretty funny.

"So Jeff thinks I'm a *wanker*, yeah?" Chris said. "It's okay, Rikayl, I've been called worse."

"I'm sorry, Chris." Fred looked daggers at Rikayl, raising the spiky feathers on top of his head. He clapped his wings with a loud snap. That seemed to be his warning signal. *Wanker* wasn't the kind of word Fred would have learned from a formal dictionary, but he obviously knew it wasn't polite. "He doesn't really understand."

Oh yes he did. Chris knew. The more he saw of Rikayl, the more he was convinced that he was a very smart bird, not a dumb teerik, but he wasn't going to argue with scientists again.

"At least he's learning to talk now." Chris gestured vaguely skyward. "And you're improving your altitude."

"I think I've reached my limit. We're not quite as aerodynamic as Rikayl is. But it's good to get out of the house. Everyone's very snappy at the moment. Very bad-tempered with each other."

"We all are, Fred. Don't worry about it."

"I'm sorry how things turned out with Gan-Pamas."

"Yeah."

"I didn't lie to you about what he said."

"Did I say you had?"

"No, but... it doesn't matter. I'm sorry about everything."

"You've all been under a lot of stress lately," Chris said. There was nobody else around for a change, so he thought it might be a good time to get a frank answer. "Fred, I know you don't want to offend humans, but how do you really feel about us giving your FTL to Earth?"

"Oh, fundamental FTL technology wasn't our invention," Fred said, as if a patent was the only issue. "We just improve it a step at a time. Are you asking if I like the idea of more humans coming to this sector, though, ones that perhaps aren't like you?"

"Yeah." That was very astute. "I think that's what I mean."

"It's a good idea. The more humans who come here, the less power the Kugin have. Being well fed and protected is very nice, but we wondered what having a choice would be like, and once we got to know you, we understood that it isn't always comfortable, but it's better."

"Okay. Just asking." Chris knew the teeriks' opinion of the neighbouring cultures and he made allowances for it now. Their purpose in life was also entirely about warfare, so like any hammer, everything they saw looked like a nail. "I wouldn't want you to feel forced into it."

"Is that because *you* don't want it to happen?"

"I've got my doubts."

"Are you the only one?"

Solomon thought the bad would drive out the good. He could tell Fred that himself if he wanted to. "I'm probably in a minority. But a lot of the people who'll come won't be like the humans you're used to." Chris stopped. There was a reason why he didn't talk much. It exposed his fears, and he wasn't supposed to have any, at least not in public. "It'd be even worse if they found out about the Caisin gate."

"But your people would have come out here eventually," Fred said. "Perhaps it would have been long after you and I were dead, but from the moment the first mechanicals landed here, nothing could stop it happening."

Fred had his reasons for wanting migration. But that didn't release Chris from his promise to the people he'd brought all this way that he'd rescue *them*, not some anonymous block of humanity he'd never met and never would. He thought he'd completed his mission. Now he felt like he was being dragged back to square one. Gan-Pamas's arrival wasn't anybody's fault — not as far as he knew, anyway — but helping other humans make matters worse would definitely be Nomad's. Opis couldn't be hidden. Tim Pham knew where they lived.

But Chris could find Pham any time, too, and pay him a visit. That was a ray of hope Chris could hold on to.

"It'll take folks on Earth a few years to get anything built," Chris said, more to comfort himself than to inform Fred. "And that's if they don't default to being assholes and start fighting over it, and if they've still got the ability to do it. So even if we knew who to hand it over to right now, they still wouldn't be here any time soon."

"But they'll come one day," Fred said. "And we have time to prepare."

"Yeah. We do." Chris nodded. He had a plan forming already. "We'll make it work."

Fred clasped Chris's wrist and shook it as if he was shaking hands. A teerik palm didn't fit comfortably against a human's, so it seemed to be the closest approximation. Chris found it oddly endearing. Fred was a nice old guy who just happened to have feathers. Whether he'd provoked Gan-Pamas or calmed things down, it would still have ended the same way.

"I know we have no other choice but to help each other," Fred said. "But if our fate has to be tied to anyone, I'm glad it's humans like you."

It was impossible not to like him. It was also hard to have these conversations when Chris knew he'd put a round in the teerik's head to stop the Jattans or anyone else taking him. But he hoped someone would do that for him if he was in the same position, so he wasn't going to feel guilty about some possible future that might never happen.

"We have our good points," Chris said. "Although you need a microscope to find them sometimes."

"*Wankaaah*," Rikayl said, one baleful eye still fixed on Chris. His pronunciation was clearer this time. He seemed to have nailed Jeff's voice pretty well, too. Chris touched his brow in a mock salute.

"I'd better be going," he said. "Lots of work to catch up on today. See you later."

He walked on through the centre of the base, heading northwest, half-wishing he could run into Fonseca because he never learned, and realised he'd let the events of the last few days drain off him pretty fast if he could laugh at Jeff's insults. But life went on, because it had to. Everyone in the transit camp had learned to do the same to stop themselves from going under. He'd thought he was an expert at it, but beneath the dumb, trivial thoughts that bobbed to the surface, darker concerns still gnawed at him in a way they never used to, the what-ifs that felt like he really did have a devil on his shoulder whispering disturbing suggestions in his ear. The angel sitting on the other side wasn't getting a word in edgewise.

The most sneaky demonic whisper was *why now*. Fate hadn't diaried the die-back lab breach, the evacuation, the APS outbreak, and Gan-Pamas's arrival so they could get all the bad stuff over with and move on. This was a chain of events. These things were connected. And the link he hated himself for seeing was Solomon.

If Sol really wanted to get people to move to another planet, and not turn around and portal back when the going got tough, die-back was a great tool to ensure it happened. It'd made folks keen to leave and reluctant to change their minds about staying, even with the prospect of heavily-armed warring aliens next door. The risk of contamination was also a good reason to pull the ladder aboard and not let anyone come to Opis. Sol had trashed Asia to defend himself, so Chris wasn't going to rule out him deploying die-back as another tactic.

Was that terrible? Well, it was, if you were stuck on Earth, and Sol had made it clear Nomad came first. He was the parent who lied about what'd happen if you didn't eat your greens, ultimately meaning well but willing to bend the truth a bit to get compliance. But what about Gan-Pamas? He didn't fit into that sequence. Fred's commune finding Opis did, though. Opis was not, as Marc put it, the arse-end of the universe. Aliens kept falling over it like it had been left in the middle of the street.

Chris couldn't work any of that out, not yet.

Jared was waiting for him at the turning into the transit camp zone. The place was a smart little suburb now, still weird enough to make Chris do a double-take every time he thought about it. Everybody living in the same places but in totally different buildings made it look like a makeover show.

"Rikayl called me a wanker," Chris said. "That's a Jeffism."

"Is that because Jeff called *you* a wanker, or everybody?" Jared asked.

"I like to believe he reserves it specially for me."

"Yeah, I can see that." They ambled along in the direction of Chris's place. "I ran into Dave Flores earlier. He says Kill Line voted unanimously that they felt safe here and wanted to stay. Okay, they don't really have a choice now. But if they had, they wouldn't have thought any different. He said it was a vote of confidence in Nomad's defence force."

"Called it," Chris said. "They're hardcore."

"So while you were out, we took a vote of confidence as well."

"I hear that's how coups happen."

"Everyone says stay, no matter what. You going to cast your vote now?"

It didn't take long to canvass the opinions of one hundred and three people, kids included. "I feel disenfranchised," Chris said.

Jared chuckled and nudged him. "Go on. I won't look. Secret ballot."

"Okay, I vote to stay too."

"So are we going to merge with Kill Line or not?"

"I don't know."

"Back on Earth," Jared said, "Doug told us we could come and live in the town any time."

Yeah, he had. It made sense back then to stay separate, but so much had changed since the beginning of the year that none of the old rules applied any more. They didn't feel much of a connection to the Ainatio community, but they'd built a relationship with the Kill Liners. Their kids had started attending the Kill Line school, and people like Chuck, who'd taught classes in the transit camp, were now teaching from time to time in Kill Line. Folks had made friends in the town, including Jared, who talked brewing with Dave and compared yeasts. It was all getting very neighbourly.

"I didn't think we'd ever have much in common with folks who hadn't been through the worst of the Decline," Chris said. "I thought that maybe the bad shit we had to do before we got there would make it too hard for them. But they don't seem curious about what we did or how we did it. Maybe they don't know enough, but maybe they really do think it doesn't matter."

"They judged us by what we did for them," Jared said. "Nobody's got to confess their past. But Kill Liners aren't dumb. They know it was hard staying alive out there. That's why they don't moralise."

"Ready for domestication, then?"

"You got me thinking about white picket fences, so I'm going to put one up next weekend."

"Okay. I'll go see Doug." Chris was going to make good on his pledge to Trinder that if they survived the showdown with Pham, they'd try to become nice normal guys with nice normal lives. He was doing his bit. But Trinder was way ahead of him and even Marc was showing signs of putting down roots. He had to up his game. "Are you sure you all want this? We've got an identity. And Kill Line's got rules."

"I thought you wanted to see if you could be Normal Chris," Jared said. "This is what we did it for. To settle somewhere safe."

It was safer than Earth. That was all Chris needed to know. "Hey, I've got a meeting with Ingram and the other guys. I'll catch you later after I've talked to Doug. You and Marsha on for movie night?"

"You bet. We've got five sequels to *Time Fixers* to catch up on and a crate of potato-skin vodka."

"Don't make me watch that *Fixers* crap. I'm asking as a friend."

"A couple of beers with chasers and you'll be laughing your ass off at it. Be there."

Normal. Normal was good. Normal was also hard work after years of forgetting what it meant. Chris went home, changed into his uniform, and hoped the session with Ingram really was about security patrols and new perimeter defences, although neither was going to help much if the Jattans worked out where their guy had been and bombarded Nomad from orbit. He couldn't think what else she'd want to discuss, though. They already had their demarcation lines and areas of responsibility. *Cabot* would deal with anything that flew or sailed, and the Gang of Three — she'd taken to using Bissey's nickname for them — would handle land forces.

"Never wanted a spaceship anyway," Chris muttered to his bathroom mirror. "Just an inside john."

Maybe Ingram was going to announce who was replacing Bissey. Chris was more worried about what mischief Bissey was going to get up to now he was officially Colony Dissident and didn't have a virtual ship to run, although Bissey and mischief didn't exactly go together.

Chris decided he looked presentable enough for a staff meeting and set off for the base again. He was a hundred yards down the road when he saw Marc approaching in one of the Caracals. Marc stopped, did a U-turn, and pulled up alongside him.

"Get in," he said. "Ingram just asked Dan if he wanted Bissey's job and Dan said no."

"No shit." Chris wasn't sure if that was weird or Machiavellian. There were no rules any longer. Few things surprised him. "Power move, or desperation?"

"She thinks he's got all the right skills."

"He's not Navy, Royal or US."

"And she's not driving a ship any more."

"Yeah, well, you have unique access to her nautical psychology."

"What's that supposed to mean?"

"You and her."

"There is no me and her."

"Right. Of course." Chris knew a disappointed guy when he heard one. That was how he must have sounded to Marc whenever Fonseca was mentioned. "So is this going to be a tense meeting now or what? Because her wardroom's going to be seriously pissed at her for not tapping one of them."

"They're all specialists she needs to keep where they are. Bissey was a seaman officer, a generalist. You know who'd be good in an XO role? Fonseca. Talking of which, stop moping around after her. She's just using you as a scratching post to sharpen her claws. Let me introduce you to the redhead who runs Water Management. She always eyes you up and she won't get bored when you talk about rocks. You two can chat about limestone infiltration rates and aquifers."

Marc might have been teasing him to get a reaction, but Chris knew it was painfully true. "I didn't realise you knew anything about geology."

"I don't."

"Do you really understand Kugal?"

"Not a syllable, mate." Marc did his half-laugh, that *huhuh* sound. "Recognise a few names, the odd word, and you know roughly what they're talking about. You can bluff the rest."

"Yeah, Sol's annoyed about that. The teeriks won't speak Kugal where we can hear them now, so he can't learn the language and work out if they're keeping anything else from us."

"Seeing as we're playing truth or dare, then, is it true you cut that bloke's ear off in prison, or did you say it to wind up Bissey?"

"True, I'm afraid."

"Balls of steel," Marc said. "But what really impresses me is you made yourself a shiv on your first day inside. Respect."

"I like to be prepared," Chris said. "Anything else I should catch up on before this meeting?"

"Haven't you seen the news?"

"No. I had other things to do."

"China's closed its border and airspace to Korea and suspended all food exports to them. So that's Korea buggered when food shortages start to bite. Russia's closed its border with them too. Not that there's much of it, but the allegation about their infected aid didn't go down well."

Chris had to say something. This was a damn big alarm bell going off. "And you still want to hand Earth the beginner's guide to FTL. It's all starting to unravel, Marc. APS states are turning on each other. It'll be fuel on the fire."

"For us or them?"

"Well, for them, but I'm kind of focused on us. There's a lot of work to do identifying planets people can colonise, but nobody's going to wait for that now. They'll bust a gut getting ships ready as soon as they can, which means they end up *here*. And the countries who don't get the data will still find out it exists, because building spaceships is a big thing to hide, and they'll fight wars to get it. So who do we decide is safe to be given the technology? Who the hell are we to decide who lives and dies, anyway? And when do we tell them about all the aliens?"

Marc pulled into a parking space outside the main building. He didn't say anything for a moment. Chris would normally jump out of the APC as soon as it stopped, but it looked like Marc wanted to carry on the conversation. He waited.

"I think we're going to have to shelve it for a while." Marc rubbed his eyes as if he'd been up all night. "Like Annis said, it's not just a matter of putting the plans online and leaving everyone to do what they like with them. There's a responsibility that goes with handing it over. And fuck knows I spent enough time arguing with Ingram about that. I didn't want to tell my own government about the Caisin gate."

"But you haven't, right?" Chris prayed Marc wasn't working up to telling him he had. "You didn't do it."

"No, I didn't. And neither did she. And I feel like a traitor every time I think about it."

"It's just the timing, Marc. It's really bad timing for Nomad."

"I know. It's always the bloody timing. The older I get, the harder I find it to slam the hatch shut and save the ship instead of the men. Sorry, that's an Ingramism. You get the idea. I'm fed up leaving people to die for some greater good. Whatever we do now, we're wrong. And we're right. And people are going to die either way." He checked his screen, grunted, and opened his door. "Come on. She's moved the meeting by half an hour. Let's have a drink while we're waiting."

Solomon must have heard all that, if he hadn't already heard it elsewhere. The Caracals were always connected and it was an effort to cut him out of the radio loop. But he didn't say anything, so he was probably satisfied and relieved, although not for the same reasons Chris was. Chris was reassured that Marc and Ingram were the sane professionals he'd thought they were and had realised the FTL plan wasn't going to help matters, at least not for some time. Solomon had doubts about the wrong sort of humans. They weren't all on the same page, not quite, but it was close enough.

He followed Marc into the staff club and the first things that caught his eye were the photos of Nina Curtis and Derek Levine behind the bar. He wondered about bringing Jamie's picture, but this was Ainatio's turf, and there was already a permanent place for Jamie back in the transit camp bar.

"Great minds," Marc said, nodding to indicate Trinder and Alex sitting at a table by the wall. "Shall we join them?"

Chris pulled up a seat next to Trinder and tried to be more cheerful than he felt. He'd make sure the conversation didn't touch on deaths or rifts in the command structure. He couldn't take it today.

"So you turned down a chance to join the Not Really Navy, huh Dan?" he said. "But blue's your colour."

"Ah c'mon, have you told everybody, Marc?" Trinder asked.

Marc scratched his head. "I don't think Rikayl knows yet, but basically, yes, because it's bloody funny."

"It's okay, I put your name forward," Trinder said. "Seeing as you're already used to serving under Ingram."

Everyone laughed. Marc somehow remained stony-faced. "I'd bring back hard tack and salt pork and make men of you."

Alex seemed more interested in the news channel on the wall screen and didn't join in. Chris looked around the club just to see who was there, then found his eyes drawn to the TV as well. Marc poked him in the shoulder.

"No, she isn't here," he said. *She* didn't need to be named. "Did she even come and ask how you were? I bet not."

"Actually, Chris, she gave me a candy bar for you," Trinder said. "But I still had it when I got zapped, so it melted and I haven't told her yet."

"Now you tell me." Chris was actually annoyed with Trinder, and then he was annoyed with himself for worrying that he'd missed another chance with Fonseca. "Great."

"Chris, put that straw down," Marc said. "It's not going to keep you afloat, mate."

"Okay, I always feel like I haven't done my homework and she's going to tell me off. I'm not even sure she realises I asked her out."

"Oh, come on. That's just bloody feeble for a grown man. Grow a pair. Ask her outright or move on."

Alex suddenly nudged Marc surprisingly hard, almost knocking over his beer. "Will you two can it? *Look*. Look who's on the news."

It took a moment for the image on the screen to sink in. It looked like a passport photo or a mugshot, and Chris knew that face all too well. Everything else in the bar ceased to exist. He felt like he'd plunged into ice-cold water up to his waist as he listened to the voiceover.

"Security sources now believe the die-back outbreak in Korea is part of an ongoing bioterrorism attack after the Mother Death environmental terror group claimed responsibility for releasing a modified version of the Martel Seven-Three-Nine virus. Police are hunting for an American refugee who arrived in Korea recently. In a statement, Mother Death said the bio-attack was 'the only way to remove human infestation and allow Earth to recover' and added: 'It's only fitting that a species which has spread like a plague to the detriment of all others on the planet should be eradicated by a plague of its own creation.' Police want to speak to Abigail Vincent, a plant genetics expert from the former United States who was granted residence by Korea in a refugee resettlement programme along with her parents, both prominent medical researchers. It's believed she brought virus-infected pollinator drones into the country. Her parents have been questioned by police and moved to a place of safety while their home undergoes biohazard tests. The Mother Death group, which rose to prominence during the Earthmother AI crisis, modelled itself on the doctrine of Dr Maryan Kellard, founder of the Human Limitation Project. Kellard advocated the extinction of the entire human species and demanded an end to space exploration that would, in her words, 'spread the human contagion to every planet it touched.' More on this breaking story as we get it."

The room was completely silent. It felt like nobody would ever speak again. It was a full ten seconds before somebody piped up.

"Hey, has anyone checked on Lianne? She's going to go apeshit."

The *Cabot* people took out their screens and started tapping messages, and the Ainatio scientists got up and left, one by one.

Chris thought he was going to throw up. He could see himself trying to be polite to Abbie and reaching for her metal flight case to put it in the Caracal, and her getting all huffy and snatching it away because she didn't need his help.

"Oh God," he murmured.

Trinder carried on as if he hadn't heard him. "What a weapons-grade bitch. I knew she was a pain in the ass, but this? How the hell did she sign up with Mother Death? She'd never been outside the campus."

"That explains why she wanted to get to Korea, not Australia," Alex said. "She could spread it further on the mainland."

"Well, this is going to complicate matters a bit," Marc said. "Pham must be in a tight spot now. He let her in. Still, at least they're not blaming Britain. Poor Barry Cho. I hope he's okay."

Alex kept shaking his head. "I never used to believe people didn't know. All these ditzy neighbours they interview when they find out there's a terrorist next door and they say how quiet the guy was and how they'd never guessed. It's true." He paused and looked at Chris. "You okay, buddy? You're as white as a sheet."

Chris couldn't stop replaying the moment he tried to pick up the flight case. Then he rewound the only other conversation he'd had with Abbie, when she'd said maybe they weren't meant to go to Opis, and asked him whether they were taking animals with them. His alarm bells had gone off but he hadn't followed up.

"*Shit.* Shit."

"I get the shit concept, Chris, but can we try to expand on that a little?" Alex asked.

"I could have stopped her."

"Yeah, we all could, if we'd known she was nuts. Why is this *your* problem?"

"The case. She must have had virus specimens in her flight case. You know, the metal ones all the scientists had for sensitive equipment. I tried to pick it up to put it in the Caracal when I took her back to Ainatio, but she wouldn't let me touch it."

There was a second or two of absolute silence again. Chris was suddenly aware that people standing around had turned to look at him. He was used to being low-profile and unemotional, a man who kept any inner turmoil battened down, but he was sure he looked like he was losing it now.

"Hey, she was cranky," Alex said. "That was her normal mode. You couldn't have guessed."

"Remember when I called you to ask about her?"

"Yeah."

"She said some weird stuff then. That maybe we were having all those problems because we weren't meant to go to Opis."

Trinder joined in the absolution. "She said negative stuff to a lot of people. She told Lianne she didn't think humans should come here because we'd only wreck the place. But a lot of the other scientists thought the same way, and they didn't join Mother Death and try to wipe out mankind."

"Thanks, Dan, but Lianne didn't have the case containing the virus right in front of her," Chris said. He was getting a grip on himself now. "I should have searched her bags."

"You don't even know for sure it was in there."

"It was. It had to be."

"Doesn't say much for APS's border inspections, does it?"

Alex had gone quiet. He rubbed the top of his nose, just above his glasses. "Well, seeing as we're recalling things that didn't sit right with us, maybe that's how the variant strain escaped from our lab," he said. "What better way to get APS's attention and screw the mission? Everyone knew APS sats monitor crops and land use. Abbie knew. It also explains the bee bots the APS technicians found. But I didn't pick up on that, either. I even suspected Solomon for a while."

"And Annis Kim," Marc said.

Chris stopped himself from saying he had as well. He also stopped himself asking Trinder if he trusted the other scientists who didn't think the Nomad mission should have gone ahead. If they weren't in this bar, their buddies were. Chris could only see potential risks now.

"Come on, we've got a meeting," he said. "Nothing we can do about her now."

But there was, although he wasn't sure Ingram would appreciate them locking down all the Ainatio staff until they'd checked them out again. Could Abbie do something like that all by herself? It didn't take much to spread die-back, so maybe she had. Chris hoped so. Nomad didn't need an enemy inside the wire on top of everything else.

"How many Ainatio people who worked on die-back are here now?" Marc asked.

Alex counted on his fingers as he walked down the corridor. "Nineteen. It won't take long to interview them all. I don't even want to think what we'll have to do if any of them are involved."

"Who says they've got to be from the die-back team to be a risk?" Chris asked.

"Access to pathogens," Trinder said. "But if Abbie managed to get biological material out of the lab, anything's possible."

Alex sounded like he was doing his best not to sigh. "You're right. Minus Trinder's people, that's three hundred and forty-nine potential suspects."

"Don't exempt us," Trinder said. "I trust my people with my life, but we have to do this by the book."

Ingram usually had the news on all day, so she'd know by now and she'd be expecting to discuss it. So much for not looking back at Earth; most of the Ainatio and *Cabot* people had drifted back to watching the news, and now they had a real excuse.

Whatever had delayed Ingram had been cut short. Her office was open and she was waiting for them, hovering in the doorway with a grim expression. There was no sneaking up on anyone in Nomad, not if you had your comms kit switched on.

"I take it you've seen the news," she said. "Have we got any more Ainatio personnel here who we can't trust, or was Vincent conveniently the only bad apple?"

"If I knew, I wouldn't be here," Chris said. "I'd be going after them. But I'm glad you're thinking that way."

Ingram closed the door behind them. "Well, we were going to discuss security," she said. "Enemies without, and now maybe enemies within."

It seemed like all the potential problems they'd war-gamed back on Earth were cropping up. They'd talked about the unidentified mole and the damage an informer did just by existing. A traitor didn't have to do anything or even be present to make people suspicious of each other and split communities. Folks just had to believe they were there.

"Lianne Maybury mentioned some of her other staff thought we'd mess up Opis and should leave well alone," Trinder said. "That doesn't make them Mother Death, but we do need to take extra precautions now and also interview all the Ainatio staff again."

"And you didn't think that was worth doing *before* this news broke?" Ingram asked.

"No, because we're not the thought police." Trinder stood his ground. Chris respected that. "But now we have a reason to ask questions of them. I was cooped up in a research centre with those guys for years. You'd be surprised how much people didn't ask and didn't notice if it wasn't their job to. Ainatio bred that kind of mind-your-own-business culture."

"If I'd known what Abbie had in her flight case, I'd have stopped her," Chris said. "Although if Seb Meikle and the others were planning to carry on working on die-back, they had a legitimate need to take a live virus with them."

"But we incinerated the lab," Alex said. "There wasn't supposed to be any."

Marc scrolled back and forth on his screen. "Funny how tooled-up aliens don't look like our biggest problem now. When we start policing our own people, things are going to get very chilly here."

"I don't think Bednarz envisioned a militarised society," Ingram said.

Marc looked unimpressed. "Well, he's dead, so he doesn't get a vote, does he?"

Ingram gazed at the TV screen for a moment but it didn't look like her mind was on it. "Bednarz was a great futurologist, but he didn't foresee everything. I think this puts sharing FTL on an even more indefinite hiatus, even though the need's now more urgent. We can't afford to put a hole in the lifeboat."

Chris didn't say a word. Solomon was remarkably silent too. He didn't pop up to offer data or helpful updates.

"The more I think about it, the more I'm inclined to say Abbie was responsible for the original biosecurity breach," Alex said at last. "We never did work out how the virus got out. All the protocols had been followed. There were no physical leaks. But if someone falsified the routine checks and smuggled something out, that would explain it. We just didn't think anyone would do it so we didn't check."

Ingram leaned back in her chair, twiddling her thumbs. "So what's the fallout from this going to be like?"

Alex shrugged. "Nobody's going to completely trust Ainatio people for a while. We're going to have to make ourselves unpopular by cross-examining Lianne's remaining team. If we're honest with ourselves, we probably won't trust the answers one hundred per cent. So we'll step up monitoring to make extra-sure that die-back hasn't snuck in. And that'll make folks nervous and upset. Sol will do more surveillance, the staff will know he's doing it — you will, won't you, Sol? — and that'll make them jumpy and resentful. People won't mix so much. There'll be a real danger of a rift between the Ainatio remnant and everybody else. I'd like to offer a solution to make sure that doesn't happen, but there isn't one. When a scientist who was all about eradicating die-back ends up deliberately spreading it, trust is the first casualty and repairing it is going to be very, very hard."

"I always had you down for Mr Positive, Alex," Ingram said.

"I'm Mr Realist today."

"Captain, what if Abbie didn't have anything to do with Mother Death, and it's just them claiming responsibility to stay relevant?" Trinder asked.

"Does it make any difference in the long run?"

"Only that it makes it harder to work out who might be an accomplice," Marc said. "But as we haven't got any more evidence at our disposal than we had when Ainatio did the investigation, it doesn't change anything. And the psychological damage was done the second the cops named her. If it all gets rolled back, it doesn't mean trust resets itself."

"I know I believed the report right away, but what if it's all psyops?" Trinder asked. "If Korea finds it's had an outbreak, its citizens start to lose trust in the authorities. That starts unravelling a lot of things across the whole of APS after the effort they've made to keep the region watertight. So they find someone to blame who's from a country that doesn't exist, because APS can't afford to get into a war with a real nation with actual bombs when it's got its hands full with die-back. And APS is held together by Korea."

"I'd say it's China stirring it, then," Chris said. "Split the APS states and there's no bloc big enough to stop them taking over again. Although my gut says Abbie did it and my brain says due process."

Ingram tapped the table. "This is all fascinating, gentlemen, but I don't think it changes what we have to rule out within Nomad."

"No, but it does mean there might never be a time when it's safe to give the whole of Earth a ticket out of there," Chris said.

"Who do we trust to do die-back screening now?" Marc asked. "The experts are all potential suspects."

"Lianne Maybury." Trinder was writing a list. "Let me go talk to her. She was blaming herself for not spotting Abbie was the informer. I'm going to take her at face value. She'll either be genuine or I'll eventually wear her down."

There'd be one way they'd find out if someone had smuggled die-back past biosecurity screening to sabotage Nomad, and Chris didn't think they'd have to wait long. Crops would die. The colony was too small for die-back to break out without being spotted, and if the aim was to kill Nomad before it consolidated itself, a saboteur would have to release it sooner rather than later.

"Don't forget the virus doesn't kill everything," Chris said. "We can live without the crops it hits. We can make sure we've got substantial bean crops and all the other alternatives. We'll be more resilient than Earth was last time. We're halfway there as it is — look at all the local plants the food techs have processed into stuff that's safe to eat. Nobody cares if it tastes like cotton wool if they're hungry enough."

Ingram gave him a baffled look. Maybe she wasn't expecting him to have an opinion on agriculture. "What if a boffin creates another die-back variant that affects other crops? Mother Death say they oppose human expansion in space. When some mad bastard tells me they plan to exterminate me, I believe them."

"That confirms we need an expert to monitor the plant lab," Trinder said. "It's going to have to be one of *Cabot*'s agricultural scientists. I know that won't improve community relations, but we can't ask the teeriks to be independent observers because they keep saying how advanced our life sciences are compared to most other intelligent species."

"I'm going to talk to Andy Braithwaite," Ingram said. "I think this is as far as we can take it for now. Solomon, have you got anything to add?"

Solomon's voice drifted out of the speaker. "I think you've covered everything. And I'm afraid I *will* be paying extra attention to my Ainatio colleagues, much as I wish I didn't have to. Perhaps more news will emerge that'll clarify things."

"I'm going to visit Doug," Chris said. "I was going to see him anyway, but the Kill Line farmers are probably our best die-back early warning system. Doug's had it on his land. He's seen it. And we trust each other."

Chris felt he was back to normal now — calm on the surface, not so calm below, but he'd moved on to the problem-solving stage. He always did if he let his logic sort things out. He accepted he couldn't have known what Abbie was planning, but that didn't stop the if-onlies. He used to live with those for a short while and then make himself erase them forever, but he wasn't sure if he could do that right now.

He signed a quad bike out of the vehicle compound and sat in the saddle for a moment to think things through before he called Doug. He could see people out and about on the green at the heart of the base, but instead of going about their usual business and walking purposefully because they had things to do, they were standing around in small huddles. It didn't take a mind reader to work out what they were talking about.

Damn, who was going to tell Fred? Jeff or Brad probably would, but Chris would check anyway. There was no point in keeping the news from the teeriks.

Chris got on the radio. "Doug, can I come and see you? You've seen the news about Abbie Vincent, yeah?"

"Come on over, Chris," Doug said. "Joanne's started wheeling out the cakes already. Yes, we saw the news."

"I'll be with you in fifteen minutes." Chris took a breath. "I hear you all voted to stay. So did our folks. We're not a transit camp any more, so maybe there's another topic to be discussed."

The transit camp folk wanted to stop running. They'd said so. They'd voted. They'd all come too far and lost too much to give up. Chris had always been told that was a dumb strategy, because people had to recognise when it was time to quit and not sink the rest of their lives into something that they'd already failed at. But dumb and fail and doing the same thing until they *didn't* fail was what made humans cross oceans and aim for space. One man's wasted time was another's single-minded tenacity.

Chris rode out in the direction of Kill Line but stopped halfway along the road to just look at what had sprung up since he'd arrived. He could still hear clanging metal and grinding engines nearby as bots carried out more construction work. Everything around him looked not only like it had always been here, but that it was *meant* to be here. It was an impossibility, like the whole damn Nomad project, but it didn't take any notice. What was Georgina Erskine going to make of all this? Chris decided to draw up a list of what had happened, just the headlines, because whoever had to bring her up to speed one day was going to need it.

He wasn't sure if he disliked Erskine or didn't really care, but as much as she'd be a pain in the ass for Ingram, getting the *Elcano* party revived and landed had suddenly become a lot more important to him.

He was clear what he had to do. There was a worse virus than die-back, and it was the one that made Abbie Vincent and Mother Death hate humans — no, hate *themselves* — and want to punish everyone else for existing. It was the same sickness that made some asshole release the original virus. If Abbie had seen what he'd seen in State Defence, how hard people had struggled to stay alive, she wouldn't have pulled all that hobby genocide bullshit. It was a luxury she had because she'd never had to fight for her life or watch the people she loved die right in front of her.

Chris listened to the construction sounds for a moment and checked his map to see what the bots were building. It was a permanent background noise in Nomad now and he was close to filtering it out, but it sounded close, and he looked around anyway.

A couple of flatbed bots were hauling a sheet of metal about five feet by seven. They trundled it over to the far side of the site and looked like they were heading for the housing zones. Chris started the quad bike and followed them.

He suspected he knew what it was. He just wanted to be sure.

He caught up with them just as they were unloading the metal sheet at the turning into Kill Line. Most bots didn't take any notice of people unless they had to respond to them, and Chris was used to that, but this time it felt like he was watching the real world from another dimension, here yet not here. When the bots lifted the sheet vertical, he recognised it.

It was the old Kill Line sign, as unwelcoming a message to visitors as he could imagine, just a remnant of the time when the perimeter of the Ainatio site extended further than its final boundary. The sign marked the actual kill line, the point beyond which all those ignored warnings to an approaching vehicle to stop would result in the checkpoint opening fire.

Chris hadn't realised that the townsfolk had taken the sign down and brought it with them. He watched the bots set it up in its new home and adjust it on its poles until it looked as presentable as a hundred-year-old sign could. It was plain and dented, and despite regular maintenance, the rust was showing again. But it was still a smack in the mouth on first sight.

WELCOME TO KILL LINE
STOP AND WAIT WITH YOUR VEHICLE
YOU WILL BE FIRED UPON IF YOU CONTINUE PAST THIS POINT

The top line must have been added later. Chris had never noticed that before. The actual kill line at the checkpoint wouldn't have been formally labelled like that, because it was only what the security guys called it, not a proper name. But if it was on the sign, it meant that all those years ago, someone had gone to the trouble of taking it down and getting those words embossed on it to match the rest of the lettering.

There was nothing unusual about calling a town Kill Line. Lots of place names had started as descriptions of the area or people who lived there, and they often weren't very glamorous. But Kill Line seemed to have wanted to preserve its edge. It hadn't tried to dress itself up as Badger Meadows or some other generic rural fantasy. And it wasn't weird for displaced, worried people to want to bring as much of home with them as they could, right down to place names. Even voluntary migrants did that.

Chris considered how he felt about it. Nomad Base really had become the point where unwelcome visitors could turn around and go back the way they came, or die right there. He was okay with that. They now lived in a world without rules, which meant they had to make their own, and there was no Earth colonial agency or other bureaucracy to lecture them on how to conduct themselves with aliens — or humans — who wanted to kill them.

No, the sign was fine. He liked it. He got on the radio to Solomon.

"Sol, it's Chris. Who requested the installation of the Kill Line sign?"

"Doug Brandt," Solomon said. "Is there a problem?"

"No, none at all. Just asking." Chris was content that the town still had the right stuff. These were his neighbours. He'd never felt he had any before, other than the tight-knit world of State Defence and the transit camp. "It looks good."

The bots seemed to have decided the sign was secure and properly aligned. They turned around and headed back to the base, parting like pairs skaters to pass either side of the quad bike. Chris took a video of the sign for posterity, if it ever caught up with him, and sat on the bike for a while, enjoying the spectacle of the first human town on an alien world. Before he went on his way, he walked up to the sign and put his hand on it for a moment.

Ingram probably secretly liked the name Kill Line. And she'd have to admit it was a better name than Nomad. Nomad said they were just passing through. Kill Line said they were here to stay and that they'd stand their ground. They'd come through their first battle, and they'd come through the next.

"Damn straight," Chris said. "Start as you mean to go on."

A town that had no intention of running away from trouble felt like the home he'd always wanted. Yeah, he could defend this place against whatever was coming, and he was ready to do it.

He was a Kill Liner now.

EPILOGUE

EMERGENCY COMMUNICATION RECEIVED
STATUS: ENCRYPTED
POINT OF ORIGIN: INDECIPHERABLE
TIME OF TRANSMISSION: UNKNOWN
ROUTE TO: HIS EXCELLENCY NIR-TENBIKU DALS,
TRUE HEIR OF JEVEZSYL, RIGHTFUL MEDIATOR OF JATT,
PRIMARY IN EXILE

Excellency,

I don't know when this message will reach you, if it reaches you at all. My previous signal was blocked by aliens I've never encountered before, so I'm forced to expend my emergency beacon to put this in your hands. I need to warn you of a potential threat that's entered our sector.

I believe I've located what you were looking for, but I'm now marooned on a planet at the above coordinates beyond Kugin Gate Four, which appears uninhabited except for a military outpost of a previously unknown civilisation. As I send this, their troops are searching for me. My teerik killed one of their females and was shot dead himself. I don't think he could have misinterpreted my orders to guard the ship in my absence, but he had become more aggressive and disobedient as time went on, which I believe supports our theory about the true nature of teeriks.

I now find myself without a ship. The aliens captured it, presumably to stop me escaping. I have to assume they removed its confidential data as well. They have teeriks with them, so we must also assume they know our locations, strengths, and weaknesses by now. One of the teeriks relayed a warning telling me to surrender and make amends for the killing because the aliens are warriors and they will bear a grudge. This indicates the teerik rebellion was in contact with them before the object was stolen, and the incident may well have been instigated by the aliens themselves. I would have preferred to have spoken to them and invited them to join us in ridding the sector of Kugin imperialism, but no prudent opportunity has presented itself yet.

Their settlement seems recently built and it appears to be the only one on this planet, which is why I believe this is a military outpost of a much larger empire, not their homeworld, and is either a listening station or the vanguard of an expansion into our sector. This means there are many more of them waiting to follow. They are bipedal, fast-moving, and as large as Kugin. They appear to coexist with a community of mechanicals, and another unknown intelligent species, aggressive tetrapods, which I had to evade by chemical means. These aliens are well armed and I have to assume they have vessels in orbit or in bunkers that are equally well equipped.

I can't tell if they represent the greatest threat to us since the Kugin occupation or a potential new ally, but we must try to make them the latter. I will attempt to access the object again and either retrieve it or put it beyond use by an enemy. While I wait for my opportunity, I'm observing the aliens at close quarters, so I can't remove my suit. It's overheating as a result and I'll be forced to discard it soon, and that will probably seal my fate. But while I still have obscuration, I'll gather as much intelligence as I can.

If I fail to return to Halu-Masset, it's important that you know all this before you come to search for the object. These new aliens are significant, and I urge you to overlook whatever happens to me and seek some kind of understanding with them. They represent a potential shift in the balance of power and that is an opportunity we can't ignore. I knew the risks when I took this mission, and if the end result furthers our cause, I die content.

I believe they are called Humans. Their arrival changes everything.

I remain Your Excellency's loyal adherent even unto death.
With my profound respect,

Gan-Pamas Iril
Controller of Procurement,
Government of Jatt in exile.

The Nomad story continues in
HERE WE STAND

ABOUT THE AUTHOR

Karen Traviss is the author of a dozen New York Times bestsellers, and her critically acclaimed Wess'har books have been finalists five times for the Campbell and Philip K. Dick awards. She also writes comics and games with military and political themes. A former defence correspondent, newspaper reporter, and TV journalist, she lives in Wiltshire, England.

WANT TO READ MORE?

Sign up here for news and exclusive previews of forthcoming books by Karen Traviss.

https://karentraviss.com

ALSO BY KAREN TRAVISS

NOMAD
- The Best of Us
- Here We Stand

RINGER
- Going Grey
- Black Run

WESS'HAR
- City of Pearl
- Crossing the Line
- The World Before
- Matriarch
- Ally
- Judge

(CONTINUED ON NEXT PAGE)

COLLECTED SHORT STORIES

- View Of A Remote Country

HALO

- Glasslands
- The Thursday War
- Mortal Dictata

GEARS OF WAR

- Aspho Fields
- Jacinto's Remnant
- Anvil Gate
- Coalition's End
- The Slab

STAR WARS

- Republic Commando: Hard Contact
- Republic Commando: Triple Zero
- Republic Commando: True Colors
- Republic Commando: Order 66
- Imperial Commando: 501st
- Bloodlines
- Sacrifice
- Revelation
- The Clone Wars
- No Prisoners